ALSO BY KATHRYN KRAMER

A Handbook for Visitors from Outer Space

THIS IS A BORZOI BOOK
PUBLISHED IN NEW YORK BY
ALFRED A. KNOPF, INC.

RATTLESNAKE FARMING

RATTLESNAKE FARMING

KATHRYN KRAMER

Alfred A. Knopf New York 1992

THIS IS A BORZOI BOOK
PUBLISHED BY ALFRED A. KNOPF, INC.

Published in the United States by Alfred A. Knopf, Inc., New York,
and simultaneously in Canada by Random House of Canada Limited, Toronto.
Distributed by Random House, Inc., New York.

Library of Congress Cataloging-in-Publication Data

Kramer, Kathryn.
Rattlesnake farming / Kathryn Kramer. — 1st ed.
p. cm.
ISBN 0-679-40428-7
I. Title.
PS3561.R2515R38 1992
813'.54—dc20 91-46714
CIP

Manufactured in the United States of America
First Edition

The author would like to thank the MacDowell Colony,
the Taft Foundation at the University of Cincinnati, and Washington University
for financial assistance in the completion of this book;
and Laura Fillmore for her time and generosity in reading the manuscript.

To Catharine Darcy, my first and only collaborator;
to my family, in all its incarnations;
and to Gayl Irwin Edwards, 1891–1973,
this book is dedicated.

"There are no successful rattlesnake farms in the United States . . ."

LAURENCE M. KLAUBER,
Rattlesnakes: Their Habits, Life Histories, and Influence on Mankind

RATTLESNAKE FARMING

I CASCABEL FLATS

". . . now that everybody's here," Zoë heard her sister-in-law say over the phone.

Now that everybody was here what? Nick and Ellie were going to let the rattlesnakes out of their cages? Nick was down checking on them this very moment (he and Ellie acted as if they had a new baby), while she (Zoë), Monica, and Pryce waited in the living room, pretending they couldn't hear Ellie talking on the phone in the kitchen. Whomever she was talking to. It had rung the moment they'd walked in the door. Could it be Dad? But that would be too easy.

"Nick's sister and her friend flew in this afternoon—Nick just got back with them from the airport. Monica—Nick's mother—arrived yesterday by train."

Monica hadn't seen the country since she was a girl—so she said to Pryce on the sofa. They had never met before.

"He promised us that at the latest we'd have them by Thanksgiving, and here it is nearly Christmas and he hasn't even come out to take measurements. He may be the best in town but his reputation isn't getting the job done."

Now Ellie was talking about their doors, the big topic of the day. On the drive home through the lunar-looking landscape Nick had already warned them that there wasn't going to be much privacy; the carpenter who'd been supposed to put up the interior doors was way behind schedule—only Indian blankets hung over the openings. They all pretended not to hear when anyone went to the bathroom. The news didn't upset Zoë, however. She'd *had* a plan that would have depended pretty heavily upon privacy to put into effect: stopped taking birth control pills without telling Pryce a couple of months ago (let him play Holy Ghost), but now that Rob was out of the hospital that plan was on hold—Robert Went, locked up for ten years for saying he'd killed his father, though everyone else insisted it had been an accident. By now, he'd want the child she'd have had to steal from Pryce. Learning he was out only weeks after she'd stopped the pill could be no coincidence, but now she'd had to figure out how to avoid sleeping with Pryce—they'd be out West for ten days. Then, lo and behold, no doors, and a further "coincidence": besides having no doors, Nick and Ellie didn't have a guest room. Pryce was obviously not meant to be the father.

Meanwhile her mother was gesturing like an emcee at the piñon-speckled prairie spread out before the sliding glass doors like a wild West movie set and asking Pryce if he'd ever seen anything like it. He said he hadn't. The sun still lit up the half-finished flagstone terrace, bordered by the tiny bare trees—apricot and cherry and apple—that Nick had planted. Blue mountains, unattainable, shimmered along the horizon like the border to another country. Zoë had been standing by the glass doors ever since they'd arrived, trying to believe that the scenery was real. Nick's famous rattlesnake farm, which he'd been bragging about all year—while being completely vague about what he was actually up to. After his blowup with the lab in Baltimore a year and a half ago, he'd refused to discuss his research. None of them, except possibly Ellie, knew what had happened. Now here they all were with this great mystery hanging over them (all except for Seth, but Zoë meant not to worry about that great mystery until she'd had a chance to talk further to Nick): Monica gracious and lovely to look at as usual, carefully not mentioning the fact that, though they all knew Zoë had been going out with Pryce for two years, this was the first time she'd introduced him to her family. She knew perfectly well what they were hoping.

Zoë had lived in the desert of Mexico, with its roof-high cactus and fuzzy mesquite bushes; that landscape had been exotic, but these scraggly junipers and misshapen pines dotting the plain at wide intervals were totally unconvincing, like props, Birnam Wood on its way to Dunsinane. Who *lived* out here? Did they all "farm" rattlesnakes?

The mountains were a different story, however. That serene, deep blue—if only it were possible to reach them without their changing color. Whenever she looked at them, she felt so certain. After ten years, Robert was out of the hospital. After ten years, something was about to happen.

"The Sangre de Cristos, isn't that what Nick called that range?" Pryce asked.

She nodded over her shoulder.

"Did he tell you what it means?" Monica demanded.

The blood of Christ, Zoë signed, pivoting. BLOOD CHRIST. Her mother would be able to understand that.

She laughed when Monica rolled her eyes. "Catholicism . . ."

"You disapprove?" Pryce asked.

"Oh, my Lord, the melodrama. Such grandstanding. The name of the town itself means "holy faith.' "

"No separation of church and state, you mean?"

"It reminds me of the winter we spent in Mexico," Monica said. "Seth—Zoë's father," she explained, "had a sabbatical. I was appalled by the graphic crucified Christs in the religious processions. All the women wailing and tearing their hair—I'd used to think that was a figure of speech. The first time I came upon one I thought I'd happened upon the funeral of some much loved public figure."

Pryce laughed. "You had."

Zoë began to spell BRID until Monica said, "Bridget?"

Zoë had never invented a sign for her.

We weren't appalled. We marched in them.

"Oh, you didn't . . ."

We wore mantillas and rebozos. She had signed SCARVES and SHAWLS, but Monica would know what she'd meant. *We went into the cathedral and took communion too.*

"Why, you little horrors!" Monica exclaimed, when she got it.

Ten years since she'd stopped speaking and her mother still had difficulty understanding sign language. She explained it as her way of showing faith that her daughter would speak again someday, but this was just an excuse. Besides, Zoë said to herself, she would speak if and when she was ready to.

WHY? She persisted in teasing Monica now. NOBODY KNEW. By now she didn't always translate, and she liked her mind's forming only the shapes her hands made.

"She and Bridget . . ." Monica shook her head at Pryce: she meant, *impossible to convey the depravity of those two* . . . "I'm sure Zoë's told you all about her." Her mother smiled at her. "We never knew which was the instigator."

Pryce tried to catch her eye, to indicate he stood firm with her against parental exaggeration, but Nick had just come in through the kitchen, and Zoë said to him, *Our mother is in shock because I revealed that we used to march in the fiesta parades in San* . . ., signing: MOTHER SHOCKED WE IN PARADE SAN . . .

"Ysidro," Nick finished. "That *is* shocking."

He sat down in one of the creaky leather armchairs angled to face the couch and smiled, the obliging host. With few exceptions, among them the couch, the furniture was Mexican: heavy carved wooden benches and tables or straight chairs, like the ones around the dining table, brightly painted with birds and flowers—giant versions of the miniature ones she and Bridget had used up their allowance on at the mercado in San Ysidro. Bridget had bargained the black-shawled women down to nothing—Seth maintained that no adults were as ruthless as children.

"Surely you remember them?" Monica appealed to Nick. "The women all dressed in black, the blood-splattered Jesus?"

"That's nothing, Mother. You should hear what goes on in some of the mountain villages around here. Crosses fluttering with rags soaked in red paint decorating the hillsides . . ." He grinned. "At least one assumes it's paint."

"Nicholas, please . . ."

He winked at his sister. "There's a secret religious sect throughout the northern part of the state whose members scourge themselves with cactus whips to reenact the stations of the Cross. Rumor has it they even used to crucify one of their members, though now they only tie him to the cross with ropes—supposedly."

"How civilized of them."

Pryce laughed.

"It was considered an honor to be chosen," Nick went on, sounding as if he had been, "although how much of what still goes on nobody really knows. They take their Christianity very literally out here."

"I'm sure Christ considered it an honor too," Monica said. "That doesn't make it right."

Pryce couldn't know that Monica was arguing with her dead mother, who throughout Monica's childhood had deserted her for Christ.

"The gory displays people require in the name of Faith . . . I've always found the need highly suspect. When I was in Europe on my honeymoon"—she sounded as if she'd gone on it by herself—"I came upon a collection of relics behind the Medici chapel in Florence that I still have a difficult time believing truly exists. A shard of Saint So-and-So's bone, a lock of this or that martyr's hair, all reposing on velvet cushions in immense, ornate, gold and jeweled coffers; the details of the martyrdoms duly noted in the little guidebook I'd bought on the way in—what were they supposed to prove? For years I couldn't comprehend why my husband had dragged me to see these things."

"And now you do?" Pryce asked.

Nick glanced at Zoë and laughed, and hope lunged at her throat; just because he and Ellie were married now and had moved out West didn't mean he wanted to sever connections with *everyone* in their family, and she asked him *How did you find out about that sect, anyway?* to start a private conversation, but he said "What?" and she had to spell out SECT before he got it.

"How do I know about them?" He shrugged. "It's common knowledge—what used to happen. It's only because they were harassed so much that they guard their privacy so strictly now."

She was going to ask where the villages were, precisely, though what she wanted the information for she didn't know, but Ellie picked that moment to make her entrance. "Ignacio Ortega was strung up by them, you know," she remarked. "That's how he got his limp." She sounded very cheerful about it. In one hand she was carrying a decanter of amber-colored liquid, in the other a bouquet of stemmed glasses.

Nick glanced at her over his shoulder and replied, "Come off it."

"Judith told me and Stewart told her. I'd think he would know."

Ellie addressed this to everyone as if they knew who these people were. Zoë hadn't seen her sister-in-law since the wedding two years ago, and she'd forgotten how striking Ellie was; with her short silky hair, Wedgwood-blue eyes, and that kind of caught-by-the-camera American smile she looked like an up-to-date Gibson girl. Spry but sexy. She had an incredible amount of energy.

"You know how Stewart likes a good story, El," Nick was saying. "Stewart Beauregard, our landlord," he explained. "Or whatever you'd call him. The fellow who sold us this place."

"Ignacio Ortega's the cabinetmaker who's supposed to have been making our doors this entire past year—it's thanks to him we'll be enjoying unprecedented togetherness." Ellie laughed as she clunked the decanter down on the coffee table. With her free hand she extracted the glasses from her fist one by one, then began pouring out what was presumably sherry. She hadn't asked if anyone wanted it. "Now he claims he'll descend upon us with them in time for Christmas. That'll be the day."

"Ortega built this house as a studio for Stewart Beauregard's father in the forties," Nick explained. "Jules Beauregard was a painter. The Beauregard ranch is about a mile south of here down the arroyo."

"The streambed," Ellie translated. "Since that time Ortega has become in great demand as a cabinetmaker, and it was only as a special favor to Stewart that he agreed to make the cabinets and interior doors for us. Of course we didn't realize people wait their whole *lives* for him to fulfill his promises, but now we can't just tell him to forget it, not without offending Stewart."

This was Ellie all over, involving you right away in some controversy you knew nothing about. Pryce was already totally smitten.

"I doubt Stewart would care," Nick said. "He's not that concerned with protocol."

Ellie had straightened up to head back to the kitchen but now faced Nick as if he had maligned her personally.

"Come on, Nick, you can't be serious! Ortega's family to him. Not to mention how he feels about this place." She looked at the rest of them as if they could back her up. "It stood empty after Jules Beauregard's death in the sixties. Stewart refused hundreds of offers for it, then turned around and sold it to us for a song."

"Really?" Pryce asked. "Why would he do that?"

"Stewart used Nick and me to thumb his nose at the local hierarchy, that's my opinion. The Beauregards own a tremendous amount of property around here, and Stewart's made a killing since the area came under development. A lot of the old-timers resent him for it. He'd told everyone this place had sentimental value—he'd never sell it. Then all of a sudden he hands it over to heathens like us."

"Heathens?"

"Everyone is so holier-than-thou around here. Only the chosen few make it to the inner sanctum. People would put a fence around the place to keep newcomers out if they thought they could get away with it. You'll no doubt hear plenty of complaints tomorrow night. Stewart and his wife are giving their annual Christmas party—you're all invited. That was Judith on the phone just now."

"Look forward to it," Pryce said.

Ellie dazzled him with her smile, then disappeared into the kitchen and returned with a plate of Brie and some round white crackers with tiny holes in them.

"It's worth going if only to see their house," she went on. "It's a fabulous old hacienda—a monastery originally, in the last century." She smiled. "I'm stuffing a rattler for the occasion."

"She's not joking," Monica remarked to Pryce, who replied, "I'm afraid I realized that."

"If he hasn't already, my son will soon invite you out to survey his livestock, as it pleases him to call them. I absolutely refused. Nothing will induce me to credit his hobby with the slightest reality."

"Then why won't you come out to the snakehouse with me, Mother? If you're so convinced they're imaginary . . ."

"Tell me the truth, Pryce," Monica said, "do you enjoy torturing your parents the way my children do me?"

"Well, if I do, I can't say I've found quite as ingenious a method."

"Fear of snakes is learned, not instinctual, Mother. Why not use this opportunity to get over yours, instead of clinging to old prejudices?"

"Much that is learned is extremely valuable," Monica answered primly. "My prejudices have generally stood me in good stead."

"I'm not talking just about poisonous snakes. I seem to recall your climbing on the kitchen table and screaming bloody murder when I brought a baby garter snake into the house."

"Not unlikely. Though I recall its being the dead copperhead you stored in the freezer that overcame my tolerance. He found it during school vacation, you see," Monica explained to Pryce, "and needed somewhere to store it until he could take it to science class and dissect it. Perfectly reasonable, wouldn't you say?"

"Absolutely."

"This so-called snake farming is nothing new, you know. It evolves naturally out of a long history of fascination with the wretched creatures—a fascination, you might wish to know, Pryce, that his sister has always condoned, or even shared. The thing I always ask people who are fond of snakes," Monica said, looking triumphant, "and what none of them has ever answered to my satisfaction, is, if snakes aren't to be feared, why must they always move in that revolting and unnatural fashion?"

Nick winked at Zoë. "We all know what snakes represent."

"To me they represent snakes, thank you," Monica retorted.

Zoë was about to ask Nick how many he had now—he'd "adopted" a den, he'd written, but rattlesnakes did not do well in captivity—when Ellie ahemmed and reminded Nick that they hadn't told Monica about Christmas Eve yet.

"Be my guest," he said.

"I beg your pardon?" Monica asked.

"We've been planning to attend the midnight service at our church in town," Ellie told her, distributing the sherry.

"*Your* church?"

"The one we've been going to. If you don't want sherry, by the way, there's beer, ginger ale, orange juice. And of course the harder stuff. Monica, we even dared hope you might come with us."

"You needn't look so horror-struck, Mother. We're not religious fanatics because we go to church once in a while."

"I wasn't aware I'd looked 'horror-struck,' Nicholas. Surprised, I suppose, merely. With your background . . ."

She means our early training in how not to believe. MEAN CHILD LESSON NOT BELIEVE. *Evidently it's backfired.*

"What did your sister say?"

"She said a background in skepticism isn't a background."

Monica shrugged. "I don't see why not."

"It's pretty low key," Ellie insisted. "Very nondenominational. There's not even a minister per se, just a visiting speaker or a member of the congregation who gives a talk. Christmas Eve will be equally informal. A few readings and carols and then hot cider and cookies afterwards."

She squashed a wedge of Brie onto a cracker, then sat in the leather armchair at the opposite end of the couch from Nick. Monica looked back and forth between them, shaking her head.

"I don't suppose one evening in church would endanger my immortal soul."

Pryce guffawed; she smiled at him.

Talk about melodrama . . ., Zoë signed. She rolled her eyes at Nick, but he raised his eyebrows noncommittally, pretending not to know what she meant. If that was the attitude he was going to take . . . She had remained standing by the glass doors throughout the conversation, but now drifted towards the kitchen. Not that she had any intention of going with them either. Hot cider and cookies! What a farce.

If *she* went, it would be at dusk, somewhere where the air was so still that even the dust motes hung motionless; she'd be barefoot, and the stones of the nave would feel cool after the sun-scorched dirt of the street. In an alcove of the deserted cathedral a priest would be waiting; she would kneel before him and he would lay his hands on her head and say, My daughter . . .

If you were going to give in, then give in—none of this "nondenominational" business. In the kitchen she turned on the cold water faucet, then began opening cupboard doors in search of a glass.

"Actually," Nick said in the living room, "you should be glad we're so conservative, Mother. There are nuts of every persuasion out here, from the Sikhs in their turbans to the Hare Krishnas."

"They say altitude is conducive to spiritual exaltation," Pryce said. "Think of Tibet."

"Must be the lack of oxygen," Monica remarked.

Nick, Ellie, and Pryce all laughed.

If *she* went, it would be once and for all. Lifting his hands from her head, the priest would take hers in his and gaze into her eyes and murmur, We have been waiting for you to come. All you had to do was give in. Rising, he would lead her through dusky arched corridors; their feet would fall soundlessly as they walked. There would be no way back out.

Zoë found a glass and ran water into it—the sound was of an approaching culmination. Leaning against the refrigerator, she glanced out the window at the mountains again. They were so still, and that rich, soft blue—like the visible manifestation of an interior peace. Not like the silence you had to keep because you had been afraid to speak when it could have made a difference. Rob was out of the hospital; finally she would know if he'd meant to do what he did. She wanted to tell Nick the news, but she hadn't had a chance to talk to him alone for more than a minute—though it was not impossible that he and Monica had already heard and believed they were keeping the information from her. They were always so circumspect about mentioning Rob—they acted as if *she'd* killed someone.

She sipped the water as conservatively as if it were communion. She had made it up to the rail with Bridget that time in San Ysidro but when the moment came she couldn't go through with it. "They might have been able to tell," she said, when, outside, Bridget taunted her with being a coward. "You made them suspicious of me, Zoë, the way you jumped out of line at the last minute! Did you ever stop to think of that?"

> Dear Zoë,
>
> I know I may be the last person in the world you want to hear from, but I thought you ought to know that Robert Went has been released from the hospital. My mother kept in touch with his mother, after she moved . . .

Zoë had memorized the letter in the ten days since she'd found it, seemingly inanimate, like certain miracles, in her mailbox.

> I figured your family probably wouldn't tell you, and I think you have a right to know. According to my mother (according to Sally Went), he's "fine" now, whatever that means.

Then Bridget had written about her own life. She knew Zoë knew that her husband had been killed in a freak accident (she used those words), because her mother had told her when she ran into Zoë at the supermarket a couple of years ago.

> Life was very difficult for a long time, but things are finally feeling a little lighter. It has not been easy, bringing up twins alone (!), but I also don't know what I'd do without them.

She sounded conventional and accepting, not like the Bridget who had always been up in arms about something, but that was forgivable, everything was forgivable now—at least it might be; it wasn't true that you couldn't go back, couldn't undo what had been done. People said that, but they hadn't had the courage to wait.

Zoë took another sip and continued to gaze out at the mountains, her thinking smooth as water, flowing into some larger understanding. Somewhere, off among those mysterious blue shapes, lighter and lighter blue as they receded into the sky, did the sect Nick had been talking about still carry out its rituals? Had they ever actually crucified someone? What would it feel like to have nails driven into your hands? Would they go through easily or would it take persistent hammering? And afterwards, hanging up there with your arms spread wide, feeling like Christ (who when he was crucified wouldn't have compared himself to anyone, must have been one of the few people in the history of the world to think he was having an original experience)—afterwards did you eventually go over some edge and stop feeling the agony? But what would you feel instead? Nothing? Joy?

Jesus, Charlotte had once told her, in her tone of knowing intimacy, had thought of all the people he was saving. Thinking of other people's pain kept your mind off your own. Zoë had wondered then, though she hadn't asked, if that was why her grandmother kept so many pictures of "Him" around. Everywhere you looked there were pictures of Jesus, framed in handmade-looking wooden frames whose corners were all crucifixes: Jesus magically coming up with bread for thousands, walking on the water, eating the Last Supper; and then the biggest one, of him wearing his crown of thorns, carrying his cross to Calvary, hanging at the head of her grandmother's bed like a marker above a grave. Of course in that one too his expression was gentle and forgiving and compassionate—he loved even those who slew him (though who knew if that was the way he'd really looked).

Rob would be able to love her now. He would come right up to the door on Christmas morning and say, Zoë, forget all this; it's over and done with. Ten years of silence; two thousand years of misplaced faith. His suffering was his passion too, just as "His" Passion had been her grandmother's delight.

II HARMONY

Harmony, New Hampshire, 1795: Three sea captains arrive with their wives. They've come there to retire and, along a rise overlooking the village, build three houses as large as ships. These they top with widow's walks—maybe an eighteenth-century sea captain's idea of a joke. Or maybe they plan to spy on the town, to observe the Connecticut River through their spyglasses; it's visible when the leaves come down in the fall. Zoë had been in Harmony only once at that time of year—after Charlotte died, when Monica put the house on the market. Maybe the captains had been homesick and pretended the river was the sea.

The joke was on them, however. Within five years of settling in Harmony, all three were dead, and their wives really were widows, trudging to the rooftops to glare at the graveyard across the road, wondering at their husbands' taste in practical jokes. Tempt fate at your peril, they muttered to their dead spouses. At least they wouldn't have had to contemplate their bereavement alone—they could talk to each other from the tops of their houses. Maybe they were even happier. Things would be different, now that they were in charge. Better, they might have felt, even if they'd never have said so aloud. On breezy, balmy evenings two centuries later, sitting on the widow's walk of her grandmother's house, watching the sun go down over the Connecticut, it seemed to Zoë that she could hear their voices.

Twenty years before the sea captains' arrival, the village of Harmony had tried a woman for witchcraft. It said so, matter-of-factly, in the town history, which had been put together in the 1950's by two spinster sisters named Esther and Viola Banks. They were retired schoolteachers, which was no doubt the reason the Historical Society had decided that they were best qualified to write the Authorized Version. That was what it seemed like, the way everyone took it for gospel. The whole town was in a huff one summer when Zoë and Nick were visiting Charlotte because a "real" historian from Boston who happened to be staying with some summer people had challenged the book's account—he insisted that witch trials had ended in America eighty years earlier than Esther and Viola's history claimed. In an interview in the White River paper the man said that he "failed to comprehend" why earlier researchers would have neglected the Harmony trial in their accounts, since it would mean that witch-hunts had persisted in the U.S. much later than anyone had thought. The discovery of such a case would inevitably have a profound effect on the shape of American history (though what new shape it might assume he didn't say). He pronounced the documents "authentic"—that is, he and other experts had examined the transcript of the trial and the accounts of the supposed witch's death by witnesses, and they agreed that these did "appear to have been penned" around the time of the War of Independence—however, he suspected that it was "really a case of murder under the guise of a witch trial," and that the evidence had been suppressed until recently, perhaps by descendants "eager to expunge" the record. The Banks sisters informed him that, to the contrary, all the material had been yellowing in the town clerk's office available to anyone who cared to investigate it, but he didn't pay any attention. Why you couldn't claim that all witch trials had been disguised murders, or how an entire town could conspire in a cover-up, this brilliant researcher didn't say—though Zoë had to admit that the second part wasn't totally incredible. Harmony was a town that could have known the true story of the Creation and the Fall and kept it from outsiders if it thought it in its best interest. Everyone always seemed to know more about everything than they were saying, but if you jumped to a conclusion about what they might be withholding—well, it was your own fault if you jumped off a cliff.

The witch's name was Marian Howe, and Zoë was Marian Howe's direct descendant through Charlotte and Charlotte's mother, Ida. Zoë had read the story of Marian's trial and execution until she'd memorized it; yet each time she turned to it she still believed that the outcome would be different, as if it were her own story she were reading.

"Many misfortunes [Esther and Viola wrote] had befallen the villagers throughout the previous year, and in all, it appeared to them, Marian had played a part." She had warned a farmer named Augustus Lewes (the Magoons—farmers whose sons Nick and Zoë played with—were descended from him) that his cows would take sick and "within a fortnight they had succumbed to a fatal pestilence." Another she told that his barn would catch fire and, sure enough, not long after, it had burst "all of itself" into flame. A child she had "gazed upon mournfully" was "stricken with palsy." Predicting the future was bad enough, but what really damaged her case was the testimony of "several upstanding young men" that, although her husband Asa had drowned while ice-fishing in the Connecticut the previous year and left her alone with a young child, they had proposed to Marian and she had *refused* them. How dare she! To top everything off, she claimed that *God* was the true father of her son, not Asa, and wedding another would only anger Him. Had He not murdered Asa? Blasphemy was added to her list of sins.

On one of the hottest days of 1776, in a pond back of Farmer Lewes's hay pasture, Marian Howe was drowned. There was no wind that day, and the witnesses could see the bubbles of her last breath breaking on the surface. Esther and Viola Banks *described* this. Zoë could just see them, sitting in their antimacassared-to-death house inventing the details, giggling, making thrilled gasps. Even more vividly she could see everyone standing around, staring hypnotized at the still water, as they wait for more bubbles to rise. When none do, they figure that Marian must be dead and drag her body from the pond by the rope that, with such great foresight, they tied around her waist before shoving her from the skiff into the water. They heap her into a cart and are halfway to the graveyard when (as Esther and Viola put it) "to their horror and fright" she begins coughing and spitting up water and breathing again. Some immediately proclaim it a miracle and that they ought to listen to God, but the rest say it's the devil's work, not God's, and this second group wins.

The next time, besides tying her hands and feet, they attached a sack of rocks to her and left her down for a week. The fish had "nibbled her," according to Esther and Viola, by the time the town dredged her up again to bury her in "unhallowed" ground outside the churchyard wall. Although the place she was buried had never been marked, everyone knew where it was. "Indeed, even two centuries later," Esther and Viola gushed, village children still "delight in daring each other to tread on the witch's grave."

This was all the Misses Banks, who talked the same way they wrote, in a small town newspaper's local-news voice trying to be sophisticated, had to say on the subject. To them it was a "colorful incident," powerless after two hundred years to provoke horror or grief. That Marian had been put to death (that is, mercilessly drowned while everyone gloatingly watched) for having known more than people thought she should, or believed she could, Esther and Viola evidently didn't feel it their prerogative to judge. They didn't consider Marian's testimony—that God was the father of her son—even worth commenting on. Hadn't they at least been curious why she'd said that? Was Marian's son illegitimate and she'd been trying to hide it? Was she crazy? Or the third possibility: it was true? (Of course that got Rob's vote—"His" plan for his son to save the world not having succeeded at first, why wouldn't "He" try, try again?)

A hundred years or so after the sea captains' arrival, only one of their families still lived in Harmony: the Robies—Henry and Louisa and their only child, Adam, although Henry "scarcely ever brightened his own hearth" (so said Esther and Viola) since he, like Thaddeus Robie, his father, Micah Robie, his grandfather, and Obadiah Robie, his great-grandfather, who had built the house, had "hearkened to the sea's call." It was almost 1900; electricity was "just coming into popular use"; the telephone had been "current for a brief while"; the phonograph was "about to be invented. In Harmony, an automobile was still a miraculous sight—those who had the good luck to be present will never forget the moment the first one rolled into town. It was huge and green and Judge Augustus Lowndes had bought it. The first time he took his family for an outing, he drove them off a bridge!"

More than a century had gone by since Marian Howe was drowned, and Harmony didn't conduct witch trials anymore, but this didn't necessarily mean people had stopped believing in witches. They certainly hadn't forgotten who the last witch's descendants were. Howes, they said, making it sound like a proverb, act queer. They can never just be born, grow, and settle back down like most folk. When Ida Howe was twenty-seven, and the town had decided she was to be a spinster, she disappeared for six months; when she returned she had a baby with her—her daughter, Charlotte. Could she have been taking a cue from her ancestor when she also said her baby had no father?

Ida, though, wouldn't have cared less what people thought—you could tell from her pictures. She looked brave, though not in a defiant way—just very calm, as if she never had any doubts about what was what. Charlotte had explained that eventually her mother's total indifference to people's opinion had convinced the town that she was out of her mind. Lucky for her, since this meant they could allow her to continue in her occupation of seamstress. Clearly they perceived no danger in a demented woman's sewing their clothes, whereas it would have been . . . oh, improper in the extreme for an immoral one to do so. Once, though, Ida worked as something else—which came about this way.

Ida hadn't been home in Harmony for more than a month when Louisa Robie gave birth to a son. The birth was difficult and Louisa couldn't (or wouldn't) nurse the baby. He was also colicky, which meant that he couldn't digest cow's milk.

One night the town doctor, Amos Jewell, visited Ida and pleaded with her to help. Zoë could see him sneaking up to wherever Ida was staying, looking around before he knocked on the door. "I do apologize for disturbing you," he says, blushing, "but I have come to beg your assistance. The Robie baby might perish if you refuse." Ida was probably the only nursing mother in town he dared ask, yet she must not have minded because she went, taking Charlotte with her. Most likely they took the back way, along the field road that wound around behind the captains' houses. Then Louisa made Ida swear that she would never reveal to a single soul that she had nursed Louisa Robie's son; instead they'd pretend that Louisa, not being well, needed someone to help tend the baby, and had hired Ida, who would be supposed to be grateful for such a luxurious home.

Ida kept her promise except for telling Charlotte, but it wouldn't have made any difference if she'd published the truth in a newspaper. This being Harmony, the entire town would have figured out within a week what was going on at the Robie mansion, and yet such was their native secrecy that Adam lived his whole life there without once hearing the story. Charlotte, who might have spared her husband much anguish by telling him, true to her Harmony heritage never told anyone more than he or she knew enough to ask about. No doubt everyone was delighted by Louisa's attempts to hoodwink them. At regular intervals she climbed to the nursery, locked the door behind her, and stayed there until Ida had fed Adam. People would have thought it appropriate that the two most gossiped-about women in Harmony should be living in the same house.

It must have been quite a scene: Louisa standing, her back against the door, staring at Ida, as Ida undoes her blouse and begins to nurse Adam. Louisa can't help wondering how it feels. Ida was beautiful; her photographs made that clear. She had that serene, wise-womanly look that seemed to have stopped showing up on women's faces by around 1920. Louisa, on the other hand, was gaunt and eagle-featured, and glared resentfully at the camera. What was she so angry about? Charlotte told Zoë that her great-grandmother had snipped bumblebees in half in midair with her garden shears. What baby, given a chance, wouldn't have been delighted to have Ida nurse him instead?

Did Louisa envy Ida? How did Ida feel? Were they friends? Did something happen between them that forced Ida to leave Harmony? Years later when Ida died, and Charlotte brought her back to Harmony to be buried, every week, winter and summer, Charlotte told Zoë, flowers appeared on Ida's grave, and no one needed to think twice to know who put them there. But then why would Ida have left town because of Louisa? Charlotte said she had no idea. Had she forgotten? Even though she was off her memory-obliterating medication when she told Zoë this, and remembered things she hadn't for years, there still could have been gaps. Either that or she'd been waiting for Zoë to hit on the truth herself before she'd corroborate it.

At the time of Charlotte and Adam's first encounter, Henry Robie was still at sea, though he'd already gone ashore in Bombay or Singapore or whatever grimy port city it was in whose "house of ill repute" (as Charlotte put it) he caught the syphilis that before long was going to kill him. Lonely Louisa kept herself busy just being rich, making sure she maintained her prominent, unpopular position in the town. By this time Ida had been willed an uncle's house on the Winfield Road—it was still standing, although windowless and caving in, by the time Zoë and Nick began to spend summers in Harmony. Adam and Charlotte were six years old.

One day, an early spring afternoon, Ida took Charlotte with her to the Robies' house. Although Ida hadn't lived at the Robies' for years, she still came once a month to do the family's sewing. Charlotte had often accompanied her mother to give ladies fittings—she held pins while Ida tacked up a hem, or practiced sewing with scraps of cloth—but her mother had never taken her to the Robies', and Charlotte was thrilled. The Robie mansion was five times the size of her house, and she couldn't wait to see inside and to watch Louisa Robie, stuck-up Adam Robie's mother and the richest person in Harmony, being measured for her summer clothes. Louisa, however, had no intention of having anyone besides Ida there when she undressed, and Charlotte's heart sank when Louisa ordered Adam to take "Ida's little girl" away and play with her. Charlotte hated Adam with all her might, and he acted just the way she'd expected. As soon as they were out of their mothers' hearing, he spun around and chanted, "Witch! Witch! Charlotte's a witch! Cast a spell on me, bet you don't dare."

Charlotte had heard plenty of this at school.

"I hate you!" she answered. "You're an evil pig. I wish you were dead and fed to the crows."

Adam waited, but when nothing happened he said, "You know what

I think? I don't think you're a witch at all. You have to be put to the test. Come with me."

Charlotte said she never considered not obeying—she was determined to get even somehow. Avoiding the servants, they tiptoed along the hallways. Adam filched a broom from a closet downstairs; in the library he climbed on a chair and pulled his grandfather's spyglass down from its case over the mantel. Charlotte found the library, with its walls of dark books, very gloomy, and she was impressed that Adam seemed undaunted by it. Then he led the way to the roof.

Being on top of the Robie mansion was like being on the deck of a ship—the wind blew nearly all the time and there was nothing, it always seemed, to prevent you from sailing off to the horizon. As soon as they arrived, Adam shoved the broomstick into Charlotte's hand and ordered her to fly. She said she wouldn't.

"Why not?" he demanded.

"I don't care to," she said.

"You can't, that's why!"

"I can."

"Then show me."

"I won't."

He acted as if he were going to push her off the roof but ignored her instead. Propping the broom against the railing, he raised the spyglass, through which he had been hoping to watch Charlotte disappear over the treetops, and pointed it towards the town.

"If you let me look, I'll fly," Charlotte said she'd told him.

Instead of answering, Adam turned to look in the opposite direction, towards the woods. He scanned the treeline, then lowered the spyglass towards the meadow in an arc, where something caught his eye. He held the glass upon the scene.

"Do you see something?" Charlotte asked. "What do you see?"

"Nothing."

"You're lying. Let me look!"

"I can't," he said. "It isn't right."

"*What* isn't?" Charlotte was so furious at his high-and-mightiness that she kicked him in the shin. Caught off guard, he loosened his hold on the telescope; she grabbed it and lifted it quickly to her eye and looked where he had been looking. It took her a moment to make out what he'd seen. "What are they doing?" she exclaimed.

In a clearing in the woods, which was visible only because the leaves had not yet unfurled, she saw two bodies. They were struggling. They were also unclothed. Charlotte could see enough to know that they were a man and a woman, even though she had never seen anyone besides herself or Ida undressed.

"What are they doing?" she exclaimed.

"Wrastling," Adam muttered, "with no clothes."

Charlotte began to giggle, but Adam shouted, "Stop laughing! It's wicked!"

"What is?" Amazed, Charlotte lowered the spyglass and stared at Adam; then, lifting the glass again, she looked through it at him. His eye was the size of her fist.

"It's wicked," he repeated. "*You're* wicked."

"I am not."

Suddenly Adam lunged to grab the telescope, but Charlotte thrust it behind her back. He tried to catch her, but she kept slipping away. Finally he cornered her and reached around her to seize it. She was bent back against the railing, holding the glass out over the roof, and his hands were around her wrists and his stomach was pressed against hers. Her face was just beneath his and they were glaring into each other's eyes, so that when they heard the rip of wood as the railing began to give way, they each saw the other's eyes widen in perfect mimicry of their own.

Adam managed to leap back, pulling Charlotte with him, but in her fright she dropped the spyglass; both turned in time to watch it roll down the slate shingles. Miraculously, instead of catapulting to the ground, it came to rest upon a layer of wet brown leaves in the gutter. For a while all they could do was stare at it, as if it might yet move.

Then Charlotte began to giggle again. She couldn't stop herself. Adam tried not to, but eventually he giggled too. Soon they couldn't stand up, they were laughing so hard. When they finally stopped, they were friends. As far as Charlotte could tell from school, Adam had never had any.

"I'll fetch it," he said. "The roof's not steep. We'll bring a rope and I'll tie it around me and you'll hold it."

And that was what they did, tiptoeing back down through the house and out to the barn, then up again with a tether. Lucky for them that the style of women's clothing that season took some time to fit. Adam, the rope around his waist, climbed down over the railing and retrieved the spyglass from the gutter without mishap. While Charlotte stood guard outside the library door, he replaced the glass in its case above the mantel. Then they returned the rope to the barn, where they played hide-and-seek in the hayloft until they were called back to the house.

Louisa, the next morning, discovering the broom on the roof, scolded the housemaid for dawdling on the widow's walk when she ought to have been sweeping the parlor. Adam, who overheard, told Charlotte years later, after they'd become engaged, that at that moment he felt happier than he ever had before in his short life, since he'd discovered what he'd never imagined to be possible: you could do something wrong and somebody else could get blamed for it.

III SPARTA

It was Bridget Wycliffe, not Charlotte, though, who first told Zoë about the Crucifixion. Bridget was Zoë's best friend, but since she was a year older she found out everything first.

Moreover, she went to church. Seth and Monica didn't care if they never set foot in a church again in their lives—they had had a bellyful in their youths—and it wasn't until they all went up to Harmony to visit Charlotte that Nick and Zoë set foot in one. Seth and Monica said they could go if they felt their lives wouldn't be complete without it, and Nick took to church like a duck to water because he had joined the Christian Youth Group and had a crush on a girl in it, but Zoë was disappointed; the sermons were never about the fancy, violent things that happened in the Bible, which she wanted to hear more about; they were just a lot of advice that anyone could think up for themselves. All her life she'd wanted to go to church but now that she did she felt exactly the same stale and bored and empty way she'd felt every single Sunday since she'd been born, sitting in the bay window of the living room of the house on Metcalf Street and watching other people all dressed up going by: women wearing hats with daisies and grapes on them, boys in suits, and girls in party dresses and white gloves, carrying miniature pocketbooks that matched their shoes. The fathers wore suits too and looked embarrassed. Seth never had to wear a suit because he was a college professor—"the only time you'll catch me in a suit is at my funeral," he said. Zoë had never gotten to go to a funeral either. On Sundays the stores were all closed except the drugstore, and it closed at noon; the streets were as empty as when there was going to be a parade; even the animals acted different. They crossed the streets slowly, sniffing things all the way, not even bothering to look for cars. Even when it was warm weather, on Sundays the sunlight always looked thin, the way it did in winter; the houses across the street looked like they did on cold February days when there was no snow. Nick could go over to the Tannenbaum's, but Bridget could never do anything until later. Every single Easter she got a brand-new dress. Seth and Monica might *say* Sunday was no different from any other day, but they were obviously lying through their teeth.

Now Charlotte expected her to go to church whenever she was in Harmony and Zoë had begun to dread it because of the collection plate. Each Sunday her nervousness increased. Charlotte, paying attention to the minister, was never ready on time, and Zoë had to hold the giant brass ashtray while her grandmother rushed around in her purse for her dollar bill. Zoë was always terrified people would think she was trying to steal the money. "Couldn't you just hold it in your hand the whole time?" she had urged Charlotte. "Then you'd be prepared." But Charlotte said it wouldn't be proper to clutch filthy lucre while you were listening to the word of God.

Which one? Was there one word every time that the minister just slipped in, hiding among all the others? The idea made Zoë feel sick to her stomach with listening, like playing musical chairs and trying to hear ahead of time when the music would stop. Charlotte had given her and Nick Golden Bibles, to keep them religious while they were in Sparta, and Zoë had looked at the pictures and read some of hers, but she didn't like the way the author always capitalized He for God even in the middle of a sentence, as if he didn't know any grammar. She must have missed that part about babes in a manger and wise men and Jesus dying on the cross for people's sins which the minister was always talking about in his sermons, but she still didn't think it really meant anything. Her grandmother had always had those pictures in her house, but they were scattered all over, and high up, and how was she supposed to know what they were? Was she just expected to know these things *automatically*? She only found out later that the Golden Bibles didn't go up that far. If it hadn't been for Bridget, she would have grown up in total ignorance.

Bridget only lived around the block, but Zoë liked to go to her house the back way: first climbing the Hardcastles' chain-link fence, hoping their revolting basset hound Sylvia wasn't out because, if she was, not only would she slobber all over you, she would bark when you climbed the fence on the other side and then Mr. Ogilvy might hear and come out. Myra Ogilvy was in Zoë's class at school and had a trampoline. Her mother was out of the picture. Her father, who worked at the Naval Academy although he never wore a uniform, had once chased Zoë and Myra around the house with a butcher knife, cackling like a hyena. Another time he had wrapped Zoë up in a rug and carried her down to the basement and locked her in for a long time. She'd never told Seth and Monica about it, because she had told them about the time with the knife and they had said that in the future she was to give Mr. Ogilvy a wide berth, which meant stay out of his way, but she couldn't always get Myra to play at her house. She had never even told Bridget.

Sometimes Zoë imagined what Mr. Ogilvy would do to her if he caught her crossing the yard when Myra wasn't around. Probably lock her up in the basement again but this time really torture her, gagging her with rags and tying her up. Probably he would make her take all her clothes off.

She and Bridget sometimes wrote notes to their teachers telling them they should punish them: boil them in pots and eat them, hang them naked from clotheslines with giant clothespins, beat them with spatulas and throw them off Hollister Point into the bay. "Show us no mercy," they said, and promised the teachers they would not reveal their identities in case they lived. They signed the letters, "Your evil slaves."

After the Ogilvys', there were two other backyards before the Wycliffes': the Voorheeses' and the Steinkoenigs'. How could anyone be named *that*? Why did they live next door to each other, anyway? Why did they even exist? Why did she exist and why did she live on Metcalf Street in Sparta and have Nick for her brother and Seth and Monica Carver for parents instead of living on some other street in some other town with some other family? Why did her and Bridget's fathers teach at the same college? If all of that hadn't happened she would never have known Bridget, and she couldn't imagine never having known Bridget.

Seth said that when he finished his Magnum Opus, it would answer questions like these. Mr. Wycliffe said that when he finished his, it would explain why Seth wanted to have these questions answered. They were engaged in a Continual Sparring Match, constantly trying to outdo each other in cleverness. "They're at it again," Monica and Mrs. Wycliffe said. "Boys will be boys." But they shouldn't say it. It only made their fathers worse.

All the older professors and their wives had accents; Seth said that if someone were to kill off the college's faculty, a large part of the world's wisdom would die with it. Both Mr. and Mrs. Wycliffe spoke with an English accent, although they called it "British." Why didn't they call them British muffins? Bridget didn't have an accent because she was born and raised in America, but she pronounced some words differently; she said "privacy" like "river" instead of "diver." She said this one day when explaining why her parents had built a brick wall around their backyard, although they called it a garden. "It's because we value our privacy," she said.

It made Zoë furious whenever she thought of the three of them sitting there and no one being able to see them. Besides that they were all Insomniacs and they made hot chocolate and played Scrabble with each other in the middle of the night. Seth and Monica said Bridget got away with murder because she was an only child. Because Mr. and Mrs. Wycliffe were already old when she was born, fifty-two and thirty-seven, they thought she was a cat's pajamas as a result. But it was just asking for trouble to let a child think she was God's gift to mankind. Zoë couldn't help thinking how much Mrs. Wycliffe must have loved Mr. Wycliffe to marry him knowing ahead of time that she would be a widow.

The only other dangerous part after crossing the Ogilvys' yard was climbing the mulberry tree in the Steinkoenigs', which you had to do to get over the Wycliffes' wall. Once Professor Steinkoenig was out on the porch and caught her, but he waved like telling a person to cross the street in front of his car and said, "Don't vurry, kids are like vild animals to us. Nussing zay do zurprises us." In the summer he wore long shorts and knee socks and sometimes went all the way to the drugstore in his slippers. He was terrified of germs and used his handkerchief when he had to open doorknobs, even in his own house. Seth said Professor Steinkoenig could think circles around them all. Mrs. Steinkoenig was the daughter of a famous philosopher who had invented false assumptions.

When Zoë jumped down from the tree that day, Bridget was sitting at their lacy iron table drawing mustaches on all the women in one of her mother's magazines.

"Hob-i," she said. "Hob-ow ob-are yob-ou?"

"Fob-ine," Zoë answered, "ob-and yob-our sob-elf?"

They were going over to the Tannenbaums', who lived at the bottom of a steep street that was also a dead end. Zoë was sure that sometime, when they were driving to the Tannenbaums', the brakes would collapse and the car would shoot straight into Ivy Creek, and she kept her window rolled down in case she had to swim out of the car. Sparta came to dead ends all over: Ivy Creek on one side, down to the harbor; the harbor was another side; then the wall around the Naval Academy, which was a mile long and taller than anyone could see over; the campus was the fourth side. The only way out was along Derby Street, where the gas station, the dry cleaner's, Goodwill, and Safeway were. Seth said this meant Sparta was well protected against invasion, but everyone knew that if they got attacked it would be from a bomb. At school the teachers were converting the basement into a fallout shelter, but all they had down there so far was V-8 juice, and Mr. Kefauver even made you finish whatever math problem you were on before he'd let you go downstairs when there was an air drill. She would just survive somehow.

Sam Tannenbaum was Nick's best friend, and they were practically always together, but Nick wouldn't be at the Tannenbaums' today because he was at his psychiatrist's, Dr. Macmillan's. He had started having fainting spells and asthma attacks and a couple of times had to be rushed to the hospital to get shots of Adrenalin in the middle of the night. His doctor had discovered that he was Psychosomatic.

"I faint because Mom and Dad fight," Nick told Zoë. "Dr. Macmillan explained it to me. It's like I get so worked up over them fighting that my body can't take it and I'm like a car overheating."

"How come I don't faint? I can't take it either."

"Because I'm older, and I bear the brunt. I'm like a shield. Everything affects me more than you."

"What? It does not."

"It's like when the Greeks sacrificed their children to the gods so they would win wars and stuff."

"*What?*"

"I'm the sacrifice in our family. If I got better, Mom and Dad would get a divorce."

"That's mentally insane. You're making it up."

"Ask him yourself if you don't believe me."

"How can I ask him? I never even get to see him!"

It was summer then, July or August, and it never cooled off, even at night. It felt creepy, sleeping under only a sheet. In the day the brick sidewalks were scorching hot—not that she was supposed to go barefoot anyway because of broken glass. She and Bridget spent all their money on paper supplies, for playing school with, and when they weren't playing school they put on their bathing suits and ran through the sprinkler, then lay on lawn chairs sucking root beer popsicles made in ice cube trays, until they were white and flavorless.

They had found out about sex by then, what really happened, the man sticking his penis in the woman and moving it around until the sperm couldn't stand it anymore and came out. Sam Tannenbaum's mother told him and he told Bridget. Bridget had come over immediately and said, "You won't believe what I found out," but when she finally told her, first making them go into the bathroom and lock the door and get in the bathtub and pull the shower curtain, Zoë knew it had to be true because it was so unbelievable.

Sam and Bridget were in love (Bridget said she would have fallen in love with Nick if he hadn't been Zoë's brother; he was ten times more good-looking than Sam any day), and because Bridget and Zoë were going to stay together always, they agreed that when Bridget married

Sam, Zoë would marry Archie. Zoë admitted she loved Archie, and wrote a letter telling him this. Bridget took it to Sam who gave it to his brother. He wrote back right away, saying "How do I know you're not playing a trick on me? You never showed any signs of liking me before." Zoë didn't answer, because it was true. But then one day she went over to the Tannenbaums' with Nick, and Archie made her come up to his room and shut the door.

"I've decided I'm in love with you after all," he said. "I don't want to get married, though."

"That's okay," she said.

Then they lay down on his bed and made love, although they didn't take their clothes off. She worried that the sperm could get out through his clothes. Archie kissed like a fish, with his mouth wide open, as if he was trying to eat her alive, and it was hot and hard to breathe. Her whole face ached by the time they stopped, and her cheeks were wet and sticky.

When she told Bridget, Bridget was incensed. "I was in love with Sam first!" she shouted. "You could have at least waited so I could make love with him at the same time!" Ever since then they'd been trying to think of ways for the two of them to be at Sam and Archie's without Nick. Nick didn't know Sam loved Bridget, and Sam had made her swear not to tell anyone; if she did, and he found out, he would stop going steady with her instantly. Now their chance had finally come.

Outside, on the street, the hotness made it feel as if you were just part of the air. It felt as if you could go into any house and it would be yours. You might even be someone else. It was practically too hot even to remember where you were going, and Zoë and Bridget walked slowly, talking like grownups, using lots of words like "especially" and "actually" and "indeed," and turning only their heads when they looked at each other instead of their whole bodies. Zoë didn't even like walking down the Tannenbaums' street—you might start running by mistake and run right into the water—but today it was too hot to worry about it. It was even too hot to be bored, and Sparta could be pretty boring. Even when she and Bridget tried to get lost on purpose, writing down directions—Left, Right, Left, Left, Straight, Right, Straight, Left—and then followed them on their bikes, they always ended up somewhere they recognized. Even getting on the bus at the stop on Chesterfield Street and riding it all the way out to Millbrook Heights, which they strictly weren't allowed to do, was boring once they'd done it a couple of times.

What wasn't? They walked to the harbor and watched men standing at a counter in the fish market swallowing raw clams, which was revolting, but you still couldn't stay there watching them all your life. You could get arrested for loitering. They ran to the hospital, which was only three blocks from their houses, when they heard a siren, but even when they got there in time to see the red station wagon–shaped ambulance pull up to the Emergency Room and the men take the stretcher out, they could never get close enough to see anything horrible.

That day, Sam and Archie were sitting out on their kitchen steps, waiting for them, something they never were. Mrs. Tannenbaum always had to call them at the top of her lungs before they'd come from whatever they were doing. There was something strange about the way they were just sitting there, and then, when they saw Zoë and Bridget, Archie got up and went inside. Sam stayed there watching them walk across the yard. Zoë and Bridget looked at each other.

"Whob-at thob-e hob-ell?" Bridget said, so Sam couldn't hear. "Hi," she said.

Sam said, "I called you, but your mother said you'd already left." He sounded as if he didn't believe it. "I was calling to tell you not to come over. Our grandfather died and we have to drive to Toledo, Ohio, for his funeral."

"To where?" Bridget said.

Sam stood up and made them come away from the house. "You can't come in," he said. "My dad came home early from work and he's crying. Tell Nick I can't go fishing tomorrow," he said to Zoë.

"Are you coming back?" Bridget asked.

"What? What a stupid question," Sam said. "We're only going for his *funeral.* We're not going for the rest of our lives."

Then he went back inside. He didn't even say goodbye; the screen door slammed shut like a monster swallowing something. Zoë and Bridget stood looking at it for a minute before they left. As they walked back up the street, they didn't say anything—Bridget wouldn't look up from the sidewalk. Zoë didn't know what to think. Neither of them had ever had anybody die—all their grandfathers had died before they were born—so how could they have been prepared? Yet the street looked sneaky and evil now, the houses too, the way they got higher like steps, as if the people only lived half next door to each other; the other half they lived next to an invisible house that was level with theirs. There were things you couldn't see around you all the time, things other people already knew about but never let you in on because they spied on you, waiting for you to run into the things so that they could laugh their heads off. Normally, she knew, she would have been ready, but today it was so hot it had kept her from suspecting what was about to happen and suddenly she felt that she was going to throw up. She stopped walking, wondering if she should go stand next to some bushes just in case. She thought about how she would have to crouch down to throw up under them. When she saw that Bridget was crying, she felt like kicking her.

"What are *you* crying for? He's not even your grandfather!"

"I'm overwhelmed with grief, do you mind? Just because you don't care. I'm going to St. Stephen's and pray for his soul."

"You're *what*?"

"You heard me. I doubt if it will do any good, though."

"Why wouldn't it?"

"Because he's Jewish. All the Tannenbaums are Jewish."

"So?"

" 'So?' " Bridget copied. "Jews don't believe in Jesus so why would God let them into heaven?"

Zoë had never heard of this. "How do you know the Tannenbaums are Jewish?"

"Because they are! Sam will have to convert to a Christian when we get married. If you went to church you'd know all this stuff. Even if I pray for him, Sam's grandfather will probably have to go to hell. *That's* why I was crying, if you really want to know, not just because he's dead."

"I don't believe you," Zoë said. She felt like throwing up more than ever, but she could tell now that she wasn't going to.

Bridget made a shocked face. "What! Are you serious? Don't you know that the reason a lot of professors teach at the college is because they were Jews that would have got killed in the gas chambers by Hitler if they didn't escape?"

"You mean the German Hitler?"

"What! You think there's more than one Hitler? I can't believe this! Don't you know anything about the war?"

"Which one?"

"World War Two! I really can't believe this! My father fought in it! He fought the Nazis. Have you ever heard of *them*? It's only about the most important thing in history."

"I don't care. Only idiots believe in history."

"Your father said that. He's just lying. You're always talking about how he exaggerates. I bet you a million dollars he's just not telling you. He has to know that the Steinkoenigs came over here so they wouldn't get gassed."

"He does not!"

"How do you know? Did you ever ask him?"

"He would have told me that."

"Well, he didn't."

"You don't have to be so mean."

"*You* believe in Jesus Christ, don't you?" Bridget asked, making spy-eyes. "I've never asked you."

"Yes," Zoë answered.

"Do you believe he died on the cross for our sins so we wouldn't have to go to hell?"

"Yes. What do you mean, on the cross?"

"On the cross! They pounded nails through his hands and feet and left him there for three days and he *died*."

"Who pounded nails?"

"His enemies! Although God let them. God gave his only begotten son so that whosoever believeth in him shall not perish but shall have everlasting life. I think it was very generous of him. If you don't believe it, you go to hell. It says right in the Bible that you do."

"Where? I never saw it."

"I don't know *where*. I haven't memorized the whole entire Bible."

Zoë felt like punching her, but she also felt nervous, the way she did before getting a shot. "How come you never told me before? Were you just trying to keep it a big secret?"

"How was I supposed to know you didn't know?"

"Well, I didn't."

"Is that my fault? If your parents weren't heathens you'd know yourself."

There was nothing Zoë could say. It was true. "Are all the Tannenbaums going to go to hell?"

"What do you think I've just been telling you? Yes! Unless they get converted in time."

"You don't even sound like you're sorry!"

"I am too, but what can I do about it? It's what the Bible says. It's the word of God."

"I doubt it."

"You better not doubt it."

"I'm leaving," Zoë said. "Go ahead and go to your stupid church, see if I care. I'm going home and tell Nick about their grandfather."

"Don't say I didn't warn you when you end up in the fires of hell!" Bridget shouted after her. "You aren't even baptized!"

Zoë walked normally until she turned the corner, even though she was already crying; then she ran all the way up Chesterfield Street to Metcalf; she thanked God for small favors that she didn't see anyone she knew. Nick wasn't back yet; probably he'd gone to Rexall's for a Coke after his appointment. He made her sick. Him and his Psychosomaticness. Bridget and her Insomnia. Why didn't she get to have something wrong with *her*?

There was a note on the kitchen table: "If anyone wants to know, I've gone shopping. Monica Robie Carver." Zoë stared at the note, then crumpled it up and threw it across the room, not even knowing why it made her so angry. Next she went up to the study. Seth was in his armchair by the fan, smoking his pipe, with his shirt off, reading.

"What can I do for you, young lady?" he asked.

She didn't say anything, just stood there staring at him—she hated him too—but all of a sudden he noticed and put his pipe down in the ashtray. He forced her to come to the chair and squashed her in a hug. He was all clammy. She coughed from crying.

"Zoë, for the love of Mike, what's *happened*?"

She refused to say a word until he let her go. Then she let him have it.

"Why don't you ever tell me anything? Why do you lie all the time? If it wasn't for Bridget I wouldn't know a single thing!"

"Zoë . . ."

"Why didn't you tell me about Jesus Christ getting nailed on a cross and if you don't believe it you're Jewish and go to hell? Don't you care what will happen to me? The Tannenbaums' grandfather is probably already there! Why didn't you tell me about the Nazis killing all the Jews and that's why Mr. and Mrs. Steinkoenig and the Voorheeses and the Tannenbaums all came over here because this is a free country?"

"Zoë, for Pete's sake . . ." But he was starting to laugh. He was the meanest person alive. On top of everything else, she had the hiccups.

"You knew all along, didn't you? You keep everything secret. It's not fair. I can face facts! Now I'm going to hell!" There was no point in talking to him another minute.

"Zoë, Zoë, Zoë! Come back here!" He grabbed her wrist. "What has occasioned this outpouring? Why today of all days do you wish to be informed of the more miserable chapters of human history?"

"Bridget's right, all you do is lie."

"I do not lie, Zoë. Don't ever say that again, do you hear me?"

She shrugged, and his face got even more scrunched-looking and she thought maybe he was going to send her to her room, but he just said, still sounding upset but not insane, "You must pardon me if I haven't wished to be the one to tell you the worst of which mankind is capable. Furthermore, the one thing I've tried above all others to do has been to allow you the freedom to make your own judgments, as a consequence of which I haven't wished to cram your head full of received wisdom. If I tell you what the rest of the world thinks, or even what I think, how will you be able to think for yourself?"

"But you do so tell me things, you just tell me wrong things! You said only idiots believe in history but now you just said you do."

"Well, Zoë, I expect I meant that I don't believe people learn from history. Many people think that by learning about the mistakes our predecessors have made . . ."

"Our *what*?"

"Predecessors. From the Latin, *praedecessor,—prae-*, before, and *decedere,* to . . ."

"I'm warning you," she said.

"Oh, Zoë." He was looking at her all funny. "Oh, Zoë, did anyone ever tell you that you're magnificent?"

"You have screws loose," she said. She felt bad after she said it, though. She could tell he was trying to be nice, he just didn't know how to behave. He'd never had a father to set him a good example. His father died in the Proverbial Gutter and his mother nearby. His Aunt Minerva raised him. Zoë was half named after her. He even tried to explain about Jesus Christ being crucified for everyone's sins so they would be spared eternal damnation, but she could tell he still wasn't telling her everything. Maybe he didn't know either. Because all she could think about was how could God give his own son to be nailed up in the air, and how could everyone in the world know about it but her, but then that night she dreamed she was in the refrigerator box she and Nick had made a house out of, only now the doors and windows they had cut in the sides were closed back up and she was in the bottom looking out the top, when Jesus Christ, wearing a light green shimmery robe, came to her, and he was holding a gleaming sword. He asked her, without saying any words, but she understood what he meant, if she would give herself up; he meant would she sacrifice herself to save everybody else in the world and she said yes. Afterwards it felt like sinking into the sky.

IV CASCABEL FLATS

Nick called, "Was it something we said?" and Zoë went back into the living room and curled up in the frayed striped wing chair that had been in one of the guest rooms in Harmony (the rest of the furniture that Monica hadn't sold or wanted for Metcalf Street she was keeping in storage for Nick and Zoë until they were "formally settled"); the chair was set off by itself beside the potted yucca Nick and Ellie were pretending was a Christmas tree. Shiny red, green, and blue balls and silver stars dangled from the elongated triangular branches, hooks piercing the green flesh like earrings; popcorn-and-cranberry strings were coiled among the spikes. What were they trying to prove? On the wall above the yucca hung a large unframed oil painting, semiabstract, of adobe houses. Ellie had had it back east; it was by her friend Nancy Chamberlain, Ellie's college roommate, who had grown up out here. Ellie and Nick had first visited the area when they'd flown out three years ago for Nancy's wedding.

While Zoë had been in the kitchen the discussion had shifted from high-altitude religious practices to southwestern architecture. They were all admiring the roof beams, which Ellie had instructed them to call *vigas*—they looked like varnished telephone poles. Pryce was still ensconced with Monica on the couch; Nick and Ellie were angled like outriders in the two leather armchairs that creaked whenever they moved a muscle. Pryce was his usual interested self—people took to him instantly—which made Zoë wonder why she'd invited him, especially since she had done so only after she'd heard that Rob was out. Why raise her family's hopes? Did she care more about having a child than she cared who its father was? She'd told Pryce that the gynecologist had said the endometriosis was getting worse and that if she ever wanted to get pregnant she'd better not waste any time, but Pryce wouldn't agree to a child until they'd "resolved some things"—he meant until she told him the real circumstances of "accident" and stopped "using her muteness as an excuse" not to do something with her life. Once she was pregnant she'd planned to leave him (this was before she'd heard from Rob)—she couldn't allow someone with his attitude to have any part of raising her child. She'd told him quite enough: a high school friend had been killed in an automobile crash that had left her in a coma and when she woke up she couldn't talk, which was all perfectly true in a sense—symbolically (which Rob would love, considering how he'd always detested symbols. "When is a rat not a rat? In Mr. Montgomery's class on *The Plague*.") Pryce could tell that this wasn't the whole story, however; as a criminal attorney he'd had too much practice cross-examining witnesses. She was sure that before long he'd find an opportunity to question Nick or Monica alone.

Ellie got up to turn on a light now. It wasn't dark yet, but the sun had gone down behind the blue mountains, leaving a big slash of apricot staining the sky; against it the little bare fruit trees in Nick's would-be garden looked brittle and black. Ellie, sounding like a tour guide, was explaining that though at first adobe architecture could seem monotonous, in fact there was infinitely more variation than one noticed in the beginning—the subtle differences among the earth tones of the houses, the colors chosen for the trim . . . In her opinion this was the ideal: to be able to assert one's individuality while blending in with the surroundings. In so many places the two needs—communal and personal—were at odds with one another . . .

Nick was gazing out the window; his "rattlesnake coop" lay in that direction, although down a slope and not visible from the house. In his letters he'd treated the whole thing almost as a joke—"Hey, I'm a rattlesnake farmer! What do you think of that?"—but Zoë had known the minute she got off the plane that he believed he was on to something big; one obvious clue was the way he reacted when she'd told him she hadn't been able to get in touch with Seth for over a week. "I've spent thirty years in their crossfire, Zo, and I've had it." She knew perfectly well, he said, that Dad wanted them to ruin their Christmas worrying about him—well, she could do as she saw fit, but he wasn't going to fall for it. Nick had always been cavalier about family tangles when he thought he was nearing a breakthrough. Ellie had to find it pretty ironic that no sooner did she convince him to move out West, away from his stalled doctoral research and out of family reach than he'd become obsessed with a new snakedom. From his elevated position all Zoë's concern with how Christmas by himself was affecting Seth (it was the first time he would be alone in Sparta) seemed trivial; Nick conveniently forgot that as recently as two Christmases ago when they were enduring the usual routine of traipsing back and forth in the Sparta slush between Metcalf and Courier Street, where Seth still lived in the same dingy apartment he'd rented when he'd moved out ten years ago, he (Nick) had had one of his supposedly outgrown asthma attacks and they'd been forced to sit on one of the benches in the St. Stephen's graveyard until he recovered. Ellie had been angry that he wouldn't spend Christmas with her in New Jersey—it was three weeks before their wedding—but he had told her that he couldn't abandon Zoë to the Sparta madness—Spartan madness . . . Driven mad by keeping mum. Every Christmas morning for ten years they'd woken at Metcalf Street, emptied stockings, eaten a fancy breakfast, unwrapped tree presents, trudged over to Seth's and opened more presents, stuffing themselves with coffee cake so his feelings wouldn't be hurt, returned to Monica's for roast beef and Yorkshire pudding, then gone back to Seth's for the identical meal over again later. Never once letting on to S and M where they'd come from (amazing how many years it had taken them to notice the initials' combination)—it was one thing for S & M to talk about each other if they were so inclined, but if Zoë or Nick so much as mentioned one parent to the other they felt as if they were blaspheming.

Pryce had just said that attractive as he found the plain white rooms and rounded plaster surfaces, he didn't think he could ever get used to living in a house with only one story—he thought people ought to go upstairs to sleep. Ellie pounced on this comment and exclaimed that though she'd originally had the same reaction she'd found that one could learn to experience dimension horizontally instead of vertically . . . (Whatever that meant.) Once you'd wandered through a two-hundred-year-old adobe, you felt every bit the sense of mystery you did climbing up to an attic or down to a cellar.

Monica remarked that she didn't know if experiencing mystery was one of her requirements for the house she lived in, but Ellie pressed on like some out-of-control Jehovah's Witness . . . Just wait until they saw the Beauregards' tomorrow night—their place had more atmosphere, more feeling of the past living on in the present than any place she'd ever seen. It had begun as a frontier settlement, then—as she'd mentioned earlier—in the middle of the last century served briefly as a monastery, then became the Beauregards' family seat. The first Beauregard out here had been a French priest, who supposedly got a local girl in trouble, was forced to marry her by her father, and then shot.

"Sounds like typical clerical behavior," Monica said.

Pryce gave Monica a quick look: he might not know who was on trial or for what, but he could smell tainted evidence. Meanwhile Ellie kept on about the Beauregards—their "practically mythical status in the town . . . You'd think Stewart held everyone's fate in his hands . . ." Ellie seemed obsessed by this person. She was cheery and animated as usual, yet Zoë registered some uneasiness, almost fear, on Ellie's part whenever she talked about their house's former owner. I don't know if I'd talk now even if I could, Zoë remarked to Rob, continuing the conversation she'd carried on with him ever since receiving Bridget's letter—it's amazing how much you pick up when you keep quiet.

It was irrelevant that even to think of her mouth and tongue shaping sounds into words again made her feel as if she were suffocating.

Oh, I can make sounds, she answered Rob's question. Laugh, cry, chortle, guffaw, wail, et cetera. It's just *words*.

Nick had been accusing Ellie of getting carried away by Nancy Chamberlain's gossip about Stewart—"You know how small-town sensational she is about everything," he said. "Besides, she's known him since they were kids. She may have reasons we know nothing about for painting the portrait of him she does. She makes him sound like some grasping Machiavellian character. You should be more skeptical of your sources."

Ellie shrugged. "Fine. But doesn't the same go for you? You take everything Stewart tells you at face value." She turned to the rest of them, conversational. "It was at Nancy's wedding that we first met Stewart, in fact. Nancy's father is Michael Chamberlain, the mystery writer, and he and Jules Beauregard were members of the same artsy circle. Most of them never known beyond the borders, but real celebrities locally—come out to visit in the twenties and stayed because the light was so fantastic." She looked at Nick in a friendlier way. "That was a party, wasn't it? Getting introduced to all the who's who in one fell swoop. Because we were friends of Nancy's the tabernacle doors were flung open—it was really quite amazing. If we'd tried to become acquainted with those people on our own we'd have had to serve years of novitiate."

"Does this mean you've taken final vows?" Pryce asked.

"Except at Stewart's, we haven't seen them since," Nick said. "I'm not saying they weren't friendly," he said to Ellie, "but we were all guests at a wedding. Why wouldn't they have been friendly?"

"I just meant . . ."

"Besides," he interrupted, "don't forget we'd had enough margaritas to make Charles Manson seem amiable."

"Okay, okay. All I'm trying to say is that if you don't already know someone here, it's like being a commoner trying to meet royalty. You can't get in unless you're in, if you know what I mean."

"Exactly. Which is why I think you ought to be more charitable where Stewart is concerned. He's the only one out of that whole bunch who's deigned to have anything to do with us."

" 'Deigned' is right," Ellie said. "But never mind . . ."

In answer to Pryce's earlier question—had they taken "final vows"—she didn't mean to imply that she still saw everything through rose-colored glasses, yet by and large she believed that the clichés were true—the reserved, uptight East; the open, easygoing West; out here there was no irony. It was no wonder that more people wanted to live out here than the area could support—famous actors, retired ambassadors, oil millionaires, British tax exiles, a sprinkling of White Russians . . . And, as they'd said earlier, it was the latest mecca for spiritual groupies of every persuasion. The place to come if you were looking for a cure—with a capital C, she laughed. Everything from Acupuncture to Zoomancy.

At the airport it had been irritation with Nick for refusing to worry about Seth's disappearance that had almost provoked Zoë into telling him about Rob—*that* might make him think about something besides his snakes. You don't find anything strange in the fact that a few weeks ago Robert Went was released and now our father is missing? No one would believe he meant to kill his own father so now he's going to kill mine. He's bided his time until he thought of a way to show the world that he knew exactly what he was doing, all along.

She'd thought of this simply as something to wake Nick out of his trance, but once the idea had occurred to her she couldn't get it out of her mind. Where *was* Seth? The rare times he'd travelled he'd always told her and Nick exactly where he was going and for how long, mailed them long lists of phone numbers. Ever since her "accident" their whole family had communicated with this air of suppressed emergency—a clinging to the lifeboat kind of togetherness (even if two of the four had nothing to do with each other). Before she'd left, she'd even had Pryce call Mrs. Jessup, Seth's landlady, but Mrs. Jessup had said she hadn't seen Seth since school was out five days earlier. "What does Pryce think of the family melodrama?" had been Nick's response to this information. When she'd said that he wondered why Seth and Monica didn't get divorced, Nick exclaimed, "Good heavens, why? Simply because they haven't spoken to or seen each other for ten years? This boyfriend of yours sounds pretty radical." But if she really believed that Seth could be in danger from Rob, why didn't she get someone to call the police?

Didn't anyone tell you what happened to me? she asked Rob. Even if they didn't, didn't you wonder if I was all right? Wouldn't they let you write me? I just can't believe that there wasn't some way you could have been in touch if you'd really wanted to. You ought to have known your mother wouldn't let me, of all people, know where you'd been taken.

Why wouldn't she? Are you serious? After what I said . . . Isn't it pretty obvious?

Said? Said when? All right, wrote down (she knew that wasn't the point of Rob's question); the judge read it aloud and everyone heard. I don't particularly feel like repeating it right now, if you don't mind. Besides, I can't really believe no one told you. It seems like the first thing the shrinks would have asked you about. Oh, I suppose I could have humbled myself to Bridget and asked her to try to discover your whereabouts from her mother (though at the time I couldn't be sure your mother was talking to anyone in Sparta), but that would have meant first humbling myself to Mrs. Wycliffe since Bridget had already run away to Oregon and I didn't know how to get hold of her. I just couldn't face it. There was no guarantee that, even if I had been able to, Bridget would have been willing to help me.

How did it actually happen? You mean, when did I . . . Well, Mr. Montgomery was going on with his theories—another of your "dares to the world," he called it—it was right after the assembly Mr. Curley called to announce that your father was dead and that you might be charged; Mr. Montgomery had made me walk down to the river with him. I started to tell him about Mr. Ogilvy and the photographs, about Charlotte—I never would have, except that he made me so angry, the way he talked as if he were the final authority on you and your motives when he didn't know *anything*, but as soon as I tried to talk I started choking. Then I blacked out. Simple. But what about you? What have you been *doing* in there for ten years? Did you make friends? Have love affairs? Take correspondence courses?

But she was being flip now—there was only so long you could go on without a response.

The other conversation in the room had not flagged, however. Life really was different out here, Ellie was proselytizing—you felt like you were *living* your life, instead of waiting to live it; you didn't realize you'd *been* waiting until you stopped. (Zoë couldn't imagine it.) It was hard to say what was responsible for the feeling—the climate? the space? Maybe simply looking off and seeing mountains on every horizon kept things in perspective. All she knew was that life made more sense, out here (*out here,* the phrase that kept tolling through Ellie's sentences like a summons to her "nondenominational" service). Nowhere else she'd ever been in the country even compared, although she'd be the first to admit the down side: the skyrocketing cost of real estate, the shrinking water supply, uranium ticking away all over the landscape where the government had forgotten they'd buried it—the most spiritual place in the nation and it was here that the most destructive power on earth had been invented . . .

"And you say there's no irony?" Pryce asked.

"Well . . ." Ellie laughed. She'd meant in the way people talked. They could really be themselves. Everywhere else everyone was so alienated that if they didn't continually joke about everything they'd probably commit mass suicide. Of course they—we—were anyway. If there was a chance left to reestablish the proper values this would be the place it could happen, she was convinced.

"You'll see what you think tomorrow night, when you meet the natives," she finished. "Nick may be right—that I've lost all objectivity. The Chamberlains will be there—all the old diehards. They may not be overfond of Stewart, but they come to worship at the altar of Jules's memory. Rumor has it that Stewart keeps paintings by his father locked up in the hacienda."

"Locked up?" Pryce prompted.

"Jules willed all his work to the local museum, but there's suspicion that part of it disappeared at the time of his death. From rattlesnake bite, by the way." Ellie glanced at Nick. "No one's *seen* them, but friends believe he had substantially more paintings than were discovered here in the studio. It's only recently that the museum has been making an effort to get their hands on them."

"From rattlesnake bite?" Monica repeated.

"I wondered when you were going to pick up on that," Nick said.

"Jules kept rattlesnakes here in the studio. Michael . . ."

"Here?" Monica exclaimed. She peered around as if snakes might come slithering out from under the furniture.

"Michael Chamberlain claims to have come over here once in the middle of the day to find Jules asleep with three or four rattlers curled up next to him like cats, though I'm not sure how far I'd trust any account of Michael's."

"I was going to say," Nick said. "Whatever makes a good story."

"Jules claimed that he'd built up an immunity to the venom, though evidently not enough."

Monica grimaced.

"My impression is that Jules Beauregard was one of those types you often find in any group of artists—cherished by his buddies for his eccentricities, his dearth of talent overlooked. Michael owns some of his work—it's nothing to write home about. Garish desert landscapes, but nevertheless the museum has finally decided to go after the rest of them. Anything western is at a premium these days."

"He willed them to the museum but his son won't let it have them?" Pryce asked. "Have they never heard of filing an injunction?"

"I really don't think we know the whole story," Nick said to Ellie. "Neither of us has heard anything from Stewart directly."

"Nick admires Stewart," Ellie said, "in case you haven't gathered. He thinks of him as the last cowboy—that old wild West, take-the-law-into-your-own-hands spirit, an endangered species."

For a moment she looked very tired. Nick said tolerantly, "What does it matter why Stewart was generous to us? He was. For me that's enough."

"And for me it isn't," Ellie said. "Tell them what he said when he drove you out to look at the place!"

Nick looked puzzled.

"He asked Nick if we were happily married . . ."

"Yes, that's true." Nick laughed. "I remember now."

"He hardly knew Nick. Then when Nick said yes . . ."

"I said, 'Yes, so far.' "

"He said, 'Good,' as if it fit in with his plans. You're the one who said that."

"I don't think I said 'as if it fit in with his plans,' Ellie."

"Something like that."

"What's the difference? He was selling to future neighbors."

"And he wanted to make sure our marriage was stable?"

"Did it ever occur to you that Stewart might have just *liked* me?" Nick asked. "Wanted to give me a leg up? He's not a snake in the grass!"

"Good God, Nick, what an expression to choose!"

"Somehow I don't think I want to hear this," Monica said.

"Should we tell them?" Ellie asked Nick.

"How can you not, now . . ." He sounded fed up, but Zoë suddenly found herself sympathizing with Ellie. If Nick was pulling the same attitude about Stewart Beauregard as he was about Dad . . . *I'm far too preoccupied by my highly important research to waste time on such mundane matters* . . . Well, time would tell. Meanwhile Ellie had asked if Zoë and Monica remembered her and Nick's old dog Aladdin—the dog *she'd* had since she was a teenager. She glanced back and forth between them.

Zoë nodded. Monica looked at Ellie apprehensively.

"You remember then that we had to have him put to sleep this past summer. Obviously Nick didn't tell you why."

"The dog was fourteen years old, Ellie," Nick said.

"It was February when we closed on the house," she went on, ignoring him. "We had invited Stewart and Judith out to celebrate at La Huerta, a fancy restaurant in town. Then, at one point, as if he'd just thought of it . . ."

"That's not impossible, if I may be allowed to point out."

" 'Hope you're fond of rattlers,' he said. 'Why?' we asked. 'What do you mean?' 'Your house is in the heart of rattlesnake country—Cascabel Flats.' Cascabel is Spanish for rattlesnake," Ellie explained. " 'Now you tell us,' we said. Though at the time I really thought he was pulling our leg."

"But he wasn't," Pryce stated.

"It was one afternoon in mid-April. We'd moved in early in March, so of course there wasn't a snake to be seen, and I had completely forgotten Stewart's remark. I was busy in the kitchen and Aladdin had gone outside as usual. He liked to lie on the flagstones—even in cold weather they warm up in the sun. But he must have gotten too hot because he went . . . There's a kind of crawl space under the house. I saw him through the kitchen window disappear under there. I remember wondering whether it was a good idea, if he might not have trouble getting out—he was pretty arthritic by then—when I heard this incredible howl. It sounded like a person screaming, though I've never heard screaming like that, and it just went on and on. I raced outside and around the house, screaming myself. Nick wasn't home. By the time I got there Aladdin had managed to crawl back out and was hopping around frantically, as if he were trying to shake something off, although there was nothing on him. He wouldn't let me near him, and I didn't know what to do—I was sobbing with frustration at that point as much as with fear. I got as close to the crawl space as I could without going in, but I had no idea what was down there. It was too dark to see. At the time I didn't even think of snakes—I thought of wasps, actually. Aladdin looked as if he were trying to shake wasps off himself."

She paused. No one moved.

"I just didn't know what to do," she said. "Nick had taken the car—it was before we bought the Datsun—and I had no idea how to reach him. I couldn't even think. It's the only time in my life I can remember feeling truly hysterical. I couldn't stop crying, and I couldn't catch Aladdin, who kept whining and tearing around in circles. I don't know what would have happened if the phone hadn't rung. I ran inside and grabbed it and yelled 'Nick!' into it. 'Ellie?' Judith Beauregard asks. I'm sobbing into the phone. 'Ellie, what's the matter? Are you all right? What's wrong?' Finally she says, 'I'm coming right over. Don't go anywhere—I'll be right there.' 'I *can't* go anywhere!' I scream at her, but she'd already hung up. She was here faster than a fairy godmother—she'd taken Stewart's truck and driven right up the arroyo. I've never been so glad to see anyone in my life.

" 'Get a blanket,' she told me. I just followed orders. She talked to Aladdin while I was in the house. Then she threw the blanket over him and we grabbed hold while he was still trying to get out from under it. As soon as we touched him he calmed down. He was shaking still, but we had no trouble carrying him to the jeep. You remember how big he was, but I held that dog on my lap the whole way into town. I took the blanket off so I could examine him and he began licking my hands frantically. One of his hind legs was beginning to swell up like a balloon and Judith took one look at it and said, 'Rattlesnake.' 'You can't be serious,' I said. 'Why not?' she asked. She said it was near time for them to wake up. I still didn't remember what Stewart had said, though. We finally got to the vet's and he had no doubt that it was snakebite. He gave Aladdin a shot of antivenin and antibiotics, and then kept him there for nearly a week—he had to operate on him for secondary infection. But finally we brought him home. The vet said he'd probably limp for the rest of his life but otherwise he'd be all right."

Again everyone waited. Finally Pryce gave in. "But he wasn't?"

"Physically, he was okay. He did limp, but other than that he recovered with no trouble. The snakes were still sluggish and he'd been lucky—only one had bitten through his thick coat. What he didn't recover from was the scare it gave him. It drove him crazy, literally."

"Oh, the poor creature." Monica looked accusingly at Nick.

"What exactly happened to him?" Pryce asked.

"He was afraid to go outside, for one thing. When we'd force him, he'd whimper and whine and scratch at the door until we let him in again. It wasn't only not going outside. He'd balk at shadows. Or he'd suddenly think he saw something under a table and bark at it. He had nightmares, too. Nearly every night he'd howl in his sleep. We'd have to bring him into our bed like a baby. It's sure as hell no way to spend your old age."

"The poor old fella," Nick said.

Ellie gave Nick an uninterpretable look.

"And the snakes?" Monica asked. She sounded the way she had when they were children and she'd insisted they confess every detail of a misdeed.

"Stewart was over here first thing the next morning—I have to say he *acted* very contrite. Maybe he hadn't thought it would be the dog who'd get hurt. He had a high-beam flashlight and took one look under the house and started to laugh. 'You're operating a winter resort down there,' he said. Those were his exact words. We looked. There were only twenty or thirty in the actual crawl space at that point . . ."

"Twenty or thirty! Dear God in heaven."

"But you could see where they were crawling from. It was a den—that means there can be anywhere from fifty to three hundred rattlers."

Monica moaned in a strangled way. Pryce whistled.

Ellie now sounded very chipper. "We really had only two options. Either we could kill them under there, using some kind of poisonous gas like cyanide, in which case we'd probably have to vacate the house ourselves for who knows how long and still be left with the delightful task of excavating wheelbarrows full of dead snakes. Or we could set up an exit trap and get rid of them later."

"Quite a choice," Pryce said.

"I would have left town," Monica said.

"That's what everyone says. Foolishly or not, we decided not to be daunted. If I'd known how it would hit Aladdin, I'd have insisted Stewart refund our money but right then I had no reason to think Aladdin wasn't going to be fine. So while Stewart went off to see a fellow he knew who had some snake traps, we mixed mud and began sealing up the entrance to the crawl space except for a couple of small openings. When he came back, we fitted the traps into them. Just in time, as it turned out. They began their exodus the next day."

Pryce whistled again. "And you farmed them. I take my hat off to you. If this individual was in fact playing some kind of sick joke on you, I'd say you certainly laid down the trump."

"There's no question in my mind but that he knew," Ellie said. "As a kid he'd watched the snakes leave. His father had the studio built over the ledge on purpose."

"On *purpose*?" Monica repeated. "What kind of a demented family is this?"

"Stewart *said* he'd thought they'd stopped hibernating here, but he hadn't checked for several years. He claimed he'd been going to take a look before we moved in, but it had slipped his mind."

"But of course you know better," Nick said.

"When it 'slips your mind' that you've sold your friends a house built over a viper pit, well, either they're not your friends or . . ."

"Or what?"

When Ellie didn't answer, Nick said, "You didn't see how devastated Stewart was when I told him we'd had to have Aladdin put to sleep.

Besides, it's important to remember that Stewart grew up around here. Rattlesnakes aren't the horrifying creatures to him that they are to us. To some of us, I should say." He laughed a kind of private laugh. "One of these days they'll get the respect they deserve. If I have anything to say about it, that is."

V HARMONY

On a hot afternoon in July of 1910, Adam Robie, eighteen years old, home for the summer after his first year at Dartmouth College, is sitting on the widow's walk of his family mansion. Except when it rains, he spends a large portion of his day up there, reading, inventing pithy epithets for letters he never has the energy to write, gazing through his grandfather's spyglass at the town—no one would now dare to scold him for taking it out of the library.

Adam's father, Henry, dead ten years, lies with the other dead Robies in the churchyard across the road. This summer it had annoyed Adam, as he told Charlotte subsequently, that he could not see his father's grave from the widow's walk, and, one day, when his mother had gone to Hanover to shop, he ordered the gardener to cut down the tall maple blocking the view. When Louisa demanded to know how he dared take it upon himself to do such a thing, he replied that, lest she forget, he would soon be master of the property. He reported this conversation to Charlotte, anticipating her approval. Furthermore, he added, he thought his mother's anger most . . . unseemly. When had she last visited his father's grave? Did her lapse of respect perchance coincide with the fact that she was being openly courted by that penniless sycophant, the late Judge Augustus Lowndes's ineffectual son Timothy? She, faithful to his father's memory? Pious hogwash! But Charlotte hadn't shared Adam's scorn for Louisa—she'd told Zoë she'd felt sorry for Adam's mother.

Lifting the spyglass, Adam makes out the stone spire of the Robie plot's imposing monument. Small tablets, a foot high, mark the heads of the individual graves. His father lies beside his older brother, Adam's uncle Samuel, drowned in a boating accident on the Connecticut at the age of fifteen. On his father's other side, a space is reserved for his mother. The stone is even now stored in the barn: LOUISA ROBIE, BELOVED WIFE OF HENRY, BORN 1868, DIED 19   . What if she should marry again? Then what would the stone say? Or would she be buried beside her second husband? Adam cannot help but think how much simpler it would be if his mother were dead already.

In the heat of July 1910, Adam Robie attempts to contemplate his future. He's wasted half the summer in this lethargic fashion and wonders what is to prevent him from continuing like this for the rest of his life. He does not require to be informed of the exact amount of his fortune to know that earning a livelihood is, for him, not a necessity. And he can summon no interest in any of the professions: medicine, law, government, scholarship . . . Their purposes strike him as ephemeral. What does not? What can be worth caring about for a lifetime? Eventually he will oversee the Robie shipping empire, but the truth is that it runs smoothly enough without him. He might travel, he supposes, though at the moment even that seems to demand too much effort.

A figure crossing into the circle of his sight interrupts his reverie. A young woman, carrying flowers. She is progressing along the sidewalk as lazily as his thought, and he pursues her with the telescope. Who in her right mind would choose such an oppressively hot afternoon to visit a grave? When she reaches the gate of the churchyard, she deliberates a moment, then swings it open and goes in.

Who is she? Adam wonders, though he realizes that, even if he were standing next to her, the likelihood of his being able to identify her would be slight. After Henry died, Louisa sent Adam to boarding school in Marleybone, Massachusetts; summers they spent at the seashore. This is the first extended period he's passed at home in ten years.

The visitor, having traversed the churchyard, kneels now in a far corner beside, Adam is startled to see, a new grave. No speck of grass has yet sprouted from the dark earth. How peculiar that he has not noticed it! And how much more so that his mother should not have mentioned a recent death. Harmony's population is small, and that someone should have died and he not heard of it strikes Adam as sinister. He tries to recall what family is buried in that out-of-the-way corner. His mind stretches unwillingly, not able to wake up.

The young woman prays now, and Adam feels ashamed to observe her, yet does not lower the glass. Who is she? He is distracted when, after kneeling for only a moment, she rises abruptly and strides back through the churchyard. When she regains the sidewalk, however, instead of returning in the direction whence she came, she walks the other way; at the corner of the churchyard wall she turns into the field bordering it and follows the wall until she stands opposite where she knelt before. Then she kneels again.

At once Adam knows. Marian Howe, the witch who was drowned in the 1700's, lies buried there. The graves inside the wall belong to her relatives and descendants. The fresh grave can only be Ida Howe's—she was the last of her generation. The young woman kneeling, then, must be her daughter, Charlotte.

But when did Ida and Charlotte return to Harmony? Adam has never forgotten Charlotte, and always wondered why she and her mother left town—it was not long after his father came home to die. Louisa must have known they returned and not told him. Yet why would she have kept it a secret?

But Adam does not stay to contemplate these mysteries. More animated than he's felt in months—in years—he springs to his feet and dashes down through the house and out the front door. He has run halfway across the long sloping lawn that intervenes between his house and the street before he notices that he still holds the spyglass in his hand. What a nuisance—Charlotte will guess that he was spying upon her. Well, he will apologize. If he takes the time to return the telescope to the house, he will lose her. Sprinting across the street, he pauses, out of breath, at the churchyard wall. There is no one in sight.

During the short time it has taken him to descend from the widow's walk, Charlotte has vanished. Yet how is that possible? The church lies at some distance from the shops, and the buildings between are private dwellings; can she be paying someone a visit? In the other direction a hayfield stretches to the woods.

Feeling as if a trick is being played on him, Adam wanders along the wall until he comes to the spot where Marian Howe is buried. He gazes over the wall at the wildflowers Charlotte has laid on the dark earth—black-eyed Susans, chicory, and Queen Anne's lace—and suddenly he is sad, thinking of Charlotte gathering flowers in a field for her dead mother. He thinks of how he liked her, that afternoon, over ten years ago now, when he commanded her to fly. Smiling to himself, he glances upward through the canopy of leaves at the sky; in the mottled sunlight the rest of the world with its requirements seems very far away.

Dreamily he walks on to the end of the wall, where the mowed lawn stops and the tall grass begins. Then he starts. The grass is beaten down. Someone—Charlotte!—has traversed the field; a parting is faintly visible, as if a huge serpent lies concealed, and again he breaks into a run, slowing as he nears the woods. When he sees the track and remembers that it leads to the bluff overlooking the river, he quickens his pace again. In the midst of his apprehension, he wonders what people are going to say.

Everyone will learn that it was he who goaded Charlotte into trying to fly—they will never believe that she tried to take flight on her own. That ten years and more have passed between his bidding and her compliance is of no importance. Cause and effect are plain in this timeless country into which he has wandered, where one can imagine something so vividly that it becomes true. When he reaches the bluff and does not see Charlotte, he is confirmed in his presentiment that she has leapt to her death, and he stands entranced by his certainty of this, alone on the promontory; below is the river; across it, the hills and meadows of Vermont. It is deep summer and only a kind of pervasive afternoon hum, like the sound of the heat itself, can be heard. Haze hangs over everything. All the activity of the present is taking place somewhere else.

Then, faintly, comes a cry. A moan, but as if dissipated by the heat and haze. It comes from below.

No, Adam says, though his voice makes no sound. He does not want to see her, crumpled on the ground, her limbs arrayed in horrible angles. Doesn't she know he didn't mean it? He was only a child—he can't be held responsible.

The sound rises again, broken into syllables; it might be his name. Suddenly he is suspicious. Has she lured him here somehow? What possessed him, after all, to bolt like a madman in pursuit of someone he has not seen since the age of six? He, who in every regard is so circumspect, who never acts without deliberation—of what was he thinking?

Wincing, he steps to the brink and looks down. Then he groans in relief. Charlotte is there, all right, but not in devastation as he was anticipating. Instead she's pacing wildly up and down a small shelf of beach, twisting her hands together, calling out words he cannot distinguish, clutching at the neck of her dress as if she is suffocating. How the devil did she get down there?

It is a sheer drop of several hundred feet; he supposes she might have attached a rope to a tree and let herself down that way, but, if so, the rope would remain. No, there has to be a path, that's the only explanation, yet it confounds Adam. He played along this section of the river as a child, and does not see how there could be a path down from the bluff without his knowledge.

While he stands pondering this, Charlotte disappears under the overhang of the cliff. He tries to recall if there's a cave there—perhaps a cave with another entrance up the bluff? He curses his mother—if she had not banished him from Harmony, he would *know* how Charlotte descended to where she is, and he would know what to do, which he does not. Should he scout for the path of descent? Should he call down to her?

The future is sickeningly close, all of it, all the years still to come, condensed into one suffocating weight, crushing his life out into one, only one choice. He was fooling himself, as, standing by the churchyard wall, he gazed up through the placid leaves, to think he could escape it. For this is no leisurely contemplation of possibilities; this is the real future, the next unforeseen moment, the cornerstone of ever after, which he has to position or cease to breathe under its weight. He wants to protest: he has been tricked; he isn't prepared for this; no one warned him; no one taught him what to do . . .

Then Charlotte reappears, and he gasps, horrified, for she has removed her blouse and stands unclothed from the waist up. At the same time, it no longer seems possible to him that she does not know he is there; her nakedness is too deliberate. Only once before has he seen a woman's body, and that occasion, too, was in her company; he has cherished the vision for years, bringing it forth to contemplate at secret moments, to embellish as he acquired facts to replace conjecture, and, for years, he understands now, he has been waiting to watch that scene again; ten years he has been alive waiting for this, exactly this. As she *knows*—witch that she is—as all her white skin, more than he can look at in a lifetime, confirms for him. But how can this be Charlotte?

At one now with his thought, she strides to the edge of the thumbnail of beach and examines the bushes and stunted trees that grow there. Then she snaps off a bough and twists and tears at it until the bark frays and the branch comes free. Returning to the water's edge, where small waves climb repetitively up the pebbles, she falls to her knees.

Adam, all compunction vanished, throws himself down so that he can just see over the edge of the cliff. He remembers the telescope, and congratulates himself now on the foresight he had not known he was exercising in bringing it. When he looks through it, Charlotte is near enough to touch. There is a mole on her left shoulder and he can make out the fine hair that drifts across her neck. He wishes she would turn so that he might see her breasts. He watches desirously, not suspecting what she is about to do.

Lifting the branch, Charlotte begins to strike herself, snapping it over first one shoulder and then the other. Adam winces and cries out, as if he too has been struck. He draws back quickly. Why? he whispers. Why do you do this? I did not ask you to. But when he dares to peer over the edge again, and sees that she has not heard his cry, he breathes out in relief. Through the telescope he can see that the branch she has picked is hawthorn; he can see its long spikes. Simultaneously he becomes aware of the smell of the sun-warmed grass and dirt, the gentle lapping of the water below. With one hand he grasps the telescope; with his other he digs into a clump of grass and clutches it, imagining that it's her hair.

Charlotte, he whispers, please stop.

Bright pinpricks of blood fleck her white back as she continues to lash herself methodically. With each stroke Adam groans, moving against the ground, bearing into it, no longer attempting to quell his mounting excitement. His blood pounds in his ears as, watching her, he pushes against the ground. It is a kind of love he makes, he thinks; it must be. She has to be mad, he pleads silently. Her mother's death has crazed her. It can be no crime to watch her if she is mad.

He does not know how much time passes. When at last she collapses upon the sand, he too collapses, spent, and for the first time hears his own labored breathing and tries to stifle it. He does not wait to see her rise, but gropes to his feet as if it were thick dark and blindly begins to run, back through the woods, along the churchyard wall, across the road, and up the scrupulously kept lawn of his house. What if someone should see him? What if his mother or one of the servants should accost him and demand an account of his dishevelment, his wild behavior? But no one is about; the shadowy hallway remains mercifully deserted as he stumbles up the stairs to his room. Bolting the door, he throws himself face down on his bed and weeps.

Meanwhile Charlotte also lies, sobbing quietly, listening to the river laboring at its bank. It persists, soft and patient, like an animal bewildered by the expression of human grief trying to attract attention to itself. She does not want it to, but it soothes her.

If most people on earth could have one wish, she knows that it would be to know the future. Yet how can anyone want this? Do they not realize that to know what is to come means that one lives, always, in the past? For she has seen her future, its unending shore, and after that living has meant nothing more than waiting for what has already taken place to be over.

Late in July after his freshman year at Dartmouth College, Adam Robie suddenly left Harmony and ran away to sea.

VI SPARTA

Robert Went showed up at school one day in the middle of the year when Zoë was in fourth grade. Bridget was in fifth. He started out in fourth, stayed a week, and advanced. Now we've got him in *our* class, Bridget said, as if it was the fourth grade's fault. He refused to explain why he'd come when he had. "Mum's the word," he said. "Pop goes the weasel."

Who cares? responded nearly everyone. Here comes Robert, they warned, as he charged across the playground towards them. He was fat in an unbouncy, grown-up way, and had shiny black hair that kept falling into his eyes, making him constantly snap his head sideways in order to see. If you didn't get out of his way he'd lower his head and butt you; teachers tried to tell everyone he was a lonely misfit and this was how he tried to be friendly, but kids saw through this. They knew he was sincere in everything he did.

Robert was the type of kid who, on highways, would kneel backwards in the back seat and try to drive the driver in the following car crazy. He'd just stare at him without blinking—he claimed he could not blink longer than anyone in the whole school—and there was nothing the driver could do. He might try to look as if he could care less, but Robert would know he was faking. Then, when the driver was at the height of his nervousness, Robert would stretch out his mouth into an enormous fake smile. He said he'd almost caused several fatal accidents.

Zoë and Bridget hated Robert's guts. They hated him the way everybody else did, for being the worst kid they had ever met, but they also hated him because he kept saying that the only reason they were best friends was because both their fathers were college professors. "It's so obvious you could kill a mouse with it," he said. He used a lot of expressions like that that no one had ever heard before, but that he insisted were very common. He was born knowing everything, he said, and unless some new things were invented in a hurry, he was going to shrivel up and die from boredom. "We wish you would shrivel up," Bridget said. It was hard to get used to the fact that he actually existed.

On weekends Robert liked to ride the bus out to the new shopping mall on the northern highway—he said it was a perfect place because it was too big for you to get a reputation. He'd ask to speak to the managers of stores and tell them he had seen someone stealing something. Sometimes they'd actually search the person. Once, when he was there with his parents, he managed to convince some people that he'd been kidnapped and asked them to help him escape. When Mr. and Mrs. Went came to get him to go home, the people wouldn't let Robert go. In the end they all had to go down to the police station, and Mr. Went had to go home and get Robert's birth certificate and Mrs. Went had to call their family doctor and some friends, including Bridget's mother (which was how Zoë and Bridget knew that Robert wasn't making it up—and also how they found out that Robert's father was a new professor at the college and that Robert had been kicked out of public school so that only Hollister Day was left) to come and swear that Robert was really their son. After the police believed it, the grownups really let Robert have it. They called him a "devious little monster" and a "miniature Machiavelli" who was "well on the road to juvenile delinquency" until finally he had to pretend to be hysterical to get them to calm down. (He said.) Later he heard his parents whispering about sending him to Dr. Macmillan, but that was no big deal to him. By now the whole world knew that all Dr. Macmillan did was play Monopoly with you. He got upset if you got all the railroads.

Although while Robert had been telling the story Bridget had acted sort of approving, she said afterwards that she despised him more than ever. In fact, she despised him so much it made life worth living. They decided to drive Robert insane, and they thought up the plan of constantly expressing sympathy for him, although they wouldn't tell him why they were, as if they'd secretly learned he was dying.

"Poor Robert, how *are* you feeling today?" they'd ask him. "Has a terrible weakness come over you yet?"

Then they picked a different part of his body each day and asked him about it, hoping to get the power of suggestion to work on him.

"How's your stomach today, Robert?" they'd ask.

But he'd just answer, "Mind your own stomach," and laugh like a hyena at his wittiness. Or else he'd ask them questions back: "How's your pancreas?" "How's your small intestine?" "How's your great-great-aunt-eight-hundred-times-removed-on-your-mother's-side's gall bladder?"

Their plan was a flop and so they went back to ignoring him, although they did keep him as the victim in their private religion, which they'd thought up because in Christianity there wasn't any way to get revenge on people; Bridget even admitted it. She said religion was too soft nowadays because they didn't torture people for not believing in God anymore and what was the point of being religious if there wasn't anything strict about it? Zoë agreed completely, and they thought up a lot of penances, like being nice to Kitty Angstrom at recess or stepping on worms with your bare feet. To get back at Robert, they made a Robert Went doll, stuck it all over with straight pins and then tried to drown it in the toilet, reciting the witches' speech from *Macbeth* while it whirled around and around but wouldn't flush—"Double double, toil and trouble, fire burn and cauldron bubble . . ."

It was a couple of weeks after this that Robert was hit by a moving van on Derby Street on his way home from where the school bus let him off. The driver said the boy walked right out in front of him, holding his hand up like a policeman. "There was no way on God's green earth I could stop," he said in the newspaper. He dragged Robert out from under and then ran with him in his arms seven blocks to St. Luke's Hospital. "It's a miracle it happened so close by!" all the grownups said. They also said it was a miracle the moving-van man was from Sparta so that he knew right where the hospital was. But what was such a miracle about that? The real miracle was how anyone could carry Robert so far.

The man was crying when he ran into the Emergency Room. In the paper he said he would bear the burden of guilt with him forever. Every grownup thanked their lucky stars they weren't in his shoes. "That's the worst street in Sparta," Zoë heard her mother say to Mrs. Wycliffe on the phone. "Every day I walk in the door after driving down that blasted street is a day I haven't hit a pedestrian." It was hard to tell what that was supposed to mean. Every day was also a day she didn't eat worms or stab someone—what did she mean? Anyone who knew Robert knew perfectly well that he'd done just what the driver said he had.

Robert had to stay in the hospital for almost two months. The whole fifth grade, and the fourth grade as well, even though he'd only been in it for a week, sent him Get Well cards. Once he was out of danger, Mr. and Mrs. Went came to school to get his books and find out where his class was up to in all his subjects—it seemed strange that they both had to come. After that the fifth grade took turns going to the hospital and giving Robert the assignments and picking up the homework he'd done. Then they reported back to each other on his behavior, as if he were an animal they were studying in science class. What did he do? What did he say? Did he show you his leg?

One of Robert's legs had been so completely crushed by the huge tires of the moving van that the doctors couldn't fix it and had to amputate. He had to have more than ten operations on the other leg. In a while he would have an artificial limb but for now he was in a wheelchair. He would show anyone the stump, which was still all bandaged up, and say, "Oopsy daisy," or "Easy come, easy go"—which wasn't at all like the things he used to say.

He even wrote the moving-van man a letter, and the man called Robert's parents and read them the letter over the phone. They copied it down word for word so they could read it to everyone else. "Don't blame yourself," it said. "You were just a pawn in the hands of your truck."

But that was only in the first few weeks after the accident, when Robert was still in shock. When it wore off, he stopped being so forgiving, although it was never the moving-van man he got mad at but the doctors. He knew they had amputated his leg, but he hadn't realized at first that they had thrown it away. He started having nightmares in which his cut-off leg was running away from him down a tunnel. "It was *my* leg!" he yelled at the doctors, lying helpless on his back, because they'd had to break his other leg again and put it in traction. "Did you just *throw it away*?"

"What would you do with it?" the doctors asked him. "You couldn't use it for anything."

"What business is that of yours? I could have looked at it. I could have preserved it! How do you know somebody didn't steal it and dissect it? How do you even know some *dog* didn't get it?"

When they told him, attempting to comfort him, that his leg had been burned in the hospital incinerator, he burst into such a rage that they had to hold him down and give him a shot to suppress him.

"That was my leg!" he kept yelling. "I've had it all my life!"

The next thing he knew, in rushed Dr. Macmillan with his Monopoly board, but Robert shouted to his face that if anyone so much as mentioned the words "Marvin Gardens" in his presence he would scream so loud they'd have to amputate his mouth too.

Poor Robert. Between his parents announcing everything from the rooftops and other parents gossiping and the whole fifth grade visiting, practically everything he did, said, and thought was public knowledge. This was really what made Zoë and Bridget feel sorry for him. Of course it was strange that they had put curses on him and then he had had his leg ruined, but they didn't feel *responsible*. He was still the one who had walked in front of the truck. If they'd caused his accident, he would have drowned.

Eventually, because Bridget lived closer to St. Luke's than anyone else in their class, she started taking his homework most of the time. Zoë went with her, because Bridget didn't want to be alone with Robert, even though now he was as quiet as a lamb, and also because it was the first chance she'd ever had to go inside the hospital. It wasn't very exciting, though; the only time they heard somebody screaming Robert told them it was just a kid named Clark having a tantrum, not somebody in the throes of agony.

Every time they went, Robert was always sitting in his wheelchair in the playroom of the children's ward, never doing anything. His homework was ready on a table beside him. He said hello in a faraway way and offered them candy. He had tons of it. However, he had no interest in food anymore, and was getting skinnier by the minute. "Take a seat," he said, like a grownup. He wanted them to tell him things that had happened at school. Whenever they mentioned other students, Robert said, "He's a good chap" or "She's a fine lassie." Zoë and Bridget almost choked to death from not laughing. Later they found out that he was drugged up a lot, but then they thought he'd just gotten nicer, sort of with his head in the clouds, like Professor Steinkoenig. It was as if in the fat, mean Robert Went, there had been a thin, friendly Robert Went waiting to get out.

Suddenly, one Monday, Robert came limping into school, using a crutch as well as his new plastic leg, which he couldn't walk on yet. Everybody stopped talking, but a teacher on the playground began to clap, and then everybody else clapped too. Robert Went, the new, skinny, one-legged Robert Went, *crippled for life,* turned as red as licorice and said, "What's the big deal? I just got hit by a truck." He acted nervous, though, and when he saw Zoë and Bridget he hobbled over and shook hands with them and said, "I want to thank you for all your assistance. I will never forget it."

"It's okay," they said. Everybody was staring at them, trying to figure out if they were friends with Robert now. At lunch Bridget said, "I hope he doesn't think things will be the same now that he's out of the hospital." From then on, they tried to talk to him as little as possible.

Not very long before Robert had had his accident, Zoë and Bridget had, as another part of their private religion, founded the Pipe School, a Reform School for Wayward Children. All the punishments were administered to the pupils as they went through pipes. They might be rolled in honey and forced to go through a pipe full of ants, for example. There were also the snake pipe, the razor blade pipe, the tarantula pipe, the rat pipe, and so on. However, the pupils were never repentant when they came out, and had to be punished all over again. The two of them took turns keeping the notebook where they recorded which girl got which punishment.

One day the worst thing in the world happened. Robert had joined their carpool after he came back to school, and one afternoon, when Mrs. Went was driving, Bridget forgot the notebook in the car. It so happened that that day at lunch they'd also just written a letter to Mr. Kefauver, the math and science teacher, asking him to roast them in the oven and eat them for dinner with ketchup and mustard, and it was in the notebook too. It was signed "Your evil slaves," as usual.

Bridget realized as soon as she got out of the car that she'd forgotten the notebook, but by then the car was halfway down Van Dyke Street. They ran after it until they nearly dropped dead. When they realized they couldn't catch up they set off immediately and walked all the way to Robert's house, which they'd never been to except with the carpool, and it took forever. They were way too late. Robert was sitting out on his front porch swing with the notebook in his lap.

"I already read it," he said, when he saw them. He didn't act surprised that they were there. "I know everything that's in it. Are you guys sick in the head or what?"

"That's private property," Bridget said, marching up to him and trying to grab the notebook, but Robert slid it under himself and sat on it. "Hand it over."

"You're lucky my mother didn't see it. You'd be in big trouble. I might still show it to her."

"You'd better not," Bridget said.

"It's none of your business," Zoë added. She was only on the steps.

"Which one of you is the ringleader, anyway?" Robert asked. "I might have more mercy on the follower than the leader."

"We're both ringleaders, snailbrain," Bridget said. "If you do anything, you'll regret it."

"Help, save me, I'm really terrified."

"Who do you think is responsible for making you lose your leg?" Bridget asked, narrowing her eyes. "You want something worse to happen next time?"

Zoë couldn't believe she'd said that, but Robert just said, "Now I have proof you're insane. If you don't tell me why you're writing all that stuff I swear I'll tell your parents. You'll be playing Monopoly with Dr. Macmillan for the rest of your life."

"Do you think we even care?" Bridget said. She acted totally calm. "There's nothing wrong with anything we wrote. You're the one that's insane."

"Is that so? What about that letter to Mr. Kefauver? I'll tell everyone in the whole school about it."

"Who cares?" Bridget said. "Our pupils wrote the letter. We make them as one of their punishments."

Zoë thought that was the most brilliant quick thinking she'd ever heard.

"Punishments for what?" Robert asked, scowling.

"Who knows. For whatever they did that got them sent to reform school. It's called the Pipe School because they all get punished through pipes."

"Why?"

"Because that way they can't escape, obviously."

Robert looked back and forth between them suspiciously. "Do they ever get sent back? I mean, once they get out, do they ever relapse?"

"So far no one's gotten out. But we've only been running the school for a few months."

Zoë could tell from Bridget's voice that she was about to start laughing, and she felt a laugh in her own stomach and tried to think of something tragic in order to control it.

"It seems like you need firmer measures," Robert said finally. "People will think the school is a failure if no one is ever reformed."

Zoë didn't dare look at Bridget.

"Are you the only teachers?"

"We're the headmistresses. We're both equally in charge."

"How about making me another teacher? A headmaster, I mean? I think you could use someone else."

"I don't know," Bridget said. "We'd have to have a board meeting."

"How long would that take?"

"I guess we could have one right now. Come on, Zoë. We'll be right back."

They walked out to the street and down the sidewalk and around the corner—they were practically choking by the time it was safe to laugh.

"I can't believe what you said!"

"I know. I'm a genius."

"What are we going to do?"

"We better let him in."

"He'll tell if we don't."

When they could stop laughing, they went back to the porch.

"The board has agreed to hire you," Bridget said. "As long as you're prepared to show no mercy and administer firm discipline. It's difficult to find the correct person."

"I a hundred percent understand," he said. "When's our first meeting?"

"Tomorrow, at lunch."

Then Robert insisted they swear him in. He laid his hand on the notebook and swore to punish all pupils fairly and equally. "Do you swear to uphold the constitution of the Pipe School, so help you God?" Bridget asked. "More than anything in my life," he said. "All you have to say is yes," Bridget said crossly.

Soon the Pipe School was taking up all their time. Although at first they held meetings only at school, the enrollment grew so large that they had to have them on Saturdays too. Then Robert began dressing up in a suit and tie. He thought she and Bridget should wear dresses, and he constantly was thinking of improvements.

As he had noticed right away, none of the pupils ever graduated, so he decided they ought to do something so permanent to them that they would never be able to misbehave again. They would all have operations that would leave them crippled for life.

"Scalpel," he'd order, as they all stood around a table. "Needles, scissors, knife, saw . . ." The usual operations were eye removals and amputations. They were all performed without anesthetic.

He added requests to the letters to teachers too: "Please cut off both our arms and legs and throw us in the creek." "Please cut off our ears and our tongues and poke out our eyes . . ." Since they were only letters, he said, they ought to think up the worst fates possible. They never questioned why they wrote the letters in the first place. Then, one day after school, when Zoë was home alone, the phone rang.

"Carver residence," she said.

"Is Monica there?" asked a mother-voice.

"No, she's not. May I take a message?"

"When will she be in?"

"Who's calling?" Zoë demanded, although she'd already recognized Mrs. Went, and had started feeling uncomfortable.

"It's Robert's mother. This is Zoë, isn't it?"

"This is Zoë Carver speaking," Zoë said threateningly.

Bridget said it made grownups nervous when you were politer than they were.

"Will you ask your mother to call me when she gets in, please?"

"Certainly."

During dinner, the phone rang again, and Monica went out into the hall.

"Who was that?" Seth asked when she came back.

"Sally Went. Why didn't you tell me she called this afternoon, Zoë?"

"Sorry. I forgot."

"I don't know what it's about," Monica said to Seth. "She asked if she could come over after dinner."

"Why, does she think our phone's tapped?" Zoë asked.

Nick started laughing, and Monica said, "You stay out of this. Robert's not in your class, is he, Zoë?"

"Bridget's."

"It can't be anything about school, then. I wonder what's on her mind."

"Curiouser and curiouser," Seth said, squinting at Zoë.

"What are you looking at me like that for?"

"How am I looking at you, Zoë?"

"How you *are*."

"Explain it to me."

"You're crazy," she said. "You ought to be locked up."

But she felt sick and, as soon as she could get excused, she snuck upstairs to the phone in Seth and Monica's bedroom and called Bridget. Mrs. Wycliffe answered.

"Could I speak to Bridget, please?" Zoë asked, pretending that everything was normal.

But Mrs. Wycliffe answered right away in her English accent. "I'm afraid that Bridget is busy examining her conscience, Zoë. I might suggest that you examine yours as well." Then she hung up.

After that Zoë went into her room. She shut the door without making any noise and sat down at her desk. Seth had built it out of plywood but had painted it white to look like store furniture. She unzipped her book-bag and took out her homework; she had to illustrate the armor section of her Medieval History notebook.

She heard Mrs. Went come over and after she'd been there awhile she heard Seth come upstairs. If there had been anywhere to hide, or any way to climb out the window, she would have, but before she'd even had a chance to think about it he came in without knocking and shut the door behind him. He sat down right away and just looked at her for a moment. Then he patted the bed beside him.

"I'll just stay here," she said.

"As you prefer," he said. "But I'm going to insist on your undivided attention. I've just heard something that concerns me, Zoë."

"What?"

"Maybe you should tell me."

"Tell you what?"

"I have to say I was hoping you'd make a clean breast of it, but since you don't appear to consider that in your best interest . . ."

"What best interest? What are you *talking* about?"

Seth looked down at the floor and sighed. "I'm afraid the teachers guessed, Zoë. Surely, if you didn't want to be found out, you could have disguised your handwriting. For God's sake, I was a cryptographer during the war! I'd expect a little better subterfuge from my daughter."

"Better *what?*"

"Concealment. Concealing your identity. I don't know, though. Maybe cunning is a learned characteristic in humans. Probably only in animals is it purely genetic."

She felt like when she was trying to run in a dream. He could do anything. She could never escape.

"Or maybe you were cunning—more cunning than I'm giving you credit for? What would be the appropriate response to such missives, did you feel? Look at me, Zoë."

"I already *am*!"

He sighed, full of despair. "I can honestly say I've rarely felt so disappointed by any human being. For you and Bridget to indulge in such morbid fantasies is one thing—perhaps not even so unusual for children raised in this culture, if the phenomenon could ever be studied. In that sense it's not wholly your individual responsibility, but . . ." Suddenly his voice got much louder and he pronounced every syllable separately, as if he thought she was deaf. ". . . to involve a mentally unstable boy who's just been crippled for life . . . Christ! I would have thought you had more sense." He stared at her. "Have you nothing to say?"

"What do you mean, mentally unstable?"

"You know what those words mean."

"Robert's not mentally unstable! You don't even know what you're talking about!"

"Oh? Whose idea was it to begin with? Yours or Bridget's?"

"How should I know?"

"One of you had to suggest it." Then he pretended to be all friendly and calmed down. "Look, sweetheart, I have the utmost respect for your desire not to implicate your friend, but I am not seeking a culprit, merely a clearer understanding of your actions." His voice switched again. "At this point I'd also say you have nothing to lose by telling the truth."

"I am telling the truth! I don't know!"

"Very well, Zoë. I think, then, that it would be best if you didn't associate with Bridget outside of school until you do know. I'm sure Hugh Wycliffe will share my opinion."

"I don't care," she said.

She tried to shrug, then looked quickly at her desk so he wouldn't see her starting to cry. The visors she had practiced drawing on pieces of scrap paper—they had pointy tops and narrow slits where the eyes were—looked all wobbly. They were all over the page. She had also drawn several maces and hundreds of portcullises.

Seth stood up, and she said not aloud, Please don't let him know, please don't let him know. If he figured out she was crying he'd think he'd won and try to comfort her, and it would be even worse than how disgusting and sick to her stomach she felt if he *forgave* her—as if it was all over—now.

She breathed out in tiny gusts as he opened the door. "I'd be ashamed too, if I were you," he said.

VII CASCABEL FLATS

Zoë had been thinking about this scene while Ellie recounted the history of her and Nick's advent into the world of rattlesnake farming—since Bridget's letter she must have gone over every single experience she'd ever had involving Rob, but that wasn't really why she'd recalled the Pipe School episode. It was the never-ending question Ellie's story had triggered: How could you blame someone for something if you didn't know why he'd done it? Had Stewart Beauregard known the snakes still denned under the house when he sold it to Nick and Ellie? And even if he had, did that mean he'd possessed evil intentions? Had Rob intentionally forced his father's car off the road? Had he meant for his father to hit him instead? But even that would be an incomplete explanation. Why would he have wanted that? Because he'd been so upset by Anders Ogilvy's photographs of her? And why had she shown them to him? Why had she written those letters to the teachers with Bridget? All of these questions seemed to be the same question. After all this time she still felt hot with shame when she imagined how the grownups must have construed the letters they wrote—some sick sexual perversion, even though it hadn't felt like that at all; it had felt as if it were *expected* of them. Somebody had to do it; it was something that had to be done, but how could she explain that? Especially how could she have explained that then?

When Ellie had finished, Nick naturally had to invite them out to visit the rattlesnake coop—the "major tourist attraction the place had to offer." Looking somewhat annoyed, Ellie began to collect sherry glasses; Monica, taking her cue, stood to help her. Ellie was still upset because Nick had continued to refuse to admit that Stewart Beauregard was a villain, even though she was the one who had gone on glibly talking about selling pickled rattlesnake for $19.95 a jar at a gourmet food shop in town and her plans for a rattlesnake cookbook.

Halted by the view, Zoë, Pryce, and Nick had stopped on the terrace. The sky was colorless now and the mountains had merged into a dark secretiveness, whatever it was they knew mixed now in Zoë's mind not only with the simulated crucifixions that might still take place among them, but also with the dusky cathedral whose image kept rising before her, where the faceless priest waited for her to submit to his power to forgive her—some amalgam of the cathedral in San Ysidro and the one in the city several blocks from her current temporary office job where she had lately been spending her lunch hours. Somewhere in the mix lurked the relics Monica had been shocked by on her honeymoon but never mentioned having seen before today (if she'd ever mentioned a honeymoon). It didn't surprise Zoë that her mother had chosen today to make the revelation, however. When the person you'd loved most in your life had been locked up for ten years for saying he killed his father, which he claimed he did to avenge the deaths of all the sons ever killed by their fathers, starting with the first, famous example, and then was released, and no sooner did you arrive *out here,* the "latest mecca," the new chosen land, than you began to hear about crucifixions and martyrdoms . . . Well, it couldn't be coincidence, to put it mildly.

Nick and Pryce had headed down the embankment, and as Zoë picked out the rocky pathway she heard Pryce ask Nick about his academic background—something to do with biochemistry, he knew from Zoë, but . . .

"Neurochemistry," Nick corrected him. "Potential of snake venoms for use as psychotropic agents, to be precise."

"You're kidding."

"Funny, that's what the lab said."

"Zoë said you were having trouble getting funding."

"Oh, no trouble *getting* it, trouble keeping it. I wrote the proposal that brought us the bulk of the money—unfortunately I hadn't specified exactly how I wanted to use it. I wasn't in charge of the lab . . . 'We're afraid, Nick, your priorities just aren't ours; research not showing enough progress to justify further expenditure; can't have one person going in one direction when everyone else wants to go in another . . .' "

"What direction did you want to go in?"

"Human experimentation." Nick laughed.

Zoë had come to stand beside them at the door of the snakehouse, a low cinderblock building twenty-five or thirty feet long and a third as wide, its roof slanted like a lean-to's. It had no windows but several skylights. Nick, noticing her studying the construction, said he planned to stucco it over in the spring; this had been the best they could do in a hurry. Three days, believe it or not. He and "Stew" and a couple of "Stew's" workmen were out there night and day—they had more than two hundred rattlers in gunnysacks and pillowcases—"what you'd call a powerful motivation." Nick had fished a key out of his shirt pocket and was opening the padlock.

You're afraid of thieves? she asked, when he turned around.

"Two hundred rattlesnakes, Zo." Pryce winked at her. "A veritable Fort Knox of snakedom."

"We kept only seventy of the original catch," Nick said humorlessly. He looked at them, tossing the padlock from hand to hand. "A hundred Ellie killed and froze—that's how she became an expert rattlesnake chef overnight. The remainder we took far enough away so that, unless they scattered pebbles like Hansel and Gretel, they wouldn't find their way back. As for the lock—no, I'm not afraid of people stealing the snakes, but of someone wandering in and getting hurt. I'd be sued before I could say Litigation."

"Wandering in?" Pryce looked around at the empty prairie. "People just happen by?"

"People have heard about the enterprise. The local paper ran an article about Ellie and me several months ago. Since then we've been deluged with requests to give tours, everyone from the local schools to the Garden Club. I tried it once—that was enough."

"Why? What happened?"

"Nothing. I was just afraid it was going to. I have double-weight plexiglass on all the cages, so I wasn't afraid they'd break, but the glass slides down and the doors don't have locks. Although I allowed in only two kids at a time I was still a nervous wreck. Now when people call I just tell them I'm not running a zoo. If they want to see snakes, there are plenty of other places for them to go. This is a research facility and not suitable for children."

He lectured them as if they'd made the request themselves.

"You're doing research out here?" Pryce asked. "I thought you'd had to abandon it."

"Only temporarily. I don't have the equipment to purify and store the venom at the moment, but I've been in touch with nearby universities. I'm hoping to make an arrangement with one of them."

"To work with rattlesnake venom specifically? What exactly do you hope to accomplish?"

"Oh, complete alteration of human consciousness." Nick laughed. "It's hard to say. It's difficult if not impossible to conduct experiments, but that's only made it more of a challenge. The odds are so great against the venom's being shown to have psychotropic applications that people generally prefer to continue exploration of its other uses. The anticoagulant action of crotoxin, for example, has been shown to be of use in preventing stroke—that's an isolate from the venom of *Durissus terrificus*—a South American rattler," he said, in response to Pryce's blank look. "Its effect on the myelin sheath is similar to that produced by multiple sclerosis, so it's also proven of use in studying that disease. There's some recent evidence that it acts to retard the growth of certain cancers. Naturally, cautious administrators are reluctant to tie up funds with harebrained schemes like mine." He looked at Zoë. "Well, ready set go?"

Why not? she signed. *It's just a bunch of rattlesnakes.* She made the sign for snake—the three middle fingers bent in a claw shape to look like fangs, moving forward as if to strike—then crossed two fingers to form an R.

"Is that really what you think?"

Nick reached inside and flipped a light switch, then pushed the door wide and stood back so that she could go first. Okay. She stepped past him—so he'd graduated from garter and blacksnake to rattle, so what? She couldn't believe he'd just told Pryce, a complete stranger, more about his research problems than he'd told her in a year of letters. It was just further evidence of how little he cared whether or not they really stayed in touch. She was so busy thinking about this that it took a moment before she had any comprehension at all of what she was looking at. Behind her Pryce said, "I am rendered speechless."

One entire side of the building was a living wall of snakes, not an entirely undifferentiated writhing mass but three continuous rows of snakes seemingly suspended in air—at first Zoë couldn't see anything that kept the two upper levels from falling into the lowest one—and for an insane moment she thought that the snakes were *levitating*; that somehow Nick had trained them to do this at the signal of the light's going on, but the optical illusion quickly resolved itself into three tiers of plexiglass boxes, twice as deep as they were wide, only the boxes' back half covered by a bedding of brown paper which had been camouflaged by the snakes' coloring. The cages also contained inverted cardboard boxes for the snakes to hide in. These were no simulated habitats, painted desert backgrounds and fake sagebrush; not even any rocks or dirt in the cages, which Nick had used at first when he was a kid to make the snakes he captured feel at home. He had learned the hard way that sand and gravel retained too much moisture and the snakes could get blister disease. It was impossible to tell how many snakes there were—a hundred, two hundred, five? Unquestionably there were more snakes than she'd ever seen before in her life in any one place—more than in any laboratory and even more than in a zoo, where, even if their total number were greater they were dispersed, only a snake or two to a cage, and the cages divided at the very least by opaque partitions. Evidently Nick and Ellie's carpenter had neglected to make any doors for the rattlesnakes either—what if they valued *their* privacy? Nearly every cage contained several snakes, and because the partitions between the cages were transparent, it looked as though there were three long uninterrupted tangles of snakes, one over the other, like lines of a score scrawled in a composer's heat of genius.

Zoë felt almost ill, trying to take in what she was seeing. She wasn't scared of snakes; it wasn't that—it was not being able to tell where one snake ended and another began. Even if you focused on a particular snake it was still impossible to keep it from slipping back into some kind of multiple vision. To make matters worse, they all seemed to be moving—very slowly, almost imperceptibly, in their effortless underwater way, like the unwavering progress of a soundless airplane—but moving nevertheless. A few, maybe responding to the presence of intruders, were sliding up the glass, exposing their pale undersides, flicking their dark forked tongues in and out, as they tried to gauge the spectators' size and proximity.

Zoë turned to catch Nick smiling at her in a self-satisfied way. She looked quickly back at the snakes and for the first time it hit her that they were poisonous. He'd never kept poisonous snakes at home. Monica of course wouldn't permit it and after he'd moved out of Metcalf Street he hadn't kept snakes—he'd always had easy access to a lab. Why hadn't he told her what he was doing research on? All he'd ever said was that he was analyzing the components of venom, and he'd been doing that for years.

Pryce renewed his questions, one right after another, a method he'd told her he used to catch witnesses off guard: How many snakes were there, all told?

About a hundred and fifty.

But hadn't Nick kept only fifty of the original catch?

Yes, but some had given birth and he'd bought a collection of prairie rattlers from an antivenin producer who was going out of business.

(Either very fast or very slow; both methods unnerved people. The trick was guessing which to use.)

Didn't they inject horses with venom to make the serum?

Yes.

Did Nick keep antivenom on hand?

Anti*venin*. No.

But what if . . .?

There was plenty of time to get to the hospital, Nick interrupted. The antivenin wouldn't have an instantaneous effect, and sometimes produced its own allergic reactions that were as bad as the effect of the venom. What you wanted was something like Adrenalin, to counteract respiratory arrest . . .

And he had that?

"No," Nick said. He stepped forward and tapped a cage in which three fat rattlers were coiled in tight separate circles, like staccato marks, and Zoë glanced at the index card taped to the upper left-hand corner of the cage (there was one on each): under the species name, *C. viridis viridis,* and their date of acquisition were listed their age, sex, and a record of medical treatment. This card had MITES and G.I.—gastrointestinal—on it, with dates. Could Nick tell all the snakes apart? She was still contemplating the fact that they were poisonous, though it was probably tantamount to visiting a missile silo and trying to comprehend how much destructiveness the sleek cylinders contained, and it pleased her to think how infuriated Nick would be by such a comparison—more evidence of people's warped perceptions of snakes. Western civilization had given snakes such a bad press . . . The Indians always had great respect for snakes; they believed they carried messages from the underworld . . . "Snakes don't lie!" she remembered him yelling, even as far back as when they still all had dinner together in the kitchen on Metcalf Street. Monica had said someone spoke "with a forked tongue" and Nick had erupted; Seth as usual had made matters worse by asking him if he knew that Cassandra was supposed to have secured her powers of divination by having her ears cleaned out by the tongue of a serpent—everyone knew how well her tales had been credited.

Pryce had asked Nick if he knew how to milk the snakes for venom himself (which he did) and then if he'd ever been bitten.

"Not to date," Nick said.

"But you know what the effect is?"

"Hemorrhage," Nick said, bored. The venom broke down the tissue—that was what it was for: to help the snake digest its prey. How much of an effect it had depended on a variety of factors: where one was bitten—that is to say, where on the body, though also how far one was from medical assistance; how much venom was injected; what one's overall state of health was . . .

I think Pryce wanted to know what it feels like, she interrupted. WANT KNOW HOW FEEL.

"Oh. I should imagine it hurts a bit."

"Hurts a *bit*?"

"A burning sensation at the site of injection, I've been told. Sometimes nausea and dizziness. Generally a drop in blood pressure. Occasional respiratory difficulty. As I said, the greatest immediate danger is usually from shock."

Zoë stepped closer to the cages and examined one occupied by several medium-sized, homey-looking snakes; their grays and browns were criss-crossed in an argyle-like pattern, and they were flowing over and around each other, so intertwined that she couldn't follow any single one from its wedge-shaped head to its tapering cordovan-brown rattles. When a length of snake moved, not only could you not tell which snake it belonged to, you couldn't really tell *when* it moved. Even if you could say it hadn't been moving before, and was moving after, it was impossible to detect the moment at which it went from immobility to mobility; a lower, invisible loop of its coil might already have been rippling motion into the upper length, so that when the head finally glided forward, it seemed as if it had been moving before you noticed it. It was like trying to catch the progress of the hour hand on a clock. Was this what Monica had meant by the "revolting and unnatural fashion" in which snakes moved?

"Just a bunch of snakes, huh?" Nick said.

She glanced at him. *They're beautiful.*

He nodded, mollified, and stepped away from Pryce and closer to her. "I could spend the rest of my life in here, watching them, you know."

I know.

"How can anyone not love snakes? I just don't get it."

She nodded.

"I think you're both nuts," Pryce said.

"Probably," Nick said, not turning around, and they stood together admiring his rattlesnakes, alone in the pleasure of not suspecting each other's loyalties for once. Zoë had the feeling suddenly that he'd wanted her to know what he was working on but had been nervous about telling her—but why? Memories of her old resentment? When he'd first begun to keep snakes, in fourth or fifth grade, for a year or two she'd officially refused, like Monica now, to have anything to do with them, partly because she was afraid, but more because she couldn't stand how totally fascinated Nick was by them. It had all seemed connected with his getting to go to Dr. Macmillan—he kept developing all these things that made him more interesting. She couldn't figure out how he came up with them. Whenever he was out, she'd sneak into his room and stare at his terrarium. Usually all he had were garter snakes, though sometimes he caught a blacksnake, which he'd keep until Monica found out and made him get rid of it. She was convinced that black snakes were strong enough to get out of the terrarium and she'd find one in her bed some night.

One day after school, when Nick was at his weekly Monopoly game, Zoë had gone up to his room and closed the door. Monica and Seth didn't get home until five-thirty. This time, she had determined, she would hold one of the snakes—it was unbearable to have Nick going on and on about how he was the sacrifice in their family and also showing off how he wasn't afraid of snakes; maybe she couldn't get to see Dr. Macmillan unless she had asthma attacks or walked in front of a truck, but she would show Nick about the snakes. She'd start practicing when no one was home since she knew she'd scream at first; she already didn't feel as afraid of them after watching them several whole afternoons, but she knew she would scream by reflex, and she was going to practice until she didn't react anymore. Then one day, right in front of Nick, she'd just reach into the terrarium and pick one up as easily as anything. Then he'd have respect for her. She couldn't stand him thinking she was a coward.

At the time he had three small garter snakes—or maybe one had been a grass snake—it was pale green. She had tried not to think about what she was going to do. As soon as she'd shut Nick's bedroom door and stuffed the towel against the lower crack the way Nick did when he let the snakes loose, she went right away to the terrarium and lifted off the mesh top—Nick kept it weighted down with bricks. The minute she looked at the snakes, it was as if her intestines began to writhe too. It felt as if everything in her whole body were coiling and squirming around—it made no sense that because snakes slithered they should disgust people, but they did. It had to be ingrained through inheritance. Just because snakes didn't take *steps,* the way people did. Her stomach was churning as she ordered herself to reach into the glass terrarium. She touched a loop of snake and screamed, and it shrank back into a corner—the poor thing was probably terrified to death. She touched another one, then the pale green snake; it was the color of a newborn leaf. She felt less squeamish about it—its single color made it easier to adjust to—and decided to take it out first. She could have used a ruler or brought a stick from outside, but part of the trial was to do it with her hand. She pretended that she would be put to death if she didn't do it—she had to pick up the snake and hold it or she would be horribly tortured and burned at the stake.

The first time she managed to hold it for a split second before she realized what she was actually doing and shrieked and dropped it. It wasn't the feel of it that was so horrible, but it wouldn't stay still; it tried to curl around her hand. She picked it up and dropped it several more times, screaming "I'm *sorry,* I'm *sorry*" before she finally managed to hold on to it long enough to lift it out of the cage. She took one step, then tossed it onto the bed. She'd thought it would look less creepy on the bed, but it didn't. It looked as if it had been put there to bite someone in the dark. Clenching her lips between her teeth, she forced herself to take out the two remaining snakes and toss them onto the bed too. But by the time she got back with the last one the first one had flopped off. She caught it, a miracle in itself, and put it back up, but by then the other two were escaping. Then she thought of the bathtub, and managed to carry all three of them into the bathroom, holding them out away from her and trying not to look at them, as if they were Medusa's head. The whole time she was swallowing a scream; her intestines were knotting and unknotting just as the snakes were looping around her wrists and forearms, but she wasn't going to stop now. She didn't think they could climb out of the bathtub.

After shutting the bathroom door and putting the laundry hamper in front of it (the lock was broken), she took off her shoes and knee socks—she was still wearing school clothes—and sat down on the curved rim of the tub. Then, holding her breath, she swung her feet over the edge and set them down together inside. Her toes were curled up, shuddering. But she was ready. She would get over it now or die. Now or never. There was a window over the tub, but the next-door neighbors on that side, the Flemings, had no children, and they both worked until six. They were older than Seth and Monica, and the way Monica said "They have no children of their own" always sounded weird, as if they might have someone else's. Unless one of them was home sick, no one would hear her when she screamed. And did she scream. Each time one of the snakes slid over her feet she screamed. She screamed at the top of her lungs, bloody murder, and it seemed as if she would never stop—as if she'd been keeping the screaming inside all her life and had to scream out every snake nightmare that not only she but everyone else had ever had: snakes writhing everywhere, pits of snakes you were thrown into, nowhere in the world you could go and be free of snakes—and when she screamed the poor terror-struck garter snakes tried to get away, but they couldn't; the sides of the bathtub were too slick. Then they tried to curl around her legs: she forced herself to stay still, but she couldn't stop screaming. She kept thinking of the stories about snakes slithering up inside women to eat their unborn children—not that she had any, but that was absolutely and totally not the point, as Bridget was constantly saying. She kept her knees tightly together and wished she was wearing pants with rubber bands over the ankles. All the while this was going on—the snakes exploring up her calves; they'd seemed to have gotten used to her screams by now—she kept seeing herself as she would look to someone else, a girl on the edge of a bathtub with her feet in a pile of snakes. And then suddenly it was just over. It was the most incredible thing that had ever happened to her—something inside her just stopped. One minute she was screaming and her insides were tied in a hundred knots, and then they were gone. Every single part of her body felt as smooth as it must have been before she was born. All the molecules in her body were humming with peace.

She remembered looking down at the snakes and for the first time seeing them for what they were—they didn't mean people any harm—and she could tell the snakes realized the change in her. She felt how helpless they were, how wild and innocent, pleading with her to help them get out, yet they didn't even *blame* her for being the same person who'd taken them from their perfectly comfortable, warm terrarium and imprisoned them in this freezing cold trough, a horrifying slippery surface they could get no grip on, and then every time they'd tried to get near her feet, the only warm, friendly spot on the heartless white porcelain, a ferocious shrillness attacked them from above and they were driven back to the cold whiteness—they forgave her completely, although that wasn't how they thought; they didn't think about things the way people did; that was the whole point.

She said to them, "I'm sorry, I'm so sorry," and picked first one, then the other two up, and let them slide into her lap. She was wearing a kilt and the three snakes snuggled right away into the warm wooly material. She picked up the grass snake again—the pretty pale green was the color of the luna moths in Harmony—and held it gently in one hand, letting it twine around the other. The two in her lap also began exploring, climbing up her arms and nosing under her hair. She breathed out, then listened to her breath, long and deep as if she were asleep. Was she asleep? Was she hypnotized? Snakes could do that. She thought again about how she would look, sitting on the edge of the bathtub with three snakes exploring her as if she were a tourist attraction, like a warm breathing tree; but it had no effect on her whatsoever. She could *remember* feeling horrified of snakes, but that had been another person. She felt as if the snakes really always had been inside of her, but now they had come out and were wrapping themselves around and around her arms and throat like living bracelets and necklaces, the shimmery green one and the two black ones with the gold stripe down their backs, and she couldn't understand at all how once the idea would have sickened her to death.

She laughed, and said something else to the snakes—she didn't remember exactly what anymore, but it had been something like, "You must think human beings are pretty ridiculous," and that was when Nick had come in. He *claimed* he'd knocked, though she'd never heard him; and when he saw her sitting on the bathtub, laughing and talking, his snakes crawling all over her like magic living jewelry, *he* screamed. He screamed and then shouted, "Help! Zoë's gone insane! Call an ambulance!" even though no one else was home. "Call an ambulance?" she repeated, and started laughing harder. "Oh, my God!" he was shouting. "Oh, my God, what have I done?" "Calm down!" she had to shout back. She was terrified that he'd have an asthma attack. She'd gathered up the snakes and carried them back to the terrarium and put the top on securely, while Nick kept moaning, "I'm sorry! I'm sorry! Oh, God, I'm so sorry!" Finally she had to shake him. "I'm fine, Nick! Control yourself!" When he saw that she really was all right, and not insane, he sat down on his bed and to her amazement began to cry.

"I thought you'd gone crazy," he said, sniffling. "I really just thought you'd gone crazy. What the hell were you doing anyway, Zoë? I've tried your whole life to get you to hold snakes and you would never even touch them!"

"So? I wanted to do it by myself."

"But *why*?" he kept repeating.

"So you wouldn't laugh at me for screaming. I knew I would just have to do it."

"Did you scream?"

"Yes."

"You probably screamed your head off," he said, wiping his nose.

"So what if I did?"

"The snakes might have gone into shock."

"Well, they didn't. They like me now. Besides, what are you doing home so early? You'd never have even seen me if you came home at the normal time."

"Dr. Macmillan made me leave early. He said I was trying to sabotage him."

"*Sabotage* him? You mean at Monopoly? How?"

"I just decided to let him win—I'm so sick of that game. I stopped buying properties and I wouldn't put any hotels on the ones I did own."

"What did he do?"

Nick started to laugh. "He got so furious. It was completely obvious even though he's not supposed to show he's upset with you."

"You never told me that before."

"There was practically smoke coming out of his ears."

"So you aren't going back anymore?" She felt a sudden great hope.

But he said, "I doubt it. I'm sure he'll get some new idea. No matter what you do in his office, he always thinks it means something. He's really getting on my nerves."

Still it seemed as if something had been accomplished. This was the first time he'd ever said anything disrespectful of Dr. Macmillan. Maybe now that she liked snakes too, Nick would think of her more as his equal. Twenty years later, observing his rattlesnakes with him, Zoë began to remember other things—the incredible way every millimeter of a snake's body touched the surfaces it travelled over—its entire length sometimes moving forward all at once, as if it were being pulled very slowly and carefully, the way you pulled a string for a cat. Snakes did not take *steps* as people did, who left untouched many places they might have stood. Miming, her hand stroked her arm, and Nick said, "What?" as if she'd mumbled.

I wasn't talking.

"You should see them strike—it's incredible how fast it is. Even when you try to watch it it's over before you know it. How a creature can move with such infinitesimal slowness and then at the speed of light . . . If they know something," he said, lowering his voice, "it's in the venom. I was so close, those damn idiots . . ."

She nodded, but Pryce leaned forward and read aloud the card on the cage and Nick snapped back to his genial host formality.

"C. *atrox,* five years, female; four years, male . . ."

"*Crotalus atrox,*" Nick told him. "Western diamondback—the original settlers. The prairie rattlers I've bought or traded for—or Stewart helped me bag. This great big Atrox, however, I caught." He pointed out a cage on the upper tier, a little to their left. He glanced at Zoë. "I'm expecting a lot from him."

"Would you care to elaborate?"

Instead of answering, Nick stepped sideways and tapped the door. The snake lifted its head, then elevated itself along the glass, flicking its black tongue in and out.

"Getting hungry, fella?"

"Do they *know* you?"

"Some do. The ones who've been here a while. They don't rattle anymore when I open their cages."

Would they if we did?

"Probably."

"What does *Crotalus* mean? I get the *atrox* part."

"Genus name. Atrox is arguably the most aggressive of all North American rattlers. Most deaths from rattlesnake bite in this country are from Atrox. Their venom is more toxic, ounce per ounce, and then they can inject a large quantity of it . . ."

"King of the Rattlesnakes, in other words," Pryce said.

"You have no idea how right you are," Nick said. "And I have to sacrifice one for Ellie to stuff tomorrow. I have only two left." He glanced at Zoë. "I need them."

You mean only two of the big ones?

"To make the biggest impression," he said. "I mean that's why Ellie wants them," he added, as if that hadn't been clear. "To generate the most oohs and ahs."

"At the party? Monica really meant she wasn't kidding."

"Ellie never kids about things like that. She'd be happy to slaughter the rest tomorrow."

She wants to pickle them all?

"That's a by-product. Her real interest is in the skins—that's why the bigger the better. Shoes go for a thousand bucks a pair."

"Jesus," Pryce said.

"It's hard being rich, you know, always having to find new ways to spend your money. Ellie's happy to help out. Unfortunately she already has her eye on the Tortuga Islanders I'm expecting. The more exotic the better. She has a customer who'll pay three thousand dollars for a vest."

"Good Lord!"

"She feels that keeping them is simply a luxurious hobby if we don't make money off them."

"You can't sell the venom?"

"No. Not without purifying it, which I can't do without a lab. In addition it has to be dried or frozen. Of course, that doesn't preclude my experimenting with it myself."

"Continuing your dissertation research?"

"No venom has a single effect," Nick said, as if this were an answer. "That's why so much time has to be spent discovering which enzyme is responsible for the activity."

"Which activity? I thought your research was on the brain."

"Is," Nick said, tapping his head.

Seth had always called it Nick's "Inventor Rhapsody"—"That degree of abstraction, Nicko, one expects a new Rosetta Stone or a Third Law of Thermodynamics. At least." "Look who's talking!" Nick protested. "Now wait a minute," Seth said. "I never claimed that saving the world was *my* ambition—I'm leaving that up to you kids. My job is pointing out what's wrong with it."

"There's just this slight problem," Nick said. "Got to find a way across the great divide . . ."

"I beg your pardon?"

"The blood-brain barrier," Nick said impatiently, as if Pryce should have realized what he was talking about. "It's basically a sieve that protects the brain from molecules over a certain size. Without it the brain could never have evolved to its present complexity. Rattlesnake venom's a protein—it's too big to get across."

But you've figured out a way, Zoë gestured quickly.

He looked at her and, grinning, said, "To tell you the truth, I'm a little worried about the Tortuga rattlers I'm expecting. They were supposed to be here today, but with the holiday package glut I'm afraid they're stuck somewhere. I'm not worried they'll get hungry, but if the air holes get blocked or they're left out in cold weather for very long . . ."

"Don't tell me," Pryce said. "They're arriving U.P.S."

"Actually, they're sent through the post office. Highly elaborate packing methods, needless to say. In this case it was even more complicated. They had to be shipped first to a breeder in Mexico, who could unpack them and make sure they were all right, then walk them through customs for me. You can imagine how skeptical customs officials are of packages marked 'Live Venomous Snakes.' You could ship a lifetime's supply of certain illegal substances in one of those boxes, so someone has to display the cargo to the officials' satisfaction. If they're not here by tomorrow, I'm going to have to trace them. You can imagine how delighted the post office will be to do that, two days before Christmas."

"A breeder in Mexico?" Pryce repeated. "Dare I ask how many of these . . . individuals there are? Are we to expect an explosion in the rattlesnake population in the near future?"

"I wouldn't stay awake nights worrying about it. The population's dwindling. Some species should already be on the endangered list."

"Really? I thought all these rattlesnake hunts I keep hearing about were to keep the population under control."

"That's what they want you to think."

Zoë smiled; she knew what was coming.

"The great white hunters—stamping out the last vestige of Danger . . . Makes them feel like real men, you know—blowing gasoline into the dens and then capturing the snakes when they're half suffocated and too cold to move. Real sport. Rattlesnakes aren't even belligerent, for Christ's sake. You won't find a rattlesnake breaking into your house to murder you. Rattlesnakes don't lie in wait for you in dark alleys to slit your throat. They don't lie, cheat, or steal. Only people do those things."

"I gather you feel pretty strongly on the subject."

What a genius, Rob said.

"I'm not alone. There's quite a network. Even the people who want to do them in—I'd have to include them. They've picked up the same scent, they're just not interpreting the information correctly."

"But . . ."

"I couldn't explain it to someone else, but at the snake convention this summer I could pick the rattlesnakers from the tiger- and coral-snakers a mile away, and I wasn't . . ."

"Just hold it right there. A *snake* convention? Where'd you coil up, at the Herpetology Inn?"

"All right, I stand corrected—Rattlesnake *Keepers'* Convention. Don't even recall its official name—something like the Annual Meeting of the Southwestern Herpetology Association. It's a combination lecture series and sales show—new handling equipment, latest advice on treating diseases, regulations, what have you. Every kind of individual from cobwebby anthropologists lecturing on the symbolism of snake icons to beltmakers—Ellie's side of the business. I picked up a lot of useful information, made some good contacts."

"And how could you tell the rattlesnakers, as you call them, from the other species?"

"Oh, a certain glint in the eye. The true believers . . ." Nick's voice had taken on the glib tone that Zoë knew meant he was going to back off whatever he'd been about to say. He might use Pryce as a way of channeling some information to her, but not for everything. "There's a good deal more interest in rattlesnakes right now than you realize." Nick glanced around and then leaned against the stainless steel counter opposite the cages. Various instruments were hanging on the wall above—a cleaver, an L-shaped rod, a giant pair of tongs, and other things Zoë couldn't identify. She had the impression that Nick was avoiding her eyes.

"The statistics exist if you don't believe me. Membership in rattlesnake societies up five hundred percent; subscription rates to rattlesnake magazines quadrupled; triple the number of rattlesnake festivals and hunts and meetings and books and articles . . . This all quite aside from the dramatic rise in interest for medical research, which I've already told you about."

"I don't know," Pryce said. "You're certainly the strongest proponent for the rehabilitation of rattlesnakes' reputation I've ever heard. Maybe you'll start a movement. A rattlesnake worship revival . . . You could have your own television show."

Zoë could see Nick stiffen.

"I wasn't intending to sound evangelistic." He controlled himself and laughed. "What the hell, a boy's got to have a hobby, right?" He slid along the counter and put his arm around Zoë. "What do you say? Ready for the next episode?"

She smiled at him. She felt so happy suddenly—the least tidbit of affection from Nick and her whole world brightened. Did every younger sister feel that way about her older brother? And that was when she saw it: a sister suffering from "hysterical muteness" and a brother exploring the power of chemicals to alter neural arrangements—how could she not have seen it before? No wonder he hadn't told her about his research the last couple of years. She hadn't questioned why, of all the more plausible chemicals Nick might have researched, he'd chosen snake venom; not to work with snakes, for Nick, would be not to work as himself. Her next thought was not to let him know she'd guessed.

"So, what do you feed them?" Pryce asked, as Nick opened the door.

"Mice. I've got a freezerful."

"Jesus. Snake TV dinners."

"They're quite happy with frozen food, contrary to what you might expect. And if a snake's not hungry there's no chance of the mouse's hurting it. Mice have been known to kill snakes, you know."

"You must be kidding. The snake doesn't defend itself?"

"Nope," Nick said, as if snakes were noble pacifists.

MOTHER KNOW MICE HERE? Zoë asked.

"Of course not—what do you take me for? I also haven't told her I'm expecting the Tortuga Islanders, by the way."

"Your poor mother."

"I'll be using most of the mice in the next couple of days, and the shipment I'll be picking up myself."

Nick shut off the overhead light and Zoë saw what she hadn't when they came in: there was a row of dim lights on the wall just above the cages. She pointed.

"Low-wattage track lighting," Nick said. "I can come in that way without arousing them. Plus, the lights provide a little heat."

They were outside now; Nick snapped on the padlock.

What if the power goes out? ELECTRICITY BREAK? Snakes had to be kept at a constant temperature.

"Stewart loaned me a generator. It switches on automatically if the electricity shuts off. This building doesn't retain heat very well, so it's absolutely necessary to have it. As you know, when it's really cold the snakes could freeze to death in a few hours."

They returned to the house a different way, around back to the kitchen. It was dark now, the mountains a mere blotch on the horizon and the trees hunchbacked silhouettes. Close by you could still make out the puffy bushes that looked like upside-down dust mops, and a couple of kinds of cactus: the cholla, they'd had that in Mexico—in the summer brilliant magenta-colored flowers sprouted from the tops of the thorny arms like those flowers that popped out of trick guns—and the round-bladed prickly pear.

Pryce would question Ellie first, Zoë decided; he'd have realized that Nick was unpredictably touchy and he might figure that Monica was too dippy. I've told you what I told him, she reminded Rob: a school friend was killed in an auto accident after we'd had a fight. I don't know how much Ellie can add to that, though. Nick must have told her something—a boy my sister was "fond of" went insane after his father was killed in a car crash; Charlotte—our grandmother—had just died . . . But maybe not. Maybe he refused to talk about it. He's obviously loyal to me in his own secretive way.

It didn't matter, in any case; Nick didn't know everything himself. Pryce could ask questions until the jury went to sleep and still never discover that she was the common denominator in these various deaths. Nick had been there when the D.A. questioned her (Monica and Seth had had to be; Nick didn't want to go but Monica insisted. "Your sister is going to need your support, Nick. Your presence is going to be more of a comfort to her than ours will, believe me." Zoë had been in the upstairs hall listening to them talk in the kitchen; they seemed to think that because she couldn't talk anymore, she couldn't hear), but although Nick knew—everyone in Sparta knew—that the grand jury had to determine whether or not there were enough evidence to indict Rob, no one knew anything about the most incriminating evidence of all. Somehow, between the time she'd been to see him at the bakery and he'd been taken into custody, he had gotten rid of Anders Ogilvy's photographs; otherwise the police would have found them when they searched the bakery and have questioned her about them: you wouldn't find photographs like that lying around and not ask a murder suspect (even a self-declared murder suspect) or their subject about them. ("Do you recognize these, Miss Carver? Who took them? How frequently did you pose for him? Always in this . . . fashion?") It was strange, though—even though she wanted to tell the court nothing, she couldn't lie; everything had *happened* because she'd lied, one way or another—lied or hadn't listened, which was a kind of lying, and so when the district attorney asked her if she could think of anything that might have precipitated Rob's action—he meant Rob's insisting that he was to blame for his father's death, not his stepping in front of his father's car (which could not be proved either unless the only witness, someone driving by in the opposite direction, made himself or herself known, and Rob might have invented this witness also)—she had told the truth.

First they had played her an excerpt from his testimony—they had taken a deposition from him at the hospital where he had already been taken for "observation"—and it was strange to her that he'd sounded so much like himself on the tape recorder: "Why are you trying to get me to admit that I was confused? I keep pointing out to you that it could hardly have taken me an *hour* to walk from the bus stop to the plant if I'd only been going out to *visit* my father, and may I remind you that several people, including the bus driver, remember me getting off at four-thirty. I would also like to remind you that of all the places I could have been waiting, I was waiting at the *one blind curve* between the bus stop and the plant. I couldn't have planned for there to be a car coming the other way, of course, but I'm not surprised that one was. Luck was with me. You say you haven't been able to locate the driver, but I tell you, it was a beige Studebaker—how many beige Studebakers can there be in a town the size of Sparta? Unless the driver was from out of town, but I might remind you that Stark Road is pretty much only used by local traffic, or by people going to work at the plant. You've already determined that the driver wasn't headed for the plant . . . You what? You're implying that I'm *inventing* a beige Studebaker? Give me a little credit. If I were going to invent an automobile, I'd invent something more plausible than a Studebaker. Furthermore, it's just as likely that my father might have gone over the embankment if there hadn't been a car coming—surely I don't need to remind you that there are steep embankments on *both* sides of the road? Why do I have to tell you how to do your job? Please excuse my oversight in not taking down the license plate."

They played this part of the tape and then asked her if she could think of anything that had happened recently that might have upset him, or made him angry with his father. She might pretend to herself later that she hadn't known what she was going to say in response—who could blame her?—after what she'd just heard. She happened to know that Anders Ogilvy, if no one else in Sparta, drove a beige Studebaker. Since he walked to work at the Naval Academy and never went anywhere, it had lasted all these years. He kept it in a garage off the alley behind his house. There were two possibilities.

Either Rob had figured out who'd taken the photographs—though how could he have, in that amount of time?—and had then tried to implicate Anders in his father's death in order, eventually, to implicate her; or Anders really had been driving by. That could hardly have been by chance, either; he would have had to have followed her from his house to the bakery and then followed Rob when he came out a little while later carrying the photographs; maybe Anders had been afraid she was a minor after all and *had* lied about her age in which case she actually might go to the police. When he saw Rob get on the bus he would have had to rush home to get his car and follow the bus route, although that wouldn't have been very efficient. Whichever explanation was true it meant that Rob and Anders were connected, and maybe even that Anders was the only person on earth who could corroborate or refute Rob's version of what had happened. It seemed inevitable that the police would locate the car, and then Anders, if Rob hadn't already, would lead the court to her. So maybe she answered the D.A.'s question in self-defense; then they wouldn't be so hard on her later for withholding information.

He'd asked if she could think of anything that might have upset Rob, perhaps made him angry with his father, and she'd answered, "I think he was angry with me." She wrote her answers on a notepad, then the D.A. read them aloud for the court reporter. "Angry with you?" She nodded. Then she wrote, "For something I said." She hadn't had to say that either. The seventh graders who'd been working in the bakery that afternoon had already testified that she'd come in and asked to see Rob, but she could have said he'd seemed upset but she didn't know about what, or that he'd seemed fine—she was positive by this point, even though they'd played her only part of the tape, that he hadn't mentioned her once in his testimony, let alone mentioned the photographs. But maybe she was already trying to devise an explanation in case the photographs turned up.

"Yes, but what did you say *to* him?" She hadn't been prepared for this follow-up. She tried to think up the worst insult she could. She wrote, "I told him he was impotent." "You told him he was impotent?" The D.A. repeated. "Do you mean, sexually impotent?"

When she saw the expressions on Seth's and Monica's faces she realized what she'd said. Nick was glaring at the district attorney. It was too late to take it back. She had to nod, feeling nauseated as she realized that what she'd said might be repeated to Rob. Then she wondered if she'd said it because she'd wanted it to be.

Yet what way except doing things was there to find out what your motives were for doing them? Had Rob found out what his were? Didn't she want Pryce to ask her family questions because if he found out about Rob from someone besides her it would make what had happened more real? It would be harder for Pryce then to convince her that, sad as it might be, it was over—it had been over for ten years—which he was sure to try to do once he had the facts to argue with. Did she *want* him to try to persuade her—was that why she'd asked him to come? But if that were true, that would mean she didn't want to see Rob.

When the three of them entered the kitchen, Ellie and Monica looked up. Ellie was rinsing a saucepan at the sink and Monica was squeezing lemons into a juice strainer.

"We're engaged in a heated debate about the best way to make hollandaise sauce," Monica announced. "I say you do it the old-fashioned way, in a double boiler, but Ellie insists she can use the blender."

"That *is* controversial," Pryce said.

Zoë noticed that Nick hung the padlock key on a nail above the kitchen door.

VIII HARMONY

By the time Adam returns to Harmony a year later, it is summer again: daisies and black-eyed Susans brighten the fields; the white houses are being repainted white; the first crop of hay stands ready to be cut. Adam may have sailed around the world, but Harmony looks as if he's never left.

"I visited Father's grave this afternoon," he remarks to his mother at dinner, "and took a stroll about the churchyard. Ida Howe was buried here last year, I observed. When did she return to Harmony? You neglected to mention it."

If Louisa is startled she doesn't show it.

"It occurred after you left," she says.

"Indeed," Adam murmurs. "You might have reported it in a letter."

"I shouldn't have imagined the news would interest you."

"A death in a place the size of Harmony . . . you usually inform me of such events, that is all."

"She didn't die here," Louisa snaps. "Her daughter had her coffin brought back on the train."

"Her daughter? Charlotte? Was that not her name?"

"Yes."

"She has long since returned to wherever they had been living, I presume?"

"No," Louisa answers unwillingly. "She stayed on to teach school in Harmony."

"I see. And for what reason could she wish to remain here?"

"Perhaps she wishes to be near her mother," Louisa remarks.

"Her mother's dead," Adam replies.

They sit stalemated at one end of the long, gleaming dining-room table, the unoccupied tall-backed chairs looming at their places like disapproving cabinet ministers.

Eventually Adam learns that Charlotte is living at the old Dawes place, an abandoned farm two miles northeast of Harmony from which, one morning in the 1880's (so later will relate the town history), "Ephraim Dawes, his wife Sophronia, and their four children disappeared. Their half-eaten breakfast, speckled, by the time it was discovered, with mouse droppings, still sat upon the table. No trace of them was ever found."

If you read the history cover to cover, Zoë thought, you began to get quite a strange picture of the town: a witch condemned later than anywhere else in the country, six people vanishing, a judge driving his family (very slowly, it appeared) off a bridge . . . And somehow the Robies or the Howes were connected with many of the events, as if there weren't enough odd occurrences within the families themselves: Ida Howe's unexplained disappearances and returns, Henry Robie's older brother Samuel's drowning under mysterious circumstances, the way Charlotte thought that her marriage to Adam was foreordained . . . She said Adam Robie was the one person she'd looked forward to seeing when she decided to stay in Harmony after her mother's death, only to learn that he'd taken a job on one of the Robie Shipping Company's ships and that no one knew when he'd be back. "I knew then that he'd left town because of me," she said. "But, Grandmother . . ." Zoë protested. "He hadn't seen you for twelve years!" "Dear, there are simply things one knows," Charlotte said. "One can't *account* for them." By the same means, she'd known that he would come back.

"The Wilkinses agreed to rent it out to her," Louisa says of the Dawes house, "though why the girl should want to live all that way up in the woods by herself the devil alone can know."

"The devil! I say, is she a witch like her ancestress, Mother? Do you fear she'll cast her spells on the town?"

"The town," Louisa says, "is not what concerns me."

"Oh?" Adam inquires. Their forks rat-tat against the gold and white china, one of the many peace-offerings Henry brought home from his voyages. "And what does concern you, Mother?"

"You would not be the first whose imagination has been stirred by her seeming love of solitude."

"Seeming? She has admirers, do you mean?"

"How could she not? I knew her mother. The fruit falls close to the tree."

Adam wonders what his mother would say if he were to ask her whether Ida, too, disrobed and lashed herself with a hawthorn branch. He finds that it amuses him to think she might be scandalized. He himself, he feels, can never be shocked by anything again. For a year, every time he's closed his eyes, he's seen Charlotte's white back, spotted with red, and experienced again his own rapture; when he left Harmony he vowed to himself that if, after a year, the memory did not subside, then he was bound to her forever and would give himself over to a life of sin.

"I remember Ida," he remarks conversationally. "She used to make your clothes."

"Yes."

"Why did she leave Harmony?"

"I can't imagine," Louisa says shortly. "She did not favor me with her confidence."

"How did she die?"

"In a factory accident. She was working in a mill. That is all anyone knows."

Adam is surprised. He has not been curious about Charlotte's mother, has not wondered about her death before now; he never asked himself what might have prompted Charlotte's self-chastisement. It was too entangled in his mind with his own depraved pleasure.

"Ida Howe was the only friend I ever had," Louisa mutters, looking down the table as if addressing the ministers. "And I hated her."

She looks at her son, pleading with him, but he is sure she has told him this to trick him somehow and refuses to respond. He wonders sometimes what his mother might not be telling him, yet it tires him to think of it. If what he doesn't know mattered, he would know about it, he convinces himself, and, reassured by this reasoning, he soon retires again to his lookout on the roof; the urgency he felt on first hearing about Charlotte's other "admirers" abates. What is to happen is to happen, he tells himself, and time actually seems to slow, now that he no longer rebels against his fate. For a year, waking and sleeping, he could not stop picturing Charlotte's kneeling body, stop hearing the whisper of the branch as it divided the dense, deaf air, or stop reliving his own ecstasy and shame. All his life he has asked the Lord to forgive his trespasses and not to lead him into temptation, never imagining he was praying for himself. Is this why the Lord has not listened to him? For a year he's prayed for forgiveness, but the Lord has seemed uninterested in his penitence, and Adam sees that the only way to arouse the Lord's interest is to sin further. Others might bear the blame for one's transgressions, yet he sees now what he didn't on that happy day when he was six: without one's proper apportionment, without a punishment to equal one's crime, nothing is solid, nothing can be depended on. One drifts above life, like leaves too light to fall.

This decision made, he is in eternity again, the place he stumbled into the year before on the bluff when he first recognized that an unlimited interval can pass between a cause and an effect, and now there is all the time in the world, time for the farce of encountering Charlotte on the street and expressing surprise at seeing her again, offering sympathy for her mother's untimely demise; of encountering her a second time and suggesting she come to dine; of the dinner itself, his mother on his right, Charlotte on his left, the unctuous Timothy Lowndes at the faraway foot of the table; of his speaking colorfully of the "charm" of shipboard life; of Charlotte's courteous yet adamant refusal of his offer to escort her home. It is a long road in the dark, not another house the last mile, is she not uneasy? No, not in the least. What is there to fear? Louisa looks, as the saying goes, volumes, though Adam does not trouble himself to read their titles.

Charlotte does permit him to accompany her to the end of Main Street, however. There, after thanking him for dinner, she remarks, "You'll come to tea one afternoon?"

It is not a question. Adam has to admit that he admires Charlotte Howe. She plays her part very well. If he did not know better, he could be persuaded that she does not know what the outcome is to be, that it was not she who sailed around the world with him, but someone who resembled, but wasn't she. He permits another few weeks to elapse before he obeys her invitation.

It is now well into the summer, the same kind of stifling hot day on which, a year ago, Charlotte wandered into the circle of the telescope; such weather is rare enough in Harmony that when it settles in people feel their identities shift noticeably. It was on a day such as this that Adam's uncle Samuel drowned—he and Henry were swimming in the river above the falls. Sam called to Henry that he was going to float downstream, but Henry thought his brother was joking until he turned on his back and headed into the current. Henry lunged towards him, screaming with his entire body, but already he knew that it was too late. When Sam felt the current snatch him, he sat up and waved, as if from a reclining position on a soft sofa, and shouted to Henry above the roar of the water. Henry was never certain of what he said; he thought his brother had called out either "Don't hurry, I'm in no danger," or "Don't worry, I'm with an angel." He was certain, though, that whatever he had said, Samuel had not been alarmed.

Henry's parents concluded, after striving in every way they could to induce Henry to revise his story, that Samuel's mind must have been addled by the sun—he clearly hadn't understood where he was. They became so inconsolably distraught when Henry tried to convince them otherwise that he forbore to, yet all his life he thought about it, long after he had stopped mourning for his brother. Samuel had known he was headed for the falls. And he had truly believed he would be safe. Yet it was not, Henry was convinced, because he'd expected to be miraculously kept from harm. He had been ready to die. One afternoon the time had come for his brother Samuel to leave this life and Samuel had known all about it. Henry had never encountered anything, during all the rest of his years, that had impressed him so much as this fact. Even his passion for Ida Howe, deeply as he had undergone it, had not persuaded him that watching his brother disappear was not, in life, his only real experience.

Adam's clothes are drenched with sweat by the time he has climbed the last half mile of the steep unkept road, but, despite the heat, Charlotte is out in the garden, pulling weeds. She wears no hat and her hair is half undone. Though once again he sees her before she sees him, on this occasion he does not persist in this attitude.

"Charlotte?" he asks. "Miss Howe?"

She looks around quietly, not startled, then stands, holding her dirt-covered hands palm out from her sides. She wears a plain blue skirt and a blue and white striped blouse, the sleeves rolled up above her elbows. The lower part of her skirt is stained with grass, and her forearms are streaked.

"Quite a day for a walk you've chosen," she remarks.

"I hope you are not unpleasantly surprised."

"Not at all."

She is so cordial, so like a hostess welcoming a guest, that Adam is taken aback. He expected that simply to arrive at her door was all that would be required of him, but he sees that she intends to play the charade out.

"Won't you come in?"

In the large, bare kitchen she pumps water into crockery and bathes her arms and face, then lets down her long braid, and, peering into a small mirror, repins it neatly about her head. The sight of her bare forearms raised to pin her hair transfixes him, recalling to him as it does the other occasion on which he observed them raised in that position, and what he feels is nearly terror. What if Charlotte had not been in Harmony when he returned? What if no one had known where she was? What would he have done to attract the Lord's attention then? He was not serious when he suggested to his mother that Charlotte had gone away again, the possibility having never occurred to him, but now the risk seems sickeningly present, and his recent complacency strikes him as lunatic. He feels bewildered by Charlotte's composure.

"Will you take lemonade?" she asks. "It's too hot to build a fire for tea, don't you think?" Without waiting for an answer, she begins to cut lemons. "You chose the right day to come. I baked yesterday." She smiles at him. "I must have known the heat was coming on."

Carrying the pitcher of lemonade and two glasses, she leads the way into the parlor. Adam follows with a plate of jam tarts and slices of dark, rich gingerbread. Setting it down where she instructs, he looks around him. The parlor walls have faded to the color of unripe apples; the woodwork has darkened to cream, and he wonders why the dark colors lighten and the light darken. Why does he not know the answer, and why has the question never occurred to him before? The mystery seems part of the same mystery which he now sees suffuses everything; nothing can be predicted, least of all the consequence of one's actions, and yet within this uncertainty one is nevertheless constrained to act, to assume reasons, to judge. The Lord sits silent; where does one turn for guidance?

The room is sparsely and shabbily furnished, yet feels formal nonetheless, and Adam, arranging himself upon a tattered settee, can think of nothing to say. He is still convinced that Charlotte knows precisely why he has come, and he begrudges her the explanation she seems to await.

It is she who speaks first. She has a lovely voice, light and musical. It reminds him of something—or of someone—that he cannot remember. Attempting to, he recalls instead the child Charlotte. Disguised as a young woman, she sits sedately, her hands, clean, holding each other in her lap.

"When we were small," she asks, "do you remember?"

He nods, his resentment abruptly extinguished.

"I wanted so much to go to your house again with my mother, but she wouldn't allow it. I begged her, but she refused. I pointed out to her that I had not been a nuisance, but she became angry when I insisted. She was so rarely angry that I remember the occasion very clearly."

"Why was she angry?"

"I never learned. And then that summer we left Harmony."

"I looked for you in school in the fall. I was sorry that you had gone. Where did you go?"

"Everywhere." She laughs. "Concord, first. Mother worked in a dress factory until she found sufficient private clients. Then we went to Lowell, in Massachusetts; to New London, in Connecticut; we lived in Philadelphia for a while. I forget all the places. It seemed that, as soon as she became well established, we had to leave."

"But why?"

"I don't know. I've always thought you might."

"I!"

"Or your mother."

"How could she possibly know?" Then Adam recalls what Louisa said—that Ida was her only friend—but he does not tell Charlotte this; it seems to him that he needs to marshal as many private facts as he can to defend himself against what seems to him her impenetrable serenity.

She sighs now, as if at his disingenuousness. "I don't know. I had hoped . . ." She doesn't conclude her sentence, but asks instead, "When must you return to your ship?"

Sitting in an old, brocaded rocker, she observes him. Her gaze is the child Charlotte's, matter-of-fact, unimpressed.

"But I am never returning!" he exclaims.

"Not returning to your ship? But I thought you said . . ."

"Yes, I made it sound glorious, didn't I? Foreign ports, the rolling main . . ."

"I was quite envious."

"I have no ambition to be a sailor."

"I have," she says, and laughs. "What then displeases you about it?"

"Certain experiences are better left unspoken." He is angry with her again—she is toying with him too long.

"As you like."

Once again he is reminded of the little girl, demanding her turn at the telescope. He feels outraged at her willful incomprehension.

"What will you do instead?" she inquires politely. "Will you return to college?"

"I suppose I shall, yes."

Her eyes widen in disapproval. "If I were so privileged, I should not sound so resigned."

"But Charlotte!" he begins, then forces himself to speak gently. "It does not interest me. Must I pretend to value what I do not?" Surely she must know that everything will remain ephemeral until their contract is complete. "How is it that you seem so . . . certain? Do you never feel lonely here? Such a long way from the town, and with no neighbors . . ." But this is not what he wants to say at all, and he breaks off and looks out the window. When he looks back, he is startled by her expression: it contains kindness, even pity, and Adam, trying to interpret it, believes that she must be inviting him to say what he came to say, that she sees through his pretenses and asks that he see through hers.

"You feel it, don't you?" he exclaims. "You do! I have never been able to forget you, Charlotte. And then, when I heard that you had returned to Harmony . . . Oh, Charlotte . . . But I do not need to speak it. The understanding between us is too plain."

She, however, regards him now without expression. Unable to bear the force of her measured gaze, he stares down at his hands; silence drifts into the room like snow. By the time he dares to lift his eyes again, Charlotte is looking out the window. Suddenly a soft sigh escapes her, and at this sound, rising against her will from that privacy of hers to which he means to gain access, he stands and goes to her, sits wordlessly at her feet, and lays his head in her lap. After a moment she rests a hand on his head. Closing his eyes, he sinks into a dimly remembered sweetness; it envelops him, and he falls asleep.

Charlotte, stirring, wakes him. He sits up, startled, then smiles at her.

"Adam, you must go."

"We will be married, Charlotte."

She shakes her head. He raises himself to his knees and takes her hands.

"You know it must be. We are intended for one another—we always have been. I knew it the moment I saw you again."

"Don't say that!" she exclaims. "Don't ever say that. No one is intended for anything—you mustn't say so!"

"But it's true! I beg you . . . You must be my wife—you are my salvation!"

She stares at him in fury, unflinchingly, and he buries his face in her lap. Someone comforted him once before—someone, he does not remember whom—now it must be Charlotte. He believes she knows the reasons for everything. She tries to free herself, but he holds tightly to her hands and looks up at her. They hold each other's eyes. Then she whispers, "I'm afraid. Please . . ."

"Yes," he says eagerly. "Yes, you should be." She is trembling, and he thinks he has never known such sweetness.

"Go, please," she says, but it doesn't matter; he has won. "Please go."

They proceed outside in silence, down the path to the road. At the road she says, "I will write to you."

"I will expect your letter," he replies, and departs.

Over two months pass before she keeps her promise. He has even met her in the interim; school has recommenced and he has encountered her in the street. "Good afternoon, Charlotte," he said. "Good afternoon," she replied, and that was all, but that has nothing to do with it.

During the interval, Adam experiences no impatience. In fact his spirits rise in proportion to the time that passes without his having heard from Charlotte. She will not marry him, then, after all. She will say no—she is merely putting off the disagreeable task of communicating this to him because she does not wish to wound him. When he understands this, Adam feels his lost vigor returning and strides briskly to his desk and takes out a sheet of writing paper; he will tell her she need have no worry on this score; his proposal was made impetuously; he hereby releases her from any sense of obligation to him whatsoever. As he writes he feels a great lightness. The world is his again. Time ceases to stand still. He is exonerated! He offered his sacrifice to the Lord, but it was refused. Refused . . . There is the catch. He cannot redeem himself. Only Charlotte can do that.

Sick at heart, he takes the letter, which he has already signed and sealed, and sets fire to it. He watches it blacken and curl in the fireplace.

Shortly thereafter, her answer arrives. Though the envelope is addressed to him, there is no salutation above the brief message it contains, which says:

> I am not made for marriage. Nevertheless I will marry you. I regret that it must be so.
>
> Charlotte

IX SPARTA

After the Pipe School was forced to close down, Robert didn't come back to Hollister Day for the rest of the year; no one knew what had happened to him, and the teachers kept their knowledge to themselves. Even Bridget's mother, who was best friends with Mrs. Went, would say only, "Robert is taking a bit of time off." "The slime," Bridget said. "He's afraid to face us." She told Zoë she'd heard from her parents that Robert had squealed and, furthermore, after talking to her father (the wisest man in the universe), she understood that Mr. Kefauver and Mme. Alignac had brought the letters on themselves by being too tough in class, and her father was going to talk to them and tell them they'd better lighten up if they inspired their students to cast them in the roles of ogres. Why hadn't Seth thought of that? Zoë wondered.

Bridget also said that even though they had written letters before Robert joined the Pipe School they hadn't been *malevolent*; she said Robert wanted to make the whole world feel guilty about his accident.

"What do you mean, feel guilty?"

"Just guilty," Bridget said. "He wants everyone to be crippled like him."

"Why?" Zoë exclaimed.

"He just does. To get even."

"But he walked in front of the truck on purpose! He said he did."

"I never believed that for a single minute," Bridget said, which was a total lie.

Then Bridget said she'd suspected for a while that Robert was crazy but hadn't wanted to say anything because *she*, Zoë, seemed to like him so much.

"What!"

Bridget even acted like the Pipe School had been all Zoë's idea. Had it? Zoë tried to think, but she couldn't remember. It had never even seemed like something they thought up. Seth told her there were fair-weather friends and foul-weather friends and maybe she ought to consider carefully which kind Bridget was, but she didn't see *how*. Why had he said that anyway?

He kept having talks with her, usually up in his study, though half the time she couldn't understand a word he said. "The poor goddamned human race," he kept saying, shaking his head back and forth like a rhinoceros. "Cripples wanting to cripple other cripples . . ." That was how she knew he was talking about Robert, although he never mentioned him specifically anymore. Then he'd start spouting Shakespeare. "How weary, stale, flat, and unprofitable seem to me all the uses of this world. Fie on it! Ah fie!" In the history of the world three geniuses had sprung up and their names all began with S: Socrates, Shakespeare, and guess who. That was how he knew the secrets of the human soul. If you didn't exercise constant vigilance, the evil part of yourself would come out and take you over.

The study had been an attic; its ceiling slanted down to the top of the wainscoting, which was dark wood, like Seth's pipes; he kept them in a round pipe rack on his desk. The ceiling was white. There were two alcoves with dormer windows, which Zoë liked to sit in when Seth wasn't there, pretending she was Jane Eyre hiding from her mean cousin, or just looking out at the rooftops, wishing they were close enough together so she could run across them like the Artful Dodger. She could have gone all over town dropping mysterious notes down chimneys to make people nervous. Sometimes she did her homework in the study while Seth read, sitting in his Morris chair by the floor lamp and puffing on his pipe. She loved to watch him. Sometimes for no reason he'd dump the pipe out and start it over. He'd pull the trash can close and then knock the pipe stem against the rim to get the old tobacco out; once the trash caught on fire but he just stomped on it. He took the cleaning tool and scraped the bowl; next he stuck a pipe cleaner up the stem. They came in yellow packets the color of raincoats and shaped like a glasses case, and you could make things out of them, so even if she hadn't taken any lately, every time he picked up the packet he looked at her over the top of his glasses and said, "Have you been pilfering my pipe cleaners again, young lady?" "What are you going to do?" she asked. "Call the police?" She knew he'd be disappointed if she ever really stopped stealing them.

After he shook tobacco out of the pouch into the bowl, he jammed it down with the round tool like a tiny potato masher with no holes in it. Finally he lit it, puffing with short breaths until it was burning right, making a dragonful of smoke.

When they told her the rule of never accepting rides from strangers she said of course she wouldn't except from men who smoked pipes because no man who smoked a pipe would be a criminal. "You may have a point there," Seth said. "For God's sake, Seth!" Monica shouted. But Nick backed her up. "Really, Mom, think about it. What criminal would smoke a pipe? Maybe Professor Moriarty, but he doesn't drive around kidnapping children." "That's right," Seth said. "Only the masterminds are pipe smokers." "Seth, for pity's sake," Monica said, "this is serious." "I agree entirely," he said. Zoë and Nick looked at each other. "Why is it," Monica asked, "that whenever I try to have a serious conversation with another member of my family I emerge with my sense of reality distorted?" "Criminals smoke cigarettes and cigars," Zoë said, to stop the discussion before it got out of hand. Monica had already arranged all her silverware perfectly on her plate.

Sometimes, not while he had his pipe in his mouth, but when he had taken it out and set it down in the ashtray, Seth fell asleep reading. His head dropped forward; he'd start to snore and snap it back up, but it would slump down again. Finally he'd lean his head back against the chair and really sleep. Zoë would watch him dozing off, trying not to laugh; if she laughed he woke up and said, "What's so funny?" with his feelings hurt. If she told him he'd been sleeping he refused to believe it.

When he was sound asleep, she pretended he was dead. He was a tragic figure—he'd told her he was and she knew he was right. He bore the world's sorrows in his heart but was powerless to assuage them. She wished she knew what to do to help him. She always got tears in her eyes, imagining his funeral; she and Nick would be dressed in black clothes (Monica would already have died), and people would all be looking at them, whispering "The poor orphans. All alone in the world." In public they wouldn't shed a tear. When people tried to separate them, making her go live with the Wycliffes and Nick with the Tannenbaums, they'd run away and live in the woods on wild food. Once when Seth suddenly snorted himself awake with an especially loud snore, she almost screamed.

Mostly when he was sleeping she just looked out over the roofs and planned the future. She and Bridget were going to live together; they would have a castle in England or Scotland, a villa in Italy, and a regular house in America. They would have to be apart some of the time, however, because besides the things they both wanted to be (a courtesan, a saint, and a political prisoner) Bridget was going to be a composer and a concert pianist, and Zoë was going to be an archaeologist. Bridget would go on concert tours and she would be in foreign countries noticing that hills were really pyramids. You couldn't do that in America; hills were just hills over here. If Heinrich Schliemann or Howard Carter had been born in America they would never have dug up anything. She had never heard of an archaeologist being American, but more than anything in her life she wanted to find something from the past that no one else had, something that would make some big suspicion come true. She read over and over again the descriptions of famous archaeologists finding things. There they'd be, just strolling along in the desert, and suddenly they'd get an intuition; they'd call to their helpers all digging in the wrong place, "I say, chaps, have a try over there," and they would, and that would be it. Or like when they first found the secret passage into the pyramid—she could hardly even stand reading about it. "But then, beyond the first, was another, even larger, chamber, and when at last the men rolled back the block of stone from the opening, a blast of cold air that seemed as old as time itself struck us full in the face. We stood in silent awe, breathing air more ancient than history, knowing we stood on the threshold of what had not been disturbed for thousands of years . . ." *Thousands of years.* "Then I shone a flashlight into the opening, and saw that a flight of stairs led down into darkness . . ." *A flight of stairs. Down into darkness.* Zoë kept having to put the book down while she read, feeling as if she were sinking backward into emptiness, sinking and sinking without ever stopping, and she read the sentences over and over, making the feeling come back until it wouldn't anymore: the cold air, lurking there all that time, rushing out at them, the stairs leading down, *down into darkness, stairs, down, darkness, thousands of years, darkness.* The stairs that led to the tomb, the burial chamber, the sarcophagus, the inner sarcophagus, and then, and then, finally . . . It just seemed, if you got to see all that with your own eyes, that maybe, even if just for one second, the mummy would still be alive.

Bridget couldn't fathom in the least why any intelligent person would want to be an archaeologist; she said it would be hot all the time in the places where you excavated and you'd get dysentery and have to sleep with mosquito netting, not to mention all the snakes there would be, and hostile natives, but Zoë didn't care; it would be worth it to find something no one else had ever found and, frankly, *she* couldn't fathom in the least how Bridget could practice the piano so much—from five to six every night, and Thursdays after school she had lessons—or why she got so excited about concerts, the most boring things in the universe. You had to just sit there and *listen.* It wasn't as if Zoë was an ignoramus about music—she could read music and play the recorder—their whole class had to; but she'd had a tragic experience with music and maybe that was why she didn't like going to concerts. She took her recorder book home to practice with and once she forgot to bring it back to school; because she was terrified of telling Mrs. Bridewell, the recorder teacher, she stole Zillo's, Kitty Angstrom's stuffed monkey's. Kitty had books in every subject for him with his name written in them, and she made him sit at a desk beside her and had a fit if anyone tried to move him. No one could understand why Mrs. Bridewell, who stared you into dust for nothing, allowed her to keep him there, but she did. Kitty had tried to get the teachers to give Zillo grades but they'd refused. At recess that day while everyone was outside, Zoë took Zillo's recorder book out of his desk and erased his name from across the top and wrote Zoë over it, using the same Z, but you could still see *illo* under *oë* if you looked carefully.

When recorder class came, Kitty couldn't find the book and shrieked as if she'd found a dead body, and Zoë was terrified out of her mind; she knew she would be discovered and be a thief in the eyes of the class and get expelled, but Mrs. Bridewell suddenly went crazy and yelled at Kitty to stop her ridiculous charade that very instant or she would take her blasted monkey and personally rend him limb from limb. Then Kitty started to cry and Zoë felt terrible; not only had she stolen Zillo's book like a criminal, Kitty had gotten in trouble for it.

Well, Seth was right, her evil nature had come out and now she was stuck with it; she took the book home in her backpack, then walked down to Main Street and threw it in a trash can outside of Woolworth's, first tearing off the corner with her name on it to throw away in a different trash can; even so she worried that somehow someone would find out, and she had bad dreams about Mrs. Bridewell and monkeys for a long time.

Starting when Zoë was in first grade, Monica had gone back to working part time—she worked for a lawyer—and then when Zoë was in fourth grade and Nick in sixth she went full time. They always got home before she did, and usually there was a note of instructions on the kitchen table. "Please peel half a dozen potatoes." "Nick, here's the check for the scouts' trip." "One of you, please zip around to Mike's and pick up a half gallon of ice cream—whatever flavor you prefer. Don't spend the change!" "Please take the clothes out of the washer and put them in the dryer. Low heat." "Clean your rooms! This is an ultimatum!"

One afternoon, they came home from school as usual, but on the table, instead of a short note, was an envelope that said "Nicholas and Zoë" on it. Inside was a whole letter. It began, "Dear Zoë and Nick." Why did she write "Nicholas" instead of "Nick" and then reverse their names inside?

"What is it?" Zoë asked.

"It's a letter from Mom, obviously," Nick said.

"I know, but I mean why did she write us a letter?"

"Why does she put 'Dear Zoë and Nick'?" he exclaimed. "Who did she think was going to read it? A burglar?" He held it flat on the table and they both started reading.

> "Dear Zoë and Nick,
>
> What I have to tell you is going to be difficult—for both you and me. You will be right to think it cowardly of me to do it this way; I can only hope that someday you'll understand how painful a job this is. The fact of the matter is, your father and I have decided to separate."

"What!" she said.

"They're insane," Nick said. "Sit down, I'll read it out loud."

"I was getting a Coke."

"Forget the Coke!"

"Just stop yelling!" she shouted. She sat down and he went on.

> "Although I know this will come as a shock to you, we thought it fairer to the two of you to make the situation plain, instead of having you have to suspect it and worry about it."

"What situation? What does she mean?"

"She's out of her mind," Nick said. "They both are. Men with strait-jackets ought to come and get them."

"Are they getting *divorced*?"

He just went on reading.

> "I'm sure you've noticed that your father and I haven't been getting along too well recently. However, though we discussed having one of us move out, it seemed that neither of us is ready to do that. What we've done is to agree upon an arrangement that will permit us to remain under the same roof."

"That means they're not getting divorced, then."

"Would you mind letting me finish?"

> "From now on, I'll have the bedroom for myself, and your father will move to his study. Since on weekdays we all leave the house before your father gets up, there won't be any problems in the mornings; three nights a week he has a late seminar. We haven't yet figured out the other two nights or the weekends, but perhaps your father will take you out to dinner on one of them, for instance."

"He hates restaurants," she said.

"I feel like leaving home," Nick said.

"Is that the end?"

> "Weekends will be the trickiest, but we'll work something out that we can all agree on.
>
> "I'm sorry, Zoë, Nick, that this has happened. It has to do with many things that happened long before you were born. Please believe me that if there had seemed to be any other way out of it, we would have taken it. Neither of us wants to harm you two, and we've thought long and hard before taking this step. Just remember, whatever you may think about us, that none of this is your fault."

"Why would it be our fault?" she asked.

"Look," Nick said. He showed her where the letter was signed. It said, "Your mother, Monica Carver."

Zoë turned away.

"I wouldn't cry a single tear for them, if I were you. They're zombies. They're total and complete idiots. I hope they go to hell!" But he was crying too. "You know what? I'm going to *burn* this letter, *that's* how much I think of it. *That's* how much I care what it says."

He crumpled the pages all together and marched into the dining room. She ran after him.

"What are you *doing*? The fireplace doesn't work! The whole house will burn down!"

"It can burn to the ground for all I care."

"Nick, don't!" she screamed, as he took out his matches. "Stop it!"

"It's just a couple of pages! Don't worry about it."

He struck the match and the paper flamed up right away. Some smoke billowed into the room but the paper burned up almost at once. Then he marched down the hall and opened the front door.

"Where are you going?"

"I don't know. Anywhere. I disown them as my parents. From now on I'm no relation to them at all."

"How can you do that?"

"I just did it."

They were down the front steps.

"Aren't you going to lock the door?"

"Are you kidding? I hope a thief does get in. I hope he steals everything. I hope an ax-murderer gets in and lies in wait for them."

"But shouldn't we get some stuff to take with us? Maybe there's money in their bedroom."

"I'm never setting foot in there again as long as I live."

"I don't mind getting it. Will you wait for me?"

"I don't know what I'll do. I don't even feel like staying on this street one more second."

His face looked like a mean rock. All of a sudden she said, "Nick, I'm going to throw up."

"Cut it out. You are not."

How do you know? she started to say, but there wasn't any time, and she ran back into the house and down the hall to the downstairs bathroom. She had never thrown up when she was by herself before—Seth or Monica had always been there and held her forehead. She got the seat up just in time and leaned over the water. What if her head got in it? When she stopped she saw Nick standing in the doorway staring at her. She got up, holding on to the washbasin.

"You better lie down," he said.

"I want to brush my teeth."

"Okay, but then lie down."

"What are you going to do? Are you still leaving?"

"I'll come up in a minute."

"You promise?"

"Yes, just stop arguing!"

When she got to the stairs, she looked around over the banister and saw him hold his nose and then go in and flush the toilet. In the upstairs bathroom she brushed her teeth, then went into her room, but she felt funny in there; it looked as if somebody had gotten in and done something to it, so she went up to the study instead, pulling herself up by the banister. She curled up in the windowseat with her head on the sill. She didn't even look out at the roofs.

"Where are you?" she heard Nick calling.

She didn't answer until he called two more times, then she said, "Up here."

He came in with a bottle of Coke syrup and a spoon.

"You have to take this."

She started to laugh.

"What's so funny? It's what they always give us for throwing up."

"I know. It's just funny." She let him give her two spoonfuls, trying to keep from getting hysterics. If she laughed she might throw up again. The same thing had happened the day she heard about the Tannenbaums' grandfather—she had almost thrown up on the sidewalk. Was she going to get sick every time she heard bad news? Maybe she was Psychosomatic after all—she felt happy, thinking this. Then she saw the letter on the desk.

"Look!"

"What?"

She pointed. Nick walked over and picked up the long white envelope. "It's to Dad. From Mom." He turned it over. "It's licked shut."

"We could steam it open."

"Who cares what she says."

"What if it's about us? Don't you think we ought to find out what's in it?"

Nick made a face.

"Well, I'm going to, even if you're not."

She picked it up and headed for the stairs.

"Zoë! Forget steaming it," he said. "All we have to do is make another envelope. We can forge her handwriting."

"Okay." She came back into the study and started to rip the envelope.

"Wait!" he shouted. He sounded as if there was some grave danger. "We better make sure there *is* another envelope." He looked through Seth's desk. "Okay, here's one." He sat down in the desk chair and took a pen out of the shaving mug with the broken handle that Seth kept all his pens and pencils in. "I better practice a few times. Here, give it to me. No, I mean, take the letter out of the envelope and give me the old envelope." He took it and copied "S. J. Carver" over several times, then wrote it on the fresh envelope.

"Wow! It looks exactly the same."

"Not to an expert. But they'd have to have the envelopes side by side to compare."

Then they read Monica's letter. It went on forever. It was eight and a half pages long. They took turns reading it out loud. The one who wasn't reading sat in the windowseat with the dictionary to look up the words they didn't know, and they both listened every few minutes to make sure Monica hadn't come home, even though she didn't usually get there for another hour. It was tiring, reading it. She kept underlining everything and putting commas even where she didn't need them. It was all about whose fault their marriage was, saying it had been a mistake, a very costly mistake, they should never have gotten married, she had been snowed under by him and had gotten trapped by the way he saw her, whatever that meant. But there was one extremely interesting part—it was Zoë's turn reading—and she felt like the words were going to slither off the page if she didn't read them fast enough. It was about their grandmother Charlotte, how she had hallucinations and had to take drugs so she wouldn't think about their mother's four dead brothers; she and Nick had never even heard of them. Monica said Seth tried to make her feel cruel for not letting Charlotte go off drugs, saying Charlotte's hallucinations had never hurt anybody, but how did he know? Had he been her child? She was sick to death of being told how to run her life. She was tired of his grandiose ideas—Nick looked up "grandiose"—and simply wanted to live a peaceful life without having to *think* so goddamn much about everything. It took her a good deal of courage to admit that, since like everyone else she was in awe of Seth's mind ("There's proof that she's berserk," Nick said), but life was short and she wanted to enjoy what was left of it. No doubt, she said, his position on these matters was all related to his upbringing, his parents dying when he was so young in "less than savory circumstances" and his having to be brought up by Aunt Minerva, but he refused to accept that he could never recover what he hadn't had. "Do you think *I* couldn't spend the rest of *my* life mourning *my* childhood, if I were so inclined?" she wrote. "Can you not comprehend that as a result of your never-ending grieving you're denying the very thing you long for to your own children?"

"What's he denying us?" Zoë asked Nick, stopping for a minute.

"Who knows. Money."

> "I suppose in a way we were a perfect pair, both of us carrying such chips on our shoulders. I thought we'd heal ourselves together. I thought that, when we finally had our own family, by giving our children the love and security we both had lacked, we'd somehow feel vindicated—and yes, I do mean vindicated."

She waited while Nick looked up "vindicated." It didn't make any more sense.

> "But it hasn't worked that way. We envy them. We want from them what we should be giving."

"I don't think she means money," Zoë said to Nick.

"Who knows and who cares."

> "What I have to say is this. If you decide you want to stop mourning the world and look forward, let me know. I don't intend to make a permanent move for a while. But I'm tired of cohabiting with the shades of what might have been, Seth. I want to breathe the air of the living."

That was the end, and they folded the letter and put it into the new envelope, sealed it, and set it back on Seth's desk.

"What are we going to do with the old envelope?"

"Burn it too. That was all meaningless," Nick said.

"You mean she made it up?"

Nick shrugged.

"Why didn't she ever tell us she had four brothers who died?"

"Probably for the same reason she does everything she does. Because she's a maniac. They're both maniacs."

"But what about Grandma Charlotte having hallucinations? You think Mom made that up too?"

"Zoë, stop asking me! I don't know!"

"But that would mean Grandma's crazy."

"So? Her daughter is. It's probably inherited."

"Then we'll get it too."

"Maybe *you* will," he said. "I'm nothing like them."

After that he would hardly ever talk about things anymore. Only when he was in a certain mood, which she could never tell when he'd be in. Monica and Seth kept writing letters, since they'd stopped speaking to each other, but after the first few times Nick wouldn't read them with her. Dr. Macmillan said it was unhealthy. "I could care less what Dr. Macmillan says," she told him. She kept reading them. She had no choice. She got expert at forging envelopes, then Seth and Monica stopped bothering to put the letters in envelopes. Maybe they wanted her to read them.

For a while after Seth and Monica first stopped speaking, Zoë thought something new would happen. She kept expecting that they'd run into each other and fight. Whenever Seth came home earlier than usual and she knew Monica wasn't in the bedroom yet, it felt like murderers had broken in and she was waiting under her bed for them to find her, but the few times they did run into each other they just said hello in normal voices and went on with whatever they were doing. Nick said in his opinion it was a big plot to drive their children crazy. Dr. Macmillan had told him upset parents sometimes thought their children were the root of their problem; Nick said Seth and Monica were probably sneaking up- and downstairs in the middle of the night, just pretending to be separated. He bet if they kept watch they'd catch them, and she got all excited, thinking about it, but he would never do it. She told him she'd do all the watching, she didn't mind, as long as she could wake him if she heard anything. But he still said no. She thought she'd do it on her own, then, and kept trying to stay awake; she'd fall asleep imagining hearing them and how she'd get out of bed without making any noise and then creep down the hallway with the flashlight, waiting while Seth came down the stairs. When he was almost to where she was, she'd jump up, turn the flashlight on in one fell swoop and shine it right smack in his eyes, blinding him, and shouting at the top of her lungs, she'd shout, "What the *hell* do you think you're doing?"

X CASCABEL FLATS

Zoë helped Nick set the table while Ellie and Monica finished getting dinner, which besides hollandaise sauce consisted of pork chops, broccoli, applesauce, and wild rice. For dessert there was caramel custard, which Ellie insisted on calling *flan* since the Spaniards had conquered the area in the 1500's. The next night they were going to the Beauregards'; Christmas Eve they were having lamb. Monica hadn't seen a leg of lamb like the one Ellie had in the refrigerator in ten years—she made it sound as if butchers had been holding out on her. There was a delicate moment when she opened the freezer door to find Ellie more butter, but if she even noticed the big white unmarked box containing Nick's mice she didn't mention it. Maybe because she knew better than to "ask questions at this time of year," as she'd always warned them when they were little not to do.

When they sat down to eat, Ellie lit the red candles and turned off all the lights except for one small lamp in a distant corner of the living room—no doubt she'd put rattlesnake meat into something and didn't want them to notice. Nick served the plates and then everyone passed around the side dishes: olives and celery sticks and sweet pickles; the closer it came to Christmas, the more they'd have to eat. Ellie had already taken control of the airwaves and announced that now that she had them immobilized she meant to have her curiosity satisfied: how had Zoë and Pryce met and how come this was the first they'd heard of him when—if in fact she had her information correct—they'd been seeing each other for almost two years? Pryce said he couldn't answer the second half of her question—he knew next to nothing about any of them either—but he could respond to the first: they'd met in a law library.

"What were you doing in a law library?" Nick asked.

Looking something up, Zoë answered.

"I noticed her gesturing for pen and paper to the librarian and since I'd taken some courses in sign language I decided to try out my skills."

Zoë watched Nick to see how he took Pryce's blatant acknowledgment of what everyone in their family avoided mentioning, but if it bothered him he wasn't showing it. Or he was still trying to guess what she'd been doing in the library. She had wanted *Derivation of the Civil Penal Code from Religious Penitential Customs* (they didn't have it), a book referenced in something else she'd been reading. She'd been trying to find out more about the Grand Penitentiary in Rome—not a holy prison, but the cardinal in charge of considering cases of vows and sins too grave for parish priests to deal with. Any priest could release you from a vow never to take another drink or absolve you of the sin of having been unkind to your mother-in-law, but things like committing murder or taking a lifetime vow of silence could only be handled by the Vatican. But how did the cardinal decide? She wanted to know that before she decided whether it would be worth her while to become a Catholic. (She half meant this.) She envisioned him sitting around with other cardinals in their scarlet robes and odd-shaped hats listening to some poor sap explaining why his vow had been a mistake and then debating whether or not to release him. What criteria did they use? How long the person had already kept the vow? Whether the reasons for making it had been good ones? What did a vow mean from which you could be released?

It was difficult to find out even the most basic things. She had followed numerous false leads, including her trip to the law library, before finally learning that only such things as the welfare of one's family, "great difficulty in the fulfillment of the vow," or not having made the vow freely (out of fear, for example) were considered adequate causes for dispensing one from it. It sounded so rote, written down like that, but real situations couldn't be so clear cut. She could probably make a case for the first condition, but the other two?

In the case of the second, it was easy to "fulfill your vow" when the thought of not fulfilling it turned your stomach counterclockwise. And as for the third condition—what about undergoing something first and then taking a vow afterwards so it would seem as if you'd meant to incur that fate? Had the cardinals ever thought of that? They had no power to release her, she'd known that before she started out (Rob would have enjoyed the irony of her being brought up sacrilegious and ending up feeling things only Catholics had names for); she just wanted to see what kinds of things had to happen to people before they could escape from conditions like hers. But most of the books she'd found that had anything to do with what she was interested in were in Latin, and even if she'd remembered enough from high school to read them, they wouldn't discuss the debates held in actual cases; those were top secret. If the discussions had been recorded at all, the transcripts would be locked up in the Vatican Archives. The Vatican Archives—one of the most top-secret places in the world; what information could there *be* so sensitive that probably only the pope himself was allowed to see some of it? Conclusive evidence that IT had all been a hoax? That "He" never did go anywhere after the third day . . . Evidence that the Virgin Birth had been one of a series? Maybe they had an account of the Harmony witch trial in there. *Things kept happening.*

It had made Pryce furious when she told him he'd been attracted to her because he felt like he was coming to her assistance—the savior complex (though she didn't use those words with him). "Helping people is natural—why do you make it sound like a crime? So initially I wanted to practice my sign language, so what? I wasn't attracted to *you* until I got to know you!" But her speechlessness *was* who she was; he'd never understood that—kept pushing her all the time to "seek treatment."

"I don't pretend to understand all the circumstances—though perhaps I might have a better shot at it if you'd trust me more—but I can tell when someone's stuck . . ." No, she didn't trust him—him or anyone who wanted to make her talk about what had happened. Only by remaining silent could she be faithful to what she'd seen then, the moment she'd last tried to speak—how she was responsible for everything that had happened; she knew very well that the instant she opened her mouth others would rush to contradict her. It's not your fault, Zoë! How can you blame yourself like this! Everyone's responsible for their own actions—even if you *did* upset Rob (and even there you can't convince us that you meant to, you were so upset yourself, having just discovered your best friend with your own father in a "compromising situation"; you know very well that it was only after the fact that you blamed yourself, trying to find any reason you possibly could to explain what was so incomprehensible . . .). They'd work away at her until she began to believe she was innocent herself.

"A *Messiah* complex, you have *heard* of?" Dr. Velkior always lowered his chin and looked out from under his inch-high eyebrows whenever he said something he thought would startle her.

In the end the grand jury—and everyone else—all concluded that Rob was crazy, at the very least "temporarily insane": he claimed to have killed his father on purpose only because he couldn't accept the horror of the accident, which maybe he had caused inadvertently, but no one was even convinced of that. It was a "not uncommon defense mechanism," according to Dr. Velkior, the psychiatrist Monica had made Zoë see (over Seth's objection)—not Dr. Macmillan, thank God for small favors; he would have tried to cure her "hysterical muteness" by observing whether she improved her holdings uniformly and gradually or sank all her resources into hotels on Boardwalk and Park Place. Dr. Velkior, pronounced "Velkyer," wasn't much of an improvement, however. And she had to go all the way to Baltimore to see him. "Often *times*," he said, in his unidentifiable foreign accent, "it is preferable *ourselves* to blame than terrible things to *believe* simply *happen* in this life." He put the object before the verb and emphasized every other word, as if he were giving dictation. He had a huge nose that had made Zoë understand the application of the word "bulbous," tiny ratty eyes, and a short, triangular beard—where Monica had dredged him up God only knew.

You see, it really *was* my father you wanted to kill—or maybe Anders Ogilvy, Zoë said now to Rob, as the others pursued their dinner-table conversation, but you would have thought it was up to me to decide my own father's fate, and you didn't know who took the pictures. Yet you had to do something. Maybe all the fathers did blend together in your mind, I don't know. You had said that antireligious stuff, but I never thought you really meant it. I thought you were trying to tell me something else—religion always seemed like a code to me. When you said you thought you could be the Antichrist—someone had to be—I thought it was your roundabout way of talking about your feelings for me. I'm *sorry*, but I did.

How on earth did I come up with that? Look, Rob, I don't *know*. I just thought you were so frustrated by the way nothing was happening between us. You kept complaining how the Bible was the "root of all evil"—what was the one book everyone had read? What was the major influence on everyone whether they knew it or not? Do you remember *saying* that at least? If that was the major influence and the world was the way it was—"Well, you can draw the conclusion yourself, Miss Carver." *Excuse* me for thinking that when you were talking about the "state of the world," the "inability of any two people ever to trust each other, they were always worrying what the other person's intentions were, whether Original Sin would get the better of them," et cetera, I thought you were talking about us.

To be let out of the hospital, did you have to say that you finally believed your father's death had been an accident; that you understood that blaming yourself had been an "unconscious guilt mechanism" (thank you, Dr. Velkior)? But I can see you swallowing your pride to make a false confession of innocence only if you'd come up with a plan to convince everyone once and for all that you knew perfectly well what you were doing. We always agreed that people who changed their minds about important beliefs were the lowest of the low. What better way to convince people than to kill my father the minute they let you out? What I *don't* understand is why it took you ten years to come up with this idea. What have you been *doing* in there all this time?

No, don't say that, that you've been waiting for me to tell what I knew—I refuse to believe that. So I could have said I knew who owned a beige Studebaker—the end result might have been that the grand jury believed you but then everyone would have known it was my fault that you became a murderer—I couldn't let you be punished for it even if you wanted to be; I hope you can understand that, at least. If they'd found you guilty, then I would have loved a murderer—how could I have? I loved *you*. Of course, maybe Anders wasn't even there; isn't it more likely that somehow you'd already learned that I was posing for him and had found out he had a beige Studebaker and mentioned it in court to let me know that you knew who he was? Or it could have been a completely unrelated beige Studebaker that came out of nothingness just in time to drive by when you were killing your father and then disappeared back into nothingness. The Holy Ghost in the form of a Studebaker, trying to figure out whose side of the other two in the Trinity to be on. Maybe this time you'll go after Anders, not my father, though I'm probably flattering myself; it would be me you'd want to hurt, not my seducer (which he wasn't technically, though you would assume he was, which I know I knew).

"There is a long tradition of vowing *silence*," Dr. Velkior said. "Some people think a *way* it is of closer coming to *God*. Do you *want* to closer come to God?"

"Not particularly," she wrote.

Dr. Velkior thought that if she confessed whatever it was she'd stopped talking not to say, she'd be cured, but if she told him she'd stopped talking because when you talked all you did was tell lies he'd ask her "What lies?" and she'd have to tell more. When you spoke with your hands, there was never the same gap between what you meant and what you said; the shapes had an integrity of their own that speech could never attain.

You were stupid ever to tell them the religious stuff, Rob; you should have realized you'd only reinforce what they already thought about you—paranoid schizophrenic projection displacement dissociative megalomania, nothing to it. "After two thousand years, someone had to get even"—I'm sure they ate that up. Brought experts to look at you. I asked Dr. Velkior why he said you had a Messiah complex when you'd killed your father—that was a mistake. "No, Zoë," he said—he pronounced my name "Zo-eh." "No, your friend Robert *himself* killed. To another human being *kill* the method the cleverest is of *oneself* destroying!" It wasn't that I wanted to hear his opinion, but I had to keep him from guessing that you'd talked to me about it all.

Yes, I know, Rob; there's a contradiction in my argument. First I say I kept things from the grand jury to prevent them from realizing you had a motive—I preferred you to be considered insane to evil; then I say that I didn't want to give them more reason to think you were "mentally unstable." But it's not that hard to understand. I'd believed you. I believed *in* you. If you were really capable of murdering someone, what did that make me? Wouldn't I have had to be evil too? On the other hand, if I'd trusted the views of someone who was insane, how could I ever trust anyone again? Do you wonder that I've never gone to Anders and asked him if he was driving down Stark Road that afternoon? He wouldn't lie to me—he didn't lie (though I thought he did; I couldn't believe anyone could be that unfeeling).

Having described their meeting and their "courtship" (gallantly exaggerating the ardors of his "pursuit"), their apartment, and their desire to get out of the city more frequently (such mutualities as he could legitimately claim), Pryce had gone on to talk about his job, his family, etc. (Zoë had the feeling that Nick had continued to observe her, but she couldn't be sure.) One of the amazing facts about her family was the way they never pressed her on anything—it had been Ellie who'd asked why she'd never so much as mentioned Pryce's name before. Nick and Monica and Seth had grown so in the habit of respecting her privacy—as if they had instinctively understood why she'd stopped speaking. They might not be officially mute, but they'd all vowed their own sorts of silence.

Now there came a lull, during which everyone caught up on their chewing. They had all had more than a little of the expensive burgundy Monica had bought several bottles of in town the day before—neither Zoë nor Nick had ever been able to remember the first thing Monica had tried to teach them about wine, which exasperated her no end. She, as if now that they were all on a more confidential footing she dared pose this question, asked Nick and Ellie if they really honestly thought that someone could have built a studio over a rattlesnake den on purpose—the way she put it, she seemed to be adding, "when we find ourselves over rattlesnake dens often enough without trying." Ellie said she'd bet a lot of money that yes, Jules had, if there were any way of proving it one way or another. Then more tipsy proselytizing from Nick on behalf of rattlesnakes. The rattlesnake should have been the national mascot, not the eagle. One of the early flags *had* had a rattlesnake on it, everyone might recall—"Don't Tread on Me" was the logo. The first settlers had been so amazed by this dread new serpent, which *announced* that it was going to bite you before it did, that they'd wanted to commemorate it. "A talking serpent, where else have we heard that before, boys and girls?" Nick asked, practically chortling. He sounded more and more like Seth all the time—"Find the philosopher's stone, kids; it's around somewhere. Don't waste time on anything less." Yet Nick seemed more intoxicated than could be explained by the wine; if Zoë hadn't known how he felt about drugs she'd have been tempted to think he was on something. (He wasn't self-righteous, he always explained; what disturbed him was not people's trying to medicate their way out of problems but the imprecision; until the discovery of the chemical that could restore the mind to its original balance, everything else was stopgap measures . . .)

"But then, a year or two before his death," Ellie was saying, "something supposedly happened to Jules's work. He had always drunk like the proverbial fish, but, for a period of six months in the midst of all his debauching, he stopped drinking entirely, worked like a madman, refused to see his friends . . . Irene MacKenzie, Judith's mother, was the only person he'd allow to visit him. Judith is Stewart's wife," she reminded them, for their approaching exam in Beauregard Family History. "Even Irene never *saw* the paintings, but she was convinced by the way Jules was acting that he was producing great work. Then, after those few months, the spurt was over. He started drinking again, told people he'd done what he'd been sent on earth to do, and didn't care if he never saw another paintbrush. I got all this from Nancy or Michael, of course. One doesn't ask Stewart about such things."

"Yet you think he keeps his father's paintings under lock and key," Pryce said.

"Oh, I don't think anything. I've learned not to think, where he's concerned. It never does any good."

This was so obviously untrue that Ellie had to reach for plates and start clearing the table in order to give her remark some credibility; everyone except Monica stood to help. She said, "I think I'll invoke the prerogative of my ancient years and stay put."

In the kitchen, when Pryce and Nick sortied on another dish-gathering mission, Ellie said, "Keep me company while I make the coffee, won't you? I feel as if I've hardly had a chance to talk to you at all."

She stalled any objection by crossing the room to take a white ceramic coffee pot and matching filter-holder down from a shelf. When Pryce and Nick came back, she said, "I think Zoë and I can manage from here on. Yes, I have an ulterior motive," she added when Nick and Pryce left. She waited until Zoë stopped stacking dishes and faced her. "I realize it's a little unfair, trapping you like this, but I didn't know how soon I'd get another chance. Obviously we're all on top of each other in this house."

Zoë remembered to nod. She didn't feel like hearing whatever it was, though she wasn't surprised; it was nothing new for Ellie to take her aside and "ask her advice" about some problem with Nick, in other words, to bemoan her fate. "I love him, but . . ." was usually in there somewhere. His difficulty in working as part of a research team "concerned her." His moods and uncommunicativeness made her "frantic." They'd always made Zoë frantic too, but when Ellie complained about him she usually pretended not to know what Ellie was talking about. Now she expected Ellie was going to say that she'd hoped the move out West would cure Nick of his monomanias, but instead he was worse than ever—him and his rattlesnake farm. However, that turned out not to be what Ellie had to say at all.

"I guess what I want to ask you . . ." she began. She always paved the way with questions. "How does your brother seem? I mean, does he seem different in any way? How long has it actually been since you've seen him? A year?"

Zoë fingerspelled L-O-N-G-E-R.

Ellie sighed. "I know, I'm being unnecessarily cryptic. I just wanted to find out if you'd noticed anything—if he seemed particularly tense, maybe, or . . ." She sighed again. "I don't know that you really want to hear about all this."

Zoë opened her palms: *Go ahead.* She reminded herself to say nothing of what Nick had told them earlier about his hopes for rattlesnake venom if Ellie didn't already know.

"I wouldn't hit you with it if there were anyone else I could talk to. It's just that . . ."

Ellie frowned, and Zoë was surprised to see that she'd widened her eyes to keep tears in. She had always been outraged rather than unhappy.

"There's Nancy, whom I've mentioned. I can *talk* to her, and of course she knows Nick—it's just that she doesn't really know his background. What's going on may have to do with that. At least I've had to conclude that it does." She tried to smile. "I don't mean to be so mysterious. It's just hard to get started. There isn't anyone I can talk to here," she said again. She paused and from the living room they heard Nick say, ". . . a little impatient with doing construction sometimes, but I have faith that . . ."

"He won't even tell me *that*," Ellie exclaimed, as she returned to the sink. "I don't know how to reach him anymore! He's talked to me more directly today in the presence of the rest of you than in ages. I don't know what . . . This is ridiculous. I just have to tell you."

Zoë was only a little taller, but because Ellie's head was bent she could see the perfectly straight part in her fine hair. It made her seem very young.

"I wouldn't burden you with it if it weren't for . . . if I didn't think maybe you could shed some light on things. What it is . . . the thing is . . ." She glanced at the door again and sighed. "We've been trying to have a baby for over a year now." Her eyes filled with tears again, and she laughed painfully. "I mean conceive one. I stopped using birth control pills over a year ago." She paused as if to let this sink in.

"About six months ago I went to a specialist, since it seemed to me that at my age . . . I'm barely thirty, in good health, no history of problems in my family—my sister has three children and my brother has two. All the initial tests showed nothing wrong. The next step would be for them to do some exploratory surgery, but before they do that they want Nick to be tested and so far he's absolutely refused. He was even reluctant for me to be, but I went without telling him. I felt very encouraged by what I learned. Yet now he won't even discuss the subject. I've tried to be patient—the doctor says it's not unusual for men to react this way at first, feel their masculinity's threatened, et cetera, et cetera—there's always the chance he might find out it's *him* . . ." She looked at Zoë: *Men* . . . "The doctor recommended lying low for a while, respecting his privacy . . . Typical male advice, I'm beginning to think. Why isn't Nick *with* me on this? I've never made it a question of whose fault it is, yet that's clearly how he perceives it, and he's forcing me to perceive it that way by his stubbornness. I last saw the doctor at the end of September, and Nick has yet to make an appointment although he promised he would. The fact is, my patience is wearing thin, and our relationship's beginning to feel like a stalemate."

She looked frankly at Zoë.

"Of course you can imagine what all this does to our sex life. I've been taking my temperature religiously for a long time and by now can predict within a day or two when I'm going to ovulate but I can't let Nick suspect when that is or he—well, what euphemism shall I use?—loses interest? So then I'm forced to try to appear amorous all the time in order to allay his suspicions, but, as I'm sure you can understand, one doesn't exactly feel in the mood at every moment. Especially when things are so tense between us otherwise. The last two months we've missed the peak times and of course, wouldn't you know, now the timing is right but I know that even if I can get Nick . . . Well, he won't, not without doors and with his mother and sister in the house."

What a spoof, Zoë thought; if she'd stuck to her original plan she and

Ellie would both have been trying to get pregnant at the same time, in the same house, with no doors and no privacy; both trying to prevent their unwitting helpers from knowing what they were up to. How many other women were busy right now trying to trick their husbands and boyfriends into the role of Holy Ghost? It wasn't really funny, though.

She glanced down—Ellie was digging at the tile grout with her fingernails. Ellie looked down too.

"Fancy that—I must find the subject upsetting. You know what your brother suggested the other day? He wanted to know why I didn't have artificial insemination if I was so anxious to have a child. Can you believe it? He's so afraid of finding out that he's the guilty party, quote unquote, that he'd rather deal with the emotional trauma of watching me bear a child that isn't even his!"

Zoë looked a question, and Ellie said, "You mean, would I consider that? But that's not the point! It's not an issue yet."

Zoë shrugged and tilted her head towards the living room.

"You mean, maybe it is for Nick? Well, if it is, it's in self-defense. It's not hard to figure out that this whole issue has to connect to some problem Nick won't admit he's still carrying around—I don't know what specifically, yet I've never quite believed he was as *over* everything about his childhood as he's pretended. His reluctance to talk much about the past has always seemed suspect to me, but he's always managed to speak so rationally about bygones being bygones that I was forced to believe him. At least, accept what he said. But now when I think about the things he's saying . . . He said, for instance, in regard to this 'suggestion' of his, that he didn't see what difference blood relationship makes; it's how you act towards people, not whether you're related to them genetically or not, that determines your relationship. It's not that I disagree, exactly. If it were established that we couldn't have children of our own, I'd be very sad, but I could deal with it. I could adopt a child. But it's this living with the whole thing as a hypothesis that's driving me crazy. He keeps telling me he's too busy thinking about the experiments he's planning with the snakes, but when I ask him what's more important, some research project or our children's existence he flips out on me and says things like 'Are they mutually exclusive?' Honestly, you may just think I'm hysterical, but I've even begun to wonder if he's quietly cracking up. What experiments? He doesn't even have any equipment!

"It makes me think that I ought to have contacted some of the people he worked with—maybe there's something I ought to know. But Nick was so convincing about their conservativeness; they had no imagination—you know how *definite* he can be. I hate to be thinking about my own husband in this clinical way, but if I've learned anything after living with Nick for five years it's that under his easygoing exterior he's as hypersensitive as they come. I know of course that he saw a shrink for several years when he was a kid—supposedly for his asthma, but now I've begun to wonder if that was the whole story."

She looked at Zoë. In the face of this onslaught Zoë decided that part of Nick's state of mind could be exhaustion from dealing with Ellie. But maybe she just couldn't stand the fact that Ellie wanted the same thing she did: a child. As if only one of them could get pregnant at a time. She mimed writing and Ellie said, "I'm sorry—I'm so thoughtless. Over here."

A small blackboard hung on the end of a row of cabinets. Ellie erased a grocery list and handed Zoë a piece of chalk.

"Our parents," Zoë wrote.

"Your parents? You mean the stress of their relationship was what made Nick . . . why he had to see the shrink?"

She shook her head: *Yes, but that's not what I meant.* "Why he doesn't want children," she wrote.

Ellie looked shocked. "He's *told* you that?"

No.

"But you think he's thought about it and that's the position he's taken?" Ellie's voice was incredulous.

Zoë erased the board, and wrote, "It's not impossible."

"I just can't believe that." Ellie sounded more self-confident now that she had disagreed. "To me a tell-tale sign that that's not the case is his total unwillingness to discuss it. If you really firmly believe something, if you've made up your mind on the subject, you're not threatened by someone's bringing it up."

"Maybe he's afraid you'd leave him," Zoë wrote.

"I doubt it. I really think that lately he couldn't give a damn about our marriage. He's somewhere else—and the man doesn't talk to a soul!"

"What about your neighbor?" she wrote.

"You mean Stewart Beauregard? That's a laugh."

Why?

"Oh, I don't know. Though perhaps you've noticed I have certain opinions where he's concerned. However, that's a whole other story. Maybe I'll tell you about it sometime, if you're interested . . ."

The kettle, which had peeped a couple of times, was working up to a squawk, and Ellie went to lift it off the stove. She poured water into the coffee filter.

"What's going on in there?" Nick called. "I thought you were getting the dessert, not making it!"

"Hold your horses," Ellie shouted back, more loudly than she needed. "To tell you the truth," she said, "I do feel a little as if I'm betraying Nick's confidence, but besides needing to talk to someone about this there's something specific I wanted to ask." She poured another filterful of water. "Did something happen to him when he was younger? I mean, something that could have affected . . . For instance, an illness or an accident that could have affected his fertility? You don't know of anything, do you?"

No.

"Did he have mumps?"

Zoë went back to the board. "I think so."

"I figured it was highly unlikely. I just thought . . . His resistance to being tested seems so completely irrational. So I scrounge around for reasons." She poured another filterful of water, then turned back around.

"You know, your mentioning it so matter-of-factly—that Nick might not want children—it makes me realize that I've been avoiding giving that possibility consideration." Ellie sighed. "I don't want to believe it, I guess. His tactics would seem such a cruel way of conveying that to me, yet, in fact, when I think about it, I realize we never did discuss the issue—either before we got married or after. I simply assumed. Having children has always seemed an obvious part of being married. You know . . ." She laughed. "I've actually imagined that he went secretly sometime and had a vasectomy and now doesn't want to go to a doctor who'd be able to tell me. I tried to think when he could have done it, and realized that at almost any time . . . There's not much of a recovery period, from what I know. Yet I don't know where the scar would be—I assume not easily visible, but I don't know. There isn't anyone I can ask—I haven't been back to the doctor since the idea occurred to me and I haven't had the nerve to call him up just to ask him." She hesitated. "I don't suppose you know, do you?"

No.

"I guess it doesn't much matter." She laughed. "It's not as if I'm going to get a flashlight and go prospecting for a scar when he's sleeping."

At the board, Zoë wrote, "But I don't think Nick—"

"Is capable of such premeditation? I know. Once I wouldn't have thought so either. But now I don't know." She sighed again. "I suppose I'd better get the dessert ready, or there'll be a riot in there."

Ellie stopped up the empty side of the sink, ran it full of hot water, then lowered a tin scalloped mold into it, careful not to let it down too far. She waited a moment before lifting it out and running a knife around the edges; then she inverted it onto a plate. The custard plopped loose with a squelch. Caramel dripped off the crown-shaped mold.

Looks great, Zoë gestured.

"If you said what I think you did, thanks. It's the easiest dessert in the world to make, though, really."

Ellie smiled her devastating smile, metamorphosed all at once back into her social self. When they were seated again around the table, she said cheerfully that she regretted having to inform everyone that the bed situation was going to be a little complicated. She would put the facts before them plainly, and recommended that everyone remain calm, since panic was obviously not helpful in a catastrophe . . . Nick was looking at her strangely. The couch folded out and then there was the rollaway, which Monica had used the first night in the living room; there was their bedroom, the living room, the kitchen, and the sun room. The sun room was unheated, but they had a couple of down sleeping bags that could be used as comforters. They also had a space heater that they could set up in there. If no one objected, she'd like to suggest what seemed to her the most workable possibility. Monica could have the sun room to herself—that would afford the most privacy—and Zoë and Pryce could have the couch, but of course Zoë and *Monica* could have the couch and banish Pryce to the sun room, or—she winked at Zoë—they could all sleep with Nick and Ellie . . .

Monica said she'd do whatever she was told. Pryce suggested they rotate. Zoë offered to sleep out with the snakes.

For whatever reason, everyone now seemed maniacally eager to please. For the rest of the evening they had what Rob had used to call a "unison conversation," meaning everyone sat around agreeing with everyone else, whatever subject came up: the disastrous state of the ecosystem, the corruption in high places, the dilemma of city versus country life . . . It was like the staged enthusiasm of extras in an opera party scene, appearing to be completely fascinated by whatever was going on center stage, when you knew perfectly well that they were really saying, "*God*, I hate the way he takes the high notes!" or, "My feet are *killing* me!"

XI HARMONY

By October 10, 1911, the day of Adam and Charlotte's marriage, the hills around Harmony have attained their full fall splendor. It's rained for a week previously; even the night before the wedding, Charlotte's last night at the Dawes place, she awakes to rain on the tin roof, and the sound consoles her, but in the morning the sky is as blue as a robin's egg and she knows there's no chance of escape.

Like her grandmother, and *her* grandmother before *her*, back to Marian Howe, Charlotte had inherited the curse of second sight. It skipped a generation, which was what made it a curse. Parents didn't believe their children and children didn't believe their parents. A twisted strand of descent, Charlotte said, possessed twice the strength of a single one.

That day, she told Zoë, she had begged her mother not to go to the mill, but Ida had scoffed at her fears. At the time Charlotte was studying for her teacher's certificate, taking the train into Boston every Monday morning to attend classes for the week, returning to the mill town on Friday, but that Monday, she said, she didn't leave the house; she sat all morning in a chair looking out the window. She had already endured her first horror by that afternoon when two men arrived from the mill to announce that there had been a dreadful accident. All she could say was "thank you."

"What kind of person would feel relief upon hearing of her mother's death?" she asked Zoë, horrified, when she told her this story. "My mother had met a brutal end and my most pronounced feeling was of relief!"

"Anyone would feel that!" Zoë exclaimed. "You weren't relieved because your mother was dead but because you hadn't been imagining things—I understand perfectly!"

"No, dear, the two cannot be separated," Charlotte said. "The gift of sight and responsibility for what one sees—someday you'll understand that."

After the wedding, to which Louisa had invited nearly everyone in town, Adam and Charlotte took a honeymoon trip to New York. Zoë tried to imagine what it had been like—did either of them know anything about sex beforehand? It was as if they'd had to get married so that they could be that couple they'd seen in the woods when they were six—that whole experience had hypnotized them. Charlotte said that what she remembered best was the ride they took in a hired carriage through Central Park; the leaves were still green whereas in Harmony they had already turned, which she said had made her giddy—it seemed as if it were a month earlier. She obviously meant: when she was still free.

Had any of the people she was descended from, Zoë wondered, actually *wanted* to marry each other? They all seemed to have felt duty-bound to go through with it, and then felt so sorry for each other at being trapped in the same unhappiness that they became even more devoted. It seemed so strange that generation after generation of *reluctance* had ended up producing her.

As Charlotte, driving through the park, contemplates the still-green leaves, she fancies how she will travel south, ever farther south, until she's regained her childhood and the blessed blindness most people never lose. The idea so delights her that she's almost happy, and doesn't even mind Adam's making it plain that what occurs between them in darkness bears no connection to their daytime lives. The acts that he is condemned by his sex to perform, and she by hers to endure, are never to be referred to, not by so much as an intimate glance or a pressure of the hand.

For his part, Adam pities her now; as he gazes at her, attired in demure gray silk, sitting bravely upright beside him in the carriage, her hair coiled, a soft hat mysteriously secured on her head, he secretly recalls the humiliations to which he subjects her, her cries of surrender in the shared anguish of their evil-doing. He recalls his conviction that only by marrying her could he overcome his guilty passion, but that notion seems laughable to him now.

For passion it still is, as Louisa takes in at a glance upon their return. That they behave towards each other with the politeness of well-bred fellow travelers does not deceive her. She has little doubt even before she listens outside their door that they have discovered what she has always suspected existed though never known herself. A loudness louder than their sounds of pretended protest floods her mind as she flees, knowing they will not even hear her footsteps.

Adam has not told Charlotte that, after he informed his mother of their intent to marry, she locked herself in her room for three days. He refused to plead with her; if she had legitimate objections to his marriage, let her voice them. It was the servants who finally took it upon themselves to place a ladder against her window and climb it; they discovered her, lying on her bed in a stupor, an empty vial on the bedtable. Only after Dr. Jewell declared Louisa out of danger did Adam visit her. By this time she was propped up in bed, looking quite cheerful. He had the distinct impression that she felt that she had accomplished her mission. Dismissing his inquiries as to her health, she said, "I know you wish to punish me for not having loved you as a mother should her son. I deserve to be punished, but, you must forgive me, I did not want to endure it."

"Why should my marrying Charlotte punish you?" he exclaimed.

"Oh, Adam, there are things, histories . . . Ask Charlotte who her father is."

"Of what significance is that to me? It's not her fault that she's illegitimate."

"Oh, illegitimate . . ." Louisa said. "If that were all . . ."

Adam left angry and bewildered. The truth was, he was not easy on that score. It was not, as he had said, because of Charlotte's illegitimacy, but because Charlotte insisted that she *had* no father. "It happens sometimes," she said. "Sometimes a woman can want a child so badly that no father is required. It takes *wanting*," she repeated. "People understand little the effects of longing upon the human body." "Is that how your mother conceived you?" he asked her. "She often told me how much she'd always wanted me," Charlotte answered vaguely.

At no time did Adam think Charlotte meant to deceive him; he believed, rather, that her loyalty to her mother made it impossible for her to think for herself upon this subject. This enabled him to dismiss his mother's hints and yet, after his marriage, and particularly after his and Charlotte's return to Harmony, the notion of what it is that Louisa conceals builds in him inexorably, until he thinks of nothing else, completing his hypothesis like a stone wall into which every rock must be individually fitted.

First of all there was his mother's "neglecting" to inform him that Ida Howe had died and Charlotte returned to Harmony. Then there was Charlotte's own mysterious reluctance to marry him, which, in his credulous state, he imagined had to do with her own recognition of the arcane troth they had pledged the year before on the river bank. But now he has begun to harbor a more sinister, devilish suspicion. He hardly requires the final piece of evidence, upon which he chances some months after his marriage, to elevate his suspicion to certainty.

One winter afternoon, Adam asks Charlotte if she has any money of her own. He's in the process of having a will drawn up, leaving everything to her, yet he worries that, should he die before Louisa, she and Timothy Lowndes, whom he not only despises but distrusts, will find a method of depriving Charlotte of her inheritance.

"Yes," she answers, "I believe so."

Ida has left her a bank account in Harmony, she tells him, but she has never gone to see about it—she cannot feel she deserves it.

"You see to it, if you like," she suggests. "Do with it as you think best."

Adam intends only to inquire into the amount, and, if it should prove substantial (which he doubts), to recommend to Charlotte that it be invested; but to his amazement, the sum is great. The young bank employee to whom he's put his inquiry, someone of his own age whom he does not know, explains that no money has been withdrawn from the account since it was first established nearly two decades ago. At the same time, deposits have been made regularly.

"Deposits!" Adam exclaims. "But by whom?"

"That I can't say," the clerk says.

It is unclear to Adam whether he means that he cannot, or will not. However, by now Adam believes he knows where to pursue his search. He leaves the bank and walks down the street to the offices of Lowndes and Lowndes, Attorneys at Law. After Judge Lowndes's death, Timothy became the executor of Henry's estate. As soon as he is shown into the inner office, Adam announces that he wishes to examine his father's will.

"But . . ." Timothy objects. "I can tell you whatever you may wish to know without your having to trouble yourself to read . . . why, all that repetitive language. You know how dull that can be." Lowndes peers nearsightedly at Adam.

"Thank you, but I would prefer to read the document myself."

"Perhaps if you would tell me what you wish to know . . ."

"Mr. Lowndes," Adam replies haughtily—and is pleased to note that Lowndes winces. "I begin to wonder at your reluctance. Is there a reason you wish to prevent me from examining my own father's will?"

"But Adam," Lowndes attempts again, "you have not yet officially come into your inheritance . . ."

"Do you mean to make me request permission of my mother? You know very well that she will grant it, but in her present delicate state of health I had not wished to trouble her with such trifles. You *do* know that she has not been well?"

At this the lawyer looks distressed. "Yes, certainly I have heard. How is your dear mother, Adam? I should like to visit her, but . . ." He trails off.

"Yes?"

"I confess to having felt less than welcome to do so."

Adam laughs. "Oh, that's over and done with, Mr. Lowndes. I'm a married man, not a boy any longer. If I've ever made you feel unwelcome in my home . . ."

Yet even as he speaks Adam wonders why he has always felt such involuntary revulsion for the man. What has Lowndes ever done to him that he should find him so altogether detestable? His abhorrence is irrational, and yet, as he gazes at Lowndes, who wears the same toadying but patronizing expression he assumes whenever he regards Adam, Adam recoils as deeply as ever.

". . . well, you'll forgive me, I hope," he finishes. "You're welcome at any time."

"Why, thank you, Adam."

Lowndes appears far more pleased than Adam can believe his cordiality merits. What a pitiful specimen, he thinks. No wonder no woman would have him.

"The will?" he asks.

Lowndes sighs, a strange mixture of eagerness and regret.

"I don't know that your mother . . . There will be things you may misunderstand . . ."

"If there should be, I shall ask you."

Reluctantly, Timothy Lowndes opens his safe and extracts the will. Adam takes it from him and goes off to sit in an armchair by the window, facing away from Lowndes. He is glad Lowndes cannot see him. The will, contrary to what the lawyer said, is neither very long nor very complicated. Louisa is left a yearly income, and the right to live in the mansion until her death. The rest of Henry's property he leaves to his son, Adam, with the exception of an annuity to be paid out of the estate to Ida Howe, and, after her death, to her daughter, Charlotte. "It is my wish," Henry wrote, "that my son assure that neither of them ever be in want, and increase their income accordingly when necessary."

Though Adam reminds himself that he expected no less, his heart thunders and it does not seem to him that there is enough air in the room. He pretends to be puzzling over what he's read until he is able to calm himself enough to face Lowndes. Then he rises, folds the will, and hands it back.

"Thank you," he says. "I have learned what I wished to know."

Timothy Lowndes is looking at him strangely. "The legacy left to Ida Howe—now to your wife . . ."

Adam waves his comments aside. "He was a generous man, my father. It was quite a scandal at the time, as you know . . . Charlotte's—my wife's—illegitimacy, if you'll forgive my speaking so plainly. Quite a scandal. My mother always pitied her mother. She always gave her as much sewing to do as she could, but to have gone so far as to prevail upon my father to remember her in his will . . ." He shakes his head, as if marveling at the boundlessness of Louisa's charity.

"Your mother . . ." Lowndes says, then falls silent, staring at Adam.

"To help a poor woman in need—quite the Christian thing to do, don't you think?"

"I beg your pardon?"

"I said, don't you think it was generous of my mother, to befriend a hapless soul like Ida Howe?"

"I don't believe your mother . . ."

"Yes?" Adam prompts.

He is enjoying Lowndes's predicament. He can tell that Lowndes is unsure as to whether or not Louisa has ever known of Henry's bequest to Ida. Lowndes wishes to guard Louisa against what she might not know, yet without ascertaining whether or not Adam's innocence is genuine, he cannot perceive the correct course of action.

"I merely wished to say that I expect your mother would not wish to have the source of the annuity publicly known. She has always been very modest about her charities, you know."

"Yes, of course," Adam agrees. "Charlotte and I shall certainly keep the information between ourselves. I thank you very much for your assistance, Mr. Lowndes. Of course you will bill the time to our account."

"Adam, I . . ."

On his way to the door, Adam turns. "Yes, Mr. Lowndes?"

Despite himself, Adam is surprised to see the mixture of longing, hopefulness, and bewilderment that eddies across Lowndes's heavy features.

"You . . . you should not assume that everything is as meets the eye," he says lamely.

"Oh, certainly not." Adam laughs. "We're both men here, Mr. Lowndes. I'd be a fool not to wonder why my father, never home long enough to regain his land-legs, should have bestowed such an amount upon a woman with whom he could scarcely have been acquainted in the usual course of events. Having been so often away from home, I'm sure he—how may I put this?—developed a taste for a certain variety in his intimate companionship, wouldn't you say? Who are you and I to quarrel with him?" Adam musters a hearty laugh. "Say no more about it, Mr. Lowndes. You can be sure I shan't disturb my mother by attempting to dredge up what occurred in the dim long ago. Good afternoon, Mr. Lowndes."

He turns and leaves the office before Lowndes has a chance to detain him. Outside, in the early February dark, it has begun to snow, fresh flakes come to soften the high frozen banks and the hard, rolled surface of the road. Many of the houses on Main Street have been wired with electricity, and the lights burn steadily, unflickering. It still surprises Adam to see them. He feels the dark is being denied its power.

As he strolls down Main Street towards his house, he contemplates his new position in life. He is sure now that not only his mother and Timothy Lowndes, but Charlotte as well, have known the truth about his and Charlotte's kinship and chosen not to tell him. Louisa preferred that her own son offend against the laws of both God and man rather than that Harmony learn of her husband's philandering—though no doubt the town already suspected more than enough. And Timothy not only felt professionally bound to guard Henry's confidence, but wished to protect Louisa, of whom, in his wormlike way, he was fond. All his life Adam has known that his elders kept knowledge from him—it was the source of their power—so it does not surprise him that they should wish to keep such mighty information as this to themselves, even at the expense of his damnation. This is the real struggle in life, he thinks—to own the most secrets; the striving after money and property is a mere dumb show compared to this. But if this is how it is, he can fight too. He will show them. By letting both Timothy and his mother suspect that he knows the truth and does as he wishes nonetheless, he will triumph.

Though for a moment he feels some surprise that Charlotte should also have kept such information from him—he has never considered her capable of duplicity—by the time he's turned up the walk to his front door he understands that she thought he knew; understanding as they both did that not repentance, but only more sin, could earn God's attention, she had consented to accompany him on that perilous but only true path to salvation.

A lesser man, Adam believes, would recriminate against his father, repudiate him for the lack of self-discipline his random procreation makes manifest. But Adam does not condemn him. For it seems to him that his father was trying to explain something to him. His father was bestowing upon him something finally more precious than any material inheritance—leaving him a destiny—his very original sin. How few people, Adam asks himself, can claim that? Who is to say that his conclusion was moot because his premises were wrong?

XII SPARTA (SAN YSIDRO)

Seth and Monica hadn't been speaking for a year when one day Zoë and Nick came home from school to find them in the living room, Monica sitting in Seth's lap. She had her arm around his neck and was giggling. Zoë stood staring at them, unable to believe her eyes, but Nick said instantly, "What's the meaning of this?" However, they explained nothing. Seth just said, "My son, the policeman," and Monica giggled again. It was nauseating as well as embarrassing. Then Seth said, "How would the two of you like to go to Mexico?" "Is that supposed to be some kind of a joke?" Nick asked. "It turns out Hugh Wycliffe and I have our sabbaticals the same year and they're going to Mexico and we thought perhaps we'd join them. Of course, if that's agreeable to you." "We decided that a change of scenery might prove beneficial to us all," Monica added. "We thought it time we made another effort to behave like a real family." "That doesn't mean, you'll note," Seth said, *tickling* Monica, who squirmed, "that we'll be one in fact. We merely intend to put on an excellent act." "Oh, Seth," Monica said. "Like you are now, right?" Nick said, as if he hated their guts. What were they up to? Seth said, "Assume a virtue if ye have it not. I believe that in trying to act, one becomes, whereas in trying to *be*, one acts. Make any sense to you, buddy?" "Oh, Seth, clam up," Monica said, but she wasn't mad. "Don't you dare call me buddy," Nick shouted, storming out of the room.

But in June the Wycliffes went and found two houses, while the Carvers were still up in Harmony visiting Charlotte. Nick said not to, but once when he'd gone fishing with Buell Magoon, Zoë asked Charlotte, "Did Mom ever have any brothers? I mean, that all died young or something?" But Charlotte just got a confused look on her face and said, "Curiosity killed the cat," and went back to reading the Bible. She had one in every room. What was she hiding?

While Zoë was still in Harmony, Bridget sent her postcards. They said, "San Ysidro is nestled in a circle of mountains like an egg in a nest."

"The women Mexicans dress very colorfully." "There is a delightful MERCADO where you can bargain for everything. My father says I have a mortifyingly developed talent for it." "I am taking Spanish lessons and I can already carry on a respectable conversation with the maid." The postcards sounded as if Mrs. Wycliffe had written them and Bridget had just signed them.

However, in San Ysidro, everyone talked like that. Everything was "picturesque," "delightful," or "charming," as if they were living in a slide show. The houses were white with red roof tiles that looked like pieces of broken flowerpots; right out their kitchen window were giant cacti stretching for miles. Every single morning at breakfast Monica said, "Isn't this scenery simply staggering?" and Seth would get out of his chair and pretend to fall over. "Sit down or I'll kill myself," Nick would say. It didn't do any good. He kept pretending to be angry to be in Mexico but actually he made friends immediately with some obnoxious boys four houses away named Wesley and Garson Chadwick from Mississippi who bowed and said, "Aftahnune, ladies," whenever they saw Zoë and Bridget. Nick convinced them to hunt rattlesnakes with him in the desert, but they never saw any. Later Nick told Zoë that he was glad they hadn't, because Wesley and Garson would have wanted to torture any snake they caught. Back in Mississippi they had once crucified a snake, nailing it to an orange crate slat which they stood in the ground and dowsed with gasoline before setting it on fire. They loved talking about how the snake wriggled and squirmed in agony.

In San Ysidro there were churches on every block, and Zoë agreed with Bridget that now would be a good time for her to convert. She bought a tiny gold cross at the market and wore it secretly under her blouse. They bought black mantillas to cover their heads when they went in the churches, and Bridget taught Zoë how to cross herself—top, bottom, left, right—so they wouldn't get hexed when they passed the altar. They knelt on the wooden benches, and while Bridget recited various prayers Zoë said the twenty-third psalm, which they'd had to memorize for English class.

Bridget had always known a lot about religion but in Mexico she began to learn even more. She said Mexicans were better believers than people from colder climates, and she began writing an opera called "The Deaths of the Saints," which was going to have all the saints singing arias while they were being tortured, like St. Catherine on a wheel—actually, two wheels. One was spiked, St. Catherine was tied to the other, and when the torturers turned her around spikes cut her to shreds. Bridget told Zoë she could help write the lyrics, and the best way to do this would be to act out some of the scenes; the words would just come naturally.

At the market they bought several yards of black cotton, rode Hera and Cleopatra, their burros, out to a place where the desert dipped down and no one could see them, and then wrapped themselves all in black and put their mantillas on their heads. They vowed never to marry and always to love God more than any man and to obey the Mother Superior no matter what. They took turns being the wicked heathen king who tortured them trying to make them give up believing in Jesus; he made them kiss the ground in front of him and say they believed in Allah, but they wouldn't and so he stretched them on the rack or flogged them and then at night he summoned them to his couch and had his way with them. As soon as they had children, he either cut off their heads or sold them to cannibals. Only if they would renounce their faith in the Lord Jesus Christ would their children be spared—the king even promised to make them his wives and clothe them in silk and rubies—but nothing could shake their faith. Bridget had a notebook and every so often she would shout "Cut!" and write something down. It was very distracting.

Zoë had never understood the difference between Catholic and Protestant—they were both Christian, but Bridget said if her parents found out she was going into Catholic churches she would be in a hell of a lot of hot water. (She said "hell" every other sentence now.) Her parents thought that the way the Mexicans carried on was a lot of hocus-pocus, having parades and wailing in them as if Christ had just been crucified yesterday, but Bridget said her parents just didn't understand a life of devotion.

Since in San Ysidro there were no churches that weren't Catholic, the Wycliffes attended a service in the house of some Germans who had a friend who was a minister. They were all Lutheran, which was a different kind of Protestant from Episcopalian, which the Wycliffes were, but it was okay for them to pray with a Lutheran minister. Charlotte was Congregational but the one time she visited Sparta she went to the Presbyterian church, which was almost the same thing. Zoë didn't get it. She knew the different kinds of churches had something to do with Henry the Eighth getting rid of all his wives but she didn't know what and furthermore she couldn't understand how anyone could get in an argument about religion, it was so incredibly boring.

Then one night when the Wycliffes came over for dinner the grownups all started talking about the Germans, the Von Ritters. She and Bridget weren't paying attention, but suddenly Nick kicked her under the table and she kicked Bridget. Seth was saying in an angry, mystery voice that you never knew about Germans living in South America. That was when Mr. Wycliffe went totally crazy.

"Goddamn it, Seth! Marika is Jewish! She was lucky to get out!"

"They've been here since the early thirties, Hugh! And, aside from the fact that she looks like a Saxon *hausfrau*, if she's Jewish why do they invite a Lutheran minister to celebrate the Sabbath in their home?"

"Because Franz is bloody Lutheran! How dare you insinuate . . ."

"Hugh . . ." Mrs. Wycliffe said.

"Seth, I don't think . . ." Monica said, but their fathers were already running amok.

"I don't casually level such accusations, Hugh. Do me the courtesy of acknowledging that. There are simply certain remarks . . . when he's had a few. Let's just say not what one would expect from someone married to one of the chosen people."

Chosen for what?

"For instance?" Mr. Wycliffe wasn't shouting now but his face was as red as an ambulance and his voice was nasty.

Seth sounded nasty too. "That *they* sabotaged the economy. That *they* were forming a worldwide conspiracy and would, had they not been stopped, have staged a coup . . . Is that specific enough for you? Would you like me to go on?"

"Oh, for God's sake, Seth, you missed the quotation marks. I've had innumerable conversations with Franz on the subject of the war and nothing even remotely like what you're reporting has ever surfaced."

"I'm sure he's careful with you. I let him think I might be sympathetic to—shall we say?—the other side. I played out the rope, and he convincingly hung himself. Marika was there at the time, Hugh. It was clear to me that she was trying to warn Franz . . . She'd say, 'Of course, many people did feel that,' or 'It was understandable, considering how many of *our* people did have prominent roles in business,' emphasizing 'our.' I'm sorry, but you will find it difficult to persuade me that she's a member of a race that was wholesale slaughtered."

"Are they talking about Hitler?" Zoë whispered to Bridget.

"What do *you* think?" Bridget acted like Seth was Zoë's responsibility.

"What would you prefer?" Mr. Wycliffe went on, making his lips all thin. "That she look *hunted*? Why would she claim to be Jewish if she weren't? I simply refuse . . . Seth, these are friends of ours you're talking about!"

"They're friends of ours too. But face facts, Hugh. It's common knowledge now that a butcher of thousands can appreciate Mozart and adore his children, spend the afternoon skinning someone alive and then . . ."

"Seth!" Monica exclaimed. "I *insist* that you discuss this at another time! Or go out to the study if you can't contain yourselves now."

"I agree entirely," Mrs. Wycliffe said. "This is not a matter to be settled at the dinner table, particularly with children present."

"You're absolutely right," Mr. Wycliffe said, standing up. "Monica, my apologies, but I simply will not stand for this. Lydia, you'll find me at home." He sounded as if he were playing hide and seek.

"Hugh, for God's sake . . ." Seth said, standing up too.

But Mr. Wycliffe just said, "I really have nothing further I wish to say."

Seth followed him into the living room. They heard him say, "Hugh, at least credit me with being able to know the difference between someone's own opinions and his regurgitation of others'. I haven't taught for twenty years for nothing." But then they both went outside.

Nick made the crazy sign with his finger.

"Good Lord," Mrs. Wycliffe said.

"Aren't you going to go with Papa?" Bridget asked.

"Certainly not. If your father chooses to act like a boor, he may; I need not follow suit."

"Well, *I'm* going with him!" Bridget said. "*I* won't abandon him in his hour of need!"

"You'll do no such thing," Mrs. Wycliffe said.

Bridget got out of her chair and said "I *am*," but she didn't dare go anywhere. They had to eat dessert while Mrs. Wycliffe and Monica talked about nothing, but finally they were all three excused. They hurried down to Bridget's house, but Seth and Mr. Wycliffe weren't there. Bridget was all huffy and didn't want to do anything, so Zoë just walked home with Nick.

"She's a pain in the you-know-what," Nick said.

"What do you mean?"

"She acts so high and mighty. At least we know our father's demented—Bridget thinks her father is God."

"That's true," Zoë said.

The next day they found out that their fathers had gone into town and got drunk together at a bar and made friends again, but before that she and Bridget had had a big fight about it and their friendship was ruined.

Every morning around nine, Zoë bridled Hera and met Bridget and Cleopatra where the road to town ran into the road to the desert. That next morning Zoë was about to leave the house when she heard Seth and

Monica talking in the kitchen. Nick was already gone and they must have thought she was. The way they sounded made her want to listen—since they'd stopped writing letters in Mexico, it was harder to know what they were up to. But when she got where she could hear, they weren't talking about their own secrets. Monica was telling Seth what Mrs. Wycliffe had told her the night before when they were alone.

"She suspects something," Monica said. "Hugh hasn't been himself for some time. This spring she put it off to stress—he had that extra seminar and had to correct the galleys of the Delphi book—but now that he has plenty of time on his hands nothing's changed. She's convinced there's something truly wrong. You know, we forget that Hugh is a good fifteen years older than the rest of us . . ."

"I don't forget," Seth said. "He never gives me a chance."

"The point is that he refuses to see a doctor."

"If the only symptom is shortness of temper . . ."

"Seth, not *every* ailment is metaphysical. Hugh's complained of headaches and dizziness, though Lydia thinks he hides his symptoms from her as much as possible."

"Well, perhaps it is something to be concerned about. I hope, however, that you—or she—aren't imagining that *I* could persuade him to see a doctor."

"I don't think the notion even occurred to her. She's simply tremendously worried. Can't someone be in distress without your feeling you're responsible? Lydia was a nurse, remember. If she's worried, then so am I."

All of a sudden Seth scraped his chair back and Zoë had to rush out. She started crying when she saw Hera, who brayed hello, but she made herself stop so Bridget wouldn't notice anything. She couldn't tell her that her father was *dying*. It was so horrible. Bridget was going to be *fatherless*. Her mother might marry someone else who would be really cruel to her. Zoë felt bad now for ever being mad at Bridget for thinking her father was perfect, now that he was going to die. She'd just have to be as nice to her as she could and when her father finally died she would offer to let Bridget live with her if Mrs. Wycliffe got married again, or even run away with her if she wanted.

When she met Bridget, and Bridget just sat on Cleopatra and said good morning without looking at her, Zoë thought at first that she must have found out.

"What's the matter?" she said, ready with her offers.

But when Bridget answered, Zoë realized she wasn't upset, she was furious. "Nothing at all in the whole world," she said.

"What are you mad about?"

"If you don't know then I can't tell you."

"Fine. I might as well just go home."

Bridget waited until she was riding off before she said, "I guess I just don't particularly like having your father accuse my father of not knowing Nazis when he sees them."

Zoë got down and stared over Hera's back at Bridget. "Why didn't you say so last night?"

"I wanted to find out all the facts of the matter first."

"I don't believe you. I don't think you knew what they were talking about—Nick didn't and he knows more about Nazis than you."

"Since when?"

Bridget had slid off Cleopatra and they had both started walking along the road out into the desert, leading the burros. In a little ways, the road forked. In one direction it continued until it dwindled away to nothing; in the other it climbed a hill where there were three wooden crosses, standing for the ones Jesus Christ and the extra men were crucified on. For a while they'd gone up there and if nobody was around kneeled in front of the middle cross and said "My God, my God, why hast thou forsaken me?" until once they ran into a Mexican lady kneeling there, bobbing up and down in her rebozo like someone bobbing for apples; they were laughing, although not so she could hear, but then she got up and when she went by, not even looking at them, they saw that she was crying. They didn't dare say a word until she was off in the distance.

"The fact of the matter is," Bridget said, "your father doesn't know what the hell he's talking about. My father was actually *in* the war. He saw Nazis with his own eyes. Your father has no way of knowing."

"Yes, he does, Bridget. He was in the war too. He was a cryptographer."

"Not in Germany he wasn't. He was here safe and sound the whole time. My father was actually in battles and got wounded. He would have got gangrene and *died* if my mother hadn't nursed him back to health."

"So?"

"I'm just telling you. Your father never even fought."

"So what?"

"Well, he ought to be more careful. You know what Nazis did, right?"

"Yes."

"Prove it."

"They killed Jews."

"But do you know *how*? Do you know they made lampshades out of their skin and performed horrible experiments on them like yanking out their eyes while they were wide awake to see how they would take it? Your father was saying *that's* what Mr. Von Ritter did."

"He was not!"

"He was so! I heard him!"

"He didn't say he made lampshades out of people." How did they do that?

"He said he was a Nazi and that's what Nazis did. I'm not saying it's your fault, but you ought to realize your father talks off the top of his head. He makes wild assumptions and jumps to conclusions. It's what keeps him from being a first-rate scholar, if you really want to know. He's brilliant but he has severe weaknesses. If it wasn't for them he'd be at the top of his field by now."

"What weaknesses?"

"Just weaknesses."

"You're lying."

"I'm not lying. You forced me to tell you by your pig-headed attitude."

Zoë narrowed her eyes. "You think you know so much, but you don't know everything," she said.

Bridget stopped walking—they had been leading Hera and Cleopatra—and said, "What exactly is that supposed to mean?"

"Nothing."

"It did too. What is it? Goddammit, you better tell me."

Now Zoë felt bad. "It didn't mean anything. I just said it."

"No, you didn't. I can tell."

Zoë started walking again but Bridget grabbed Hera's halter. "I'm warning you, Zoë Carver," she said. "This is your last chance for staying my friend and I mean it. I'm sick and tired of all your big secrets!"

All what big secrets? What was Bridget talking about? She was just mad because Seth knew something her father didn't. If she'd just *admitted* it, maybe Zoë wouldn't have said anything.

"Okay, but you're not going to want to know. Don't say I didn't warn you."

"What *is* it?"

"Okay! Your father might have something wrong with him, that's all. I mean that's making him get upset about things. I heard my mother telling my father this morning. That's why he walked out of our house last night, if you want to know the truth."

Bridget squinted, but then she said, "You're just making it up to get back at me. Nothing's wrong with my father."

"Yes, there is. He gets dizzy and has lots of headaches."

"Everybody has headaches, big deal."

"Not like he does. Your mother's worried about him but he won't go to a doctor. I didn't want to tell you, but you made me."

Bridget didn't say anything for a minute, but then she shouted, straight in Zoë's face, "Oh, yes, you did! Yes, you did! You've been waiting! You've been dying to tell me! Don't try to pretend you haven't! And you know what I think you are? You're a *worm*! That's even too good for you. You're a snake. You're a slimy, sneaking snake! If you were smaller, I'd step on you! I'd crush you under my foot. That's what you deserve!"

All of a sudden she burst into tears and turned her back and climbed onto Cleopatra.

"I didn't *want* to tell you!" Zoë shouted.

"You did! You did! You did!" Bridget screamed. "You *loved* telling me and I hate you! I hate you forever! Don't come near me again as long as you live!"

Then she turned Cleopatra around and galloped away. Zoë stood there, staring down the road. Was Bridget right, that she'd wanted to tell her? When she rode Hera home, she forced her to walk and brushed her for a long time in the paddock, trying to understand how she could have wanted to do something without knowing it. She knew she'd been mad, but had she really wanted to hurt Bridget? Zoë knew that if she told Seth about the fight he would try to make her think it was all Bridget's fault, but she didn't know anyone else to talk to and she had to know once and for all—was she really evil inside? Had Seth really not known what he was talking about last night? She was so sick and tired of being brainwashed. She'd always known he had weaknesses, but now she was just going to have to face it. She went to the little building he used for his study and kicked the door.

"Come in," he called. He was sitting at his typewriter.

"What are you doing?" she asked sarcastically. "Working on your Magnum Opus?"

"Afraid not. I'm coming to the conclusion it will take a greater man than I to explain how we came to settle for this vale of tears. I'm writing a letter."

"To who?"

"To *whom*. To Hugh Wycliffe, if you must know."

"Why? Are you too weak to walk as far as his house?"

"Very amusing, Zoë. Have you come here solely to insult me?"

"Would you mind answering just one question? How do you know that Mr. Von Ritter is a Nazi?"

"Ah," Seth said, tilting his chair back. "I wondered if that would come up. Have you and Bridget been fighting about it?"

"None of your business."

"What *is* it with the two of you?" he exclaimed. "Must you replay every item of world controversy? Can't you accept the fact that your elders sometimes disagree? Never mind, I can see you're on a crusade for answers. As to the specific question, whether Mr. Von Ritter is a Nazi—which I didn't say, if I may be allowed to point out . . . You've formed some idea as to what a Nazi is, I take it?"

"I wouldn't have if it was up to you."

"Not living up to my job description again, is that it? The answer to your original question, Zoë, is that of course I don't. Know for certain that Mr. Von Ritter had Nazi sympathies, that is. It's difficult to know *anything* for sure about other people. I merely suspected . . . There are certain things Franz—Mr. Von Ritter—has said to me . . . I wasn't preparing to turn him over to Nazi-hunters—I wasn't accusing him of having participated, in any case. But Hugh and I have talked it over. I assume that what matters to you is that we parted amicably. Yes?"

"Why didn't you fight in World War Two?"

"I beg your pardon?"

"You heard me."

"Well, Zoë, you already know how I spent the war."

"Not exactly. Were you even *in* the army?"

"To the best of my knowledge, yes, I was in the army. I had that great privilege for the last three years of the war, in fact."

"Then why didn't you go to Germany?"

"Because the powers that be decided I would be more useful at home, learning to decipher codes. I was in Florida first. Then in Alabama. But I've confessed all this before."

"Did you decipher any top-secret messages?"

"Zoë, the damn fool army spent eighteen months training me to be a German cryptographer, then decided that since the theater of operations—that means where the most fighting was going on—was moving to Japan they'd send me to a different school to learn Japanese. By the time I could have translated *War and Peace* into Japanese and back again the war was over."

"So you really didn't do anything."

"If in your book 'doing something' means shooting someone or being shot oneself, then, no, I didn't."

"Could you have fought if you'd wanted to?"

"I suppose I could have requested active duty. I don't know that it would have been granted me, but it might have been."

"Why didn't you?"

"Because I had no particular interest in having my head blown off, or blowing anyone else's head off. I realize that that may seem a dishonorable reason to you. For myself, I'm neither proud of it nor ashamed of it. I did my 'patriotic' duty. I was called up. I endured three years of sensory and intellectual deprivation for the sake of my country. If they chose to waste my time and talents, then that was their decision. I was theirs to do with as they wished. I'm sorry to have made you ashamed of me, but you may as well face up to the truth. If you want to leave home immediately, I'll understand. Except for target practice, I handled a gun only once during the entire war."

"When?" She didn't even know why she bothered asking.

"I was assigned to guard a prisoner." He laughed.

"A prisoner!"

"A Chinese *shopkeeper*, Zoë—poor son of a bitch."

"Did you capture him too?" She felt a tiny ray of hope.

"Zoë, sit down for a minute, will you? That is, if you can spare the time. I'd like to tell you a little story."

She didn't want to but she sat down in the only other chair in the study, a leather one with a tiny round seat and an enormous back, spread out like a fan. People coming up behind you wouldn't know you were in it—if you had a pistol you could turn around and blast them.

"Something nobody much likes to remember about our history, Zoë, is that while the Germans were rounding up Jews, we were rounding up the Japs. People of Japanese descent that is—some, people who'd lived here all their lives. After we declared war on Japan—we did that after they bombed Pearl Harbor in Hawaii—our government, our great Land of the Free, Home of the Brave American government, decided that everyone who looked the slightest bit Oriental ought to be investigated, so we arrested them and some were sent to our very own concentration camps and incarcerated until the war was over."

"What did they do to them? Did they make lampshades out of them like the Nazis?"

Seth stared at her, and suddenly she knew she'd done something wrong. He didn't even get mad though, which made it worse; he just got a look on his face like he was about to cry.

"Did Bridget tell you that?" he asked very quietly.

"You mean it's not true?"

"Oh, it's true enough. That little . . . *viper*." But that was all he said.

He turned around and looked out the window. "There is nothing I can do, is there?" he said, not looking at her. "There is not a goddamn thing I can do."

"About what?" She felt pretty nervous now.

"Zoë, *everything* is true." He turned back around. "Everything horrible you can imagine and more that you can't. Can't you just take it on faith that evil exists? This is a perennial problem between the two of us, I know. Must I crack open the earth and show you the hellfires myself? Can't you understand that I don't want to be the one to inform you about these things?"

"No," she said.

He sort of laughed then, sounding sad, which made sense if you were insane. She knew he liked her, he just had never been trained right.

"Besides," he said, "if I'd told you, you probably wouldn't have believed me. You're always going to want to experience things for yourself. But I'll make a bargain with you anyway. From now on I'll tell you whatever you want to know, but you have to promise not to be angry at me for not having told you things you learn from other sources. Is it a deal?"

"I don't know," she said. She stood up.

"Well, you think about it. Meanwhile, I'll tell you the story of my one prisoner of war. That is, if you still want to hear it. Do you?"

She shrugged.

"Look, Zoë, the tale may not boost me in your estimation, but at least you should be ashamed of me for the right reasons."

"What is that supposed to mean?"

"It was after I'd been sent from Florida to Alabama," he said. She sat back down while he was talking. "I'd been studying Japanese for seven or eight months, and could form a rudimentary sentence and understand two thirds of the radio broadcasts. One day I was sent to a small town way out in the country. It was so hot—I simply can't tell you how hot it was. Five times as hot as the hottest days in Sparta ever get. It was like being inside a dryer. Simply breathing was exhausting. And I was being sent to arrest a storekeeper of Japanese descent—or so I'd been told.

"I drove out with another man from the base—he didn't speak a word of Japanese—didn't speak English either, for that matter. All the way out in this damned jeep—nearly eighty miles in an army jeep is no picnic, let me tell you—my companion, his name was Burt Rilestone, kept saying, 'If he makes a move, he's dead meat.' 'Rilestone, I am in charge of the mission, you'll be so good as to remember,' *I* kept saying. 'Flush it, Carver,' he said."

" '*Flush* it, Carver'?"

"You like that, do you? After an interminable amount of time, we got to the town. It wasn't hard to find our dreaded foreign spy—he was sitting out in front of the only grocery store in town, fanning himself with a newspaper."

"He was?"

Seth held up his hand.

" 'What may I do for you gentlemen?' he asked, when we drove up. Rilestone leaped out of the jeep and stuck his gun in the fellow's face. 'Hands up!' he shouted. I was so infuriated—I jumped out of that jeep and knocked the gun away from Rilestone so fast he didn't know what had hit him."

"Why did you do that?"

"He was sitting in the dirt looking up at me in amazement. Suddenly he started shouting. 'I get it, Carver! I get it! You're on *their* side. Well, shoot me then! Shoot me and get it over with! Just don't do any of those Japanese torture games with me.' I turned my back on him and looked at the storekeeper and shrugged. He didn't smile, but he nodded ever so slightly and said, 'I will bring you gentlemen something cool and refreshing to drink.' He stood up and walked with great dignity into his store. I *worshipped* him. If it had been as simple a question as being on his side or 'ours,' well, there's no uncertainty in my mind as to whose I'd have chosen."

"You mean you'd have betrayed your country?"

"Zoë, will you please please *listen*? When the storekeeper left, Rilestone recovered his senses and jumped up and began screaming, 'You're lettin' him git away. You're derelictin' your duty.' By now people were coming out of the nearby houses to stare at us. 'Rilestone,' I said, 'if you say one more thing—one more single thing—I'll bind and gag you and leave you out in the heat to melt. Is that understood?' "

"What did he say?"

Seth chuckled. "He just stared. He'd thought I was a mild-mannered milksop, a lily-livered eggheaded pantywaist. I was having a swell time. I had his gun and my own now, and to further show him what an ass he was, when the storekeeper—Mr. Chang was his name, I soon found out—came back, I set the rifle against the wall beside Mr. Chang's chair. Rilestone became apoplectic—about to explode—but he didn't dare say anything. I guess he thought Chang was too stupid to see the gun and if he didn't make any mention of it then maybe Chang wouldn't notice.

"The rest of the interview didn't take long. I explained to Mr. Chang what I'd been sent for and apologized for the boorishness of my government. His government too, of course. We conveniently forgot that the Constitution protected his rights as well as those of individuals with European features. He listened very courteously, and then said, 'You are not responsible. Do not perturb yourself.' I tell you, Zoë, I felt as if God had come right down from heaven and given me absolution. 'May I be allowed to pack a few items and to arrange my affairs?' he asked. I told him he could have as long as he needed. He then went off down the street and I had to level the gun at Rilestone to prevent his following."

"Were you going to shoot him if he tried?"

"It wasn't a possibility," Seth said. "I had never loaded my rifle. Rilestone didn't know that, however, and sat quite respectfully on the chair Mr. Chang had vacated. While he was gone, several of the neighbors came by and wanted to know what the story was. I told them and they said that it would be very hard on his daughter when she heard—she was away at college. Her mother had died just a year ago. I decided right then and there that the moment I got out of the army I was going to head straight to wherever she was and propose to her."

"You did? Did you?"

"No." Seth laughed. "That is, I headed there, but I didn't propose. That's another story, however. By the time Mr. Chang came back I'd learned that he was generally loved in town, and—what amazed me, although it shouldn't have—that although everyone deeply regretted his having to be arrested, *no* one doubted its necessity. Evidently they did not find it the least bit implausible that this fifty-year-old Chinese storekeeper, out in the middle of the Alabama tobacco fields, could be masterminding a dread attack against our native shores. That's when I lost whatever faith I still had in the human race. Except, maybe, in Mr. Chang."

"But why was he in Alabama?"

"For the only reason he probably could have been. He'd fallen in love. He'd come to America when he was twelve, had been educated, gone to college, and at a dance somewhere met a girl from Alabama. They were married, much to the horror of her family, but settled in Chicago. They had two children, one of whom died of scarlet fever at the age of five. When his wife's parents died, she inherited their house and her father's general store and since it was right smack in the middle of the Depression they went south. People disapproved of them on principle but liked them in fact. Then, the year before, Mrs. Chang had had a heart attack and died. By then Chang was running her father's store and he just stayed. Earlier that year, his daughter had left to go to college—the same college your mother and I went to—though, as I said, that's another story."

"It seems like the same story to me."

"On the drive back to the base, Chang and I never mentioned the fact that he was a prisoner and I his captor. I remember we discussed philosophy. I'd been reading a lot, but unsystematically, and he had a much more disciplined mind than I. He'd studied almost everything, it seemed, and had a phenomenal memory. He had been teaching at the University of Chicago when the Depression hit, and because he was low man on the totem pole he got bumped. Of course our discussion drove Rilestone, whom I'd made sit in the back, stark raving mad. He was convinced we were talking in code, and mumbled to himself without ceasing. Finally we got back to the base. Chang was marched off—in handcuffs, mind you—and I didn't see him again for several days. During that time they interrogated him. I don't know what all they could have asked him, but they managed to satisfy themselves that he was dangerous enough to be shipped off to one of the camps. I, your father, was chosen to escort him there. I was the best student in Japanese and the idiot in charge would not be convinced by anyone that Chang wasn't from Japan. Or maybe that was a front—maybe because he'd taught physics at Chicago they thought he was selling nuclear secrets to the enemy. *I* don't know. Rilestone had tried to convince the C.O.—the commanding officer—that I was in league with Chang but evidently made such a fool of himself that they sent him off for three weeks of R and R—rest and relaxation. So one steamy day Mr. Chang and I were put on a train to Mobile. We were supposed to fly to Utah from there. Since the flight wasn't until the next day, we went to a hotel. It's one of the mysteries of how the army operates that they could have incarcerated this fellow in solitary confinement and grilled him under a dangling light bulb and then paid for him to stay in a plush hotel suite with room service. Believe me, we lived it up. And no one ever said a word to me later about the charges.

"Then somehow the plane tickets got messed up. To this day I don't know why we were being sent in a commercial plane, unless it was because there weren't enough prisoners from that part of the country to make it worth the army's while to fly Mr. Chang out in one of their own transports. The airline became suspicious of us and called the base, but even the C.O.'s reassurance wasn't sufficient to get them to let us have our tickets—everyone was so spy-crazy in those days. Washington got involved, and so naturally that slowed everything down. For four days Mr. Chang and I sat on the veranda of a lovely old hotel in Mobile, Alabama, drinking mint juleps and discussing the categorical imperative until we began to be convinced it could be defined only in terms of each other."

"*What?*" Zoë said. But he wasn't even listening.

"When we were bored with that, we'd go out to a movie. We saw every movie playing in Mobile at least three times. I'll never forget *The Song of Bernadette*, alas. I was under orders, of course, never to let Chang out of my sight—they'd given me handcuffs to restrain him, if I needed to sleep. They hadn't bargained for the fact that I'd be spending more than twenty-four hours with him, but even before I knew it myself I told him straight out, 'You want to escape, escape. The gun's not loaded.' I showed him the empty chambers. 'Thank you very much,' he said, and that was all either of us ever said about it."

"Why didn't he try to escape?"

Seth shrugged. "Where would he have gone? He was damn visible in Alabama, you know. Besides, he knew that if he tried to escape that would only confirm his guilt in the minds of the high mucky-mucks. And he didn't want me to get in trouble. The most honorable man I've ever met, Zoë. I even felt a little honorable myself in his company."

Seth stopped talking and she was afraid he was getting all worked up again so she asked quickly, "Then what happened?"

He looked out the window a minute, and said, "Eventually the airline was satisfied we were legit; we flew west and I turned him over to the camp authorities. He shook my hand and asked me to write to him when the war was over." Seth smiled, but he looked really sad. Then he said, "Do you remember that girl, Xiao Smith, who spent a couple of nights with us a few years ago?"

"Kind of."

"She's Mr. Chang's granddaughter. I did write him at the end of the war but didn't receive any answer to my letters. Then I had to wait until I was discharged from the army and could locate his daughter to find out what had happened to him."

"Did you still want to marry her?"

"Yep."

"Why didn't you?"

He laughed. "She was already married. A contingency I hadn't considered. Suffice it to say that we became friends and wrote over the years. When her daughter was at a camp one summer in Virginia, Lucy thought it would be nice if Xiao spent a couple of days with us. Maybe Nick would remember her better than you do."

"But what happened to Mr. Chang?"

"Oh, Zoë . . ." he said, as if he had just noticed she was there. "He died in the camp. There weren't enough blankets to go around and he got pneumonia. I'm sorry."

"He *died*?" Tears came into her eyes; she couldn't help it. "He really died?"

"I'm sorry, Zoë. I wish I could have given you a happy ending."

"But I just don't understand why Mr. Chang didn't try to escape! You could have helped him. Couldn't you have just gone off in the woods or something?"

"That's a question I ask myself almost every day of my life."

She didn't know what to say after he said that. She felt so sad for Mr. Chang and for Seth too, carrying his guilt around all these years; had he ever told anyone else that story? She wished she could have brought Mr. Chang back to life. It made her want to tell Bridget she was sorry before it was too late, yet she knew Bridget was never going to forgive her. Instead she told Seth it wasn't his fault that Mr. Chang had died; he was just following orders.

"Thank you for that, Zoë," he said. "It's the children who bestow grace, not the other way around."

Then one day about a week later Bridget just came to the front door and knocked. Zoë had seen her coming through the window and her heart was pounding like crazy. She wished someone else could open the door, but she was the only one in the house.

"Hi," Bridget said, all normal.

"What are you doing here?"

"Can I come in?"

"You want to?"

"No, I'd rather just stand on your doorstep for the rest of my life. Of course I want to come in. What do you think I am, a Fuller Brush salesman?"

She came in and sat on the couch. Zoë sat on the other end of it.

"I came to tell you I'm not mad anymore. What you did turned out to be a blessing in disguise. I was so upset after you told me about my father that he noticed and then I couldn't help telling him and once I'd told him my mother got on him and we absolutely *insisted* he go to a doctor. They took some tests and found out he's allergic to some medication he's been taking for some problem with his phlebitis or something. He never even connected all his dizzy spells with the medicine, can you believe it? Now my parents are saying Dr. Mitchell is a terrible a-s-s, and they never, I mean but never, use that word unless they really think somebody is the scum of the earth. My mother even wants to write a letter to the medical board of Sparta, but my father is trying to persuade her not to since he says it's as much the fault of his stubbornness as it is of Dr. Mitchell. The doctor here gave him different medicine and he says he feels like a new person! Isn't that unbelievable? And it's all because of you! If it hadn't been for you getting mad and telling me and then me getting all upset and telling my father and forcing him to go to the doctor he really could have died! He could have died! Do you realize you saved his *life*? I forgive you everything you ever did and I apologize for everything bad I ever said to you, and I hope you'll forgive me because I want to go back to being friends forever."

"You do?" Zoë said. "Really?"

She was extremely happy but she was also more confused than ever. You did something that seemed fine but turned out to have been horrible, but when you did something wrong on purpose it turned out to be a blessing in disguise. How were you supposed to *know*? And if you didn't know, how could you be safe doing *anything*?

A few weeks after this, one day when they were bored, she and Bridget forged a letter to Bridget's mother from Mrs. Went saying Robert had held up the first grade at gunpoint, demanding that all their legs be cut off, and Mr. and Mrs. Wycliffe actually fell for it, rushing right over to Seth and Monica to show them the letter, and then they all sat around moaning, "Oh, I always knew the child was unhinged," "Poor Sally and Ted," until Seth the sleuth finally noticed that the postmark was drawn on with a pencil, not stamped. But for a few hours they'd been in a real uproar.

XIII CASCABEL FLATS

In the morning they were going into town, this mythical place where everyone always said what they meant . . . Zoë wasn't sure that she wanted to see it. Ellie needed to pick up a few last-minute items for the Christmas Eve and Christmas dinners, and she also—it was after breakfast and Nick, accompanied by Pryce, was out slaughtering the snake she was going to bake for the Beauregards' party (she had decreed that under no circumstances, that is, certain guests in the house, could Nick use the freezer for euthanasia as he usually did)—wanted to run by Ignacio Ortega's shop to see if Nick's Christmas present, a Spanish-style chest she'd ordered back in March, nine months ago, was in fact going to be delivered that afternoon as promised. They—Zoë and Monica—would have to help her think up some ploy to get Nick out of the house when the chest arrived. She thought she would store it in the sun room, throw a blanket over it, and forbid Nick to go in there until Christmas morning.

Had Ellie convinced Nick to "try" last night? But Zoë had been too busy convincing Pryce *not* to, to listen for Nick and Ellie. The lights were off so all she could do was push him away. "I can be quiet," he kept whispering. "You can't imagine how quiet I can be." God knows what she'd have done if there had been any doors. She was back on her regular cycle and the next couple of days would be the peak time for conception. She wondered if Pryce suspected that she'd stopped taking the pills, he'd been so persistent; maybe he was willing to be a father after all if he thought it was the only way he could keep her. On the other hand, how could he have known? For two months she'd been flushing a tablet down the toilet every morning right on schedule.

When Nick and Pryce came back in, Nick was in a bad mood and said he'd "prefer to sit this one out" when Ellie asked him if he were ready to go. She followed him into their bedroom and when Monica went into the sun room to get her pocketbook, Pryce told Zoë that Nick had dashed outside and vomited after he'd decapitated the snake. He'd come back in just in time to save Pryce from picking up the head.

"Did you know that the head can still bite after it's cut off?" Pryce exclaimed.

Zoë nodded, worried about Nick.

"Your reaction is certainly mild considering I came within half an inch of having to be rushed to the hospital!"

Before Zoë could respond, Ellie returned; she slumped against the counter, looking at Zoë and shaking her head: *Remember what we talked about last night?*—that is, Nick's supposedly shaky mental state. They heard Nick come out of the bedroom and go into the bathroom, brush his teeth and gargle. Monica came back in, but no one said anything else until Nick reappeared.

"Shall we take the Chevy?" Ellie asked.

"Whichever you prefer," he said.

So she'd convinced him to go; was that evidence of anything? He drove and Monica sat in front; Ellie, Zoë, and Pryce sat in the back. It was colder than the day before: the sky was a flat gray and snow had been predicted. The blue mountains looked pale and the ones north of town were a menacing fir green splotched with bare, dun-colored patches. To Zoë the stumpy asymmetrical trees on either side of the road looked like giant sloppily pruned bonsai. When houses started showing up they were all the same squat blandness as Nick and Ellie's—bunkers with windows. All around them, the salmon-colored earth showed through the misshapen trees like a scalp. The place seemed no more recognizable as a part of the country she'd lived in all her life than it had yesterday.

Nick caught Ellie's eye in the rearview mirror and said he thought he'd detour a little on the way into town in order to show their guests some of the more picturesque neighborhoods.

"That's a good idea." She beamed at his reflection.

Complying with some unwritten law of cause and effect, Pryce laid his arm across Zoë's shoulders.

I hope you realize what I'm up against, Rob, she said. Pryce isn't you, but he does love me and wants the best for me. Despite what he says, I think that if I did become pregnant he'd want the child. It was one thing to wait when you were locked up, but now that you're out . . . What's keeping you? Not hearing from you is completely unbearable. I can conceive only in the next few days. Why should I wait when you haven't even given me some kind of sign?

When Nick turned off the main road, the streets grew narrower and the houses closer and closer together; then they actually joined: one garden wall connected to the next, all painted the same bland ocher—it was impossible to tell where one property stopped and the next began. Probably no one had doors out here; Ignacio Ortega must have thought Nick and Ellie were joking when they'd ordered them. Out *here*, we're into togetherness, you know? We don't try to make our separate peace. Down tiny alleyways even more buildings were visible, but whether they were attached to the larger houses in front or were separate residences wasn't clear; it was like not being able to tell which snake was which, and Zoë felt the same queasiness she had in the snakehouse. Even though they were hideous, she preferred the isolated lumps outside of town. But, wouldn't you know, Monica had exclaimed that she'd finally recognized what the place reminded her of: an old European fortress town, and Ellie had exclaimed back "Yes!" as if Monica had given the correct answer on a quiz. Now they were practically singing a duet about the architecture, Pryce chiming in occasionally on the refrain: everything looked so *human; out here* you had no neat rows of houses, each protected by its own lawn from involvement with its neighbors, and scarcely a right angle to be seen—no feeling of nature tamed or tortured, wood chopped down and sliced; the buildings grew right out of the earth. Thank God Nick interrupted this demented hymn.

"Most of these babies go for upwards of five hundred grand, I'll have you know. Hard to believe for a lot of mud and straw, isn't it?"

"But it's *authentic* mud and straw." Ellie laughed.

"Strange how what was once utilitarian becomes the aesthetic, isn't it?" Pryce asked.

Where did you come up with this joker? Rob exclaimed. *He* doesn't have to talk like this—he wasn't raised by the Guardians of Western Tradition the way we were!

Come on, she said, don't be so hard on him. If you'd spent the last ten years having conversations you'd find yourself making these statements too. Taking these *stands*. It's impossible to help it. Why do you think I don't talk?

But Rob had stopped listening, as if reproving the disingenuousness of her question. Or maybe he didn't have much of an attention span—shock treatments could do that, couldn't they? Or medication. Well, when they were together he could stop taking it.

Meanwhile Ellie pointed out houses once occupied by "famous" people none of them had ever heard of. Her happily married and settled tone seemed to imply that she and Nick had worked things out after all and that Zoë shouldn't hold her to her earlier distress. Downtown, in the area Ellie called the "plaza," Christmas lights and banners were strung across the streets like anywhere else in America, but in the center of the snowless square an *adobe* crèche had been set up—naturally they'd have their own version of Christmas *out here.* Nick had his window open and as they waited at a stop light for people who looked like refugees loaded down with all their possessions to drag their shopping bags across the street, they could hear the Salvation Army stand on the corner playing "It Came upon a Midnight Clear" while the Salvation Army man shook his bell lethargically. Zoë tried not to listen to the words—even this tinny rendition could make her feel like crying.

I can't fight it without you, Rob. Two thousand years of hope is more than I can stand up to on my own.

"There's the cathedral, by the way," Ellie announced.

Zoë glanced up the street, shocked to see it looming straight ahead of them like an ocean liner about to run them down. It was so huge and so completely different in style from the square adobes surrounding it that it looked as if it had come from somewhere else and would leave when its business here was over.

Bless you, my child, the priest would say. I promise not to be merciful—have faith.

Some people might think that not having been able to speak for ten years should be enough, but the priest would know that something more lasting was called for. Poor Rob—the more he'd tried to convince the judge and jury he deserved to be punished the less they'd believed his story. Only the innocent could be martyrs. Had he decided that not being believed was his real punishment? Was that why he'd decided to go along with his "keepers" finally?

He would have had to admit he'd been crazy or they wouldn't have let him out, yet she still couldn't believe the Rob she'd known would betray himself like that.

The cathedral was missing its steeples, Ellie pointed out, if they were wondering what looked odd about it. "Well, we'll just have to have a steeplechase," Pryce said. Universal groan. Had they simply got sick of building it or what? he asked. "I don't remember the explanation," Ellie said. "Maybe the workers felt antagonistic—there'd been no priests for a long time and people had grown used to administering their own ceremonies . . ." Zoë wondered what Monica would think if she knew that her daughter had spent every lunch hour for the past month in the cathedral down the street from the high-rise where she was working, typing the same form over and over for an insurance company; sure that at any moment she would be exposed for an infidel, she slouched at the far end of a pew, thumbing through the *TV Guide*–like daily prayer program, spying on the people who knelt on the red-imitation-leather–padded benches, trying to guess what *they* prayed for. Monica found "public displays of emotion" so "distasteful." Maybe the priest was in this cathedral here—not that the "priest" would necessarily have to be a priest; anyone who could make the punishment fit the crime would do.

While she'd been thinking this, Nick had parked the car and now they were all walking down the street, looking in windows, two days until Christmas: Zoë knew there were things she wasn't seeing. Why had she not cancelled her plans to come out West after hearing from Bridget? Not only not cancelled them, but invited Pryce to come along? Bridget might have given Rob her address; now he would have no way of getting in touch with her. It was no coincidence that the cabinetmaker who'd been pretend-crucified had stalled on the doors to keep Pryce from sleeping with her, yet why *pretend*-crucified? To indicate that Rob had failed at *his* martyrdom?

She knew everything had to signify *something*, yet to figure out what was like trying to complete a jigsaw puzzle when the pieces could fit in more than one place and the picture wasn't of anything recognizable anyway. Like thinking in high school about the connotations of her family's names (Mr. Montgomery–inspired, and she'd been ashamed to tell Rob she'd fallen for it, he was so scornful of anyone thinking symbols were anything real)—trying to think what it *meant* that she was named Zoë, Greek for "life," Greek for "Eve," not only Zoë but Zoë *Minerva*—did it mean she was wise about life? (Maybe Seth and Monica had hoped she would be.) Did it mean she would make war on life? *For* life? It was like trying to read a sentence with the verbs missing. And Nick—"Nick" could stand for St. Nick, Santa Claus, the spirit of giving, but it could also mean *Old* Nick, the devil. *Seth* had been one of Adam and Eve's sons. Her grandfather was named *Adam*. But then *she* would be her grandfather's wife and Seth would be their child, which made no sense symbolically or any other way. Monica had been christened Harmony but had changed her name. Everything meant *something*, but nothing added up. (And these were just their first names.)

Now they were all walking a gauntlet of seated Indians selling turquoise and silver jewelry laid out on scarves and blankets on the sidewalk—necklaces, bracelets, and earrings, and those disgusting string ties that made men look like giant boy scouts. Ellie doubled back and told Zoë and Pryce that after this they'd go investigate a few shops, then she and Nick wanted to treat everyone to lunch at one of the local watering holes. Nick was going to slip off to the post office in a few minutes. She gathered he'd told the two of them about the new boarders he was expecting. While he was gone she'd dash over to Ortega's—she told Pryce about the chest; she ought to have her head examined for ordering it after Ortega's dallying with the doors.

Zoë had already decided to go to the post office with Nick in order to consult about Seth, but now she wondered if she should check out Ortega and his religious limp instead. Did he limp on the same side as Rob? Maybe it wasn't Rob who was supposed to father her child but Ignacio Ortega. How old was he? However, it might be a while before she had another chance to be alone with Nick; if something happened to Seth and she hadn't done anything . . . It would be ten years ago all over again. Nick's mood was not improved by having to wait in line at the post office nearly forty-five minutes only to be told that even though they could put an emergency tracer into the system there was no guarantee that what with the holiday crunch the next stop down the line would pick up on it.

"Well, that's just great," he said, as they left the building. "Our no-fault society. Jesus Christ."

At one time frustration like this would have automatically launched him into an asthma attack, but now he just walked fast, fuming. Zoë wondered if she was going to be able to talk to him about Seth after all—not if he stayed in this frame of mind—but he startled her by bringing up the subject himself.

While they were standing on a corner for the light to change he said, "You and Dad actually have conversations in Morse code on the telephone?"

She faced him, eyebrows raised: *How did you know that?*

"Pryce told me when we were out sacrificing the snake."

Dad speaks English.

"Well, I assumed . . ."

They crossed the street and Nick gestured towards a bench set back from the sidewalk as if they'd agreed that they would sit down somewhere. When they were settled he said, "I guess we're going to have to discuss what to do."

Zoë nodded. She tried to calculate how best to convince Nick of the situation's gravity, but couldn't think, then took a breath as if about to speak and signed, *I got a letter from Bridget recently.* LETTER B-R-I . . .

"Bridget Wycliffe? I didn't know you heard from her."

Nick's voice was flat.

I didn't until a few weeks ago.

When she didn't elaborate, Nick said, after waiting a moment, "Well, it so happens that there's something I have to tell you too. I got a letter—that is, you got a letter—from Robert Went."

A letter? Zoë repeated silently. She closed her eyes and opened them again, but otherwise she didn't react. She knew Nick had said this only to get even with her for having caught him still feeling touchy about Bridget even though they'd gone out for such a short time.

"It was addressed to Metcalf Street first," Nick continued, watching her.

She tried to process the possibility that he might be telling the truth.

"You think I'm making it up?"

If it was addressed to Metcalf Street, then Mother knows. If the letter *was* real, Monica and Nick had probably *discussed* whether or not to tell her.

"No, not necessarily. It wasn't forwarded. The first address was just crossed out. He must have been going to mail it there, then found out you'd be out here. As far as I know, the only people who could have told him are Mom and Dad. Besides me, but he would have had to contact them to find out where I was."

Zoë watched him, unable to move.

"I don't think it's Mom," Nick said. "Why would he have addressed it to Metcalf Street and then talked to her? That leaves Dad. I think that's part of the reason I was so annoyed yesterday when you told me you hadn't heard from him—he must be up to something. There's no return address, although the envelope is postmarked Sparta. I take it this is the first time he's written to you, then."

Zoë still couldn't process this information. *Why didn't you tell me yesterday?*

Nick smiled disarmingly. "I don't know, really. I guess it's . . . Well, you always act as if you're the only one who can comprehend Dad's motives—it bugs me. I meant to tell you at the airport. Later I didn't have a chance."

She decided to ignore this for the moment. *If there's no return address, how do you know it's from him?*

"It says, 'Robert Went, At Large.' "

Despite herself, she laughed.

"You can see I didn't make it up."

She shrugged. *Someone besides Rob could have mailed it.*

"What else?" Nick looked startled. "What do you mean? You think he was *there?*"

Zoë suddenly felt much better. At least there was *something* Nick hadn't known.

That's why Bridget wrote—to tell me he was out.

"*What?*" Nick exclaimed. "Did you say what I think you did? Robert Went's not in the hospital anymore?"

Right.

"And that's what Bridget wrote to tell you?"

She thought none of you would tell me.

"Who does she think she is?"

Well, would you have?

"Would I have told you?" Nick shrugged. "Maybe not, if I'd known."

There you go.

"I said *maybe* not, Zoë. What else did Bridget say?"

HUSBAND ACCIDENT. ALREADY KNOW.

"She has two kids, doesn't she?"

BOYS SAME.

"Twins, right. Is she still living in Seattle?"

WHERE LETTER FROM.

They watched people walk by. Then Nick said, "Actually, I haven't told you quite everything. I confess I asked Mother if she'd heard any news about Robert recently."

What? Zoë began to sign almost randomly. *Goddamn it, Nick I . . .*

"Take it easy, Zo. I didn't tell her anything."

But you just came out and asked her? NO INTRODUCE . . .

"I got around to the subject in the usual way. Whenever she hasn't seen me in a while she always asks me whether I know if you're in any kind of treatment—that I should tell you she'd be happy to pay for it, but she doesn't dare mention the subject to you . . ."

You never told me that before!

"So I'm telling you now." He laughed. "Since this seems to be True Confessions Week. When I asked her if she ever heard anything about Robert, she looked insulted. 'Why should *I* hear anything? You know very well that Sally Went left Sparta a decade ago and if she communicates with anyone it's Lydia Wycliffe.' Of course the devil in me wanted to ask her if she hears anything from Lydia—do you think they speak when they run into each other? They must run into each other. Maybe they just spit and growl."

Zoë smiled grudgingly.

"That's why I'm sure it must have been Dad who gave Robert this address."

Or Bridget.

"How would she have got it?"

From Dad.

Nick looked away. When he looked back, she asked, *Where is the letter?* WHERE LETTER? She might recognize Rob's handwriting—at least she'd know for sure that he'd sent it.

"In the back of my sock drawer."

Did you tell Ellie about it? The sign they used for Ellie was "E-marry."

"No."

What about Stewart? She spelled out his name.

"Stewart Beauregard? Why on earth would I tell him?"

She shrugged.

"Ellie must have put some bug into your head about him," Nick said, disgusted. "I don't know *what* she has against him. He's never been anything but helpful to us—he's never once lorded it over us about the house. Ellie thinks he had some devious aim in mind when he sold us the place, but I think he was just sick of thinking about it, frankly. Everyone finagling for his favors. I didn't even know he had the property! I was working on one of his construction crews, and we got in the habit of having a few beers together. One day I mentioned that El and I were looking for a house and he said he knew of one."

Zoë nodded.

"I didn't even know who he was when I first met him! He was actually working on the crew—he does that on occasion, disguises himself as a mortal. Then one day he wasn't there and I asked the foreman if he'd called in sick—the foreman was highly amused. That was how I found out Stewart paid my wages. Ellie talks as if he has some ulterior motive for everything he does, but he's just a guy who happened to cash in on a trend at the right time. He's been very encouraging to me about my research as well." Nick gave her a mischievous look. "It helps to have a little boost now and then when you're trying to readjust the world's conscience, you know."

Are you talking about the venom?

"Think of the expressions, Zo. Your conscience 'gnaws' at you; guilt 'eats away' at you—that's neurotransmitters you're talking, sweetheart." He embarked on a soliloquy about amino acids and blocked neural pathways. He stopped suddenly to ask, "Is this also the first time you've heard from Bridget since . . . I just assumed it was, but maybe . . ."

YES.

"You've never told Pryce about any of this, have you?"

NO.

She expected Nick to comment, but he simply nodded. His mind was clearly somewhere else.

"I know there are things you've never told me either—things about

Rob, maybe other things too. I'm not asking, it's just . . . You know, Zoë, I've thought about a lot of things since I've been out here. It's strange, it's almost the first time I've even had time, since—I'm sorry, Zoë. I'm sorry I'm so bad at talking about it. I guess I'm afraid you'll think it's an intrusion."

She shrugged: *go on.*

"I sometimes think you still blame yourself for . . . well, I don't even know what exactly. It's just all seemed so clear to me lately. Maybe the time, maybe the distance—after all it's the first time I've ever lived more than fifty miles from home." He looked at her. "Strange, isn't it, to be thirty years old and never have lived away from home? You see, I think you mixed everything up. Because so much happened at once you thought it was all connected . . ."

It was.

"Yes and no. Obviously you were connected to everything because you knew all the people, but that doesn't mean the events were connected. It's a common fallacy."

Think what you like, Zoë said to herself—I was still the common denominator. I kept everything secret, whereas if I'd said something . . . "I mean, how could you foresee how things would turn out? You did what you could given the information you had. We never have enough information so how *can* we do the right thing? You can't ascribe moral value to biological weakness. Hey, Zoë . . . What's the matter? Why are you crying? Hey, I'm sorry! I didn't mean to upset you. Rob never killed . . . never did it on purpose."

She shook her head and wiped her eyes. People passing by would think they were having a lovers' quarrel. Nick patted her arm.

It was on a back road, she signed impatiently. *He knew his father always took this particular shortcut home from work. It wasn't like he just happened to be crossing some street and his father came along. He timed it! He took a bus out to the place! The driver testified!*

Nick nodded. He had scarcely been watching her hands. "The thing is," he said, "after He threw them out, she stopped trusting what she knew—I'm not sure *he* ever did know. If I could be sure where she was bitten—maybe it doesn't matter, although the quicker it makes it to the brain the better, I'm sure." He glanced at her. "It had to be hormones that took it across. It just couldn't have been anything else. Even if the fruit had fermented, I don't think the molecules could bind."

What molecules? What are you talking about?

He acted surprised by her question. "Alcohol, what do you think? Even though that would be the more plausible explanation. For one thing, alcohol deludes one into thinking one has everything figured out so it makes sense that it locks into the site intended for the real receptor—same thing with morphine, as I'm sure you know. Almost identical structure to the body's natural painkiller. Unfortunately doubt like everything else will be found to have a biochemical makeup; when everyone kept saying she'd done the wrong thing, that continual influence obviously mutated the substance of clear thinking she otherwise might have passed down after the first bite—I'm talking about its biting her, not her the apple, you understand."

Oh, of course.

"I think I could have isolated it if they'd let me use the protein separator another few months, but they said there was no point since I couldn't perform useful experiments on animals and even if there were human beings crazy enough to let me try it on them at the very least I'd need to use the PET scanner and you know how much those cost.

"It's possible, of course, that it was something that was always meant to be repeated with every individual—I mean, administered from outside—and if that's the case then my job will be easy. All I'll have to do is find out which species it is. At this point I've pretty much narrowed it down to the Tortuga or the diamondback." He grinned at her. "Of course I'd prefer it to be the diamondback—call it latent patriotism."

Oh, definitely, call it that.

How gullible did he think she was? She seriously doubted that molecules hitched rides on each other that way. Why was he trying to get her to believe this insane story? Sure, Nick, an injection of diamondback venom will reverse the Fall.

Remember the *Fall*, Rob? Mr. Montgomery, *Paradise Lost*, the "mistake that made us what we are today"?

Nick was turning out to be his father's son after all: wild talk about the universal alkahest when what you probably needed was a socket wrench.

I think Rob may be after Dad, Zoë said, to put an end to this discussion. R-O-B MAYBE KILL DAD. She hadn't kept silence for ten years only to have Nick tell her she wasn't responsible for what had happened.

He looked at her as if he couldn't remember who—or even what—"Rob" and "Dad" were. But he could as easily be pretending. The tactic was genetic. He said politely, "That's a shame."

No one believed him the first time, now he wants . . .

"How *could* they believe him?" Nick said in disgust. "No one else knows what they're doing. But it makes no sense, don't you see? It contradicts every known evolutionary principle. We evolve to adapt. Every other species acts instinctively to ensure its survival. Why are we different? Why don't we simply *know* the right thing to do? Only a radical mutation can explain it. Only a radical remedy can reverse the trend."

The thing is, now that I know he wrote to me . . . NOW KNOW WRITE . . .

"Maybe it's not too late. One can only hope it's not too late." Then Nick said, "Are you talking about Rob?"

What if there were no return address *in* Rob's letter? It could say, "Hi, Zoë, had a great decade. Wished you were here." He could have sent one of Anders Ogilvy's photographs of her, ripped into a hundred pieces. She'd assumed he'd destroyed them, but maybe he'd simply hidden them somewhere—a secret cupboard or passageway. The house on Mulberry Street where he'd had the bakery was old enough to have had one.

"I can see now why you're worried," Nick said, sounding like someone from another culture trying to understand the customs of the one he was visiting, "but you know there's no point in jumping to conclusions until you see what Robert has to say. He may be emigrating to Australia, for all you know. Isn't that where they used to send convicts? Here too. We're all descended from criminals. People who can't foresee the consequences of their actions." He sounded as if he were quoting a definition. "Do you see what I mean, Zoë? It's our national heritage. No wonder no one could believe Robert knew what he was doing. Even I didn't think so at the time, but now I . . . Poor guy, he must have been furious when the prosecutor wouldn't press charges."

Nick had completely forgotten that ten minutes ago he'd told her Rob *hadn't* known what he was doing.

"You were always much braver than I was, I think. You always knew what Mom and Dad were up to, for instance, and sometimes I could stand to face up to it, but a lot of the time I couldn't. We're a nation of cowards, I think. Refusing to look the rattlesnake in the face. That must have made it pretty tough on you sometimes."

Robert was the sanest person I ever met, Zoë said. She made sure Nick understood exactly what she'd signed, but nothing fazed him.

"I'm sure you're right. I'm sorry I was so out of it at the time. Although except for the stories about the accident he lost his leg in when he first came to school practically everything I heard about him came through Bridget, so it's no wonder . . ." He stopped. "Do you *want* to see him?"

Yes, she said. *No. I don't know.* Had she really said that?

"Well, that's understandable. You say Bridget didn't know where he was?"

She didn't say.

"Well, you'll see, Zoë. You'll read the letter and see. If I forget when we get back—it's in the top right-hand drawer of my dresser, under the socks. Safest hiding place in the universe. My dresser's the one to the left of the door when you go in the bedroom. We better rejoin the troops now, don't you think? They'll be suspecting us of going AWOL."

Where would we go?

"Good question." He laughed. "To an Islamic country? Where else can you get away from it? 'Goddamn secular holiday,' he complained, quoting Seth. " 'Always dangerous to detach symbols from their origins. They get loose, you know, kids, they create havoc.' "

They were laughing hysterically before they were halfway down the block. Nick's grip on her arm was friendly and protective. As they came in sight of the others waiting in front of the restaurant, Zoë noted that, still, neither one of them had so much as mentioned calling the police.

XIV HARMONY

In the back of one of the black Bibles Charlotte records the birthdays of the children who aren't born: Henry Micah, February 9, 1912; Thaddeus Obadiah, September 18, 1912; Llewellyn Asa . . .; Samuel Adam . . . (though it is not she who says they never lived). She has her first miscarriage the winter after she and Adam are married, and though she tells Adam it is her fault for having neglected to communicate to the child how much she wanted it, at this point she still seems to understand that it is dead. Adam pities her in her grief even though he knows the child's destruction to be divine retribution, and eagerly he agrees to Dr. Jewell's suggestion that he take Charlotte on a tour of Europe—new sights should lift her spirits. They are supposed to leave from New York on April 2, 1912, and Adam waits until mid-March to tell Louisa that they are going; but this turns out to be a mistake, since it precipitates another of her "attacks." (Charlotte told Zoë that Adam refused to admit that his mother had tried to commit suicide—that is, until he had no choice.)

Once again Adam refuses to enter Louisa's room; there's no telling what, in her delirium, she might reveal and thus force him to act upon. Though her condition is grave, he nevertheless plans to leave Harmony without delay. He and Charlotte can spend the time before their ship sails revisiting sights in New York; however, to his astonishment, Charlotte refuses to leave Harmony until Louisa is out of danger. Furthermore, she insists upon tending the invalid herself. Two days before their ship's scheduled departure, Louisa cheerfully waves them off at the train station. This sight tempts Adam to think that his wife and his mother have all along been colluding, yet ever since she conceived his child, his wife has begun to seem wholly innocent to him; it has even occurred to him to doubt that she *knows*—she mournfully remarked to him that she particularly regrets the loss of their child since it, at least, would have had a father. Adam can scarce credit her with the wickedness of taunting him with such comments if she knew that *theirs* was one and the same.

Charlotte somehow forgot to mention to Adam that, while she was raving in her fever, Louisa kept clutching her hand and calling her "Ida." But then you'd need a chart to keep straight who'd told what to whom when—it was like Rob's equation, X minus something equaling the number of people thinking secret thoughts about each other, or whatever it was. People keeping secrets, it was never even clear why, in Harmony simply habit, the thing to do since time began, as if they were trying to get even with God for having kept secrets from them.

Zoë wished she could have seen her grandparents together; it seemed to her that so much would have been made clear then—Adam and Charlotte disembarking at Southampton after an uneventful crossing on the morning of April 10 in the midst of a great hullabaloo enveloping the docks, for that evening the S.S. *Titanic* was to set forth upon her maiden voyage.

"How sad that the ship will go down," Charlotte muses, as they are driven along the quay. "The greater number of its passengers will drown."

"Charlotte!" Adam exclaims. "How can you say such a thing?" Yet then he adds gently, "Never mind about the ship." ("Your wife is delicate," Dr. Jewell told him, "and the loss of the child has unsettled her mind. If you are patient, and do not cross her, she will the more quickly recover herself.")

"I say such things because I must," she replies, "even though I no longer expect to be believed."

On the morning of April 15, when newsboys thrust newspapers at them shouting, "TITANIC SINKS! Read all about it! HUNDREDS DROWNED!" Adam spins around to his wife in horror.

"How did you know?" he whispers. "How?"

She shrugs. "I don't know—I knew."

He is afraid to ask her anything else—does she really know the future or was her prediction a morbid fancy that happened to come true? For the rest of their stay in England he tries to shake the sinister feeling the incident has left him with, yet all of their subsequent sightseeing—to the Cornish coast; to the castles and grand houses whose very architecture seems to convey complicity in his illicit marriage . . . even their quiet moments together, when they enjoy an ample English tea or read to each other from one of their favorite writers, E. A. Poe, whose gruesome tales, to Adam's amazement, entertain Charlotte—all is filled with an oppressive uneasiness.

However, when in Paris (exploring the catacombs in the Bois de Boulogne), Charlotte complains of dizziness and subsequently confesses that she has conceived a second time, his nervousness is replaced by exhilaration. His lugubrious thoughts dissipate. For the first time he even permits himself to think that he might have imagined everything. Whoever Charlotte's father *was*, it could not have been Henry—it must have been his mother's insinuations and Timothy Lowndes's devious looks that encouraged him in such unhealthy speculations, he tells himself. He finds an American doctor who assures him that there is no need for them to return home; Charlotte is in excellent health; they may certainly tarry in Europe until the end of the summer. Charlotte, recognizing Adam's hopefulness, hasn't the heart to tell him that this child will not live either. She must allow him his joy—soon there will be no more chance of that.

However, when a few months have passed without incident, and her nausea has abated, even her mood begins to lighten; she takes pleasure in visiting the sights—they have travelled the length of Italy and back and are now in the Alps, where they find relief in the cooler weather—and for the first and only time in her life, Charlotte wonders if she might not have been tricked by grief into dooming herself, if it is not a temperamental predisposition common to her sex that sketches dread in the lineaments of truth, and that other world begins to fade—the world in which Ida is still alive and in which her first little son, whom they meant to name Henry for Adam's father, is healthily growing. For the first and only time, Charlotte forgives herself for living on without them. She even permits Adam to discuss redecorating the nursery, hiring someone to assist in caring for the baby, choosing a name for it. They decide on Thaddeus, if a boy; Louisa, if a girl. They both agree that Adam's mother will be pleased.

In Zurich, in mid-September, a few weeks before they are supposed to sail home from Le Havre, Charlotte goes into labor and the baby is born dead, at not quite six months. Adam, who is more afraid to enter his wife's room after the doctor leaves than he has been afraid of anything in his life, cannot distinguish relief from horror when he discovers Charlotte to be entirely calm. It seems to him that she *pities* him as he kneels beside her bed and weeps, yet it is not, he incredulously feels, because she shares his grief.

It is true that Charlotte is sorry for her husband in his anguish, yet she is puzzled that he cannot see little Henry, two years old already, leaning eagerly over his baby brother as he lies contentedly in Ida's lap. Ida sings to them, sweet soft songs Charlotte remembers from her own childhood. Quietly she begins to hum along. Adam stares at her, amazed, then breaks into even more violent sobs.

"Forgive me, Charlotte! Forgive me! Oh, but how can you?"

"For what should I forgive you? You have done nothing wrong."

"Oh, you don't know. My God, it's true! You don't know! Oh, Charlotte, how shall I live with myself?"

By early October Charlotte is pronounced well enough to travel and before the end of the month they're home, just a little over a year after their wedding. Louisa, to whom Adam has written of the second pregnancy and then of the stillbirth, greets them uncertainly. Their moroseness causes her to chatter. Much has happened: a scandal involving the minister; a new bridge to be built across the Connecticut; the burning of the Dawes place—it appears to have been struck by lightning. Oh! And Timothy Lowndes has proposed to her, she exclaims. Is that not utterly ridiculous?

"No, why?" Adam asks.

"Oh, Adam, don't be absurd!" she scoffs. "How could I consider marrying a man like that!"

Adam consults with Dr. Jewell, who, though expressing deep regret at Charlotte's misfortune, assures him that it is still nothing terribly unusual; there is no reason not to hope that she will soon bear a child successfully. He points out that she carried this one three months longer than the first. Adam finds himself unable to speak of Charlotte's strange equanimity.

During the next three years, Charlotte conceives twice more and twice more miscarries. After the last time, the prognosis is not good. Dr. Jewell and specialists in Hanover, New York, and Boston all advise Adam that it would be dangerous for Charlotte to undergo another pregnancy. They no longer consider it likely that, under the best of circumstances, she could now bear a child, and at this date another miscarriage, besides endangering her physical health, might well damage her mental state, which they judge to be precarious, beyond repair.

Thenceforth Adam and Charlotte sleep in separate rooms, a decision by Adam which Charlotte never questions. Her acquiescence leads him to conclude that she is grateful for the arrangement.

In fact, she does think it natural—the children make such a lot of noise tramping in every morning to greet her, and no amount of scolding seems to prevent them. "Four boys making a racket! Who can sleep through that? Your father needs his rest," she explains, when they ask her why he no longer shares her bed.

Whether because his marital relations have been suspended, or for soi-disant patriotic reasons, in 1917 Adam enlists in the navy. He's only twenty-five years old, but perhaps because he's been at sea before (or perhaps because he's rich), by the time he's sent abroad he already bears the rank of commander. During his year or so overseas, every month he writes to Louisa and Charlotte (letters Charlotte showed to Zoë)—he is stationed at Brest; he has a cold; he's been invited to dine at a château . . . Charlotte said she'd read the letters to the boys: Henry, who was ten during the war, and eight-year old Thaddeus—Thaddy—were old enough to interest themselves in details of the fighting. The younger two—Llewellyn and Samuel—didn't really understand where Adam had gone; all they wanted to know was when their father would be coming home.

Louisa, during this interval, recovers full control of the household. Her daughter-in-law, though perfectly restored to health, it suits her to treat as an invalid. Having by now stunted whatever affection she might have been developing for Charlotte during her own illness, she confides to her acquaintances her great sadness that Adam should be burdened with an infirm wife. Of course her son is too honorable to divorce her, although Louisa doubts Charlotte would protest. Thus, unless Charlotte should die young, permitting Adam to remarry, the Robies, it must be accepted, will die without issue. Almost she would prefer for Adam, she hints . . . and then later, to acknowledge . . . But how can one suggest such a thing to one's own son?

However, when Adam returns to Harmony late in 1918, bearded, fierce-looking, bearing the rank of captain, Louisa realizes that the idea of suggesting anything whatsoever to him is absurd. Though he is polite to and considerate of both herself and Charlotte, except for the hour each evening when they dine they do not see him. During the day he shuts himself in the library, finally interesting himself in the business of his shipping concerns; he travels to New York and Boston. He doesn't tell his mother and Charlotte his fears that if he does not make some clever and timely decisions, they will not survive the lean economic years that he, along with only a few others, suspects are soon to come (as if he has learned from Charlotte the art of divining the worst). He convinces the company directors to diversify their operations; at his urging the Robie Shipping Company becomes Robie Shipping and Transportation, since it has bought out a railroad company; then Robie Enterprises, when he purchases one of the largest lumber operations in the West. These are only the first of many strategic decisions. As the twenties wear on, and businesses around them begin to falter, the men who first warned Adam that his wild schemes would bring ruin to the shipping company begin instead to assert that he is an entrepreneur of genius.

Meanwhile Charlotte has taken up sewing, designing beautiful boys' clothes; Louisa arranges for them to be sold at a shop in Hanover. She herself has embarked upon gardening, and her iris and roses are the admiration of Harmony. Too bad the Robie women have nothing more useful to do with themselves, the town remarks, as the decade with its difficulties wears on.

For over six years then, they live like this, during which time Charlotte has much to occupy her. The children grow like asparagus—it is difficult to keep track of their ages. Llewellyn and Samuel are eleven and seven now; they were born only a few months apart, but Llewellyn grew much faster—and the sewing! What it is to keep four boys supplied with clothes! It seems that no sooner does she complete a garment than it disappears. When she questions her sons, they look ashamed, but never offer any explanation. Of course she can never bear to be stern with them for long—what mother could? That is a father's job, after all, and even if their father chooses to ignore them . . . "We knock at the library door," they complain. "We knock softly and we knock loudly, but he never lets us in."

It is not for the money, of course, that Louisa sells the beautifully fashioned suits and shirts that Charlotte makes and leaves folded in the sitting room as if expecting them to be taken; it's to reassure herself that Charlotte has gone politely mad. Else why does she never ask what's become of her sewing? Louisa tells herself that she's doing a kindness to Charlotte; if Adam were to suspect how deranged his wife has become, it would not go well with her. Besides, Ida would want Louisa to treat her daughter gently. And, although Louisa is not sure that Ida ever did anything to deserve her kindness, Louisa is incapable of feeling other than devoted to her.

"Why?" she asked her, standing sentry with her back against the closed nursery door. "Why did he love you and not me?"

"I don't know, Louisa," Ida said.

"Why did you force him to go? If he'd stayed, at least I would have been able to see him. Maybe he would have come to love me. Why did you have to send him away?"

"You know as well as I that such an arrangement would not have been happy, Louisa."

"But why then?" Louisa asked repeatedly. "Why you and not me? Am I so ugly? Am I so undesirable? Why did he shudder at the thought of my embrace?"

"You're not ugly, Louisa," Ida said gently. The baby obliviously sucked. Louisa could hear it. "You know that has nothing to do with it. Henry should not have married you."

"No, of course not. He should have married you, but you wouldn't have him. If it hadn't been for your pride, he would never have considered marrying me! And then to lie to me as he did . . ."

So incessantly did Louisa ask herself how Henry could have loved Ida and not her, so brutally did she repeat this question, that she eventually felt she understood; she became Henry, in order to understand; she imagined what it was like to be Ida's lover, to cover her lovely face with kisses, to adore her—one had no choice but to adore her, Louisa felt that herself. At such times she did not feel that it mattered, whether Henry loved her or Ida, whether she or Henry loved Ida. She gazed dreamily at Ida, who gazed dreamily at the small face pressed against her breast.

"Describe it to me," Louisa said softly.

"Describe what to you?" Ida asked.

"Henry . . . when he embraced you . . . Tell me."

"Louisa," Ida said, "why do you torment yourself?"

The baby was asleep and Ida stood to lay it in its cradle. She bent to kiss her own child, sleeping nearby, then sat back down in the rocking chair, closing her blouse but not buttoning it. "He was a man, that's all." She looked at Louisa oddly. "Surely you know yourself, in any case."

"I *don't* know," Louisa said. "I never knew. Now you know the truth."

"But, Louisa . . ." Ida laughed. "You have a son. What can you mean?"

"I know I have a son. I still tell you that Henry never came to my bed. Not once. Oh, at first, after our marriage, I thought it was merely shyness that constrained him. Shyness or inexperience. I said to myself that when he grew used to me he would overcome his awkwardness. But then—how blind I was for so long!—I learned he loved *you*! But because you would not marry him, he married me to spite you. To spite *you*. I was merely the instrument of his revenge."

"I don't know," Ida mused. "Perhaps you are right. I know that Henry can be spiteful."

"To spite *him* I took a lover of my own. What a lover! Timothy Lowndes—to think I imagined that Henry would be jealous! Do you know what he wrote to me after Adam was born? 'I am delighted to congratulate you on the birth of your son. Now we are both safe in our indiscretions.' " Louisa sobbed with anger and hatred.

"Louisa, Louisa!" Ida cried softly. "Don't distress yourself so! Come to me!"

In a daze Louisa knelt beside Ida's chair. Ida embraced her and settled Louisa's head against her knee. "There," she murmured, "there." It was what she said to their children as they nursed.

Gradually Louisa's sobs lapsed and she took Ida's hand and pressed it to her lips. Ida stroked her cheek. "There," she said, "rest, dearest." Louisa looked up at her, but Ida's eyes were closed. Louisa felt as if they were both asleep, or in that half-sleep where nothing is proscribed. Later it seemed to her that she must have thought that. Maybe at first Ida *had* been asleep.

Louisa waited a long time, hours it felt like to her, studying Ida's face, her half-open mouth, her closed eyes, until she could no longer remember not having been looking at Ida's face or feeling any sensation other than longing to dissolve the last boundary between them. Carefully then, surreptitiously, she drew back Ida's blouse and bared her breast; a drop of milk stood on the extended nipple. Louisa touched her finger to the drop and then brought her finger to her tongue. She tasted nothing, but the gesture inflamed her, and within herself she cried, I love you! I must love someone! She froze when Ida lifted her hand, but all Ida did was to bring it down again and smooth Louisa's hair. Louisa didn't dare look up now, yet slowly she lifted her head and inched nearer. Finally, delicately, soundlessly, she closed her lips around the nipple.

"There," Ida moaned softly. She reached to cup her breast and lift it: Louisa sucked harder and felt the thin milk come.

"There," Ida said again. "You're very hungry."

Louisa swallowed, and Ida continued to murmur and sigh. She *was* Ida, Louisa thought; she was Louisa and yet she was Ida; and she was Henry—she forgave Henry—and she was Adam; she was Ida's child as well. She knew that Ida knew this; it was the thing Ida had always known. It was why Henry loved her. It was why anyone could not help but love her.

"Good girl," Ida soothed her, her fingers tight against the back of Louisa's neck. "You were very hungry. This was all you needed."

In 1925, the year before Monica's birth, Charlotte was thirty-three years old. How *had* her mother come to be born, Zoë wondered, when there hadn't been any pregnancies for years? Unlike the majority of women in Harmony, who by that age were thick-waisted and slowing down, Charlotte had stayed wiry and spry—maybe because she rode horseback regularly; except in the winter, when the snow was too deep, she'd said, her favorite afternoon activity was to ride to the Dawes place. After the house burned down only a small barn was left, but Charlotte kept a quilt in it so that she could spread it across the tall grass and take a nap.

Maybe one day, having slept longer than usual, she wakes to the sound of a voice. In fact it's Adam, talking to her horse, which she allows to graze unrestrained while she sleeps. Maybe he's received some bad news from his shipping offices in the afternoon mail and has decided to take a ride to think out his strategy. Coming unexpectedly on Charlotte's horse, he's afraid that something has happened to her. When she stands up sleepily, he jumps.

"Ah, you're here!" he exclaims. "I had feared . . ."

"I was asleep," she says.

"I saw only the horse."

"Yes, he eats while I rest."

Who knows what they really would have said to each other—probably stood there in awkward silence. After all, they'd scarcely been alone together for half a decade.

"Well, how are you?" Adam inquires stiffly.

"Oh, in tolerable health. And yourself?"

"Quite well, I'm grateful to say."

Then another silence, after which Adam asks, "Do you know who I am?"

"Of course," Charlotte says, amused. "You're Adam Robie."

"I don't mean my name. I mean who I am in relation to yourself."

"You are my husband." Charlotte laughs her sweet laugh. "I am your wife."

"I . . . Oh, Charlotte!" Adam is overwhelmed—the last few years Charlotte has seemed so distracted—but now she is once again the calm, self-possessed young woman whom he visited in this same place so many years ago. All he can think of is how long it's been since he's spoken tenderly to her. He takes her in his arms and holds her tightly. "My God, how I've missed you! How I love you!"

"I love you too, dear," she says.

"Do you? Oh, do you? But how much? How dearly?"

In 1925, he wouldn't have exactly come out and asked her to go to bed with him. And she'd have had to reply something vague—vague yet clear to him, since in those days language could be used like that.

"All that you want," she says—something like that. "However much you like."

"My beloved Charlotte," he murmurs.

She smiles.

"May we meet here on occasion? I would like to enjoy your company away from my mother's scrutinizing eye—I had not realized how it oppressed me."

"Certainly," she says. "Whenever you wish."

Charlotte said she was glad that her sons did not feel about her as Adam did his mother, though she never said so for fear of offending him.

XV SPARTA

The fall after Mexico, Robert was back in school. However, when everyone asked where he'd been for a year and a half, all he'd say was that he'd been called away to be an attaché to the Court of St. James (which no one would have believed was an actual court if Gustina Rudd's father hadn't been in the Foreign Service and told her about it.) Even Mrs. Wycliffe had no information—or wasn't letting on if she had. Robert kept saying they were all going to find out someday how right he was about everything and went around singing things like "Cockles, and mussels, alive, alive-oh," as if it meant something deep. When Zoë and Bridget ignored him he said, "Why, if it isn't Mr. and Mrs. Snoot! How are you today, Snoots?" After a while he just pretended to take off a hat and swept a Three Musketeers' bow whenever he saw them. Then he made friends with some other weird boys and stopped bothering them. By the time Zoë noticed him again, he hardly even limped.

She was in tenth grade now, Bridget in eleventh. Nick was a senior. Zoë had joined the drama club, even though Bridget had said she wouldn't stoop so low. The latest profession she aspired to was acting—she'd given up concert pianist (too much travelling), senator (too much shaking hands with strange people), and astrophysicist (too many equations). However, you'd need the memory of an elephant to keep track of all the careers Bridget had decided were for her. Who knew how long being an actress would last? Zoë still wouldn't have minded being an archaeologist, but nowadays you had to *train* to be one and then spend your life excavating potsherds with a fingernail file, which she couldn't exactly see herself doing. Nothing else excited her yet, though. She had to admit that although Bridget might be fickle, at least she did things, which was one reason Zoë had decided to try out for the school play. Except for playing the fake duke in *Huckleberry Finn* in fourth grade she'd only worked on scenery. Of course, since Bridget had already had two small parts in a local *repertory* company's productions, she wouldn't touch a school play with a ten-foot pole.

The play they were putting on in the spring was by a girl in eleventh grade named Laura Jenkins; it was called *The End of Slavery*. Mr. Montgomery, the drama and English teacher, insisted they all read it before they try out. Its cast of characters included a blind girl, a convict, a nun, a lion tamer, an organ grinder (with speaking parts for the monkey and the lion), and a demented individual who believed he was King Arthur reincarnated. The opening line, delivered from a pitch black stage, was, "I would rather die than serve you." When the lights went up, the audience saw the lion tamer and the lion on stage; they weren't supposed to be sure which one had spoken. Mr. Montgomery called this "purposeful ambiguity," but that was only because he was madly in love with Laura Jenkins, who had breasts the size of balloons.

The plot was crammed with totally unbelievable coincidences, but Laura refused to change a word, claiming that when you were fighting against injustice you couldn't worry about petty problems like that. She had the brain of a lizard, but because he was so busy ogling her proportions, Mr. Montgomery was unaware of this. Usually his main criticism of students' plays was that they were "implausible," but he insisted that Laura's play was a "melodramatic spoof," and therefore didn't have to "bother about verisimilitude." Laura, the poor moron, was wounded that he called it a spoof, but he also—*no* one could believe this—said she had a "flair for the medium" and was a "master of dramatic pacing." She just smirked and said, "Why, thank you, Mr. Montgomery." He was even allowing her to help direct it.

The truth was, however, that although everyone scoffed at *The End of Slavery*, everyone still wanted to be in it. The characters would be a gas to play, even if the plot was ridiculous. The whole point of it was that all the characters who were captives—the blind girl of the convict; the lion and the monkey of their trainers; King Arthur of his mental-hospital keeper, the nun (since he wasn't violent mere nuns could take care of him, Laura had thought it necessary to explain to them)—all found an opportunity to escape at some point yet chose not to. The blind girl was whacked on the head by a falling vase, which miraculously restored her sight; the monkey learned to unlock his chain when the organ grinder was asleep and then he freed his friend the lion; King Arthur realized he in fact *was* King Arthur time-travelled to another century, but that if he pretended he didn't think so anymore, he would be allowed to go free and could then look in earnest for a way to return to Guinevere and Merlin and the Knights of the Round Table.

In the beginning of the second act, when the convict, the lion tamer, the organ grinder, and the nun insane-asylum keeper were all sleeping—actually, *put* to sleep by sleeping pills the monkey had stolen from a pharmacy (talk about unbelievable)—all the prisoner characters held a meeting to discuss how they would turn the tables on their captors. The lion would crack his whip and force his tamer to do pirouettes on a stool; the monkey would make the organ grinder dance; King Arthur would put the nun behind bars and tell her she was just fantasizing being a nun; and the blind girl would make the convict wear a blindfold and see how he liked it. They kept having these meetings and yet every time they made a date to carry out their coup, something happened to prevent them. At least, that was what they claimed at their next meeting.

For a while it wasn't clear what was going on, but eventually it became obvious that they were attached to their captors. The blind girl had fallen in love with the convict; the lion liked his tamer; the monkey couldn't live without the organ grinder; and King Arthur realized that it would ruin the nun's day if she didn't get to say to him, "And how's the king this morning? Did Your Majesty sleep well?" She had a pretty dull life.

In the end they all, one by one, accidentally revealed to their captors that they had been free for ages and had just been humoring them. Their captors, moved to sobs by this revelation, saw the error of their ways and repented. In the final scene all the characters stood facing the audience in a big semicircle, holding hands and singing "We *Have* Overcome," with all the lyrics slightly rewritten. It went, "We have overcome / we have overcome / we have overcome our sla-a-a-very / O-oh deep in our hearts / we do believe / you too can overcome this way."

Mr. Montgomery said that the implications, though far-reaching, were obvious, so they never actually discussed the meaning of the play in class. Everyone except Mr. Montgomery and Laura, of course, realized that there was a huge flaw in the theme—who would ever sacrifice themselves like that in real life?—but Mr. Montgomery just said things like "Dramatic license" when this was pointed out to him.

Despite all this, Zoë still had an urge to play the blind girl. She'd practiced being blind many times, walking around the house with her eyes shut, opening them only when she thought she might be about to trip over something. It had always seemed to her that blind people would make purer judgments. If you fell in love with someone when you were blind, for instance, it would be because of the kind of person he was, instead of being attracted to someone because he was good-looking or was good at sports, or even because someone walked a certain way or danced a certain way. She'd always felt that *Jane Eyre* would have been better if Mr. Rochester hadn't gotten his sight back in the end.

However, she didn't know if she had a chance. For one thing, the blind girl was one of the two biggest parts in the whole play (the other was the convict), and Mr. Montgomery would probably give it to someone with more experience. For another, he had an extremely bizarre way of having people try out. You had to stand up in front of the whole drama class and ad lib for five minutes. He timed you. Hardly anyone made it past three. This was the main reason Zoë had avoided trying out for plays since fourth grade when there'd been a different drama teacher. It didn't help to prepare beforehand, because Mr. Montgomery could tell if you had and would bellow, "No! Not canned! I said something off the top of your head! Off the top!"

Everyone in the school agreed he was totally whacked out. He cut his hair in a flat-top despite the fact that flat-tops had gone out of style several centuries ago, and he dressed in black pants and tight army-green T-shirts, which always had enormous sweat spots under the arms. He smoked like a chimney all through class, even though the headmaster had told him not to. "It is not my intention to curtail your personal liberties, Jack!" they had all heard Mr. Curley shouting at him in the hall after catching him in the act. "It's a question of fire insurance!" He just came back in and lit right up again. No one knew why he didn't get fired; possibly because all the plays he put on brought Hollister Day good publicity.

Zoë was shaking so hard when it was her turn that she could hardly stand up. In spite of the no-preparation rule she had planned something to talk about—San Ysidro; it seemed like the only thing she'd ever done unique enough to be interesting—but when she turned around to face the class it seemed like such a stupid idea her mind went completely blank. However, suddenly she was talking anyway—it must have been an automatic reaction to the last time she was in front of an audience, because she was speaking a line from her role as the duke in *Huckleberry Finn*, "I wash my hands of this," in a perfect English accent, and then the next thing she knew she was being Mr. Wycliffe talking to Seth about the universe, and Seth answering. They were having their eternal argument about whether the world was "reducible to stable variables" and what this had to do with the "problem of good and evil" and how, in the "wake of the breakdown of the self" they all felt the "irrelevancy of moral choice." She was amazed that she remembered this much, just from half-listening at dinner. She threw in a truckload of adverbs—"consequently," "categorically," "absolutely," and "indubitably," the way they always did—and had them insult each other's favorite philosophers. "My friend, Descartes is a pantywaist!" "How can one possibly have any respect for the thinking of a man who sounds like a sort of pasta?" (talking about Spinoza). Et cetera.

She had no idea how she was doing; she heard the class laughing but that didn't necessarily mean anything—they could just as well be laughing because she was making an incredible fool of herself. Suddenly Mr. Montgomery honked "Time!" and she stopped, thinking he must have stopped her because she was so terrible. But then, as she walked back to her place, he looked her straight in the eye and said, all pent up, "Thank you very much, Miss Carver" (he called everybody, even in the lower school, Miss and Mister), and she was so embarrassed she practically tripped trying to sit back down in her desk. Someone near her whispered, "You were great!" and she said, "Thank you," but she couldn't look up yet. Mr. Montgomery *never* complimented people on their performances.

There were a few other people, who didn't do very well—they kept laughing and having to start over—and then Robert Went went up. He just stood there, and everyone started being nervous that he was frozen from stage fright, but then suddenly he pointed his finger at them like Uncle Sam and shouted, "Food! You're food! You are what you eat! Think about it! How many of us have ever really taken that old expression seriously? Do I *look* like a peanut butter and jelly sandwich? Do I *look* like a piece of fried chicken? Do I *look* like fried eggs and ham and toast and orange juice? Of *course* I don't." People were rolling their eyes at each other, but Robert seemed totally oblivious of how idiotic he sounded. Zoë had to admit he did, but she was also amazed at how handsome he'd gotten. She hadn't looked at him this long since she and he and Bridget had all been friends.

"Does Elwyn look like a cream cheese and olive sandwich on whole wheat just because he's eaten one for lunch every day since he was born? Evidently not. But the point I'm trying to make is that the name of food is taken in vain. That saying I mentioned earlier isn't an isolated incident. Let them eat cake, Have your cake and eat it too, An apple a day keeps the doctor away, Two peas in a pod, A bird in the hand is worth two in the bush, A stitch in time saves nine . . ."

"Those aren't *food*," someone said, but Mr. Montgomery turned around; if looks could kill . . .

"Actually, if you want to get down to it—get down to what? The world is full of stupid expressions. Early to bed, early to rise, Rats desert a sinking ship, No man is an island, No man is a rat, A cat may look at a rat . . . However, I *am* straying from the subject, aren't I, ladies and gentlemen? Our subject today is whether or not we are what we eat. Well, yes! Yes, I say! You're surprised? You accuse me of contradicting myself? Do not be perturbed . . ." (he pronounced it "pertur-bed"), "I'll soon explain it all to you. You see, it's like this." He stopped talking. He said to Mr. Montgomery, "Dramatic pause."

"Thank you for making that clear, Mr. Went," Mr. Montgomery said.

"My pleasure." Then Robert said, "You see, everything in the world is in disguise. I don't know how many of you may have noticed that. But think of it. Really, if you ask your mother what's for dinner she ought to say, 'Ground beef patties in white-flour air buns' instead of 'Hamburgers.' "

People were starting to snicker. Partly because now that they realized he was saying things on purpose, it was funny, but partly because it was Robert, Robert Went—Mr. Scholar, Bridget called him—reporting how he'd refuse to open his mouth in class unless he had something totally brilliant to say; he'd even say to teachers who asked him a question, "I'm afraid I have nothing of note to offer." Bridget had said that if he got answers wrong on a test he looked like he was going to commit suicide. But now here he was going on like a maniac.

He said, "You think that's amusing, do you? The truth is, even *that* wouldn't be honest. To be really honest you'd have to say ground-up cow flesh and wheat and yeast and so on. *In fact* . . ."

He paused again. Actually he was sort of plagiarizing her talk, and she glanced at Mr. Montgomery to see if he noticed, but he was just sitting there like a statue.

"Protein cells and fat tissue and hemoglobin!" Robert shouted at the top of his lungs. "Amino acids, atoms, protons, and neutrons! Subatomic particles!

"Do you see?" he asked in a normal voice. "Basically, there *is* no difference between Elwyn and a cream cheese sandwich. The difference, such as it is, is purely superficial. Just remember, at night when you say your prayers, that it's entirely an accident that you're you instead of a . . . a . . . radish!"

Then he said, "Applause. Thank you, thank you," and sat down. Now everyone checked out Mr. Montgomery, but he was featuring his usual non-expression.

"Thank you, Mr. Went," he said. "I believe I've heard from all of you now. Class dismissed, as they say. You'll find the parts posted on the bulletin board in the hall in the morning."

"That really bugs me," Archie Tannenbaum said, as they were filing out. "What does he do, say eeny-meeny-miny-mo? If he hasn't decided already, what's going to happen between now and tomorrow?"

The next day (Zoë and Nick and Bridget rode to school with Sam and Archie Tannenbaum now—they had their parents' old blue Buick), they all hurried inside to look at the bulletin board. The others were in front of Zoë and she couldn't see the board. Suddenly Bridget screamed, "I don't *believe* it!"

"What?" Zoë exclaimed.

"Look at this! Look!" Bridget grabbed her and pointed. There, at the top of the list, was "Zoë Carver" beside "Blind Girl." Underneath it, beside "Convict," was "Rob Went."

"Rob!" Bridget exclaimed. "Who the hell calls him *Rob*?"

"Mr. Montgomery, obviously," Archie said. "Wouldn't you know *I've* got the most idiotic part in the whole play."

"Archibald" Tannenbaum was down at the bottom opposite "Monkey."

"Typecasting," Nick said.

"Shut up, Carver."

"He sure as hell doesn't know what anyone's name is," Bridget said.

"Well, all I can say," Archie said, "is I may have a meaningless part but at least I don't have to kiss Robert Went. Excuse me, *Rob*."

Bridget goggled her eyes. "You have to *kiss* Robert?"

"It's just a play, Bridget," Zoë said, but she could feel herself starting to turn red.

" 'It's just a *play*,' " Archie mimicked. "She doesn't just have to kiss Robert, she has to kiss him *long and hard*. It says so in the script. It says *overwhelmed with passion*."

"Is that true?" Bridget asked. "No, don't answer me. I might lose my breakfast. Come on, Zoë. This calls for an emergency meeting. Please excuse us, gentlemen. This is a crisis."

Zoë went with her, although she was frankly getting a little sick of Bridget ordering her around.

"You're going to quit, I presume," Bridget said when they were out of earshot, but talking as if she still had an audience. "You can't possibly be considering kissing Robert Went. I don't care if it's on Broadway! Robert Went is Robert Went. I don't think I could *look* at you anymore if you kissed him."

"Then don't. I don't care. I think you're being ridiculous. It's just a play. I'm not saying the idea of kissing Robert is particularly thrilling, but the blind girl's a great part. I'm not giving it up just because Robert is playing the convict."

"I can't believe you," Bridget said.

"Besides, how do you know Robert isn't different now? You haven't said two words to him for five years."

"I'm in his *class*, dearest, in case you forgot. I have the great pleasure of seeing him every day of my life. I don't *need* to say two words to him. I know his utterly repulsive personality by heart."

"What's so repulsive about it?" Zoë asked. "Anyway, what do you care? It's not as if *you* have to kiss him." The bell rang then, but at recess Bridget was still harping on it.

"You know, I've been thinking. You know how Mr. Montgomery has a reputation for assigning students parts playing opposite someone they hate in real life? No one's ever known for sure if he knew what the hell he was doing—he's so out of it he might just not know who's friends with whom—but *I've* always been sure it was just because he has a warped sense of humor. If I had any doubt before, this convinces me. Do you remember those letters we wrote to the teachers once?"

Bridget mentioned them as casually as if they discussed the subject all the time.

"What about them?"

"We wrote some to Mr. Montgomery, remember? It was back when he was only teaching English."

"I know when it was."

"Well, the teachers found out who wrote them, remember? You do remember that?"

"I'd appreciate it if you'd stop talking to me as if I were an idiot."

"Don't act like one, then. Don't you see that Mr. Montgomery thinks it's *funny* to make you play opposite Robert Went? He'll be laughing up his sleeve at you the whole time!"

"That's crazy. Besides, even if he remembered that stuff, I don't think Mr. Montgomery would do such a thing. He cares too much how the play turns out."

"I think it's *exactly* what he would do. You can't deny he's enough of a pervert. He lives alone with *guppies*, for God's sake! What *else* does he have to do at home except contemplate revenge?"

"Contemplate Laura Jenkins," Zoë said, laughing. Bridget was furious that she wasn't taking her seriously. "You're the one who said he's wilting away for her in English class. Frankly, I think you're mad because I got such a big part. If you really want to know the truth, Mr. Montgomery picked me because I did well in the audition. Actually . . ." She laughed. "I pretended I was your father, talking to my father."

"You *what*? What the hell did you say?"

"You heard me."

"Well, you're completely wrong about me being mad that you got a big part. *Frankly*, I'm delighted that you've finally developed an interest in life. But *frankly*, since you mention it, I object to having my father impersonated so that *you* can end up starring in a play with that sick slime Robert Went. Not that you *could* really impersonate my father, of course."

"Oh, why don't you just relax."

Bridget couldn't believe her ears. "Well, I have only one thing further to say to you, Zoë Minerva Carver," she said, sounding as if she were in third grade. "I was hoping you'd see the light, but . . . If you take the part, I want you to know I'll consider it a great disloyalty to our friendship. I thought we'd agreed always to uphold each other's likes and dislikes, but now I see that *I* was the only one who took the vow seriously."

With that she marched off. But there was no point in trying to talk sense to Bridget when she was like this. She completely refused to listen to reason. And her father could still do no wrong. Sometimes Zoë wondered if she would have even *liked* Bridget if they hadn't already been best friends.

After about a week of being standoffish, Bridget brought it up again. She was willing to let bygones be bygones on one condition: if Zoë promised never to mention the play or Robert Went.

"Fine," Zoë said, shrugging. Some people don't *need* to advertise every single thing they're doing in life to the whole world, she felt like saying, but she didn't. It would only piss Bridget off again. Actually they weren't spending that much time together, anyway. Bridget had gotten involved in a play at the college—she was a stagehand and an understudy—and Zoë was busy with her own rehearsals. She and Robert (whom everybody in the class had started calling Rob, first to mimic Mr. Montgomery and then because he said he preferred it) didn't talk to each other except when they were speaking their lines, and everything went fine until they had to start rehearsing the love scene. It wouldn't have been any big deal if Bridget hadn't made her self-conscious, she wasn't *that* unsophisticated, but now she kept thinking how Rob was really Robert Went, one-legged Robert *Went*, and she couldn't get over feeling squeamish. Laura Jenkins was complaining and Mr. Montgomery was making sarcastic remarks about "virgin actors" having to lose their "dramatic cherry"—it was disgusting.

Long before Mr. Montgomery said it was appropriate, Zoë started having stage-nightmares and who knew what would have happened if Robert—Rob—hadn't decided they should take matters into their own hands.

About a month of rehearsing had already gone by. One day in the garden where the upper grades ate lunch, Robert came over to her—he must have been waiting for a time when she wasn't sitting with Bridget, who was sick that day, which he would have known—and said, "Hello, I'd like to introduce myself. I'm Rob Went. I'm the person playing opposite you in *The End of Slavery*—I trust you're cognizant of that fact?"

"So, what is it?"

"May I take the great liberty of sitting down, or is this bench reserved?"

"Feel free."

"Feel free . . . You're ordering me to feel free? That's a tall order, though maybe you meant it to be a short order . . ."

"Just sit *down*."

"Why, thank you, don't mind if I do."

He sat and she turned sideways to face him.

"I'd like to make a suggestion," he said. "I realize that for some reason altogether obscure to me you find it reprehensible to extend to me the courtesy of addressing me as a fellow human being, but I wonder if you might not consider lifting my sentence—I'd enjoy observing someone lifting a sentence, wouldn't you?—bestowing a reprieve upon me, shall we say, in the interests of High Art? Obviously you agree with me that *The End of Slavery* is a masterpiece."

"Oh, obviously," she said. She couldn't help laughing.

"Glad you share my opinion."

She had already noticed the way he smiled. Sort of mischievous, as if he was telling you not to take anything he said too seriously. It was actually sort of sexy. Too bad he was Robert.

"Here's what I was thinking, okay?" He seemed to expect her to answer.

"What?"

"Do you want to hear my brilliant idea or not?"

"More than anything in the world."

"I can tell. Well, here it is, anyway. I was thinking we could rehearse privately. Maybe after school or something."

"Where?" she asked.

She must have looked really grossed out because he said, "Don't worry, I'm not trying to find some devious way to get you alone. I just thought maybe it would make it easier if we talked to each other outside of our parts. I don't like having to do that love scene any more than you do, you know."

She didn't say anything. She felt insulted, even though a minute before she'd been suspicious.

"Did you think I *did*?"

"Who knows," she said.

"You must really think I'm a pervert if you'd think that. Even if I didn't disapprove of love scenes in general I'd have to be off my rocker to want to kiss some girl who won't even speak to me, in real life or out of it. I mean, what do you think I am?"

"Nothing. You never enter my mind."

She couldn't believe the way they were talking, squabbling like ten-year-olds. She never talked to boys like that.

They sat silently for a minute. Everyone in the garden was looking at them.

"Well?" he said. "What's your answer? I haven't got all day. What a stupid expression, 'got all day.' Sometimes I can't get up in the morning for thinking about all the stupid things people say. Does that ever happen to you?"

"Not exactly. But I know what you mean."

"Well, what's your answer?"

"Where would we rehearse?"

"I assume at one of our houses—assuming you live in one."

"No, I live in a cave."

She was thinking of the time in ninth grade when she'd had a party and Seth had made bizarre remarks to everyone. "You must be the plumber's son," he'd say, for example, which he thought was hysterically funny because no one in their school would have a plumber for a father. Never again.

"If your house is a problem, we can meet at mine. My parents don't come home until six-thirty. As you probably recall, I have no siblings."

" 'Siblings . . .' Mine don't usually get home before five-thirty. However . . ."

"Don't worry, you don't need to explain insane paterfamiliases to *me*."

" 'Paterfamiliases' . . . That's only fathers."

"Well, pater and materfamiliases, then."

"Besides, my brother is usually lurking around."

Zoë wished Bridget weren't home sick. She had this evil desire for her to walk by right then.

They agreed that she'd come over the first afternoon there wasn't a rehearsal, the day after tomorrow. Zoë had been looking forward to it, but as she rang the Wents' doorbell she suddenly felt like running away. However, Robert acted as if it were normal she was there.

"Would you care for a beverage?" he asked, after taking her jacket and hanging it up in the closet.

"A *beverage*?"

"A beverage, a libation, a thirst-quencher, a drink . . ."

"I *know* what it *means*."

"What seems to be the problem, then? Are you bowled over by my generosity?"

"Not exactly."

He was walking down the hall into the kitchen. "Do you want a Coke or not?"

"Couldn't you have just said Coke in the first place?"

"No doubt I *could* have. However, I didn't, and now the opportunity is gone forever. Another of life's many tragedies. What's your decision? I can take it."

"Okay. Sure."

He poured two Cokes into tall glasses with ice.

"Care for a straw?"

"A *straw*?"

He turned around. "Is it against the law? Or are you just hard of hearing?"

"No, it's just that . . ."

"Just what?" He sounded as if he were really angry.

"I'm sorry. It's just that no one I know has straws in their house. I mean, since they were little."

"Where should they have them? In their trees?" Suddenly he started laughing to himself, sounding like the old Robert Went. Forget the idea that he had changed. She must have been crazy to agree to come over to his house by herself. Bridget was right.

Then he suggested they "retire" to the living room. His parents had a sort of big wooden bench with pillows on it for a couch. Besides it, the only places to sit were four plain wooden rocking chairs. The only picture was a big one over the mantel of some men in a rowboat on a stormy ocean. Robert noticed her looking around.

"I'm not responsible for the decor of this room, by the way. My mother has this thing about Shakers. They thought everything should be plain. My father, who is an idiot—although you'd have to know him—says, 'Well, we live in Sparta. I suppose we should live like Spartans!' That's his idea of a sense of humor."

Zoë made a sympathetic face.

"I recommend sitting on the couch. It's actually more comfortable than it looks if you rearrange the pillows. We could go up to my room, but I haven't cleaned it since the Dark Ages."

She sat on the couch and he sat down on the other end and started right in about his parents again, how they were always in foul moods when they came home from work so he tried to have everything ready. He made dinner and the second they came through the door he poured them drinks.

"I didn't know you knew how to cook," she said.

"Why should you? You don't know anything else about me either."

"I meant that I make dinner sometimes too. Or Nick does. Half the time my parents are on strike."

"What do you mean on strike?"

"Who knows," she said. "Just having their heads in the clouds and forgetting about mundane things like meals. Once my mother told Nick and me that wild animals are on their own after a few weeks, as if we were supposed to go out hunting."

"I really think there's something about having kids that drives people insane," Robert said, disgusted. "I'd stake my life on it. Just think what the world would be like if a cure could be found. That's the one thing I like about the Shakers. They didn't believe in having kids. They only adopted them. However, when I pointed out to my mother that she wished she was a Shaker because that would mean I wasn't really her son, she almost had a litter. How could I *think* such a terrible thing—didn't I know she'd lay down her life for me, blah blah blah. You know how they get."

"Tell me about it."

"When you finally catch on to how crazy your parents are, they send *you* to a psychiatrist."

She didn't want to say she knew he'd been, so she said, "My brother used to have to go to Dr. Macmillan."

"I'm not surprised. He has half the children in Sparta in his clutches. He used to have me, you know."

"Did he make you play Monopoly with him? He made Nick."

"For a while. Then we switched to chess. He wanted me to think he was letting me win but that was a joke. I happen to be close to master level. When he couldn't stand it anymore he talked my parents into sending me to cripple camp."

"What? Are you kidding?"

"It was the summer after my leg was amputated."

She almost said, Well, it wouldn't have been before, but was glad she didn't.

"Mr. and Mrs. Went decided I wasn't 'adjusting' well so all of a sudden they ship me off to this place in Vermont. It was in the mountains—its real name was something like 'Disabled Youth Recuperation Sanitarium,' one of those totally fake names. Ages eight to fifteen, I think. Everybody had had something happen to them. Who but an imbecile psychiatrist would think that the best thing for you when you've just been crippled yourself would be to send you somewhere where you'd be surrounded by lots of other cripples?"

"God, how stupid."

"The other kids were okay, it wasn't that. It was just the idea. They thought if they could teach me to water-ski on one leg all my so-called problems would go away. They could have cared less that I didn't have the slightest *interest* in water skiing."

"I really can't believe this."

"I know. The counselors kept making speeches about how we were just as good as everybody else until you felt like puking. It never occurred to anybody that we weren't until they started mentioning it. We all had nicknames for each other—mine was Pegleg—and the counselors got all hot and bothered about that. They constantly corrected you for saying 'cripple' instead of 'handicapped,' but I hate that word—it's so fake—it sounds like you're likely to beat someone in a race if you don't give them an advantage. They were always down on me about being a 'negative influence.' It was before they had the Special Olympics but some genius there already had the idea and kept trying to make us play cripple sports. Can you imagine anyone besides a moron wanting to play wheelchair basketball? Anyway, I got expelled after three weeks."

"You got *expelled*?"

"That's what my parents said. I'm probably the only person in history to get expelled from cripple camp, at least according to them. The counselors said I was a 'rabble-rouser.' They said I brought down the general morale."

"That's horrible."

"I didn't care at all. I was happy to get out of there. Except for the fact that it meant being here, of course. Since I'm the only kid my parents managed to produce and then one of the only two *legs* they managed to produce goes up in smoke, they couldn't stand it. That's why they sent me to a special school for a year. They can't bear the idea of going through life being the parents of only one leg."

Zoë couldn't help laughing, but Robert laughed too. She rearranged some pillows to get more comfortable.

"Some of the things they did, you wouldn't believe if I told you. When I came home from cripple camp I found out my father had given my old bike away without asking my permission. In the first place, I could still ride it, but in the second place, you'll never guess who he gave it to. A blind eight-year-old!"

"What? That's insane!"

"No kidding. When I asked him what on earth he did that for, he said he thought the kid could ride it in big parking lots on the weekends. I asked him if next he was going to give our old car away to a blind eighteen-year-old so he could practice driving it around parking lots on weekends—you can imagine how well that went over."

"I can't believe this! They sound completely warped."

"They seemed to think that because I lost a leg I couldn't even brush my teeth. If they ever had *been* rational human beings, they had suddenly given it up. Then they started having to talk to people about it all the time. It got so I couldn't go anywhere with them because they'd have to tell everyone I had only one leg."

"Are you *serious*?"

"I know. Once, for instance, we were in this restaurant, you know, Maison Charles? Down by the harbor?"

"You ate there?"

"Years ago. Wait—of course! I know exactly when it was: after they took me out of school, before they sent me to cripple camp. They thought I wanted to. After my accident, so called, I started to like cooking so they thought it would cheer me up to go out to a fancy French restaurant. I didn't require cheering up, but in their opinion I did. I presume they thought that if they cheered me up enough, my leg would grow back."

"They sound even more nuts than my parents."

"They make any other parents in the universe look as sane as cucumbers, believe me," he said. "Anyway, we go to Maison Charles. It's decked out like the *Titanic* inside. It's got candles all over the walls and there's about three tablecloths on every table, don't ask me why, and everything, absolutely everything, is in some special shape, even the *ice cubes*, for Christ's sake. The whole menu's in French, of course, and here's where my parents start going off the deep end. They think because I've taken French for two years I'm going to speak French to the waiter."

"Oh, God."

"As it so happens, French is the one subject I'm lousy at. Maybe it's because I've never been able to stand Madame Alignac's attitude, who knows. Eel foe *etrah* fronsay poor vrayma com-pron-dra lay fronsay . . . *Spare* me. Anyway, it was a stupid idea to take me to any restaurant. I liked cooking, but I wasn't very interested in eating at the time. Maybe you remember."

He glanced at her and she said, "You gave us all your candy at the hospital."

"I think all the sedatives they gave me did something to my tastebuds. They were still trying to weaken my willpower so they could convince me I'd had an accident—I mean, instead of doing it on purpose."

Zoë acted unsurprised that Robert had said this.

"Anyway, so I didn't like eating. You would think this would have pleased my parents since it meant I wasn't fat anymore. But not them. 'What's happened to our Robert? You used to love apple pie. You used to love corn on the cob. You used to love stuffing your face like a fat slob . . .' Not eating, though, I'd started thinking about food for what it really was. What meat was, bread, even ice cream. That's what I was talking about the day I had to foam at the mouth to impress Mr. Montgomery. I know it was idiotic, but it was all I could come up with. Actually, some of the stuff you said in your audition made me think of it."

She nodded. She didn't mind once he admitted it.

"I thought you were brilliant, really. Does your father honestly talk like that?"

"Sometimes. When he gets going. He and Bridget's father egg each other on."

"I'd rather have your father than mine. At least he's crazy in an interesting way. I've heard my father talk about him, actually. We saw him and Mr. Wycliffe once on campus—before my dad quit—and he said to my mother, 'Here come the practicing metaphysicians.' He was being sarcastic, but it was probably because he was jealous."

"Why did he quit?"

Robert's father had left the college the year after they were in Mexico.

"He was, quote, sick of everyone acting like it was the Fort Knox of Western Tradition—you know, the way they act like there wouldn't be any problems in the world if only everyone had read Plato."

"Tell me about it."

"He's basically a research scientist, and he wanted to do something more practical. His brilliant solution was to work for the government. Anyway, what I was saying—basically all I wanted to eat were fruits and vegetables because they were the only foods that were themselves. As you can imagine, this was already driving my parents wild because they had come to the conclusion, using their brilliant powers of deduction, that I was trying to starve myself to death. I wasn't, I hope I don't need to say. The point is, they should have known better than to take me to a restaurant. Maybe they thought that if all the food was in French I would be fooled. Boy, were they barking up the wrong bush."

"What did you do?"

"I don't remember every single detail. I just remember eventually getting furious and yelling and my parents being mortified. I think it was because—no, I know, it was because I didn't believe the chef was French. None of the waiters were, which was a relief, but I just couldn't see the point of having everything in French if nobody there was French. It sounds stupid now, I realize, but I was incensed then. I may even have been slightly hysterical, I'll admit. I remember what got me the most. My parents said it was for *atmosphere*. I asked them what would happen if people started putting everything in French just for *atmosphere*. Stop signs, for instance. It could cause all kinds of accidents. What if the president of the United States started making speeches in French, just for *atmosphere*? They maintained I was upset because I didn't know what all the things on the menu meant, and maybe that was true, but it was beside the point. I'm almost done with this story, by the way."

"I don't care. It's fine."

"It was like an existential crisis for me. I felt like there was no way of knowing *anything* for sure. Do you know what I mean? Not only that, but I felt as if my parents were in on it. Whatever I ordered off the menu, unless I already knew what the words meant, like *es-car-go*, how would I know if what I asked for was what I got?"

"You mean, they could substitute something else?"

"You don't exactly take your French-English dictionary to a restaurant with you. Besides, I realized that even dictionaries could be fake. There would be what the words really mean, which you'd know if you lived in France and could see people pointing to things, and then there'd be what the French pretended they meant to foreigners. Do you see what I mean?"

She nodded. It reminded her of Seth and Mr. Wycliffe's arguments over the "fundamental unknowability of the universe."

"Then I had a great revelation and realized it could be the same in English. How do we ever know that the words for things are the real words? We're not *born* speaking English. We don't come out of our mothers and say, 'Hi, Mom. Hi, doctor and nurses.' We have to wait to be told what everything is called. How do we ever know we've been told the truth?"

"Yeah, I know. It's just that most of the time you forget about it."

"To conclude the Restaurant Tragedy . . . What happened was, I marched into the kitchen. I decided I had to see for myself if the chef was really French."

"Was he?"

"I think so. Either that or he did a great French accent. I didn't get much chance to talk to him, though. A couple of waiters strong-armed me."

"They *did*?"

"We had to leave. That was fine by me. The part that drove me insane, though, that made me finally realize what lost causes my parents were, was that as we were going out I overheard my father saying in a stage whisper to the maître d' that I had an artificial leg."

"What? What an idiot!"

"That's the understatement of the year. Actually, I tend to forget sometimes, I'm so used to him." He looked at her. "Can I ask you something?"

"What?" Suddenly she was nervous—she felt like it might be anything. Had she ever had sex, why had she and Bridget written those letters, did she want to see his leg? She glanced down and noticed that his hand was really close to hers on the couch.

"Have you ever found out something about your parents you wished you hadn't?"

"I don't know. Like what?"

"Well, anything, I guess. But, specifically, something really horrible you'd rather not know but can't tell them you know but nevertheless can't stop thinking about?"

"I don't know, exactly." She thought about Charlotte having hallucinations, and all the things Seth and Monica wrote to each other, but maybe that wasn't the kind of thing he meant.

"It doesn't matter, I guess. I still need someone else's opinion about this. There's not really anyone I can tell about it. I don't know you that well, obviously, but it seems like you've had a lot of practice with insane parents."

"What did you find out?"

"It wasn't that long ago. First I have to explain that there's this heating vent between my room and the kitchen. If it's open, I can hear whatever's going on down there. Usually my parents remember this. When they're approaching classified information, they go into the living room. 'This is sensitive territory, Sal,' " Robert mimicked. " 'Let's take our discussion elsewhere.' Then I have to get out of bed and try to hear over the banisters."

"You do that?"

"Of course. Don't you? How else can children find out what they need to know?"

He seemed to think it was the most normal thing in the world. Her heart began pounding as if she were about to jump off a cliff.

"My parents write notes," she said. They'd started writing again after Mexico. "They don't talk to each other about big things."

"Notes would be easier," Robert said calmly, as if she hadn't just told him something she'd never told a single soul besides Bridget. "You could read them at your leisure instead of having to get out of bed when you'd rather be sleeping."

She wondered if he kept his leg on in bed. Wouldn't his parents hear him if he hopped?

"But the time that I'm talking about they didn't leave the kitchen. And yet what they were talking about . . . Maybe they were just too upset. That's what I can't figure out. The thing is . . . Well, here's what they said. My parents think my accident ruined their sex life."

She couldn't believe what he'd said. "They *said* that?"

"My mother said my father identified himself with me and so when I lost my leg he lost his masculinity. She means his sex drive. He said it was *her* fault because she was afraid of giving birth to another one-legged child."

Zoë tried not to laugh, but Rob said, "Go ahead and laugh. You have to laugh or you'll kill yourself. When I heard them, I thought of calling in the crazy wagon. However, this is my dilemma, I can't decide whether they meant me to overhear them or not."

"You mean you think they said it there on purpose? But that would be . . ."

"I wouldn't put it past them."

"But why would they? That would be so cruel."

"That's what I can't figure out. What would be their motive? When there's a crime, there has to be a motive. I've thought about it a lot. I can't believe it was an accident. It's the one and only time I can remember them not going into the living room when they had something private to discuss. I would have heard what they said anyway, but I don't think it would have bothered me the way it has. I would just have considered it another one of their lamebrain ideas. I've thought about it a lot now and my conclusion is that they want me to feel responsible. I really think that's what it is. But what the hell do they expect me to *do* about it? That's what I don't get. I can't grow a new leg, can I? What do you think? Do you think they want me to leave home? Maybe they want me to kill myself."

When he said that, she couldn't help it, tears came into her eyes. She looked out the window for a minute.

"Not that I mind leaving home, of course."

"I think they're extremely warped, Robert. I think that from now on you should try not to listen to a word they say. Especially if you think they're saying things for your benefit."

"Benefit . . ."

"Well, your non-benefit."

"I'm glad you think so. By the way, do you mind calling me Rob?"

"Sorry."

"No apology necessary. I've discovered I enjoy having a new name. It seems peculiar that no one ever called me that before."

Well, Rob was a normal person's name, Zoë thought but didn't say. Robert Went had hardly seemed *normal*. But she wouldn't have wanted him to misunderstand her. He seemed perfectly normal now. Actually, he seemed really nice.

Neither of them said anything for a few minutes. She looked around the living room, trying to imagine what it meant to have your sex life ruined. She wondered if Robert had ever slept with anyone. Would he take his leg off? What kind of person could his mother be who would furnish a living room only with rocking chairs?

"Do you mind if I ask you something?" he asked, in a curious voice but as if he already knew the answer.

Was he already going to ask her to make love with him? It seemed sort of soon. What would she say? It would be like sacrificing herself, the way Beauty did for the Beast, not that she minded. Then she felt bad for thinking that. He really was pretty nice. It wasn't even that she didn't like him—it was just that the *thought* of it was so weird. It was strange to have the thought and the experience be different things. Imagine if Bridget saw her now.

"Why did you and Bridget Wycliffe suddenly stop speaking to me five years ago?" he asked.

"What?" Zoë exclaimed.

"Or whenever it was. Wait, of course! I know when it was—it was right before I got waltzed off to cripple camp! Would you mind telling me? I'd really like to know."

Now that she'd adjusted to what he was talking about, she stared at him. What was he up to? He'd turned them in and now he acted like he didn't know what had happened.

"Are you pulling my leg?" Then she heard what she'd said. She could feel herself blushing. "Sorry."

"About what? Oh, you mean that expression? Don't be an idiot. You'll make me feel like I'm back at camp."

"I'm sorry."

"Stop being sorry! And the answer is, No, I'm not pulling your leg, speaking of stupid expressions. So what was the story?" he asked again.

"Do you mean you really don't know the reason we stopped speaking to you?" Did he have amnesia?

He was beginning to look disgusted.

"I mean, I'm not saying you're making it up," she said. "It's just that it's hard to believe, since all this time . . ."

"One minute you're my friends and the next minute I get this spiteful letter from you."

"Spiteful letter?" Zoë tried to think back. But they hadn't written him a letter.

"Don't tell me you don't remember it."

"We never wrote you any letter."

"Come on. It's a classic. Here, hold it right there."

He went out into the hall and she heard him clumping upstairs. Most of the time you couldn't even tell he limped unless you watched closely. When he came back down he had a wrinkly-looking envelope, and he took the letter out at once and started reading it.

> "Dear Robert,
>
> Who do you think you are?
>
> You are the most treacherous slimy traitor the world has ever seen. Judas Iscariot and Benedict Arnold were nothing compared to you."

"I never wrote that," she said.

"Well, you may not have *written* it, but you *signed* it. Don't try to squirm out of it that way."

"I'm not! I just . . ." She was trying to understand what this meant. Bridget had written Robert a letter? But why would she have done that without telling her? And why would Robert still be pretending after all this time not to know why she had? So what if Bridget had written him? He had still turned them in.

Zoë looked at all the rocking chairs. They gave her a creepy feeling, as if they were empty because they had refused to let anyone sit in them.

> "We thought we could trust you, you serpent. Now we know you for the Mesopotamian monster you truly are!"

"Mesopotamian monster!"

Robert managed to keep a straight face.

> "If you think we will ever speak to you for the rest of eternity, think again, you worm.

"It's signed 'Z. M. Carver and B. P. Wycliffe.' "

"Can I see it?" Zoë asked.

Robert had written things in the margins: beside "Who do you think you are?" he'd put "Robert, who did you think?"; beside "Judas Iscariot and Benedict Arnold," "Prove it"; beside "Mesopotamian," "Babylonian?" "Egyptian?" and "Sumerian?" although "Sumerian" was crossed out.

"I was planning on writing a rebuttal, although I never got around to it."

"It's Bridget's handwriting, but—I know you won't believe this—I never saw this letter before in my life."

"Look, all I know is suddenly I get this letter and you're not speaking to me. Now you say you never wrote it."

Zoë stared at him. "But you turned us in! Why don't you mention that part? I admit I don't know why Bridget wrote you on her own—though probably it was because we weren't allowed to see each other out of school for a whole *month*, but you're still the one who turned us in."

"What are you talking about? Turned you in for what?"

"For the Pipe School! For all that stuff! The letters! Why are you making me say it?"

"You mean the letters we had the pupils write to the teachers? Why would I turn you in? I did it too."

"How should I know? Maybe because you wanted to get us in trouble. Maybe because you thought it was a sick thing to do and felt guilty."

"Felt guilty about that? Are you crazy?"

"Bridget said you told your mother. Then your mother called my mother. I know that for a fact because I answered the phone."

"But, Zoë," Robert said—it was the first time he'd said her name—"just because my mother called your mother doesn't prove that I *told* on you guys. That would never stand up in court. My mother never said a single solitary *word* to me about the Pipe School, I swear to God. Try to think back. What happened first?"

"Your mother called! Next thing I know my father is trying to make me feel like a worm for leading you astray."

"Leading me *astray*?"

"How could we be so irresponsible as to mess up someone who was already mentally unstable . . ."

"Me, I take it."

"No! *He* meant you. Really, Robert—Rob—I never thought any such thing."

"Okay, okay. So what happened next?"

"He told me the teachers had recognized our handwriting, but then Bridget told me later you'd confessed. We weren't allowed to see each other out of school for a whole month. The weird thing is, we never really talked afterward about what happened. I guess I was so embarrassed that I didn't want to."

"Embarrassed about what?"

"Just all the stuff we wrote to the teachers." Zoë could feel herself starting to blush again. "I just felt . . . My father made me feel like I was really sick in the head."

"God!" Robert shouted. "What is *wrong* with them? Do they all want to drive their children insane? I'm *never* having children! Never in a million years!"

"You wouldn't have to be like our parents."

"You can't help it. Something happens to your brain when you have children. Some chemical goes haywire. If you want kids, you can always adopt them. There are plenty of orphans."

Zoë wasn't really listening, though. What *had* happened, if Robert hadn't turned them in? Even if Bridget thought he had, why would she have never told Zoë about the letter she'd written to Robert? Zoë suddenly remembered the time in Mexico when Bridget had accused *her* of always keeping secrets—had Bridget thought Zoë had turned them in? But it wasn't like Bridget to keep such a suspicion to herself. Had *Bridget* turned them in but pretended Robert had? But then why would she have accused Zoë of keeping secrets? Seth had said the teachers guessed and then Bridget had said it was Robert who had clued them in; but had *she* really been the one and all these years kept that huge secret? It was the only explanation that made sense, but Zoë could make no sense of it. Why would Bridget have written the letter to Robert if she knew he hadn't betrayed them? Had Bridget gone *crazy*? Had she really *believed* that Robert was the culprit? And then . . . All this time Zoë had believed that she was a sick, horrible person to have written those letters but now here was Rob saying that that was ridiculous . . . Zoë couldn't take it in. Who *was* Bridget? Who was *she*?

She looked around the living room; the rocking chairs looked as if they were about to start rocking. It was like that day a long time ago, reading Monica's letter announcing that she and Seth were separating, and like the time before that, hearing that the Tannenbaums' grandfather had died—her stomach started thinking instead of her brain. Couldn't she hear bad news without getting sick? Or was it only a *kind* of bad news that made her sick—learning that things had not been what she'd thought, and not because she'd been mistaken about them but because someone had kept *something from her* . . .

Without meaning to she'd started to take quick deep breaths, one after the other. Maybe she should put her head on her knees.

"Zoë, what are you doing?" Robert asked.

She raised her head. "I'm . . ." she started to say, but Robert's face looked out of shape, like a face on a balloon. "I think I just need to . . ." She stood up but that made the whole room wobble. "I think I'm . . ." she said.

The next thing she knew she was lying on the floor, looking up at Robert, who was kneeling beside her. For a moment she had no idea where they were, but then she realized that they must be in *The End of Slavery*, except that it had to be the real performance, since no one else was around them—oh God, she couldn't remember what her next lines were, or even what scene they were in! Robert said in a concerned voice, "Are you all right?" Where in the play did he say that? She tried to communicate to him by shaking her head very slightly that she'd had a sudden bout of amnesia, then remembered Mr. Montgomery's saying that if that ever happened just to say anything, anything at all, and it would get you back on track again. Rob obviously wasn't catching on; he kept looking at her in a worried way, terrified that she was going to ruin the entire scene. Zoë tried frantically to remember her character, the blind girl, and what she would be doing in this situation, lying on the floor with the convict looking at her; if Robert—that is, Louis, the convict—was looking at her so directly then they had to be in that part of the play after he'd discovered she wasn't blind anymore, but she didn't see how it could be the love scene because in that they were standing up. However, she had to do something in a hurry.

"Louis, kiss me!" she said in a loud voice and reached up to put her arms around his neck. When he bent down she could whisper to him that she'd forgotten her lines and he would realize what had happened.

Robert stared at her. "*What* did you say?"

"What?" Zoë murmured. She lifted her head and saw the rocking chairs and Robert's living room and no audience. What had happened? Had she really *fainted*? She scrunched up so that she was sitting with her back against the couch. "I can't believe it! I thought we were in the play!"

"Come on, you're kidding, right?"

"I fainted! I've never fainted before in my life! When I woke up and saw you looking at me I thought we were in the play . . ."

"You're putting me on."

"Why would I do that? Do you think I would say 'Louis, kiss me' if I didn't think we were in the play? I couldn't remember my lines, so I was trying to signal to you, but when you didn't figure it out I said, 'Louis, kiss me,' so that you'd bend down and I could whisper that I'd forgotten my lines. This is so weird."

"Oh, very."

She'd been so excited that she'd fainted that it took her a minute to hear the tone of his voice.

"Are you mad? What's the matter?"

"Nothing."

"Robert! You think I was faking?"

"I'll admit the possibility occurred to me."

"But why would I . . .?" Suddenly it dawned on her what he must be thinking. "Do you mean you thought . . .?" He refused to meet her eye. "You think I was trying to trick you into kissing me! That's it, isn't it? You think I pulled that whole thing just to . . ."

"Shut up," he said. "Just shut up."

" 'Shut up!' " She'd never been more surprised in her life. "But you're the one who . . ."

"You're crazy to think I would even think of such a thing. Why would *I* think *you* could possibly want me to . . . I mean, excuse me . . ." He sounded more and more sarcastic. "How would I even *dare* think such a thing? How could I forget I'm a *cripple*! How could I forget that no girl in her right mind would ever get anywhere near me? Please excuse my lapse into insanity."

"But, Robert! *Rob* . . ."

"How could I, a lowly cripple . . . How could a person with only one leg ever dare to think a person with two legs might be *attracted* to him? God, I ought to be put to *death*."

"Robert," she said, laughing, "that's totally insane! I never thought any such thing!"

"Not only a cripple, but *insane*. I shouldn't even be allowed to *breathe*."

"Robert, come on, why are you getting this way all of a sudden? I never thought anything like that." That might not be exactly true, but she certainly didn't think that now. "I really did think I was in the play—I don't even know what happened. One minute we were talking, and then I felt sick. The next minute I'm lying on the floor with no idea where I am."

"Fine," he said. "Forget it."

"Besides, I do so think you're good-looking. I even *like* you, now are you satisfied? Bridget doesn't know anything."

"What's she got to do with it?"

"Because it's because of her that I've thought you were a creep all this time! Obviously she was afraid that if we got together we'd find out what she did."

"Well, it worked."

They looked at each other.

"I just can't believe she kept something like that secret all these years. It's so weird."

"I'd say so," Rob said. "Why don't you ask her about it?"

"Ask her!"

"Why not? Don't you want to get to the bottom of it?"

"Yes, but . . . I just can't see coming out and asking her about it."

"Then I will. I think she deserves her comeuppance. Whatever that is."

"No, don't do that! Please! She'd never forgive me."

"Never forgive *you*!"

"Please, Rob, just let me handle it. She's already so suspicious of me for having anything to do with you."

"Suspicious . . . Well, I guess now you know why."

Zoë sighed.

"Well, we haven't exactly gotten any rehearsing done, have we?" Rob said.

"Not exactly."

"Tell me honestly, do you like the play at all?"

"I don't know. I guess I like a few parts."

"Name one."

"I like some of the lines. The lion's and the monkey's."

"You like 'I could have eaten you in one bite but my merciful nature stayed my hand'?" He mimicked Mr. Montgomery. " 'Purposeful mixing of metaphors to produce a state of disorientation in the audience . . .' Laura Jenkins doesn't know a metaphor from a hole in the ground."

"No, where he says, 'Henceforth, whenever you gaze upon me, remember that I serve you by choice.' "

"It all sounds pretty corny to me. The worst is in the scene where we vow eternal love to each other. It's one big cliché. 'My beloved, you've released me from my bondage. I thought I was free when I escaped from prison, but now I'm truly free at last.' Then you say, 'I've broken the fetters with my love,' et cetera. The whole audience is going to throw up. Don't tell me you like that line?"

She shrugged.

"You do like it! You've got to be kidding!"

"I don't *like* it, it's just not as bad as the others. Anyway, what's wrong with it?"

"It's totally and completely unbelievable, that's what's wrong with it. Would you ever say that to someone?"

"It all depends."

"Come on. Say it then. I mean, say it to me as if you really mean it."

"You'd have to really feel it."

"We have to really feel it in the play. Come on, rehearse it."

" 'I have . . .' I can't without you saying your line first."

"Okay. 'My beloved, you've released me from my bondage. I thought . . .' "

"You're not even trying to be serious."

" 'Zoë, my beloved . . .' I mean, 'Anne-Marie, my beloved . . .' "

"Why do you think it's so unbelievable that her loving him turns him into a better person?"

"It's not just loving him! It's staying his prisoner because she loves him, not letting him know that she could go free because it would hurt his *feelings* to learn he'd even flubbed up his job as a captor . . . Give me a break! What person in his right mind would do such a thing? We're supposed to believe that if the captors didn't just *happen* to discover that all the prisoners were willing victims the prisoners would never have told them? Come *on*. Not to mention all the coincidences, like Anne-Marie just *happening* to get hit on the head with the vase and recover from her blindness so she can see Louis and fall in love with him in the first place."

"No, she doesn't. She falls in love with him *before* she sees what he looks like. That's the whole point. Remember when she says, 'Are you handsome? I'm sure hordes of women before me have fallen head over heels in love with you'? If someone falls in love with you when they're blind you know they really love you for yourself instead of how you look."

"Since I don't plan on anyone falling in love with me I really haven't given it much thought."

"I don't think you *plan* on someone falling in love with you, Robert. Rob, sorry."

"Why?" he asked. "Are *you* in love with me?" When she didn't say anything he said, "Don't worry about it. Someday I'll meet a girl with no hands."

"Cut it out."

He squinted at her. Then he said, "Why are you getting all worked up? Haven't you ever heard of an inferiority complex before?" He sort of smiled. She couldn't believe he'd just come out and said that—she would never have said such a thing in a million years.

"Anyway," he said in a friendly voice, "I have a plan. I thought we could make up new lines. At least for the love scene. At school we'll rehearse Laura's lines but here we'll rehearse our own. Then on opening night we'll use ours."

"That would be pretty mean."

"Ha! It's pretty mean to make any self-respecting person recite such idiotic lines. Instead of swearing eternal love to the convict, Anne-Marie can shoot him. She can say, 'I knew you were a creep by the sound of your voice but when the vase restored my sight I realized you were the ugliest thing on the face of the earth! I'm going to put you out of your misery! Bang!' " He started cackling his old Robert Went laugh.

Zoë smiled.

"Maybe we could even convince some of the other captives to screw up their lines too. I bet you the Federal Reserve Archie Tannenbaum would. I heard him say he'd like to bite the head off his trainer."

"That's just because it's Mike Janacek."

"I know, but don't you think it's a good idea?"

"It would ruin the whole idea of the play!"

"Precisely, my dear Watson. It needs to be ruined. As I've just explained to you, it's the sickest idea I've ever heard—that someone would choose slavery because they pitied their captors. I'll bet you anything Laura Jenkins's family is from south of the Mason-Dixon line. If you listen closely, she even has a drawl. I'm sure she's sorry the Civil War ever took place."

"Maybe," Zoë said. But she couldn't stop thinking about what they'd said before. Did Rob want her to like him or didn't he? This whole plot about sabotaging the play made it seem as if he'd go to any extreme to get out of having to kiss her.

XVI CASCABEL FLATS

All through lunch at some crowded little place that everyone eating there seemed overwhelmed with joy to find themselves in, Zoë kept worrying about Seth and about not having pressed Nick to do something. She *had* to convince him to take Seth's disappearance seriously. However, no sooner had they returned from lunch than up drove a rattletrap old pickup and lo and behold the mysterious landlord himself got out, and that was the end of talking to Nick for a while. Stewart Beauregard hardly looked like someone trying to take over a whole town, Zoë thought (at lunch Ellie had ranted on about how he now owned half of the plaza and was trying to buy the huge old Holy Faith Hotel on the plaza's northwest corner); he was shorter than Nick and somewhat stocky, with straight dirty-brown hair and watery, nearsighted-looking blue eyes; his posture wasn't great. He said "Pleasure" when Nick introduced him to everyone but didn't offer to shake hands and seemed somewhat taken aback when Pryce held out his. He told Ellie he'd come to "borrow her husband" for half an hour—Judith had "commanded" him to move some furniture. Zoë didn't know what she'd expected, but Stewart sounded basically like everyone else from the twentieth century, though he spoke in such a soft voice you had to strain to hear him. It was difficult envisioning him as the subject of continual gossip and fascination.

"You need Nick to help you move furniture?" Ellie repeated incredulously.

"If he doesn't mind."

"Of course I don't mind," Nick said, giving Ellie a look. "Be right with you, Stew."

Though Ellie forced Stewart to come to the house, he insisted on staying just inside the door, keeping one hand in his pocket and with the other restlessly stroking the metal runner. He didn't meet anyone's eye and in general seemed very nervous. More socially awkward than anything else—the result of being scrutinized all the time? Whatever the case,

Zoë could hardly believe that this was the scheming millionaire land baron of Ellie's stories. When Nick came back from the kitchen Stewart gave him a quick look and mumbled, "Never told me you had a *sister*, Nick."

Nick had stopped at Zoë's side, and she signed, *They like to keep me a deep, dark secret.*

"She said that's typical of me." Nick grinned.

"That isn't what she said," Stewart objected in a peeved tone. He kept giving her rapid, searching looks while everyone else stared at him—did he know sign language? Was he actually *annoyed*? Had he meant to make a joke and it had backfired? But what joke? He wasn't smiling, and for an instant he almost did seem like someone who could have sold a house built over a rattlesnake den without telling the buyers, but then he grinned at Nick as if remembering his manners and said, "In fact I don't think she was talking about you at all!"

Nick laughed, as did everyone else, with a certain amount of relief. Weird guy. He made Zoë uncomfortable and she took a step towards the hallway, meaning to slip into Nick and Ellie's room while everyone was occupied and get Rob's letter, but Stewart called, "Hey, miss, like to come along with your brother?"

She turned and looked at him. Hey, *Miss*? Who called anyone that? Yet she found herself thinking that he'd known what she'd been going to do and was trying to stop her. She glanced at Ellie and was shocked to see the open hatred on her face, but the next moment Ellie was chattering about the new menu at Ocho's, the restaurant where they'd had lunch: how vastly the food had improved since they'd fired their drunken chef . . . "You don't say," Stewart said, but Ellie kept on—how jammed the downtown had been, last-minute Christmas insanity; Stewart had done all *his* shopping, she hoped . . . It was as if she kept talking because she couldn't believe the hostility she'd been feeling.

"One sec, Stewart," Nick said, and now he went into the bedroom; had he realized what she'd meant to do? Zoë wondered. Stewart watched Nick go, not even pretending to pay attention to Ellie anymore, but she immediately switched tracks and asked him a question so he'd be forced to respond to her. Did he have any idea what had become of Ignacio Ortega? His shop had been closed—no sign, no explanation—when she went by this afternoon.

"Still after your doors?" Stewart shrugged. "Might run into him tonight—Judith will have asked him."

As Nick came out of the bedroom and winked at her, Zoë was suddenly convinced that something must have happened between Stewart and Ellie that Nick didn't know about. Could they have had an affair? But how could Ellie have been attracted to him?

Nick had changed his sweater—so he hadn't gone for the letter after all, but Zoë felt too conspicuous trying to get it now. Despite Stewart's creepiness she was curious to see the place whose grandeur Ellie kept extolling; besides she'd be more likely to get another chance to talk to Nick if she went along. As he slid open the glass doors, Stewart told Ellie he wouldn't "keep her husband long"—just as long as he needed him. Most people would have smiled, saying that, but Stewart just gave Ellie one of his quick stares. Zoë heard a slight accent in his speech now, not exactly a drawl, more a lengthening of certain syllables, as if he were stretching the words out. It was almost hypnotic, combined with his soft voice. Did he speak so low on purpose? He squinted whenever he looked at anyone as if he had trouble seeing, but Nick had just been telling them at lunch how, out riding, Stewart could spot a rattlesnake a hundred yards away when all he, Nick, saw were rocks and sagebrush.

Outside—evidently they were all going in the truck, a faded turquoise round-fendered old Dodge—Stewart hoisted himself into the driver's seat and Nick held the passenger door open for Zoë. She climbed up and slid over—the cab smelled of motor oil and dirt, reminding her of Buell Magoon's truck in Harmony, but she could also smell Stewart: some combination of warm flannel, stale cigarette smoke, and a faint sweet smell, maybe aftershave. Nick had pulled his door shut and Stewart was reaching to turn the key in the ignition when Ellie came running out of the house shouting, "Nick! Telephone!" When she was nearer she panted, "It's the post office."

"Oh, Lord. Sorry, Stewart."

When Nick got out Zoë moved back towards the door and for the first time Stewart smiled in what seemed a natural way.

"I can see why Nick didn't let on about you," he said.

What is that supposed to mean? she signed. She didn't believe Stewart could really understand her, and the insolent way he talked made her want to be rude to him.

"Wouldn't have been any need to sell him the place then, him and his *wife*, would there? S'pose we all make errors in judgment now and then, though, don't we? I'm no different from anyone else, am I? You certainly wouldn't say I'm any different, would you?"

Zoë stared at him. Was he for real? What was he saying?

He said impatiently, "Don't give me that. You knew right away what

I'm like, don't pretend you don't. They've told you all kinds of stories, haven't they? I know quite well I'm a favorite topic of conversation, but you knew better than to believe what they said, what *Ellen* said."

Zoë moved her head vaguely, trying to decide if he were genuinely insane or just putting her on.

"Good," Stewart said. "That's good." He nodded to himself, stroking his thigh with his palm, down and up, down and up, watching her.

I don't see how he could hurt me, she surprised herself by saying to Rob. He's just showing off. He's made a few lucky guesses—he can't be sure he was right.

"Why do *you* think people talk about other people?" Stewart asked, sounding for the first time as if he really wanted an answer. "It's my observation that they'll go to any length to pretend everything's not perfectly clear. The more they make things a mystery, the better they feel. Why do they do that? Like to make up stories about how I control what happens in this town."

Do you?

"Disappointed in you," he said, frowning. "I thought we understood each other, you and I. Don't disappoint me—I really can't stand any more disappointments. Not now, not after all I've been through. You and I both know where things stand; it's other people who can't face it. I'm only helping things along. Nothing wrong with that, is there?" He lifted a hand and laid it on hers where it rested on the seat. She froze. "I know you wouldn't be thinking I'm talking just to talk. I know you're too intelligent to make that mistake."

Zoë felt paralyzed—Stewart seemed so oblivious of conventional behavior that she almost felt gauche calling attention to what he was doing—but before she had decided what to do he had taken away his hand and said, "Be careful. You'll disillusion me in a moment, Zoë. That is your name, isn't it? Zoë?"

He pronounced it with distaste, as he had "wife" earlier, though this seemed different—as if he disliked the fact that who she was had to be contained by one sound—and for a moment his eyes were focused. "Good," he said for the second time. He had both hands on the steering wheel and was facing forward. "You do know what's going to happen, don't you?"

To happen? When? she signed, but he wasn't looking at her. Did she really believe that he would have been able to understand her if he had been? He seemed so strangely *condensed*, as if present simultaneously in some other dimension, measuring everything against something. She still felt nervous and on the one hand was thinking that Ellie had been more on the mark about Stewart Beauregard than Nick had, but on the other she felt alert in his presence in a way she hadn't in years, since . . . No, it couldn't be. It simply couldn't be. If Stewart was the reincarnation of anyone from her previous life, she *insisted* that it be Rob.

Now they both turned to look back at the house—as if trying to get away from something, Zoë thought.

Well, I waited for you, Rob. What did you expect me to do? (This after they'd gotten back together and were hashing it all out.) I only had so much time. How could I know how you felt about me? As I already told you, it was one thing when you were locked up—it was as if time had stopped. But knowing you were out . . . You could have had a girlfriend, how could I know? I could have been the last person you wanted to see.

But, Zoë, I wrote you a letter! Would I have written you if I didn't want to see you?

How should I know? You could have been writing to tell me not to think that just because you were out you ever wanted to lay eyes on me again.

The others would be dying to know how she and Stewart were managing in the truck by themselves all this time—Zoë was surprised that Ellie hadn't trumped up some excuse to come out. Finally they had to turn back.

"Dislike me?" Stewart asked quickly. His gaze kept clouding and clearing.

Why should I?

She was surprised how some uneasiness seemed to leave him at this, as if he *had* understood what she'd said. He lifted his hand to touch her again, differently this time, she could tell, but then shook his head, admonishing himself, and laid his hand back down. But who knew what would have happened if Nick hadn't come back just then. Though a moment ago she would have felt relieved to see him, now she felt annoyed by his timing.

"Sorry to be so long," he said, as he swung open the door. "Did Zoë tell you . . ." Then he stopped, mortified.

"Yes, she did."

"She . . . Well, that's good."

Zoë felt like telling him to get over it already; at this rate she'd be talking again before he had adjusted to the fact that she didn't. She slid back next to Stewart, who purposely didn't budge. As he started the engine, Nick said, "I can't believe this but some kid in Las Cruces they hired to help out over the holidays didn't believe the label on the box and decided to investigate. One of the snakes got loose. They've managed to confine it to a room, but they claim, which I can't believe, that they don't know of anyone who can catch it and get it back in the box. They say they'll give me until the end of the day to get hold of someone or they're going to shoot it. I remembered meeting someone at the convention who lives down there, so I gave him a call but he wasn't home. His wife said she didn't know if he'd be back before the post office closes. She said she'd call a couple of people who might be able to help and would get back to me—Christ! The post office! 'We've got Christmas presents that have to be delivered, Mr. Carver,' " he mimicked. " 'You're holding up the U.S. postal system.' They blame *me* for not making the box impossible to open! I responded by threatening them with a lawsuit for negligence if the snakes aren't in perfect health when they arrive."

What if they call when you're not here? Zoë asked.

"Oh, Ellie will deal with it."

"You like snakes as much as your brother?" Stewart asked. As he shoved the truck into reverse, the gear shaft pressed against her knee and he let his hand rest there as long as he dared. Without moving, Zoë tried to let him know that she didn't mind. Then he laid his arm along the back of the seat behind her, and she tilted her head back until her hair touched his sleeve. Turning to look over his shoulder, he held her eyes. She looked away first.

How much does he like them? she signed.

"Seems like everything's going haywire at once, doesn't it?" Nick said, not seeing her. "We've got other things on our minds besides the snakes," he added to Stewart. "I thought we might try calling Sparta while we're out of earshot. Our father," he explained.

"Who art in heaven?"

"I certainly hope not." He mouthed so that only Zoë could see, "I got the letter for you."

You did? Where is it?

"You want it this minute?"

No, that's okay.

"Why?" Stewart asked.

"We don't know where our father is," Nick said, not even registering this. "We're trying to do a little detective work. In fact . . ." He looked at her. "What about the Wycliffes? Dad must still see Hugh on occasion."

I don't think we ought to involve them.

"No?"

Would you want to talk to them?

"I guess I see what you mean."

Let's just wait. Maybe the letter will tell me something. Why was Nick suddenly so eager to call, anyway? Because his new snakes (and maybe his experiment) were in jeopardy? Because he'd sensed the attraction—if that was even the word for it—between her and Stewart?

"Are you *worried* about your father?" Stewart asked. He had stopped the truck before turning onto the highway—he was looking at her.

"The truth is, we're trying to decide how worried to be," Nick answered. "There's no reason to believe something really disastrous has happened, but on the other hand we'd be irresponsible not to be concerned."

"Have you called the police?"

"Well, we have a few avenues to explore first. We'd feel pretty foolish if we put out an all-points bulletin only to find he's gone off to some South Sea island to get even."

"Get *even*?"

"It's the first time one of us hasn't been with him for Christmas."

"He cares?"

"That's what we don't know. But let's forget the melodrama for a while," Nick said to Zoë, as if she'd been the one to suggest calling. "You have a great treat in store for you."

How do you know? Then she realized he meant seeing Stewart's house, not reading Rob's letter. She felt irritated now that he'd thought to go after it—why was he in her business all of a sudden?

They stayed on the highway only a short time before they turned off onto another dirt road and headed back towards the blue mountains.

I thought you said Stewart lived only a mile away.

"As the crow flies. As the arroyo runs. How far is your house from mine by road, Stew?"

"Seven."

They were descending into a small river valley now, with some real trees in it—large, white-flaked trunks and graceful, dangling branches like weeping willows'.

"You should see this place when it's green, Zoë. What a paradise. I'll never forget the first time I saw it. I'd never been particularly bothered by the aridity of the countryside the way some people are, but when Stewart first led me down here I realized that I hadn't even noticed how much I'd missed green. My heart was in my mouth. Of course"—he laughed—"it wasn't only because of the natural splendor. Stewart was doing ninety. I was trying to follow in the Chevy."

"Give or take fifty," Stewart said.

They grinned at each other across her, and Zoë was reminded once again of driving around Harmony with Nick and Buell—she felt that free suddenly, pre-Rob free; Buell had just gotten his license and whenever he didn't have to help with haying they'd take off—go into Hanover and mess around or explore back roads—though they never stayed away for long, not wanting Charlotte to be lonely.

She tried to imagine Stewart's valley in bloom; after the desert even the leafless trees seemed like flowers. Then the road sloped up again and Nick said, "Hold it at the top for a moment, Stewart, do you mind? Let Zoë get the full effect."

"The full effect?" Stewart repeated. Nevertheless, he put the brake on and the truck slid to a stop at the next rise. They were poised above another, tinier valley, extending to the edge of a gully. Built right up to its edge, a huge three-sided adobe house enclosed a courtyard, which they could see only because they were looking down on it. You could tell the house was old by the way it had slumped down into its surroundings. All along the side facing them ran a veranda, its plain round wooden pillars wrapped around by bare vines, like veins, dry and gray now, but in the summer covered with flowers. Clematis and wisteria. Roses. Hundreds of kinds of flowers, all blooming simultaneously. A miracle. Though not when Father Jules first arrived. Then there had been only the plain, scarcely windowed building that now formed the right side of the horseshoe—deserted, utterly silent except for the sun-warmed wind which was like silence, blowing. Father Jules had fought his disappointment. "This is it?" he asked his guide. "I had thought . . ."

"Something, isn't it?" Nick said. "Didn't I tell you?"

What was happening? How did she know these things? Zoë scarcely noticed as Stewart, releasing the brake and shifting into neutral, let his forearm rest for a moment on her thigh. The truck coasted down the rise; Stewart parked it and they climbed out and crossed the veranda through an enclosed arched passageway that bisected the front of the house and led into the courtyard. In its center stood an empty fountain surrounded by low bare rosebushes; the rest of the courtyard was laid with flagstone. All this Zoë took in without paying attention, for she'd already known how it would be: on the fourth side lay a low adobe wall with a rusty iron gate in it leading to nowhere; it had been Father Jules's one indulgence—he had carried it with him all the way from the monastery he had begged not to be made to leave; if I am going to that godforsaken land I must be allowed at least one souvenir of civilization. Afterward he had laughed at the memory, both at the abbot's astonishment when he had asked, having been promised one small, easily replaceable fixture from the monastery, for the garden gate, and at having used the expression "Godforsaken." God-forsaken . . . It was where God *lived*. Though that was nothing he could have written to the abbot, his former superior.

Zoë moved slowly across the courtyard, shocked, staring: for out beyond the low wall were the mountains, the blue mountains she'd longed for ever since she'd first laid eyes on them, though she'd known very well that she could never reach them, yet here they now *were*, closer, so much closer than ever before, and yet still blue, the same deep blue they'd been at a distance. How was it possible?

"Pretty breathtaking, isn't it?" Nick asked.

She turned, startled. Stewart had disappeared.

"It's the foreshortening of the view that makes the mountains seem so near—how it's telescoped by the walls. At least that's what Stewart insists. The son of a painter . . . I still can't convince myself there's not some kind of mumbo-jumbo involved. But come to the edge; you'll get a better sense of how far away we still actually are."

Yes—when she approached the edge, she saw that the gate opened onto steps leading down to a small terrace from which a rough track disappeared into the canyon—from here the mountains stood at their usual distance.

"An escape route, that's what it always makes me think of," Nick said.

But Father Jules had known there was no point in trying to escape. There were many of them and one of him and they were younger, and stronger, and moreover they had horses. For all he knew they might have even had justice on their side. He could no longer tell. The distinction, once so clear to him, between right and wrong was obscure to him now. He could see only what people did, and what they didn't. He did not know how he could ever explain this to the abbot.

"Well, shall we?" Nick asked, gesturing towards the house.

What?

"Where were you? I've been talking to you for the last minute."

Had he? What was happening to her memory? Who was Father Jules? Moving like a sleepwalker, Zoë followed Nick into an immense kitchen: it had a flagstone floor like the courtyard's, but polished to a dark shine; white walls; and in the corner a small fireplace—Nick and Ellie had one like it in their bedroom. On all the counters and on the walls immediately above them were dark blue tiles with white birds on them, caught in midflight. Zoë had an instantaneous vision of them coming to life, fluttering about the room as weightlessly as butterflies, and then, when she opened the door, taking off for the mountains—as if they were actually imprisoned in the designs made of them. Everything in the room had been added long after Father Jules's time, except for the fireplace, where he had thought about burning the letter he had written to the archbishop telling him about Carmela, but had reconsidered—if he hid it someone might find it someday. He did not think Carmela's father or his men would search the house and even if they did they would think what he had written a monstrous lie, the confession of his clever, clever method of seducing an innocent, foolish young girl. The windows onto the courtyard had been added—they were large—but the small ones on the north side were original. The ceiling was low. There was little furniture in the room—several carved wooden benches (had Ignacio Ortega made them?) and, in the center of the room, a long, wide-planked table, worn very dark, gleaming. It was the first thing Father Jules had ever built with his own hands. Dough had been rolled out on one end, and cookie cutters in the shapes of stars were fastened in it. However, there was no one in the room.

"Hello?" Nick called, then said to Zoë, "This is the oldest part of the house. It was supposed to have been the refectory, I think. You were in the room when we were talking about this place yesterday, weren't you? Can't you just see it? Lots more tables like this one with monks sitting at them slurping soup?"

She smiled. It had been Father Jules's dream. But then Carmela had arrived, and he knew that thenceforth nothing would be as he had planned. Of course he hadn't believed her at first—bearing God's child . . . How could he? Everything he had been taught since he could first pronounce the words "Seigneur" and "Sauveur" had impressed on him the fact that it had happened *once*; by definition it had happened once and any hint of suspicion that that might not be true amounted to the gravest heresy; one could worship and admire but never experience or know; one lived *here* and *that* was *there*, and one might die holding out one's arms longingly and crying for the holy symbol to be made flesh again but it never never could be. Only when you died could it come to life for you. By the end he understood very well why Carmela was afraid to let anyone know the identity of her child's father—this father who wanted to lift his son from life and make him into something else, leaving behind only a rumor to tantalize survivors.

The world You have made is full of wonder—why is that not enough for You, Lord? prayed Father Jules as Carmela's father with his posse led him to what he knew would be his death. Look at this! All around us, this sky, these mountains—I could look at them forever and never be tired of them, why cannot You? Is it possible that You *envy* it, this earth You have created? That You vie with it for our allegiance? But it was only at the end that he understood this, that which he had fought for so long but which Carmela had understood from the first. How it saddened him, that he should have regained his sight only when he was about to die.

Then Stewart came back in with Judith, the woman who'd saved Aladdin the dog's life. (Temporarily.) She was attractive, in a fragile refugee-like way—big dark eyes and dark hair wispily curling around her delicate face. Zoë felt sure that Stewart didn't love his wife, so she'd expected her to be lacking in some obvious respect; however Judith was not only attractive, but friendly and warm—she came right up to Nick, took his hand in both of hers, and said, "Merry Christmas—a little early." And then, "You must be Nick's sister?" She shook her hand too. "How nice that you could come out for Christmas. Are you enjoying your visit so far?"

Zoë nodded—Stewart looked amused—and Judith said brightly, "Not everyone does like it out here. Some people take one look at all this space and get right back on the plane; it's too wide open for them—they feel unsafe." She laughed. "I don't know from what." Then she asked Nick earnestly how Ellie was—she sounded as if Ellie had been ill, or in an accident.

Had Stewart told Judith she couldn't talk, Zoë wondered, to spare her embarrassment? That didn't seem likely. Yet it was obvious Judith knew. It must have been Ellie. Had Judith told Stewart before about her muteness and he pretended not to have known? But why would he have done that? Was this an example of how sparsely Stewart and Judith communicated or of how insignificant Nick and Ellie really were to them? And why would Nick have never mentioned her existence? Did having to tell people about her really upset him so much? After their brief intermission from competition before lunch his "sensitivity" again bugged her—*she* was the one who couldn't talk; why did he still have to try to steal center stage?

When Stewart and Nick went off to move furniture, Judith said, "Let me stick another sheet of cookies in the oven, and I'll show you around the house."

Zoë nodded, gesturing an offer of help.

"Oh no, I'm all set, though that's very kind of you. But this is the last batch. I've made three hundred already!"

She was making *bisochitos*, she explained, a Mexican cookie flavored with anise—it was traditional *out here* at Christmas. She kept up a patter while she arranged the dough stars on the cookie sheets, careful to ask only questions that could be answered by yes or no—had Ellie and Nick taken them into town yet? Was it crowded? Had they had lunch at Ocho's? Ellie had mentioned she wanted to take them there . . . Judith looked over every time she asked a question as if she were doing the crawl and turning her head out of the water to breathe.

Suddenly Zoë remembered Rob's letter—why hadn't she taken it from Nick? How could she have forgotten about it for even one moment? How could she not have read it immediately? Just gone into the bedroom and taken it out of the drawer and read it? Stewart wouldn't have physically prevented her—if he'd meant to prevent her at all, which now seemed ridiculous. What had she been *thinking*? Ten years she'd waited to hear from Rob and now she finally had and she was finding excuses not to read his letter? She wished Judith would stop chattering. People often did when they first met her; she was used to it and mostly it was entertaining in a perverse way but right now it was keeping her from thinking clearly; Stewart must have been *counting* on Judith to distract her. Yet the moment he had gone off with Nick the atmosphere had thinned and she had begun to think clearly again—if Judith would just be quiet. Words like "fiendish" and "malevolent"—words she'd never used in her life—were occurring to her in connection with Stewart. But she was overwrought. Where *was* Rob? Just because for a moment in the truck she'd had an urge to lay her head on Stewart's shoulder—all right, more than that, something she preferred not to think about, which she'd have thought her experience with Anders Ogilvy would have cured her forever of wanting—was Rob reminded, too? Was that why he was staying away? But she refused to think about Anders Ogilvy. If Stewart was an updated version of anyone, it had to be Rob. He was the one who was out of the hospital, he had written to her—why had she let Nick go off with the letter? Had something finally been about to happen with Rob when she began to pose for Anders Ogilvy? Now was she . . . She had meant to say, was she finding another impediment? But what did Father Jules have to do with this? Why were his memories leaking into hers? Was it because Rob had been released or for some other reason? Was Father Jules the priest who was expecting her? Would she see Samuel again now?—who she still could never believe had been her own, dead, great-great-uncle, come back dripping wet in the middle of the night . . . Sometimes it happens that way, Charlotte said; I always saw the future but I know the sight can turn in the other direction. I don't know which is worse, dear.

For ten years Zoë had experienced no other incident of the "Howe family curse"—if that was what it was; she had begun to think of that first time as a dream. She had wanted to be reassured that it had not been, but now that her wish seemed at last to be coming true she felt extremely uneasy. Why should it happen only after she'd met Stewart?

Judith was saying, "Actually, I should supervise the furniture-moving for a moment. Would you mind waiting here in case the timer goes off before I get back?"

What? What was Judith talking about? But it had been a question so Zoë nodded and smiled.

"Thanks so much. I shouldn't be long."

As soon as Judith left, Zoë went to the window over the sink and looked out, hoping to see—she didn't even know what. The tension was increasingly unbearable. Off to the right were a small barn and a paddock. She hadn't noticed them when they drove in. Nick and Stewart and then Judith after them had gone into the front part of the house. Zoë followed and looked through the doorway: it led into a long formal dining room—a huge carved table, surrounded by heavy, carved chairs. An intricate tin candelabra hung above it and, on the walls, tin sconces with red candles in them. Sideboard, china cabinet—all were in the heavy Spanish style. Some religious paintings on wood. Zoë stepped inside to look more closely at them, even though she knew they were too old to be Stewart's father's. French doors opened onto the courtyard—they probably had some other name for them, *out here*. The door to the next room was nearly closed. She could hear the others a room or two beyond. The place was endless, much larger than it had seemed from outside.

Returning to the kitchen, she saw that the door on the other side—the one Stewart and Judith had come in through—was ajar. It was divided into two sections horizontally like a Dutch door, though permanently joined. She crossed the kitchen and looked in.

A step led down into a small sitting room, informally furnished in an ordinary way: a comfortable-looking striped slipcovered couch and matching pudgy armchairs. On a faded blue table, beside the couch, a telephone. The door beyond was also open and led to a hallway, covered by Indian rugs, that ran the length of the courtyard. The doors on the interior side of the hallway were all closed. Probably bedrooms.

While she was standing there wondering which room was Stewart's, he came back into the kitchen. She didn't need to turn around to know who it was. A kind of babble, like voices of several people arguing, broke out in her mind.

"Looking for anything in particular?"

Of course, she said, turning. But as soon as she looked at him the noise subsided and she was amazed how happy she was to see him. But he was immediately annoyed.

"No—I've told you. Don't pretend. You know better than to think I wish you well."

I don't believe you.

"I won't lie to you."

That could be a lie.

Was there such a thing as conducting a trial by proxy? Who substituted for whom was complicated, though: Anders Ogilvy, assuming he really had been driving by in his beige Studebaker at the moment of the accident, could clarify Rob's actions—had he appeared to step in front of his father's car intentionally?—so in that case she would want Stewart to stand in for Anders; on the other hand, Anders could never clarify Rob's motives; for that she'd want Stewart to be Rob. Even if she couldn't decide, Stewart's behavior to her in the present would elucidate the past. She had to know, and she had to know now, what Rob had done and if he'd been aware of what he was doing. She certainly had to know before she saw him, and she might even have to know before she read his letter. Wouldn't that be what he'd want?

The grand jury refused to indict you—the more you insisted you should be tried, the less willing they were to do it. I'm only doing what you'd want, Rob.

Stewart was looking at her with dislike. "We both know what's going on, but you want me to take all the blame."

Blame for what?

"Not now. They're coming back."

But . . .

"Don't think I'm unaware that things could have been otherwise," he said quickly. "Remember that. You're the one who wants it this way."

What way? she signed quickly, but Nick and Judith had come back in now. There couldn't have been much furniture to move, if they were finished already. Why couldn't Judith have helped Stewart herself? Rob's letter had to be either in one of Nick's back pants pockets or in his shirt pocket under his sweater. Meanwhile he was in the middle of telling Judith a story—they'd stopped by the table so he could finish it. Someone else he'd met at the Rattlesnake Convention. Was he some kind of clown, that all he could talk about anymore were rattlesnake anecdotes?

"He sang them to *sleep*?" Judith had asked.

Zoë was out of patience with him. His grand schemes. She couldn't believe she'd told him Rob was out.

The timer went off and Judith took the cookies out of the oven while continuing to listen to Nick.

"No, in fact they crawled all over him," he said, "looking for the sound. Eventually they'd settle around his neck; he said they could feel the vibration coming through his windpipe. He said that the only time he got into trouble was when he was handling a large Adamanteus alone in his house, and it curled around his neck so tightly that he could scarcely breathe."

"Heavens," Judith said, sounding not at all alarmed.

Nick glanced at Zoë and Stewart.

"Unfortunately each time he either stopped singing or tried to lift it off it constricted—he said it's the only time he's ever known a rattler to do that. The Adamanteus is the largest rattler besides the Atrox," Nick said to Zoë. "It's the Atrox's eastern equivalent."

It was probably just a boa with . . . B-O-A WITH . . .

"With a rattler's head stapled on, you mean?" Nick laughed happily.

Then she was annoyed with herself for having cooperated with him even this much. He knew she was referring to the time the police had almost been called to throw him off the property of a little country zoo near Harmony; what he didn't realize was that the incident now seemed absurd to her instead of admirable. "The World's Most Venomous Snakes," had read the ad. "Completely tame! Come and pet them!" She and Buell and Nick had gone to check it out. Nick had figured out immediately that the snakes were ordinary garden snakes and black-snakes painted to look like cobras and coral snakes and rattlers. He was mad enough about that, but what really incensed him was when he told people and they said, "Shh—don't let the kids hear." "You mean you *want* your children to think it's all right to pick up poisonous snakes?" When people tried to avoid him he went up to the pens, where the littler kids were allowed one at a time to pick up tiny garter snakes, practically dead from exhaustion, and said, "They're not real, you know. They're not really poisonous. Don't believe what your parents tell you." She and Buell had been pulling him away, but he refused to leave. "It's *wrong!*" he kept shouting. "If they pretend harmless snakes are poisonous, then they'll pretend poisonous snakes are harmless!" Only when the manager came out and threatened to call the cops would he go. They'd planned to return soon in the middle of the night and turn all the snakes loose, but right after that he'd jumped out of the Magoons' hayloft and broken his leg. She'd always thought he was a hero for wanting to save the snakes, but now he seemed foolish; he just couldn't accept the imperfect, snake-suspecting world, the way everyone else had to.

"So here he is singing for his life," Nick went on, in his overeager voice, "when the doorbell rings. He knew who it was—a girlfriend he'd had a fight with he really wanted to apologize to—if he didn't he'd never see her again. Your classic sitcom dilemma. If he opens the door the visitor might startle the snake into biting and, as you know, if you get it in the neck or the face from such a big one you might not live to tell about it; besides, even if the snake didn't bite, it wouldn't allow him to stop singing long enough to explain what was going on. Anyone want to guess what he did?"

"I can't imagine," Judith said. "Wrote a note and slipped it under the door?"

"Judith guesses that he wrote a note," Nick said, like a game show host. "That's what I guessed too. Stewart?"

"Couldn't begin to tell you."

Nick nodded. "He thought of writing a note, in fact—there was even a letter slot he could have put it through, but, for one, he didn't think there was time, and, for another, he didn't think his girlfriend would believe him. What he did will seem the obvious solution once I mention it. But to have had the presence of mind to think of it under the circumstances . . . He got out a tape recorder, singing all the while, brought it close to the door, and then sang to his girlfriend an explanation of what was going on. 'Hold on, dearest, there's a rattler round my throat . . .' "

Judith laughed. Stewart was looking at Nick incredulously.

"At least, if she didn't believe him, he figured she'd be entertained enough to stand there until he could open the door. Then he rewound the tape and played it back. Smooth as silk, the snake slid right off and curled around the tape recorder. He got his hook and slipped it into a bag before it had a chance to say Encore."

"And she was still there?" Judith asked.

"The girlfriend?" Nick laughed. "Funny, I can't remember that part."

"Didn't you want to make a phone call?" Stewart asked.

"What?" Nick said. Then, "Not sure I see the connection, but . . . You up for it, Zoë?"

"You can use the phone in here."

"Thank you—I think." Nick led the way into the sitting room. When he'd shut the door he said, "Stewart's in a weird mood. I've never seen him like this. Jumpy. I don't get it. It must be the prospect of entertaining."

Why couldn't Judith help him move the furniture? she asked.

"Oh, her back's sore or something. I don't know."

Do you have the letter?

"Mais oui, madame." Nick pulled it from his hip pocket and handed it to her. She breathed a little when she held it in her hand, though she still felt too irritated with Nick for the dippy way he acted around Stewart to really react to having it. As he'd told her, the return address said only "Robert Went, At Large," and her address on Metcalf Street had been crossed out and Nick's out here added. On the bottom of the envelope was written, "Hold for arrival." With a feeling of nausea she did recognize Rob's handwriting—either that or an excellent imitation. Bridget could have forged it. She might have been up to her old tricks where Rob was concerned. Wasn't that more likely, in fact? How could his handwriting still look so much like it had then? And that would have been the sample Bridget would have had to copy from—probably stolen a paper of his back in the dim, dark days of English class, just on general principles, in case she ever needed it.

They had both sat down on the couch, and Zoë set the letter against the lamp on the end table and looked at it.

"I'm sure you'd like to have some privacy when you read it," Nick said. When she didn't contradict him he said, "Well, let's call anyway and then I'll leave you alone."

I'm not ready to read it just yet.

"You're not ready . . . Really? Well, it's up to you. Do you know the number or shall I call information?"

She signed the last four digits. Nick knew the exchange. "Three, four, nine, seven," he repeated. "I'll charge it to my number." He spoke to the operator, then sat listening. Finally he hung up. She sat very still.

"I suppose I could try Mrs. Jessup," Nick said. "You don't happen to know her number, do you?"

No.

He called Information. Again Zoë waited nervously while he dialed, but Mrs. Jessup didn't answer either.

"Probably out Christmas shopping." Nick laughed, then looked uncomfortable.

Maybe he and Mrs. Jessup ran away together.

"Of course—why didn't I think of that? Well, we'll try again later. We can sneak away during the party, if we don't get a chance at home. By then you'll know what Robert's letter says, too."

He acted as if he had a right to know. In the kitchen he told Stewart that if Stewart had no further use for him, they'd be heading home.

"Right," Stewart said, not looking at her. "Let's go."

"Actually, I thought we'd walk—if you'd like to, that is, Zo."

Whether it had been Nick's reason for wanting to walk back or not, they hadn't gone more than ten paces up the miniature canyon he kept calling an arroyo before he was talking about Stewart and the snakes again. The whole thing had been so fortuitous—his running into Stewart,

Stewart's offering them the house, then the snakes . . . It was enough to make a person believe in predestination.

"You seem to have made quite an impression, by the way," Nick said, interrupting himself. "He wanted to know all about you when we were in the other room—why I'd never mentioned you . . ."

Why didn't you?

"I don't know. It's strange, isn't it? It's not a fact I generally conceal." He gave her such an affectionate smile that despite the irritation she'd just been feeling with him it took all her willpower not to believe that he was innocent.

XVII HARMONY

Charlotte and Adam meet secretly at the Dawes place that whole summer and fall, hoodwinking Louisa. Embracing in the tall grass, Adam thinks again of the couple they caught through the spyglass as children, conjoined in the spring woods as if in the pristine time before the world began. He is amused now when he recalls his six-year-old's opprobrium. Where did he learn it? Certainly his mother never spoke to him of such things! It seems to him that it is only now, as with Charlotte he enacts the tableau himself, that he understands how entirely shameless it is.

The weather turns cold, and Adam is wondering how he and Charlotte will now prosecute their dalliance when she begins to complain of tiredness and prefers to stay home in the afternoon to nap. Adam asks if he should call in the doctor, but Charlotte tells him she isn't ill, merely sleepy—she doesn't like to tell him that the boys, jealous of all the time she's been spending with him, have begun to visit her early in the morning and to insist that she play with them. By the time afternoon arrives, she's too worn out to do anything. Henry, Thaddeus, Llewellyn, and Samuel (Llewellyn is older than Thaddy now)—sometimes they rush in when she's barely awake to show her something they've found—the last blackberries, late mushrooms, apples . . .

Do they never sleep? she wonders. They jump on the bed, their cheeks ruddy, their hair mussed, their clothes smelling of outdoors. "Shh!" she cautions them. Sometimes their father is asleep beside her—on occasion he slips into her room after Louisa has gone to bed, waiting until he hears her go downstairs in the morning (she is an early riser) to tiptoe back to his own room.

The boys always laughed at Adam, Charlotte said: "Look, his mouth is wide open! A fly could fly in! And how he snores—he sounds like a wild beast!" They wanted to pull his beard, to tickle him on the nose with the late asters they'd picked for Charlotte until he sneezed, but she couldn't allow this. "You mustn't wake him," she scolded. "He is your father. He needs his rest."

Charlotte's favorite story about that time she'd told Zoë more than once: one morning the boys had burst in with a string of freshly caught trout, and their enthusiasm was so contagious that she exclaimed, "Oh, let's eat it at once!" She'd suddenly become possessed of a tremendous appetite. "Yes, yes!" they clamored, so she put on a robe and all five of them tiptoed down the stairs. It was barely dawn, and even Louisa wasn't awake yet. While Henry and Sam cleaned the fish, and Thaddy and Llewellyn set the table, Charlotte built up the fire and melted butter in two large frying pans. She had just put the fish on to fry and was slicing bread when Louisa appeared, darkening the door like a storm cloud.

"What do you imagine you're doing?" she demanded.

"Frying trout, as you can see," Charlotte told her. She said she'd learned not to be nettled by Louisa's petulant ways. "Did the smell wake you?" she asked politely, as Louisa stood in the doorway glaring. "Don't *gape*," Charlotte admonished the children, who had stopped their chores to gawk at their grandmother. It was true Louisa was quite a sight, Charlotte recalled, laughing—her nightcap askew, her voluminous nightgown blooming around her under the influence of the breeze unfurling gently up the cellar stairs.

"What smell?" Louisa cried shrilly, but at this the children collapsed completely.

"She must sleep with a clothespin on her nose!" Thaddy shouted.

"And cotton in her ears!" Llewellyn exclaimed.

"The fish, of course," Charlotte told her calmly. "It's so appetizing—I wonder it doesn't wake the dead."

"What have you set all these places out for? And for whom is all this bread sliced? To whom were you speaking?"

Louisa looked absolutely crazed with indignation, and the children were chortling and guffawing—it was all Charlotte could do not to join them.

"She's crazy!" they bellowed.

"She's out of her mind!"

"Let's burn her like a witch!"

"Let's set her nightgown on fire!"

"She's merely a bit grouchy," Charlotte whispered, bending down so Louisa wouldn't hear. "Come, boys, speak more respectfully to your grandmother," she added aloud. She didn't like Louisa to think she couldn't discipline her own children.

However, Louisa had fled—to hasten upstairs and pound on the door of Adam's room, it must have been, since that was the first time Adam had realized there was something awry in Charlotte's mind—but what happened *then*? It made Zoë crazy the way that Charlotte's stories would just break off and she'd have to piece everything together from so many different sources, or just get it out of the air somehow.

Unable to rouse him, Louisa goes in, but Adam is not in his bed, nor has his bed been slept in. Sick with foreboding—and with something else she dares not let herself think about—she hurries down the hall to Charlotte's room and flings open the door. Adam lies sound asleep on his back, an arm flung out across the side of the bed where Charlotte lay.

Louisa's mind writhes. How long has this state of affairs been transpiring—and under her very nose? Her mind coils and springs, coils again and springs further. How long? How long? How long have they been living as husband and wife without her knowledge? Keeping it from her on purpose, it is clear . . . Deceiving her, deceiving her; never letting her forget her own sin, her repudiation by Henry, without which she would not have sinned . . .

The agitated tangle of her thoughts devours her brain; if she does not smooth them out she will die, and suddenly she shrieks. She stands beside the bed, screaming and screaming. Adam sits bolt upright and cries, "Charlotte! What is it?" When he realizes that it is his mother who stands there, he leaps out of bed and grabs her by the shoulders. She collapses in his arms, sobbing, but he shoves her away, shouting at her, "Where is Charlotte? What's happened to Charlotte?" When Louisa will not speak, he seizes the pitcher of water from the washstand and flings it into her face.

"Where is my wife?"

Suddenly the tangle in Louisa's mind disentwines, but if her sobs change tone Adam doesn't notice.

"She's mad!" Louisa says, weeping. "She's lost her mind. I found her just now in the kitchen, talking to no one! She's set the table for five and sliced an entire loaf of bread! When I asked her what she was doing, she replied that she was frying fish!"

Unconvinced that his mother can be telling the truth, Adam pushes past her and hurries downstairs. By now Charlotte is sitting at the head of the table, offering an invisible platter to invisible companions. Sick at heart, Adam stares at her, yet in the moment before she notices him manages to regain control of himself. "Charlotte?" he asks gently. She looks up, and he sees uncertainty cross her face.

"I am sorry—I did not mean to wake you."

The fear in her voice breaks his heart. By a great effort of will he continues to speak quietly.

"I woke because you were not there, dear. Will you not return to bed?"

"All right," she replies, staring, confused, at the table. "But . . ."

"Never mind," he assures her. "Breakfast will wait."

She nods and lets him take her hand and lead her upstairs, past Louisa, who stands open-mouthed on the landing, into her bedroom, whose door he shuts. He helps her back into bed and then sits beside her, stroking her hair. For the first time since he's known her, she begins to cry.

"What is it, darling? Charlotte, what's wrong?"

"Oh, Adam," she falters, "don't hate them. Please don't hate them. It is not their fault."

"Hate whom?" he asks.

"Why, our children, of course! Whom did you think I meant?"

Adam can scarcely even begin to think about this, let alone how to reply, but finally he ventures, "I love you. Why would I hate our children?"

"Then you love them?" she gasps. "You love them as you do me?"

"Yes, Charlotte, I love them," he lies.

Now she cries from relief until she falls asleep in his arms.

When she awoke later in the morning, Adam told Monica (the only time he *ever* told her anything about her mother, the summer before she went to college), she appeared to have no recollection of what had happened; she had regained her usual composure, although she did seem somewhat distracted. After the midday meal, she went back to bed again to rest.

This time, while she slept, Adam forced Louisa to tell him everything she knew—which chiefly had to do with the clothes Charlotte made and Louisa sold—demanding to know how on earth she'd imagined that she had the right to keep this information from him.

"In her own way," Monica wrote Seth, "my paternal grandmother was a sick woman too. She allowed her son's 'sinful' union to endure beneath her roof; by not exposing it (after, of course, allowing it to take place to begin with), she must have felt she'd earned the right to exercise some control over their lives."

After his confrontation with Louisa, Adam had stormed off to see Dr. Jewell, and since old Dr. Jewell wasn't in he had to be content with Dr. Jewell's son Eldridge, Dr. Jewell, Jr.—younger than Adam by half a dozen years. Adam had never felt any confidence in the "whippersnapper," but since his father wasn't due back until that evening and Adam couldn't bear to wait that long to talk to someone, he'd decided that Dr. Jewell, Jr., would have to do.

After listening to Adam's story and studying Charlotte's medical history from his father's files, Eldridge Jewell inquired if it were possible that Charlotte be pregnant. Adam (so Monica told Seth) unbelievably replied that he did not see how—she was almost thirty-four years old, after all. "He was astonished to hear that women could conceive at fifty," Monica wrote. "Obviously he had had no idea that he was endangering his wife's health or he would never have returned to her bed." It struck young Dr. Jewell as quite plausible that a pregnancy might induce an episode of the nature that Adam described, considering Charlotte's history.

Eldridge Jewell could not lecture Adam as his father might have done, but he seemed to be trying to vanquish him with Greek and Latin terminology. After he'd explained that the word "hysteria" derives from the Greek for "womb," Adam lost patience.

"I think it would be best if your father examined Charlotte when he returns," he said. "She is accustomed to him."

Adam was terrified to think of how another pregnancy—which numerous doctors had already sworn could never be carried successfully to term—might permanently unsettle Charlotte's mind. He thought of Charlotte's sewing young boys' clothes for years—a melancholy enough pastime, to be sure, but was the occupation necessarily evidence of an unbalanced mind? Yet that morning he himself had witnessed her presiding at a table set for five, and she'd told him she'd been afraid that he didn't love their children . . .

That evening old Dr. Jewell stopped by to examine Charlotte and confirmed his son's suspicion—Charlotte was now between three and four months pregnant. However, to everyone's astonishment, Charlotte refused to believe it. She told Dr. Jewell that she had four children already—it would be beyond her capacities to care for a fifth. She recited their names to him quite matter-of-factly. It was impossible, Dr. Jewell said, to predict what was going to happen. If she'd consent to remain in bed . . . But she was clearly not to be persuaded on that score, now that the nausea and exhaustion were passing. He really couldn't say how the loss of another child would affect her mind. The only recommendation he could make was that Adam do his best not to contradict her; at least that way he wouldn't precipitate a crisis.

"Can you imagine what my poor father must have suffered?" Monica wrote Seth.

"What about your poor mother?" Seth wrote back.

Throughout her entire pregnancy Charlotte never once admitted what was happening. Dr. Eldridge Jewell, meanwhile, had managed to insinuate himself into the household—he was fascinated by Charlotte's mental state. His eagerness to study her case repelled and frightened Adam, and yet Eldridge Jewell was the only one of all the doctors who'd examined Charlotte who believed it possible that she might have a successful pregnancy. As every day went by, he told Adam, there was less cause for worry. Already Charlotte had carried this child longer than any of the others. The mind worked upon the body in mysterious ways, he said, and who were they to know what methods Charlotte might have of healing herself? Perhaps it was necessary to the continued health of both mother and child that Charlotte deny what was taking place inside her. Having read about psychoanalysis, Dr. Jewell, Jr., was convinced that in Charlotte's past lay hidden a dreadful dark secret, and that it had formed the basis of her illness. ("Can you imagine how my father must have felt?" Monica wrote. "He must have been terrified that Charlotte would give him away. Even though he'd decided that my mother had no idea that they were siblings, it seemed to him that her body could have been secretly rebelling against giving birth to her brother's child, and that somehow Eldridge Jewell had discerned this.") The four miscarriages, Dr. Jewell insisted, were clearly not sufficient in themselves to cause such imbalance of mind.

As Charlotte's pregnancy advances, Adam feels a yearning affection for his unborn child that he has never experienced before for any living creature. At night he curls against Charlotte's back, an arm over her belly, feeling the child impatiently kicking, and tells it to be patient, to wait until it is time to be born; when he is sure that Charlotte is asleep, he lays his cheek there, and whispers to it that he loves it, assuring it that as soon as Charlotte sees it she will love it also—she needs only to see it. He still blames himself for the deaths of the first four—though not anymore because they were the children of his sin with Charlotte; he sees, rather, that he did not love them enough; he did not believe in them and so they died. Charlotte had to do all the believing herself, and that is why she no longer has the strength to believe in this one. Through his secret communion with his not quite living child Adam begins to see life in a different way, and it strikes him for the first time that children are separate beings entirely, with no concern whatsoever for what their elders have done, right or wrong, and cannot be influenced by their sins or wrongdoing. The sins of the fathers, he thinks, are only said to be visited on the children by the *fathers*; the children need not accept them. He tells Charlotte silently that he understands now the loss she's suffered, and promises henceforth always to share her sorrows with her. If this child too should die, then he himself will lay another place at the table for it. Every night as long as they live their five children shall dine with them; they shall love them, and let the world be damned.

Adam, reversing his earlier position, now condemns Louisa for having kept the truth from him—Louisa, Timothy Lowndes, his father, perhaps Dr. Jewell—how can they have known and not told him? Is not the primary duty the old owe the young to tell them what they do not yet know, but need to, in order to act rightly? Everyone who should have carried out this trust on his behalf neglected it. Instead they left him to guess it, to absorb it through hints, dark looks, unexplained congruities. They allowed him even to imagine that he was somehow *privileged* to be endowed with such an original sin. Sin, he thinks, is unavoidable, yet it is perverse beyond expressing to feel indebted to someone for it. He, Adam vows, will never lie to *his* child—and it is then that the harsh fact hits him. How can he *not* lie? How can he *not* perpetuate this sordid inheritance of deceit? He cannot harm his child in the way that to confess the facts would so indelibly harm it. Perhaps on his deathbed he will be able to murmur the truth—but he is not even sure of this. How could he witness his child's disillusionment in him?

Louisa, meanwhile, perseveres in her own plans. Whenever she can manage to be alone with Charlotte she murmurs, "Who is the father? You need not fear that I will tell Adam."

When Charlotte gazes at her in bewilderment, Louisa says, "Oh, you may give up your pretense with me. I'm on your side. Our lives have been more similar than you know. Do you think I don't know what it is to have a husband who does not desire you? I do not blame you for seeking another's embrace. I wish to help you, Charlotte."

Charlotte never replies to these sallies. She merely sews quietly; the boys are outgrowing everything, and she has more to do than she has time for.

One day, when Charlotte is nearly eight months pregnant, as she and Louisa sit together in the back parlor in the late afternoon, Louisa, who has been reading the Bible aloud as Charlotte sews, sets down the book and says abruptly, "I am out of patience with you! I have tried to befriend you, but you think you do not need a friend. I wash my hands of you! Go on pretending it's not happening—you'll know soon enough that it is. And do you know what, Charlotte? When I hear you scream, I'll laugh. I tell you, I'll laugh. I hope it splits you in two."

Charlotte glances in amazement at Louisa; she is shocked to see that Louisa's face is contorted with hatred.

"You'll cry to God for mercy for your sins, but He will not listen. You'll beg Him to let you die to end your agony, but He will not. The others—your torturers, your jailors—will tell you to hush; they'll rip the bed clothes off you and hold your legs up and push on your belly. When you try to fight them off they'll tie your hands to the bedposts because you are nothing! Do you understand that? You are not alive anymore; they care only for the creature inside of you. You are only a receptacle. All those months it feeds upon you, a parasite, sapping your strength, bloating you, and then when it's ready it discards you like a useless shell. It doesn't care if *you* live, so long as *it* has life. Neither do the others. When they've finally pulled the child from between your thighs and you lie in your own blood, they hold the child aloft; they exclaim over it; they say how much it resembles its father; they say won't its father be proud, they must hurry to bathe it so he can come in to marvel at it. And then do you know what they do? Do you? They leave! They leave you all alone, lying in your blood; they don't even untie your hands. They forget to untie your hands!"

Charlotte is staring now at Louisa, who is no longer looking at her. Her face is as flinty as ever, her expression as harsh and unforgiving, but tears have run down her cheeks, leaving traces like water that has trickled prehistorically over rock.

"I couldn't bear the sight or sound of him. They brought him to me while I still lay on the bed and untied my wrists and laid him in my arms; they wanted me to give him my breast to suckle. As if it wasn't enough for it to have used me to force its way into the world, still it must feed on me, batten on me, and I felt its blind mouth opening and closing against me and I screamed. I shoved it from me and screamed for them to take it out of the room. They didn't ask me to feed him again. He would have died if it hadn't been for Ida."

Charlotte starts. "Ida?"

"Ida Howe," Louisa says impatiently. "She came to nurse him. Her own daughter had just been born and she nursed both of them. She told me I would feel differently about my child when my memory of the pain subsided, and I have heard other women say they forgot all about the pain as soon as it was over because they loved the child; they loved its father. But I loathed its father, who was not my husband, and I loathed my husband more, for letting me go to the bed of another. They both played upon my weakness. All I wanted was to be loved—it is all anyone wants—but Henry did not love me and he was happy when Timothy courted me. I allowed Timothy's attentions only to make Henry jealous, but he did not care. He told me, 'You are free to do as you like, and I to do as I do.

Neither of us shall reproach the other.' When the baby was born, I was at Henry's mercy, and he knew it. After that he wasn't even circumspect or private—he would tell me about the woman he loved, and how much more beautiful she was than I. 'If she would have married me,' he said, 'I would never have given you a second look.' He played the proud father, but said to me afterwards, 'You may pass him off as mine, so long as I need have nothing to do with him.' And people wonder why I have never been able to love my son! Dr. Jewell wondered why I refused to give him my breast. That was why Ida . . ." She glances at Charlotte and, looking at her strangely, adds, ". . . why you had to come.

"Yet when I watched you feeding him—feeding my child—I envied you. You looked so peaceful, and I wondered if I had made a mistake—if I would not have grown to love him if I had let him take his nourishment from me. One day—I never told you this, Ida," she says shyly, "but one day, while you were in the garden, I went up to the nursery. He was sleeping and when I lifted him he did not wake. I sat down in the rocking chair, where you always sat, and I unbuttoned my blouse. I held the baby's head close to my breast just as you did and even in his sleep his mouth fastened on it. I swallowed my revulsion, but then he stopped sucking and began to whimper. I gave him my other breast and he tried to suck there but again stopped and began to cry bitterly.

"I had forgotten, of course, that I no longer had milk. And I was in such a rage then, I wanted to kill him. That was all I wanted. I sat there, my breast still bare, and plotted how to murder my son. Though he was no longer mine—you had stolen him from me. I schemed how I should kill him, somehow so that it would seem to be an accident. I could smother him, I thought, but I feared there would be signs. Poison, I then thought, but I did not know how to procure any without arousing suspicion. I could let him fall, pretending to slip while descending the stairs, but the thought that he might merely be crippled, and live to accuse me, prevented me."

Louisa smiles strangely, privately. Charlotte watches her, but Louisa is not looking at Charlotte any longer. Dusk is descending and the sitting room has grown dim, yet neither stirs to light a lamp. Louisa's fingers twist like captive snakes in her lap, but when she speaks her voice is trancelike.

"I couldn't let it happen again. You understand, don't you, Ida? I couldn't endure it another time."

Charlotte gazes at Louisa, then asks quietly, "How did you kill the others?" She speaks in a conversational tone, and Louisa replies similarly.

"There were two," she says. "I had tried to refuse Timothy my bed but

I could not. He told me he would let the entire town know who Adam's real father was if I denied him. He's a mean-spirited man, is Timothy—don't be fooled by his meek manner. The first time I waited until I thought the child was large enough, then took a syringe the veterinary used for the horses; I filled it with lye and injected it through myself into the child. It was born, dead, within three days. It was painful to me, but not as painful as the first time, and knowing it was not alive I cared little that I suffered in being rid of it. I think Dr. Jewell suspected me. Then I was lucky and did not conceive again for five years. You had left Harmony by then. That time, I made sure not to let anyone know I had conceived, since I suspected Dr. Jewell of having warned the servants that I should be watched closely. For four months I opened a vein in one of the horse's legs to bloody rags lest they suspect. By then I was desperate—I knew I could not try poison again. Finally I could think of nothing else to do except throw myself down the stairs. I broke an arm, but was lucky, and miscarried. You can imagine how I rejoiced when Dr. Jewell informed me that I would never be able to have another child. You understand why I had to do it, don't you?"

"Yes, I understand," Charlotte says. "Yes, Louisa."

She speaks gently, but there must be something in her tone that alerts Louisa, for she looks up sharply. It is now too dark to see clearly, but nevertheless Louisa leans forward.

"Ida?" she queries.

Charlotte says nothing.

"Ida?" Louisa repeats, her voice quavering. "You are Ida, aren't you?"

"You know who I am." Charlotte speaks quietly. "I do not judge you, Louisa."

"But who *are* you?" Louisa demands again. She rises to light a lamp. When she sees Charlotte, she whitens, and opens her mouth as if to take in more air. But her eyes widen and grow wild and she cries out, "You're not Ida! You've tricked me!"

"I didn't trick you, Louisa. I'm Charlotte, Ida's daughter. Your son Adam's wife. You know that."

"You!" Louisa hisses. Fear and anger distort her face. "You forced a confession from me! You bewitched me!" She gives a low cry and falls to her knees, sobbing wildly. "I told you! I told you everything! You're the devil! I've always known it! You're the devil!"

"Louisa, calm yourself!" Charlotte exclaims, and rises to go to her, but Louisa stumbles to her feet and runs, staggering, from the room.

That was the last time Charlotte saw Louisa alive. She hanged herself in the horse barn later that night. Dr. Jewell couldn't give the exact time of Louisa's death, since her body wasn't found until ten the next morning. The time of death could have been anywhere between midnight and four o'clock.

At first, Adam tried to keep Charlotte from finding out how Louisa had died, but she heard the servants talking. After Louisa's body had been taken to Taplin's Funeral Parlor, Charlotte told Adam what Louisa had confessed to her—except for the news about Timothy Lowndes. She couldn't see any point, she told Zoë, in telling him something that would only upset him for no reason; he was so proud of being Henry Robie's son.

Zoë didn't say anything when her grandmother told her this, but it was one time when she wondered if there weren't something devious in her grandmother after all. She seemed so totally innocent, and yet she'd sat there, letting Louisa think she was Ida, knowing Louisa would never have told her those things otherwise; when Louisa ran out Charlotte hadn't gone after her to see if she was all right; she had let her husband die believing he was someone else's son. Even if she never suspected that Henry was her father (which seemed almost impossible) she was certainly casual about her decision to keep such important information to herself. It seemed to Zoë that her grandmother, even if she'd never realized it, must have resented her husband—his mother too—for never having understood how agonizing it had been to lose four children. She'd found her own way of taking revenge for the guilt and pain that had driven her into a world of fantasy because she couldn't stand to stay in the real one.

Adam would have discredited Charlotte's story as another product of her diseased imagination, he told Monica, except that when he mentioned it to the elder Dr. Jewell, Dr. Jewell said that he'd always suspected something along those lines. Moreover, Charlotte seemed more levelheaded than she had in a long time. It was as if there were only so much sanity to go around in any one family, and when Louisa relinquished her claim upon it, Charlotte could stake hers.

Then, at the beginning of May, a little early, Charlotte is safely delivered of a daughter. Throughout the nearly thirty hours she is in labor, she is weirdly calm. When the baby is finally placed in her arms, she looks at it tenderly, and when Adam enters the room and sees this he is so overwhelmed with happiness he can't speak. Charlotte's first words dispell it.

"It is sad for a child to be without a mother," she says. "I will try to be very good to her."

Later, when Adam and Dr. Jewell have left her alone, the boys tiptoe into the room and peer with great solemnity at the sleeping infant their mother cradles in her arms.

"We will take good care of her, too," they promise, "the poor orphan."

"You are good boys," Charlotte praises them. "It is very generous of you to share your mother."

She tells them that the baby will be named Harmony Ida Robie after the town and after their grandmother.

"Harmony Ida!" they sing, dancing about the room. "Harmony Ida! Harmony Ida Robie!" They list all the things they will teach her—to fish, ride, swim, find birds' nests . . . They vow to protect her from all harm. No girl, Charlotte thinks, could ask for more devoted brothers.

XVIII SPARTA

The End of Slavery was an unmitigated smash. You could tell the difference between polite parent clapping and sincere clapping, and this was undoubtedly the latter. It was the third and final night of the performance and, standing on stage, holding hands with Rob and with Rhonda Armitage, who had played the nun, bowing each time the heavy red curtain shot up again, Zoë was already almost crying. The audience was clamoring, "Author! Author!" and then Laura Jenkins came out, all dolled up in a fancy green and blue striped dress and matching blue high heels, and everyone cheered. She even had blue eye shadow on. Mr. Montgomery dashed out on stage with a big bunch of roses and kissed her and everyone went crazy. It was amazing how people could seem to be cheering at the top of their lungs and then you'd find out they actually hadn't been. How loud *could* they get? Then Rob's father standing ovationed—ovated, that was what Rob called it—so of course everybody else had to stand too. "Oh, Jesus," Rob groaned. His parents had been having conniption fits ever since they'd found out that their one leg was going to be on stage. Seth and Monica had come opening night.

When the curtain came down the fourth time and stayed down, thank God, Zoë raced ahead of everyone else to the dressing room. She just wanted to grab her clothes and get out of there before she had to talk to anyone. She had nearly made it; she had turned the corner of the last hall when she heard the clump-slide, clump-slide of Rob's hurrying after.

"Hey, hold on! Is the place on fire? What's the matter?"

She didn't answer but he followed her right into the girls' dressing room.

"Zoë, what's the story? Aren't you speaking to me?"

"Oh, God, everybody's coming!"

He looked at her, then said, "One way to fix that," and shut and locked the door.

"Now they'll *really* know something's going on," she said, but she sat down at the dressing table and hid her face in her arms.

"So let them."

Footsteps came closer and someone tried the door. "Who's in there?" Rhonda shouted, pounding.

"Just hold your horses!" Rob shouted.

By then other people were also banging and yelling. "What's going on in there?"

"Take a slow trip to Outer Mongolia!"

Zoë couldn't help laughing, and Rob sat down beside her on the old piano bench, facing the opposite way, and nudged her with his shoulder.

"I know. You're so moved by the characters' nobility."

"It's just because the play's over," she said.

Rob didn't answer, but after a minute he slid around to face her way on the bench and put his arm around her shoulders.

"How can you cry over the stupidest play in the universe?" he asked, but in a nice way. He patted her hair once or twice, and she leaned her head against his shoulder for a second. He didn't seem to mind. They just kept sitting there.

"What the hell are you *doing* in there?" Rhonda shouted.

"*Unwinding!*" Rob shouted back.

Zoë laughed again. Then she sat up. "What am I going to do? I'd rather die than face them now."

"Perhaps there's a less desperate solution." He looked around the room. "You could disguise yourself, although that probably wouldn't work. They're almost that dumb, but not quite. Hey, wait a minute—I've got it! You can climb out onto the roof! I'll wait long enough for you to go around to the other side of the building before I let the plebeians in."

"But how will I get down?"

"As soon as I've changed I'll get a ladder from the maintenance shed and come and get you."

"What if it's locked?"

"I'll break the door down. Don't *worry*. Just wait on the side by the science lab."

"All right."

It was an insane idea, but that was the only kind she had any interest in at the moment. She dried her eyes and they moved the piano bench beneath the smallish, high-up window and with Rob making another step with his hands she managed to get through and jumped down to the roof.

"You okay?"

"Fine."

"I'll count to ten. Go."

She was on the roof of the veranda that went around three sides of the mansion. It wasn't steep at all, and the administration had had to take down all the rose trellises because students were always trying to climb onto the roof and crashing through the trellises and breaking arms and legs. However, the silvery sandals that Laura Jenkins had forced her to wear in the last act after Anne-Marie regained her sight and cared about her appearance kept coming off when she tried to hurry. If she took them off, though, the sharp gravel pierced her feet. Finally she reached the windows of the lab and sat down with her back against the wall to wait. She thought of all the mice and hamsters and snakes inside, curled up, waiting in terror for the next science class to start. Mr. Weyland, the science teacher, also brought in run-over animals, even cats, if they weren't too far gone and made the class dissect them.

Why was she thinking about that now? Her mind was a trampoline—she came down for a minute but then bounced right off into the ozone. She hadn't been on a trampoline since Myra Ogilvy had suddenly gone away to live with her mother in fourth grade. One minute she'd been feeling as if everything was over, she'd never be that close to Rob again, and then the next minute she found out he loved her and she was so happy she felt like jumping off the roof. I love you, she said to the night air. I love you, Rob. Soon she would be telling him.

Who cared what anyone else thought? About them, about anything. Why Seth and Monica and all her ancestors were so sick in the head and whether she was going to end up like them and why Nick wasn't on her side anymore; why Bridget was not to be trusted and why everyone changed their feelings about things as they got older except for her. It was immaterial now. It felt as if nothing—even huge buildings—were really stuck in place or weighed very much, and furthermore Rob would know precisely what she meant. He said it was easy for him to believe in invisible things, growing up around a father who always talked about neutrons and protons as if they were household pets, but that it was amazing *she* had managed not to get brainwashed. Everyone was always trying to convince you that what you couldn't see wasn't there, just because they'd given up. They recognized the truth when they were kids but then most people became lazy cowards and convinced themselves that the way the world was was the way it had to be. "You watch," he said. "In five years all our so-called peers who are now ranting and raving about the terrible state of the universe, people starving, injustice, even Archie Tannenbaum and his protest marches—they'll be saying, 'Well, it sure is a shame, but that's life.' Mark my words. 'Mark my words . . .'

Shut up, Robert," he said to himself. When she was with him, she knew that what he said was true; she just wished she could not be so influenced when she was on her own.

It was a clear, breezy night, only three weeks left of school. At the end of June she and Nick were going to Harmony for two months. They'd started going by themselves after Mexico. Monica and Seth had had another whole humongous correspondence about it. Monica found it "increasingly painful to spend time in her mother's presence," and considering that she thought Charlotte "scarcely noticed whether she were there or not" she'd just as soon remain in Sparta. "Let the kids go. Their company seems to cheer her up. No doubt I simply remind her—as much as she's capable of being reminded, that is—of things she'd rather forget." What things? Her mother's dead brothers? The notes went on and on, but they never went into enough detail. Monica and Seth argued about whether they should take Charlotte off her medication (medication for what?)—Eldridge Jewell (Dr. Jewell) thought no harm could come of it, but, as Seth knew (Monica wrote), her opinion of him was not of the highest. (Why not?) Seth wrote back, "Is it really fair to keep your mother a lobotomized automaton for the rest of her life? How can it hurt anyone even if she does lapse back into her harmless fantasies?" Monica said he didn't know what he was talking about. It was all very well for him to "deliver judgment from on high," but he wasn't the one who'd "felt the effects. They weren't 'harmless fantasies,' Seth—they were full-fledged psychotic hallucinations. You didn't spend the first years of your life believing you had four invisible brothers who loved you more than life itself only to find that your mother had invented them!"

The last couple of years Bridget had come up for two weeks in August but this year she wasn't going to because she was in a summer production with the rep and then some old friends of her parents from France (her father had fought with the man in the war, of course) were coming for a month with their son, who was thinking of going to college in the U.S. Zoë didn't really care, seeing how full of herself Bridget was lately, but she'd already been feeling sad about leaving Rob. She'd been trying to think if there was some way for him to come up, although in a way she couldn't imagine him in Harmony—she couldn't see him hanging out with Buell and Dwight Magoon, helping with the haying, going swimming in the witch pond and the Connecticut. Even aside from his leg, he seemed too citified. She felt bad thinking that, though. However, if they started things up before she left, then wrote letters all summer, by fall they'd be more in love than ever.

She watched the dark trees swaying in the breeze. When there wasn't any wind, you could hear the bay sloshing down at the pier. The school was five miles from Sparta on a peninsula called Hollister Point—named after a Senator Hollister, who had built the mansion as a summer retreat for his family when Sparta took a lot longer to get to from Washington than it did now. He'd had seven children, but his youngest daughter had died of tuberculosis and after that he would never come out to the summer home anymore. Near the end of his life he supposedly went off the deep end and thought that his daughter, who had been buried in a cemetery in Washington, would never rest in peace if she weren't buried out at the Point, because she'd loved it so much out there, and he'd been caught in the middle of the night digging up her grave like Heathcliff so he could move her coffin. It was probably just a story, but everyone pretended that her ghost haunted the school and that you'd see her if you hung out there at night.

Zoë thought about the story now, as she watched the trees, but she didn't feel afraid. Had the same trees been there? What kind were they? Oak? Not that it mattered. To botanists, maybe, but there weren't any botanists on the roof. "Botanist on the roof, meet Fiddler on the roof . . ." How old had the girl been when she died? Had she been old enough to be in love? It wouldn't be so sad to die if you had loved someone. She wouldn't even mind dying right now—not that she particularly wanted to, but she wouldn't mind.

She had no idea how long it had been when she heard someone dragging something across the grass. She got up and stepped carefully to the roof's edge. Rob said, "Ahoy there," and propped the ladder up against the gutter. She threw her sandals onto the lawn, and he held the ladder while she climbed down. The grass was nice and soft, so she carried her shoes in one hand while, with the other, she lifted one end of the ladder to help Rob carry it back to the shed. "You carried this all the way by yourself?" she exclaimed. "It weighs a ton!"

"Fathers," he said. "I nabbed a couple. I told them we needed it to take down lighting. Gullible city. They brought it to the side door for me and then I dragged it from there. Fortunately the maintenance shed wasn't locked."

"I'll say. I can just see spending all night on the roof. What did they say in the dressing room?"

"Nothing. They thought I'd been having a psychotic episode. They didn't know you'd been in there."

She laughed, imagining people thinking that Rob had locked himself in the girls' dressing room. Hadn't anyone wondered where she was? When they had stuck the ladder back into the shed, he said, "Well, now what are you going to do?"

"I thought your parents wanted to take you out."

"I already told them I'd decided to go to the cast party."

"Are you?"

"Am I what?"

"Going to the cast party."

"Are you?"

"I don't know. I guess I don't really feel like it."

"My sentiments precisely. It's bad enough being with our fellow actors when they're dressed up as monkeys and nuns—who wants to see them as their real selves? All they'll be doing is rehashing the play. I'd like to erase it from my life as soon as possible."

"You would?"

"Wouldn't you?"

"I don't know. I guess."

"Well, what do you propose we do instead? Want to go for a walk?"

"Sure."

"We could go down by the water."

It didn't bother her that everything they said was so mundane. Once he kissed her they would be able to say whatever they wanted. They headed across the lawn past the two brick and marble cupolas with Doric columns that the Hollister children must have played in or Senator Hollister and his wife must have sat in to drink mint juleps on summer afternoons. Maybe he'd carried his daughter who died out to lie in it when she was sick.

They crossed over the little pagoda bridge between two sections of the rose gardens and walked out onto the playing field. From the far end of the field a path led down to the bay. She was carrying one shoe in each hand, but now she shifted them into the hand away from Rob so that if he tried to hold her hand he wouldn't find a shoe in it. However, he didn't.

She listened to the difference in their footsteps, her even ones, so that she had to concentrate on one foot or the other for there to be a downbeat, and his more lopsided ones, which she had to be careful not to copy through listening to so closely. He would have noticed if she had.

The dark grass was cool but not wet, and in the far corner of the field Rob suddenly said, "Want to take a breather?" Her heart started beating like crazy—this was it, but she just said "Sure," and he lay down on his back. She lay down beside him, close enough so that he could reach her but not so that she'd be being forward and then they lay there, side by side but not touching, looking up separately at the sky. It was crammed with stars.

Rob said, "I can't stand those people who always have to point out which constellation is which."

"I know."

"What do they think they're trying to prove? The stars aren't even *there*, did you know that?"

"What?"

"We're just seeing light that started out somewhere else years ago. It takes that long to get here."

"I don't believe you."

"Swear to God."

"You don't even believe in God."

"I can still swear to him, can't I? Besides, God is probably like the stars. He, or she, or *it*, may have really existed but by the time the concept got to us the original was somewhere else. I do *think* about God on occasion, you know. I mean, I'm not religious, exactly, but I do have occasional fits of reverence."

" 'Fits of reverence . . .' "

"I think the religions people have now are on their way out. The Bible itself basically says so. Whoever wrote it knew Christianity would self-destruct in a couple of thousand years."

"What are you talking about?"

"Armageddon. The Apocalypse. The Second Coming. What's the matter with you, haven't you read the Bible?"

"I've basically only read the Old Testament." Why was he bringing all this up now?

"No wonder. I'm going to have to have a talk with your parents, not giving you a proper religious upbringing."

"Go right ahead."

"I will. First thing Monday morning."

He didn't say anything else, and she hoped he wouldn't keep talking. She felt how he would turn on his side and she would have her eyes closed and then when she opened them he'd be looking into them and would touch her face with his hand, saying her name, and she would smile and he'd tell her he loved her. She would say "I love you, too, Rob," and then he would kiss her. Or maybe she would say "I love you" first but only after he'd looked into her eyes and then when she said it he'd be so overwhelmed he would kiss her passionately.

She waited, sometimes with her eyes closed, sometimes with them open, looking up at the sky, but she was concentrating so intensely on when he was going to kiss her that after a while it was as if her thoughts came loose and she forgot all about him. Everything was waiting. The grass, the trees at the edge of the field, and above them the stars, like pinpricks in dark cloth which a light beyond sparkled through. Everything was breathing—breathing but using her breath. Why were they waiting? What were they waiting for? Didn't he love her after all? But she knew he did. It felt like she loved him with everything around them; the way people said they loved someone with all their heart, she loved him with the smell of the grass, with the fluttery wind in the trees standing on the sidelines like spectators, with the stars flickering. Didn't he *know* that? Didn't he feel it? Why didn't he kiss her? This last time on stage, when they'd had to "embrace, overwhelmed with passion" she had pretended it was really him she was kissing, not Louis, and she was sure he had guessed, the way he'd looked at her in a quick, careful way when they'd let each other go—it was Rob looking at her, not Louis, and it was as if all of a sudden he'd *realized*, but then the play had ended and they would never play those parts again. And now here was their chance, their only chance, but he didn't move. Why didn't he move? Why? It felt as if her whole body was listening to him; she could hear him breathing, and every time he breathed deeper her heart beat faster, but he never moved. They just kept lying there, without speaking, looking up at the stars, until something had not happened. They lay there until the moment that could have changed their lives forever and made the whole universe different had gone by. They must have done it on purpose.

Rob spoke first—he said, "I suppose we should be heading back; it's getting sort of late," yet he sounded so far away, so *hopeless* that she suddenly thought, Was it *her* fault? Was she supposed to have done something? Had he been waiting for her to make the first move?

Oh, Rob, I'm sorry, I'm so sorry! But how could she say it? What if he said, Sorry about what? But why hadn't he hinted? Why hadn't he given her some sign? Instead they had let the time slide by, just lain there and watched it slide by in the sky, and now they could never get it back.

Walking off the field, she wished they *could* die; not die the way she wouldn't have minded, earlier, waiting for Rob out on the roof when everything was full of hope, but die because there was nothing left. She wished they could be found lying on the wet cold grass in the morning; at least then other people would know they'd been together. Mr. Eggert the maintenance man would find them; he would call Mr. Curley first—no, the police, then the headmaster, who would call their parents. Seth and Monica would draw together in their sorrow. The whole school would come to their funeral. Would they have just one funeral? Bridget, of course, would try to prevent it.

Thinking about Bridget only made her feel worse. She had really been looking forward to the day when she could tell Bridget she was in love with Rob and that he loved her back—when Bridget reacted disgustedly she'd just say, "Bridget, I really could care less what you think. We know what you did five years ago, ruining our friendship then; we're not going to give you that pleasure again." She would have been completely invulnerable. Not that she intended to give Bridget any details, the way Bridget did every single time *she* went out with someone. Now she had this boyfriend from the college and she liked nothing better than to tell Zoë exactly how far they'd gone. Zoë had planned how, when Bridget asked her what she'd done with Rob, to say, "That's private." It would *kill* Bridget. But now she couldn't say anything. Bridget would be able to tell if she made something up.

The school was dark and locked now. It looked heavy and cruel, part of the end of things. Its whiteness was like a sheet over a corpse. Since it was so far out on the peninsula, no cars would be heading into Sparta until they got to the highway, which was almost two miles. It was late and all the people who lived out on the peninsula would either be home or coming home. It was only when they stepped onto the gravel driveway that Zoë realized she'd forgotten her shoes. Rob offered to go back for them but she said, "Don't bother." "What's eating you?" he asked. "*Nothing*," she exclaimed.

As they walked they didn't talk except when she'd occasionally step on a pebble on the paved road and say, "Damn it," and Rob would say, "I *offered* to go back for your shoes." "I know! Just forget it, all right?" "How can I forget it when you keep swearing every other minute?" By the time they got to the highway and started hitchhiking, she could tell he couldn't stand her; when they finally made it back to town after four different rides they didn't even say good night. It was Saturday, and all day Sunday and Sunday night went by without either of them calling the other—ever since they'd started rehearsing they'd seen each other every weekend and talked on the phone most days they didn't; they hadn't only talked about the play, even though that was the ostensible reason they called. Rob would ride the bus in from where he lived and they'd go to the drugstore and get sodas or go over to the campus and shoot pool in the game room or go down to the harbor and sit on the docks—all the things she'd used to do with Bridget before Bridget started spending all her time hanging out with more *impressive* people.

Now not only didn't she have Bridget anymore, she didn't have Rob either; how she was going to get through the rest of the year she had no idea. On Monday she almost pretended to be sick, but she was afraid if she did she'd feel worse; it would be better just to face it than to spend all day thinking about it. She felt as if everyone in the whole school would know what had happened; Rob had probably called up various people and told them how she'd had this big fantasy he loved her just because he'd been nice to her when she was upset and how awkward it was for him. Well, he didn't need to worry. She wasn't going to embarrass *him* again.

What happened, however, was even worse. As soon as she got to school people started making suggestive remarks and it was clear that they simply assumed she and Rob were going together. It was so awkward she couldn't believe it. She tried to avoid him but at recess they happened to be standing near each other and she heard Mike Janacek, Laura Jenkins's boyfriend, say to Rob, "Hey, man, why don't the two of you go to the drive-in with us some weekend? We'll get a six-pack, live it up . . ." Rob knew she'd heard and looked over at her and shrugged. She felt a moment of hope until she realized he just didn't want her to embarrass him. She didn't know what to do so she just shrugged back. When Mike had gone Rob came over and said stiffly, "I'm sorry. I didn't know what to say. 'Excuse me, but you've made a terrible mistake'? Don't worry, I'm sure he'll forget all about it." "I'm not worried," she said. He just walked off.

After that she started having dreams about him all the time. They'd be out in the field and Rob would lean over and kiss her. Walking along the road to town they'd hold hands. In other places she'd never seen he'd embrace her tenderly; he'd lie beside her and kiss her; he'd stroke her hair. She hated waking up after them.

Finally, about a week and a half after the play, Rob called her up and asked her out. They'd hardly even said hello since that Monday. He sounded strange, as if they'd never talked on the phone before and didn't even know each other.

"I wondered if maybe you wanted to go to the movies or something," he said.

"What movie?" she said. "I mean, sure."

"Don't do me any favors," he said.

"What are you talking about?"

"Nothing. Forget it."

When she met him downtown, though, things were more normal. After they got the tickets, since it was still early, they walked up to the

Statehouse and sat on a bench and he said, "I hope you realize that you and I are madly in love, by the way."

"What?"

"According to the rabble." When she didn't say anything, he added, "I am completely not a democrat, if you know what I mean. I think there's a case to be made for absolute monarchy—with me as king, of course. That would be a first, wouldn't it? A king with one leg. Imagine such idiots as we're surrounded with being able to *vote* in a couple of years."

"Why? I mean, why them in particular?"

"It's a terrifying prospect, that's all. I shudder to think."

She couldn't figure out what he was up to. He only used tacky expressions like "shudder to think" when he was angry or making fun of someone but what did *he* have to be angry about? She refused to cooperate with the way he was trying to get out of everything.

The movie they saw was *Women in Love*; it was embarrassing watching the sex scenes and the naked wrestling parts with Rob, but afterward he just said he doubted that D. H. Lawrence would have been very happy about the film. "Why not?" she asked, and he was starting to tell her, sounding more like his old self than he'd sounded since before the play was over—he could get worked up over things that had nothing to do with him—and they were about to go down and sit on the docks when they saw Laura and Mike come out of the theater; they had their arms around each other's waists and Laura's hair was all messed up.

"Here comes trouble," Rob said under his breath.

Naturally Mike spotted them right away and waved. Rob nodded at him but when he looked at her he rolled his eyes.

"One vote apiece," he whispered. "Remember."

She laughed and he said in a low, serious voice, "We have to do something about this."

"About what?" she asked, but then Mike and Laura were there, and they all stood around, and then Mike suggested they get a six-pack and all drive out to Stover Beach and look at the moon. He winked at Rob and she thought for sure he was going to say, "No thanks, Mike, not tonight," but once again he shrugged and looked at her. Why was he always leaving things up to her? "I don't care," she said. "If you want to." "Do *you*?" he asked. What did he mean? Did he mean did she want to make out? That was all anyone did at Stover Beach. She'd never been there, but Bridget had kept her fully informed—"Once we drove in and we saw someone's derrière gleaming through a car window at us like the moon."

She had never been able to get the picture out of her mind. Bridget said, "Of course, all the high school guys do is brag about how far they got the next day." She laughed her new laugh. "Sam Tannenbaum told me that if he were a girl he'd join a convent."

"What kind of stuff do they talk about?"

"Just how far they can go, whether you'll blow them or not and so on."

"*Blow* them?"

"Give them blow jobs."

"What does that mean?"

"You're really living in the Dark Ages, aren't you?"

"Just tell me."

"Oh, God," Bridget said. "It's when you suck a guy's dick until he comes."

"*What?*"

"You heard me."

"What do you mean, until he comes?"

"You *have* to know what that means."

"I know, I mean I guess, but, I mean, in your *mouth*?"

"I think it would be sort of interesting, actually."

"You mean you'd *do* it?"

"I don't know. How should I know? The situation hasn't exactly yet . . . arisen." Then Bridget cackled like a banshee.

"Come on, you old stick-in-the-mud," Mike said now. He grinned at Zoë. "You old stick-in-the-muds, plural."

"*Sticks*-in-the-mud, actually," Rob said.

"Oh, God, Mr. Grammar. Go dangle some participles, why don't you?"

Rob rolled his eyes at her, intending Mike to see this time, but he said, "Oh, what the hell, Zoë, let's mingle with the common folk. But just for a little while, okay?" he said to Mike. "With all the enemy troops about we don't like to be out very late."

"Sure, man, we'll just have a squint at the view and come on home."

On the way Mike drove by a package store, went in and came out with the beer. He waved his fake I.D. at Rob. "I know where you can get one if you want one."

"I'll let you know," Rob said.

When they got out of town Mike handed a couple of bottles and a bottle opener back to them. Rob opened one and took a swig.

"I didn't know you drank beer," she said.

"When in Rome . . ."

He offered it to her, and she took a sip. She hoped he wouldn't keep passing it to her.

Before they were even there, Laura was pressed so tightly up against Mike that three more people could have fit in the front seat. She was nuzzling his ear—they could actually see her sticking her tongue in it.

"Whoa there, woman!" Mike said, then turned and winked at Rob.

Rob gave him a sort of lopsided smile. Then he leaned over and whispered to her, "This was a grave error."

Mike looked over his shoulder again and said, "Don't mind us."

The instant the car was parked Mike turned to Laura and said, "Okay, sweetie pie, you asked for it," and they began making out like crazy and soon disappeared from view and Zoë and Rob heard noises of unzipping and both of them moaning. After a second Mike sort of sat up again and glanced at them once more over his shoulder, a zombie look on his face, and said, "Take your time, don't you?" But then he arched his back and closed his eyes, saying, "Oh, baby, bad girl," and then leaned forward again. They heard more clothes being rearranged and then more smacking and slurping noises besides all the moans.

Were Mike and Laura actually *doing* it? But how could they be in that position? For several minutes she and Rob just sat completely frozen, but then he took hold of her arm and whispered, "Come on."

For one insane moment she thought he meant, Come on, they should do the same thing, but as she was giving in to the idea—this was how it was going to happen, this was how she was going to make love for the first time, in the back of Mike Janacek's *car* while he and Laura Jenkins were making sound effects in the front seat—Rob was opening the door as quietly as he could, not that anyone could have heard anything over the slurps and groans coming from the front seat. When they were safely out and he'd shut the door she couldn't help glancing back; what she saw was worse than anything she could have imagined in her worst nightmares. Laura's head was going up and down but then, while she was watching, suddenly they both did a flip-flop and then Mike's white *rear end* was going up and down over Laura's *face*. It was everything Bridget had said, and more. She couldn't help staring, but then she heard Rob say softly, "Pigs."

He had turned and was walking away fast, which made his limp more obvious. She caught up with him but didn't say anything. When they were out of the parking area he said, "I'm really, really sorry, Zoë. I should have known. I guess I thought that if we went once they'd stop bugging us. I'm sorry you had to go through it."

His voice sounded really tragic.

"Don't worry about it," she said. "I'll recover."

It was true she'd felt disgusted at first but now she didn't. She wondered why. She kept seeing Mike's white bottom going up and down, like a ball someone was bouncing, and it was what Bridget had told her about—he'd been giving Laura a blow job; he'd had his thing in her mouth and was forcing her to suck on him until he had a climax. Except it wasn't as bad for some reason actually seeing it as imagining it when Bridget talked about it. She even wondered what it felt like. Did Laura like it? She must have or she wouldn't have started everything. Mike seemed cruel yet masterful. Zoë kept thinking of the way he had just turned Laura over and knelt above her, making her do it; he even called her "baby," groaning with ecstasy. Zoë felt as if a fuzz had been cleared off her thinking.

Everything seemed completely different than it had only a week ago when they'd lain out on the playing field and she'd wanted Rob to kiss her. She'd wanted him to kiss her more than she'd wanted anything in her life, but did that mean she'd wanted him to do what Mike was doing to Laura? Did she want *Mike* to do that to her and not Rob? What was Rob thinking? Did it really disgust him or did he just think it ought to? It seemed kind of cowardly either way.

"Well," he said, "we certainly seem to have a penchant for getting stranded on country roads in the middle of the night."

"You can say that again," she said.

"We certainly seem to have a penchant . . ."

"Very funny."

He was acting so infantile. Didn't he ever want to do anything except make smart remarks? When they got back to town he asked her if she still felt like going down to the harbor, but she said she was kind of tired—maybe another night.

"Suit yourself," he said.

"What's that supposed to mean?" she asked.

"I was under the impression I was speaking English."

"Oh God."

"Well, thank you, I had a delightful time."

She almost said, Oh, shut up, but she just said, "Good night. Thanks for the movie. See you on Monday."

There was only a week of school left now. She felt sort of empty, but better since she'd realized it was Rob's problem, not hers. Maybe Bridget had even been right about him. She was in a kind of depressed yet calm state, but then on Tuesday, during phys ed, when everyone was heading into the locker room to change into their hockey uniforms, Laura Jenkins came over to her and said—it was the first time she'd seen her since the weekend—in a voice so people could hear, "Just like to *watch*, huh? What's the matter, are you *frigid*? Think you're too good for everyone? Why don't you let Rob go out with someone who'll give him what he deserves?" She walked away before Zoë could say anything. Everyone was staring, including Bridget. Zoë didn't even dare look at her. Even though people came up afterward and told her Laura was an asshole, she knew what Laura said was true, and after that everything was much worse than it had been in the first place. She saw that what had really happened was that she'd made Rob so uncomfortable he couldn't act naturally. He hadn't been uncomfortable because he thought she was a sex maniac but because he thought she was a cold fish. But now it was way too late to fix anything.

The worst, though, was that there was no one, *no one*, she could talk to about it. Some girls could talk to their mothers, but the idea of talking to Monica about blow jobs was like asking the president questions about Kotex. Once she might have asked Bridget's advice but now Bridget would just lord it over her. Once she could have even asked Rob—not specifically, exactly, but he would have told her what he knew—but now she could hardly even say hello to him without feeling all ashamed.

The strange thing was, he didn't seem annoyed with her; in fact he was being really nice and kept calling her to do things, even after school was out until she left for Harmony, but she couldn't get over thinking he was just doing it because he felt sorry for her. She couldn't believe she'd once felt more comfortable talking to him than to anyone except Bridget when they were younger.

The last night before she left, they went to another movie—it was a scary and disgusting movie about a woman sleeping with a devil and having his baby and eating raw liver, but it seemed to Zoë to be about everything that she already had on her mind, how abnormal and perverted she herself was. Outside it was beautiful, and they walked down to the docks, looking in all the store windows on Main Street along the way, and it felt more peaceful than it had felt anytime since that night after the play. Rob said a couple of times that he'd miss her, and she didn't think he was just saying it entirely to be polite.

"I'll miss you, too," she said.

"You won't forget me, will you?" he said, then sort of laughed as if to show he didn't really mean it.

"Why would I forget you?"

This was after they'd walked back to Metcalf Street and were standing on the corner before saying goodbye.

He sang "La donna è mobile, we have no soup today . . ."

"Right," she said.

"Well, see you in September."

Then he walked off down Chesterfield Street towards the bus stop. They hadn't even discussed writing letters.

XIX CASCABEL FLATS

As they walked up the sandy streambed, stepping over gray, honeycombed dead cacti and rocks covered by lichen the color green that copper turned when it corroded, Nick told Zoë he'd be the first to admit that no one had discovered the *seat* of conscience or even demonstrated conclusively that there was a physical basis for it, although the research conducted over the past ten years on genetic defects common to some types of violent criminals was promising—maybe the phrenologists would be proven right in the end, you never knew. But sometimes you just had to take a leap of faith. Whereupon he *winked* at her.

It wasn't that everyone had been good and now was evil, he didn't mean to imply that; it was that no one knew which was which. Either you felt that you weren't responsible for anything or that everything in the world was your fault.

"Mutation, yes," he said, as if she'd said something. "Blame time, blame pollution—electrical, chemical, auditory, visual—it makes no difference. It's *survival*—for us, choosing the right course of action is survival. As I told you before lunch, that capacity *has* to be programmed into the organism. If not . . .

"They had it right on the flag, you know—'Don't Tread on me'—but they lost their courage." He stopped walking. "Come on, Zo, stop giving me that look. It wouldn't be any stranger than any other major scientific discovery—they've all required people to get over some inherent bias, haven't they?" He laughed. "Our padre should be happy, don't you think? For years he's badgered me about wasting my time on the small picture; now here I finally am with an idea, with capital letters—what's the matter? You're a skeptic too? I thought I'd left all of those behind at the lab."

When she didn't respond, he said, "I suppose I am asking a lot. It took me a while to believe it myself. But the climate, the terrain—they're identical to the so-called Holy Land's—which I'm not the first to notice, by the way—and then those guys up in the hills still acting everything out . . . It could have been *here*, don't you see? It's just one of those ideas so outlandish it has to be true, know what I mean?"

Like the person you love killing his father?

Nick looked startled when he understood but said, "Well, why not? This summer I went back and reread that first chapter. It doesn't say much, you know. Not a single mention of what *kind* of fruit it was—that was what started my speculations: could it have been fermented? But that seemed too fortuitous. Then I wondered if there could have been something about her *condition*, quite aside from what she ate, that might have affected her susceptibility, or, more technically, the accessibility of the brain to the venom. I concluded that the fruit was just a smokescreen—the explanation given by someone not wanting us to have the full information . . ."

He debated, then grinned.

"Ellie's been trying to get pregnant, I expect she may have told you. As a result I've been unusually conscious of her menstrual cycle, and that's what brought it all home to me. She'd always talked about changes in mood before, but I'd never paid much attention. I thought she was exaggerating, to be honest, blaming whatever state of mind she was in on hormones. But now I started listening more closely. She probably assumed that my questions manifested greater sensitivity to her on my part—which made me feel like quite the creep, let me tell you. What she told me fit my hunch, though. One thing she didn't like about taking the pill was that it seemed to make her mildly depressed all the time. She got depressed otherwise, but she felt more in *contact* with things. On the pill, she felt as if she couldn't *think*. And then, she said, there were a few days somewhere in the middle of her cycle, right before the progesterone started—when she wasn't on the pill, that is—when she felt terrific. Incredibly clear-headed. All the things that fogged her thinking the rest of the time just seemed to dissipate. You might not think so," he added confidentially, "but she's often in turmoil about something—what she said to so and so, should she have done such and such . . ."

Zoë couldn't believe Nick was saying this to her. Did he think she was deaf and blind as well as dumb?

"Maybe you already know what I'm talking about, but what struck me as most remarkable was her conviction that this brief span of days was the way she really *ought* to feel—that the rest was a kind of clouding. The question I then asked myself was this. What if some substance were induced into her system at the time that she felt most clear-minded that could *permanently* adjust her to that state? No one really knows, after all, what *use* the human female reproductive cycle is. Something that dramatic—it stands to reason there's some explanation for it besides Nature's showing off how subtle she can get. My next step was to call up a friend who's done a lot of research on the neurological effects of hormones and ask him if there were a chance that varying amounts could affect the permeability of the blood–brain barrier. Let's just say that nothing he told me led me to doubt my hypothesis. That's when I began taking Ellie's birth control pills."

You did WHAT?

Nick laughed at her expression.

"She threw them away when she decided to try to have a kid, so fortunately she can't have any idea I'm using them. She'd just bought almost a year's supply. At first I took only one a day, but then I realized that was absurd and doubled the dose. I started feeling a little sick to my stomach sometimes, but nothing like the visionary effects she described. You can understand my problem, though." He grinned. "I could hardly make an appointment with a gynecologist and ask him what brand of pill might be most likely to produce the desired effect."

No wonder he didn't want to go for a sperm count.

"Finally I decided just to go all out and I doubled the second dose. I have only another couple of weeks' worth of pills left, so if I'm going to do anything I'm going to have to do it soon."

He started walking again, as if whatever else they might discuss were insignificant enough to be settled while they were in motion. Zoë was getting cold—the pines leaning out over the high eroded banks had dropped long scraggly shadows across the gully—however, they were almost back; she could see the slanted roof of the snakehouse. She didn't follow Nick, forcing him to turn.

Couldn't taking all that estrogen affect your testosterone level? she signed. She fingerspelled the names of the hormones.

"That's the idea," he said.

But isn't it kind of unfair to Ellie to let her think that . . . NOT FAIR ELLIE SHE THINK . . .

"Oh, I see." Nick looked embarrassed. "You mean she'll think it's because of her I've lost my sexual appetite? Did she tell you that? No, don't answer—I don't want to know. I suppose you're right. But it's only been a few months and as soon as I've conducted the experiment I'll be back to normal." He laughed. "Or some facsimile thereof. It seems appropriate somehow to conduct the experiment at Christmastime. Considering what that whole adventure was supposed to accomplish . . . What, Zoë? Have you seen the proverbial ghost? What is it?"

Nothing, she signed. But that wasn't true; she'd just realized that she'd left Rob's letter sitting on the table in Stewart's sitting room.

"Are you sure? You can tell me, you know."

Nick would never believe it had been an accident.

It's when you can get pregnant, she said. She didn't know a sign for "pregnant" so she pantomimed.

"Pregnant? Who's pregnant?"

No, I meant that that's when you think clearly. She spelled "fertile." *When the progesterone starts.*

"Oh, I see. Of course. I should have realized that."

Why should you? Why should you care? You don't have to get pregnant in the next six months or face the possibility of never being able to have a child.

She signed more quickly than even Nick could follow, but he had picked up on the tone.

"Ellie did talk to you about it, didn't she? Last night, I bet, while you were making coffee. I thought so. Well, that's her side of it."

What other side is there?

Zoë had felt sympathy for Nick when Ellie was going on about it, but at the moment she felt none whatsoever. He was just like Pryce, refusing to let her have a child until *he* decided it was the correct time. Before lunch she'd almost told Nick about the endometriosis but now he was the last person on earth she'd confide in.

"I think you mean to say you understand how Ellie feels," he said. "What can I tell you, though? I'm just not ready. I have to figure things out first. I'd think that, coming from the background we do, you could understand why the prospect of fatherhood doesn't have me turning cartwheels with eagerness."

She didn't bother answering. She'd heard it too many times—I have things to do first; I'm not ready; I want to be sure you love me. They were all the same. Yes, even Rob! All his years in the hospital—what else had it been but that? Staying locked up until everyone understood what he *meant*. Nick had to see *clearly* before he could be a father. Pryce had to know what she was hiding. They had to be sure the world was perfect before they would risk being fathers.

The way Nick carried on—this supposed plan to inject himself with rattlesnake venom when he thought he'd taken enough female hormones to carry it to his brain—even if he were right about the molecules' being able to make it through, he had no proof that they had receptor sites. He was playing with her, that was the only explanation she could think of. He'd have to be completely off his rocker otherwise, which she refused to believe for a minute. It was just the same old one-upmanship; once he'd laid eyes on the letter from Robert Went he knew she was going to be keyed up and he couldn't stand it. The idea that she might get more attention than he did . . . *He* was the one whose career had come to a screeching halt, who had had to move to the land of New Age nitwits, who'd been sold a house over a rattlesnake den by a supposed pal . . . He had been counting on a lot of sympathy, and here she came with worries big enough to make his seem insignificant. She could even see what he was up to in deciding to be concerned about Seth; that way he took over the problem. That's one for Nick Carver, ladies and gents, did you *catch* that masterful underhand?

Since she didn't talk, he would even the odds by saying only what he *didn't* mean—oh, very clever. More than clever; if you thought about what he was saying it was cruel: he had discovered the mind-altering substance that once and for all would straighten everyone out; they'd know right from wrong, good from evil, upright motives from nefarious ones; they'd know what things they were responsible for and what things they weren't . . . It was only when he'd seen how upset she was by the news of Rob's letter that he'd started talking about his rattlesnake in the garden theory. He'd guessed that she was afraid to read Rob's letter without knowing if Rob had really done what he'd claimed or not—otherwise how would she be able to interpret it? Yet ten years of silence to protest not knowing Rob's motives could be made completely pointless by Nick's magical solution. It would be like undergoing years of excruciating treatments for a terrible illness only to be told when you were almost better that there was a new miracle drug that could cure you instantaneously. What would all that suffering have been *for*?

But it occurred to Zoë as they were starting up the embankment that someone else might say she was no different from Nick; she'd refused to talk because she didn't know whether Rob was a murderer or not. Refused to trust anyone since she'd trusted him and then hadn't known whether or not he was to be trusted. Refused to go on with life, just as Nick had.

She knew she hadn't left Rob's letter behind by accident; she might as well admit that she'd wanted Stewart to find it and read it. Then she could be more certain of Stewart's subsequent behavior attesting to Rob's guilt or innocence. Rob couldn't have said very much, in any case; the envelope wasn't thick. Yes or no. "Yes, I really did it." "No, I didn't."

Nick said, "I assume I can trust you not to tell Ellie what I've told you. If she found out what I've been up to it would rock the boat unnecessarily."

Rock the boat unnecessarily! Did he have no idea how *miserable* Ellie was? Was Nick so afraid of his sister's cornering the distress market that he couldn't pay attention to his wife?—though was she any different in this respect either? When was the last time she'd been concerned about Pryce's feelings? But why were she and Nick like this? Still competing to be the "sacrifice" in their family . . .

When she and Nick came in through the glass doors, the living room was empty; Pryce was in the kitchen with Ellie, pretending not to be squeamish about helping her stuff the snake. She was chopping onions and celery; he was breaking bread into little pieces in a bowl. The headless snake, rattles still on, lay stretched out flat on the counter. It had been slit and gutted. Its head, resting in a small glass bowl, looked like one of those pet turtles they sold in dimestores; the snake's tongue protruding could have been the turtle's little head.

It depressed Zoë to see the snake lying there, headless and limp, its alertness all gone—Nick had said that they could always tell when he was going to kill them. The ones he'd had for several months didn't rattle when he took them out to examine them for sores or to milk them but as soon as he opened the cages to bring them into the house to freeze they went into an attack coil and rattled desperately. It had to be one of life's more bizarre experiences, he said (trying to be flip about it)—standing with an ear against a refrigerator freezer, listening to the rattling becoming slower and slower until it stopped.

Zoë pointed. *What is she going to do with that?*

"She wants to know your plans for the head," Nick translated.

"Reattach it, of course," Ellie said.

"Of course," Pryce said.

"Where's notre mère?" Nick asked Ellie.

"In the bedroom, wrapping presents. Strictly off limits."

When they went back into the living room, Monica called, "Is that you, Nick? Is your sister with you?"

"No, I lost her in the desert. Of course she's with me, what do you think?"

"I wouldn't venture to say, dear."

"Oh, brother," Nick said under his breath.

You think Dad could have called?

"Could you ask her to come in here a minute?"

"She's right here, Mother!"

Wouldn't Ellie have told you?

"Eventually," he whispered. Then, at a normal level, "I have to jump on the phone to Las Cruces and see if Mrs. Peterson has been able to reach anyone. It's after four already. I guess I'll have to use the phone in the kitchen."

"Zoë, can you spare me a moment, please?"

She signed to Nick and he called, "She'll be right there, Mother." He returned to the kitchen and she quickly tried to imagine other things Rob might have said:

My dearest Zoë, For ten years you've never once been absent from my thoughts. Of course, I realize your life may not have been at a standstill during that time the way mine has . . .

My dear Miss Carver, I don't know whether or not you bear any recollection of my existence; indeed, it seems to me to have been in a previous life that I knew you . . .

He'd be upset when she told him some of the personalities she'd imagined for him—how could you think I would have turned into such a *creep*, Zoë? You must have thought I was a creep before, otherwise I just don't see . . . Rob, it was imagination, okay? How could I know what you were like? A person's basic *personality* doesn't change, Zoë. But, Rob, you were in a mental hospital! So? So!

He wanted to talk about everything now—it was exhausting sometimes. Of course she was six months pregnant too; that didn't help her energy level.

Unwillingly she moved towards the bedroom. She had a feeling Monica was going to quiz her about Nick. "Is anything bothering your brother, dear?" That had always been her tactic. Divide and conquer. She was sitting on the edge of Nick and Ellie's bed, gifts still in their bags, wrapping paper, ribbons, bows, and gift cards strewn all around her. One leg was folded under her, the other dangling—even visiting family she wore skirts and stockings and fancy shoes. Her expensively cut, tastefully streaked hair fell forward around her face, making her look very girlish.

"Be with you in a minute," she said, as if Zoë had had an appointment, then finished the card she was writing.

Men were always pestering Monica to go out with them, but she said they were all "crashing bores" (an expression she'd picked up from Lydia Wycliffe in the days when they were friends); that, or "dimwits." "Dimwit" she used for men she'd thought she might "at least be able to enjoy having dinner with," before they said something revealing that they "possessed the intellectual acumen of a summer squash."

She said now, "I suppose it would have been more sensible to do this at home, but things get so bumped around in baggage compartments. I've always thought that part of the fun of Christmas is having beautifully wrapped presents."

But you took the train, Zoë gestured.

"Why did I come by train? Oh, a whim, I suppose you'd call it. I haven't been on a train since I was in college, and I haven't gone so far overland since I was a girl—my father thought I should see the country. There were more trains then, of course."

You never told us about that.

Monica stopped tying a bow and paused, her finger on the knot. She looked at Zoë, her eyebrows slightly raised.

I said, You never told us about that.

Monica sighed. "I'm not following, Zoë."

Zoë shrugged—*Forget it*—but to her surprise Monica didn't seem annoyed. She said, "It's so long ago. I've always loved trains, though. I took the train to college. I had a sleeping compartment on the way to Chicago—I changed there for Centuryville. My father bought the tickets and he always had me leaving on the next train out, but I used to change my reservation."

What for?

"The train arrived in Chicago in the early morning. I'd change my reservation to that evening. Then I'd spend the day in town."

You did? What did you do?

Monica smiled fleetingly at her. "I rode the escalators at Worman's Department Store."

What?

"Hours and hours. Eight floors up and down, gazing at all the merchandise. It was so soothing—I could have stayed there forever. It was the only time in my life I'd felt completely independent. No one ever asked me to stop." She looked at her daughter. "But I can't imagine why you're interested in this." She finished her package. "I asked you in here because I need your opinion. I bought a sweater for Pryce—I want you to tell me if you think he'll like it."

You did what?

"There are only a few sizes, you know. I bought a large, figuring that if he couldn't wear it, Nick could. But do you think he'll like it?"

She lifted up a brown sweater with a beige and gray argyle pattern down the front. It looked like the crosshatching on the diamondbacks.

It's fine.

"Are you sure? There's still time to get him something else."

It's fine, but I don't see . . .

"Well, Zoë," Monica said, "when you bring a boyfriend home for Christmas, it would be rather unfriendly of your family not to make some gesture of welcome, don't you think?"

The wrapping paper she was using was dark green with a diagonal pattern of gilt bells. There were gold ribbon and gold bows to match.

Did you bring all this stuff on the train with you too? PAPER ON TRAIN?

"Yes, why?"

Did you think they wouldn't sell wrapping paper out here? THINK NO PAPER HERE?

"No, dear, but I didn't know if I would have the opportunity to purchase any."

Dear Zoë, I was so shocked and upset to hear that you haven't been able to talk for ten years . . .

Dear Zoë, Remember me? Robert Went, baker and father-killer? I'm a free man! They made a big mistake and let me out from behind bars and you know what the first thing I'm going to do is, don't you?

Dear Zoë, I would really like the chance to explain. I have never cared if anyone else understood what I did, but I have always cared that you did. I hope this reaches you, and that you'll answer . . .

"Dear, could you do me one favor before you go?"

What? What is it?

"In my purse—in the sun room—there's a pen. This one's running out. Could you get it for me?"

Such a familiar request: Get my purse, it's . . . upstairs in the bedroom; in the kitchen; in the living room, I think; come to think of it, maybe I left it on the hall table . . . Like fetching the scepter or the crown. It was years before they were allowed to get things out of it themselves. Her old, harmless purses Monica had let Zoë and Bridget have for dress-up.

"Don't be afraid to rummage around in it," Monica called after her. "I don't know exactly where *in* it the pen is."

The purse itself was on top of Monica's suitcase, sitting beside the neatly made rollaway. It was soft, mahogany-colored leather now, not the shiny black trapezoids from days of yore. Zoë lifted the flap and tried to see in, but couldn't—it was too big, so she did what she'd done as a child: dumped the contents out on the bed. There were the usual things—wallet, credit-card case, change purse, makeup case, hair brush, peppermints, nail file, a couple of pens in fact, a pack of cards (had Monica played solitaire on the train?), a small spiral notebook, and a long, plain envelope. Zoë leafed through the notebook, nothing in it, then opened the envelope: Monica's train tickets. Out of habit, she took the ticket out and looked through it. She was about to put it back when she glanced at the destination on the return and saw that it wasn't Sparta—that is, Baltimore, the nearest train stop. After Chicago, it said "South Bend." South Bend, *Indiana*? What would Monica be doing in South Bend, Indiana? Zoë stared at the ticket while she began to replace things in the purse. Monica had been acting so giddy—her unprecedented chatting about her past, her gregariousness to Pryce . . . Monica had always been polite to her children's friends, but not convivial like this. Zoë had no idea where in Indiana South Bend was, but Centuryville was in Indiana. Centuryville was where Monica and Seth had gone to college—it was a small enough town that the train probably wouldn't stop there anymore. Could Monica be going to Centuryville for some reason? A college reunion? But why would she have said nothing about it?

When it hit Zoë, she couldn't believe how slow she'd been. What a fool—of course! Monica was going to meet Seth! That's where *he* was already. Why, those conniving, deceitful . . . Obviously he was spending Christmas with the Changs—that is, the Smiths: Lucy Chang Smith and her husband, David; they'd probably drive with Seth to South Bend to meet the train after New Year's, have a big celebration. "A neat trick of deluding the children, don't you think?" Uproarious laughter over the spiked eggnog.

Zoë felt as if she were becoming invisible; she couldn't believe that after all this time she'd fallen for their same old trick—letting you "discover" information you then couldn't use because of the method by which you'd discovered it. Oh, Seth and Monica might *claim* that the reason they'd never told her and Nick anything was because they hadn't wanted to "impose their problems on their children"; they'd wanted them to "have the opportunity to experience the world first hand," which was impossible anyway, with everyone who preceded you in life constantly trying to imprint their version of it in your mind. At the least S & M could have told them *that*. Instead all they'd accomplished by their supposedly uninterfering attitude was to turn their children into spies in their own household. And how ingeniously Monica had set it up, getting *her* to bring up trains (no doubt she'd already been planning it when she bought the wrapping paper), then making that remark about travelling with her father; she'd known perfectly well that Zoë would say, How come you never told us about it before? Which would give her a perfect opportunity to mention taking the train to college, thus putting Centuryville in Zoë's mind. Oh, how very very clever.

Here she and Nick had been, worried about Seth, but also feeling ridiculous for the things they'd been imagining. Oh, what brilliant parents they had! In fact, of course, it was so obvious now that only people brought up to be blind, deaf, and dumb as they had been wouldn't have seen it. Seth must have told Monica about Rob's being out, or vice versa—they would have guessed the conclusion Zoë would jump to when she didn't hear from Seth. What could please them more than for her and Nick to wonder if they wanted their own father to be dead, if that was why they weren't making more of an effort to find out where he was; that was what they'd always wanted, for their children to suspect themselves of deep dark evil motives. "It will always come out," Seth proclaimed. "Evil will always come out in the end . . ."

Zoë could hear them, planning it out on the phone: "Whatever you do, Seth, under no circumstances tell her or Nick you're going anywhere . . ." How deliciously they were floating now on the cloud of their children's suspicions. It set you free—to be suspected of something you could never be accused of. She must have known that her whole life.

Good God—had Rob? But that was too much to worry about now. She tried to think calmly and logically. What end result did Seth and Monica hope for? Would they go so far as to move back in together but pretend they hadn't? She and Nick had always joked, all those Christmases when they'd trooped back and forth between Metcalf and Courier streets, wishing they had clones who could celebrate Christmas for them—just think! they'd say. We could make two of each of us and tell S & M that we had had it with the other: "From now on we're going to spend the whole day with you!" And meanwhile they (Nick and Zoë's real selves) would be off on some South Sea island, lying on the beach, sipping mai tais, whatever those were. They'd joked about how S & M were on the phone with each other as soon as they were out the door, laughing hysterically over how they'd pulled the wool over their children's eyes. "We've really made them believe we don't love each other anymore! Isn't it incredible? There's no end to their gullibility!"

They could love each other only if it were a secret, a secret their children knew but could never mention because they would be punished for the means they'd used to discover it. Or—was it possible? But under the circumstances—what circumstances? *These* circumstances—they could be thinking that if they upset her enough she'd forget she couldn't talk, and yell at them! Had they really been acting out of generosity, all these years? Yes, even when she could talk just fine, they'd known somehow; they'd always been preparing for the moment when she would need to be shocked out of speechlessness—all these years they'd been sacrificing themselves, preparing for her moment of extremity, when really all they'd longed for was a normal family life, everybody sitting around together after dinner, telling each other about their day, what they were looking forward to, what was troubling them—they'd longed for that but they'd given it up for their children's sakes, they'd sacrificed their dream of a happy home, knowing how much more *useful* it would be to the kids later in life to have grown up in an espionage ring. They'd be so much better prepared for the world.

"Zoë!"

She swung around; Monica was standing in the doorway.

"I've been calling you for the last five minutes! I feared one of Nick's creatures had escaped and taken a bite out of you. What have you been doing in here all this time?"

Well, this time, for once, she wasn't going to let them get away with it. Enough was enough. She looked bitterly at her mother.

So you and Dad are getting back together—how nice for you. Don't tell me you were saving it as a surprise for Christmas. How you must have been enjoying watching Nick and me trying to hide from you the fact that we were worried about him—I bet you've had a wonderful time laughing at us up your sleeve . . .

She was signing sloppily as well as fast, and she knew Monica would understand little of what she was saying, but at least she was saying it. Even if it were only practice for when she'd make her real accusation, she was still saying it.

"Zoë, what on earth is the matter?"

Monica sat down beside her on the rollaway, but Zoë jumped up and gestured wildly.

Don't touch me! Don't lay a hand on me!

Monica rose and pulled back the curtain over the sun room door.

"Nick! Nicholas! Please come in here."

"He's on the phone, Monica," Ellie called back.

"Please ask him to call back. I need him in here. We're in the sun room."

"Mother, I'm on the phone to Las Cruces!" Nick shouted. "For God's sake, it's an emergency!"

"So is this, Nicholas!"

It's not an emergency! Leave him alone! But in another second he was there.

"What the hell couldn't wait two more minutes?" Then he saw Zoë's expression. "What is it? What's happened?"

The fear on his face was so great that in the midst of everything she had the urge to laugh.

Don't worry, you can claim this one too. You can stop pretending to feel sorry for me . . .

"Maybe *you* can understand," Monica said. "She's clearly furious at me but won't slow down enough so that I can figure out what she's saying."

If you'd ever bothered to learn to understand me, you could have. But you had to pretend you didn't because you had such faith I'd speak again someday. Well, let me tell you; if I do it will be because I decide to, not because you or anyone else wants me to . . . Then she decelerated and signed to Nick: *She's going to meet Dad in Centuryville.*

She'd spelled out "Century . . ." and Monica said, "Centuryville? I was telling her earlier about my trips there by train in college . . . Zoë, is this the usual thing?" Monica turned to Nick again. "I refer of course to our supposed failure as parents to make full disclosure . . ."

"She said you're meeting Dad out there," Nick interrupted.

"What on earth . . .?"

I found your ticket. Don't tell me you didn't tell me to go searching through your purse so I would find it.

Now that he knew what was going on, Nick looked shocked that she was talking to Monica like this. He repeated only, "She said something about a ticket."

"You looked at my train ticket?" Monica asked her. She seemed bewildered. "Nick, what is this all about?"

"Well, are you?" he asked flatly.

"Am I what, Nicholas?"

"Meeting Dad in Centuryville?"

Monica stared at them both. Then she shook her head. "I really don't know sometimes . . . How did I produce two such Grand Inquisitors as you? Where on the Lord's green earth did you come up with such an idea? Have you both ingested some intoxicating substance while you were at your neighbor's?" She sat down on the rollaway. "No! I am *not* meeting your father, my former husband, in Centuryville, Indiana! All right?"

He's not your "former" husband. You've never even had a legal separation! Besides, if you're not going to meet him, whom are you going to see?

Nick started to translate but Monica held up her hand.

"I got the first part, at least. Yes, you're correct, Zoë, technically we're not divorced, not in legal terms, but it never seemed necessary to either of us to undergo the unpleasant procedure of having a judge pronounce upon what we ourselves already knew, and . . ."

Oh, knock it off. We've heard this all before.

"So why *are* you going there?"

"To visit old friends."

Who?

"You never said anything about it when we discussed the dates of your visit."

"I hardly see . . ." Monica began, but she sounded more embarrassed than angry. This in itself was incredible. "I don't cross-examine you about the company you keep, do I? You expect me to respect your privacy at all times. Surely I deserve a similar consideration from you?" She actually seemed to be pleading with them.

Nick looked at Zoë and shrugged. She shook her head, afraid she was going to cry—once today was enough—and pushed past Nick out of the sun room, through the curtain; how perfect that there were no doors in a house full of secrets. It was amazing that the roof didn't blow off from the pressure of them. She didn't believe Monica; how could she? And yet she suddenly ached to; it felt as if it were the only thing she had ever wanted—not always to have to be on the lookout. She was so tired. Ever since they'd arrived it had been nothing but secret after secret: Ellie's from Nick, Nick's from Ellie, hers from Pryce, now Monica's from them . . . It was Christmas!

Tantalizingly, like a slide shown quickly and then replaced, she could glimpse a different view: Monica going to Centuryville for some reason that had nothing to do with Seth; Seth had written to tell her (Zoë) where he was going, but the letter for some reason hadn't reached her before she left; Robert would have heard what had happened to her and written to say that he was sorry—it had taken him ten years to learn to forgive himself for his father's death; for years he himself hadn't spoken to anyone. That was a strange coincidence, wasn't it? Literally for the first two years he had just sat in a room, looking out the window at nothing. He ate only because they threatened to force-feed him if he didn't. He would have killed himself, he said—his hands were dying to do himself injury—but that would have been the easy way out. Instead he had had to sit there and suffer, which was punishment but not blame, which was what he'd done it for—to be blamed, to be officially guilty, but instead they kept insisting he wasn't guilty; he wasn't evil; locked him up for ten years until he admitted it—and who knows, Zoë, maybe it's even true.

She kept thinking of her mother, before she had been her mother, riding that escalator up and down in the 1940's, her one great escape—except, how ironic, every time she went up, she came back down again. Over and over she tried to get away; every time she boarded the Up escalator she must have felt, This is it; now, *this* time, it will keep on going, it won't come down . . . But every time it did, and then suddenly she was a mother who had never had a mother of her own. Zoë felt so sad. It was all just so sad.

She wandered into the kitchen; Pryce was inserting the stuffing now and Ellie was sewing the skin back together. She glanced up and said, "After it's baked I pull the thread out and it still holds together."

"She bakes the snake *coiled*," Pryce said. "She props it up in striking position. Do you bake the head, by the way?"

"I parboil it very lightly in vinegar water and attach it afterward."

"What about the venom?"

"I cut the sacs out, but in any case the heat would destroy it. Besides, it's not poisonous if you eat it. It has to get into the bloodstream. Only if you had a cut in your mouth or a stomach ulcer could swallowing it do something to you."

"Well, that's a comfort," Pryce said.

The phone rang; Ellie answered.

"Hold on a minute." She laid the receiver on the counter and went to the door of the kitchen. "Nick, it's Simon Peterson on the phone."

"I'll get it in the bedroom," he shouted back.

Ellie hung up when she heard him on the extension. It wasn't a minute before Nick returned, his lips pressed together. He headed straight for the back door and grabbed the key to the snakehouse off its nail.

"Nick, what's *happened*?" Ellie exclaimed.

"What the hell do you care? Maybe if the shipment gets here soon enough you can cook the rest of them too." He slammed the door on his way out.

For a moment they all just stood there. Then Ellie turned back to her preparations and Pryce went over and laid a hand on her arm.

"Something must have happened to the snakes. I'm sure he didn't mean to be unkind."

But Ellie exclaimed, "Damn it! God *damn* it!"

For a second they thought that she'd messed up what she was doing with the snake, but the next moment she threw the needle down on the counter and ran past them out of the room, crying. In a second she was back, looking at them, appalled.

"There's nowhere I can go in my own house! Monica's in the bedroom! What the hell am I supposed to do?"

She was crying openly now. Pryce said, glancing at Zoë—*you'll understand, won't you?*—"Ellie, let's go for a walk. I think you could use a breath of fresh air. Let me just wash this stuff off my hands."

"Maybe *you* can console Nick," Ellie said to Zoë, sobbing. "I'm sure he doesn't want *my* comfort."

They went out through the back door but headed down the driveway. When they had disappeared around the first curve, Zoë went down to the snakehouse. She knocked; when there was no answer she pushed open the door. Nick was sitting on the stool with his forehead pressed against one of the glass cages. Without turning around he said, "They shot him—they shot the snake." He looked at her. His face was clenched. "You won't believe what those assholes did. Some fool of a postal clerk who came in for the night shift talked big and convinced them that he could bag the snake—he did it all the time as a hobby, he told them. If this was *true*, which I doubt, it's clear he didn't count on its being so big. It bit him on the arm. They rushed him to the hospital—he's going to live, unfortunately, the jerk. Simon tells me they want me to pay for the guy's medical bills! Then they add insult to injury by killing the snake that their own ineptness provoked into biting. What the hell did they think was to be gained by shooting it? It makes me feel like going down there and blowing up the whole place. It's their own damn fault for not teaching their people to believe labels. Simon and Lincoln—his son—arrived twenty minutes after it was all over, and half an hour before the deadline they gave me. They'd have had the snake safely back in its box in five minutes. What absolute jerks! And now *this*."

What do you mean?

"Look," he said.

He pointed at the cage in front of him. Zoë saw now that one of the small prairie rattlers it contained was lying in a peculiar position, an ungainly half coil, partly upside down. Its head was extended as if it were stretching, but there was no movement.

"Amoebiasis," Nick said. "It can happen very quickly. I suspected she might have it—she was a little lethargic this morning, but I was hoping against hope that I was imagining things. It's highly contagious, and I'll have to kill the other ones in there and sterilize the cage. I ought to isolate all the snakes, but I don't have enough cages."

Do you want some help?

She didn't want to watch him kill them, but she didn't feel right leaving him to do it alone. She could sympathize with him when there was something she could do to help. She moved back against the door as, one by one, he lifted the writhing snakes out with his L-shaped hook, pinned them on a board by pressing them just behind their heads, then brought the large cleaver down and guillotined them. She winced. He knocked the heads off into an empty coffee tin he evidently kept for this purpose.

She didn't feel squeamish—just sorry for the snakes, and sorrier for Nick, for having to carry out their sentence. It all seemed part of the whole miserable state of things.

Nick took a black plastic bag from a stack of them on the shelf above the counter, shook it open, and slid the still twitching bodies in. He tilted the can and the heads rolled into the bag; then he knotted the top. As he wiped off the board he glanced at her and said, "I guess you haven't had a chance to read Robert's letter yet, have you?" He didn't want her to say anything about the snakes.

Not yet.

"If you want, when I've finished cleaning up, you can stay here while I go back to the house."

She frowned. But what the hell—why not tell him? Add one more piece of information to the mass already knotting in his mind. He could think what he liked about her motive; the deed was done. Stewart would have read it by now if he were going to.

I can't, she signed. *I left it at Stewart's.*

Nick stared at her. "You what? Where? How could you have done that?"

I set it on the table while we were calling Dad.

"But, Zoë, why didn't you say something earlier? When did you realize you'd left it?"

What difference does it make?

"Jesus Christ, Zoë! You haven't heard from Robert in ten years, and you act like . . . How could you just forget the letter? And after all the stuff you've been suggesting about Dad . . ."

Well, now we know where he's gone, what difference does it make?

"Where who's gone? You mean Dad? Zoë, we don't know anything! You're inventing this whole situation just because Mom happens to be stopping off somewhere on her way back to Sparta."

And didn't tell us.

"Why should she? I think she's right—she's entitled to some privacy. Look, why don't I call Stewart? Better yet, I'll just run over in the car and get it."

What for? I'll get it tonight.

"But, Zoë, I think we ought to . . ."

Nick, it's my letter! I should never have said anything!

"What?"

She repeated it.

"Maybe not, but you did. Now you can't just . . ."

Rob's letter is none of your business!

Nick looked at her, shook his head, picked up the bag of snakes, and headed for the door. Then, as if he'd just thought of it, he turned and said, "How can you say such a thing? You want me to believe our father's *life* may be threatened and then tell me that whatever the guy who may be threatening it says in a letter is none of my business? If you invented the whole idea just to get to me, that's one thing, but if you're serious then you damn well better expect to be *taken* seriously. Make up your mind which it is."

XX HARMONY

Embarked at twenty on a quest to ascertain who'd made her world what it was, Monica was forced to conclude that, had she been born dead, her mother would have known how to love her. She would also have never had to be hospitalized.

"Perhaps it is possible, from a dispassionate point of view," she said to her friend Del, one afternoon in Centuryville, Indiana, "to feel sorry for her, but as her daughter I cannot; I endured too much. To this day, I miss my brothers."

She had informed Del, whose unquestioning acceptance of her version of events irritated her, of her father's discovery when she was four that the playmates she prattled about had not been imagined by her but were his own unbreathing children, whom he had believed finally laid to rest at her birth.

"As I recall, his face took on the appearance of a death mask. When my mother finally returned from the hospital, I didn't recognize her either. Now, of course, I sympathize with what he must have been experiencing, but at the time . . . well, I was a child."

"How very painful for you," Del said cautiously. "To lose your mother in such a . . . complicated way."

"You know I believe there's no sense in lamenting the past, Del," Monica said. His expression reminded her of a spaniel's. "I didn't believe my father or the doctors who told me she'd suddenly fallen ill. I knew she was in perfect health. My single solace lay in plotting with my brothers how to murder our father. My mother, you see, had informed me that he didn't love them—he had used to, but after I came to live with them I became his favorite—therefore I should be careful never to mention them around him. Do you know how loyal children are?" she asked. "How blindly and completely loyal? And inevitably to whatever version of events they encounter first. The great gentleness my father showed me during my mother's absence—almost two years, mind you—only hardened my resolve never to trust him. When I think back on it now . . . What my poor father must have suffered! To have his wife declared incurably insane and then to have his daughter turn against him. He must have been a saint to remain so patient with me. It wasn't until after my mother returned, and sat day after day with a vacant expression on her face, reading the Bible, urging me to pray for my sins, that I was finally, grudgingly, able to accept his affection."

"But how did you come to accept the fact that your brothers weren't alive?" Del ventured to ask.

"The doctor took me for a drive one afternoon. He had to pay a house call in Amber, nearly ten miles away. I was seven or eight. He had a beautiful roadster, and he had the top down. He catechized me. At the time I liked him very much and talked to him freely. I told him how distressed my brothers had been at my mother's disappearance, but now that she was back it wasn't any better. When I tried to talk to her about them—even though my father had told me not to—she said I had no brothers. They were imaginary. They had never existed. She recited these facts in the toneless voice of children declaiming the Declaration of Independence."

Del smiled, then wondered nervously if he should not have. However, Monica seemed not to have noticed.

"The doctor was quite ingenious, I realize in retrospect. He never contradicted me; never told me my brothers weren't real, but somehow persuaded me to articulate my own understanding of the fact that, although they were still my brothers, they weren't the *same* as I was. I suppose I must have been ready for a means of honorably dissociating myself from them. By the end of our drive, I had come to understand that, although *I* could tell the difference, my mother couldn't, and that that was what had made her sick.

"Unfortunately," she added—her tone of wry amusement made Del wince—"it turned out that my mother no longer believed I existed either. When my father found this out—back she went to the hospital for more shock treatments. I have to say in his defense that he couldn't have known how brutal they were. This time she stayed for four years—we visited her once a month. She learned to acknowledge me, though not, I realize as I think back on it, because she remembered me, but because she had memorized my identity. She had become so eager to please. Now, of course, I know that she would have said anything the doctors told her to, to escape the shock treatments. If my father had known what they entailed . . . But I'm sure he couldn't have. I only recently, myself, had any idea. I saw a film—I don't mind admitting to you that I found it difficult to watch when the iron-hearted nurses strapped the patient onto the table and shoved the piece of rubber into her mouth . . . She even looked a little like my mother—that same soft hair, that gentle expression . . ."

"Oh, Monica . . ." Del said.

"I simply hadn't realized how violent the treatment was," she said sharply. She turned away from him and spoke to the trunk of the giant oak tree under which they were sitting on the well-tended grounds of Century College.

"Of course I'd never tell my father. To this day I don't believe he has any conception, though I don't mind admitting that I experienced a certain resentment as I watched the film. I wondered how my father could possibly have allowed his wife to suffer such helpless agony, but later, of course, I realized that he was in no way responsible. If anything, it was for my sake that he felt obliged to take whatever the doctors told him was the best course of action—not our local doctor," she added, implying something Del could not catch. "He told me not long ago that the happiest years of his life were those after I was born and before he discovered that my mother still persisted in her fantasy life. He'd thought all that had vanished at my birth. She had some difficulty believing I was really hers in the beginning, evidently, but that too, he had thought, had been overcome. He admitted to me that he sometimes found himself wishing he hadn't interfered; in a way her departure from sanity was harmless enough. But of course he had my welfare to consider—what the effect on me would be of growing up with an invisible family. You do agree he had no choice, don't you?"

"I don't know," Del said. "He might have considered what it would be like for you to grow up without a mother. At least before the hospital she was happy. She loved you. I'm sure in time you would have made your peace with your brothers' being pretend."

"My father couldn't risk that. He did the best he could under the circumstances. None of this was easy for him, you know. Imagine how lonely it was."

"I'm more concerned with how lonely it was for you," Del suggested.

"You needn't be. I've managed quite well. Many people in the world have undergone far greater privations than I—we would all do well to remember that. I've never known hunger or want of any sort. My sufferings are hardly worth mentioning."

Del refrained from asking her why she spoke of them so incessantly then. He merely said, "Suffering's a part of the human condition. Who's to say who suffers more than others?"

"When she came home the second time," Monica said, "I was eleven.

They had tried a new medication and she was more alert now. She sewed again—until I left for college I never owned a store-bought dress. Of course I needn't tell you how I longed for one. She worked in the vast flower beds my grandmother had planted—they truly are stunning. She read the Bible and attended church devotedly. She quoted to me incessantly from the Scriptures—we would all be rewarded in heaven for our losses on earth. The more we suffered, the better off we would be. Such a devious and clever philosophy. My father and I were both very gentle with her, so life was relatively peaceful, if a bit restrained. Then, when I was twelve, I went to boarding school, and came home only for the summer and Christmas vacations."

She seemed to have come to a dead end, and Del, watching her face, saw stealing over it a forlorn uncertainty.

"Did you enjoy boarding school?" he asked quickly.

"Oh, it was like any other, I expect. Not coed, of course. Susanna Percy, whose family keeps the house next to ours in Harmony as a summer home, attended the same school. She's my age. I spent all my Easter vacations with the Percys in Boston. They lived in an elegant old brick house overlooking the Charles, and we used to go boating—row to Cambridge and back. The only blight on my otherwise perfect happiness during those visits was Susanna's insufferable younger brother, Marsh. Marshall Winton Percy the Third. He was the size of Napoleon and five times as conceited. When he was fifteen, he decided he was madly in love with me. I never had any peace after that."

"How old were you?"

"Sixteen. He made my life an absolute hell."

"I suppose fifteen-year-old boys will do that," Del offered.

"I pushed him down the stairs," Monica said. She laughed, embarrassed. "He cracked his skull and broke two ribs and his wrist. It wouldn't have amounted to much, but he developed some swelling on the brain and had to be in the hospital for weeks. At one point it seemed he might die."

Del was incredulous and looked it.

"I didn't do it on purpose," Monica protested. "He lay in wait for me one night on the landing and tried to kiss me and as we struggled I shoved him and he went head over heels."

Del smiled at her. "I feel adequately warned."

"Oh, Del," she said.

But what did she mean by that?

"As you can imagine, I've been persona non grata with the Percy family ever since. Even Susanna hardly speaks to me anymore. Except, of course," she added, "to inform me that I'm as crazy as my mother. I needn't tell you it hasn't been pleasant having them next door all summer, particularly since I had to explain to my father why I no longer spent all day, every day, with my good friend Susanna."

"How did he take the news?"

"He was bewildered, I think. How could his darling daughter be so violent? I'm sure it appeared seamy in some way. I think he thought that Marsh must have attempted a good deal more than a kiss."

"I admit I . . ."

"You'd have to know Marsh, before you'd be qualified to judge," Monica said. "He's unredeemed slime. The only good thing he ever did for me was to give me my name."

"Your name? What do you mean?"

"My real name is Harmony—I thought I'd told you that. Harmony Ida. It was Marsh who distorted it into 'Harmonica'—something else I despised him for until Susanna thought of shortening it to 'Monica.' When I came to college I decided to make a clean break. Coming from Harmony is enough—I don't need to be named after the place."

It was May 1945, and Del, badly wounded in early 1943 after one week overseas, had come back home to Centuryville, Indiana, to attend college. To save money he lived with his sister and widowed mother, who took in boarders. He had fallen in love with Monica Robie the moment, in October 1943, their freshman year, that he met her, and had thought that from then on life would be simple, but it hadn't turned out that way: she did not love him back. Yet neither would she let him go; if he took out other girls, she behaved so disdainfully to him that he could not bear it. And the way her face lit up sometimes when she saw him . . . One day he'd confessed his dilemma to Monica's roommate, Annie Ewing, who told him she'd already discerned his feelings and assured him that Monica was merely shy and would, one day soon, come around. He was not sure he believed this, but he allowed himself to hope.

Monica belonged to a sorority—Sigma Omega Phi. Joining it was the thing to do, so she had done it, and, outwardly, she seemed like all the other girls. Like her "sisters," she dressed for everyday in skirts and sweaters; for jewelry wore a single strand of pearls. To class they wore saddle shoes and bobby socks; to dress up, high heels. They wore lipstick and curled their hair. Yet they minded each other's business in a manner to which Monica could not become accustomed.

"Delmore Holland's head over heels in love with you," Annie said to her. "What's more, you're in love with him back. Everybody in the world knows it except you. You go crazy with jealousy if he dates someone else."

"I most certainly do not!"

"You're practically going steady with him."

"I am doing nothing of the sort."

"If that's true, which I sincerely doubt, it's because you've scared him off. He's too modest to put himself forward where he thinks he's not wanted."

"Well, he isn't wanted! I can't stand the way he looks at me so adoringly—like a dog!"

"Someday you're going to be sorry if you throw him away," Annie said testily, but in fact she was kind-hearted and persisted in believing that Monica was simply shy and inexperienced. She plotted ways to bring these two charmingly shy and inexperienced people together.

Annie owned a car—a snazzy 1939 Zephyr. All spring of their freshman, and now of this, their sophomore year, on sunny Saturday afternoons six girls—sometimes seven—would arrange themselves in the car, wearing culottes and white blouses, tucked in, and go for drives in the country. Centuryville was not large and it didn't take long to escape into farmland. When they began their drives in early April the fields were bare but ploughed, the earth dark. Tall narrow farmhouses with porches stood back from the road in islands of lawn, elms standing sentry at their borders. Each Saturday the spring had advanced a little further; the trees flowered and leafed, the corn and the wheat began to sprout, and the cows seemed to be lying down more, either because they were hot or because they didn't have to look so hard to find enough to eat. In September, when the girls came back to school, the second growth of corn would be ten feet high, the tassels turning brown, and everything would look slightly worn, as if to be looked at so long were as tiring as doing the looking.

To Monica the countryside never seemed quite believable. She couldn't understand why the houses weren't by the side of the road. The land was not snug, as it was around Harmony, and if people were out driving on those long flat stretches and got caught in a snowstorm and it started to drift, they sometimes froze to death. This past Christmas, her father had offered to buy her a car to keep at college, but she had said no, thank you. She wasn't sure that someday she wouldn't simply sit down in it and head out into that flat, unreal country until she had driven too far ever to come back.

On the drives with Annie, she generally claimed a seat in front by virtue of her status as Annie's roommate. Today she was sitting on the far side by the door. Shirley Bridges sat between Annie and herself. In the back were Penny McNeal, Jean Oyler, and Jean Bolender, whom they called "Bolie" to distinguish her from Jean Oyler. As they reached the edge of town, Monica tied her triangulated scarf more securely under her chin and turned her face up to meet the wind. She closed her eyes and listened to the radio. Though it was turned to its top volume, Duke Ellington was barely audible singing "Don't Get Around Much Anymore."

Their habit was to drive for perhaps an hour, then stop in one of the tiny farm towns that popped up out of the flat countryside like jacks-in-the-box—places with random-sounding names like Elmira, Corliss, and Melodyville—to have a soda at the drugstore. Besides the five-and-dime, hardware, and grocery, it would be practically all that was there.

Today, after they'd squeezed themselves into one of the two booths in the back of Harvey's Drugs in Corliss, their subject of discussion was the upcoming Sadie Hawkins dance at Sigma Omega Phi. They were all members of the planning committee and it was their job to determine the theme of decoration. Someone suggested hearts and flowers; another a red-white-and-blue motif—after all, it never hurt to remind people that they'd recently won a war—but the objection was raised that they already possessed quite enough patriotism and the discussion soon lapsed into consideration of whom they meant to invite. The druggist, carrying the sodas on a tray and sliding them across the table said, "All righty, now—here's your three chocolate, two vanilla, and one root beer float. Any of you girls can't get a date for that dance, I'll go. I may not be as spry as I used to be, but I'm polite."

"I may just take you up on it," Annie said, and everyone, including the druggist, laughed. Everyone, that is, except Monica. When the druggist, who judging from his graying hair and sideburns appeared to be nearing fifty, had departed, she said in a low voice, "I don't see what's funny. Stranger things have happened than girls our age dating men of his. Sometimes we even marry them. I think it's unkind of you to make fun of him."

They all stopped sipping their sodas to stare at her.

"But, Monica," Annie exclaimed, "he wasn't serious! We were only joking."

"I think it's detestable that you'd think a man unattractive simply because he's older."

"But, Monica . . ."

"Even if he laughs at himself. How do you think he feels right now, inside?"

Simultaneously they all looked at him. The three with their backs to the front of the store turned their heads; the druggist was dusting bottles in the window display. In the silence of their observation they could hear that he was humming.

"He certainly doesn't sound in any distress to me," Jean Bolender said.

"You can't judge anything by that," Monica said scornfully. "You can't expect him to weep in public. He has a job to do."

Shaking her head, Annie reached across the table to feel Monica's forehead.

"I'm perfectly well," Monica said. "It's the rest of you there's something wrong with, I'm beginning to think. If you'll excuse me," she said to Shirley Bridges, who sat next to her in the booth and was staring at her in disbelief, "I'd like to get out. I intend to take a walk."

Shirley looked at the others, who began to protest, but Monica said, "I asked you to let me out, Shirley."

"I declare. Suit yourself," Shirley said and slid out of the seat.

"Thank you," Monica said primly. She picked up her pocketbook and walked out. She was careful not to return the druggist's glance when he looked up. By the time she had shut the door behind her, she knew she was crying. She didn't look back but walked as fast as she could out of town, not the way they'd come, but in the direction they'd been heading.

"Damn it," she said, when she reached the edge of town, which took only a couple of minutes. "Damn it, damn it, damn it! I *can't* be in love with him."

She was thinking not of the druggist, whom she'd already forgotten, and certainly not of Delmore Holland, but of Eldridge Jewell—"young Dr. Jewell," as he was still called in Harmony, even though his father had been dead for several years and he was in his late forties, only five or six years younger than Monica's father.

"I don't love you, I don't love you, I don't!" Monica shouted at the foot-high corn and the crows already scavenging.

"Damn crows!" she exclaimed. "Damn cornfields! Damn Indiana!" She continued on, cursing and sniffling.

That past summer, not long before she'd left for her second year at Century College, she had come down with a cold and at her father's insistence had gone to see Dr. Jewell. Her father didn't like Dr. Jewell—for reasons that had to do with Dr. Jewell's overzealous interest in her mother's "condition," he was not her physician—but thought him "competent enough" to treat a minor illness. Monica knew perfectly well what Dr. Jewell would tell her—take naps and drink liquids—but before he told her, he would have to listen to her heart, peer into her ears, eyes, and throat, take her pulse and blood pressure. Ask her if she was suffering from headaches, stomachaches, or pains of any kind. "No," she'd say. "No. No. No. No." But she went nevertheless, to please her father.

In the examining room, Monica climbed onto the table, and sat with her legs dangling. Besides her father, Mr. Percy, Susanna's father, and Verne Magoon, who mowed the lawn, Dr. Jewell was the only man over twenty she'd ever had anything to do with.

"I've left my stethoscope in the lab, Harmony," he said—though she'd told him her name was Monica now, he couldn't seem to remember. "Mrs. Fletcher is out for the afternoon, so I'll have to get it. If you'd just undo your blouse . . ." he said, as he went out. When he returned he found her sitting on the table, unclothed from the waist up.

"Harmony, I didn't mean . . ." he began, and blushed.

"Didn't mean what?"

"Nothing. Never mind." He began to move briskly around the room, collecting instruments.

She sat oblivious, waiting; she felt no more embarrassment at being undressed in front of Dr. Jewell than she did in front of her dogs and cats. He moved behind her then, placed a hand on one of her shoulders and asked her to breathe in and out deeply.

"Say 'Ahhh,' " he said.

"Ahhh," she said.

"Again."

"Ahhh."

"Again."

She closed her eyes and relaxed. His warm hand on her shoulder seemed to be holding her up, and the stethoscope was pleasantly cold here and there on her back.

"Do you hear something?" she asked, when it seemed to her that he was taking longer than usual.

"Hear something?" he repeated. "Oh, no, not a thing. That is, besides your heart. Pays to be thorough, that's all."

"There isn't anything wrong with me, you know. It's just my father—if I sneeze he thinks I'm going to die."

"He loves you, that's all," Dr. Jewell said, venturing around to the front of her.

Monica put her hands behind her to support herself, then leaned back. He replaced the stethoscope, pressing it against her chest.

"More deep breaths, please."

She closed her eyes again. "Breathing like this always makes me sleepy," she murmured.

"Does it?" His voice sounded far away, somehow helpless. He moved the stethoscope here and there. She felt like a piece of land being surveyed, and suppressed an urge to giggle.

"Do you ever listen to your own heart?" she asked.

"Oh, every once in a while. Just to make sure it's still beating."

"I don't think I'd want to hear mine," she said dreamily. "I don't like to think how it always has to keep going."

"It's built to do that. Everything in the body is designed to do what it's supposed to."

"I suppose so," she said, starting as she realized that his warm hand was covering her breast. Then she told herself not to be silly; he must be lifting it to place the stethoscope beneath it; she hoped he hadn't noticed that he'd surprised her. She didn't want to appear foolish. To show him that she thought nothing of it, she let out her breath languorously and leaned her weight back even more heavily onto her hands. Feeling a cool touch on her breast, she breathed out "Ahhh" again, before she noticed that the feeling differed from that of the round, hard stethoscope. What was it? Her eyes, under her closed lids, roved through her body, testing hypotheses. But now the coolness was warm. Barely opening her eyes, she looked down; Dr. Jewell was touching her breast with his tongue. Quickly she closed her eyes again, shocked. Whatever she did, she couldn't let him see that she'd noticed. She was terrified of embarrassing him. But what should she do?

While she debated this, he moved his mouth to her other breast, and kissed it, then began to move back and forth between them, as if to be sure of being fair. Suddenly he let out a sigh. He had forgot himself! Monica didn't dare open her eyes. What would he do when he realized what he was doing? She had heard of men "losing control of themselves," but she had never heard what to do about it. How mortified poor Dr. Jewell would be if he discovered that he had done so in her presence! And meanwhile he forced her concentration back and forth, as if swinging a watch to hypnotize her. How could what he was doing make her feel like this? He flicked the ends of her breasts with his tongue, first one, then the other. She felt as if he were a guide into unmapped territory—wherever he touched she had to follow. It amazed her that there should have been a whole geography, right there in her own body, that she'd never even known about—but that he had. She felt full of respect and admiration for him. What an intelligent man he was to know about her what she'd never even known about herself! She squeezed her eyes even more tightly shut, as if this would keep him from noticing that she'd noticed.

When he took the end of her breast more firmly in his mouth and pressed it between his lips, she wanted to grab his head and force him to stay there, as if she might get lost were he to let go, yet she didn't dare move, even though her wrists burned from supporting her weight. Whenever he left one breast even to move to the other she wanted to cry out, "Don't! Don't stop!" but she bit her tongue to force herself to remain silent. Then his mouth began to wander farther up towards her neck, then down again to her waist, and she felt as if she had entered a great forest with paths leading off in myriad directions; she couldn't follow all of them and yet she had to, if she were ever to find her way out. Dr. Jewell's fingers were fumbling at the waist of her skirt, and, not intending to, she sighed impatiently, and he lifted his head and looked at her—at least she imagined he did, since she still didn't dare open her eyes. But then she felt his arm around her shoulders and he was gently pulling her along the leather-padded table until her legs could stretch out, easing her down on her back. He lifted her skirt and tugged at her underwear; she raised her hips so that he could slide it off.

Then suddenly his mouth was somewhere else, in between her legs, where no one had ever touched her, where she never even touched herself, and she cried out in surprise, but the next moment in gratitude—how immensely intelligent he was to have known how to locate this place she'd been striving to find without even knowing she was looking for it.

Very cautiously, she reached down to stroke his head. She had meant to be delicate, hoping he wouldn't notice, but her fingers of their own volition tangled themselves in his hair. She didn't see how it could be her own body that transmitted the sensations she felt. What a vast territory it was—boundaryless. How could it have been capable of feeling all this and she not known about it? She still kept her eyes pressed tightly closed as if this would prevent Dr. Jewell's noticing her hand in his hair, but finally her body rebelled and she forgot caution altogether, moving in response to him; and then her voice joined the revolt and she heard it say, "Don't stop! Don't ever stop! Please don't stop!" and then she didn't even hear it.

Now, almost a year later, here she was, walking along the straight paved road that stretched across the Indiana landscape from nowhere to nowhere, the bars of white paint on the macadam like huge, detached piano keys narrowing to the vanishing point ahead of and behind her.

"I hate you, Eldridge Jewell!" she screamed. "Go to hell! Just go to hell!"

Now she began to feel better. She rummaged in her pocketbook for a handkerchief but, not finding one, held each nostril closed in succession and blew out the other onto the ground, the way Verne Magoon did when he didn't think anyone was watching. She untucked her blouse and used its tails to wipe her eyes and then rubbed her nose with her shoulder. These actions also improved her mood. She went on walking, but more slowly, and after another minute or two turned around and headed back towards the town. She hadn't gone more than a mile, she thought, but already in this flat country the buildings were a mere smudge on the horizon. Would Annie and the others have left without her? She wondered but didn't care. Whether or not she ever returned to Centuryville did not concern her.

Eldridge Jewell had a wife and four children. This was not something Monica had given any thought to one way or the other until he pointed it out to her. He did so a week after the afternoon in his office—a week during which she'd kept a regular watch from the widow's walk with the family telescope until she suspected him of keeping under cover. She had no choice but to take direct action. When she'd made up her mind what to do, she walked across town; it was near suppertime and he was locking the door to his office, located in a wing of his large house. Mrs. Jewell was sitting on the front porch. Monica waved to her.

"I'm afraid I've just closed up shop for the day, Harmony," Dr. Jewell said in a hearty voice.

"I'm called Monica now," she said.

"Monica, Harmony. Whatever ails you—can't it wait until regular hours?"

"I'm in pain," she said loudly.

"Eldridge, for heaven's sake, open up!" called Mrs. Jewell. "You know Harmony Robie wouldn't seek you out special if there wasn't a good reason."

Dr. Jewell mumbled an inarticulate reply, but he had no choice but to unlock the door and lead Monica through the waiting room into the interior office, shutting all the doors behind them as they went. There, he sat down dejectedly at his desk. She remained standing.

"Why haven't you been to see me?" she demanded.

"Been to see you?"

"You could have come to my house. Nothing could be easier. Father's always in the library, and Mother notices nothing."

"Harmony, you don't know what you're saying."

"Monica!" she corrected him angrily.

"I confess I've been waiting in terror for you to denounce me for my deplorable lapse of . . . propriety. But what you suggest—if indeed I understand your meaning—it's out of the question!"

"What is?" she demanded.

He didn't answer at first but then he implored her. "I'm so ashamed.

I should never have done what I did—I can't think how it happened. I've never done such a thing before—never even contemplated it. I feel as if I've betrayed my own daughter. I've known you all your life, and you trusted me, and then . . ." His voice cracked, and she glared at him.

"Don't *you* cry!" she exclaimed. "Don't you dare cry! I'll scream if you cry!"

"Oh, Harmony, how can I hope for you to understand? Listen to me—you must listen to me! It's as if there's another world alongside ours, where one has everything one desires—you're too young to know about it; you don't know yet that you can't have everything you want in this one. Most of the time there's no door between those two worlds, but last week . . . I can't expect you to understand, but it was as if the door were suddenly open. I thought I could go through. I thought I could do whatever I wanted."

"But you can! At least you can with me."

Feeling fondly towards him for his foolishness, Monica began to unbutton her blouse, but he cried out, "Whatever are you doing? Stop! Don't do that!"

She stopped. "But I thought you wanted . . ."

"You torture me," he said. He added, "Don't you know I have a wife and four children?"

"What does that have to do with it?"

"What does that have to do with it? It has everything to do with it! Quite aside from the disparity in our ages."

"I could care less how old you are," she said. "I love you!"

"You don't know what you're saying. These things are always found out. In a town like this . . ."

"But I'm leaving soon. No one would know."

"You'll be back. Besides," he added, looking at her, his tone changing, "I don't know that if we were to . . . I don't know that I could restrain myself."

"You mean you want to do *more*?" she asked tremulously.

"Of course I do," he said. "What do you take me for?"

"But that's what I want!" she cried, as he hushed her. "I want you to do everything! Everything you want to—everything you can think of!"

"You don't know what you're saying," he said again. "For one thing, there could be consequences."

"Oh, you mean . . . But you're a doctor," she reminded him triumphantly. "You know how to prevent that."

"Harmony, don't tempt me! It's out of the question."

"But *why*?"

"For all the reasons I've mentioned! I'm a married man and a father; I'm nearly three times your age; I've known your family all my life. If your father were to find out he'd ride me out of town on a rail. If he didn't shoot me first. If the town found out, it would be the end of my practice. I have a wife and four children to feed!"

"I'm tired of hearing about your wife and four children!" Monica shouted, as he pleaded with her again to lower her voice. Then a new idea occurred to her. "Wouldn't it end your practice just as quickly if the town found out what you did in here last week?"

"I can't believe you would be that vindictive. I've told you I blame myself, though . . ." He paused. ". . . you seem to have taken no little pleasure in my . . . misdemeanor."

"I will tell only if you don't do as I say."

"How can you be sure anyone would believe you?"

"Enough people would believe me. I'm not the kind who tells stories. My father would believe me, and he's never liked you very much."

Dr. Jewell started to protest, but she interrupted him. "What's your answer? I have to be home for supper."

He was silent for a moment, then sighed. "What is it you want me to do?"

She came to stand right next to him. "What you did before—and everything else."

"Very well," he said. "If you're sure that's what you want."

"It's the only thing I want in the world! You know you want it too!"

Glancing up at her impassioned face, Eldridge Jewell wondered if in fact the door between worlds might not be kept permanently ajar. He stood up and she threw her arms around his neck and kissed him, exclaiming, "Oh, I love you! I love you!" He kissed her back. He couldn't remember that anyone had ever felt so violently about him. Harmony—Monica Robie. Who would ever have thought? Coming from that somber household . . .

They arranged that on Friday, the day after next, when he drove out to the country to make house calls, she would be walking along the Groveton Road. Only three weeks remained until she left for Centuryville, and he promised to meet her twice a week until then, more if possible.

That Friday, as Monica walked along in a blissful haze, waiting for him to drive up behind her, she felt sure that six meetings would suffice for Eldridge Jewell to recognize that they could not live without each other. "Eldridge, Eldridge," she said softly in sing-song. "Eldridge Jewell. Eldridge Jewell." She kicked a pebble along to keep time. Finally she heard a car.

"Hurry," he said. "Get down on the floor."

"What?" she exclaimed.

"In case someone should see you! Do as I say!"

"No one's ever on this road," she said, but she obeyed nevertheless.

Soon he took a turn-off and she sat up. They followed an old logging track until it became impassable. As soon as they climbed out of the car, she walked towards him, undoing buttons, but he said impatiently, "Not here, Harmony." She followed him through the woods until, entering a small clearing, he said, "This should be far enough."

She approached him again, but when he still did not move to embrace her, she instead took off her clothes and then trampled a space in the tall grass and spread her clothes across it. She lay down and waited for Dr. Jewell to undress.

"You aren't too shy, are you?" he said, as he sat down, clothed, beside her. Gingerly he laid a hand on her stomach. She closed her eyes, sighing happily, but then opened them again.

"You are going . . . You are going to do everything, aren't you?"

"I'll do everything. I promised, didn't I? Only please don't talk anymore now."

"I might not be able to help it," she retorted.

When Monica was almost back to town, she saw Annie's car coming to meet her. Annie was alone in it, however. She stopped opposite Monica, who crossed the road in front of the car and got in. Annie didn't at once drive on.

"What got under *your* bonnet?" she asked.

Monica shrugged.

"Did you truly think the old geezer's feelings would be hurt?"

"Yes, partly."

"What's the other part?"

"The other part's private."

"I don't call that a very nice way to talk to a friend," Annie said, but she backed the car up until she came to a field gate and could turn around.

"I don't see why it isn't," Monica said, when they were headed back to town. She raised her voice so that Annie could hear her above the wind. "Friends don't have to tell each other everything."

"No, they don't. But they should keep what they don't tell to themselves!"

"Mostly I do," Monica shouted. "Sometimes by mistake something slips out. I can't help that."

Annie didn't say anything else, but she was convinced that she had been right sometime back to accuse Monica of being in love. The others were waiting in front of the drugstore. They were sucking on Smith Brothers cherry cough drops; none of them said anything particular to Monica, but they behaved kindly to her. If she had paid more attention to other people, she would have realized that they'd talked about her after she left and devised an explanation for her behavior that would enable them to treat her generously.

On the following weekend, on a soft postwar evening around eight o'clock, Annie and Monica came down the gleaming curved staircase of their sorority house. Both wore strapless evening gowns with wide skirts, pearls around their necks, and charm bracelets. They carried slim evening purses decorated with sequins. Each had an arm around the other's waist. It was the night of the Sadie Hawkins dance and they were leaving to pick up their dates. Annie, as usual, would drive. Jean Oyler and Penny McNeal were waiting for them at the foot of the stairs.

Since the drive into the country, Monica, in the interests of peace, had made her roommate a partial confession. She loved someone, she said, although she also hated him. She hated him, she explained, because he had made it impossible for her to love anyone else yet wouldn't declare himself. Monica, correctly judging Annie, despite her often free and wild talk, to be deeply conservative and moralistic, not only didn't tell her that the man she loved was already married, but let her think he was simply another student at the college. She thought that if she told Annie this much, Annie would finally leave her alone.

Monica's confession, however, had merely confirmed Annie's suspicion that Monica could mean no one else but Delmore Holland—it added up too neatly. The poor shy doves, she thought, and took it upon herself to rectify matters.

"Whom are you taking to the Sadie Hawkins dance?" she asked Monica the day before.

"No one," Monica said, surprised. "I don't even know that I'll go."

"Supposing I find a date for you?"

"I don't . . ."

"Be a sport, come on. I promise it will be someone you'll like. If you don't, you won't have to go out with him again. You'll just dance the night away and forget your troubles. Please, Monica? Let me do this one thing for you."

"Oh, why not," Monica said, sighing. What did it matter what she did, when Eldridge Jewell didn't love her?

Annie then hurried off to set Del on the right track. He listened unbelievingly while she scolded him for not having seen through Monica's dissemblances.

"She must have meant someone else, Annie. I know you intend well, but I don't think . . ."

"Nonsense, Delmore! Whom else could she mean? You two have misunderstood one another, is all. You're shy and she believes you don't care for her."

"I don't see how she could."

"That's just your trouble!" Annie exclaimed. "Won't you trust me, Del? All you have to do is don your finery and be ready to go at seven-thirty tomorrow night."

"Well, all right, Annie. If you insist. But if she's not pleased by your choice, don't say I didn't warn you."

"She'll be pleased, Del. Don't you worry."

As Annie, Monica, Jean, and Penny drove through the spring dusk, they joked about who Annie's choice would be.

"My swain," Monica said. "He's probably one of those science egg-heads who doesn't know how to talk to anything besides a Petri dish."

"He has buck teeth and thick glasses, didn't I tell you?" Annie teased her.

"He's fat and bald and pushing forty," Jean contributed.

"And reeks of garlic," added Penny.

How narrow-minded they were, really, Monica thought. Eldridge Jewell was no thin rail; his glasses were as thick as anyone's, and his teeth, if not exactly protruding, were not precisely straight, either. And he'd said goodbye to forty before any of them was in high school. She said all this to them silently. And, she added, lying naked in his arms in the woods I was happier than I've ever been in my life. She'd like to see the way their eyes would pop out of their heads if she told them the truth. Suddenly she looked around.

"Where are we going?" she asked Annie.

They were heading away from the area in which all the college residences were located, towards a part of town not usually inhabited by students.

"We told you," Annie said, laughing. "He's fat and bald and pushing forty. Not only that, he's a drunk and he has three wives."

"Annie," Monica asked grimly, "are you going to Del's?"

"Of course I'm not! What makes you think that?"

"Because he's the only person I know who lives out this way."

"You don't know everyone in Centuryville, do you?"

Monica let her proceed a few more blocks before saying icily, "Annie, stop this automobile. I'm not going to the dance with Delmore Holland. You've tricked me."

"Don't be silly, Monica," Annie said. "He's expecting us."

"That's just too bad. You never should have asked him. How could you?"

"But you said . . ."

"Said what?"

"You said you were in love, and . . ."

"You thought I meant *Del*? Are you crazy? Annie, stop right now!"

"But, Monica," Annie shouted, "he's in love with you too!"

Annie had turned down the street Del lived on. Monica knew he had to sleep on the sofa because his mother needed the rent money his room brought in, and if he wanted to study at home he either had to wait until everyone was asleep or go down into the dank, unwindowed cellar. It wasn't wired for electricity, and the kerosene lamp made him sick to his stomach. On top of that he worked as a night watchman from four until midnight three times a week to pay his tuition and help his mother. His situation would have melted a heart of stone—besides, he would lay down his life for her; she knew that. But she didn't have a heart; Eldridge Jewell had it, and until he let it go she'd feel nothing for anyone. It was as plain as that. Wishing wouldn't change it.

"Annie," she said evenly, "if you don't stop this car right now, I'll jump out."

She sounded so matter-of-fact that Annie paid no attention, but kept on down the street, raising a hand to wave to Del, who had descended his front steps when he saw the car. Next thing Annie knew, Penny McNeal was screaming, as Monica swung open the car door and jumped, tottered like a marionette for a few steps, then rolled along the pavement.

Annie screeched the car to a stop and Del, who'd seen it happen, came running. Monica was sitting in the road, delicately feeling her arms. Their entire length was scraped raw.

"What in hell happened?" Del shouted. "What happened?"

"What did you *do* that for?" Annie yelled, standing over her. "You stupid fool! How could you do such a thing?"

"I warned you," Monica said. "I told you I would. You just wouldn't listen to me."

XXI SPARTA (HARMONY)

The train for White River Junction, Vermont, left Baltimore at seven-thirty in the morning. Monica had driven Nick and Zoë to the station. As soon as the train pulled out, Nick told Zoë, he intended to relocate to the smoking car—daring her to criticize him. Monica raised Cain if she caught him with a cigarette. They were in their seats, watching her pace up and down the platform, scanning the windows; neither of them tried to attract her attention.

"She looks harmless enough," Nick said. "We'd have no way of knowing if she weren't our mother."

She was dressed in a pale pink, almost lavender-colored skirt and matching jacket made out of raw silk and underneath it a white blouse with tiny purple stripes. She wore white sandals with high heels and a narrow-brimmed white straw hat banded with a lavender ribbon; her short, naturally curly dark blond hair fluffed out from under it. She looked pretty sharp. Too bad neither of her children had inherited her looks, Zoë thought. They both had straight dull brown hair and the nicest thing anyone had ever said to her about her appearance was that she had the kind of features that would "age well." Thrills. Monica had to be boiling hot—it was already ninety—but she would never take her jacket off somewhere like a train platform. How had she gotten to be so proper? Had she always been this way? She'd had hysterics when Zoë came down at five that morning wearing blue jeans. "You will never leave the house like that to ride a train as long as I'm alive," she said. Zoë had settled for a dark blue sleeveless dress with a white collar that had been a birthday present from Charlotte, intending to change in the train bathroom once they were on their way. It looked like something a new-fangled nun would wear.

Nick was about to tap on the window, but Zoë suddenly cried, "Don't! Wait!" She felt as if she were on the verge of discovering something about their mother. Then, as they watched, a man approached Monica and asked her something. Maybe the time—except she didn't look at her watch. She thought for a minute, then said something. He nodded while she talked. What could she have to talk about? Wasn't she at all concerned that the train might leave at any minute? In fact it gave a jolt and suddenly both she and Nick started pounding on the window—Nick even called, "Hey, Mom! We're here!" though she couldn't hear and was no longer looking for them.

The man nodded and walked off, and Monica spotted them and came to stand below the window. They couldn't hear what she was saying over the noise of the engine.

"What?" they both shouted back.

She was saying two words—on the second word her teeth came down on her lower lip as if she were biting it.

Zoë and Nick looked at each other, then back at Monica and shrugged. Nick pointed at his ear and shook his head. She seemed annoyed, as if they weren't listening. Once again she shouted the words.

"I think she's saying, 'Have fun.' "

"Have fun?"

"Watch," Zoë said.

Monica opened her mouth the same way again and Nick said, "Hey, I think you're right!" He yelled, "We will!" and she nodded and smiled. At that moment the train jolted back, then caught itself and slid forward. Other people walked along the platform, keeping pace with whomever they were seeing off, but Monica stood still, waving at the train even when they could barely see her by craning their necks.

"I can't believe she's still waving! Do you think she even knew it was us?"

"God only knows," Nick said.

Was Monica *relieved* that they were leaving? It seemed to Zoë that she'd never realized before that their parents existed when she and Nick weren't with them. She settled back in her seat—Nick was by the window. The trip would take twelve hours—four to New York City, then seven to White River Junction. There was an hour layover in New York, although they didn't change trains. Every year Monica made them promise not to get off, and every year they disobeyed her.

Zoë looked out the window past Nick at the gray backs of buildings, and thought about Monica soundlessly shouting "Have fun! Have fun!" It made her seem so helpless somehow. What if she'd been trying to warn them of a tidal wave about to break on top of them? But why did this make her feel sorry for her *mother*?

"I'm going to change," she said, standing up to pull her suitcase down off the rack.

"Don't you think you should wait?"

"What for? You think Mom will have spies at the next stop?"

"I just thought maybe you could stay until they take our tickets."

"Can't you give them to them?"

"Forget it."

"I just don't see . . ."

"I said forget it!" Nick began to cough. When he didn't stop, Zoë shoved the suitcase back and sat down.

"Are you all right?"

He kept coughing, not answering.

"Are you starting to have an attack?"

The attacks weren't as bad as when he was younger, but they could still be pretty scary. They didn't have to rush him to the hospital, but that was because he had new drugs; they came in little pipe-shaped things he sprayed in his mouth. But if he had a real attack he had to stay home from school recuperating afterward. A couple of days ago, Monica had taken her aside and asked her to "promise not to aggravate" her brother—she didn't want him to have an asthma attack away from home. When Zoë protested, Monica said, "Just don't go on and on at him about things, will you promise me?"

"Give me a break, Mom. He's the one who goes on at me! Why do I have to be the one . . ."

"Because you don't have a disease with life-threatening complications," Monica said. "Take this seriously, Zoë! I simply think Nick may be on edge. I'm not sure why. All I'm asking is that you think before you say things. He's not as resilient as you are."

"How do you know whether I'm resilient or not? Anyway, what things?"

Now here was Nick coughing and wheezing and starting to look panic-stricken when they'd only been on the way for five minutes. Was Monica *right*? Did she aggravate Nick? Just because she'd wanted to change her clothes . . . ?

"My sprayer . . . ," Nick choked out. "I packed it, but now I don't remember where—Zoë, I can't breathe . . ."

"Calm down. You'll make it worse." She opened the old canvas purse Monica had handed down to her; she was carrying the tickets, all her money for the summer in traveller's checks, a hairbrush, a paperback copy of *Crime and Punishment*, which Rob had said she ought to read, a package of dried apricots, and an extra sprayer for Nick. Monica had given it to her the night of the briefing. She hadn't wanted to "make Nick nervous" by suggesting he carry one on him.

"Here," Zoë said, handing him the sprayer. "Just breathe in slowly."

He looked both furious and amazed, but he accepted it and sprayed three full sprays into his throat.

"You're only supposed to do two and then wait," Zoë said. She tried to take it back, but Nick closed his fist around the sprayer, resting his head back against the seat. His breathing deepened almost immediately. The people across the aisle were leaning over and asking if everything was all right.

"He's fine. He has asthma attacks sometimes, that's all."

"You don't have to tell the whole world," Nick muttered.

Zoë managed to keep herself from saying anything back. Nick stayed still with his eyes closed; in a minute the conductor showed up and she gave him both tickets.

"Boyfriend asleep?" he asked.

"He's not . . ." Zoë started to say, but the conductor had already moved on to the next seats.

Nick opened his eyes and looked at her, making Groucho eyebrows. Then he asked, "How'd you get hold of this?"

"Mom gave it to me. She thought if she gave it to you you'd worry."

"I would have worried less if I'd had it on me. The coughing only got so bad because I started to panic."

"Are you positive?"

"What do you mean, am I positive?"

"I thought maybe I'd brought it on."

"Are you insane?"

"Mom said I aggravate you."

"Jesus Christ, don't you know better than to listen to them? God, I'll be so happy to get out of that madhouse."

He was starting college in the fall and was going to live in the dorm.

"Are you going to take a pill?"

"I don't want to be a zombie the whole trip. They're just to calm me down. Now that I know I have the sprayer, I'll relax."

"I hope so."

"Don't be supercilious."

"I'm not!"

" 'I hope so.' Sounds pretty supercilious to me."

"Sorry."

After a minute he said, "What are you getting all depressed about? It's no big deal."

"You wouldn't understand."

But she was still wondering if Monica had been right; maybe it was why Rob hadn't been interested in her—she had some big flaw in her personality that everyone else could see but she couldn't. Monica said she aggravated Nick; Nick said she was supercilious; Laura Jenkins said she didn't give Rob what he deserved . . . Was she selfish and inconsiderate? It was true she'd thought only about what *she* wanted from that very first night lying out under the stars—but how was she supposed to know what Rob wanted? How could you see outside yourself?

"Try me," Nick said.

"I don't want to talk about it."

"Don't tell me. Romance. Come on, who is it?"

"You don't tell me things like that."

"So?" He laughed. "Get it off your chest. Otherwise it will fester inside and give you cancer. Cancer can be caused by unrequited love, you know."

"Oh, right."

"It's common knowledge."

She went and changed into her jeans. Nick didn't say anything about moving to the smoking car—at least she didn't have to try to argue him out of that. He started crowing about his great escape in the fall.

"God, I can't believe I'm going to have to live alone with them," she said.

"Come on, Zo, someone has to be there for them to drive crazy."

"That's what Rob says." She laughed. "He thinks something happens to people chemically when they have children."

"Rob?" Nick said. "Rob who?"

"Robert Went." She blushed. She hadn't been thinking about what she was saying. "Everyone calls him Rob now."

"Robert Went? I didn't know you were friends."

"We were in the play together."

"I'm aware of that fact, but according to Bridget you nearly quit because you had to kiss him."

"According to Bridget? Since when are you so chummy with Bridget?"

"We were in the same Greek class this year."

"I know, but . . ."

"I have to admit I was surprised to discover that Bridget was actually an intelligent human being. Here all these years I thought she was just my kid sister's obnoxious best friend."

"Thanks a lot."

"You're welcome. However, let's not change the subject. The real news in this conversation is that you're friends with Robert Went. Robert Went over the edge."

"You're really out of date." No one had said that for years.

"Crazy as a loon."

"He is not crazy."

Nick made spy-eyes, as she and Bridget used to call them.

"Did you go *out* with him?"

"None of your business."

Suddenly he started grinning like a maniac. "You did! I can't believe it—my sister dated Robert Went! Zoë and Robert—excuse me, Rob—sitting in a tree, K. I. S. S . . ."

"I don't see what the big deal is."

"She doesn't see what the big deal is, going out with a lunatic. My own sister . . ."

"You don't even know him."

"You don't have to know him. He's got that wild look in his eye."

"I can't believe you're so prejudiced."

"Besides, Bridget's with him every class period. She's supplied me with inside information."

"Such as?"

"I can't really remember specifically."

"I think you owe it to me to tell me what she said."

"I *owe* it to you?"

"What makes you think Bridget knows what she's talking about? She may be in Rob's class but she never has anything to do with him."

"Fine. Forget I said anything."

Nick looked out the window as if the view were fascinating, which it wasn't, but suddenly Zoë could see as clearly as Nick could what he was looking at: what he wasn't telling her and why Bridget had been weirder than ever lately, why Nick had seemed "on edge" to Monica. She waited until he turned back around.

"I think you're keeping something secret yourself. You're going out with Bridget, aren't you? Don't bother trying to deny it. I can tell by your expression."

She could see him debating, but finally he said, "So? Is there some law against it?"

"Have you gone out a lot?"

"What's a lot? We went out a few times."

"Are you going steady?"

"How could we be? We'll be in Harmony all summer."

"Are you going to write letters?"

"I more or less doubt it."

"Why, did she jilt you?"

" 'Jilt . . .' Where did you get *that* word?"

Zoë had said it off the top of her head. "You mean it's true?" she exclaimed. "Bridget broke up with you?"

"Could we just drop the subject?"

"I can't believe this!"

"Look, Zoë. If I tell you will you promise not to bug me about it all summer?"

"Sure. Of course."

"Okay. We went out four times exactly. I wanted to keep seeing her, but she didn't want to, okay?"

"Why not?"

"You're already breaking your promise!"

"I promised not to bring it up after this, but you haven't told me anything."

Nick groaned. "Christ. She was going out with some guy from the college at the same time. When she told me she didn't want to keep seeing me she said that she was attracted to men with more experience. Quote unquote."

"What? What a jerk! She really said that? Were you upset?"

"I didn't plan to kill myself over it, if that's what you mean."

"I just can't believe this. When did it happen?"

"About a month ago. Can we drop it now?"

Right in the middle of rehearsals for *The End of Slavery*. Well, that figured. It would hurt Nick's feelings if she told him that Bridget had gone out with him to get even with her for becoming friends with Rob, but it was obvious that that was what had happened. Yet in that case Bridget would have wanted Zoë to know she was dating Nick. So what . . . ? Was Nick really *hurt* because of Bridget? Maybe Bridget hadn't been able to carry out her revenge because she couldn't stand it that Nick was so inexperienced. Probably over the summer Rob and Bridget would run into each other and talk about how screwed up she and Nick were. Neither of them knew what to do when they went out with someone. If it hadn't been for the proof of their own existence, they'd have had to conclude that Seth and Monica had never heard of sex, let alone done it. Zoë felt disgusted by herself and Nick—and that conductor had thought he was her *boyfriend*!

For the rest of the trip they both avoided talking about sensitive subjects. Nick read James Bond and she read *Crime and Punishment*, which was pretty slow, and she couldn't figure out why Rob had been so thrilled by it. As the trip went on, she felt as if she and Nick were being sent into exile from Sparta because neither of them knew how to have a relationship. She couldn't believe she had to spend the whole summer with her *brother.* But when they finally arrived in White River Junction and Verne Magoon was there to meet them in Charlotte's station wagon (Charlotte had never learned to drive), and Buell, Verne's grandson and their friend, was with him, she began to feel better. At least everyone in Harmony didn't know her and Nick's reputation.

"How you *been*?" Buell said.

"Oh, okay. How you been?"

"Keepin' outa trouble."

"What kinda trouble?" Nick asked.

They always immediately started talking like him.

"Any kind I could think of," Buell said, winking at her.

"Your grandma's been sit'n on the po'wch all day," Verne said. "She's not too eager to see you."

"Guess not," Nick said.

Though Charlotte seemed to enjoy their company, you couldn't really have a conversation with her—she'd forget what you were talking about from moment to moment. She spent most of her time on the front porch in her white wicker rocking chair sewing or reading the Bible, or else just staring at the graveyard across the street. Her husband and her mother were buried there, but there weren't any markers for her dead sons. By now Zoë knew that her mother's "brothers" had been miscarriages.

Charlotte said grace at every meal and every morning after breakfast read them the "lesson" she got from some schedule at church. Listening to her grandmother's gentle, resigned voice gave Zoë her flat Sunday feeling—everything seemed to be just an empty shell. It was the same way she felt about herself when she thought about people in Sparta talking about her and Nick and how they didn't know anything about anything.

Strangely enough, Sunday itself was when they had the best time with Charlotte. Maybe because then it was just there, instead of leaking into all the other days of the week. Mrs. Magoon, Verne's daughter-in-law, who did the cooking and the cleaning, was off except for coming by in the morning to make sure that Charlotte took her medication; they went to church, but afterwards they always went out to dinner at The Blue Rooster, the only real restaurant in Harmony. It had a buffet every Sunday: ham and turkey and roast beef; baked beans, cole slaw, potato salad, Jello with fruit in it, spiced apples, sweet pickles, corn relish, homemade rolls, date bread, and banana bread; then for dessert lots of kinds of pie, depending on the time of the summer: strawberry-rhubarb, raspberry, blueberry, custard, lemon meringue, apple, blackberry . . . There was always a tall four-layer devil's food cake with chocolate frosting and an angel food cake with lemon frosting standing up in peaks. She and Nick ate like pigs, and Charlotte always laughed when they puffed out their cheeks or held their stomachs and oinked. She ate hardly anything herself—whatever drug she was on must have suppressed her appetite; that was what had happened to Rob after his accident.

"I think Buell Magoon likes me," Zoë wrote to Bridget, who'd started corresponding as if they'd never had a falling out, "though of course nothing can get going with Nick the watchdog always around."

At one point she wrote Bridget that Nick seemed sort of depressed and she thought maybe he was carrying a torch for someone, but Bridget knew how secretive he was, et cetera—to give Bridget a chance to tell her; however, Bridget didn't confess anything. She did write back with various schemes for how Zoë could get to be alone with Buell, but Bridget didn't understand what things were like in Harmony—she and Buell couldn't just go off somewhere. Mainly Bridget complained about how bored she was. "What a hellhole of a town this is," she wrote. Her "paramour" from the college had "had the nerve to go home for the summer," and if that wasn't bad enough, she was going to have to "be all hostessy to this French creep and his family" who were coming to visit. "If my mother tells me one more time that his name is pronounced 'Bear-narrh' not 'Bernard,' I'm going to commit hari-kiri, or whatever it's called. You don't know how lucky you are to have a parent-free summer."

Bridget was the first one to mention Rob.

> I don't know how to put this, exactly, [she wrote], but he swims *without his leg*. I mean, he walks out on his artificial leg, which is a little weird, but no big deal, but then he takes it *off* when he goes in the pool. I don't want you to think I'm a bigot or anything—I mean, I think he's entirely entitled to swim in this or any other pool in the universe, with or without his leg, but what gets me is that I think he does it on purpose to make people uncomfortable. He's constantly making remarks about it, like he's the only mermaid in the pool, or he has to take his leg off so it won't get sunburned, or if he catches someone looking at him he says really loudly, "Don't worry, it's not catching." I think he's gone off the deep end. (No pun intended.) Don't get me wrong. I feel as much sympathy for him as anybody (except you, I guess, since you're probably the only friend he's ever had), but I think it's weird that he's always trying to call attention to himself. It's like he's bragging about having only one leg, do you know what I mean? Did he ever act like that with you?
>
> I hope I'm not offending you, by the way. I don't know how you feel about him these days, but I asked him if you guys were corresponding and he said no, so (unless he's just not telling me, of

> course) I didn't think you'd mind if I wrote you about him. But maybe you don't give a damn. Just say the word and I'll never mention his name again.

In one way Zoë wanted to write, "God, that's really weird. I hate to say it, but I honestly think he's acting that way because he thinks I rejected him," and then Bridget would probably tell her about Nick and they could get back to genuinely being friends, but she didn't; she couldn't just throw Rob to the wolves like that; make a sacrifice out of him to appease the wrathful god Bridget. Besides, it would just confirm Bridget's suspicion that nothing had ever really gone on between them. Then something happened in Harmony that made her stop thinking about Rob and Bridget altogether.

Nick wasn't allowed in the Magoons' hayloft because his allergies might set off an asthma attack, but it frustrated him no end, and every summer at least once he finally couldn't stand it and would go up anyway, then have to be rushed to Dr. Jewell for an Adrenalin shot. Monica was always furious when she heard, though less it seemed because Nick had disobeyed orders than because she didn't "enjoy being forced to use Dr. Jewell's services." According to her he was a "small-town quack" and she'd only take her family to him "under duress"; unless it was an emergency, if they needed a doctor she had Mrs. Magoon drive them to Dr. Mervyn in Hanover.

This summer Nick controlled himself until almost August. Then he said he was going to try it—he hadn't had a single problem since the train, and besides he had the sprayer. Zoë knew there was no point in trying to prevent him so they went up with Buell and started swinging from the rope tied around a rafter, jumping into a pile of loose hay, and Nick actually seemed okay for a while. She was almost beginning to believe he'd been right when suddenly he coughed a couple of times and then before they knew it he began turning bright red and then practically purple.

"Zoë!" he croaked in this panicky voice. "I can't breathe! I can't breathe!"

"I knew it! You stupid idiot! Get your sprayer!"

He started rummaging through his pockets, but it must have fallen out in the hay. Yet before she and Buell could start looking for it Nick had staggered towards the second-floor doorway that hay was unloaded into and jumped right out of it. (Later he told her that the attack was the worst one he'd ever had.) She and Buell started screaming for Verne, Jr., and Dwight, who were loading the manure spreader, and then Mrs. Magoon, who happened to be home, thank God, had figured out what the story was (she was used to it by now) and came running with a cup of the strongest instant coffee she could make that would still be liquid. Before Nick had the sprayer it was what they always gave him to help him breathe until they could get him to the doctor. However, it turned out that this time he'd also broken his leg. Needless to say, there would be no more Nick in the hayloft that summer. He was going to be in a cast for six weeks minimum; Monica wanted them to come home early, but fortunately they managed to convince her that Nick would only be more uncomfortable in ninety-five degree-, ninety-nine-percent-humidity-Sparta.

Though Zoë kept Nick company most of the time, playing chess and checkers and gin rummy, sometimes she still went to visit Buell, who was too busy now with haying to come over.

One afternoon she found him hosing down the milkhouse—the milk truck had just come and he was rinsing out the empty bulk tank. She waited until he'd finished. By then she had made up her mind.

"What else do you have to do?" she asked.

"Nothing till milking."

"Thought I might go up in the hayloft," she said.

"What you goin' to do up there?"

"Look for mischief."

"Think you can find it by yourself?"

They climbed into a hideout they'd been building the day Nick had had his attack, and she curled up in a corner. She was being pretty obvious, she thought, but Buell said, "Now what?"

"I don't know."

"How about hide and seek? Remember how to play that?"

"If you want to."

"Only one thing," he said. "Whoever gets found before counting to twenty has to do something the other person says."

The first couple of times she found him before she'd counted to twenty, she didn't make him do anything; she told him she was saving up his penances. When he found her, he said, "Guess I'll just save mine up too." But his next turn he pretended to stumble into her hiding place; he grabbed hold of her and she fell down with him.

"Not lettin' you get away this time. Now you got to pay up."

Then he kissed her. She kissed him back. They went on kissing, while the whole time she was thinking how *normal* it was, even though she hadn't kissed anyone since Archie Tannenbaum in third grade. Why hadn't it been this easy with Rob?

She and Nick were leaving in a few weeks, but in between she and

Buell went off together as much as they could. It was amazing that Nick didn't suspect anything. She wouldn't have been surprised if he thought she was totally sexless. Rob evidently did. She even snuck out a few times after Nick and Charlotte were in bed; she and Buell would go into the old horse barn where there was still some moldy hay, or just out into the fields, even though they were usually wet by that time. The only problem was, Buell didn't seem to want to do anything except kiss her. He felt her breast once, but through her clothes—it could even have been an accident. She got up her courage once and asked him, didn't he want to do more than kiss? It felt so uncomplicated, lying out in the fields under the stars—what should have happened that time with Rob after *The End of Slavery* but hadn't. But Buell said it wouldn't be right.

"You mean you're not attracted to me," she said.

"You're crazy if you think that!" he exclaimed.

"Then I guess I'm crazy."

Buell even told her he loved her; he said if he was older he'd ask her to marry him, and she said, "Then why don't you want to fool around?" But he just laughed. He said he respected her too much, but obviously there was something about her that turned men off. She had been feeling kind of scornful of Rob, for not being as masculine as Buell, for being citified and full of complexes, but now it began to seem to her that Buell just didn't have as strong a character. She'd been able to persuade him to kiss her against his better judgment, though he'd balked when it came to going all the way. She started feeling guilty for being unfaithful to Rob. If she'd just had more will power—if she'd shown him she was true by writing letters—then when she got back he might have decided she was worthy of him after all. How could she have been such an idiot as to leave Sparta for the whole summer? All she'd done was to prove to Rob that she wasn't interested in him! How could she have been so stupid?

She could hardly stand the last few days in Harmony and the whole way home on the train all she could think about was what an unbelievable jerk she'd been; she hoped to God it wasn't too late. Then practically the first thing Bridget told her was that Robert Went had quit school and opened a bakery.

XXII CASCABEL FLATS

There were already so many cars that they had to park halfway up Stewart's driveway and Ellie was anxious about the snake. Under the tinfoil on the platter she carried, the poor thing was coiled and propped into striking position with toothpicks browned in butter so they'd be camouflaged.

The Beauregards' hacienda was lit up like something out of a fairy tale. All along the roof edges and in the windows faint lights were flickering—it made Zoë think of an ocean liner, what it would look like passing soundlessly by across a dark ocean. It was very mysterious and beautiful, and she hoped Ellie wouldn't start up again with the social commentary she'd given them on the drive over (Stewart liked to mix and match; the party would be a real melting pot; *out here* was a kind of a microcosm of the many forces waging war throughout the U.S., even though people moved out here because they felt they could escape them . . .); however, all she said was, "I hope I don't drop this."

She was obviously depressed. Since Nick had rushed out of the kitchen after learning of his Tortuga rattlesnake's execution she'd hardly spoken to him. It was he who now informed the rest of them that the lights were called *farolitos:* "little lanterns"; they were candles in brown paper bags weighted down by sand. It was traditional out here to decorate the rooftops and walls with them at Christmastime; on Christmas Eve everyone walked around town looking at them—it was quite spectacular. He and Ellie planned to take them on the tour prior to the Christmas Eve service. The lights were symbolically meant to guide Mary and Joseph on their way to Bethlehem.

"I should have known," Monica said.

The air was thick and moist with unfallen snow. As they neared the house a wild, half-sweet smell of woodsmoke that Nick said was burning piñon became practically edible in the air. Guests were entering through the door on the right side of the archway—a *maid* opened it: black uniform and white apron. She tried to take the tinfoil-covered snake from

Ellie, but Ellie insisted on carrying it to the kitchen herself; the maid accepted the rest of their coats instead.

The very long room, which Zoë hadn't ventured into earlier, was already crowded. Most people were standing, clutching glass cups of frothy eggnog. Another maid, holding aloft a platter of hors d'oeuvres, threaded her way among the guests. Zoë picked Stewart out immediately; he was leaning against a wall beside one of the fireplaces. There were two of them catty-corner to each other, both bright with crackling fires. Stewart, still wearing the jeans and flannel shirt he'd had on that afternoon, seemed to be the only person in the room who wasn't dressed up, though the styles varied: men were wearing anything from suits to tie-dyed shirts; women, long skirts with embroidered Mexican blouses or conservative dresses of velvet or silk. Everyone seemed to be loaded with Indian jewelry. Stewart was seemingly fascinated by the conversation of a man with shoulder-length gray-blond hair wearing a black leather vest over a turtleneck, who was pounding his fist into his palm. Stewart looked so innocuous that Zoë couldn't believe the things she'd been thinking about him since that afternoon—that he was the "real thing" (whereas Rob had been a weak imitation); that he would carry out the task that Rob—or Anders Ogilvy—had left incomplete, though her mind veered off from thinking in any detail about what she might mean.

As they moved forward into the room, she heard a person talking about "body quadrants." Someone else said, "More people commit suicide during the Christmas holidays than at any other time." "That makes sense." "The soil around here is full of uranium—no one has any idea what effect that has on brain waves." "The point is, the West is over—it's *over.*" She wished that Rob were there—she'd love to hear his comments—but she might as well face the fact that he wasn't going to make it in time. (In time, at least, to be the father of her child.)

They had almost made it to the punchbowl when Judith, wearing a blouse embroidered with giant red flowers and a short black velvet skirt, hostessed up to them and with a welcoming smile announced that she'd "deduced" Monica's and Pryce's identities. She shook hands with Pryce. She said, "Nick, I think you know quite a few of these people—Nancy's here somewhere. And there's Michael, over there in the corner with Stewart." At that moment Ellie reappeared, still wearing her coat, and exclaimed, "Judith!"

"How are you, Ellie?" Judith asked.

She spoke more coolly than when she'd greeted the rest of them—did Ellie notice? If so, she didn't let on. She was cheerfully telling Judith that the kitchen staff were ready to rebel—she'd told them it was a rattlesnake, and not to look if they were squeamish, but they hadn't believed her. She was surprised Judith hadn't heard the screams from here.

"What snake?" Judith asked, frowning.

"Stuffed, Judith—not alive. I told you I was bringing a surprise."

"I had no idea that was what you meant."

"Well, if you'd rather not serve it . . ."

"Perhaps not," Judith said. "Let me think about it."

Pretty blunt. She went on talking to Nick, then took him off to introduce him to someone named Dan Bingham who had some connection with the university. Pryce took Monica's arm and steered her on to the punch table. Ellie stood staring after Nick and Judith, then suddenly said, "Could we talk for a minute, Zoë?"

Sure. Go ahead.

"No, I mean privately. How about over there? No one's sitting in that windowseat. Unless you want a drink immediately . . ."

She shook her head: *It's fine.* As they walked over, she didn't have to look to know that Stewart was watching them. The room was electrified with it—the party chat was like cells his wordless messages travelled over. "It's only out here that I feel centered." "I knew the moment I saw those mountains that I never wanted to let them out of my sight." "Christmas feels different, too—more organic." "I honestly feel sorry for the rest of the country." "Phil, let me introduce Abby and Josh—Dan Bingham's children. They're home from college for the holidays." "Just don't tell everyone about it—they'll want to move out here." "With the number of nuclear strategists up in the hills, I'm sure we could find a way to secede."

Ellie had taken off her coat and stuffed it behind her on the windowseat and sat down. Then she laughed.

"It's getting to be a regular thing, our evening tête-à-tête, isn't it?—not that I object, though I wish the subjects were different. Well, I may as well get to the point before someone interrupts us. I hope you won't think this is too weird of me, but I feel I should say something to you about Stewart."

About Stewart? Zoë should have seen this coming.

"You've gathered by now that I'm not his biggest fan. I sometimes even think he's the devil incarnate, though it's one thing to believe it in the abstract—to hear about people like that on the news . . ." She laughed. "You never think it could be someone you know."

Zoë frowned. *People like what?*

Just what are you up to? Rob asked. Big deal you spent ten years not talking—it hasn't made you any smarter.

It was beginning to make her uncomfortable, the way he was responding—or not—on his own.

"I know, I know—I wouldn't blame you if you thought I'd gone off the deep end—but, Zoë, honestly, I'm not trying to be patronizing. I just feel I should warn you."

Warn me? Warn her off, was what Ellie meant.

"Maybe I don't need to—maybe you aren't in the least susceptible, though I . . . Look, whether this is the product of my overactive imagination or not, I hope you know enough not to trust Stewart. I don't know what private vendetta he's carrying out against the world, but at the moment he seems to be trying to accomplish it through our family. I wouldn't like to see you become the next victim."

Zoë raised her eyebrows: *Victim!*

"I'm sorry—I know it's not fair of me to do this when there's nothing you can write on. Let me go get something."

No, just go ahead, she gestured.

"Are you sure?"

Go on.

"All right, but only if you promise to stop me if you want to say anything. I mean, anything involved—I can understand sometimes, you know." Ellie smiled tentatively. "Maybe I'm being absurd—you don't find him the slightest bit interesting—but this afternoon I was sort of getting the impression . . ."

When Zoë didn't respond, Ellie went on.

"From what I can see, I'd say that Pryce loves you. I also get the feeling that it may not be mutual. Am I being unwelcomely personal?"

Zoë shrugged.

"I'm not trying to pry, honest, Zoë. I know you're a private person. I wouldn't say this if I didn't feel . . . If what I said is true, it could make you more vulnerable to Stewart's manipulations."

If what's true?

Ellie misread. She looked around to make sure no one was within hearing.

"Okay, I guess I'm hardly being fair. Invading your privacy like this, while . . . If I keep being so mysterious, you're not going to believe me. It's just . . . Okay." She laughed. "I've told you all my other secrets. Why not this one as well? I know you'll keep what I say to yourself." She let out a long breath. "Okay. Basically, Stewart came on to me. I don't mean once, either, but over a period of time. Now I'm sure he must have noticed right away that Nick and I were having problems. We'd already started having difficulties about . . . what I told you last night. For all I know, Nick may have even told Stewart about it."

Zoë must have looked skeptical—she was thinking that Ellie would do anything to keep her away from Stewart—but again Ellie misinterpreted.

"Don't think I mean Stewart made suggestive *remarks*. I mean he made a crusade of it. He'd come by when Nick wasn't around—this was at the place we lived before—claiming he was looking for Nick, although he had to know Nick was working. It didn't bother me at first—I figured he wanted to be friends but was too awkward to come out and say so. He seemed like he needed someone to talk to. That myopic gaze—he can look so fetchingly helpless. I'd heard what a big deal he was in town from Nancy, but like you probably, when I first met him I couldn't believe that *he* was the focus of so much gossip. I just figured he was a shy fellow who found it a relief to talk to someone who wasn't in awe of him. I didn't think it was anything more than that in the beginning, though now I see that even then I was making up stories about him to suit myself. He makes people do that, you know.

"So, anyway, things went along like that for a while. I'd invite him in for a beer, he'd put his feet up, make himself at home. One beer, another . . . And he'd talk to me. At first about work, the changes happening to the town, how he was sick of everybody minding his business for him. How could he single-handedly save what everyone else wanted to destroy? Of course I was the soul of sympathy. Yes, it's lonely at the top, poor Stewart, et cetera, et cetera. Then he became more personal. Marriage. How confining marriage was. How he and Judith had been together for so long, all their lives, more or less, and though he couldn't imagine living without her, he often felt impatient, did I understand? Did I ever feel like that? Pretty blatant, but believe it or not I still thought he just wanted a confidante."

Zoë nodded unwillingly.

"I'm pretty terminally dense in some respects, I guess, but, to be honest, nothing like that had ever happened to me. I had nothing to compare it to. Of course, eventually even I began to get the point. At first I answered evasively, but pretty soon I began to trust him. Besides, I told myself, there wasn't a married person alive who hadn't felt dissatisfied at some time or other. What harm could there be in admitting that? I figured he was attracted to me, and I certainly found him attractive—that quiet intensity of his. There wasn't anything wrong with that. And I was finding it such a relief to have someone to confide in about Nick. Stewart went on and on about Judith, how fond he was of her—his exact word—but he couldn't really talk to her. The familiar story. I told him about my problems with Nick—our personality conflicts, my impatience with his moodiness, the way he just disappears on me sometimes into these . . . *states.* Eventually I even told him about our difficulties having a baby. I didn't tell him Nick had refused to be tested—that seemed disloyal to Nick—and in all my conversations with Stewart up to that point I really hadn't been trying to blame Nick for anything. I presented every problem as our problem—the modern way, you know.

"This went on for a couple of months—Stewart coming at first once a week, then twice or three times. But then there began to be those silences. The old who's-going-to-make-the-first-move silences. That was when I realized I had to make a decision about what I would do if and when. Each time after he left I told myself I had to ask him not to come again—things were heating up too much—but of course I never did. All this time, by the way, he's making increasingly suggestive remarks. Well, suggestive is the wrong word. He was pretty up-front about it. Didn't think it made sense that one should have to love only one person; you made these promises to people before you knew who else was out in the world—was it fair to make people keep promises made in ignorance? I found I couldn't disagree with him. I'd been with Nick since I was fairly young also, and I certainly wouldn't choose someone with Nick's temperament again. Don't worry . . ." Ellie smiled. "I'm not telling you anything I haven't told Nick. I tell you, I was really beginning to think Stewart was falling in love with me. No one had looked at me like that for so long—so desirously. I finally couldn't stand it." She laughed. "I'd completely forgotten how nondescript he'd seemed to me in the beginning. I'd been agonizing about whether it was a terrible thing to do or not, was I somehow justified because Nick had basically lost all sexual interest in me—I even imagined that *he* was having an affair. I *hoped* he was—that would get me off the hook. Finally I decided I was just making too much out of the whole thing. Stewart seemed to be getting impatient and I thought, what the hell, we'll have an affair, get rid of all this tension, and then we can get back to being friends." She shook her head. "What I thought was the beginning of the end was really only the beginning. Christ, what torture I went through."

Torture?

"You probably want to know what happened, after all this buildup. The answer is, exactly nothing. Once I'd made up my mind, I went out of my way to show Stewart that I was available, but now he didn't seem to get it. I turned all kinds of mental somersaults, trying to figure out if he was simply shy or what was going on. Finally one day I came out with it. And I made a fool of myself—I still cringe whenever I think of it."

Ellie shook her head. "It was only a couple of weeks after we'd moved in. The rattlesnake episode was over and it was before I'd realized that Aladdin wouldn't recover. Even though I still couldn't believe that Stewart hadn't known about the snakes, I'd talked myself into thinking that his forgetting to tell us was all part of his manly, untamed nature. That day he'd been sitting in the living room most of the afternoon—I'd been trying to write some letters and was a little irritated at being disturbed—and he was going on and on about how he wanted a different life and what a relief it was to talk to me about it, et cetera, et cetera. Finally I spun around and said, 'Stewart, do you want to go to bed with me or not? If we're going to, let's do it and stop hinting around.' I was exactly that direct. I don't know what got into me—I've never been the aggressor before. I suppose I was just too frustrated at that point to worry about being ladylike. I say this, and then I sit there. Stewart's looking at me, then smiles that swallowed-the-cat smile he has and says, 'What makes you think I want to do that, Ellen?' As if he'd just met me and didn't know I had a nickname. Christ. But I was so blind that I *still* didn't get it. I thought that was his coy way of saying yes. I don't mind admitting to you that I was ready by that time. It felt as if we'd had two months of foreplay. He was sitting on the couch and I went right over and sat down next to him and put my hand on his knee."

Ellie shook her head and laughed angrily.

"He stiffened as if I'd given him an electric shock. I looked at him and he had the stoniest-looking face I'd ever seen—cold, cold, cold like you wouldn't believe. More than cold—inhuman. Needless to say, I took my hand away. Took my hand away . . . Moved across the room! But I was pissed, I tell you. 'What the hell have you been doing here, all this time?' I screamed at him. 'Don't tell me you haven't been driving at that all these weeks!'

" 'I really don't know what you're talking about, Ellen,' he said. I was *furious,* but the more I berated him, the nastier he got. Finally he says, 'You have a vivid imagination, Ellen.' I'm screaming at him by this time. Then he says, 'I can see I'm not welcome here,' stands up, and leaves—just leaves! Walks out the door. Twisting every single thing that had happened, assuming not one iota of responsibility for anything. And that was the last time I've seen him alone—believe me, he's made sure of that."

Ellie waited and Zoë nodded, frowning slightly. Among other things, she was thinking that Ellie must assume she felt no allegiance to Nick whatsoever. Didn't it occur to her that she might have qualms about keeping Ellie's would-be infidelity in confidence? She and Nick had their sibling rivalry, but that was none of Ellie's business.

Ellie looked at her for a minute, then exclaimed, "I hope you don't think I'm exaggerating things, Zoë. That's Stewart's whole trick! Arousing feelings he never means to satisfy, then making you think you imagined everything. I honestly don't know what sadistic pleasure he derives from it. At this point I don't even want to know. I've wasted enough time trying to figure it out. That's part of the trap—you think if you can just understand him it will change things. I don't know what rage he's trying to relieve and I don't care. Has he said anything to you about me?"

Zoë shook her head.

Strictly that was true. However, his attitude had been clear enough.

She glanced over Ellie's shoulder and, relieved, flicked her chin back: *Someone's coming.* Ellie swivelled, smiled at Pryce approaching with three cups of eggnog, then went on quickly, "I didn't like you to think I bore him a grudge for no reason."

Zoë nodded, sorry for Ellie. She couldn't believe Stewart would treat someone he respected the way Ellie claimed he'd treated her. She must have ascribed motives to Stewart he'd never had. Didn't Ellie know that you couldn't trust what someone *said*?

"If I'm completely off where you're concerned, then forget what I've told you. I felt I had to say something—you seemed so skeptical."

I understand. What else was she going to say? "What's going on between Stewart and me is completely different"? "It has to do with things that happened years ago, things that have never been finished"?

"You certainly are cozily ensconced here," Pryce remarked as they took their cups from him.

"Oh, I've just been chewing her ear off, poor thing. She's been very forbearing."

Pryce glanced at Zoë to see if she were offended, then said affectionately, "She is." He added, "Speaking of having one's ear chewed off—I was detained by your friend Michael Chamberlain. Stewart introduced us. So he could escape, I think."

Zoë glanced over at the fireplace—how long had Stewart been gone? She'd felt certain that he'd been observing her and Ellie. She was anxious suddenly; where was he? Surely he knew there was no time to waste.

"Apparently Michael's writing a mystery story about the penitential sects around here," Pryce said to Ellie. "Did you know that?"

"How strange—no. He's never mentioned it."

"When he found out I'm a lawyer he corralled me. Some legal details he needs help working out. I said I'd go back." Pryce looked at Ellie. "My impression is that the story's based on Stewart's father. The main character is a painter who happens to witness something incriminating at one of the ceremonies which he reveals in his paintings but subsequently his paintings disappear. Sound plausible?"

Ellie shrugged. "Everything does sound plausible where the Beauregards are concerned."

Pryce and Ellie smiled at each other. Evidently they'd become good friends while stuffing the snake that afternoon.

"Oh, and you'll be interested to hear this," Pryce continued. "The local museum finally filed an injunction against Stewart this afternoon."

"You're kidding!"

"In response to one filed by Stewart this morning. Evidently there's some property dispute—do you know about that? He's seeking to have one of the city's water reservoirs shut off as of the first of the year."

"What?"

"Apparently his great-grandfather gave the city a ninety-nine-year lease to land on which it then built a reservoir. I suppose the document's been moldering away at the courthouse and no one would have remembered it if the city hadn't suddenly received a letter from Stewart's attorney giving notice that he doesn't intend to renew."

"But how can he do that?" Ellie exclaimed.

"I don't think he can, in the long run. I don't know the particulars of the water laws out here, but I know Stewart can't own the water. I'm sure the city or the state will be able to exercise the right of eminent domain. Nevertheless, Stewart could tie things up for quite a while and cost the city a fortune in legal fees. Clearly they filed their injunction as a retaliatory measure, hoping he'll settle out of court."

"I shouldn't imagine Stewart would enjoy having the issue of his father's paintings decided in public," Ellie said. "I'm amazed, though. If it's the reservoir I think it is, he could cut off two thirds of the city's water supply."

"He won't be able to do that, Ellie."

"Maybe not—but to think of having the chutzpah to try it! I told you one should never underestimate him," she said, glancing at Zoë.

"I'm sorry I won't be around when it comes to a head. It might be pretty interesting."

"Why won't you be? If Stewart's trying to shut off the water by the first of the year . . ."

"Both sides will ask for postponements. It could take months before it actually comes to court, though I bet it never will. They'll settle. Well, I'd better go back. I promised Michael I'd only be gone a minute."

"I'm glad you had a chance to meet him," Ellie said. "If you can stand not getting a word in edgewise, he's interesting. He knows more lore about the area than anyone else I've met here." As Pryce left she continued, "I wonder how many people have heard the news. Strange to think that Stewart's guests might know the city's suing him for illegal possession and vice versa. Probably all dying to talk about it but afraid he'll overhear them."

Zoë would have liked to ask Ellie why Stewart wouldn't let the museum have his father's paintings—if she'd given a reason when she mentioned the story yesterday Zoë hadn't heard it—but it wasn't worth searching for pen and paper. Looking around the room, she spotted Monica talking to one of what seemed to be an endless supply of tall, sincere-looking men with beards, dressed in Mexican wedding shirts and wearing those revolting string ties that made them look like overgrown boy scouts. She wondered if Michael Chamberlain were divorced. At this moment Judith Beauregard bore down on them from the direction of the kitchen. She bestowed a rueful smile upon them.

"Ellie, the most dreadful thing's happened—I'm afraid it's your snake. One of the caterers set out to put it in the oven—she thought she'd warm it up. I'd told everyone not to touch it, but I suppose they weren't paying attention. When she took the tinfoil off, someone who wasn't there when you told them what it was . . ." Judith laughed, and laid her hand on Ellie's shoulder. "Well, she reacted very quickly. She grabbed a spatula lying at hand and knocked it off the platter. If she'd thought half a minute she'd have realized that no live snake would have stayed nicely coiled up like that under a piece of aluminum foil, but she reacted instinctively. I'm afraid the head came off. Otherwise it seems all right. Do you think you might be able to put it back together? I do think I'd prefer not to serve it—it doesn't quite seem in the Christmas spirit somehow—though I appreciate the gesture. You'll be able to use it at home, won't you? I thought you'd want to repair it right away." She laughed again. "The whole kitchen is talking about the crazy gringa who would stuff a rattlesnake."

Ellie gave Zoë an incomprehensible look and went off with Judith. Zoë slid farther back into the uncushioned adobe windowseat and gazed out at the room, sipping eggnog. If Pryce noticed she was alone he'd be sure to come over to run interference for her with anyone who might try to strike up a conversation, but he had his back to her, listening to Michael Chamberlain. Maybe Michael was trying to smoke Stewart out with his mystery novel—what could the paintings reveal that Stewart would want to keep hidden? What could happen at the secret religious ceremonies that could incriminate *Stewart*?

"Interrupting something?" Stewart asked. He smelled as if he'd just come in from outside. "It looked like it needed interrupting." Then he leaned forward, blocking her view of the room. Speaking rapidly, he said, "You know I don't give a damn what people think—though I can guess what Ellen told you. What I want to know is if you believe her." Now he sat down, letting one of his knees press lightly against hers. "You're going to tell me what you know sooner or later—why do you fight it?"

What I know?

"Don't pretend you don't know what I'm talking about."

She shrugged. Okay. *What were you in for? Whom did you kill?*

"Not like that, not now," he said irritably, fingering the cushion.

What did he mean? Had he figured out the sign for kill? It was pretty graphic, and she felt stupidly nervous for a moment. Embarrassed, as if she'd been flirting.

"I know you don't *want* to tell me," he said. "The things people say about me—they don't understand. You know better than to believe them."

No, she gestured, thinking suddenly, No! I don't want to tell you—I don't want to! She felt so confused. A little while ago she'd felt completely invulnerable—it had been very clear to her how everything would go—but now she was all tangled up in his wiles again. Did this mean she believed Ellie?

"You'll be repaid—I'll give *you* something."

Without meaning to, Zoë sighed, and she saw a new look come into Stewart's eyes—a disturbed gentleness, immediately followed by angry resistance. So that was it—he was afraid he was going to fall in love with her. She kept herself from smiling by looking away and around the room.

"Why do you bother?" Stewart exclaimed. "*They're* not real—you know that. I don't know what they are here for."

When she looked back he whispered, "I'll give you a chance to talk. You'll be able to say everything, I promise."

As she watched him, wondering, it seemed as if the air in the room were clearing, as if the thoughts of everyone else present had evaporated; everything was very fresh, lucid, untangled. Then the air felt warmer, sweeter; there were currents in it, which bore the scent of hundreds of flowers—Father Jules knelt down. He closed his eyes but when he opened them the Virgin was still there, watching him from her grotto in the mountains. Then abruptly Zoë could see only Stewart's face, his eyes narrow and avid.

I'm not ready, she protested. She didn't even know whom she was talking to anymore. Rob wasn't anywhere. I'm not ready for this yet—there's some danger.

Charlotte had told her someone would try to take from her what she knew—and she wouldn't be able not to give it. Zoë had been disappointed, having hoped for something more specific. It was the night after Samuel had visited her, shivering in the wet clothes in which he'd drowned. But Charlotte had said that that was all she could see. "It's no use, but I'm warning you because I never warned my mother." Yet Charlotte was dead.

Stewart was studying her. Then, unforeseen, his hand flickered to her head and lit upon her hair. It slipped slowly down to her neck and then away.

Before she had a chance to reconsider, she said quickly, *You don't love . . .* She didn't want to spell out "Judith." *Your wife,* she finished. Then she waited. He was impatient again, though.

"You'll *have* what you want—I told you! Why won't you believe me?"

At that moment Judith and Ellie came out of the dining room. Ellie saw them right away and began to turn back, but then Judith signalled Stewart and Ellie had no choice but to follow her. Zoë shrugged, opening her hands: *He came over—what could I do?* (Though why did she owe an apology to Ellie?) Stewart had stood; Judith was telling him that her mother's car wouldn't start—would he mind driving over to give her a lift? Remarking to Zoë that he "trusted they might resume their conversation before long," Stewart excused himself. Judith said, "I'd better get back," and also left.

"Well, you certainly seemed to be deep in conversation," Ellie said. "I'm sorry, but I have to ask. Were you talking about me?"

No. Not at all.

Ellie wasn't convinced.

What do you expect me to do? Zoë signed. *You always confront me when I can't communicate with you . . .*

"I'm sorry, Zoë. I'm really on edge. After what Judith told me just now—I don't mean about the snake—and then to come out here and see you chatting so chummily with Stewart . . ." Her eyes filled with tears. "It's all getting to be too much."

What is?

"What did Judith say? Oh, I'll tell you—God knows, I have to tell someone! I'll explode if I don't. But I can't talk here. Could we go into the courtyard for a minute? It's not that cold out. Would you mind?"

Zoë could feel Rob's objections—why wouldn't he just *say* something? If he was so concerned about her, why wasn't he here? It was all very well to tell her to watch out, but he wasn't here!

She followed Ellie into the dining room, where the table was spread with a white tablecloth, waiting for the food to be set out. Plates, silverware, and napkins were already arranged on a sideboard. Ellie opened the French doors and they stepped out; they sat on the stone rim of the empty fountain. It wasn't cold outside, just cool after the crowded party room. The night seemed even softer than when they'd walked down the drive. Ellie, trying to control her voice, said, "Judith's pregnant. That's what she told me, whispering to me while I was putting the snake back together. All that work and she won't let me serve it. That's minor, though. I'm the first person she's told—she hasn't even told Stewart!"

Zoë stared at her. Whatever she'd been expecting, it hadn't been that.

"She's not certain he'll be pleased! She means to wait as long as possible. You see, she did it without telling him."

What?

Ellie was gratified by Zoë's surprise. "She—I could hardly believe this—but . . . She tricked him! Judith, the picture of holy innocence. She punctured her diaphragm and stopped using spermicide. She got an extra diaphragm so she could keep an intact one in the medicine cabinet. Not that Stewart would notice. She said he's squeamish about such things."

They sat there separately contemplating Stewart's squeamishness and what this might mean.

"She told me all this very matter-of-factly, as if it were something every woman did to get what she wanted. Aside from the fact that it seems so completely out of character—I mean, don't you agree? Doesn't Judith seem like the last person you'd imagine being devious like that? I know you don't know her, but just the way she looks—that utter candor in her face, that madonna-like serenity. Do you know what I mean?"

She didn't, but she nodded. Judith didn't seem particularly innocent to her. She was trying to process this new information: Judith was pregnant. What did that *mean*? Did Stewart truly not know? Even though he might not love Judith, he might love his child—it could be what Judith was banking on. And he might not go through with things if he found out Judith was expecting. Wasn't this actually Judith's clever way of warning her to stay away from Stewart? *Your sister-in-law was enough; don't think I'm going to sit by while . . .*

"What I can't figure out is why she decided to tell me," Ellie went on. "That's what I'm most upset about. I think she did it to get even."

You mean for what Stewart. . . ? She pointed back at the room where they'd sat on the windowsill. Ellie understood.

"Yes, I think that she must have suspected something. I didn't think she did, but I may have underestimated her. I don't suppose I was particularly observant at the time. I can't be sure, but she said—Zoë, I can't even realize what I'm saying yet, because if what she said is true . . . My whole life may be over. I'm sitting here calmly and my whole life may be over!"

She turned wildly. "I don't know what to do! I just don't know what to do! Nick and I can't have children!" She began to sob. "Judith said . . ." She looked at Zoë frantically. "She said, as if it had just occurred to her as she was in the middle of telling me her news, that she hadn't thought, perhaps it was painful to me. I've confided in her, and at first I thought she meant because Nick and I were having such trouble, and of course that was true, it would have been upsetting, but . . . oh, Zoë, I don't know how to say this!" Ellie's voice was unsteady and strange. "We *can't* have children. Nick must have told Stewart and Judith saw fit to tell me. She didn't know I was learning this information for the first time—I can't believe that. It would be too evil. She probably thought I acted as shocked as I did because I was surprised to know she knew it. Yet—this is what's so distressing—I mean, it's not what's so distressing; what's so distressing is the news, but what makes it worse is how unsympathetic Judith seemed. I mean, she said she was sorry, but—oh, maybe I was too upset to gauge her reaction. Zoë, I can't go back in there now! I really can't! What am I going to *do*?"

Zoë nodded, trying now to sort out *this* news.

"It's the lie, Zoë! It's the lie! Here I've been exhausting myself, checking my cycle and at the same time trying to hide from Nick that I was lest he become overly self-conscious and all this time—all this time, he's known! He's known that nothing would work. He's known there was no point to it."

Ellie was choking on her sobs. Zoë moved closer and laid a hand on her arm.

"He must have gone to be tested without telling me. But it's not that—even that I could forgive. I can imagine how terribly upset he must have been. It's that he told someone else without telling me, and for that person to be Stewart Beauregard . . . How can I ever forgive him?"

Zoë wasn't sure what to do. She didn't believe what Judith had told Ellie; either Stewart had made it up or Judith had. Or, more likely,

Stewart had misconstrued something Nick had told him. She couldn't believe that Nick would have known he couldn't have children and have kept it from Ellie. It would be better for Ellie simply to ask him if what Judith had told her were true.

She squeezed Ellie's arm, mimed writing something, then went inside through the kitchen. She was relieved to see that Judith was not there. The women putting the food together, all wearing uniforms, looked up but didn't say anything as she walked into the sitting room. In the drawer of the end table—no letter on it anymore, of course—were pen and paper. She took them out, then sat on the sofa and quickly dialed Seth's number, let it ring five times, and hung up. It was possible that he could be asleep—it was eleven his time—but she doubted it. Outside, she sat back down beside Ellie, who was trying to stop crying, and wrote, "I don't believe Nick would tell someone else before he told you. He probably said something to Stewart that Stewart misunderstood."

It took Ellie a moment to register this, but then her face brightened.

"Do you really think that could be it?"

"Either that or Stewart assumed it from what you told him."

"I hope to God you're right, that's all I can say. I don't see how I could forgive Nick, if he'd done that. You've been very sweet to listen to all of this—I don't know what I would have done if you hadn't been here."

"Why don't you ask Nick about it?" she wrote.

"Ask Nick! What do you think I've been trying to do for the past six months!"

No. "Tell him what Judith told you."

"What if it's true? I couldn't pretend for the next week that everything was fine. At least this way I can keep going on the hope that it's not true."

They were silent for a short while. Zoë was starting to feel cold. Ellie said vulnerably, "Are you sure Stewart wasn't talking about me?"

"He talked about himself," Zoë wrote.

"About himself?"

It was easy enough to nod. Ellie's voice filled with relief.

"Oh, don't tell me—how sick he is of his reputation—don't people have better things to do with their time than to talk about him . . . No one realizes what a responsibility it is, being the focus of so much attention . . . I can't tell you how many times I've listened to *that* lament."

At that moment Zoë glanced over into the corner of the courtyard and was surprised to see a woman: pregnant, far along in her pregnancy, leaning against the door to the kitchen, barefoot, wrapped in a black shawl and wearing a long colorless dress. She seemed not to have noticed them.

Who. . . ? Zoë gestured, looking at Ellie. But Ellie was gazing in the same direction and obviously saw no one.

Then Zoë heard the woman crying—sobbing in the empty pure way people did when they were alone. Then abruptly she stopped and peered up at the sky.

"I didn't know they would *kill* you," she said, as if defending herself against an accusation.

She was speaking in Spanish but Zoë found she could understand her even though she remembered little from the year in San Ysidro.

"Up to the last moment I never believed they meant to. I thought it was a trick to make you admit to being the baby's father. They told me you admitted it—so why did they have to kill you?"

The woman seemed to fade until she looked much older—she was no longer pregnant.

"Oh, Padre, so much has happened since last I spoke with you. I want to tell you. I want . . ." She wrung her hands, as if searching for something to hold on to. "I was so careful not to let anyone know the truth. I thought I would be safe that way—I thought my son would be safe. But now—oh, Padre! Now I am afraid that that is what He wanted me to do! This way it is even easier for Him—He can claim my son in secrecy. I cannot fight back. My son is a troubled boy, Padre, and it is my fault for not having told him the truth. I should have known that he would discover it on his own and that afterwards he would never trust me. Oh, Padre Julio, why did I not tell my father I loved you? He would never have shot you then, that I know. If I had told *you* that, would you have accepted to be Joseph? Together we could have prepared the boy; we could have warned him. Oh, but there are too many fathers in this life, too many fathers, and none of them here!

"Oh, Padre, can you hear me? Do you believe me? Do you forgive me?"

XXIII HARMONY

Though Seth Carver didn't hide from his classmates the fact that he'd spent most of the Second World War in Alabama, he was still a veteran and a military aura emanated from him—at least he knew the sorority girls imagined it did—maybe because of his excellent posture, which recurred at intervals throughout his life. "Shoulders back, head high, kids," he would exhort Zoë and Nick, self-consciously impersonating a traditional father. "You don't want the world to think you're ashamed of being born in a body, do you?"

He knew that his classmates were curious as to why he'd chosen to attend Century College in Centuryville, Indiana, when, as he'd let it be known, he'd been offered fellowships at top universities; why he was so contemptuous of everything; and how he had come to know Lucy Chang Smith, a premedical student in her last year who had married her chemistry professor.

Very tall—almost six and a half feet—lanky, cadaverous-looking at times (there was a picture of Seth and Monica taken shortly before they were married; their lips were very dark in their pale faces, and Zoë thought that they looked as if they were about to face a firing squad, their expressions were so desperate and defiant), with his hair slicked straight back and a pair of old-fashioned round eyeglasses—one of the few possessions he'd inherited from his father and which he could see better without—Seth knew he was the era's caricature of an intellectual. Yet he was also one of the college's best athletes; he was not subject to the bashfulness and awkwardness people expected from someone of his ungainly physique—rather, he enjoyed the reputation of being "fast," and it pleased him to contravene people's expectations. It was assumed because Monica Robie was seen with him frequently enough during this, his freshman and her junior, year so that people could legitimately speak of them as a pair, that she must have acquiesced to his "demands," a rumor that Seth did nothing to dispel. One of his principles, he had told Monica, was never to contradict what people said about you. "Let them erect monuments," was how he put it. "It's their own grave they're commemorating." In the same breath he added that he would do her the favor of telling her something it might take her a long time to discover on her own: the only people who earned his respect were those who he felt had a more interesting claim on misery than his own. "Is there anything you wish to tell me?" he asked.

"People who are truly miserable," Monica retorted, "have no need to boast about it."

"Ahh, very clever," he said. "Miss Robie has a talent for repartee."

"Furthermore," she added, "I don't think you believe you have any claim on misery at all. That's what makes you so angry all the time."

"Oh, is that so?" Seth replied.

He admired Monica Robie because she was unimpressed by him; he could tell that she thought his "soldierly" poses silly—his purposeful slouch, his cigarette dangling from his lower lip as he talked. At the same time it seemed to him that they shared a belief in the necessity of inventing a personality for oneself that could manage one's encounters with the world. He understood, as Monica's friends had been unable to, her impatience with the upright, kind, all-around *decent* Delmore Holland, who everyone knew loved her and wanted to marry her. People like Delmore believed in "true selves" and wanted to love other people for them, and these were precisely what he and Monica, Seth assured her, didn't possess.

The war had affected many of Monica's friends; girls had come back upstairs from telephone calls weeping to pack and go home; others had looked up in horror and disbelief while reading a letter. They had lost friends or brothers; some, fiancés or boyfriends; a few, fathers. Several boys from Harmony Monica knew by name had been killed, but she didn't remember their faces. As girl after girl earned her 'badge of sorrow,' Monica felt the only real grief of her adult life—losing Eldridge—recede into ever deeper privacy. The single war death with which she felt any connection was, bizarrely, that of Marshall Percy III, yet even that she didn't think it right to claim publicly. She wondered why Susanna had written to her. The Percys had not spoken to her since what she always thought of as "Marsh's accident." "I thought you would want to know . . ." the letter began. Was Susanna capable of sarcasm at such a time? "Even though you have no brothers, I am sure you can understand . . ." Monica had confided to Susanna the existence of her mother's imaginary sons, her own imaginary brothers . . . Was Susanna being cruel? Monica had never realized that people's behavior was open to interpretation, and she didn't like learning this.

She replied, "I am puzzled as to why you wrote to me, considering my status in your family; however, you have my deepest condolences." She had debated between "deepest condolences" and "heartfelt sympathy," but had decided that the latter had a false ring to it.

She heard nothing else from Susanna, but that next summer, of 1946, she had been in Harmony only half an hour when Susanna came over from next door.

"Thank you for your letter," she said. "I wrote you because I still feel that you're my closest friend. I realized how stupid it was of me not to speak to you because of what happened between you and Marsh. I'm sure he was quite unbearable. You see, having someone close to you die makes you realize certain things, and I hope you'll be willing to be friends with me again."

"I am not unwilling," Monica replied, relieved not to be contending anymore with multiple views of Susanna. Susanna had known Monica for a long time and did not feel rebuffed by her stiffness. She flung her arms around her; Monica awkwardly returned her embrace.

"We must tell each other everything," Susanna said enthusiastically when they had taken up their watch on the widow's walk, and were sipping from huge glasses of lemonade into which they'd poured shot glasses of gin. "What excitement has taken place in your life since we last spoke? It's been ages."

"Not much," Monica said, which to her mind was the truth. As far as she was concerned, only one thing had happened: she had fallen in love and been spurned. Even the war was secondary.

"Tell me the truth now," Susanna teased. "I bet you have a boyfriend."

"No," Monica replied.

"Come on," coaxed Susanna. "Don't you even date someone?"

"Yes, I suppose I date someone."

"Well, who? Don't torture me like this! Name names!"

"I mainly date Seth Carver. He's twenty-four years old and studying philosophy, history, and science. He's a veteran."

"Oooh, how interesting he sounds! Are you ready to go down the road with him?"

"Down the road?"

"I mean, do you want to marry him?"

"Of course not. I don't want to marry anyone."

"I don't believe you, Monica, dear. Everyone wants to get married. You must not have met the right man."

Monica's silence implied that she knew otherwise, and Susanna pressed. "Are you sure you're not just discouraged because he hasn't gone down on his knees yet?"

"I certainly hope not," Monica answered. "Seth Carver could never ask anyone for anything."

"He couldn't? Why? Is he moody?"

"I wouldn't describe him as 'moody.' He can't stand people to think he might want something from them. Yet he likes for people to wonder about him. I think he likes to be thought of as harboring a secret sorrow."

"Is he cold and calculating, then?" Susanna could not fit Seth Carver into any category she had developed to explain men. They were either pushovers, moody, cold-and-calculating, or nice, although sometimes they seemed to have vacillating temperaments.

"Yes and no," Monica answered. "He's too angry with the world to be calculating. But he can be cruel—it's how he feels sure he's having an effect on you."

"What's he so angry about? He doesn't sound very nice," Susanna added.

"He isn't," Monica answered. "He doesn't aspire to niceness. He aspires to truth—eternal, not personal, as he keeps telling me. Niceness gets in the way." She was a little surprised to hear herself saying all this.

"Dear me," Susanna said. "You certainly seem to understand him. I often find men a puzzle. One minute they seem to want nothing more in the world than your sweet love and the next they don't want to be bothered. Do you understand it?"

"They hate you to have a hold over them. They don't like to admit what you can make them do when they're overwhelmed by desire."

"Overwhelmed by desire!" Susanna exclaimed. "I think you love Seth Carver!"

"Love Seth! Susanna, if you only knew . . ."

"Knew?" Suddenly a light dawned in Susanna's eyes. "Have you. . . ?"

"Have I what?"

"You know. Had a love affair with him," Susanna said, blushing. "Of course, you don't have to tell me if you don't want to."

"A love affair? With *him*?"

Susanna, still blushing, inquired if Monica had ever "done that" with anyone, and Monica, after debating a moment, decided to confide in Susanna. Eldridge was becoming a phantom, and she needed to tell someone about him to bring him back to life. And Susanna, unlike Monica's friends in Centuryville, knew Dr. Jewell; that Susanna would be stunned and revolted bothered Monica not at all. At first Susanna simply refused to believe it.

"You're trying to pull one over on me—you know I'll believe any old thing!"

When at last she did believe it, she exclaimed, "With him? You really did it with him? That old goat?"

But Monica was so calm and proud that Susanna became gratifyingly envious.

"You mean you *wanted* to?"

"He's skillful—he's a doctor, you know."

At last, most satisfying of all, Susanna was indignant.

"How could he make you love him like that and then turn around and ignore you! The nerve of that man! I guess they don't get any nicer when they get older. Men and their 'morals'! What did he do when you saw him the next summer?"

"He decided to risk that I wouldn't tell on him. He said he'd deny it if I did—people would believe him instead of me. All he'd have to do was to remind them I was my mother's daughter . . ."

"Meaning what? That low-down swine!"

"I knew that if I could see him in private I could persuade him to be my lover again, but he made sure—he still makes sure—that I never have a chance. If I pretend to be sick and visit him at his office, he has his nurse stay in the room with us. If I wait on a road for him to go by on house calls, he drives right past me. I can't figure out any other way of catching him alone."

"Do you still think that if you could, he wouldn't be able to resist you?"

"I have no doubt whatsoever."

"Truly?" Susanna asked. "But what do you *do*?"

"All I have to do is begin to undress—and I mean begin. Once I'd been to a tea with my mother and so was all dressed up and I'd only drawn off my glove when he went wild. I can understand it may be hard for you to believe, Susanna," Monica said, smiling at Susanna's wide-eyed expression, "since you know him only as Dr. Jewell, but he—Eldridge—he's very passionate. And, you know, his wife never allows him to watch her undress. First she gets under the covers, then she lets him come in."

"I believe you," Susanna replied fervently. "But what does he do, once he . . . once . . ."

"It's not so much what, Susanna, it's how *often*. He wants to over and over. I think sometimes . . . four or five times . . . in the space of an hour. Sometimes even I had to beg for mercy."

"You *did*? What would he say?"

"He'd say," Monica said, closing her eyes, "he'd say, 'Harmony, I *can't* stop. I warned you, I'm not responsible for myself in your presence.' " She opened her eyes and looked directly into Susanna's. "But then I wouldn't want him to anymore. Stop, I mean."

"Oh, you wouldn't!"

"He's ruined me for any other man, Susanna. I'll never love anyone else."

Susanna nodded in hopelessness and delight. Then she shamefacedly confessed that she was still a virgin.

"I'd rather be unhappy in love, like you," she said. "At least I'd know what all the fuss is about! I can't say I feel very *inspired* when Kurt kisses me."

Kurt Fulwyler was her fiancé.

"He's probably not very experienced," Monica said. "All Eldridge has to do is look at me and I feel as if I'll expire from impatience."

"Well," Susanna said, "Kurt wants to wait until we're married. He's kind of strict about things like that."

This summer, for the first time that Monica could remember, her father was not well, and an even greater melancholy than usual pervaded the household. Monica could not bear to imagine a world without her father in it—he was her bulwark against the bland oblivion of Charlotte's existence, which she was convinced would, without him, quicksand-like suck her beneath its surface.

Meanwhile Seth was sending her long letters from Detroit, where he had found a summer job on an assembly line. He discoursed interminably about his "despair at life's inequities"; his "lack of confidence in the possibility of remedying the world's problems." . . . Susanna, with whom Monica shared Seth's letters, exclaimed, "Why, Monica, he sounds like a Communist!"

"Does he?" Monica replied. She shared Harmony's instinctive distrust of pontifications and a specific response to Seth's complaints surprised her.

"Well, you sure have tricky taste in men," was all Susanna could think of to say.

But then Seth began to slip personal confidences in among his disquisitions, as if to test how closely Monica were reading them.

"Did I ever mention that both of my parents are dead?"

"Did I ever tell you that my mother is incurably insane?" Monica wrote back.

"Did I ever tell you that my father died in the proverbial gutter, drunk as the proverbial skunk, leaving me the proverbial orphan?"

"Did I ever tell you that for the first years of my life my mother imagined that my four 'brothers,' whom she miscarried before I was born, were still alive? They took her for shock treatments."

Monica liked this game and wondered who would win.

"I was raised by my Aunt Minerva, who had nothing in common with the goddess of that name, unless it was her warlike demeanor. She still believed that cod liver oil could root out all evil, and forced her faith upon me with missionary zeal."

"Until my father caught us at it, I used to celebrate my four brothers' birthdays with my mother—I believed every child had siblings she couldn't see. It was on my brother Thaddy's (short for Thaddeus) twelfth birthday—their ages, unlike those of the average person, went both up and down—that my father walked in on us. Mother was serving cake onto six plates. All six of us were talking. I'll never forget the expression on my father's face as long as I live."

"What do you mean, all six of you were talking? I was seven when I went to live with Aunt Minerva, working every day after school and all summer in her grocery, to pay for my 'upkeep,' which she insisted was at least as large as the gross national product. She was my father's older sister, and never forgave him for leaving me on her hands. My mother had died when I was too young to remember. 'That was when the fool took to drink,' she assured me. 'I have never held much truck with true love.' "

"Your aunt sounds like the wicked stepmother. I mean, I'd tell Mother things the boys had said, and she'd tell me the same. 'Lewie (short for Llewellyn) says he wants to go fishing,' for example. Father must have been listening at the door before he came in. He said to me, 'Leave the room!' No explanation, just 'Leave the room!' I obeyed, but went outdoors and listened beneath the open window. I heard many 'How dare you!'s and 'To befuddle your own daughter's mind in this manner!'s. I had never heard my father so much as raise his voice to my mother and I was terrified. I screamed at him to stop. She was sent to the hospital in Concord the next day."

"How bewildering it must have been for you. No doubt Aunt Minerva meant well; it is one of the aspects of life that most appalls me—that one's intentions can be good and yet so ultimately harmful. May I pay you a visit? I will be free from the factory in late August, and there will remain two weeks before the opening of college . . ."

Perhaps, had events not taken the turn they did, the sections of their letters in which they responded sympathetically to each other might have gradually grown in length and substance until they equalled the sections in which they competitively detailed their misfortunes, but a new calamity arrested them in their initial circumstance.

Monica's father had been growing weaker, and though she insisted that he visit Dr. Jewell, and then doctors in Hanover, they could find no explanation for his failing health other than a slight anemia, for which they prescribed calf's liver. He seemed unperturbed by his increasing lassitude, however. "When our time comes, it behooves us to accept it," he admonished her. Or, "The Lord works in mysterious ways, Harmony."

"Don't say that!" she exclaimed. "Don't give in like this!"

But later she thought how ironic it was that he'd made that statement, for her father's illness proved her means of reintroducing Eldridge Jewell to his addiction.

It was early in August, and she was returning from a swim in the river with Susanna. On her way upstairs to her room to change out of her bathing suit, she stopped in the library to check on her father. At first she thought he must have gone out into the garden; then she saw his feet and legs contorted beneath the desk. He had slumped from his chair onto the floor. "Papa!" she screamed. "Papa! He's dead! My father's dead!"

However, by the time the cook and the maid had come running, she had discovered that he was still breathing, and had pulled him out from under the desk.

"Call the doctor! Hurry!"

Adam was breathing, but had not regained consciousness when Dr. Jewell came panting into the room. He knelt beside Adam and took his pulse and lifted his closed eyelids. He listened to his heart with his stethoscope.

"Stroke," he said shortly. Monica stood stone-faced, looking down at Eldridge Jewell kneeling beside her father. "I'll call an ambulance."

"Shouldn't we drive him to the hospital ourselves instead of waiting?"

"There's no hurry now."

"Is he going to die?" she asked. "Will he wake up?"

"I'm sorry, Harmony, I can't answer those questions. His condition is stable now—what will happen later . . . I wish I could tell you."

He went into the hall to telephone the hospital. Then he came back into the library.

"I'll stay with him until they come," he said. "There's no need for you to stay."

"Of course I'm not going anywhere," Monica said wrathfully. To the servants she said, "Mother must be out in the garden since she hasn't heard. Please make sure she doesn't come near the library."

When she had shut the door behind them, she observed Dr. Jewell. He would not look at her; instead he fussed with his patient, repeatedly taking up his wrist to calculate his pulse, laying a hand on his forehead.

She still wore her flowery wet bathing suit—only the flounce had dried—and her hair was damp.

"Are you afraid of me, Eldridge?" she demanded.

"Harmony, at a time like this . . . Your own father lies here, unconscious . . ."

She said nothing further, but she was thinking carefully. In fifteen minutes the ambulance arrived. When the attendants had lifted her father onto the stretcher, she said to them, "I won't ride with you since I understand there's no immediate danger. I'd like to change my clothes, and Dr. Jewell has offered to bring me in in a little while."

He had done no such thing, but she was right in predicting that he would not contradict her in front of others. When the ambulance had gone, and he returned to the library to fetch his bag, she followed him, quietly locking the door while his back was turned. Running on tiptoe across the thick rug, she took one of her great-grandfather Henry's swords down from where it hung, crossed over another sword, above the mantel. Below the swords, forming an abbreviated hypoteneuse, hung the first Thaddeus Robie's spyglass in its leather case. Eldridge Jewell turned to see what she was doing.

"Harmony, what on earth. . . !"

"Quiet!" she whispered loudly. "Do as I say and I won't harm you."

"Harm me! Harmony, have you gone mad? What do you . . ."

"I said, be quiet! Come across the room, away from the windows. No one will see us there."

"See us . . . Oh, no! Oh, no, you don't . . . If you think that . . ."

She walked up to him and plunged the sword a half inch into the flesh of his upper arm. Blood ran from the small wound.

"Harmony. . . !" he said, in a strangled way.

"There is not a thing I fear. You had better believe that. Your life depends on it."

"My life!"

"No harm will come to you if you do as I say. Otherwise, I'll kill you. I know how," she thought to add.

"I can't believe you're serious!"

"Then you're a fool." She moved to stab him in the other arm, but he shouted, "No!"

"Hush!" she exclaimed. "If you make any more noise, I *will* kill you!"

She was pleased to see that he was beginning to believe her. "What do you wish me to do?" he asked despondently.

"You know what."

"But, Harmony, I can scarcely . . ."

In reply, she pulled the strap of her bathing suit off her right shoulder, then took the sword briefly in her left hand and pulled off the other strap. Switching hands again, she tugged at the zipper on the side and then slid the suit down to her feet and stepped out of it.

"Harmony, no! Please, not here!"

"No one will disturb us. If they do, I'll tell them to go away. You'll tell them I'm upset and that you're comforting me."

"Harmony, please! I promise—I'll meet you somewhere, but not here! It would be my ruin."

"You know I can't trust you to keep your word, Eldridge." However, she could feel the way he was looking at her beginning to change. "Don't tell me you don't want to."

He didn't reply, but neither did he back away when she moved closer, holding the sword down at her side. She undid the top button of his shirt.

"Oh, never mind," he said petulantly. "I can do that myself."

She sat on an ottoman with the sword laid across her knees, watching him. He turned his back when he took off his pants.

"I know you're ready. Don't be ashamed. Oh, Eldridge," she sighed, "how can you think it wrong?"

"It just is, Harmony. You know it is. And especially at a time like this . . ."

"You said yourself that there's nothing we can do for him. Besides, he's my father, not yours."

"It seems awfully cold-blooded of you, Harmony. I don't know . . ."

"If I am, it's your fault! If you hadn't been so unkind to me I wouldn't have had to resort to such violent measures. But never mind. Let's not be angry with one another."

She laid the sword across the arms of the leather-covered wing chair behind her and stood. She walked to within a few inches of him and looked him right in the eyes.

"I'm warning you," he said, as he had many times before, his hands rising towards her like magnets. "I won't be responsible for my actions . . ."

"No," she murmured, "I know you won't, Eldridge. It's all my fault, I know it is."

That was on a Tuesday. The following Monday, Adam Robie died without ever having regained consciousness. The funeral was held on Wednesday. Charlotte sat in the church, uncomprehending. It was only when they stood beside the open grave, before the coffin was lowered down into it, that she appeared to understand what was happening. However, Monica was not sure whose funeral her mother thought it was.

"I'm sorry," she heard her murmur under her breath. "I could not prevent it. I tried, but I could not."

It was then nearly the third week in August. Day after day, Monica climbed to the widow's walk and sat in the August heat, keeping an eye on her father's grave with the spyglass through which several generations of Robies had tried to discern their destinies before their destinies caught up with them. She responded sullenly to Susanna's blandishments, delivered from the rooftop across the way.

"Leave me be, please, Susanna. I want to be alone."

Even Eldridge Jewell's visit to her on the roof, and his offer, timidly proffered, to comply with her every wish, if this would comfort her, afforded her no relief. She could feel no pleasure that, for the first time, he was the one who asked, and she the one who refused.

"Harmony, be a little consoled," he said. "Your father never suffered."

"I am not thinking about my father, Eldridge. I have been waiting to grieve for him, but I feel nothing. Do you know why I sit here like this, day after day?"

He signified that he did not.

"It's because I've learned something that I wish I hadn't."

"And what is that, Harmony?"

"I've learned that you can want something for too long. When that happens it doesn't matter if you get your wish. What you get isn't what you wished for. You get the outward form but the inward part, all the feeling of it, has been drained out of it by wishing."

"Harmony, it pains me to see you so unhappy. I even . . . Harmony, I do love you, you know. I never thought I would say this, but if you want me to leave Cora and go away with you, well, I will! I just will! What do you say to that?"

"Didn't you hear what I said? It's too late, Eldridge. I've waited for you too long. I still want you, but all the wanting has taken me into a place where you can't follow. Don't you understand? And it's not only what I long for—it's everyone, everyone in my whole family! That's our curse. My mother wanted a child, but by the time she finally had one, she couldn't love it. My father wanted her to know I was hers, but when she believed it it was too late to make any difference to him."

"You're grieving, Harmony. You don't believe me, but it will pass."

"I'm not grieving!" she cried. "This isn't grief! Grief would be *easy* compared to this. You know nothing, if that's what you think."

The next day Timothy Lowndes came to call, to read Monica her father's will and to deliver a sealed envelope from him. Monica listened politely to what her father's lawyer said—it came as no surprise that she was wealthy, or that she was now her mother's guardian; she wished he would finish so that she could go back upstairs to the widow's walk and read her father's letter. Finally Mr. Lowndes stood up. He walked feebly and leaned on a tall cane.

"Harmony," he said, "I don't know what your father has written to you, but I have known your family all my life. I knew both of your grandmothers. I may even know a few things your father didn't. If there's anything in his letter that causes you any consternation, I hope you'll ask me about it. I've always been very fond of you."

"Thank you," Monica said. She had hardly ever spoken to him before; her father had held no high opinion of him, she knew, and she dismissed his remark as another of the fanciful statements people felt called upon to make following a death. She was not to recall his offer until several years later, when she heard from an attorney in Hanover that Timothy Lowndes had died and had made her his heir. And by then of course she couldn't ask him anything.

Monica opened Adam's letter while the August trees moved stealthily all around her, as if they already knew what the pages she held contained. Despite the breeze, the air was bleary and thick. As always, such weather in Harmony unnerved everyone—it was as if the weather from somewhere else had descended upon the town by mistake. But whose mistake? That was the sort of thing the dreary sluggishness of the atmosphere caused people to wonder about. On days like this in Harmony, Monica asked herself questions she didn't permit herself at any other time. Why her parents weren't happy. Why her grandmother had hung herself from a rafter in the barn. Why her other grandmother had been cut to shreds in a factory accident. Who her mother's father was and why no one knew or why everyone pretended not to know. Why her father's uncle had drowned in the Connecticut when he was fifteen—she had heard the story: he had allowed his boat to drift over the falls. Why it had been one of her ancestors, of all the people it might have been in the town, who had been drowned for being a witch, the last person put to death for witchcraft in the United States. Surely this was more than a common number of disasters. Surely the universe must be trying to express something, using her family as its language. She tried to translate the events of her own life. Why could she not stop mourning her imaginary brothers? Why had she pushed Marsh Percy III down the stairs? Why had she never thought to protest when Eldridge Jewell had laid his hand where his stethoscope had been? Why had she risked her life by jumping out of the car on the way to Del's house the night of the Sadie Hawkins dance? Why was she considering marrying Seth Carver when she didn't love him?

Before, Monica had convinced herself that such questions possessed no answers, but now she wondered. What if in fact the answers were contained in her father's letter? She looked at her name written in his baroque but precise handwriting—"For Monica, upon my death"—and opened it.

"Your mother and I . . ." "I always knew it was wrong . . ." "Forgive me . . ." "Forgive us both . . ."

The words seemed to spring at her all at once; she tried to force them back into their syntax, but they slithered free again. Too many facts—or was it one fact, one large fact? How could a fact have a size? She heard a sort of a shriek, a horrible, guttural noise; without knowing she'd made it she leapt up, terrified, and shoved the sheets back into the envelope, anxious now only to make decisions, to take actions of her own, as many as possible, to counteract those that bore down on her out of the past; the less explicable her actions were to everyone else the better they would serve.

A few days later, she saw a green Plymouth pull into the driveway. She watched it through the spyglass until it disappeared around the side of the house. Then she raised the glass and centered it on her father's grave, staring at it until she heard Seth climb through the hatchway.

"Monica?"

"Hello."

"Monica, you didn't . . . I didn't . . ."

Seth stepped onto the roof and took a seat in the chair beside her. "A woman downstairs . . . your maid, I presume," he said, sounding now more like the Seth she remembered. But then he was speaking again in his artificial, stricken voice. "She told me. Monica, I'm so sorry. If you'd told me, I wouldn't have come."

"Why wouldn't you have come?"

"Well, I mean, if you'd wanted me . . . Oh, Monica," he said. "I'm so sorry about your father."

To her amazement Seth had tears in his eyes. What right had he? Without a word she handed him her father's letter, which she had never reread but kept with her, caged in its envelope, as if to prevent its escape. Even before he'd read it, Seth correctly interpreted her gesture as a dare—and a retaliation. When he had finished the letter, he knew that theirs would be a contest for life. With this one envelope, Monica had amassed years of credit entitling her to be "Most Suffering and Therefore Least

Guilty"—and Seth knew that she would not willingly share the championship with him. On the drive back to Centuryville, somewhere between Turnip Hole and Nectarine, Pennsylvania, perhaps prompted by the memorable names, Seth proposed. He said, that is, "We can be married if you like."

"I had thought we would," Monica said, and then added, before Seth had a chance to look gratified, or annoyed, or regretful—however he'd been going to look, "But do you know what irks me? It's that everyone will think I'm marrying you because my father is dead."

"There's no difficulty about that," Seth said. "We won't tell anyone. We'll wait until no one can suspect there's any relationship between the two events whatsoever."

"*You* don't suspect there is, I trust."

"I've already told you that I don't believe in cause and effect, Monica."

"You don't believe in so many things," she said. "It's not easy to remember them all."

Around the time they reached Banquo, Indiana, and after Seth had finished reciting "Out, out, damned spot. . . ," they'd decided to be married in June of the following year, the day after Monica graduated.

XXIV SPARTA

Whatever factory turned out unbelievable events certainly went into production that fall—the fall after the last summer Zoë and Nick were in Harmony together. First there was Robert and his bakery; it seemed to be the only topic of conversation in Sparta. Every time you turned around—Hey, did you hear about Robert Went? Somehow I can't see Robert making A-clairs—probably putting arsenic in them. Any unexplained deaths in town recently?

When Zoë had first learned about it, she'd been sure people would be asking her all kinds of questions—she'd gone out with him, after all—but when school started everyone seemed to have completely forgotten that she had ever known him; it was bizarre. It was as if she'd stopped existing. It was as if he had; the Robert Went who'd stepped in front of a truck in fifth grade had returned from the dead and swallowed up the eleventh-grade Rob Went who'd been a "great guy," a "real card"; about whom people said, "He's all *right.*" Now they said, "What can you expect? It's like the seven-year locust—the insanity was dormant. *I'm* not surprised to hear he's done such a screwball thing." What got to her the most was how smug they were about it, as if they'd known all along that this (whatever "this" was) was his true personality and they'd been waiting for it to reappear. She knew perfectly well that he'd opened the bakery somehow because of her; yet she knew how insane it sounded—"Robert Went quit school and opened a bakery because of me." What? people would exclaim. Run that by me again in plain English. You're as crazy as he is! What got her was not even that Rob had done something outlandish and unexpected, but why a bakery. What did that *mean*?

Everyone knew the basic facts: somehow Rob had convinced a V.I.P. at the Sparta National Bank to give him a loan (*he* has to be out of his mind, people said. Who could Robert give as a reference? Attila the Hun?) and was renting a narrow little house on Mulberry Street which had used to be a hat shop, owned by two elderly sisters everyone said (wink, wink) weren't really sisters. He was living upstairs. Everyone who'd been to visit him—the bakery wasn't opening until October—said all he talked about was dough and frosting.

Did you know he's hiring all seventh-graders to work after school? He had to file a special petition to get around the child labor laws. Do you know *why*? He says he wants to build their self-confidence through baking. Does that sound like Robert to you? He really went this time.

Why had she not simply gone down to Mulberry Street right away and asked him what the hell he thought he was doing? But at the time it had seemed unthinkable to visit him until she'd figured out what he was up to.

So the bakery was one thing. Then there was coping with being the only one at home. Nick never set foot in Metcalf Street if he could help it, and though he made an effort to see her elsewhere—took her out to dinner at The Chinaman or to rock concerts in Baltimore with him and his roommate—she felt unable to talk to him about Rob and it made her feel lonelier. Meanwhile Seth and Monica acted as if they'd been hit over the head by falling objects and developed entire new personalities. Monica started making dinner every night, tried to take Zoë shopping for clothes, and gave her the third degree about friends and school. "You don't seem to see as much of Bridget as you used to, is that an accurate perception?" Seth oozed good cheer, whistled "Oklahoma" and "With a Little Bit of Luck" or roared old army songs like "The Caissons Go Rolling Along." Whenever he ran into Zoë in the hallway he'd get this idiotic amazed look on his face and would exclaim, "Well, if it isn't a pleasure to run into you!" Or he'd make some remark like "Defied the laws of gravity recently?" or "Discovered the universal solvent yet?" "Yeah, right," she always said. "Oh, I understand," he said. "Don't want to let the cat out of the bag until you've got all your data in order." "Unlikely," she said. Were they *happy* that Nick was out of the house? Had her and Nick's relationship driven *them* crazy? But *that* was crazy. To be quite honest, by this point she wouldn't have cared what was going on in their demented brains if it wasn't that it all seemed too coincidental for it to be coincidence: Rob quitting school, Nick leaving home, Seth and Monica acting like they were tripping. She didn't imagine that they'd gotten together and plotted to drive her over the edge, but it was plain that *life* was trying to tell her something. Then Mr. Montgomery and his oracular pronouncements got into the act. She had him for English now, and he started asking her to stay after class. He'd been wondering if she could "shed any light" on this "Rob Went business"—he had the impression the two of them had become fairly good friends during *The End of Slavery* last year. "Sort of," she said guardedly. She was gratified that someone had noticed, but why of all people did it have to be Mr. Montgomery, who ate tuna fish and miniature marshmallow sandwiches—no one knew if he'd had a tragic love affair or was queer or what; he could be like Jake in *The Sun Also Rises*—there had to be some reason that it was his favorite book. He'd said in class that he believed in asking students only questions he himself wanted to know the answer to; he didn't approve of teachers who "conceived of learning as an Easter egg hunt." But what exactly was he asking via his interest in Rob? Zoë knew Rob would hate the fact that she was discussing him with Mr. Montgomery.

"I ran into our friend Mr. Went yesterday at the bank," he said one day. "He was seeing about his mortgage on the house on Mulberry Street."

"He's *buying* it?"

"Precisely my response," Mr. Montgomery said, leaning back in his chair until he bumped against the blackboard. She was sitting in a front row desk. "What is the fellow up to, I've been asking myself. I have to confess that it worries me. Have you gone to see him, Zoë?"

"No."

"Would I be invading your privacy if I asked why not?"

"I really don't know why."

"Well, I hope that at least you take Rob's enterprise to be more than the benighted prank most of your peers treat it as. If Rob is playing a game, it's a deadly serious one."

"What do you mean?"

"I'm not sure what I mean, Zoë. It's always a cause for alarm when someone deliberately ducks his potential, but there's something more in this than that, if only we were clever enough to see it."

He smiled. His teeth were all tobacco-stained, but he had a nice smile anyway. She'd started to say that she understood about not wanting to fulfill one's potential; it was too *planned,* if he knew what she meant—doing what everyone expected—but he waved a hand and said, "Oh, I don't worry about you. But Rob I suspect of acting to a script. If someone doesn't stop him he may follow the plot to its bitter end."

"What do you mean, follow the plot?"

"Sensitive people in this day and age," he said, "anguished at their powerlessness, often turn their energies against themselves." He leaned towards her across his desk, supporting himself with his hands as if he were getting ready for the hundred-yard dash. "We've been trained to blame ourselves for not being able to end suffering," he said, jabbing her with his eyes.

She looked back, wanting to ask him if every baker in the world was blaming himself for not being able to end suffering. Obviously Rob thought the world was a disaster; who in their right mind didn't? It had never seemed like he was *anguished* about not being able to change things. But mainly she was thinking that you evidently had to drop out of school and open a bakery or almost choke to death from asthma for anyone to worry about you. I don't think it's the world he's upset about, exactly, she felt like saying.

"Rob has always metabolized people's scorn and bewilderment into some necessary nutrient," Mr. Montgomery said. "Perhaps you and I are missing the obvious. Would you consider the possibility that Rob might still be revenging himself on everyone for his early loss?"

"You mean his leg?"

"With someone like Rob who shadowboxes his way through a conversation, one is always tempted to believe he knows what he's up to, but he just may not."

"What do you mean, shadowboxes?"

"Dodges and feints against an imaginary enemy. Deflecting potential criticism. You must hear that continual self-irony."

"I guess."

"Did he ever let down his guard with you? Was he ever able to speak unselfconsciously?"

She didn't say anything.

"What's going on in that mind of yours, Zoë?"

"It's too hard to explain."

Mr. Montgomery fixed her with his eyes again. "Why not give it a shot?"

She shook her head. "I can't." Everything she thought of saying sounded like a line from some stupid late-night movie: Once I thought we really loved each other but then I found out I was wrong and nothing has ever seemed the same since . . . I didn't show Rob how I felt about him so he doesn't want to be the same person anymore . . .

Mr. Montgomery looked at her for another minute, then opened his drawer and took out his cigarettes. She was surprised he'd gone this long without one. He lit it, then said, "Let me go so far as to say this, Zoë. If there's a message in what Rob's doing, I'd lay odds that it's directed at you. I don't wish to frighten you, but in my opinion you're the only one who can save him."

"I *know,*" she said.

In the meantime there was also Bridget's love affair to deal with, news of which started out like a fresh chapter in a mystery that *appeared* to be about a completely different subject, though you knew that by the end you'd get a clue as to how it connected to the main one. One Friday afternoon they were sitting in Bridget's backyard at the white iron table a couple of weeks after school had started. Bridget's parents were in Washington seeing some new mummies at the Smithsonian, and Zoë and Bridget were drinking vodka tonics. Zoë was beginning to get a headache.

"Remember that French guy I mentioned?" Bridget suddenly asked. "Bernard?"

Zoë ought to have guessed from the casual way Bridget brought it up that something she didn't want to hear was coming. "What about him?"

"Well, ahem . . ." Bridget made a big thing out of gulping her drink first and sighing. "I went all the way with him," she said.

She was looking off into the distance. Zoë stared at her. "What?"

"Swear to God. Not just once, either." Bridget laughed. "Actually, every chance we got. For a while anyway."

"I didn't even know he was our age," Zoë said finally.

"He's nineteen."

"Nineteen!" It was one thing for Bridget to date someone older, but this was different.

"He's thinking of going to college over here—his grandfather knew my father during the war . . ."

"I know. You told me. Where did they sleep?"

"You mean, where in the house? His parents stayed in my room and I slept up in the study. Bernard . . ." Bridget pronounced it the French way. ". . . slept on the rollaway in the basement." She smirked. "It was quite convenient."

Zoë ignored this for the moment. "Did he speak English?"

"A little. He had an unbelievable accent. Mostly I spoke French."

"You *did*?" Somehow this made it all worse.

"So could you have. After ten years of Mme. Alignac with her *eem-peh-cah-bleh akh-sohn* from Tours we damn well ought to be able to. Besides, we didn't do a lot of *talking*." Bridget laughed again, like Vincent Price. "He was quite experienced. He'd already made love with lots of women, particularly in Scandinavia. He spent several summers there working on farms. They're not all uptight about sex there. I mean their society isn't. He also . . ." Bridget lowered her voice. "He also slept with his mother's best friend. Seriously. She seduced him. Her name was Félicie."

"What?"

"He was only fifteen."

"That's pretty disgusting."

"Why? I think it's adventurous. He was pretty funny, actually, telling about it." Bridget laughed privately. "She really had the hots for him—he pronounced it the 'otts.' I taught him some American expressions. What was really ironic, over his spring vacation his parents had to be out of the country so they asked Félicie if Bernard could stay with her! That was after she'd already seduced him the first time. Félicie's not married. The whole time his parents were gone, Bernard and Félicie spent every instant in bed. She's a journalist or something, so she doesn't have to go to an office. He said she couldn't get enough of him. It was a big relief when his parents finally came home. Can you believe it?"

"Who knows," she said. What did Bridget mean, "She couldn't get enough of him"? Did she just grab him whenever he came near or what?

"She was in love with him, but he wasn't in love with her. He was glad he'd learned all the stuff she taught him in bed, but he didn't want to keep seeing her. She, however, *definitely* wanted to keep on seeing him. She got hysterical when he tried to tell her it was over. He said he was even afraid she might try to commit suicide."

"You're kidding."

"She didn't, but she told his mother she couldn't be her friend anymore and refused to tell her why. Naturally Bernard's mother suspected that something had happened while he was staying with Félicie so she cross-examined him, but he didn't confess anything."

"When did he tell you this?"

"What do you mean, when?"

"I mean, before or after you . . ."

"I don't remember. What difference does it make?"

"He could have been trying to impress you if he told you before."

"You mean so I'd think what a great stud he was?"

"I guess you must miss him a lot," Zoë said.

Bridget had pulled the lime out of her glass and was sucking on it. Now she spit it back.

"Oh, I don't know. We weren't getting along very well by the time he left."

"You weren't?"

Zoë felt more hopeful, hearing this.

"He told me I was insatiable."

"Insatiable?"

"*Insatiable,*" Bridget pronounced in French. "It's the same word."

"I know, but what did he mean?"

"What do you think he meant? He said I was like Félicie. He said he'd thought I'd be different because I was younger but I was just as 'sex-starved' as all the other women he'd been with."

"They were? I mean, he did?"

Zoë had visions of Bridget snaking her legs around him and stroking Bernard's chest with long painted fingernails, like sex symbols on T.V.

"I told him he was a stuck-up prig who thinks he's God's gift to women. It's true, he is."

Zoë must have been looking as if she didn't believe her, because Bridget said again, "It's the truth. He likes to get you to fall madly in love with him and then keep you begging."

What did Bridget mean, begging? Did she go down on her hands and knees, pleading with Bernard to make love to her?

"I think he's probably queer too, if you want to know the truth, although he doesn't know it."

"It seems like you think all men are queer." Mr. Montgomery. Rob. Now Bernard.

"I'm beginning to wonder, I can tell you. I think the person whose pants Bernard really would have liked to get inside of were Sam Tannenbaum's. Everywhere we went, he'd say, 'Oh, let's *anh-veet* Sam, tu veut pas?' As you know, Sam and I aren't particularly friends anymore, so it was pretty awkward. Everytime we'd see him Bernard would shake his hand as if he hadn't seen him for years. He'd put his arm around his shoulders and whisper things to him."

"Maybe it's normal to do that in France."

"Well, it's not normal here. Besides, it wasn't just that. It was the way he'd seem to get turned off if I wanted to fool around too much. He kept saying things like 'You women are all alike,' and he'd act grossed out if I got too passionate."

"That's weird," Zoë said. She thought of Buell, refusing to go all the way because it wasn't "right." She sympathized with Bernard, however. She could see how revolting it would be to have the person you were with get all oblivious because they were so overwhelmed with passion.

"Sometimes I really feel fed up with men, do you know what I mean? Sometimes I can really understand why women become lesbians."

For one insane moment Zoë thought Bridget was going to make a pass at her, and she was trying to figure out what she would do when Bridget said, "Don't worry, I don't mean I'm going to, I'm just saying I can understand it. I get so sick of men—not even men, *boys*—acting like they're the Holy Grail. At first they act like all they want in the world is for you to be interested in them, but when you finally are they get turned off."

Zoë tried to think if this was what had happened with Rob. Was what Bridget said true? But then there must be something creepy that women did if so many men felt that way. How did you tell if you were doing it?

"Do you have a picture of him?" she asked.

While Bridget was gone, Zoë drank the rest of her vodka tonic. She felt like getting totally drunk. When Bridget came back, Zoë tried not to act surprised. She had expected some incredibly handsome French type, but Rob was a hundred times better-looking than Bernard. Bridget said now, all confiding, "I *wanted* to tell you right away when it happened. After all you're my closest friend in the world and we've always told each other everything. I just felt too weird putting it down on paper, does that make any sense?"

"Of course," Zoë said.

"I also thought you might get mad at me."

"Why would I get mad at you?" Zoë immediately forgot everything she'd just been feeling.

"I don't know. I just thought . . . Never mind."

"That's ridiculous."

"I'm glad you think so."

Zoë thought of her conversation with Nick on the train, but she put it out of her mind. She couldn't deal with it right now. She and Bridget both had another drink and then went inside and boiled hot dogs. When dinner was ready they left the lights off and lit candles.

"So, have you seen Robert?" Bridget asked, when they were sitting on the couch eating.

"No," Zoë said. She felt incredibly casual about it. Her mind was all over the place. She was remembering when the three of them had argued about if they were a law firm what order their names would be listed in: Went, Wycliffe, and Carver; Carver, Wycliffe, and Went; Wycliffe, Carver, and Went, Attorneys at Law.

"Do you *want* to?" Bridget asked.

"Yes and no." Zoë could remember being upset about Rob but it seemed silly now. "I don't want to see him if he's going to be weird."

"How do you mean?"

"Oh, just be all sarcastic. I'd still like to be friends with him, but I don't know if he wants to be friends with me."

"Did he write you at *all*?"

"Not one single letter."

"And you didn't write him either?"

Zoë shook her head.

"Well, if you want my opinion, you should stop wasting your time. He really hasn't changed that much, if you think about it. Once a fruitcake, always a fruitcake. Only now he's *making* fruitcakes."

Bridget started her cackling laugh. "Besides, all this stuff with the twelve-year-olds working for him. He's probably seducing them all, I bet you a million dollars. He probably bribes them not to tell by giving them all the cream puffs they can eat."

Bridget's parents were due back at ten, so around nine-thirty Zoë left, but instead of going home where she might have to deal with Laurel and Hardy she walked down to the water. It was five blocks from Bridget's house to the harbor, two blocks closer than from hers. Down Pearl Street, across Chesterfield, another block to Main. Then stores until the fishmarket, everything closed up now, even the drugstore. The Harbor House would be open but it was farther down Arch Street near the Yacht Club. Mulberry Street, where Rob's bakery was, was one of the little streets that went off from the harbor like spokes. She didn't know yet if she were going to walk up it or not.

She crossed the empty square where Harbor, Academy, and Arch Streets ran into the lower end of Main. In the daytime Harbor Place was always clogged with cars. Now there was a car only every few minutes, the headlights splashing against the big windows of the stores like searchlights: Woolworth's, the jewelry store, Roentgen's Toy Shop. Across the street, the liquor store and McCullough's Shoes.

Zoë sat on the edge of the pier, leaning against one of the big posts, dangling her legs down over the water. Taking deep breaths of the salty fishy air, she pressed her thumbnail into the huge cigar-colored timber; it was so soft you could make a mark on it with the end of your finger. The posts stood every ten feet or so along the pier—supposedly they were still solid in the middle; the Harbor Authority was always sticking ice picks in them to make sure. What would happen if they gave way? Would Sparta be flooded? It was a nice thought. There was a rock jetty underwater near one end of the pier; the top showed when the tide was out, but she couldn't see it now—the streetlights were off a ways.

She could see the water, though. Gray and greasy, with bits of trash floating on it, or snagged against the dock. Out a little ways, however, among the small motorboats and rowboats that people used to ferry themselves to their yachts, it didn't look so scummy. The white sides of the boats shone in the reflections of the streetlamps.

Across the harbor, catty-corner from where she sat, lights were still on in the houses at the end of Harbor Street. Their windows looked so calm and welcoming, glowing there like a haven across the water. She wished Rob lived in one of those houses and were waiting for her to come home. He would come to the door from time to time to see if she were in sight.

A car drove by, sweeping her with its headlights—she wondered if it had noticed her. Suddenly she became very aware that she was sitting alone on the dock at night. She'd always been with Bridget or Nick and then with Rob. No one knew where she was right now. She must be really upset. Was she drunk? But she didn't feel upset. She felt quite calm, in fact.

At first, when Bridget had been telling her about Bernard, she'd felt as if everything were totally hopeless. Bridget really had done everything now; she (Zoë) might as well give up thinking she'd ever be able to have a life of her own. Every step she took, Bridget would always have taken before her. It was hard to believe that she'd been considering telling Bridget about Buell Magoon—Bridget would laugh. But then, as Bridget had gone on, raging about how stuck-up Bernard was, how he'd got what he wanted and then dumped her, Zoë had been glad that at least Rob couldn't feel that about her.

She thought about what Mr. Montgomery had said—that Rob was "acting to a script," "following a plot to its bitter end," "blaming himself for the world's anguish"—and at this moment it also seemed clear to her that this was Mr. Montgomery's *idea* of Rob; he wanted to believe it for some reason of his own, but that didn't mean it was true. Rob was just Rob—nobody knew why he'd opened a bakery. Maybe he was sick of school and wanted to be a baker, had anyone ever thought of that? He liked to cook; no one knew that, did they? If they'd asked her she could have told them, but they were too busy scrounging up their old opinions of him to bother.

She looked at her watch—it was past ten already. She'd better head home. Monica might decide to call Bridget and then Zoë would have to explain what she'd been doing. Monica seemed to think she had hundreds of boyfriends, and Zoë didn't want to give her more ammunition to load her theory.

It was dark enough now that Rob wouldn't see her unless he were sitting outside, which was unlikely, since he supposedly got up at five o'clock every morning to bake bread. (The bakery was opening in three weeks—he had sent coupons to everyone at school giving them half-price on their first order.) She walked up Mulberry Street—upstairs in Rob's house there was a light on—and Zoë stepped back into the shadow of a house across the street. Rob's house was a tiny yellow clapboard squashed between two taller brick ones. It was older than they were, and slanting, as if it would have fallen down if it hadn't had the brick houses on either side to support it. To the left of the door there was a small bay window where the hat ladies had used to hang hats. Would Rob display pastries there?

He was supposed to be calling the bakery "Went's Baked Goods." The sign wasn't up yet, but on the door Rob had already hung one of those charts that had the days of the week printed on it—the storekeeper filled in the hours. Zoë felt a sudden urge to read it and crossed the street and sidled up to the door. Under "Open," Robert had written "Eight" six times, Monday through Saturday; "Six" under "Closed," Monday through Friday; "Two" under "Closed" for Saturday. Opposite "Sunday," across the time compartments, he'd written "Ha Ha." One "Ha" in each compartment. Zoë was so surprised when she read it that she laughed aloud, then heard herself laughing and raced back across the street into the shadow again. Someone might be spying on her out of one of the darkened windows and think her behavior suspicious and call the police. She couldn't have cared less, however, now.

Rob had only put up the sign so that he could write "Ha Ha" after Sunday—Zoë knew she was right. That was the single reason and probably even the reason he was opening the bakery in the first place. Zoë also knew that she was the only person in the world who knew the real reasons why Rob did things.

XXV CASCABEL FLATS

Zoë and Ellie sat on the fountain until Ellie announced that she felt able to face the world again. Zoë told her she thought she'd stay out another few minutes.

"Is everything all right with *you?*" Ellie asked, as she stood up. "I'm so self-absorbed at the moment . . ."

Fine. Go on in.

"Well, if you're sure . . ."

Ellie went through the French doors; Zoë couldn't have been sitting there for five minutes when Stewart came out.

"I had to look for you," he said, sounding peevish, the way he had that afternoon. "Come inside. I want to show you something."

In the air something stirred, and Stewart said, "What? What is it?"

I think it's your ancestor, Zoë signed, although this time she didn't see anything. GRANDMOTHER PAST PAST.

Stewart shrugged. "Play games now if it amuses you. You *will* tell me."

He had taken her hand and pulled her to her feet—bringing her along with him, she thought; she'd picked up the pad and pencil she'd brought out from the sitting room but he said, "You won't be needing those," and tossed them into the dry fountain. He led her to a door on the far side of the courtyard. Zoë heard the woman hiss at her, but she couldn't stop now; she had to see what was going to happen, didn't the woman understand? She took a last look over her shoulder as Stewart opened the door, which hadn't been locked; was this where he'd come when he'd been outside earlier? Inside he didn't turn on a light but the windows gave enough illumination so that she could see that on either side of the room stood a narrow bed; they had heavy wooden headboards carved into the shape of a fan; the mattresses were covered with Indian blankets, white zigzags against what looked like a red and gray background. The beds were divided by a bare table with a chair pulled up to it.

Stewart knelt beside one of the beds, reached beneath and felt along the frame. He removed something—Zoë couldn't see what; it was too small to be a knife or a gun, however, because he kept it in his fist. Then he led the way into the adjacent room, an office or study, but he didn't stop here either; in the next room he did turn on a light. Zoë was surprised that he'd risk their being seen, but then she saw that, although there was a door onto the courtyard, the only windows faced towards the mountains—this then must be the last room on this side of the house. It was another scarcely furnished bedroom, this time with only one, not quite double, bed. Stewart knelt by this bed also—for a moment she thought he was going to pray—but he reached underneath and dragged out a trunk. His father's paintings, of course—she should have guessed. He unlocked it—he'd had the key in his hand; that must have been what he'd taken from under the bed in the other room.

Lifting the lid, Stewart said, giving her his quick, piercing glances, "Easy for someone to get hold of these, you know, if anyone had wanted. All talk. I'm going to have to destroy them, but I wanted you to see them first. I know you won't say anything to anyone."

There was nothing in the room to write with, but the windows were fogged up. On the nearest one, intending to write "How do you know?" Zoë wrote instead, "Ignacio Ortega." She stared at the name.

Stewart stood up to read it. He snapped, "What do you know about Ignacio? No, never mind, there's no need for you to tell me. It had to come from your brother's wife."

Zoë held her arms perpendicular to her body.

"And what of it? That tells you nothing."

"It's not true?" she wrote, on a fresh pane.

Stewart didn't answer, and Zoë thought she'd clear the window and try to look out—maybe see the woman again—but instead found herself writing something else. "You were there." Stewart was standing right beside her and she looked up at him, amazed.

"How did you know that? Who *told* you?"

She didn't know what she'd meant. *No one.*

"You're going to tell me!" he exclaimed.

He stalked into the next room and she heard him wrenching open drawers, muttering to himself. Then he went farther, the door onto the courtyard slammed, and when he returned he had the pad and pencil he'd thrown into the fountain. She took them from him and wrote, "No one told me."

Faster than she could see it happening, Stewart hit her across the side of the head with the back of his hand. She staggered and dropped the paper, then put her hand up to her cheek.

"What," he sneered, "you're not going to scream for help or run out of the room? What does it take?"

He raised his hand again and Zoë recoiled but didn't take another step. When Stewart let his hand fall back to his side she released her breath and stepped towards him. She was not going to be scared off this time. She turned her mouth up to meet his and he pushed frantically into hers, his hands fumbling at her sweater. Meanwhile he was walking her backwards toward the bed, but the trunk must have caught his eye. He shoved her away and exclaimed, "What do you *want* with me?"

Before she could think how to respond he was bending over the trunk, taking out a canvas, unrolling it on the bedspread.

"Hold this side," he said, refusing to look at her.

But she knew now that, whether he wanted to or not, he was going to have to play his part, and she sat compliantly on the edge of the bed and rested her palm on the lower corner. As Stewart unrolled the canvas, the feet appeared, crossed at the ankles and nailed to the wood—no, they were tied—no, they were *also* tied, and only one foot was nailed. Before she could remark on this, Stewart had unrolled the rest—the man on the cross wore baggy grayish-white trousers that came down just over his knees, and no shirt—but all she could look at was the face, the eyes just come awake with the horror of what was happening to him.

"My father's best work. A pity it can't be exhibited, isn't it? It's so—what would be the appropriate word? Realistic? Lifelike? Gives you the feeling it really happened this way, doesn't it? He has his eyes open, for one thing—so many crucifixion scenes, the eyes are closed. My father was always struck by that."

He knew she couldn't answer unless she let go of the corners.

"People wouldn't speak of him as a minor, regional figure anymore, would they? Whatever they thought of him, they couldn't dismiss him the way they do now. Jules Beauregard the irascible drunk. The crazy rattlesnake-keeper. The widower crazed with grief. Grieving so much he couldn't stand the sight of his own son. Don't think I don't know what they say. Ready for the next one?" He still wouldn't look at her. He rolled the canvas from the top down. She tapped his arm and pointed.

"The feet?" he asked, glancing at her swiftly. "Yes, he forgot the nail in one of them. Never said he was perfect. Just a great painter. A genius for finding the right subject."

What did he mean, Jules had forgotten one of the feet? Hadn't there been only one nail, through both of Christ's feet?

Stewart had set the rolled canvas in the open trunk lid and picked up another. It and the next few were all close-up studies of parts of the first canvas, several of the face: the eyes frozen wide, trying to see what couldn't be seen.

"All right," Stewart said softly, sinuously. "What was it like? Tell me. What did it feel like? What was going through his mind?"

Zoë shuddered. He grabbed her by the shoulders and when her hands came off the canvas it rolled back up with a snap. She kept shaking her head. She thought he was going to hit her again but after a moment he let her go. "You're lying," he said. "You know." He began to unroll another canvas.

There were several of the top half of the crucified figure—fake-crucified . . . Jules had used Ignacio as a model, used his face for Christ's? Zoë looked at the hands, and noticed for the first time that they were tied with rope only, not nailed. So Jules had painted the false crucifixion—except that there was a nail through one of the feet. Why? When Stewart rolled up the canvas she went to pick up the pad of paper and the pencil, still on the floor by the window, and wrote, "Why aren't there nails through the hands?"

"Couldn't reach that far."

But they had nailed Christ to the cross before they stood it up, hadn't they? Wouldn't the sect have followed suit? She had no chance to point this out, however. Stewart was rapidly unrolling, then rolling up the paintings, one after the other, holding his arm across the lower edge of the canvas while she stood beside the bed. He seemed to be reminding himself that they were as he remembered.

"Did Ignacio know your father was there?" she wrote, again surprised when she saw what she'd written.

Stewart looked at the paper.

"You tell me," he said.

Now the paintings were of longer views: the cross was situated on top of a small hill, surrounded by the low stunted pines; there were splotches of snow under some of the trees. Jules had painted the scene as taking place at night.

In the last painting Zoë thought she saw two figures near the edge of the circle, the larger seeming to be dragging the smaller into the trees, but Stewart had rolled it up before she had a good look at it. Now he was returning the paintings to the trunk. She sat back against the footboard and watched him. His hands were trembling—good, she thought. He *ought* to be afraid. It wouldn't mean anything if it cost him nothing. But then, when he shut the lid and looked at her, his face was so full of fear and resentment that she pitied him; he was so helpless, hurt, and lost—she would hide from him as much as possible what he had to do. Why had his father made him watch?

Watch what?

She saw the hands again, the wrists tied. The feet again, tied at the ankles, one foot also nailed to the wood. She breathed in sharply.

"What? What is it?" He seized her by the shoulders again and glared at her. "What?"

She shook her head: *Not yet. You have to wait.*

Furious, he ripped the sheet of paper off the pad and crumpled it and tossed it into the middle of the bed. She was waiting for more violence but suddenly he strode to the window and pressed his face against it, trying to see out. Zoë gasped at the same time that she heard a gasp outside, and then a terrified scream, quickly losing volume. She ran to the window, pushing Stewart out of the way—the woman had fallen! She'd been watching them and then Stewart had frightened her. Her little boy was screaming now, and Zoë leapt to the door onto the courtyard but it was locked. Before she could reach the next room, Stewart had grabbed her.

"What? Who's out there? Who is it?"

She shook her head, struggling to free herself, but he held onto her.

"Tell me!"

No!

But already Zoë couldn't hear the boy crying anymore. Had he fallen too? Had the woman fallen all the way into the canyon or only to the intermediate ledge below? Could she hurt herself when she was already dead?

Zoë stood still, waiting for Stewart to release her, thinking of Samuel. Was it her task in life to send the dead to their final rest? She only half noticed the wistful look come into Stewart's eyes before he banished it and said, "I don't feel sorry for you—why should I? I told you before that you'll get what you want."

He knelt to lock the trunk, then shoved it back beneath the bed. Zoë sat down and wrote on a fresh piece of paper: "You want me to tell you why you want to destroy what you love but you can't stand it when I do. So why . . ."

He was reading over her shoulder, leaning into her. He let out a scornful breath. "I don't need you to tell me that." He held up the key to the trunk. "You want this? You can bring them all in and show them. Invite everyone. That meddling mystery writer with his 'hunches.' The newspapers. It won't make any difference. I see now that they'll never know. How can they, when you don't? They don't even know that you're capable of knowing."

He had sat down beside her and laid a hand on her knee but she shook it off, went to the window, and as if absently tracing a design wrote "Hypocrite" on a fogged pane. Stewart followed.

"No," he said, smudging the word out. "A hypocrite pretends to be better than he is."

She took up the paper again. "You pretend to be worse."

"Now you're entertaining yourself."

"Cold-blooded, too." But she felt disgusted with herself—this was artificial now.

"That means you depend on a source outside yourself for heat. I don't do that."

Zoë indicated herself: *You think I do?*

"You prove your own point." Stewart drew her to sit with him on the bed; he took the pencil away and held both her hands. "So what did your sister-in-law tell you?"

Zoë looked at parts of his face. His lips were thin and finely etched; his nose was slightly crooked. His eyes weren't dark, but she couldn't tell the color. She didn't know what he looked like anymore—she didn't know if she'd recognize him if she saw him again. She looked at his hands instead. His thumbs stroked hers over and over.

"They wonder why I sold them the house, don't they?"

She nodded. She felt his leg against hers and then his hands in her hair, lifting it free from her neck, smoothing it back from her face.

"It was the anniversary of my father's death," he said quietly. "Every year on that day I drink as much as possible—don't talk to anyone if I can help it."

Even though he was right beside her she could hardly hear him.

"I used to sleep at the studio, the night before. Last year—a year and a half ago—I didn't, I don't know why. Usually I don't leave the property all day, but this time I felt like it. For the first time in my life I knew what people mean when they say that they don't know what to do with themselves." He kept stroking her hair, as if to calm her, as he told his story.

"I always drank—I used to drink as a memorial to him, but I'm not much of a drinker, can't get drunk in a satisfying way. I give myself a headache and want to go to bed. This last year, for the first time, it had an effect on me. Maybe I was sick. As I said, I slept at home, surprising hell out of Judith, got up and hurried off to one of my rehab jobs.

"It was raining heavily, an all-day rain—it rarely does that here, especially in summer—so I knew the crews working outside would have stayed home. There was a condo complex in town I knew would be working, so I went there. Ran into Nick. I'd never seen him before, though his wife says we met at a party before they moved out here. I began to talk to him. Talked to him as if he'd been a friend, and I don't have friends. I don't ramble on."

Zoë glanced at her hands; they were now clasped in her lap.

"For the next few weeks, I kept working on the crew. Nick didn't know I owned the whole development. He thought I was his friend. I sold him the studio so he'd keep thinking that. Look at me."

No.

"I said, look at me."

He took her face in his hands and turned it. She closed her eyes.

"Look at me. Look at me."

She forced herself to open her eyes.

"It was for you. You know that, don't you? I've been waiting for you. I was using Nick to get to you. Tell me you knew that."

Yes.

"I can do what I want with you, can't I? It's what you want, isn't it?"

Yes.

"We both thought that happiness could never happen to us in this life, didn't we? But now it will always be with us. Being as one with another—I believe that—but it's not something we can have. We can see it now, you and I, but we mustn't try to grasp it. That way, we'll know what it is all the time."

She moved to kiss him, but he drew back.

"Come on," he said. He crumpled both sheets of paper and put them in his pocket. He took her hand as if they were friendly lovers, and they went back through the adjoining rooms. He replaced the key under the bed-frame. When they stepped out into the courtyard, it was snowing, and they both stopped and turned their faces to the sky: huge porous flakes hurtling soundlessly down through the dark, urgently coming into focus.

"Look at it," Stewart breathed. "Will you just look at it?"

He put his arms around her and they stood there like that, the snow falling on them, like a promise being kept.

"What are you thinking?" he whispered. "You know you can tell me if you want to."

She tried to kiss him again, but he pulled back.

"Don't you want to? You know you want to."

Why did he look at her like that? So tenderly . . . It wasn't fair if he didn't mean it. She didn't know what she was doing. She swallowed, then opened her mouth: I . . . What people always started by saying, impressing themselves upon the formless universe, but before any sound could issue a vise clamped onto her windpipe, her body seized, and she gagged. Then she burst into tears.

"I'm sorry, Zoë," Stewart murmured. He held her closely, running his hands up and down her back. He laughed softly to himself. "It must be the snow. Snow does something to me. Or you do. Before the effect wears off . . ."

They kissed finally, the snow settling on their closed eyelids. Her face grew wet with melting flakes. Then he was whispering something in her ear, holding her head against his shoulder so that she couldn't pull back. He repeated it.

"Ellen's out here. Just wanted to warn you."

What? Now he let her turn. Ellie was standing beside the kitchen door where the woman had been standing earlier—how long would she have watched them if Stewart hadn't seen her? Zoë despised her at that moment—would she never accept that it was not *she* whom Stewart wanted? And anyway she already had Nick! Ellie kept on staring, not saying a word. Stewart put a hand on Zoë's back and moved her with him towards the door, whispering to her as they advanced, "Only you know me. Don't let anyone convince you otherwise." They stopped. "You going to let us in, Ellen?"

"You can go in," Ellie said.

Stewart looked at Zoë.

Go ahead, she gestured.

He raised his eyebrows but then shrugged and went on inside. As soon as he'd shut the door, Ellie stepped up close to her.

"You little bitch," she said. "How could you *do* such a thing?" Sobbing in a forced way, she brushed past Zoë and stood facing the fountain.

Zoë stayed where she was. After a minute Ellie turned and said, "I'm sorry, Zoë. I had no right to say that. It's just that after everything I told you—I'm so on edge, and then to come out and see Stewart kissing you . . . You must understand that it seemed as if you'd done it on purpose to humiliate me. You didn't say anything earlier. If you'd even given me a hint as to how far things had already gone . . ."

How could I say anything?

Ellie said, "I'm sorry, but I honestly think you sometimes say things on purpose so that people can't understand you, even when you know they're making an effort. You use not being able to talk against other people—you enjoy making them feel guilty for not understanding you."

Zoë stared, then turned to go inside—she wasn't going to give Ellie the satisfaction of a response—but Ellie grabbed the doorknob.

"It won't kill you to listen to me for one more minute. I think at least you owe me that—all that pretending you did earlier. Obviously you were laughing up your sleeve at me the whole time."

All I did was kiss him, Zoë signed. She felt giddy and impatient now, as if she were drunk.

"I'm sure Stewart had his own version of what transpired between the two of us to regale you with. Oh, I know, it's highly unfair of me to go on like this when you can't respond, but I can't say I feel very guilty about it. You're so accomplished at making the rest of us feel like fools, as if there's something suspect about anyone's trying to say anything—as if you're somehow purer than the rest of us for not getting over whatever . . . whatever caused your condition. I can't believe you're not aware of how idiotic one feels sometimes, talking in your presence. I suppose I'd never have had the gall to say this except that I feel you've declared your hostility towards me by what you've done.

"Tell me, why have you never even tried to do something about your condition? You must realize how it tortures your family. Your mother would do anything for you—so would Nick. But you've never even tried! Of course it's scary, but we all have fears we have to overcome. I'm not trying to minimize what you're up against—granted Nick's never divulged the details, but at this point I think the cause is irrelevant. At least I'd have more respect for you if you'd made an effort instead of being so holier-than-thou about it. What are you waiting for? At this point nothing's going to happen on its own. Or don't you care?"

Ellie was staring at her—Zoë felt too stunned even to be outraged.

"And what will you say to Pryce when he asks you where you've been all this time? Or are you going to lie to him too? Oh, don't worry, I'm not going to tell on you. I'll keep your guilty secret."

Her guilty secret? *I'll tell him Stewart showed me his father's paintings,* she signed.

Ellie shrugged irritably.

Stewart . . . Zoë indicated where they'd been standing. She drew a square in the air and mimed a painter brushing paint from a palette, making a stroke on the canvas, the drawing back and calculating perspective. Next she made the sign for "father," which she knew Ellie knew. Her arm was trembling—it was like being forced to speak calmly as a child when you were torn apart by sobs . . . Calm down! If you don't tell me what's wrong, how can I *help* you?

"Stewart showed you his father's *paintings?* Oh, that's very clever."

You asked me what I was going to tell Pryce.

"What?"

She repeated it twice.

"You're going to make up a story about the paintings to tell Pryce?"

Not make up.

"And what, if I may ask, do you plan to tell him the paintings are of?"

Zoë couldn't believe it, but she heard herself laugh as she stepped away from the doorway, stretched out her arms and hung her head.

"Crucifixion scenes? That's clever too. You got that idea from listening to us talk about Ignacio. That and Michael's new book. Well, there's no point in going on with this." Ellie reached to open the kitchen door but kept her hand on the knob. "I'm sorry if I was harsh—it's not that I don't believe the things I said and I'm not sorry I said them, though I wish I'd picked a different time and manner. But you're making fun of me, Zoë. You sat there storing up all the things I told you, things I haven't told anyone—I had no one to tell them to . . . You must have thought I was a real jerk for giving you such ammunition. And last night too . . ." Ellie shook her head incredulously.

"Don't tell me you haven't always resented me—the fact that I made Nick happy. We might as well be honest about it, particularly since I may be losing him. I . . ." Her voice broke and she turned. "I'm going in. This is getting nowhere."

She opened the door, waited a moment for Zoë to protest, then shut it.

XXVI HARMONY (CENTURYVILLE)

At two o'clock in the morning the night before her wedding, Monica found herself standing on a bridge beside Delmore Holland; since shortly before ten they had been pacing like sentries back and forth across Centuryville, keeping watch on the last hours of her freedom. Seth, who had always claimed to have no friends (other than Lucy Chang Smith), had suddenly found it imperative that he spend his last unwed evening with his "chums." Monica did not object, though she wondered if an attribute of marriage were its capacity to cause a person suddenly to dissent from his most firmly stated convictions—though she felt herself unlikely to succumb to this temptation.

Del had bought her dinner at the Centuryville Inn, whose rooms wealthy parents occupied when they came to visit their children at college. Monica's father had stayed there before they took their train trip across the country, so Monica knew what a meal there cost and that Del had used up a week's earnings on it. Yet she felt no compunction about this, since it would be the last time in her life that she'd enjoy herself. Del would have years to pay himself back for the expense.

It had been at approximately half past ten that evening, on the first of their noctambulations across Centuryville, that Monica had imparted to Del the news that her father's letter had contained. As if in passing—the information slipped into a subordinate clause.

"Wait a minute," Del said. "What did you say?"

"You heard me," Monica said. "If you want me to talk about it at all, I have to keep moving. It seems much worse if I stand still."

This tussle had been reenacted numerous times until a short while ago when they'd come to an exhausted halt on the bridge; now they were staring down at a small slow stream they could barely see. Del, having laboriously pieced together her parents' story from Monica's cryptic replies to his questions, asked, "Have you told Seth this?"

"He read my father's letter."

"And what does he say?"

"Del, as far as I'm concerned, it's over and done with. I regret that my parents were so saturated by their religious and cultural upbringing that they felt that what they had done was wrong, but I don't *blame* them. I pity my poor father, feeling obliged to announce his shame to his own child. My mother chose the easy way out, taking refuge in insanity."

"But, Monica," interrupted Del, "how can you say that? Four children died before you were born!"

"That's happened to many people. Besides, if my mother had been able to face what she'd done, as my father had, she would probably never have miscarried."

"But, Monica," Del tried once more. How often had he said those words?—"But, Monica . . ."—protesting statements he could not believe she truly meant. He was convinced furthermore that she wanted him to object; there could be no other reason that she continued to seek his company. And ever since she'd announced her engagement to Seth, a month ago, she'd sought it more than ever, repeatedly informing him how much she cherished his friendship, how lonely she would feel without his companionship, even though she wouldn't be moving away for another year . . .

"But, Monica," he'd pointed out, "you'll be with Seth. You won't be lonely."

"Yes, of course," she said, "but you know what I mean."

"I can't say that I do."

"It's just what I've decided to do, that's all."

To date Del had managed to contain his distress at Monica's plans, but now, as they stood on the bridge—not resting anymore so much as waiting, it seemed to Del, for the other to take the initiative in saying goodbye forever—he could not give up his last chance to convince her not to make a lifelong mistake.

"Monica," he pleaded, "don't marry Seth. He doesn't love you—you know he doesn't. I've kept quiet as long as I thought you were in love with him, but now I don't believe you love him either. Tell me you do, and I'll leave you alone."

Monica sighed, looked at him, then back at the water. It seemed to carry some explanation along with it, present but always moving away from her.

"Did I ever say I did?" she murmured.

"But then, Monica, why, *why* are you marrying him? That's a logical enough question, isn't it? In this day and age people marry for love—try to, at least. Don't they? So why. . . ?"

"I haven't any idea, nor any interest in, what other people do. Isn't it enough for you that I've told you the truth?" But then she relented. "I'm sorry, Del. I shouldn't snap at you, this night of all nights. I know you care for me."

"Oh, Monica," Del said, laying his head on his arms.

Cautiously she touched his back, then slid her hand to his neck and let it rest there.

"Del, don't cry over me. I can't bear it."

"But, Monica, I love you!"

"You say that as if it were all the explanation that's ever needed for anything!"

"Isn't it?"

I loved Eldridge Jewell, she thought. What good did that do me?

Del straightened and brought her into his arms. She put hers around his neck and they stayed in a long embrace.

"I love you," he murmured, sounding annoyed with himself, as if he meant something else but this was all he could think of to say. "Do you have any idea how much I love you?"

He was so busy telling her that he didn't even hear her at first when she told him she loved him too. But, did she or was she simply so hungry to say it to someone that she'd allowed herself to believe it for a moment?

"*What* did you say?"

She wouldn't repeat it.

"I hope I heard what I think I did. I thought you said you loved me."

"Well, I do," she said crossly.

"Oh, Monica . . . Monica!"

He kissed her exultantly, then took her by the hand and led her to the end of the bridge and down the grassy embankment to where it leveled off by the edge of the stream. She didn't resist when he sat down and pulled her down beside him. He took her in his arms again and they lay back and Del murmured to her again as they kissed. "My darling," "my love," "my dearest sweetheart"—terms no one, not even Eldridge Jewell in the height of his passion, had ever used to her. "I do love you, Del," she said simply. "I really do."

Yet there must have been something in her tone—some intent to reassure or persuade—that unsettled him, for he propped himself on an elbow to look at her.

"What are we going to do about Seth?" he asked frankly, though he had the sickening feeling, even as he asked the question, that he was bringing to an end what had only just begun.

"What do you mean, what are we going to do about Seth?"

"I mean . . . You're not still thinking of marrying him!"

"Of course I am. That's the way it has to be."

"Has to be, says *who?*" Del shouted, and Monica said "Shh" even though there were no houses near and no one on the road.

"How dare you tell me to hush? You're telling me you love me but you're going to marry another man! Tomorrow! Hush? I ought to scream until I wake up every single person in this godforsaken town and let them hear what you've just told me!"

"Life is complicated, Del," Monica said, sitting up and hugging her knees. "I wouldn't have told you if I thought you'd carry on like this. Honestly I wouldn't."

"Do you mean you didn't mean it?" he asked hopefully.

"Oh, no. I wouldn't lie to you, Del. I never lie to anyone. But I can't marry you. It just isn't meant to be."

"But, my God, why, Monica? Why?"

"I don't know. What does it matter why? I suppose because it would be so . . . I can't explain it. It would be as if we were to drift down this stream here together and never be seen again. I don't know if you can understand, but that's what it would feel like to me."

"That doesn't sound so terrible."

"It does to me. I don't want to do that. I always want to know where I am."

"And you will if you marry Seth?"

"Yes."

"Then I don't believe you," Del said. "I think you must really love Seth and are simply trying to spare my feelings. Or else . . . Is it . . . You know, if there's something you're ashamed of telling me . . ."

"Something I'm ashamed of?"

"Sometimes things happen . . ."

"Oh, so that's it." Monica laughed. "No, nothing like that." She didn't tell Del that she and Seth had never been lovers. "We didn't decide this suddenly. We decided it last summer, driving back from New Hampshire. We just didn't tell anyone until recently, because . . ."

"Because what?" Del asked, alert.

"Oh, because Seth is so private about such things. You know how he is."

"That's not what you were going to say," Del said.

Monica didn't answer. She was thinking of how her mother had called her upstairs the evening after her father's funeral as the whole town swarmed over the house, eating the food they had brought themselves, or that Vera Magoon had cooked under Mrs. Percy's direction—Mrs. Percy having known what to do about everything, after her recent practice burying Marsh. Charlotte had beckoned to Monica over the railing of the stairs, then led her into her bedroom and asked her to sit down.

"I know that I should know who you are, my dear," she said, "but I'm so preoccupied right now—could you remind me?"

"Certainly," Monica said. "I'm just a neighbor. Susanna—Susanna Percy. My family summers next door."

Since Monica had gone to college Charlotte's memory, already weak, had nearly refused to function. Monica was used to her mother's not knowing who she was, but this was the first time she had pretended to be someone else.

"You don't look quite as I remember," her mother said, "but never mind. I did think you were someone of whom I could ask a question. May I?"

"Go ahead," Monica said.

"Could you tell me whose funeral this was? I was . . . You know, I was married once," she confided. "Could it have been my husband who died? We quarrelled, you know. I don't remember why. Is he dead?"

"Yes," Monica said, "it was your husband's funeral, Mrs. Robie."

"I thought it might be," Charlotte said.

She sat there, looking sadly at her hands. For the first time since she'd been a child, Monica pitied her mother—felt for her as might have someone who didn't know her, who hadn't grown up enveloped by her emptiness—as Susanna might have. Her poor mother—she'd lost her whole life.

"Where are your children, Mrs. Robie?" Monica asked gently. "Do you hear from them often?"

Charlotte looked at her. "My children? I have . . ." She shook her head, sadder than anyone Monica had ever seen. "I have no children."

"But, Mrs. Robie, I thought you had four sons. I . . . My brother Marsh knows them well. Don't you remember? Thaddy and Llewellyn, Henry and Sam? I always liked them so much—they were such lively companions."

Charlotte still looked confused, yet a strange light had come into her face.

"They're all doing well, it seems," Monica went on, "making their way in the world. One's at sea. Another lives in Boston—he's a banker. Marsh often sees him. Another went out West and works on a ranch. Another is a scholar. He teaches in a university. A very famous university. I . . . I'll tell you a secret, Mrs. Robie. I love him. I think we might be married someday. How would you like that? Then you'd be my mother too."

"Your mother? You would be my child?"

Charlotte had begun to weep softly and Monica knelt beside her chair and clasped her hands.

"Don't cry, Mrs. Robie. Please don't cry."

"I wasn't a good mother," Charlotte said. "My sons would have written to me otherwise."

"I'm sure that's not the reason, Mrs. Robie. It's boys—my brother's the same way. My mother despairs of his ever becoming a correspondent, just ask her. I'm sure you were a wonderful mother, Mrs. Robie. They were lucky to have you."

This scene had sped through Monica's memory as she sat on the bank of the dark stream, but she tried to banish the feeling it aroused in her. She couldn't go on pitying her mother—she couldn't; there would be no end to it. It was her father she felt sorry for—his years of loneliness—what right had she to be happy when he had never been?

She looked up at the overcast sky, at where stars should have been flickering. She wondered if her marriage would change when she and Seth had children. She found it difficult to imagine loving an amalgam of herself and him.

Then she thought of Del's having children with someone not her, and of their two families meeting someday in the future, at a college reunion perhaps. Their children could become friends. Discussing among themselves, they would put two and two together and realize that once Mr. Holland had loved Mrs. Carver. "How odd," they would say to each other. "We were almost brother and sister." This scenario comforted Monica; the years in between did not seem so bleak and long.

Del had sat up too and was staring at the little river, moving past so quietly. Although she could no longer remember what he had said, he had been the last to speak. She spoke now as if he had been privy to her train of thought.

"We'll see each other again, Del. Our children will be friends. We'll smile about this night someday, believe me."

At ten the next morning, Annie woke Monica, who otherwise, as Annie pointed out to her, might have slept straight through her own wedding! They were to meet Seth and his companion at the judge's house at noon. In a daze Monica let Annie do her hair, help her dress, even manicure her fingernails. Against Annie's protestations, she had chosen a pearl-gray silk dress to be married in. At the last minute Annie slipped out to a florist's and bought a small bouquet of violets—she thought that Monica might at least consent to carry that.

As it happened, Monica protested nothing. Annie told her she looked pale and ought to wear a little rouge and she let Annie rub it into her cheeks. Annie said that even a justice of the peace expected a bride to wear something in her hair and Monica stood meekly while Annie pinned a piece of white lace across her coiffure.

"Does Seth have a ring?" Annie inquired.

"I don't know. I never thought about it."

"Well, *he'd* better have thought about it."

On their way to the justice's house, alarmed by Monica's somnambulistic expression, Annie pulled her car to the sidewalk and stopped.

"Monica," she said, "you know you don't have to do this. There's nothing shameful about changing your mind. Lots of people have at the last minute, you know. Better to stop now than to do what you might spend years regretting."

"Annie," Monica said, "please start the car. I know Del put you up to this, and I know you mean well, but of course I'm not going to change my mind. Everyone spends years regretting something. It's better to choose what you will regret."

Annie was so shocked that she couldn't say a word; she started up the car, drove the three blocks to the J.P.'s, and before Monica noticed it, she was married. Annie, then Seth's "old army buddy Sal Cipio," kissed her. The justice of the peace shook her hand and called her "Mrs. Carver." She was Mrs. Seth Carver now—she could have stationery printed. Deliverymen and workmen would call her Mrs. Carver. Monica had forgotten that her name would change—it had changed once before, but she had changed it on purpose. Now it had changed all by itself. Where was Monica Robie now? Could she be with her brothers? Seth's name, however, had not changed.

Outside, she and Seth got into his car and Annie and Sal got into Annie's. That also was different. She had arrived in Annie's car, but was departing in Seth's. Now, whenever there was a choice, she would always ride in the same car as Seth. So many things were clearer now. They were on their way to Lucy Chang Smith's house for their reception. Maybe they had married in order to visit her, since Seth had never taken her to Lucy's with him before.

"How did you make friends with her?" Monica asked Seth suddenly. He'd been driving along slowly, much more slowly than he usually drove, whistling a tune she didn't recognize. Seth knew many things about which she knew nothing, but so far he hadn't insisted she learn about them. She hoped that, now that they were married, he wasn't going to start. She would refuse, and there might be a fight. She was prepared to fight with him, but not over something about which she had no intention of ever changing her mind, and she couldn't think of anything, right now, about which she intended changing her mind.

"Friends with whom?" Seth asked.

"Lucy Smith. How did you get to know her?"

"Oh, a science class, I believe. I forget exactly."

He was lying. Monica studied her new husband's profile, understanding that he was debating with himself whether or not to say something else. She was surprised to discover him in a lie, but she was not uninterested.

"I'll ask Lucy," she said.

"No," Seth said, glancing at her. "Don't do that." He took his right hand off the wheel and reached across to her. "I would, in fact, be very grateful if you wouldn't. I'll explain it all to you later, I promise, but there's not time now. All right?"

"You don't have to tell me anything," she said, looking down at his hand on her knee.

"I realize that, but I want to. I didn't think I would, but I do. It's important, I think. If we're to have a shot at a real marriage . . ."

"A real marriage?"

". . . we can't start out by keeping secrets from each other, can we?"

"But there's privacy, isn't there? Is privacy the same as secrecy?"

After considering this a moment, Seth answered, "To my mind the distinction should be drawn between those things not confided to another that could not affect the other and those things not confided that could. Of course, it may be difficult always to know which is which."

"It's not the truth but the suspicion that another purposely obscures it that can drive a person to madness," Monica said, as if reciting, and Seth, already applying his principle, did not point out to her that this was what her father had said in the letter, in which, among other things, he had accused himself of having caused her mother's illness.

"Do you believe I obscure the truth?" Seth asked, interested. "I've always wondered. I'm not sure that believing in the existence of truth isn't in itself a way of obscuring it."

Monica's answer—if it was an answer—took him by surprise.

"Do you desire me?" she asked. "Do you want . . . You've never said."

"Yes, right now I do, yes," he answered. "Of course."

"That's not why we married," she said. "Not to satisfy a passion. So I wondered."

"Why did we marry then, in your opinion? Since you seem to have thought so much about it . . ."

"To think clearly, isn't that the reason? To be free of . . ."

"Free of what?"

"I don't know," Monica said. "Just free."

"Interesting," Seth said. "I thought I married you because I loved you."

"I hope that's not true." Monica spoke with such vehemence that Seth stared at her. "The car," she said calmly, as it swerved. He straightened it out. "I thought you married me because you envied me for having more to grieve over than you do. That's not the case?"

Seth looked bleakly ahead of him. "If what you say is true, Monica, then I'm a cold-blooded bastard. I hope to God it's not. I won't deny that what you call envy may have been an emotion I've experienced, but I wouldn't say that I'm proud of it. I wouldn't like to think that it's my only feeling for you. One can begin with one feeling but end with another, don't you think so?"

When she didn't answer, he said, "It's going to be a hell of a marriage if we're going to fix such a fine lens on each other all the time. There has to be a little . . . haze, for lack of a better word."

"No one can make that happen," Monica said. She didn't add that she never wanted to feel that again. When she'd loved Eldridge, there'd been all the haze anyone could have wanted. It was very agreeable, the way all the corners and sharp edges of things had softened, as if something had actually changed out in the world, not solely in her view of it. But then her father had died and a cold harsh light had illuminated everything. She was used to living in its glare now; she never again wanted to have to readjust to it. She felt that to be scrupulously honest with each other was the only gift that she and Seth could make to each other that would even begin to compensate for their not being in love.

Later she wondered how she had ever imagined that it would be possible to maintain that clarity—as she made her way through the endless unprogressing years, her thoughts hopelessly confused: her own among themselves, hers with Seth's, later both of theirs with the children—but how could she have known? She knew that when she had envisioned being married to Seth, the future had appeared to her as an infinite suite of rooms through which the two of them would wander, engaged in their separate pursuits, meeting at prearranged intervals to converse politely across the distances. Not loving each other, they would be comrades in their unrequited longings for people not present, and, if they shared a bed, it would be in the same spirit of diffident friendliness. She had even imagined that, after a time, a new kind of feeling might arise—not the consuming passion she had felt for Eldridge Jewell, not the affectionate gratitude she experienced for Delmore Holland, but a lucid, stalwart companionship like that which soldiers in battle felt for each other, an acknowledgment of mutual need and support that transcended temperamental differences. When they spent most of their honeymoon viewing relics in shrines throughout Europe, this had seemed somehow to cement this understanding; it was as if Seth meant to suggest that in marriage as well as in religious persecution, if you didn't recant your most cherished beliefs, you ran the danger of dying for them.

Yet none of Monica's expectations were borne out. From the start neither she nor Seth could seem to remember that the other was not the person they wished for; instead Monica found herself believing that Seth could be Eldridge if only he tried, and she knew that he believed she refused out of obstinacy to admit that she was the woman he truly loved. Instead of wandering through spacious chambers, they occupied a house that was a jumble of hideous, cramped rooms and vicious passages: no windows anywhere, vile-looking furniture in revolting colors, fabric torn, upholstery spurting out, finishes gouged, legs and arms missing; and the two of them crouched behind doors, waiting to spring out and catch the other out of disguise. At the least sign that their longed-for beloved's true identity seemed about to emerge, they responded with such fervor—and then with such rage when the similarity dissipated—that at times it seemed that they might even succeed in molding each other into the desired shape. There followed the moments when they realized how they had been twisting each other, and the agonized searches into themselves to locate the grafts of the imposed personality, in order to tear them loose. Yet in this frenzied disengagement they also ripped away parts of themselves they had long been convinced were purely their own, and thus little by little they felt themselves disappear, and none of their various attempts to arrest this vanishing process—to live apart (albeit under the same roof); to live together, but in a foreign country—proved of any avail.

But that June afternoon in Centuryville, all of this was yet to come. Seth had listened rigidly while Monica had explained to him that only unrelenting honesty could make up for lack of love—they were out in the country now and nearing the turn-off to the farmhouse where Lucy and her husband lived.

"Have you finished?" he asked, his voice swollen.

He sounded as if he couldn't wait to be rid of her company, but then, in one of those rapid switches that always convinced Monica she was right to think that hardly anyone said what they meant, he stopped the car by the side of the road, pulled her into his arms and kissed her. She surprised herself by responding passionately. Annie and Sal drove by, honking the horn and shouting. They pulled apart.

"Never tell me again that I don't love you," Seth said harshly. "If you can't promise to do that, I will leave right now."

"Fine," Monica said. "Just don't tell me you love me when you don't."

"Believe me, I won't," he said, and they kissed again.

"I don't want to wait." He was fumbling at the hem of her dress.

"Where can we go?" she asked.

They looked around. As usual only cornfields, freshly green, stretched for miles.

"Nowhere," he said.

She suddenly wondered if he'd ever had a girl before—that was how she thought about it, "had a girl"; it was a possibility that hadn't occurred to her.

"We can lie down in the back seat," she said, smiling at him.

"You *are* bold," he said.

"There's never anyone on this road. Besides, what business is it of theirs? We can do whatever we want. We're married." She began to laugh.

"What's so funny?"

"I just realized that we were married."

"Well, that's a start."

"Come on," she said.

They clambered into the back seat. Monica arranged herself beneath him.

"I never imagined it happening quite like this," Seth said.

"Better that way," she answered. "Everything's better when it's not what you expect."

As he began to grapple with her clothes, she was more than ever sure that Seth had never "done it" before. She would never have suspected this, from the languorous, bored way he always behaved around women. She decided to act shocked at some of the things he was doing—to give him confidence. Maybe in time he would know as much as Eldridge. She pretended to be as aroused as he was. Afterwards, she felt a little sorry for him, he was so content. Their clothes rearranged, they sat for a while in the back seat, holding hands. Seth said, "I want to tell you—it's not right not to tell you. I've loved Lucy for a very long time. I still love her, although I've accepted that it will never be requited."

Monica nodded. "I'm sorry."

"I just wanted you to know. It didn't seem fair not to tell you."

"It's all right. I love someone else too."

"You do?" he asked, amazed. "Who? Delmore Holland?"

"Delmore . . . No. No one you know. Someone in Harmony. He's married too."

Seth still looked astonished. "You conceal a lot, you know that?"

"So do you."

"All right. I guess that means we're even." He kissed her on the cheek. "We should go."

She nodded, and then they climbed out of the car and straightened their clothes. Back in the front seat she leaned over and tilted her head to see her hair in the rearview mirror. Seth started the engine and they drove down the road to their reception.

XXVII SPARTA

One Sunday morning in early November, Zoë went out to get the Sparta *Sentinel*; it was waiting on the frosty brick steps, a fact that never ceased to amaze her. As she rolled off the thin red rubber band, she aimed as usual for the open front door, but even though for once it went through she forgot to wonder what she'd done right this time because Rob was staring up at her. There he was, smack in the middle of the front page, wearing a tall white chef's hat, standing in front of a huge oven, taking out loaves of bread shaped like railroad cars with a giant wooden paddle.

Feeling ill, Zoë took the newspaper upstairs to her room and shut the door. It was only a little after eight. On weekends Monica usually slept until nine and Seth hardly ever got up before noon. She sat on her bed and spread the paper all the way open across it. The caption under the picture said, "Young Entrepreneur with Staff of Life." And, in smaller letters: "Photo by Marietta Frank. For article, see page 9." Zoë opened the paper. The article was by Marietta Frank too. Inside was another, smaller picture of Robert, this time squeezing frosting onto a cake in the shape of a witch. The caption said, "Robert Went, proprietor of Went's Baked Goods, plans many specialty items." Zoë didn't know if she felt like laughing or throwing up. The idea of Rob "planning many specialty items" sounded so completely bogus—could he truly talk like that now?

> The new bakery that opened last month on Mulberry Street in Sparta quickly had customers agreeing that this is no ordinary business. "It has a special atmosphere," remarked one satisfied patron, in between bites of a "Napoleon," this bakery's version of a chocolate éclair. But that's not strange at Went's Baked Goods, whose logo might well be "Nothing is what it seems."
>
> If you ask for an éclair, you are just as likely to be served a blueberry muffin. If you request a cruller, chances are the baker will provide you with an apple turnover. But are customers annoyed by these shenanigans?
>
> Far from it! Said one pleased patron, "I like not knowing what I'm

going to get. Usually in a bakery it's so hard to choose. Here you can't get what you ask for, so you don't have to worry about it."

Robert Went, the ingenious proprietor of this novelty business, explains the appeal another way.

Was this article for real?

"When I was young," (Mr. Went has a way to go before reaching twenty) "I always hated going to bakeries because I never knew what things were called. It was humiliating having to say, 'Uh, I want one of those round things with red in the middle and white around the edges,' and even then the clerk would never get it, so you'd have to explain further. 'Uh, no, duh, not *that* red and white thing, that oblong one, yeah, the one shaped like a football field . . .' It was enough to take away your appetite!"

Even pointing is of no avail in Went's bakery. Continues Went, "All attempts to exercise choice will be foiled in my establishment. People who enter my bakery must relinquish all hope of getting what they think they want."

Marietta Frank, whoever she might be, obviously hadn't a clue that Rob was quoting *The Inferno*.

Robert Went—Rob, to his friends . . .

What friends was she talking about? Zoë felt like decking this reporter—Marietta Frank, what kind of a name was that? She sounded like she was wearing a tutu. "Rob, to his friends . . ." No doubt *she* now considered herself one of his "friends." They probably sat at the little bakery tables and ate imaginary éclairs and drank imaginary coffee; no doubt they were having an affair, doing all kinds of inventive things like spreading frosting on each other and licking it off.

. . . Rob, to his friends—is a young man who thinks carefully about everything he does. "This is the first existentialist bakery in history," he says, grinning mischievously. (Went refers to the philosophical movement popularized after the Second World War by French philosophers Albert Camus and Jean-Paul Sartre.) "Scratch that," Went says. "This is probably an anti-existentialist bakery; the ones already out there are the existentialist ones."

For most of us it may require a big leap of the imagination to see what a French philosophical movement could have to do with Sparta, U.S.A. (though, as Went likes to point out, most pastries are of French origin). However, for Went this kind of thinking is habitual. "When you grow up hearing your father arguing on the phone with other fathers about Wittgenstein and Hegel," he says, "you can't help it." Went's father,

> Theodore Went, is a former college professor who has since gone to work for the government. His work is in the "highly sensitive but perfectly obvious vein," according to his son.

God, Lois Lane Frank had really fallen for him hook, line, and sinker. It would have been funny if Zoë could have been sure that Rob was pulling the wool over this idiot reporter's eyes.

> Although Went credits his background with an important role in his development, he attributes his special interests to an accident he suffered at age ten. Hit by a truck on Chesterfield Street, he lost a leg. The months he spent in the hospital, he says, gave him much time to think. "Everyone should do it at least once," he says. (Future patrons of Went's Baked Goods be warned: its proprietor possesses a wry sense of humor.)

That sounded more like Rob. Nancy Drew Frank seemed to have missed the point again, though—Rob wasn't joking. He'd walked in front of the truck on purpose.

> Went speaks as frequently of the philosophers Sartre, Nietzsche, and Kierkegaard as most teenagers do of the Beatles or the Rolling Stones. Yet don't fear a gloomy lecture when you visit Went's Baked Goods. The atmosphere is anything but somber. Went's assistants are all under fourteen. Despite the burdensome paperwork required to employ minors, Went says it's worth it. He hopes to show that teenagers can hold responsible positions in society. "We do not simply freak out, make out, and drop out," states Went. "Besides," he adds, "they don't try to boss me around."
>
> He would have preferred to hire "all crippled children," he claims (Went expresses a distaste for the word "handicapped"); "however," he says, "area hospitals were less than cooperative in providing names . . ."

He'd gotten that phrase about teenagers from some magazine article last year about "Today's Youth." "Today's Youth—Angry Innocence or Disillusioned Sophistication: Is There a Difference?" The whole article had been like that—they'd all made fun of it at school. "How are you this morning?" "Oh, disillusioned and sophisticated, how about you?" "Angry and innocent, actually." But maybe Rob took this stuff seriously now. He sounded as if he'd had a lobotomy.

> Whether one agrees or disagrees with this baker's philosophy, no one who has made his acquaintance is unimpressed. Says Jarvis Cornford, chief loan officer of the Sparta National Bank, "I was completely bowled

> over by that young man. I wish all our clients talked as sound business sense as he does."

Rob? *Business* sense?

The article ended,

> He looks like a younger and thinner Clark Gable, he possesses wisdom beyond his years, *and,* it seems, he knows how to turn a profit. The world may be this young entrepreneur's oyster—or should we say "éclair"?

Zoë slapped the paper shut. She stared again at the picture of Robert grinning in his tall white popover hat, and tried to guess what he was really feeling. Since that night on the docks six weeks ago, when she'd felt sure that things between her and Rob were going to be fine, she hadn't wanted to risk losing that feeling by trying to see him. Now she heard Monica, earlier than usual, get up and go into the bathroom, and, suddenly in a panic, she rapidly folded the paper back together. She couldn't face Monica; she had to get out of the house before Monica came out of her room. Quickly she took off her slippers and pulled on her boots; then she collected all the money she had in the room—about eighty-five dollars (Monica had decided to double her allowance)—stuffed it, her hairbrush, and *The Plague,* which they were reading for English, into her purse, and tiptoed down the stairs. She left the paper on the hall table, and scrawled on the telephone pad, "I'll be out most of the day. Zoë."

Then she grabbed her coat, hat, and gloves out of the hall closet, and rushed out. It was cold, gray, and drizzly, typical Sparta November weather, and as she hurried down Chesterfield Street she thought that if Seth and Monica had only *told* her that she could expect to be miserable most of her life then at least she wouldn't feel that things were wrong all the time; she wouldn't always be blaming herself for having made some terrible mistake. But Seth and Monica were too busy trying to figure out why they weren't happy themselves, which they undoubtedly were doing because *their* parents had spent *their* lives doing the same thing, all the way back to Adam and Eve.

Zoë had come to the bus stop, but when the bus hadn't arrived after a couple of minutes she grew nervous that someone might see her waiting and walked down Pearl to Main, planning to go up Main towards St. Stephen's Circle to sit in the graveyard until she planned what to do next. By the time she got there, however, she'd already made up her mind. She walked over to Derby Street to the Greyhound Station and bought a ticket to Washington. The trip took about an hour; by the time the bus pulled into the Washington terminal she was starving. She planned to spend the day in museums—it would be warm and the chances of running into someone she knew were minuscule—but first she had to eat breakfast. After walking only a few blocks she found a diner squashed between two skyscrapers—as if a caboose had gotten stuck there. It reminded her of Rob's house, propped up between two larger houses. What a coincidence. The diner was half empty and no one paid any attention to her. She ordered French toast and orange juice and coffee and took out *The Plague* and started reading where she'd left off. She was hardly in the mood for rats and plague symptoms, but she had to have read to page two hundred by tomorrow—in case she ever went back to school, that is.

Was she having a nervous breakdown? Was this the kind of thing people did when they had one? Why hadn't she gone to see Rob? Had she been living in a fantasy world? That was what had happened to Charlotte. She had been so miserable in real life that she'd gone into an imaginary world and never come back. Well, if she went crazy that would give Seth and Monica something besides themselves to talk about for once. Oh, Zoë? No, I'm sorry, she can't come to the phone, she's a raving lunatic. Yes, that's correct, she's in an insane asylum. Zoë laughed aloud, then heard herself and looked around to see if anyone had noticed. She really must be going insane—laughing aloud to herself. Yes, it is, it really is a pity, a bright young girl like her . . . Well, of course we miss her, of course we wish it hadn't happened, but, after all, one can't help what happens to one's children; of course one is obliged to shelter and feed them, but beyond that . . . Well, yes, thank you very much for calling. I'm sure Zoë will be happy to know that you were concerned about her—if she ever returns to her senses, that is.

Who had called? Rob? Bridget? Archie Tannenbaum? Mr. Montgomery? Who else would care? Then Zoë shook her head in disbelief. She'd just been seriously wondering, trying to *remember,* who had called her parents to find out how she was. She *was* insane, if she was thinking like that. It wasn't so hard to go insane, really; people had the wrong idea if they thought it meant that you had to rant and rave and *act* out of your mind; all you had to do was to lose contact. You lost contact and then you couldn't convince anyone that you had because they couldn't understand unless they'd lost it themselves and if they'd lost it then they couldn't communicate either. You'd just go farther and farther into your own mind until you couldn't even talk. It came from spending more time thinking about people than being with them so that after a while your imagined version of them was more real than they were. She could even see how, once you'd noticed this discrepancy, you could be around someone all the time and it could still be there.

Feeling very nervous suddenly, Zoë paid the bill and hurried back up the street to the bus station. She was in no mood to wander around looking at great art. It was unbearable waiting for the next bus back to Sparta, and throughout the entire trip she kept feeling as if Rob were leaving that morning on an ocean liner and she were going to miss even saying goodbye to him. But when she turned down Main Street from St. Stephen's Circle on her way to Mulberry Street what she had been feeling seemed ridiculous and she headed instead for the Naval Academy. It was the only place in Sparta where she could be sure of not running into someone she knew. The Academy had visiting hours on Sundays, but only people not from Sparta went there unless there were a parade, and there was no reason they'd be having a parade today. Veterans' Day wasn't until next week.

She walked around the grounds until she found the library—she'd used to go there years ago with Myra Ogilvy when they'd been waiting for her father—whatever it was he had done there. The main area was full of midshipmen studying whatever they studied—how to sink ships, God knows what. She ignored them. She could really care less what they thought she was doing there; if anyone tried to tell her to get out she would tell them to go to hell, she was an American citizen and this was U.S. government property and if they wanted to argue with her, then take it to the Supreme Court.

She found a little desk by itself down at the end of an aisle in front of a window, and she put her stuff down and sat and looked out—the window gave a view of the parade ground. She took a deep breath—it felt as if she hadn't been breathing all morning. For the first time since she'd seen the paper with Rob staring at her she felt calm. No one knew where she was but nothing could happen to her here. She was surrounded by books and it was peaceful and quiet. The sun came in across the desk and she stretched her hands out into it, then set her bag on the floor and folded her arms and laid her head down on them, her face turned towards the sun. She was thinking how weird it would be if she fell asleep and didn't wake up until after the library was closed, but it was only three.

It really happened. She woke up and it was dark out—lights were on in the buildings across the parade ground. At first she didn't think anything about it—she just pushed her chair back and stood up, but the scraping sound was very loud and she realized then that the only lights on in the library were the little ones over the book alleys. As quietly as she could, she stepped down the narrow aisle of books—she couldn't believe it: the library really was closed. The big tables in the main study area were all bare and gleamed where a ray of light either from the stack-lights or from a lamp outside hit their surfaces. She went out among them, running her hand along their tops. It still seemed like a joke, though, as if someone were warning her that she shouldn't imagine things she didn't want to happen. Suddenly she had the feeling that someone was watching her and for the first time felt scared; then she got even more scared wondering why she hadn't been scared before. She looked up at the balcony that ran all around the room; the second-story wall was lined with books too. She remembered, then, having been up there once with Myra Ogilvy and being afraid. In fact she had had nightmares about it, she remembered now—she would be trying to make her way around the balcony and it would start tilting, trying to tip her off, to slide her into something horrible below—what had it been? Had she had it before or after Mr. Ogilvy had chased her and Myra with a knife and locked them up in the basement? Either way, what did the dream mean? She had had it several times.

You got up to the balcony by a staircase in the corner, she remembered now, back behind more rows of books. It had used to give her the creeps too—it was a rickety wooden circular stair, which looked as if it had been there for hundreds of years, even longer than the rest of the building; as if it had been left standing from the ruin of an earlier building, and the library had been built around it. And then they'd built the Naval Academy to go with the library. Zoë wondered if the stairs were unsafe, but they weren't roped off and there wasn't any warning sign on them. She started up and the center pole squeaked loudly, but other than that the structure seemed stable. When she'd made it to the balcony, she realized that she had been holding her breath. Was there someone up there?

She decided to walk all the way around—it would be an exorcism; she would make herself do it—and she set off, taking careful steps, keeping close to the bookcases. If the balcony could hold the weight of all those books then her weight would hardly be enough to pull it loose from the wall. She tried glancing down over the railing but the vertigo that struck forced her to look up immediately. But why? She wasn't afraid of heights. She wasn't nervous on Charlotte's widow's walk, for instance, or on bridges or even at the top of the Washington Monument. It must just be because she couldn't figure out what made the balcony stay up. There were no columns or supports under it.

She had made it to the first corner now and started along the second side. All the books were large—encyclopedias or reference books? She couldn't read the spines—there were no lights on up here. Maybe the volumes were some kind of naval records. She hadn't looked over the railing again, but merely thinking about it nauseated her. Realizing that she was two whole sides away from the staircase didn't help either. She was about to turn the corner when she suddenly almost screamed. There was a *door* right in front of her. She hadn't seen it before because she'd been avoiding looking at anything besides the books. A door, Jesus Christ—what the hell was a *door* doing up here? It had been lurking there, the whole time, waiting for her to get to it—to whatever or whoever was behind it. When she turned the next corner, whatever it was could spring out at her. How was it that she hadn't remembered the door from before when she'd climbed up there with Myra, Myra leading the way and putting her finger over her lips as if she were going to show her a secret. As if she were going to show her a secret? Why had that come to mind? *Was* there something behind the door that Myra had shown her, something so horrible that she had blocked it out all these years? Some deep Freudian guilt memory?

But what could Myra have shown her? A dead body? Someone hanging from a rafter? Someone doing something obscene? Two midshipmen having sex? But how could Myra have known ahead of time that something was going on, unless it went on nonstop, and how could something like that go on nonstop? Had it involved her father? Creepy Anders Ogilvy? Had he done something to them? To *her,* Zoë?

Zoë walked to the door and opened it. She couldn't see anything, but she felt along the wall inside and found a light switch. It didn't matter at this point if someone saw the light from outside and came to arrest her; she would still have had time for the memory to come flooding back, the horrible memory of whatever it was that had warped her for life. After that how could she possibly care if she went to jail?

When she had turned the light on, however, she saw that there weren't any windows in the room. It was hardly a room, just a small cubicle with a desk, a lamp, a telephone, and a tin of ballpoint pens that all said "U.S. Naval Academy" on them. Now what? She sat down at the desk to look in the drawers but they were locked. Was she going to have to force them open in order to experience her revelation? What could she use?

She looked around—the room could have been either a private office or an interrogation chamber. She felt bored now, deflated. No great revelation was forthcoming, that was obvious. She'd worked herself up over nothing. What a weird day: a trip to the nation's capital for breakfast, then the afternoon spent, *asleep,* in the Naval Academy library; waking up to find out that she was locked in; remembering her childhood nightmare; thinking she would discover its original source, and then finding herself in this bland unused interrogation room off the balcony. Nothing there at all. Just a typical Sunday.

She felt depressed, but also more practical. For the first time since she'd woken up she started thinking about the actuality of being caught in the Naval Academy library on a Sunday night. Not only that, she was probably even locked in the Naval Academy itself. For the first time she looked at her watch: it was six-thirty. She thought she remembered that the gates open to the public all closed by about six (or at least you'd be stopped by the guard). She could get out of the library—she doubted it had an alarm—but how the hell was she going to get over the six-foot wall?

Suddenly, before she lost her courage, she picked up the phone and dialed the operator for information; a switchboard operator came on instead and asked her what extension she was trying to reach. She hung up, hoping the operator hadn't noticed where the call had come from; after a moment she picked up the phone again and dialed nine. That was what you had to do at the college. Thank God, the dial tone changed. She dialed zero again and this time a real operator answered. Zoë requested the number of Went's Baked Goods and copied it down on the blotter with one of the Navy pens. Whosever office this was could try to figure out how Went's Baked Goods' telephone number had come to be written on his blotting paper. She hoped it was Anders Ogilvy's. It would serve him right. Rob answered on the first ring.

"This is he," he said.

"What's that supposed to mean?" she asked.

"Who is this?" he asked.

"This is she," she said, trying to sound as pompous as he had, but then she started to laugh.

"*Zoë*?" he asked.

"Rob?" she replied, still laughing.

"Zoë! Are you all right? What's the matter?"

It seemed funny that he sounded concerned—that he would automatically think something must be wrong for her to call him.

"Nothing. I'm fine. It's just that I happen to be locked in the Naval Academy library."

"You're *what*?"

"I got locked in here. I fell asleep and I guess they don't check very carefully—some national security, right—or else they did it on purpose, though I can't imagine why they would do that, but, anyway, I woke up and it was dark and I was locked in here and I was just wondering, I don't think it will be a problem getting out of the *library,* but I thought you might have some ideas about how I could get out of the Academy. I was thinking that maybe the best thing would be to go down to the water and try to steal a rowboat and row around to the harbor, but I feel sort of nervous about how far I'd have to go out in the river before I could head back in, and I don't know if the current would be strong or not and besides it's pretty cold out . . ."

"Can a person get a word in edgewise?" Rob shouted.

"Sure. Of course," she said. "I'm sorry. I didn't mean to . . . I mean, it's just that I . . ."

"Zoë!" he shouted into the phone.

She jumped, then asked "What?" Her voice sounded so meek.

"What the hell is going on? You have me worried."

"I have you *worried*?"

"What! You don't speak English anymore either?"

What did he mean, "either"? She didn't answer and he said, "Do you swear to God, you're really in the Naval Academy library?"

"Yes," she whispered. Her voice was acting very peculiar suddenly. Don't make me cry, she said silently. Please don't make me cry. What exactly was she praying to, her *voice*?

"How do you tell if you're having a nervous breakdown?" she asked Rob. "What are the signs? Are there any? Do you know?"

"You get locked into the Naval Academy library on a Sunday night and then call up a friend you dumped six months ago and start babbling as if you'd just talked to him yesterday. That's one very common sign. It's in all the medical books."

"Oh," she said. "Well, that's a relief." Then she said, "I didn't dump you. I think it was the other way around, frankly."

"You think the shoe in the hand is better than the bird on the foot, do you? Look, we'll go over the fine points later. For now we need to establish exactly what *degree* of nervous breakdown you're having. You can talk—more or less, anyway. Enough to fool the average peon, let's say. Can you walk? Are your motor faculties in any way impaired?"

"Not that I know of." She was about to start laughing hysterically or start crying hysterically; she couldn't tell which.

"Good. Can you control your behavior to any extent? That is, once you're out of the library you won't start singing the West Point theme song at the top of your lungs or anything, will you?"

"I don't even know what it is."

"That's small comfort. You could think you did. Besides, I'm sure you know the Marine Hymn. 'From the halls of Montezuma to the shores of

Tripoli . . .' " He began to sing it. "Though why *those* are the words to the Marine Hymn and why it's a *hymn* I couldn't tell you if my life depended on it. Fortunately, it doesn't . . ."

"I think nervous breakdowns are contagious," she interrupted.

"Yes, I'm sure you're right. Everything else is. We better talk as little as possible until we're somewhere where it won't be dangerous to have a complete mental collapse. I've got a plan. Do you know that gate all the way up at the end of Academy Street? Right before the bridge?"

She nodded, then remembered that she was on the phone. "Yes, what about it?"

" 'What about it?' she says. It's just extremely charming, that's all. I thought that since you'll be spending some time in the grounds, you might enjoy having a look at it. Meet me there in half an hour, you moron."

"What good will that do? It will be locked."

"O ye of little faith," he said. "It may be locked but I doubt it will be guarded. I go for walks a lot late at night when I can't sleep, and . . ."

"You do? So do I. Or I did once. Once I . . ."

"Hold your horses, will you? 'Hold your horses . . .' Jesus Christ. Hold whatever goddamn animals you feel like. I've never seen that gate guarded yet. By the time I get there, I'll have devised the rest of the plan. Okay?"

"Okay."

"No, no, you're supposed to say, 'Roger,' and then I say, 'Roger, over and out.' Don't you know anything? Haven't you ever played Escaping from the Naval Academy before?"

"No," she said.

"Zoë, you are making me *very nervous,*" Rob said, in a sing-song voice.

"I am?"

"I have this strong urge to . . . never mind," he said. "You'll really be there in half an hour, won't you? This isn't a hoax, is it?"

"What were you going to say?"

"Never mind—I'll tell you later."

She was smiling. "What time is it now?" she asked.

"You don't have a watch?"

"Of course I have a watch. We're supposed to synchronize them. Don't *you* know anything?"

"Sorry, I forgot." He sounded as if he'd been holding his breath and had just let it out.

It was only six-forty. She was amazed—it seemed as if a lot more time had gone by since she'd called him. After they'd hung up, she took one last look around the room, but besides being positive that there really wasn't any revelation to come from it—she'd never seen anyone or anything in there, dead, alive, or otherwise—she wouldn't have believed it if she'd had one. Revelations were imaginary. Rob was real.

She turned out the light and went back onto the balcony, shutting the door softly behind her. The wood flooring of the balcony creaked.

She walked around the two sides she hadn't been on yet, feeling slightly queasy, but nothing like before. Back downstairs, she checked out the entryway; it was brightly lit and she'd be a sitting duck if snipers had their eye on it. She wasn't in the mood to get shot at right now. Better see if she could get out through one of the windows.

Back at the table where she'd been sitting she inspected the window—it opened outward with a latch, but there was a screen on the outside and besides, it was too near the door. She'd still be in the light. She picked up her purse and returned to the center of the room. All along one side were tall windows that didn't open at all. She went back into the stacks in the opposite direction—yes, here were more of the smaller windows. The screens seemed to be fastened in place only by little latches on the inside, and she finally managed to get one back through a window sideways. It was quite a drop to the ground, but at least this side of the building was dark. She threw her purse down first—now she had no choice but to jump. She remembered from gym class to bend her knees, and although she fell forward she wasn't hurt. She scrambled up, grabbed her purse, and ran around the far side of the building, then stood, panting, thinking of the safest way to get to the gate from there.

She snuck along in the shadows of buildings, even hid once in some bushes, thinking someone was coming, but in fact she didn't see anyone—the entire Naval Academy must have been eating dinner. Some national security, she thought again—she could have blown the whole place up if she'd wanted. She'd never realized how easy it could be to take over an entire country.

Rob had been absolutely brilliant. He had tied several sheets, and baker's aprons when he ran out of sheets, together to make a rope, and he'd knotted loops in it for footholds. He stuffed it through the bars of the gate—there wasn't room between the gate and the archway to climb over, so she'd have to climb over the wall. She threw one end of the sheet-ladder back over to him and when he had a secure hold he whistled. There was still no one around. "If someone comes along," he whispered through the gate, "tell them we're practicing maneuvers. We're midshipmen disguised as ordinary human beings." She started laughing as she climbed. She kept expecting at every moment to be zeroed in on by a spotlight and shot dead. But nothing happened at all. It would almost have been disappointing, if she hadn't been so happy to see Rob. There he was, when she got to the top, which fortunately wasn't spiked with barbed wire. He had the other end of the sheets around his waist and was bracing himself against a tree.

When she got to the top, she suddenly had such a strong feeling of déjà vu that she exclaimed, "Hey, I already did this!"

"Did what?"

"Jumped down from this wall."

"Oh, great. You drag me out of my nice warm house, making me think it's an emergency, and then you tell me you've done it all before."

"No, I don't mean like that. It's like a déjà vu, only stronger—like a real memory." She felt she'd never seen anything so clearly in her life as this picture—herself jumping down from a high wall, everything the same—the texture of the bricks, the chill November air, escaping from the Naval Academy . . .

"Well, Zoë," Rob said, "can we discuss it when we're both at the same level? Or do you prefer to continue speaking from on high?"

"Okay, okay."

She jumped down and he pulled the sheets back over and bundled them up.

"Hi," he said.

"Hi, how are you?"

"You know, I'm really going to sleep soundly in my bed from now on knowing how vigilantly our shores are guarded."

"Isn't it incredible?"

"I can't believe they locked you in there. Haven't they heard of the separation of church and state?"

"What are you talking about?"

"I don't know. It's Sunday, you're a civilian, you should have been at church . . . Oh, forget it. I'm just making conversation."

"Give me a break. You never make conversation."

"Well, I was babbling then. Would you accept that explanation?"

"Not exactly."

" 'Not exactly,' she says."

"Why are you quoting me?"

They had started walking down Academy Street towards the harbor.

"Why am I quoting you? Why does anyone quote anyone? Generally because that person's words have made a great impression. 'To be, or not to be, that is the question.' "

"Rob . . ."

"Don't tell me, you're warning me. If I don't shape up . . ."

"Have you gone crazy from inhaling too many dough fumes?"

"Dough fumes . . . What a unique expression. I seriously doubt that those two words have ever before been used together in the history of the English language."

She stopped walking. "Can I ask you a question?"

"Fire away."

"What were you going to say earlier?"

"Earlier when?"

"On the phone. When you said you had an urge to do something."

"Oh, that." He shrugged. "I think the moment's passed."

She stared at him, then exclaimed, "It *always* has!"

He gave her a quick look sideways, but just kind of grinned and said, "Come on, Zoë, let's go home."

XXVIII CASCABEL FLATS

Snow had already covered the road by the time they left the party. No one had talked on the way to the car, but now Monica said, "At least we'll have a white Christmas." What did she mean, "at least"? But Zoë felt too tired to think about it; she closed her eyes and listened to the slapping of the windshield wipers and the fizzy whirring of the tires.

At home even before they were out of the car Nick announced, "I'm going to tell the creatures good night"—he sounded as if he thought someone meant to prevent him. Zoë motioned to Pryce that she would go with Nick. As she followed him down the embankment she kicked the light, fluffy snow. She wondered how much Ellie had told him. It made no difference to her, she was just curious. When she'd gone back inside after Ellie's diatribe, intending to try Seth again, she'd walked in on Ellie and Nick in the sitting room.

"Jesus Christ," Nick swore. "Forgot the bloody key."

Zoë stood where she was until he came back, letting the snow wet her face—second time that evening—savoring her complete lack of anxiety; it was as if everything occurring now were already memory.

"Why the hell didn't you stand under the overhang?" Nick exclaimed.

What? What difference did it make to him?

He hadn't waited to see her reply but had opened the door and gone in. He turned on the overhead light and scanned the bank of cages, then leaned close to the big Atrox, which appeared to be asleep. It lay in a loose splayed coil, its spade-shaped head resting like a crouching frog on a section of itself that would have measured several feet away had it been stretched out.

"You told Ellie what I told you this afternoon, didn't you?" Nick said. "After you gave me your word . . ."

What?

"Don't lie, on top of it. Ellie interrupts a conversation I'm having to pull me aside to announce that Judith is pregnant but hasn't told Stewart yet. Then gives *me* the third degree. What have I told Stewart about our so-called problems? I ask her what this has to do with Judith's pregnancy and she insists that I've been keeping something from her, but won't say what. Don't tell me you didn't tell her about the birth control pills."

I didn't.

"I'm sorry, I just don't believe you anymore. I don't understand what you're up to, Zoë."

She shrugged. *Stewart showed me his father's paintings,* she signed. S-T-E-W SHOW ME FATHER PAINTING. It would be interesting to see what he said to that.

"What?"

She repeated the gestures.

"Stewart showed you his father's paintings? Cut it out, Zoë."

They're of Ignacio Ortega. She spelled out the first name.

"You can make up a better story than that."

I suppose you think I forged Rob's letter, too.

"What did you say? You read the letter? What did he say?"

I forgot to ask Stewart for it.

"You forgot . . ." Nick looked totally disgusted. "Zoë, I've had enough—I'm going in. If you decide you want to put your cards on the table, fine. Otherwise just leave me out of all this. This private melodrama you're acting out—Robert Went going after Dad, but you won't read his letter; this fantasy about Mom scheming to meet Dad after New Year's . . . Grow up, why don't you."

She stared at him, then exclaimed, *Why don't you just say it? You think I made it up—Robert getting out! You think I wrote a letter to myself and sent it out here! You probably think I wish Dad were dead! You've been suspicious of me our whole lives—no doubt you think I've been pretending not to talk for ten years!*

In her anger she had forgotten that it was impossible ever to say what she meant and had been signing so vehemently that she'd thrown herself off balance and had to catch herself against the cages. A few of the smaller snakes twirled themselves into coils and rattled, but the big Atrox merely lifted its head and measured the air with its tongue. Nick, who for a moment had looked as if he wanted to hit her, stared at the large chubby judicious snake. It seemed to calm him.

"Look, I didn't catch everything, but I get the gist. You obviously resent me because I've managed to extricate myself to some degree from our familial mess and don't want to be pulled back into it."

Right, Nick. What's your great scheme for the snake about, then? She pointed at the fat diamondback. *Purely hypothetical?* She signed "imagine." *Taking your wife's birth control pills? Lying to her when you know how much she wants to have a child? Just a little Christmas skit you dreamed up?*

Nick wasn't even fazed. "What does that have to do with our family?" He laughed. "It's two millennia of guilt I'm trying to eradicate—I don't have *time* for my personal problems."

And they said Rob was a megalomaniac. She had spelled most of the last word before Nick got it.

"I never got too much of what his reasons were supposed to be, to tell you the truth. It was too nerve-wracking watching you write all your answers and then having to hear them read aloud by those assholes to concentrate on much else."

Oh, poor Nick.

He stared at her, then said, "Go to hell, why don't you? Just go to hell."

He stalked out of the snakehouse and slammed the door. Zoë stood still, staring at the snakes. Her mind was ricocheting—she felt as if she'd let one of the snakes out of its cage and were waiting to see what it would do. Maybe it would lunge and sink its fangs into her. Yet, wrought up though she was, she could take that possibility no more or less seriously than anything else that might happen. No one ever believed her. What difference did it make what she did? She looked at the diamondback, a series of overlapping concentric circles that reminded her of the child's toy made up of round plastic tubes stacked in order of size on a post. What would it feel like to have it curled up in her lap?

It was almost one o'clock—they'd left for the Beauregards' at eight. She must have been with Stewart for over an hour. Was it possible that Pryce hadn't noticed? She padlocked the door and climbed slowly back up the embankment. Everyone else was in bed; Pryce had opened out the couch and was lying on top of the covers.

"Snakes all tucked in?" he asked.

She nodded, grateful for once for his good nature, hoping he wouldn't ask her anything. She'd had enough confrontations for one evening. But when they were undressed and under the covers, he said, "Anything you want to say to me?"

About what?

"I don't think that's quite the politics of it. Didn't you go off somewhere with Stewart Beauregard?"

Ellie told you that?

"Not at all. I saw you talking to him in the windowseat and then the next thing I knew you'd vanished."

Ellie asked me to go outside with her.

"So you were with Ellie—were you with her the entire time?"

Why don't you ask her?

"I'm asking you."

All right, no. Stewart showed me his father's paintings. After brushing her hand with two fingers for "paint," she sketched a square as she had done earlier for Ellie. As always when she had an extended conversation with someone, the person speaking seemed stolid and negating in contrast to her continuous fluidity. *That* should have been the common way to communicate, instead of alienating speech. You *were* what you said when you spoke with your hands, instead of *indicating* what you meant. Why did she even bother to think about speaking again?

"Are you serious?" Pryce asked now. "He's had them in his house all this time?"

Yes. Was he humoring her?

"Why did he show them to you?"

He thinks I can tell him something about them.

If Pryce got this, he wasn't curious about it.

"Tell me this. Did you arrange with him beforehand to meet him privately?"

Arrange with him when? WHEN?

"This afternoon when you were over there."

No. What makes you think. . . ?

"I don't see why you're surprised by the question. Ever since you laid eyes on him—or he laid eyes on you—you've been acting strangely. You have a perfect right to talk to whomever you wish for as long as you wish, but the man strikes me as absolutely unhinged. Doesn't he make you nervous? You're so sensitive to other people's moods."

I am? What did Pryce mean? *Did I say that he didn't?* she gestured.

"Well, then, Zoë . . ."

Pryce stopped, thinking. He had taken her hand and was playing with her fingers. She would have been surprised at his equanimity had she not reminded herself that he was trained to be cool when he was trying to find out something.

"Are you *interested* in him?" he asked. "Because I . . ."

She waited.

"Well, because . . ." He sounded reluctant. "The thing I've realized . . . I'm sorry, Zoë. I've been realizing that I'm not jealous."

Jealous about what? What do you mean?

"I mean that I'm not jealous. I find that my predominant feeling is one of concern about you."

But that's . . . She was going to say that it was a sign of how generously he loved her, but before she had a chance he said, "Zoë, I think what it means is that I'm not in love with you anymore. I'm very sorry. I know that this isn't the best time to say such a thing, but it's just . . . Well, meeting your family, seeing how you are around them—I realize how little you feel for me."

What do you mean, how I am around them? She was trying to understand what he was saying.

"How they feel about you means everything to you, Zoë."

What? Are you out of your mind?

"If Nick looks at you cross-eyed you sink into a depthless depression. If your mother's impatient because she has trouble understanding you you act as if it's the end of the world."

What!

"You feel that way about Ellie too—to a lesser extent, I admit, but even her opinion counts more than mine does. The strange thing is, I think that if we were already married, so that you could consider me your own flesh and blood, you'd love me just as much as you do them. Unfortunately it doesn't work that way."

Why not?

This wasn't what she'd meant to say, but she didn't know what she'd meant to say. Her throat felt very tight and she felt sick to her stomach. Was Pryce *breaking up* with her? This was something that in her wildest dreams she'd never imagined happening.

ELLIE THINK STEWART TRY TRAP ME, she said. What she meant was, I can't help it—help me. I can't help myself. But Pryce had to be able to translate or his help would be useless. She didn't know the sign for "seduce" and when she made the sign for "trap," two fingers like a forked stick against her throat, she poked too hard and started to cough.

"Come on, don't try to slough off all the responsibility onto him. I grant you the guy is out of his tree, but no one's forcing you to have anything to do with him."

Oh, no?

"What does that mean?"

This would have been the time to tell Pryce the truth—about Rob, his being out, his having written, her being afraid to read his letter because of what it might not contain; about Anders Ogilvy, the missing evidence of the Studebaker driver; about Charlotte, her own participation in Charlotte's death; about Bridget, Bridget's desperate attempts over the years to get her attention, she still wasn't sure why . . . Pryce would have been the perfect person to tell, too. He was smart, he was kind, he was trained to sort out complicated tangles of events and assess everyone's degree of responsibility for them—but she couldn't tell him. Something else still had to happen; even if not telling him meant losing him, she couldn't say anything. Besides, if he couldn't understand without her saying anything, his understanding was meaningless.

"Zoë," Pryce said, "I may not be the world's best judge of character but I'm not the worst, and I would swear on a stack of Bibles that Stewart Beauregard is no playboy."

Wasn't that just the point?

"When Ellie carried on about him yesterday, I thought she was exaggerating to make a good story. When I met him, I thought that, if anything, her descriptions of him had been too mild. I might not have said this were it not for your seeming so drawn to him, but, Zoë, I've never met anyone—and this includes so-called hardened criminals—who made my skin crawl the way he does."

Don't you think you're the one who's exaggerating now?

"Zoë, I simply . . ." Pryce sighed. He was looking at her in such a sad way—she'd never seen him look like that. She slid down into the bed and embraced him.

"Zoë, sweetheart . . ." he murmured. "I just . . ."

They kissed and she began to think that they might make love. Hurriedly she revised all her plans—this wouldn't be so bad, really; Pryce was right, she would feel differently about him if he were already a member of her family, and what better way to become an automatic member than by fathering her child?—but then he said, "I'm sorry, Zoë, I can't right now. I don't feel comfortable after what we've just been talking about. Let's go to sleep—we can talk again tomorrow. Whatever may happen, I do care for you very much. Good night." He kissed her and turned away.

Later—she had been sleeping fitfully and it must have been four or five in the morning—something awakened her: a sound, something in addition to the refrigerator's soft muttering in the kitchen. Carefully disengaging herself from Pryce, Zoë sat up against the back of the couch, pulling the covers up as far as possible—it was cold in the room. She could make out all the furniture—the glass doors weren't curtained and although there was no moon the whiteness of the still-falling snow was bright.

Then something gave. As if with the last push of a creature struggling to be born, a barrier fell away and something new existed in the room. She had not known the barrier had been there until it dissolved—though now she recognized that it had begun to dissolve earlier in the evening when she'd seen the woman she had guessed was Stewart's ancestress in his courtyard, or even earlier, when the priest's thoughts had occupied her mind. She knew where she was now, and she held her breath, waiting. She had not been there for over ten years.

"Not yet," someone said.

"Then when?"

She turned around but couldn't see anyone. In fact the voices—a man's and a woman's—came from near the doors. The man's sounded closer—as if he were within the room and the woman without.

"I don't know when. Maybe never."

Samuel? Zoë whispered in her mind. But she knew it wasn't.

"You'll have to stop coming by if all we can do is have this argument," the man's voice said impatiently. "I'm not going to show them to you—I may never show them to anyone. I had to discover if a certain thing were true—I know now that it isn't. I don't owe anything to anyone."

"But you do. That's what you don't understand, Jules."

Zoë knew who they were now: Jules Beauregard, Stewart's dead father, and Irene, Judith's mother, in a younger incarnation. Ellie had mentioned her.

"It's not yours anymore, once you've painted it. Not when you've been possessed like this. Something's working through you—you're only the instrument. You don't own what you make any more than a parent owns a child."

"That's where you're wrong, Irene."

"Frances would have wanted you to show them—she always hoped that you'd find what you were looking for someday."

"Don't throw that at me, Irene, or the conversation stops right here."

"All right, all right. At least promise me that you won't destroy them," Irene pleaded. "Maybe you don't want them to be seen in your lifetime, but they may be very important to someone someday. You can't foresee what life your work will have."

"I'll promise no such thing! It's my work—I can do whatever I choose with it."

Zoë's attention to this conversation was distracted by sounds of private laughter and increasingly rhythmic sighs, and she heard something thudding, like a bed-frame hitting the wall. Then she realized that the sounds weren't coming from near the doors any longer but from farther away. Had Jules stepped outside? But the sounds were coming from within the house; then she almost laughed—it was Nick and Ellie, "trying." Now she didn't hear the voices—had she dreamed that part and only now woken up? But she was sitting up in bed.

Their cries—or Ellie's—were louder now; how could Pryce sleep through it? Ellie had to know they could hear. Ellie *wanted* her to hear. Zoë slid back down and pulled the covers over her head.

If she had become pregnant that time with Samuel, what kind of child would she have given birth to? Half-ghost, half-human? Was one strain dominant? Maybe it wouldn't have been a child at all she'd have been impregnated with—though that sounded so clinical, like "inseminated"; wasn't there any other word for it? What had they called the Virgin Mary's "insemination"? Was there a religious name for it? None of the terms suggested any choice in the matter. Quickened, maybe; what about that? Especially if not with a child but with whatever Samuel had known when he went over the falls, though he didn't remember, didn't believe he was dead even after she'd told him. Had he "rested in peace" afterward? Was that why he'd left his shoe? In some places people were buried without shoes.

Even under the covers she could still hear Nick and Ellie's labored breathing. Was Monica awake? It had been only when Zoë got out of bed the next morning and saw the shoe that it had occurred to her that Charlotte might have overheard, but when she told her Samuel had been there, though Charlotte wasn't surprised, she didn't seem to be hiding anything either. And she slept in the back wing of the house.

On his wedding night, Henry had told Louisa how he had helplessly watched his brother drift over the falls. As he climbed into bed beside her and she turned to him, arms outstretched, eyes shy with happiness, he had said, "Louisa, now that you're my wife there's something I must tell you . . ."

She was alarmed—what could he be about to confide? He had fathered children out of wedlock? The family wealth had dwindled and they were destitute? Nevertheless, obedient wife, she composed her face and stifled her impatience in order to receive with understanding whatever he might have to say. When he announced that his brother Samuel, at fifteen, had allowed himself to be carried over Harmony Falls, knowing that he would die, she was bewildered. She knew that Samuel had drowned, and though she understood it was significant that he had taken his own life and not been drowned accidentally, she didn't see why Henry was telling her so now. "He didn't mind, don't you understand?" Henry kept repeating incredulously. "Yet it wasn't that he was eager to die."

The light from the oil lamp was flickering and beginning to smoke, but Louisa forced herself to ignore it.

"But if he wasn't tired of living . . ."

"No!" Henry exclaimed. "That's just what I don't mean! He loved living! He was full of joy. Can't you understand? He believed that death wasn't death!"

"He believed in life after death?"

Louisa struggled to comprehend what her husband of a few hours was trying to tell her. She could not but think that he meant to communicate how he felt about her but could find no other manner in which to do so.

"No!" Henry shouted. "You simply don't understand!"

She shrank back.

"It was all life to him! There was no difference! If he had wanted to die—if he had thought he were going somewhere else . . . He loved life more than anyone!"

Henry's eyes were wild, as if his thoughts were live things, thrashing within his mind, and he were begging her to release them.

"Henry, dear, why does it still trouble you so?"

He looked at her incredulously. "You can ask me that? You, my *wife*? Louisa, if you do not know . . ."

"But how could I know?"

"Well, you should!" Henry exclaimed. "You would, if we had a proper marriage."

He used that as an excuse to leave her bed, never to return. If the person nearest and dearest could not release one from this indomitable vision—someone dying who believed he would not die . . . Henry was accusing Louisa, among other things, of not being Ida, which Louisa did not yet realize. Ida had explained to him that his memory of Samuel continued to trouble him because he did not know why Samuel had let himself drift to his death, and when you could not understand for what reason someone dear to you had died, it was often impossible to go on living. For the first time in all those years Henry had thought he glimpsed peace.

"Do *you* know?" he asked, childlike, it not mattering what her answer would be, only that it should satisfy him.

"Yes, but I don't need to know."

"But I do. What is it? What was the reason?" Henry looked at her trustingly.

"So many attempt to live another's life," Ida said, admonishing him. "You must overcome that temptation."

"Yes," Henry said. "Yes, I can—because you tell me to." He felt Ida's certainties billowing around him, protecting him from the sickening absence that had occupied his mind ever since he had helplessly watched his beloved brother disappear.

But to his alarm Ida cried, "No! That's just what I don't do! You must not take comfort from me—you must not!"

To spite her for this betrayal he had married Louisa.

It was quiet now in the house and Zoë pulled the blankets back from her face. She wished that she'd got out of bed under cover of Nick and Ellie's noises; now they would hear her. She wanted to be outside in the whiteness—to walk in the falling snow until the voices had finished talking; too many voices, all trying to speak through her, to live through her, demanding not to have suffered in vain.

If she'd become pregnant that first time with Samuel, would she have given birth already? Why should the gestation period necessarily be nine months when a ghost fathered your child? What kind of child would it be and what would it take to give birth to it? What kind of labor pains?

She was shivering—the air had changed somehow in the room. Maybe Nick or Ellie had opened a window. Or Monica—except that the sun room windows didn't open. Eventually Ellie intended to use the room as a greenhouse. But the air smelled different—Zoë smelled pine trees and felt a wind blow across her face. A child gasped and someone said, "Shh!" There were other voices, conferring quietly. "Dad, what are they. . . ? Why are they. . . ?" Then again, "Shh!" The father. Sharper now, angrier. "Are they going to *kill* him?" "No! Now quiet, or they'll hear us." The other voices diminishing then, footfalls softening. The child's voice again, a boy's, shocked. "They're *leaving* him up there!" "Only for a moment. Now stay here. Don't move and don't make a noise or you'll be sorry—is that understood?" Overlaid on their voices were other voices, speaking Spanish, arguing. "Padre . . ." someone spat out contemptuously. A different voice said, "Es *mi* hija." She's *my* daughter. A new wind, cool, but promising heat, like the early morning of a hot summer's day, eddied into the chilly night.

Horses restlessly shuffled; a voice cracked curtly. "Basta, Padre. Andamos." Let's go. The sun had risen and bloomed; the air was quiet with the threat of approaching heat. The dust that had scarcely settled during the night rose in small cyclones to pursue the horses as they pounded the dry, hardened road. No water. No water anywhere. The crops were dead, the wells were dry. To find even enough to drink the villagers had to ride the long miles to the river and the water there was murky, brackish, and rancid, its level lower than anyone could remember its ever having been. Yet, all this time, in the priest's yard, flowers bloomed. All summer long, all through the hottest days of the drought, they prospered. The villagers had spied down his well to see if by some chance it had not run dry like everyone else's, but they had found no water in it. Yet when Emilio,

Carmela's younger brother, had lain watching the house through an entire day, he had observed Carmela drawing full buckets of water from that same well. Others had taken his place and seen the same. Some had witnessed rattlesnakes slithering across the parched earth to sip water from her cupped hands. The priest had been blessed by a miracle but he was not sharing it with them.

What has he ever done for us? they reminded each other. Interfered with us—thinks that when he puts on his robes we should forget what we have known our entire lives, that if you do not endure at least a part of what our Savior suffered then your soul will wander eternally, your voice will join with all the voices of the lost whose wailing, disguised as wind, makes the living shudder in their beds and cover their ears. The priest cannot absolve us—he has no power to bargain for others with God.

Out of the cold night wind came a groan. "Ten piedad, ten piedad . . ." Have pity. The child was sobbing, fighting himself in order to make no noise. Sobbing under his breath. Steps, the father's voice. Low, angry. "Shut *up*!" The child was silent, in rage and fear. A little ways away, someone groaned again. Then the child and his father were running through the trees. Behind them, shouting. "Stop them! Don't let them get away!" Arguing. More shouting. "Forget *them*—get him down!"

XXIX (CASCABEL FLATS)

It was more than one had any right to expect, Father Jules thought—the bougainvillaea swarming the walls, clutching hold of cracks in the adobe. Brightly colored flowers blessed the whole of the decrepit building, thirty years old and already crumbling, as if no structure were to be allowed to remain in that place, not even the earthen buildings that least of all disturbed the harmony of this, His most cherished country. Though "harmony" was the wrong word; harmony implied the existence of elements that only through intention could be kept in concordance, and Father Jules did not think that the Creator had made this land in the same way that He had made the rest. It could not be the artifact of anyone's conscious intention, not even His—was that blasphemy? Perhaps He had dreamed it, then woken to find the earthly residue of His dream—and to know that a more profound mystery existed beyond any mystery He might create. No wonder that the Franciscan friars had wanted to build their monastery there, and no wonder that it could not last. The people in the villages nearby had been happy when the monastery was abandoned the first time; they had never recognized their God in the Franciscans' benevolent deity, and now here was a new priest, sent by the archbishop to persuade them all over again that they could not conduct their own sacred affairs. It was bad enough that this same archbishop had swallowed up the adobe church in town with a new stone cathedral designed to look exactly like all the cathedrals where he came from; the building made them think of a buffalo come to graze among a herd of goats—no wonder its cornerstone had been stolen; and now he had burdened them with yet another priest and they were supposed to be grateful . . .

Father Jules had learned very quickly that they felt these things. He had done his best to be unobtrusive, not to censure them for their private rituals and penitential rites (some of which he knew about, some of which he guessed at) as he knew he was supposed to do; he had known as soon as he climbed down from his horse that first afternoon after the slow ride from town and looked west at the blue mountains, opening up out of the desert like a fan held in the hand of God, that he would teach them nothing; he had come there to be instructed, not to instruct.

Now he stood in the dooryard, awestruck as always by the profusion of flowers—purple clematis and tangerine-colored roses, hollyhocks nearly as blue as the sky, crimson morning-glories, purple lupins, and bright white daisies, colors not to be seen in the old world, all blooming together regardless of season. Even the ragged cactus plants in the bare dirt before the doorway were covered with fierce yellow flowers. He noted that it would be a brilliant day again, the sky as deeply, evenly blue as it had been every day for the past three months, and he thought on the strangeness of the fact that it was the man who had guided him here who was now going to shoot him. In the same thought he understood that then the rain would come, the magnificent threatening clouds that the people had been praying for would loom over the mountains to the east and roll across the blank blue of the sky; as soon as he finished dying the storm would drench the parched earth, pelt it with hailstones as large as peas and then crabapples, mesmerizing and intoxicating everyone with its violence.

Inside it was dark. He could see nothing at first. If they had wanted, they could have crept in through the other door and been waiting for him: a man could be shot without knowing who pointed the gun at him, but they were not so craven; and besides they would be hoping for a confession of guilt from him, that they might execute him in good conscience. Father Jules did not think he was afraid to die; nevertheless—as the objects in the room that had been his home for the last two years emerged from the darkness—he felt drawn with sorrow: he would never see the child; he would never again be among the villagers, with whom he would gladly have joined in procession, dragging one of the rough-hewn wooden crosses to their Gethsemane, if only they would have allowed him to; never again would he wake to that sky.

Carmela was at her mother's—he had taken her to within sight of the house before dawn after ten-year-old Emilio, Carmela's youngest brother, had tapped on the window and told him the men were coming for him. Carmela and Emilio's father, Gustavo; their uncles Mauricio and Rodolfo; their uncle who was their mother's brother, Panceto Aguilar; and many others—they would be riding over when the sun had climbed above the hills. Emilio had heard them say the priest had to be deprived of life like a mad dog. He wanted to know, could he go with Father Jules when he fled into the hills? He would be useful to the priest, he said; he knew how to fish and trap rabbits; he could buy food in the villages—no one would think anything of a ten-year-old boy.

Tears had come to the priest's eyes as he thanked Emilio, and he had called upon God to bless him—though what God it was to whom he prayed he did not any longer know; but he did not intend to flee and told Emilio this.

"God's will shall be done," he said, "and He has sent me no sign to leave the monastery."

Father Jules persisted in thus naming the single adobe building, even though he had known as soon as he'd arrived that others would never join him.

"But I am the sign!" Emilio had protested. "I am sent in time to tell you to leave!"

"You are sent by your own goodness of heart," Father Jules said, smiling. "That is all. If I ran away, Emilio, my flight would further prove to your father and your uncles that I am guilty."

He had been able to persuade Emilio to leave only by convincing him that his father and uncles could not really intend to shoot him—they merely threatened to out of anger; he would speak to them quietly and make them listen to reason. As he said this to Emilio, Father Jules almost believed that it was possible.

Together they had awakened Carmela, which he had hated to do—she slept so restlessly now, in her seventh month—and told her (he and Emilio had agreed upon this) that her mother was ill and needed her. He had accompanied her to within sight of her father's house (Emilio had gone ahead to admit his mother into the ruse) and then he had come back and waited for the sun to rise, on this, the last day of his life. He had lain down outside on his back, and, as he had known it would, his mood lightened along with the firmament; he watched, rapt, as the sky assumed its color: gray, then the roseate flush, then, imperceptibly (although he knew he perceived it), the blue again, dependable, reassuring, deepening gradually to the rich, compelling hue for which he had never found a satisfying comparison until the day he had seen the Virgin Mother in her grotto and observed that the sky exactly matched her robe. When he looked at that sky, it did not seem to matter very much whether or not the God he had always credited with its creation had forgotten him or not. But then he had thought of Carmela's God, and the thought had brought restlessness to his limbs and he had stood and begun to walk nervously up and down along the edge of the gorge beyond the refectory.

Now, later, inside, he could not sit still; he paced up and down the room, went to the door, looked out, looked back at the room, and cursed himself for not having asked Emilio *when* they were going to come for him. They would not harm Carmela; he did not fear that, nor that they would harm the child. Once the baby was born, she would be a mother, and that would be more significant than the fact that she had no husband. Particularly if he, the presumed father, had been justly put to death. And she would not grieve for long; he knew she cared for him, but as a protector, not as a lover; and she was eighteen years old—only seventeen when she had come to him half a year ago with her story. But he had promised not to tell her story.

Father Jules wondered if the archbishop would learn how he had died. Several weeks ago he had written down everything Carmela had told him and then had folded the papers and sealed them with the official seal of the order, but the mail coach had not come by since then and he had not dared trust the packet to a rider. Now he would have to burn the papers; he could not bear the thought of what he had written being read and mocked at by those who wanted to kill him, even though, otherwise, he bore them no malice. In preparation, he placed more sticks on the fire that Carmela had insisted on building for him in the corner oven before he took her to her mother's. He then loosened the adobe bricks behind which, in the thick wall, he had hollowed out a hiding place for the papers. Even Carmela did not know of it. He broke the seal and drew the thick sheets out of the envelope he had made of a scrap of muslin he had stolen from Carmela's sewing basket, and set them on the plain, heavy table that with its two benches was the only furniture in the long, low room. However, before reading over what he had written, he would make himself coffee—even the Savior had eaten a last meal—and he set the kettle on the fire. When it boiled, he poured it over the grounds left from the night before, thrifty as always, then laughed at himself for considering thrift at a time like this. Perhaps he was not as resigned to death as he had supposed. He pulled a chair near to the open doorway, so that as he read he could keep an eye on the track that led down towards the monastery from the main road. He skipped over his introductory paragraphs and began to read where the story commenced.

"From the first I could never really believe that she lied," he had written, "even before the Virgin appeared to me."

It had been so difficult to write those words, to know how they would strike another, detached from the images in which they were dressed for him.

"My faith is shaken, your Grace; I seek your counsel."

When Father Jules had first arrived, the priest he was to replace had maundered about the country and its crazy, literal beliefs: "They stubbornly refuse to comprehend that they are meant to live the idea, not the thing . . ."

"Carmela said to me," Father Jules read over, " 'It was an angel who appeared to me too. It came while I slept. I woke and it told me. The next month, I did not bleed.'

" 'But why have you come to me?' I asked her. 'If, as you say, you do not wish anyone to know?'

" 'I am afraid,' she said. 'If they find out, they will kill him. They will think he is born to be sacrificed. Yet I cannot lie—no one has ever believed me when I lied.'

" 'But our Savior gave His life that we might live—so that it need never happen again.' So I dutifully told her, your Grace. She corrected me as matter-of-factly as if I had misnamed one of the flowers growing in the yard.

" 'No, Father,' she said. 'You do not hear about it because the other women say nothing; afterwards they give themselves to a man and he believes that he is the father of their child. We have seen what happens to the children of women who admit that they conceived alone. But those women can lie, Father; I cannot.'

"Your Grace, I did not believe her. I did not think she *lied,* but neither did I believe her to be in her right mind. I tried cajolery, I tried sophistry; nothing availed; Carmela never departed from her story in any particular. If at that time I had been more familiar with the people she lived among perhaps I would have understood her fear; that is to say, in other places a woman who claimed a virgin birth, and was believed, might be destroyed as a witch, but here . . . Your Grace, *here,* I have come to think, they do not accept the Holy Story as *singular;* at the very least they wish to participate in it. And, your Grace, I must admit that I myself no longer understand the teachings of the Church in this. Why do we not wish them to aspire to what our Lord felt? We exalt martyrs, do we not? Must martyrs be *chosen,* is that the reason? They may not choose themselves?

"Your Grace, Carmela wished me to tell her father that she had been assaulted; to choose a young man of the 'parish' to accuse—her father would believe *me,* she said; he would force the man to marry her and her child would have a father.

"Naturally I refused. How could she ask a man of the cloth to lie? I demanded. And if she truly believed that the Lord had chosen her, why did she not accept His will? Yet, at the conclusion of our conversation, I made what I have come to see as my first mistake: I offered her the protection of the monastery. (As if I kept battalions at my command!) She had begged me to hide her; she insisted that no one would think of looking for her here, and though I knew that this was absurd, I did not have the strength to refuse her. I hoped also that, were I to permit her to stay a short while, I might gain her trust and learn what had truly occurred. That was my second mistake. Had I gone at once to her family and told them either what she had told me or what she had told me to tell them they would never have had a reason to accuse me. Perhaps the habit of the confessor was too strong in me, I don't know. But I did not so much as send word to her family that she was safe. My foresight, it seems, deserted me, although, in truth, even if someone had suggested to me then that *I* might fall under suspicion, I would not have believed it. Yet when Carmela was finally discovered here, nearly a month later, and already four months with child, no one—perhaps not even I—found it possible to believe I was innocent.

"Your Grace, it is true that I never knew Carmela as a man knows a woman, yet I will not say that I did not desire to be her child's father. If that be a craving of the flesh, it is one, then, to which I succumbed. As the child's presence became evident, I longed to be its protector; she placed my hand upon her belly when the child first began to stir. Forgive my impudence, your Grace, but I felt that I was able to understand something in the Scriptures which I never had before been able to understand: how it was that Joseph could be helpmeet to Mary.

"Oh, your Grace, this country! You who have lived here longer than I—do you not see how like it is to the Holy Land in its terrain and its climate? How often have I not asked myself the secret of its power without being able to discover the answer! Is it in its proportion? The incomparable presence of the sky, the impression it gives one of being directly visible to heaven? Heaven . . . The very idea of it expands here, do you not find it so, your Grace? If our Holy Father in Rome could but see this country, I cannot but think . . . yet it is not for me to pursue this thought. I can speak only of what I myself have undergone. It is only since I came here that my soul has attained its completion. I admit that I did not know if I could bear it at first—I cowered before such immensity, the ever-present reminder of eternity, from which it is impossible to turn away. It can drive men to madness—is that blasphemy? I don't know. Yet I defy those battened on the cloistered, civilized faith of the old country to persist in thinking that we, mankind, are the crowning achievement of God's creation. We were put here to admire, that is all. To husband it, to believe in *its* life. If we do not—if we refuse this trust—it will die. And we will die. That, if nothing else, is clear to me now. The Creator created out of loneliness, not out of love.

"I was, after all (as no doubt you will wish to remind me, should I still be among the living when you read these pages), sent here to preach the Gospel to these priestless peoples, to bring them a vision of God achieved beneath stone arches, impressed upon one through tinted glass windows. But instead it has been they—and their land—who have taught me.

"Your Grace, this is a country crazed by belief. Not only for Carmela, I now think, but for everyone, there is no difference between *here* and *there*. Perhaps it is because of the way eternity lies spread out over everything, like a veil through which one must learn to recognize anew the everyday. Those of us in our well-kept gardens, our stately cloisters—how could we know what it is to live with this? I pray you to believe I write only in a spirit of humility—a humility I would never have learned had I not been sent to this place. I sorrow, but I am grateful.

"Since Carmela came here, your Grace, the flowers have not stopped blooming. She came in March; it is now nearly August and from the earliest daffodils (the bulbs I carried with me from Lyons), to the latest roses, all are still in full flower. Everywhere there is drought but here nothing dies. But that miracle now seems incidental—it merely forms the backdrop, as it were, to what I have to tell you. But I must hasten to complete my story. Carmela has gone walking with her little brother, the only one of her family not to desert her, and they will soon return.

"A week ago Carmela's father came to me and said, 'A man understands how these things happen. Here we are not afraid of your Church. Marry my daughter, and all will be forgiven. You will join our brotherhood and confess your faith as we do. Marry my daughter,' he said, 'and we will welcome you into our family. We will protect your honor against all who seek to degrade it.'

"We spoke for a long time, sometimes in anger, sometimes in amity. We each of us wished to do justice to the other, but were bound by our separate codes. I was a priest, I told him, and had not nor ever did intend to break my vow of chastity by word or deed. I swore by all I held sacred that I was not the father of Carmela's child, but then, as is natural enough, he wanted to know who had that honor and I had to say I was bound not to tell him. 'Carmela does not wish it to be known,' I told him.

'Let me see her!' he raged. 'Let me talk to her.' I agreed only if he would speak to her in my presence and promise not to abuse her. Then I summoned her from where she hid, down among the cottonwoods by the dried-up stream, but of course the interview availed him nothing, as I had known it would. Carmela sat mute as a marble madonna, her hands resting on her belly, as if to calm the child. In the end he abandoned any hope of persuading her to confess and departed, threatening retribution if she did not repent.

"It was after he left, in the early evening, when the sinking sun strikes the western mountains with bolts of gold, that I saw the Virgin for the first time—yes, your Grace, the Virgin, our beloved Mother of Christ. I had walked out to the edge of the ravine behind the monastery and knelt to ask God for guidance. Carmela was in the house, preparing dinner. I held aloft my joined hands, as I have since I was a small child and first taught by the brothers who schooled me how to pray. Was I wrong to keep secret what Carmela had told me? Should I have written at once to your Grace to ask for guidance? It seemed to me that Carmela had been sent as a trial of my faith, but I did not comprehend what was required of me. Should I guard her secret at the expense of her honor and my own? Should I request my superiors to consider the possibility of a second incarnation? (Forgive me, but already I could imagine your distressed laughter, your Grace, your tone of concern as you discussed me with your confidants.) Did Satan tempt me to doubt the uniqueness of the very events upon which our Church rests: the birth and death of our Savior Jesus Christ?

"At that moment, a ray of sun directed my eyes to an opening in the far mountains, and there I saw a grotto, gilded by the light, and in the grotto knelt the Virgin Mary in a blue dress the color of the sky, bathing the Christ Child in a little spring which spurted out of the grass like a fountain. All at once the sun struck her full in the face, and she looked up with a distracted expression. Then she saw me.

" 'Hello, Father Jules,' she said, speaking kindly but a trifle impatiently, as might any mother preoccupied with her child, 'What do you wish of me?'

"As you might imagine, your Grace, I was at first unable to reply, but before long her friendly and unaffected manner enabled me to confide in her as in an old and trusted acquaintance. I told the Virgin Mother Carmela's story, that is, whom she believed the father of her child to be, though not why she wished it not to be known. I said instead that Carmela feared no one would believe her. Before the Virgin would answer me, she asked me if I doubted Carmela.

"I said, 'Forgive me, Mother of God, but I cannot. Yet how can it be true?'

"At this she was surprised. 'Why can it not be?' she replied.

" 'Because it . . . Because . . . It has already happened!' I exclaimed. 'If it can happen over and over again . . . Forgive me, Holy Mother, but how then can it have meaning? For it is upon the suffering on the Cross of your Son that our hope of salvation lies.'

" 'Suffering on the Cross!' she repeated, astonished. 'Of what do you speak?' She turned anxiously to look at the baby Jesus splashing in the fountain.

" 'Of the Passion of our Lord. God gave his only-begotten Son so that whosoever believeth in Him . . .'

" 'Not *my* son!' she cried, snatching up the baby and holding Him to her. Frightened, our Lord began to whimper. 'Now see what you have done!' she accused me.

" 'I beg your pardon,' I said. 'I did not realize that you did not know . . . that it had not already happened . . .'

" 'That what had already happened—*what*?'

"You can appreciate the position in which I discovered myself, Father. I spoke with the Virgin Mother, but, it appeared, at a time before the Crucifixion had taken place, and I did not know what to say to her. If I told her what I knew, might that not alter what was to come? Might she not take measures to prevent from occurring the single most important event in the history of mankind, the event upon which our Faith is founded? I was deeply bewildered—so caught up by the responsibility thus thrust upon me that I did not consider how absurd might appear my considering that I, a simple priest, could reform nearly two thousand years of human belief. I said nothing, yet she knew I kept something from her and demanded I tell her what it was. I crossed myself, and she asked me why I kept repeating that peculiar gesture. Commending my soul to heaven (not knowing where else to commend it), I told her, then, what it signified. As I spoke, she clutched the Christ Child until He wailed.

"When I had finished, she drew open her smock and nursed the baby. Not until He was comforted did she speak to me. 'It is an evil story,' she said sadly. 'A terrifying one, but I know that it is not impossible. This child's father is capable of anything. In His solitude He despairs—I am not surprised to hear that I am not the only one He has gotten with child. He cannot bear to admit that the world He created is not perfect.'

" 'But your Son, our Lord Jesus Christ . . .' I began, meaning to tell her of His teachings, of what He had meant to the world. *Lose thyself and thou shalt be saved* . . . But she interrupted me.

" 'My son!' she exclaimed. He was playing now in the grass at her feet, picking wood violets and trying to eat them. 'What does my son know? He is a child! I forbid you to speak of him in this way!'

"I said, 'But, Mother of God. . . ,' and for the third or fourth time she objected to my addressing her as that. 'But, Mother of God,' I said, 'I still do not know what to do.'

" 'Do you mean for the young woman Carmela?' she asked, sounding impatient now. 'But is not your role clear? You must marry her; you must be the child's father. You have said yourself that you have wished this!'

" 'Yes, Virgin Mother,' I said, 'but I have sworn a vow of chastity.' (I did not think, your Grace, that I should attempt to explain centuries of ecclesiastical custom.) 'Besides,' I told her, 'I exalt the Father. How could I presume to usurp His place?'

"At this, however, our Lady became exasperated; she said she had heard that before; had men learned nothing in all the years since . . . She looked nervously at the Christ Child, playing in the grass. 'Learned nothing?' I repeated. 'Learned nothing about what?' 'Why, about His nature!' she exclaimed. 'And what it is theirs to do!' But at that moment the sun dropped from the grotto and our Lady was lost from sight. I saw again only the delphinium blue mountains, and then Carmela came out of the house to call me to dinner.

"And that is the end of my story, your Grace. I do not know what to believe, or, I should say, what not to believe. Am I mad? Is Carmela mad? Yet my vision was not a dream. I am not ill with fever. I believe everything—and nothing.

"Of you I beg only this, your Grace. Before you repudiate me, come here; kneel in this spot where I have knelt, pray where I have prayed, here where, as I believe you must know, there is no proper boundary between what happened once and what happens every day, between heaven and earth, between God and man. Pray here for my soul."

"Such arrogance, Father Jules," Father Jules said to himself, as he now refolded the pages, reinserted them into their muslin envelope, and replaced it in the cavity behind the bricks. He did not notice that, during the course of his reading, he had decided not to burn the pages after all. He wondered, now, if Carmela would ever tell anyone the truth.

He said again to himself that he was not afraid to die. He felt, in fact, that there was some justice in it. Soon after his arrival in this God-haunted country, he had recognized that he was extraneous; no one here needed him to intercede for them with the divine; and yet he had refused the one role that had been offered him. He had told the Virgin Mother that he could not usurp *His* place as father by playing Joseph to Carmela's Mary, but the truth was that this refusal had had more to do with his sense of his own incapacity than it did with humility. Yes, perhaps at moments he had felt love for Carmela's unborn child—but to feel that *always*? To believe *always* in a relation that could never be other than imaginary? To take on the endless responsibility of believing in what he would have never felt, seen, or experienced directly? For a mother it was easy; how did any father do it? Believing in the Holy Family was nothing compared to this.

Now Father Jules left the room for the last time. He carried outside with him the small china bowl from which he drank his coffee and walked once again to the edge of the ravine; perhaps the men had, unseen and unheard, already crept up behind the building and would shoot him in the back, and his body would tumble forward into the gully. Yet he knew they would not let him take his end unaccused. As he gazed at the mountains to the south—nearer and smaller than the mountains to the west, though no less beautiful—he could feel no distress that he was about to die. His life of the past two years, since he had come to this rich and austere land, had possessed a rightness and inevitability that made it impossible for him to question anything that happened to him. It seemed to him now that his previous understanding of the principal events upon which his faith rested had been simpleminded to the point of idiocy. Like most young men in training for the priesthood, he had sometimes had to struggle to believe at all, had had to fight himself in order to accept the necessity for chastity and obedience, for the suppression of youthful spirits; but now, to doubt *not* that Jesus of Nazareth was the Son of God nor that He had died on the Cross but the *explanation* for these things . . . Nothing in all his earlier life had prepared him to grapple with such questions.

And now there was no time—he heard the sound of horses galloping towards him. He took one last look at the western mountains, where the Virgin had appeared in her grotto, and then turned to meet his accusers. The men had ridden to the front door of the refectory. "We know you are in there," called a voice he recognized as that of Gustavo Muñoz, Carmela's father. "Be a brave man and come out. We will not shoot you down like a dog, even though that is what you deserve."

Father Jules tossed the cold dregs of the coffee onto the ground, then, carrying the bowl in one hand, walked around the building.

"Gustavo, there is no need to insult me," he said quietly.

The men, startled, turned abruptly, and several of them drew pistols, as if they had thought that he might have a weapon aimed at them. There were more of them than he had expected: besides Gustavo and his brothers and Panceto Aguilar, there were Gonzalo Oñate, José Ruiz y Vargas . . . Gustavo told them to put away their guns.

"We will discuss this quietly," he said. "At first. So, Padre," he said, addressing him in Spanish, "you found it lonely in your monastery. It is not so unusual. We have seen it happen before."

This was the same conversation Gustavo had conducted with him months ago, repeated now for the benefit of the others, and Father Jules saw no need to answer.

"I will even say," Gustavo said, "yes, I, her father, will even humiliate myself so far as to believe that you did not betray my daughter—she has always been a silent and mysterious girl. I believe she may well have been the one to entice."

"That's not true," said Gonzalo Oñate, in a voice like a cactus, but the others laughed at him; everyone knew that he had always wanted to marry Carmela.

"Carmela has come, and you have made her welcome. That at least you do not deny."

Gustavo's voice was as soft and caressing as a sheathed knife.

Father Jules sighed. "Of course I do not deny it. But I have already protested my innocence, Gustavo. We have never lived as husband and wife, and I am not the father of her child."

"No, indeed," broke in Gonzalo. "No, of course you did not live as husband and wife, for how could you? You are not married."

The others laughed again, but this time in a rehearsed, watchful way.

"You understood me," Father Jules said.

"And soon you will understand me," Gonzalo said, in his cactus voice. "Now, enough talk. You will come with us."

"Come with you where?" Father Jules asked, but now they would not speak to him. He saw that they had brought an extra horse with them, and they warned him to mount without trying to escape or they would shoot him without first letting him say his prayers.

"Please do me the favor not to insult me," he said again. "I am not a coward. Besides . . ." He laughed. "Where on earth would I go? You know I am no horseman."

"That is true," said Gustavo, in a friendly tone, "but you will learn. Everything can be learned, Padre."

Nevertheless they did not trust him, and kept his horse surrounded as they rode. What did Gustavo mean, he "would learn"? Were they planning for him something other than what he had imagined? But what? They would not tell him where they were taking him, though they were headed towards the village, and confined their talk to lewd jokes about him and Carmela until Gustavo exploded at them that she might be a whore but after all she was still his daughter. Thereafter they rode in silence. After twenty minutes it was clear to Father Jules that they were taking him to Carmela's house.

"Please," he begged them, "I do not want her to have to see . . . It will be difficult enough for her as it is."

"She will see nothing she has not seen already," Mauricio remarked, and they all laughed heartily.

"Why not admit you are a man like other men, Padre?" Gustavo asked him, still in the friendly tone Father Jules did not trust. "Would it not be easier? We will all like you the better for it."

"I am not a man like other men," he said simply.

No one spoke to him again until they reached the house. It stood at some distance from the village, though it was as plain and unadorned as all the other houses. When they drew near, all dismounted, and Carmela's younger brothers and sisters, including Emilio, came running out and led away the horses. Then Carmela appeared, supported by her mother. For a month now, her legs had hurt, and she had had difficulty walking. Her face and eyes were swollen and there were bruises on her neck and arms. She looked at him stone-faced, and this frightened him more than anything.

"Carmela! What have they done to you?"

He stepped towards her, but one of the men grabbed his arm and held him back. Father Jules turned to Gustavo.

"Are you a monster? To treat your daughter in such a way. . . !"

Gustavo shrugged. "What do you know about having daughters? We will see how you like it when it is your turn." Again there was the falseness in his voice.

Even in the midst of his anger, it occurred to the priest for the first time that Carmela might give birth to a daughter instead of a son. How was it that he had never even questioned her assumption that it was a son she bore?

"I told them," she said to him. She spoke to him, but she would not look at him.

"What have you told them?"

"What they wanted to hear," she said. "That you forced me to your bed and took my virginity. Then you bewitched me, so that I would not tell anyone. You made me come to you day after day. When it was clear that I was carrying a child, you told me that if anyone asked I was to say it had been conceived upon me by God."

Father Jules stared at her.

"Quiet, Carmela," Gustavo said impatiently. "He knows well enough what he has done. He should be grateful we do not hang him. If it was not that I know your ways, Carmela . . . I am not so quick to say who did the bewitching. Let us be done with this. Panceto, are you ready?"

"Yes, my friend."

Then Father Jules remembered that Panceto Aguilar was the member of their brotherhood who officiated at marriages and christenings when there was no priest to be had.

"Stand beside my daughter now," Gustavo ordered Father Jules. "There is no need to touch her or look at her. Panceto will marry you, do you understand? My daughter shall have a father for her child."

Father Jules glanced once more quickly at Carmela. Did she want this? If she did, could he . . . Would he have the courage for the insuperable task then? But now Carmela's mother went into the house and came back carrying two shawls, one white and one black, and he understood. Ignoring Gustavo's orders, he watched as Carmela's mother draped the white shawl over Carmela's head and shoulders. Carmela would still not look at him. Then they were both forced to kneel and Carmela was asked to repeat her vows first. She refused and her father lifted his hand to strike her, but Father Jules cried out to him to stop and said, "It doesn't matter, Carmela. Do as they say. I will not be here."

Still she refused to speak the words so he said, "Carmela, think of it as a kindness to me. For one moment, let me be your child's father. Let him know that I wished I had been able to stay."

She looked at him now, afraid, and he whispered, "What is it? Tell me—you have never looked at me like that before."

The others seemed bewitched—they did not move or speak. They permitted Carmela to move closer to him.

"Should I have lied sooner?" she whispered back. "It seemed so clear to me before, what I should do. Now I do not know."

But before Father Jules could answer Gustavo exclaimed, "Enough foolishness! Take your vows and be done with it or I shall kill you both! My patience is ended."

Carmela, with a last look at Father Jules, spoke the necessary words. Father Jules ritually entrusted his soul to heaven and promised to be Carmela's husband. As soon as Panceto had announced that in the eyes of God and man they were now married, Carmela's mother took her daughter by the arm and led her away. Father Jules watched her go. In the doorway to the house she twisted free and turned.

"Carmela!" Father Jules cried out. As he heard the men cock their pistols, he saw Carmela's mother slipping the white shawl off her shoulders to replace it with the black one.

XXX SPARTA

Robert opened the door of the bakery. He dumped the pile of sheets on one of the customer tables and left the door open while he went behind the counter to pull the light switch. "And God said, Let there be light," he said.

Zoë looked around. There was an empty glass display case with paper doilies on the shelves, a cash register, and six tiny tables like the ones they had in ice cream parlors—round, with a kind of black wire tripod holding them up—two in front of the windows and two each against the other walls.

"Well, it looks like a real bakery," she said.

"What are you, Inspector of Bakeries?" Rob asked, returning from behind the counter to retrieve the sheets. "I've heard of you undercover pastry agents, lurking around in the middle of the night, trying to sniff out frauds. You want to see my cream puff license?"

"Just make sure you don't use it for something else."

"Jawohl, Herr Commandant. I keep thinking I have to get you to change out of your wet things. I seem to think I pulled you out of a river. Now why would I think that?"

"Rescue, Naval Academy, naval, water, drowning?"

"Plausible. Just barely plausible. Come on."

His arms full of sheets, he led the way into the kitchen. It seemed to be entirely made out of steel: ovens, sinks, counters . . . If it hadn't been for the pots and pans and stacks of bread tins it would have looked like an operating room.

"I could think I saved you from drowning because I'm losing my mind. When you never talk to anyone besides seventh-graders and salivating customers it's difficult to be sure of your sanity. I hope you'll tell me if you think I'm slipping. You would tell me, wouldn't you?"

She smiled.

"*Some* people might say I was out of my mind to tear all the sheets off my bed and out of my laundry hamper and race off to rescue some person who got herself, God knows how, trapped inside of the goddamn Naval Academy . . ."

"Are you telling me the sheets weren't clean?"

"Especially when I haven't heard from her in months."

"I haven't heard from you in months either."

"So?" He had leaned against one of the steel counters. "Neither of us has heard from the other in months. We've established a fact and, as we know, facts are few and far between in this universe. Would you like something to eat? This is a bakery, you know. There are, therefore, foodstuffs in it. Chiefly carbohydrates, it's true, but I do have eggs and milk. Of course, I have regular food upstairs. Meat and vegetables. O.J. All your basic food groups. Assuming you're hungry."

"I haven't eaten since breakfast, so I guess I should be hungry. I ate breakfast in a diner in Washington, D.C."

"Why did you do that?" Rob asked, starting up the stairs. It was less than a yard wide, built inside the wall, with wide boards and high steps, like the one from the kitchen to the upstairs back hall in Harmony. It turned twice. "No, don't tell me," Rob said, ahead of her, invisible. "You probably spent the night in the Pentagon."

"I just felt like going somewhere this morning," she said loudly. If Rob made the connection between the article about him appearing today and her trip to Washington, he wasn't mentioning it.

The stairway opened out into a narrow hall—everything was miniature in this house. Directly facing the stairs was the bedroom; all the covers were torn off the bed—the blankets and the bedspread were in a heap on the floor—and the light on the bedside table was on with a book, face down, beside it. It looked like a Bible but that was hard to believe. Next to the bedroom was the bathroom, then the kitchen, and, at the front of the house, the living room. Rob turned on a floor lamp by an armchair. The room reminded Zoë of the bedrooms in Harmony: the wallpaper was patterned with violets on a lilac-and-white-patterned background, and the curtains were the same white filmy ruffled kind that Charlotte had had.

"Needless to say, I'm not responsible for the appearance of this place," Rob said. "I don't mind it, though. At least it's a change from my mother's Shaker mania. I hardly spend any time in here, anyway. I have to be up by five in the morning. I'm usually asleep by ten, unless I have insomnia."

She nodded. It was strange how he took it for granted that now he was a baker.

"Here, give me your coat. What do you want to eat? How about tea? Or a glass of wine? Do you like sherry? I keep a lot of liquor for baking. You wouldn't believe the trouble I had to go to to be allowed to keep that stuff here, since I'm under eighteen."

"Maybe some tea."

"What about to eat? Want a Napoleon? A cheese Danish?" She was about to say yes when she realized that he was being sarcastic.

"What would I get if I said yes?" she asked. "That lady Marietta Frank said you called everything something else."

"You read that? That *dame* . . . Frankenstein would be more like it. Someone should do the world a favor and send her to Outer Mongolia."

"Why did you let her interview you?"

"*I* don't know, Zoë. Something came over me, I guess. She exaggerated everything."

"She sounded like she was in love with you."

"God, spare me."

"How old is she?"

"Who knows? Thirty? Forty? Twelve? What's the difference?"

"Well, I mean, was she old?"

Rob turned around and looked at her, just for a second.

"Ancient," he said. "Practically in a wheelchair. So what do you want? I can make you a hamburger. Or scrambled eggs."

He draped her coat over a chair. There were two flowered chairs and a flowered couch. They didn't completely match the wallpaper.

"Maybe some bread or something."

"Bread!" he exclaimed. "Talk about eating coals in Newcastle." But he got up and went next door into the kitchen. She heard him running water into a kettle and lighting the gas stove with a match.

"Bread, huh?"

"Sorry."

"Want some cheese with it?"

"What kind?"

"Picky, aren't we? Well, I think it's just Velveeta, actually."

"You eat that stuff?"

"No, I keep it on hand for visitors."

He brought in a loaf of sliced rye bread and the package of cheese, a plate, and a knife. "Are you sure this is all you want? The tea will be ready in a minute."

"This is fine."

When he left again, Zoë opened the cheese and cut some off. The minute she bit into it, she realized she was starving. She ate an enormous bite of bread next, chewing as fast as she could, so Rob wouldn't see her with her mouth stuffed.

"What do you take in your tea?"

She swallowed. "Do you have cream and sugar?"

"Do I have cream and sugar . . . What do you think this is, a drugstore? How much sugar?"

"One spoonful." When he didn't say anything she called, "How come you're not asking me what size spoon?"

He came in walking normally, carrying two teacups on saucers, and set them down on the coffee table beside the bread.

"I can't believe you didn't spill it. I spill it all over the saucer, even if I walk like a zombie."

"Don't look at it. I learned that trick carrying coffee across the bakery. It must throw your balance off to look at something while you're moving."

"Very interesting."

"It's weird. It seems like one of those things someone could tell you along with 'Don't play with matches' and 'Look both ways before you cross the street.' Of course, they didn't tell me that after you look both ways you're not supposed to step in front of a truck."

He gave her a kind of strange look. Why had he brought that up? She wondered.

She was blowing on the tea—the hot cup felt comforting in her hands, and she felt so happy to see Rob again that nothing seemed very real. She hadn't even been listening to what he'd said next.

"Male cats and hamsters eat their offspring if they get half a chance. At least that's honest." He twisted a piece of Velveeta off the loaf and ate it. "When you do something nobody can believe you're doing, it's as if you're invisible—do you know what I mean at all?"

"Are you talking about why you opened the bakery?"

"It was so weird, Zoë. I happened to be looking for a summer job. I had no intention of spending the whole three months reading Friedrich Nietzsche by the swimming pool—maybe you remember, I was doing an extra-credit project with Mr. Montgomery—but the only things available were fishing or picking vegetables, neither of which I can do. All the ice cream jobs and gas station jobs had been snatched up. I was about to give up when suddenly, flash of inspiration, I looked over from the Help Wanted column to Business Opportunities, and that's when I saw this bakery for sale. All the equipment, that is. Some guy about a hundred miles from here—a town called Minksburg, up towards West Virginia—have you ever heard of it?"

"I've heard of West Virginia," she said, but Rob didn't laugh.

"The man was retiring. I called him up and told him I was interested—I guess I managed to sound old enough not to arouse his suspicions. I made an appointment to see him the next day. Of course, you realize I didn't have the slightest idea how I was going to get up there. As you know, I took Driver's Ed this spring and got my license but they had a special car fitted with hand controls."

She nodded.

"My parents couldn't afford the controls on our car—so they said. They're just afraid I'll smash it up. I called the bus station, but they laughed me off the line when I asked if there were any buses to Minksburg. To make a long story short—'To make a long story short' . . . Remind me never to use that expression again in my life—I stole my parents' car. I took the bus out to where my father works—I'd filched my mother's keys from her purse the night before. I knew that if I could actually drive it, I could get out to Minksburg and back before it was time for my father to come home from work. He's more reliable than Greenwich time. Fortunately, the car's an automatic. It turned out to be a cinch. I stuck my fake leg out over the front seat and drove with the other one. Good thing I didn't lose my left leg. I was amazed how easy it was—in fact, I couldn't believe I'd gone to the trouble of learning to drive with hand controls."

"It seems pretty stupid they wouldn't realize you could drive an automatic."

"Up until this time, the whole deal had been a gag. I was so convinced the guy wouldn't believe I was serious about wanting to buy his business, and then that I wouldn't be able to drive the car, but here it was all going so smoothly. I kept waiting to be stopped, do you know what I mean?"

"You mean by cops?"

"No, just by something. It was so totally ludicrous. But nothing stopped me. I tried telling myself I was being irresponsible, that it wasn't fair to trick this unsuspecting retired person—I ought to call the guy and tell him I'd lost interest. Besides, I was sure that the instant he laid eyes on me he'd curse me for making a fool of him."

"But he didn't?"

"It was completely nuts, Zoë. You would have died laughing. Here I am, limping into this tiny bakery in this tiny town like I've just been wounded—I hardly limp at all normally, but I'd strained my hip socket or something, sitting in that weird position in the car for so long. I could have taken my leg off but that would have required that I take my pants off and then . . . Well, I'll spare you the details."

"I can take it."

He looked at her, but said only, "This guy's about seventy years old, fat as a mountain, and puffing on a cigar—I nearly choked to death. After I told him who I was, he said, 'I'm Pete. What happened to you?' I told him the truth—more or less. I said I had an artificial leg and got stiff driving. You have no idea how having a fake leg raises you in people's estimation."

Zoë laughed. Rob seemed surprised that she was laughing, but then he laughed too.

"Next thing he says is, 'You're really the fellow who called about the business? How old are you?' All suspicious. This was where I'd expected to admit I wasn't serious but now I felt that I had to convince him I was. I said, 'Eighteen,' and then—get this—I told him that I'd come into an inheritance and wanted to use it to start a business that could give young people in Sparta some experience. I went on about how hard it was to find a summer job—it was pitiful. I could tell that he didn't completely believe me, but who dares contradict a person with only one leg? I told him my father had died in the Korean War and my mother of cancer when I was in fifth grade and since then I'd been a ward of the state, shuttled from one foster home to another, and then suddenly, a year ago, a rich uncle of my mother's I'd seen only once or twice in my life had died and left me a ton of money. 'One of those real fairy tale endings,' I said to him. People tend to believe you more when you sound skeptical yourself, have you noticed that? Then I told him, before he could get a chance to cross-examine me and see the holes in my story—while I was talking I'd realized that if my father had been killed even at the very last minute of the Korean War I couldn't have been *born,* but obviously he was even more oblivious about dates than I am—I told him that I'd given what I was doing a lot of consideration, thought about many kinds of businesses, but really had my heart set on a bakery. I told him—you should have heard me—that bread was the staff of life and although man couldn't live by bread alone he sure as hell couldn't live without it. I could tell he liked it when I said 'as hell,' so naturally I started throwing it in every other word; I even stooped to using the kinds of expressions I utterly despise—things like 'you bet your bottom dollar' and 'until hell freezes over.' I even referred to my supposed father's supposed death as 'kicking the bucket.' People are insane."

She smiled at him—she loved him so much.

"You should have seen me, Zoë. I was really something. I told him that what I liked about baking was how basic it was—how it teaches you not only what steps are involved just to make something as simple as the slice of toast you have every morning of your life and never think about, but teaches you patience. As everyone knows, I said, there's no way to make dough rise faster than it wants to. He got so enthralled he let his cigar go out, thank God. He said, 'You know, it makes me so happy to hear you say all this. It's what I've felt all my life, but I never thought I'd hear a youngster say the same things.' Naturally he launched into the lecture about what's wrong with us young folk. I let him roll, and every time he started running out of steam I'd throw in some more poetic observations about bread. It was quite a scene, believe me."

"But how did you get the money?"

"Well, first good old Pete and I shook on the deal. I told him I'd have my lawyer call him within the next couple of days. I told him I'd had a lawyer ever since I came into my inheritance. All the way back to Sparta I was depressed, though. I mean, I thought he was sort of a jackass for believing me, but on the other hand I felt like a creep for deceiving him. I thought how he'd really despair of 'us young folk' if he found out how I'd lied to him. I didn't have the slightest idea what to do. I managed to get the car back to Stark Road just in time; then I took the bus all the way downtown and limped around the harbor. I went into the Harbor House and had a sandwich and a cup of coffee. I was pretty miserable. I decided that what I'd done was completely inexcusable, and I was already mentally composing a letter to poor old Pete—I didn't expect him to understand but I hoped he might find it in his heart to forgive me. Blah blah blah. It sounded like I was breaking up with him. Then I left—I think I left about an eighty percent tip, I was so upset—but I couldn't bear the idea of going home. I knew my parents would be wondering where I was, but I couldn't stand the idea of sitting down with them at dinner and listening to them argue about who had had the worst day at work. I decided to walk over to the college—I thought I'd sit on the grass for a while—and that's when I walked by this place. It was for sale."

"I remember seeing the sign."

"Emily had bad arthritis—that's why they had to sell it. She couldn't sew things on hats anymore. Emily was the shorter one," he added. "Anyway, the same thing happened as when I looked at the newspaper—Zoë, I can't tell you how bizarre it was. One moment I'm standing on the street, looking at the For Sale sign, and the next minute I'm inside, surrounded by these hats you wouldn't believe, asking Emily and Delia how much they want for the property. I fully expected them to tell me to talk to their real estate agent, who did I think I was, barging in after the store was closed, was it some kind of prank, et cetera and so forth, but they took me seriously. They were even dumber about business than I am, if that's possible. I got the impression that they weren't concerned about money. I told them that it had been my lifelong ambition to have a business of my own and this seemed like the perfect-size place to start out with.

"You should have seen the consternation on their faces. They thought I wanted to take over their hat shop! They looked at each other and then Emily said, in this incredibly polite way she has—I don't know if you ever knew them—'But, my dear, are you quite certain you would enjoy hatting?' "

Robert cracked up.

"When I explained to them that I wanted to start a bakery, they got really excited. Anyway, to try to get to the end of this . . . They said that if I could get a mortgage they'd ask for only a thousand dollars down. I said no problem and told them I'd be back in the next couple of days to make everything final. I went home feeling drunk. I couldn't imagine how I was going to get hold of the money, but I wasn't worried anymore—even my parents didn't get on my nerves, I was in such a euphoric mood. The idea of being able to tell them I was moving out, that I was going into business for myself, that I was going to open a bakery—I was so happy I could have levitated with no trouble."

"I know what you mean," Zoë said.

"It was like I'd gotten into some parallel universe—as if I was Robert to some higher power. The next morning, as soon as my parents left for work, I headed down to the bank. There I ran into the world's single most gullible human being, Jarvis Cornford. He acted—the only word I can think of is bewitched. He listened to my story, how I was out of school—I lied about that too; what was he going to do, ask to see my diploma?—and wanted to do something worthwhile with my life and this was what I'd decided on. I laid it out as if I'd thought it over for years. When I finished, he said, 'How much do you figure you need, son?' I almost said, 'Everything you've got, pop,' but somehow I managed to say, 'On my best estimate, approximately twenty-five thousand.' I'd already discovered that he got nervous if I mentioned precise figures, but if I said that the bakery equipment was *around* six thousand, or the house was for sale for something *like* twenty, he didn't care.

" 'You say around twenty-five?' he asked. 'Around that,' I said. 'Sounds reasonable to me. How soon do you need it?' 'Oh, I don't know, exactly. I need to get back to these people in the next couple of days, but I don't suppose I need the cash at once.' He liked it if I used other words for money besides money. Like cash, or bucks, or greenbacks. He liked greenbacks the most, was my impression. 'Say, a few weeks or so?' he said. 'Or so,' I said. It was like some kind of a dance. He makes this move,

I make that one. It was as if I'd been born knowing how to do it. Then I stood up and he leaned across the desk and shook my hand. 'A real pleasure doing business with you, Mr. . . . ?' 'Went,' I said. 'Robert.' I couldn't believe he'd agreed to lend me twenty-five thousand dollars without knowing my name."

"Maybe he's a shyster."

"I don't think so. I got the money, normal interest. The first thing I did when I left the bank was to find a lawyer. I went down Main Street and into the first law office I saw. It was a little tiny one piled up with books, a real Uriah Heep hangout. I didn't care, though, I just needed someone for paperwork. I told the lawyer what had happened and asked if he'd take care of the legal details for me. He was by far the most skeptical of everyone I'd run into—in fact, he insisted on calling Mr. Cornford while I sat in his office, just to make sure I was telling the truth. But I guess Cornford must have chewed him out for not believing me, because after he hung up he was more polite. I don't think he liked me one iota, however. I think he suspected that there was something untruthful underneath. For one thing, he was a criminal lawyer before he moved to Sparta—where, as everyone knows, no crimes are ever committed—so he had a lot of experience sniffing out people's lies. He moved here because he likes to sail, if you can believe that. However, I think he was hard up for business, so he agreed to represent me.

"And that's pretty much the whole story. In August I took the high school equivalency exam and got my G.E.D. Emily and Delia moved out and I moved in. They already owned a totally furnished house in North Carolina—that's where they've retired to—so they wanted to leave all this furniture. Which is why we're sitting in this room being suffocated by all these flowers."

"What was it like telling your parents?"

"That I was moving out and opening a bakery? Wonderful, incredible, fabulous, magnificent, fantastic, superlative, superlative, superlative."

"What did they *say*?"

"They refused to believe me at first. Even after I showed them the mortgage and the loan agreement, they still did. My father couldn't understand how a minor had been allowed to sign without someone else's signing with him."

"How were you?"

"The lawyer signed with me. It seemed pretty fishy to me, but he said it was perfectly aboveboard—who knows if it is or not. Probably he's the real owner of the bakery, but who cares? What's he going to do, put a lien on the crumpets?"

"It's pretty incredible," she said.

"Isn't it? I tell you, though, Zoë, if you can figure out what people want to believe, they'll think you're incredibly wise and do whatever you want. I hate to think that, but it's true. What amazes me, frankly, is how I kept knowing exactly the right thing to say. It's not as if I've ever been a particularly tactful human being, so where did this talent come from? These amazing statements just kept coming out of my mouth."

"Have you figured out what I want to believe?" she asked, then immediately wished she hadn't said it.

"Have I what?" He looked startled.

"Nothing," she said. "Never mind."

"I hate that," Rob said after a moment. He looked at the floor.

"Are you mad?" she exclaimed.

"Why should I be mad?"

"I didn't mean anything, Rob. I just said it!"

But he went on staring glumly at the rug. Finally he said, "I can't believe you think I'd lump you with everyone else. You're the only person in the entire galaxy whose intelligence I respect. How could you think that?"

Only the galaxy? she almost said.

"But I didn't . . ." Then she started getting angry too. "You think I just *know* how you think about me? How could I know? You've never said anything!"

"What was I supposed to say? 'I highly respect your intelligence'? I thought it was obvious."

"Forget it."

"I never noticed you telling me how you think about me."

"Could we drop the subject?"

"Fine. Consider it dropped." He carried the plate of bread and cheese into the kitchen. Should she go home? She was trying to figure out if he had been justified in getting annoyed back, but when he returned he seemed to have already forgotten what they were talking about.

"It's a good thing you called me," he said. "I think I'm starting to go a little crazy here. It was a gas for a while, but now it's turning weird. This fake Robert Went has started to take over. That article you read—I could have said anything to that dame and she would have swallowed it. It's not even that I totally lied, but I keep expecting more resistance from people. If it had been you, you would have kept contradicting me. You would have automatically known when I was trying to get away with something.

"The thing is, I'm afraid I'm going to forget. I'll keep acting like this invented person, Robert Went the baker, and then one day it'll be too late and I won't be able to stop being him. As it is it's only when I see someone like you—'Someone like you . . .' You!—that I realize I've been acting. But what if you hadn't called me? What if you hadn't fallen asleep at the Naval Academy? I can't believe that my entire identity depends on someone else's falling asleep in the Naval Academy library."

"Why?" she asked. "I feel the same about you." It was true—it was only since she'd jumped down off the wall and said hello to him that she'd realized how distant she really had been from everyone.

"I have to fall asleep in the Naval Academy library for you to remember who *you* are?"

"You know what I mean."

"Well, not exactly I don't. I haven't noticed you walking in front of a truck or opening a bakery lately just because it's something you can't imagine doing."

"So?"

"What do you mean, 'So?'?"

"I don't know!" she exclaimed. "It's just . . ."

"Just what?"

She didn't even know how to begin to explain. He sounded like he wanted her to rescue him but if she rescued him, who would rescue her? Two people couldn't both rescue each other. If one person wasn't a stationary point, they would both float all over the place. She couldn't see any way to tell him how she felt about him without drifting off.

She said instead, "Well, if you feel that way, why don't you quit running the bakery?"

"That would be a logical step. On the other hand, it could make everything worse. Right now, even though I have to be this fake self, it's as if I have something to hang on to. I don't know, Zoë—I get freaked out sometimes. I feel as if I'm trying to avoid my fate, but like all the poor saps in Greek tragedies, everything I do winds up leading me right to it."

"What fate do you think it's leading you to?"

"I don't know, but I don't think it's going to be a happy one."

Zoë didn't say anything, but she was starting to feel the way she did about Nick, that Rob was just trying to be the center of attention.

"I also feel as if everybody else already knows. They know and they're not telling me."

"I'm not," she said.

"I know, but you're not part of the equation."

"What equation?"

"God, how weird!" Rob exclaimed. "That was a stray remark, but it's actually true!"

"*What* is?" He was beginning to get on her nerves.

"I mean, there's really an equation. That is, I invented one. Hold on, let me get the diagram."

"What diagram?"

He rushed down the hallway to his bedroom and came back with a Bible—it *was* the book that had been lying on his bed.

"One day when things were slow downstairs I made this equation about people thinking about each other," he said.

"You read the Bible now?" she interrupted.

"Evidence."

"Evidence?"

"I'll get into that later. Right now I want to show you this."

He took a folded sheet of paper from between the pages and spread it out on the coffee table. There were several clusters of points with lines drawn between them, connecting each point to every other point and then a formula, which she looked at to see if it was one she recognized:

$$2x(x-1) + (x-2).$$

"X equals the number of people present," Rob said.

"Present where?"

"Anywhere. In a room, say. It was looking at the tables downstairs that gave me the idea, actually. Of course, this is a highly hypothetical situation. It assumes that every person is (a) thinking about every other person present, and (b) wondering what every other person present is thinking about him. Or her. I know it's too simplistic, because in real life the numbers would never be constant, but it gives a general view. That's just the first half of the equation. Say there are five people present. Two times five is ten times five minus one, four, is forty—that's forty *simple* strands."

"Simple what?"

"Thinking in one direction, or thinking *about* one direction. Either one is a strand. Of course you then have to factor in what everyone is thinking everyone else is thinking about everyone else. That's x times x minus one times x minus two: $[x(x-1)(x-2)]$. And obviously that's only the beginning. You can always take it up a level: what everyone thinks everyone else might be thinking *they're* thinking everyone else is thinking about everyone else."

"I think I'm lost. What does the equation equal?"

"That's what I mean. There's absolutely no way you can keep track of it, don't you see? That's why you can only be free by living your life as a fake. It's a sacrifice, but at least nobody can define you. The more they try to, the more they're defining a fake. That's what I was saying earlier.

That's why I stepped in front of the truck—the time I wrecked my leg," he said, as if he'd done it more than once. "It seemed so weird to me that there were all these cars and trucks barrelling down the street and all that kept me from getting run over was the fact that I stayed on the sidewalk. Your parents tell you to look both ways before you cross streets, so you do; but how do you really know what will happen? It wasn't as if I'd seen some kid getting run over, and even if I had, how could I be positive that the same thing would happen to me? I was in fifth grade and I blew a fuse."

"I know," she said, "but what does that have to do with all those equations?"

"Trust me—everything. It's so important not to give in. That's the main thing in life—not to give in."

Zoë nodded, but she felt depressed. Something had happened while Rob was talking; he'd changed somehow—been multiplied to some other power, as he'd joked. Nothing he was saying was that different from what he'd been saying earlier, but the way he talked was different. He didn't really seem to be talking *to* her anymore.

"The feeling I had when I saw the ad in the paper—of the bakery for sale?"

She nodded, feeling sad; she loved him so much—she knew she would never love anyone else like this as long as she lived, but he seemed so out of it—was it because she'd gone away for the summer?

"It was the same feeling I had before I stepped in front of the truck. The identical feeling. And now the thing is, I wonder what I'm going to do the next time—because I'd have to do it. I wouldn't have any choice."

"I wouldn't mind feeling something like that," she said.

"Yes, you would, Zoë. You don't know what I'm talking about if you think that." He looked off into the distance, although the shades were down and he could only be looking at the wallpaper.

"Sometimes I get this feeling," he said. "I'm afraid that the next thing I have an urge to do will be horrible. I'll get hurt again, or someone else will. Sometimes I have dreams—dreams is not the word. Nightmares. Nightmares you wouldn't believe, stampeding through my sleeping brain. They're always about the same thing, but I can't remember them when I wake up. Just the feeling. It scares me."

"I don't see why you couldn't stop yourself if you're thinking about it in advance."

"But that's what I'm trying to tell you—nothing I do makes any difference!"

She sighed. He looked at her, thinking, then said, "Okay. Okay, I'll say it."

Suddenly she could hardly breathe, but when he started talking she knew it wasn't what she'd been hoping for.

"Zoë, you're going to think I'm completely insane, but I have to tell you this. I have to tell someone or I think I *will* go insane. You promised earlier that you'd tell me if you think I'm going around the bend, so when you hear this . . ."

"When did I promise that?"

"Look," he went on, ignoring this, "you can call the men in white coats if you want, but sometimes I think—just let me tell you what I think before you run out of here screaming, can you do that?"

"Why? Are you going to murder me?"

"I hope not," he said. "No, of course I'm not going to. Was that supposed to be a joke? I love you. You're the only person in the world I love. I'd be a madman to think of murdering you. But I have to tell someone what I'm thinking. I don't know, Zoë. Sometimes I think I really am going crazy in here. Maybe I spend too much time alone with dough. Dough fumes—what was it you said? It's not as if I ever had tons of friends, and I certainly didn't have any great admiration for the teachers, and when I decided to quit school I felt like for the first time in my life I'd be able to think clearly, but I know I felt closer to normal back then. Even though I think all school does is brainwash you, at least I was brainwashed to be like everybody else."

He stopped and looked at her. She just stared at him—she couldn't arrange a single expression on her face.

"What it is, more and more I think I'm here on earth for some specific reason—I don't mean the way people say every life has meaning. I mean, I sometimes think I was *sent* here, the way—and I know this will sound totally crazy—but the way Jesus Christ was sent—or the way people say he was. I have a lot of problems with that, as you know. At the same time—and if you think I should be behind bars, you're probably right—sometimes I think I *am* him, or the Antichrist, sent here to balance out the first time. I agree with a lot of what Nietzsche says, by the way, about God sneakily making everything into symbols. It's time for a change. Not that I think I'm God, don't get me wrong, but I think I'm supposed to even things out. I know, I know, don't look at me like that, but every time I manage to convince myself I'm just an insane megalomaniac this voice starts saying, 'But you know something major's supposed to happen around now. How do you *know* it isn't you? It has to be someone, why shouldn't it be you?' Then I wonder if it's a devil talking to me, or an angel! And Jesus Christ—so to speak—I'm not even religious."

He stopped talking as if he'd finished solving a math problem. But she couldn't even think about what he'd said—it seemed so obvious that he was babbling because he'd said he loved her and was too nervous to say it and then be quiet. He had said she was the only person in the world he loved, and then instantly started raving about being the Antichrist, whatever that was supposed to be, exactly. They didn't get to Nietzsche in Humanities until spring. For months the only thing in the world she'd wanted was for Rob to tell her he loved her, but, now that he had, he'd said it as if it were totally obvious and he'd already told her before. Did he think he had?

"Do you think I'm completely off my rocker?" he asked.

She shrugged. "I don't see what the big deal is, frankly. Plenty of people have thought that besides you. I had a dream when I was only four years old about Jesus coming after me in a refrigerator box and asking me to be killed to save mankind. Probably most people have some experience like that sometime in their life."

"Oh, really?"

"Why shouldn't they? Everyone knows it's predicted that Christ is supposed to come back in two thousand years. Why shouldn't people suspect that he's come back as them? It's the most natural thing in the world."

" 'The most natural thing in the world . . . ,' " Rob mimicked. "Well, I don't think it's natural at all. I think it's sick. Not that I actually believe you—I don't think most people think that. I can see why you might—you're the kind of person God would like to get his hands on, just like me, but . . ."

"Mr. Montgomery said that you were trying to sacrifice yourself," she said.

Rob stared. "He said *what*?"

She didn't repeat it.

"Well, aside from the fact that I can't believe you discussed me with that idiot, that's the exact opposite of what's happening. Haven't you been listening to anything I said? Sacrificing yourself implies that you want to. All I said was that I'm *afraid* I'll do something—if there's nothing to stop me. What the hell am I doing running a bakery, for God's sake? But there was nothing to stop me! Don't you understand at all? Pete, the man I bought the equipment from, came down last week to visit me. He acts like the convict in *Great Expectations* who's so proud he made Pip a gentleman. He made me go out to the Harbor House with him for dinner and he'd brought his Instamatic and got the waitress to take our picture. It was the worst experience of my life, but there was nothing I could do about it. And now—I'm trying to *tell* you—all these thoughts I keep having . . . I'm not trying to be interesting, I swear, Zoë. I wake up in the middle of the night terrified."

It was so strange the way he looked at her, as if she could explain it to him. She didn't want to keep talking about it. It was giving her the creeps. He didn't act like Rob anymore; he acted like—she didn't know what.

"What's the first thing I do when I move in here? I start reading the Bible. Emily and Delia left one—they left boxes of things they said they didn't want anymore and told me to give whatever I couldn't use to Goodwill. Mostly cooking stuff—I think they were trying to help me out. And so here's this Bible, and one day I start reading it. After a while I can't stop—like your grandmother. Every single thing is in it—all of the explanations for why we are the way we are. Think about it. What's the one book almost everyone in the world reads? The Bible. Think of all the things people say that come out of the Bible. It's a cliché factory, which is reason enough to be suspicious of it. It's translated into a zillion languages. It's in every motel room. It's like germ warfare. When you're trying to find out the reason for something, you look for the lowest common denominator. They make people *swear* on the Bible.

"Things are bad, Zoë. They're a lot worse than I even thought when I first started thinking about it."

"Rob, what do you *mean*?"

"I mean God, God the Father, don't you get it? Don't you see? It's so typical I can't believe it."

"*What* is?"

"Fathers making sons feel responsible for their failures—it's what they *do*. You know that line parents trot out when they punish you? 'It hurts me more than it hurts you'? You're supposed to feel sorry for *them* that they have to watch you suffer! It's obvious that the people who wrote the Bible just wrote about what went on all the time. They made it symbolic, but it's what everyone's always been doing to their children. The problem is, once it was in the Bible, everyone could say, So big deal, what's wrong with it? God did it, why shouldn't I? You know what I think, every Sunday when I see people walking by here on their way to St. Stephen's? There go a bunch of people to worship a murderer—a murderer and a liar. And then if you don't agree that it's the most wonderful story you've ever heard they burn you at the stake. Or torture you to death. Am I right?"

"Yeah, sure."

"You don't agree with me," he said, sounding really sad.

"I didn't say that."

"I think there's very little hope, Zoë. As long as everyone keeps counting on the next life, the end of the world will have to come before people realize what's really going on."

"You sound like you want it to happen."

"I don't *want* it to happen. I just think it's inevitable."

"Well, death is inevitable. Why not kill yourself right now and get it over with?"

"Would you like that?"

"Rob!"

"Well, sometimes I feel that way, I really do. I can think of only one way out."

"What?" he forced her to ask.

"Someone has to get revenge. That's the only way."

"Revenge for what?"

"What do you think? What I've just been talking about!"

"Oh," she said. She couldn't stand being there anymore. She pretended to read her watch. "Well, it's getting pretty late."

"It's not even nine o'clock!"

"I really think I should go."

"You could stay here," he said.

She couldn't believe he'd said that now. "Here where?"

"What did you think I meant?"

"What did you mean?"

"I guess I meant whatever you think I did."

"If you can't even *tell* me . . ."

"Are you *angry*? Zoë, what's the matter? What have I done?"

"If you don't even know . . ."

He looked like he was really upset, but all she could think of was how much she wanted to go home—she couldn't figure anything out with him there staring at her.

"I have to go, Rob. Really. I've been gone since this morning. My parents will call the police."

"Let them."

"I can't. I really have to go."

"Are you going to come back?"

"You mean tonight?"

"Tonight. Anytime. Please, will you promise? Something's going to happen—something . . ."

"You keep saying that, but you don't say what!"

"Zoë, don't. Please don't give me a hard time."

She couldn't believe it—he sounded as if he were about to cry.

"Rob, I just . . ."

"You don't understand, do you? I tried explaining it to you tonight and all it did was make you end up hating me."

"I don't hate you! How can you say that?"

"But even if you do, when you're here I feel safer. It's as if I can stay back from some edge when you're here."

XXXI CASCABEL FLATS

By eleven o'clock the next morning the snow had stopped, the last clouds were shredding, and everything glistened blindingly. Nearly a foot had fallen and huge raggedy clumps clung to the piñons like unpicked cotton. Jays swooped and chattered, brilliant blue against the snow like pieces of the sky.

"That's more like it," Ellie said.

Everyone was still lounging around the breakfast table, trying to muster the energy to embark upon the day's projects. Monica was going to begin the stollen for Christmas a.m. and the rolls for Christmas Eve dinner. Besides the miraculous leg of lamb, they were having oyster stew. Incredibly Ellie had managed to secure fresh oysters, which, besides the roast for Christmas Day, still had to be picked up; she would take care of it when she went into town to deliver the fruitcakes she'd made weeks ago.

Nick had taken the box of mice out of the freezer when he first got up and emptied them out onto a cookie sheet so that they would thaw faster. They were individually wrapped in tinfoil, and reminded Zoë of those chocolates that, for no intrinsic reason, were distinguished from the others in a box. Nick had stashed the tray in the oven.

Pryce had asked Ellie if she'd care for some company on her appointed rounds.

"Love some," she said. "*Need* some, in fact." She meant she still hoped to pick up Ignacio Ortega's chest for Nick. She then reminded them that they'd be going into town that evening to look at the illuminated houses—she'd do everything short of employing physical force to persuade the three of them to come along. She guaranteed them an experience like none they'd ever had before—and it would be a hundred times more picturesque now that it had snowed. She didn't insist that they come to church, though she'd hazard a guess that they'd probably find the experience pleasant—some of the same people who'd been at the party would be there: Michael Chamberlain and Nancy and Greg; Frances

MacKenzie; possibly Judith—you'd have to take a cattle prod to Stewart to get him inside a place of worship . . . In any case, they could take both cars.

Pryce said he was perfectly happy to adhere to the whole program, though it depended on what Zoë wanted him to do. He looked at her.

It's fine with me, she said.

"Really?"

Had he been hoping she'd say no so that they could come back alone after the light-viewing? He had been so sweet to her all morning; she could tell he felt bad for what he'd said the night before—he was in the zone where a few words from her could change everything back again. Last night she had been ready to revise her plans, but he hadn't been ready then and in the steadfast brightness of the morning she saw that there had been a reason. What hurt you saved your soul—that was the rationale people ascribed to, at least. Was Stewart going to do that? He'd be at the service tonight, despite what Ellie had said; if Zoë had had any doubt about this it was dispelled by what happened after breakfast. She had gone out with Nick to give the snakes their Christmas mice, and he was about to unlock the door when they heard a loud thumping and clattering coming down the driveway.

"Stewart," Nick said. "He plows us out. Usually he's over here at the crack of dawn, but I suppose he figured we wouldn't be in a hurry today and decided to wait until the snow stopped."

What if there'd been an emergency?

"What did you have in mind? The Subaru has four-wheel drive."

She was holding the tray of mice. While Nick took off the padlock, she kept an eye on the house—like the snakehouse, it was snow-frosted—but Stewart never appeared; she heard the truck turning around and heading back up the driveway. She had been so convinced that he would be eager to see her after last night that at first she couldn't believe he'd gone, even though she realized that he wouldn't have wanted to risk running into Ellie, especially when he could count on seeing her (Zoë) that evening in a less scrutinized place.

Maybe it was the snow, the emptied-out way you sometimes felt when the sky finally cleared after a big snowstorm, but suddenly she felt uneasy—had she been inventing everything? Even the snakes didn't reassure her; yesterday she had felt on the verge of being able to read their spirals and parabolas and infinity signs, but today they were meaningless scribbles and she had no patience with their shifting hieroglyphs. Why had Nick had to mention his crackpot theory? (Assuming he even believed it himself.)

"You want to help or do you feel squeamish?"

I'll help.

Nick was in a great mood, their contretemps of the night before seemingly forgotten. He and Ellie had obviously patched things up. She had been very friendly this morning too, Zoë knew, trying to get her alone so that she could apologize for her accusations in the Beauregards' courtyard—but a rapprochement with Ellie would only make what she had to do more difficult.

"Take the cages with only one snake, to begin with," Nick said. "Slide the glass down an inch or so and tip the mice in. It says how many they get on the cards."

Zoë had noticed the numbers on the index cards before, but had thought that they gave the number of snakes in the cage. Now she saw that on the big Atrox's cage was written "3." She began to unwrap the white mice; they were limp as when first killed, but cold and somehow heavier. And unscathed, unlike the mice that the barn cats in Harmony left lying around when they'd caught too many to eat. Their tails had been neatly wrapped around their hindquarters—did someone stand in an assembly line doing that?

Where do you get these from? WHERE MOUSE FROM?

"Some place in Texas."

What, the Dead Mouse Supply House? DEAD MOUSE SELL PLACE?

"An outfit that supplies labs. They're delivered by refrigerated truck."

Wouldn't it be more of a Christmas present if you left them wrapped?

Nick laughed. She watched him drop a couple into a cage containing two knotted prairie rattlers; when the mice hit, the snakes disentangled instantaneously like a magic Boy Scout knot. One reared and the other inched cautiously forward.

"They're relative newcomers. I caught them this fall. First ones I ever caught all on my own."

WHERE?

"Right here." Nick made a dismissive gesture, as if finding them by his own house didn't count. "They must have escaped in April—though I didn't think any had. Maybe they were the advance guard."

SNAKES KNOW WHAT HAPPEN? Usually Zoë liked not translating her thoughts, but this morning, instead of reaffirming her sense of her integrity, it made her feel as if a part of her mind were busy with something it didn't want her to know about.

"I can't imagine they didn't. They seemed bewildered to find the entrance blocked."

WHERE GO IF NOT CATCH?

"Looked for another den, I expect."

TRY COME IN HOUSE?

"Not once they'd sensed our presence, they wouldn't."

REMEMBER J-U-L-E-S?

"Jules? A memory of a human being who meant them no harm—yes, I suppose that would be enough of a shock to alter the genetic code."

THINK J. THINK SAME YOU POISON?

"Did Jules share my ideas about the venom? Who knows? He was trying to build up immunity—that's all I've heard. I presume so that he could handle them in their untamed state."

She would have liked to know if Jules had painted the crucifixion scenes before or after he'd started letting the snakes bite him—if the truth he thought he'd learned had been taught him by his venom injections, the venom itself an antivenin, as Nick imagined; an antidote to two thousand years of mistaken thinking—though, how ironic, you couldn't give up the idea that you could save others by sacrificing yourself without causing yourself intense pain either. At least, she imagined it would be intense.

"I think I owe you an apology, Zoë," Nick said, pausing with a foil-covered mouse in each hand. "Ellie said you told her what you did me—that Stewart showed you Jules's work. She had the same immediate reaction I did—of course you know that. But, talking about it later, neither of us could think of a good reason why you'd make it up. I didn't even know that the museum had filed an injunction against Stewart when you and I were talking last night. It doesn't seem outlandish to me in the clear light of day that hearing that news could provoke him to take such an unprecedented step."

Nick unwrapped the mice and slipped them into a cage, then turned towards her again.

"I'm finding myself in the awkward position of having to admit that I may have been wrong about Stewart too." He laughed. "I don't know how much more humbling I can take in any twenty-four-hour period. I'm seeing a side of Stewart I've never believed existed, although Ellie's always maintained it did. The way he behaves around you, for instance—it's as if he's fascinated by the fact that you can't talk. Everyone noticed how he lit up when he met you yesterday. It's as if—this is pretty bizarre—but I actually think that Stewart somehow imagines that because you can't talk his secrets will be safe with you. It makes no *rational* sense, but I'm beginning to think that rationality is not his strong suit.

"You know," he went on, when she didn't reply, "if he did show you

Jules's paintings, there's the legal angle to consider. You can provide the first confirmation that the paintings actually exist. Pryce would be the one to know, but it seems to me that if someone has a legal right to them and you know where they are and don't say anything, you could be accused of withholding evidence."

Before there's a trial?

"It wouldn't hurt to ask Pryce about it."

CHRISTMAS EVE!

"You mean nothing will be happening, legally speaking? That's true."

Nick tipped another mouse into a nearby cage. Its occupant lunged and sank its fangs into the unresisting lump.

"Hungry, weren't you, fella?" Nick asked fondly.

Zoë had undone the latch at the top of the big Atrox's compartment—it was looping restlessly around the space—and was about to slide the plexiglass down when Nick exclaimed, "No! Not him!"

YOU TELL ME FEED SNAKES ALONE.

"Yes, I know, but not him."

WHY?

"Oh, all right—give him one. It's not fair, everybody else eating except for him."

She had thought Nick wanted to feed the big diamondback himself but now realized that he must want to keep the snake hungry for his experiment. But why? He couldn't milk more venom because it was hungry.

THOUGHT YOU WAIT UNTIL WE LEAVE, she said, signing slowly.

"Wait for what? Oh," he said, looking embarrassed. "That. Well, I am."

Was he afraid now that he'd slept with Ellie that he'd be increasing his production of hormones that could interfere with the experiment? Was he feeling foolish for having told her as much as he had? His hypothesis was fantastical, and she couldn't rid herself of the suspicion that he was pulling her leg for some elaborate private reason, but on the other hand there was the ironclad logic: if you believed something enough, it would happen; if it didn't happen, you hadn't believed enough.

When she slid down the glass, the Atrox glanced at her but otherwise didn't move. She dropped the snowy mouse onto the brown paper bedding; the snake quivered and then, if it were possible for a snake to do so, turned its back on the mouse. It curled up so that its triangular head was aimed in the opposite direction.

Nick. Zoë tapped him on the arm and pointed at the cage. *Something's wrong with him.*

Nick looked at the snake, alarmed. He tapped the glass but the snake wouldn't budge.

"That's strange. I know he's hungry. God, he can't be sick too!"

Nick took a long fork off the wall behind him—the type used to roast marshmallows, except that the handle had been bent at a ninety-degree angle. Zoë soon saw why: he could reach into the cage with the fork while keeping his hand outside. He speared the mouse, and she looked away; she hadn't been squeamish about anything else, but there was something about a fork with a dead mouse on the end of it . . . If Monica saw that, she'd realize that Nick's rattlesnake farming was more than simply a demented hobby. Nick gave the mouse instead to a fat prairie rattler in an adjacent cage, who right away inched over to it and seized it in its jaws. Then Nick unwrapped another mouse and dropped it into the Atrox's cage. As soon as he'd slid the plexiglass back up, the Atrox nosed around and glided over to the mouse and began the same process as the snake next door.

"Well, I'll be damned."

I'm insulted. INSULTED. Index finger jabbed between a V-sign made by the other hand. Without taking note of the fact, Zoë had begun to translate again.

"Try feeding some of the others. I'm curious now how they'll react."

Every other snake, large and small, male and female, prairie and diamondback—all accepted the mice from her right away.

"Very interesting," Nick said. "Very, very interesting."

Zoë looked at the reluctant rattlesnake with its pleasant crisscross pattern, brown and gray scales that looked like the overlapping white flakes on the inside of milkweed pods. It was so familiar-looking somehow, as if it reminded her of something, yet it didn't remind her of anything besides itself. Nick was wiping off the fork he'd used to spear the mouse with.

"Somebody picks up serpents and they do not bite him—who was that?"

Someone in the Bible?

"Where else?"

Isn't it "he who is without sin"?

"I thought that that was who casts the first stone."

They looked at each other and laughed.

"Such a religious upbringing we had."

Didn't we?

When they went back in, Monica was washing dishes at the sink. On the counter the dough for the stollen and for the dinner rolls was rising in two large ceramic bowls covered with dishtowels. The house was quiet.

"Ellie and Pryce left already?" Nick asked.

Monica shut off the water but didn't turn around.

"Your father called," she said.

Nick looked at Zoë, his arm still raised to hang up the key to the snakehouse. Monica faced them now, waiting.

"Well." Nick hooked the key on its nail. He seemed to be trying to recall the comment appropriate to the situation. "Did he leave a message?" He knelt to unbuckle his boots as if to protect himself from Monica's answer.

Monica gave a brief, explosive laugh. "I suppose you might say that." She turned back to watch the dishwater drain out. "He asked me for a divorce."

Nick stood up. "He did *what*?"

Monica faced him again, as if prepared to take whatever was coming to her. "You heard me, dear. Your father wants a divorce."

"He called now, out here, to *ask* you that?"

"He has the papers all drawn up. He wants to send them here. I keep the house, he makes no financial claims." Monica laughed again in the same awkward way—of all things she sounded *embarrassed*. "That would have been ironic, wouldn't it? After all his stubbornness about not using my money. I would have enjoyed that."

Zoë and Nick simply stood there, Nick with his boots half unlaced; Monica was drying her hands on a small checked towel and smiling at them in an affectionate and undemanding way they didn't remember ever seeing.

"You *two*," she said.

The spectacle of your own mother lying through her teeth was really quite spellbinding, Zoë told herself. She wanted to sign to Nick not to believe her, but she couldn't take her eyes off Monica.

"I suppose that your father's requesting a divorce after all this time does come as somewhat of a surprise," Monica said hesitantly. "His timing *is* rather extraordinary. On the other hand I don't know why it should particularly surprise you that he call while I'm out here. It's the kind of attention-getting device he's always used."

"Attention-getting?" Nick repeated stupidly.

Monica looked astonished. "What has your father ever tried to do his whole life except get everyone to wonder what he's up to?"

Did he explain why he decided to ask you right now? Zoë asked.

"Oh, my. Yes, dear, he did. He wants to propose to Lucy Smith."

"What?"

What?

"She was in college with us."

"We know who she is!"

"David died not long ago. He was quite a bit older than she. Your father has always loved Lucy, you know. He told me so the day we were married."

"He told you . . ."

He felt responsible for her father's death in the internment camp, Zoë signed. FEEL RESPONSIBLE FATHER DEATH PRISON.

"He told you that?" Monica asked, when she'd understood.

In Mexico.

"In Mexico?"

Because of a fight I had with Bridget. I think he thought he could have done something.

"Yes, that's true. He generally did feel that. About everything. Though I never knew about Lucy's father . . . That's interesting."

"Interesting!" Nick shouted. "You finally learn the reason for years of unhappiness and all you can say is 'interesting'?"

"Is that the reason? I don't know that there was any one reason, dear."

"For God's sake, Mother, aren't you even upset?"

They were all three of them standing with their hands at their sides, Zoë and Nick with their coats and snow-covered boots still on, Monica dangling the dishtowel. It reminded Zoë of a game of Old Maid, everyone trying to guess who held the incriminating card.

"Upset?" Monica seemed puzzled by the question. "It's time for it to happen, don't you think? I simply never had the ambition to set the wheels in motion."

Zoë scanned her mother's face, beginning to think that the incredible might actually be true—what a strange feeling *that* was. Yet she had always expected to greet this news with enormous relief—a feeling of immense liberation—and now it was as if her preoccupation with Seth and Monica's unhappiness had grown too vast, too far beyond anything personal, like the figures of myth who endured, abstracted, as configurations in the sky, for their divorce to have any effect on her personally.

Monica continued to look perplexed; she studied them as if there were something she wanted to tell them, but if they didn't ask her the right question she wouldn't be able to. Had Seth said something else? About Rob?

"Excuse me," Nick said. "If no one minds, I'm going to sit down."

He clumped between them into the living room. They both followed, inadvertently sharing a mistrustful glance. Nick had tracked snow across the rug. Zoë sat down in the wing chair and Monica at the other end of the couch from Nick. She was still carrying the dishtowel, which she now laid across her lap and began to fold.

"I think you should know that Dad is missing," Nick said.

"Missing?" Monica exclaimed. "How can he be missing? I just now spoke to him!"

"Zoë's been trying to reach him for ten days. He doesn't tell either of us he's going anywhere and then suddenly he calls, out of the blue, and asks you for a *divorce*? And it just happens to occur the only moment you've been alone in the house since you got here? How gullible do you think we are?"

"Nicholas, I don't know what you . . ."

"Zoë and I have been worried *sick* about Dad! Of course you and he have known all along that Robert Went has been released from the hospital, haven't you?"

Monica, shocked, looked back and forth between the two of them. "Is that true? Zoë, is that true? No, Nick, I had no idea. You think I would have kept such information to myself? Why on earth didn't one of you tell me?"

Nick looked hysterical—Zoë felt very calm. She signed to him, *You know, I think she really might be telling the truth.*

"Just you keep out of this!" he shouted.

What?

"Who told you?" Monica asked.

Zoë began to spell "B-R-I-D. . ."

"Don't say *anything*!" Nick cried.

"Bridget?" Monica said. "I should have guessed. I always suspected that Lydia heard from Sally Went. Remarks she'd let drop—intentionally let drop, I should say."

Let drop? *Since when do you see Lydia?* YOU TALK L-Y-D . . . ?

Zoë glanced at Nick—did he think she was deserting him? She was only trying to get to the bottom of things.

"I run into her on occasion, Zoë. A town the size of Sparta one can't not run into people from time to time."

But you speak to her? YOU SPEAK . . . !

"What do you take me for? One can't simply not be civil to people because . . . I've tried to put that all behind me, Zoë."

"Put it behind you!" Nick shouted.

"Nicholas, I hardly . . . What are you implying?" Monica shook her head. "Zoë, dear, are you all right? No wonder you've seemed on edge."

I told Nick about Rob.

"Even so . . ." Monica glanced at him as if to say, And have you been of any help? "Do you mind if I ask if Bridget told you anything other than the fact of his release?"

She said he's fine now. SAY HE FINE NOW.

"Oh, very helpful."

"He called you," Nick said. "Robert. He called you or Dad."

"He called us?"

"He wrote to Zoë out here. He had to get the address from one of you."

"He wrote to you, Zoë? Is that true?"

"One of you had to give Robert this address," Nick insisted.

"Well, it wasn't I."

"Where was Dad calling from?"

"I assume from Sparta, Nick. It didn't occur to me to inquire."

"But it was long distance?"

"So far as I could tell. What are you suggesting?"

"Maybe he already has the papers drawn *up*," Nick said bitterly. "Maybe he's on the way to Las Vegas and wants to drop by and have you *sign* them."

Monica looked completely bewildered. Then Zoë thought of something.

When did Dad decide to propose to Lucy?

"When? Recently, is all I know."

When did he hear that her husband had died? WHEN HUSBAND DIED?

"That happened six months ago at least. Why? What are you driving at? What's with you two? I'd have thought you'd be relieved that your father and I are finally doing the sensible thing."

The postmark on Rob's letter was dated only a couple of weeks ago, about a week after Zoë had heard from Bridget. Time enough for Bridget to hear that he was out and write to her; time enough for Rob to make it to Sparta . . . Zoë almost laughed, the sequence of events seemed so obvious now.

Does Dad think Lucy will say yes? she asked.

"He didn't seem overconfident. I expect he fears that she may think it a bit late in the day to start trying to be happy."

"But *he* doesn't think so," Nick said.

"The answer must be no, I'd say."

"And what about you?" Nick went on belligerently. "Do *you* think it's too late in the day?"

"I don't know, Nick. Sometimes I do, sometimes I don't."

"But you'd be willing to give it a shot?"

Again, astonishingly, Monica looked embarrassed.

"I suppose it all depends."

"Depends on what?" Nick exclaimed. "What the *hell* is going on around here?"

"Depends on Delmore," Monica said. "An old college friend. I feel free to speak of it now. He's invited me to visit him in Centuryville. That's where he's from. He lived in Chicago until five years ago when his wife and eldest daughter were killed in an automobile accident. He and the other two children went home—they're both in college there now. He says it's strange to see them doing the very same things we used to do."

"We? We *who*? You and him?"

"What was that, dear?"

Monica was feeling very lightheaded, as if she were waking from a long, Rip van Winkle sleep. The sunlight sparkled on the snow. What season had it been when she'd stopped noticing the seasons?

"We dated. Of course I was madly in love with Eldridge Jewell—I never gave poor Del half a chance."

"Eldridge *Jewell*?" Nick repeated in a strangled way. He was beginning to look the desperate way he had when he'd been about to have an asthma attack. "Dr. Jewell from Harmony?"

"I never told you about that?" Monica said dreamily. "Well, I suppose I wouldn't. I was always so circumspect about my private life."

Who did her mother think she was talking to? Zoë wondered.

Does he want to marry you? she asked. *Is that why he invited you to visit?*

"Who, dear?"

It reminded Zoë of listening to Charlotte talk about her four sons—you had to be careful not to jar the person back to self-consciousness—but Nick exclaimed recklessly, "Delmore Holland! Whom did you think? Or does Dr. Jewell want to marry you too?"

"He's proposed every Christmas since Cora died," Monica said, shrugging. "That was eight years ago. I'll be surprised if his card isn't waiting when I get back to Sparta."

But you'd rather marry Delmore? Zoë went on calmly. Fortunately Nick was now stunned into speechlessness himself.

"Oh, I don't know, dear." Monica sighed. "Such a nice man, but I don't know . . . Your father used to call him 'Dulmore.' " She laughed. "There'll never be another man like your father. We may not have been happy, but we weren't bored. I don't know how many married couples can say that."

But at this Zoë forgot herself. *You want another man like Dad?* she gestured emphatically.

Monica laughed again. "No, no, I didn't mean to imply that, Zoë. But he's a great man in his way. I've never known anyone with his integrity—I don't expect I ever will. He'll cling to principle even if it should destroy him. One has to admire that."

What principle? What are you talking about?

"I suppose believing that the world is broken beyond repair."

Then why did he try to convince Nick and me to repair it?

"Children don't know everything about their parents, dear," Monica said, not having understood. "Your father still wants his chance at a little happiness, like everyone else. He'd like to have the weight of the world taken off his shoulders. He's embarrassed to ask for help, that's all."

Monica gazed out at the white desert, bound on the horizon by those elegant mountains. Such a royal blue today.

Her sweet children—they were always so outraged about something. She smiled, remembering the time when Nick, at five, had insisted on pulling Zoë the three blocks to her nursery school in his red wagon; he'd been in the car when she'd been pulled over for a malfunctioning turn signal and had decided it was unsafe for Zoë to ride with her. Where had they come from, those two? With their insistence that their parents behave a certain way—how could they have been born into the world with such particular expectations? And yet along with the outrage, that blind, unsuspecting love—how could anyone love her like that? Don't, she'd always wanted to plead with them, don't *trust* me, as they ran to her for comfort or threw their arms around her neck and kissed her.

Now here was Nick, her son, terribly upset with her for she knew not what reason. Zoë, on the other hand, seemed relatively pleased by the news of the impending divorce. So odd—Monica would have predicted their reactions the other way around. But then they never did do what you expected. Parents had to learn to let their children go—couldn't children do the same for their parents? Was it possible that Nick had been hoping all this time that someday she and Seth would be *reconciled*?

He said something now and left the room. She and Zoë listened to him slam the door.

"Oh lord, Zoë," she said, "you'd better go after him. What has him so upset? He's scaring me."

What else is new?

Zoë hadn't moved.

"What did you say?" When she wouldn't repeat it, Monica exclaimed, "Oh, Zoë, you're still *jealous* of Nick? For heaven's sake, what *is* it with the two of you! You adore each other, you always have, and yet you continually suspect each other of getting more than your share of misfortune! I cannot comprehend it!"

You can't?

Zoë looked at her mother.

"You're suggesting that I should be able to?"

What did you and Dad do in all your letters but compete? Where else could Nick and I have learned it?

"You read our letters?"

Of course we read them! What did you expect?

Monica was shaking her head again, but she seemed more amazed than angry. She said, "Zoë, can we take this up at some other time? I simply can't bear to think of your brother out there by himself with those poisonous creatures."

Okay, okay. She stood up. *I'll go check on him, but you don't have to worry—he's not going to do anything.* Mentally she emphasized "he."

As she headed down the embankment, she was thinking that if Monica married Delmore Holland, they could have a double wedding with Seth and Lucy. Delmore and Lucy both had two children—that made six children and four parents—quite the crowd when they all got together. It would be irrelevant if the house *had* doors—there'd be so many of them in every room. They'd all have so much to say to each other anyway that they wouldn't want to miss anything anyone said; if there *were* doors they'd have to prop them open. "Your parents did *what*?" "Oh, yes, thousands of pages, over the years . . ." "You should have started a postal service—say a nickel for each trip up or down stairs. You'd have been set for life." They would stop gossiping only long enough to realize that if their parents had never married the wrong people, none of them would have ever existed.

XXXII (CASCABEL FLATS)

Once Stewart had discovered the letter (not long after his marriage to Judith when at her request he undertook to remodel the kitchen) that his paper ancestor, Jules Beauregard, had written to the archbishop but concealed behind an adobe brick, he understood things about himself that had never been clear to him before. He had known since the time he was small that people *wanted* to believe in his—Stewart's—existence but that he might never meet anyone who had the courage. He didn't concern himself with whether the priest's story were literally true or not; it was enough that it confirmed for him the knowledge that he'd been put on earth for a reason, made sense of earlier events in his life, and pointed him towards his subsequent actions. Though unsure what these specifically would be, he knew that they would be devoted to convincing people—even if that were only one other person—to relinquish the fond belief that everything in this life, however painful and unhappy, was designed with the ultimate best interests of humanity at heart. He was here to conclude a cycle, yet to accomplish this would require that someone recognize him for what he was, and to date he had never met anyone who did not subscribe to the notion that he was a creature of circumstance.

He had been only four years old when his mother died; people said he had adored her and had never recovered from her loss. He had not even cried when told that Frances was dead (of a ruptured cerebal aneurysm, it was learned at the autopsy), and people implied that if Stewart would permit himself to mourn her, he would be able to live a life alternating between hope and despair like everyone else's.

Stewart recalled very clearly insisting to his father, after his mother's death, that he could still see her.

"By the fountain—yes, she is—she is too! Brushing her hair!"

When Jules, and Rosario and Ignacio Ortega, didn't agree that they also saw her, Stewart screamed until they said, "All right. All right, Stewart. We see her. Yes, she's there."

"Really? Really you do? You promise? Cross your heart?"

They swore, whereupon he shouted, "Liars! Liars! She's dead! I made it up. You lied! You lied!"

He knew then and there that no one was to be counted on—if they had not the heart not to tell a child what they thought the child wanted to believe.

Jules had wept and left the room. Rosario exclaimed in Spanish. Ignacio said, "You ever do that again, Stewart, I will personally hit you. Very hard. Do you understand me?"

"No, no, I don't understand you! I don't understand you! You are a liar! All of you are liars!"

Ignacio hit him. Rosario cried, "Stop! Stop it!"

Ignacio said, "He knows right from wrong. He is asking to be reminded."

Ignacio had not hit him very hard despite his threat, but there was truth in what he'd said and for the time being Stewart had let himself be comforted. Yet the episode, though it earned Ignacio Stewart's lifelong respect, did not alter his behavior towards his father. Whenever Stewart saw Jules he told him that he had seen his mother, how pretty she looked, how nice she'd been. Or else he asked him, "Why did you kill her? Didn't you like her anymore? You had no right to kill her."

Dreading the sight of his son, Jules began to leave the house for the studio in the morning before Stewart awoke and to return after he'd gone to bed. Yet the accusations—accusations that in his misery he felt were somehow justified—pursued him and he began to drink. Even Irene MacKenzie, Frances's best friend and the only person besides Ignacio and Rosario with whom Jules would speak during his first, intense period of grief—even she could not persuade Jules that Stewart needed him.

"He's a child!" Irene would protest. "He's too young to understand death, Jules. You have to help him understand."

"He's not a child, Irene," Jules would reply. "He merely pretends to be one. Besides, who can understand death?"

Though Rosario, too, tried to persuade him not to abandon his son, Jules soon slept at his studio as well; Rosario took him something to eat once a day. He hung blankets over the lower part of the windows so that no one could look in. Once Rosario found a dead rattlesnake flung outside the door and she screamed and pounded on the door until he yelled at her from inside to go away. Usually, the dish she had brought the last time stood on the doorstep empty.

Meanwhile she and Ignacio had moved into the main house with Stewart, and for the next seven years this arrangement continued. By this time, Ignacio, who was blacksmith as well as carpenter for the ranch, directed all its operations. Rosario was in charge of the house. After Ignacio, at Jules's request, had built a kitchen and a bedroom onto one end of his studio, they saw him at the big house rarely. He would appear without notice, drunk, and inquire with hearty joviality as to Stewart's welfare.

"Quite the young man you're getting to be!" he'd exclaim, slapping him on the back. "Can you shoot a rattlesnake between the eyes yet? What's the trouble, aren't you being trained properly? Ignacio, bestir yourself at once."

"Si, señor," Ignacio replied, doing his best imitation of a servile Mexican, which delighted Jules—it let him feel that Ignacio appreciated his sense of humor.

After Jules's visits, Stewart had begged Ignacio and Rosario to promise that they would never allow his father to take him away from them. He told them that Jules came in the middle of the night and tried to frighten him—stories that reduced Rosario to tears, though Ignacio was not fooled. However, he said only, "You must be respectful of your father. I do not like this behavior, Stewart." Inarticulately Stewart felt that Ignacio recognized him and yet could absorb the knowledge into himself in such a way that he could still love Stewart, whereas everyone else could love him only by pretending to themselves that he wasn't what he was. In his feeling for Ignacio, Stewart suspected, lay the only power that might have the possibility to tempt him from the path laid out for him.

Ever since Stewart was five and Judith two, they had been inseparable. Shortly before her death Frances had prevailed upon Jules to allow her dear friend Irene, impoverished and recently widowed, to live rent-free in a ranch hand's house a half mile away from the main house. Once Judith went to school, Irene drove the two children into town and was always waiting for them in the parking lot when school let out.

On the Friday afternoon before Easter when Stewart was eleven, he and Judith left the building to find Irene arguing with Jules, who was leaning against his pickup; Irene was gesticulating rapidly.

Stewart heard, "I am not *drunk,* Irene! I'm as sober as an undertaker!" He puffed into Irene's face. "Is there any other reason you can invent to prevent me from taking my son on an expedition if I choose to do so?"

"But where are you going? Why won't you tell me where you're going, Jules?"

"Because it's secret, Irene—don't you understand? S-e-c-r-e-t. That spells 'none of your business.' "

Stewart had turned to head back into the building when his father saw him.

"There's the culprit now!" he exclaimed. "Come on, Stew, hop in. We're going for a ride."

Stewart walked back as slowly as he thought he could get away with. His father was wearing a clean checked cowboy shirt with his jeans instead of the dirty pullover he wore the rest of the time, and he had on cowboy boots instead of filthy white sneakers.

"Where are we going?" Stewart asked.

"Didn't you just hear me tell your protectress that it was a secret? You'll find out when the time is right."

"How long are we going for?"

Stewart looked at Irene. She shook her head, which he understood to mean, Don't cross him; it will only make it worse.

"Can I go?" Judith asked. "I want to go with Stewart."

This infuriated Jules.

"No! Enough of this nonsense!" he bellowed. He took Stewart by the arm and propelled him to the passenger side of the truck. "Hop in."

Stewart obeyed, although when his father left to go around to the driver's side, he considered leaping out and running away as fast as he could, but where would he go? It would be only a matter of time until Jules caught up with him. Besides, he felt an enlivening excitement: he had always expected that his father would attempt to destroy him one day, and he was glad that at last he could stop anticipating it.

As Jules settled himself behind the steering wheel, Stewart wondered if his pocket knife were sharp enough to kill a man and if he were strong enough to stab his father if it came to that. He noticed then that, not only was Jules neatly dressed, he was freshly shaven. He *didn't* seem drunk, either. He began to ask Stewart how school was going, as if they had this conversation every day. His father didn't even know that he was in the sixth grade. "Mind your own business," Stewart considered saying, but he was afraid of his father, of his intent purpose and spruced-up looks; instead he responded in monosyllables and stared out the window.

Jules drove through town and headed north. When they hit the highway, he began to sing army songs, the kind of cheerful tunes that made it seem that going to war was a jolly thing to do, and Stewart wondered if his father had gone crazy and planned not merely to kill him but to do so in some sickening and drawn-out way, such as tying him to horses and letting them tear him to pieces, or skinning him alive. These were only the first possibilities that occurred to him. At school, as everywhere where children gathered, he regularly heard of new methods of killing; in town one day a lady had buried her infant upside down in a big flowerpot, only his feet sticking out—she told her other children that it was to help him grow bigger. When they protested that he wouldn't be able to breathe, she held their hands in the flame on her gas stove until they promised never to say that again. Children knew that these things happened all the time and that their elders conspired to keep this knowledge from them; what surprised Stewart was not that his father planned to do away with him, but that he should have dressed up to do so—that and let Irene see them go off together.

After a little while they turned off the paved road and headed up into the hills, and Jules's jaunty singing subsided to a whistle. Stewart was beginning to think he knew where they were going. Occasionally he had been with Ignacio and Rosario to the village where they grew up and lived before they moved into town, though his father didn't know this.

The road was narrow, winding, and rocky, but Jules drove fast, spinning the tires on sandy ledges and fishtailing out of turns. Once, despite himself, Stewart shouted, "You're going off the road!" but Jules just laughed.

Every now and then a village rose up around them—sloped tin roofs; long shuttered windows with sills scarcely a foot above the ground. Perhaps three trees in the entire village. A few scrawny dogs sniffing along the empty streets. In one a rusted gas station pump stood before an open doorway that gaped blackly; Stewart didn't understand where everyone was. He wondered if Irene would tell Rosario and Ignacio what had happened and if they would come looking for him—though how would they know where to go?

As they crested the next hill, his father finally stopped whistling and slowed down, and Stewart saw that he was looking out the side window of the truck like a sailor staring out to sea. Following his gaze Stewart saw, at a short distance, a bare stony hill crowned by three white crosses. The one in the middle was biggest. Then he knew that they were on the outskirts of Ignacio's village.

Jules turned to him and said, "Which would you rather be? Christ or one of the thieves?"

"What thieves?" Stewart asked; he knew the story perfectly well—Rosario made him read the Bible and go to Mass with her—but he thought it was a trick question.

"Would you prefer to be punished for a reason or punished for being born?"

"I'd prefer not to be punished at all," Stewart said.

"Ah, but that's not an option."

Now they were coming into the village, and here there were a few people on the street—two women chatting before a house; two girls Stewart's age skipping rope—who all looked up as the truck approached, and suddenly Stewart wanted to roll down the window and shout for help, but they had already gone by. He saw more women and children, but no men, and considered whether or not to jump out if his father didn't stop; he knew where Ignacio's sister lived—she might protect him. But then Jules pulled the truck into a dooryard and stopped, and Stewart recognized Ignacio's sister's house. She came out to welcome them, speaking to Jules in Spanish: "My brother said you would be coming." "¿Cómo estás, Miguela?" Jules said.

In the house Stewart tried to be polite to Miguela, as if this would help to keep him safe. He was torn between wanting proof that his father meant him harm and wanting to escape. It was true that he already knew what he knew, but after all he was still a child, with a child's fantastic longings and a child's reflexes of fear. Miguela was preparing dinner and he exclaimed enthusiastically about everything: how delicious the cooking smelled, how pretty the house was . . . But Miguela told him to go out the back door and play with Enrique and Dolores, her children. He found Enrique walking about the dirt courtyard on his knees, while Dolores pursued him, hitting him lightly over the shoulders with a juniper branch. He was repeating a phrase Stewart knew: *Señor, ten piedad de nosotros . . .*

"¿Qué están haciendo?" What are you doing? Stewart asked, when they didn't notice him.

"Hi, Stewart," Enrique said in English. "Did you come to see the procession?"

"What procession?" he asked.

"Los hermanos. Tonight they make their walk."

"Do you mean los Penitentes?" Stewart exclaimed.

He had heard of them—everyone had heard of them—the men who walked barefoot until their feet were cut to shreds, or beat themselves over their shoulders with whips. He realized that this was what Enrique and Dolores had been pretending to do. Some of his schoolmates' fathers or uncles were in the brotherhood, but no one who wasn't knew for sure where the processions went or what the penitents did when they reached their destination. Nobody who wasn't in the society was allowed to watch.

"Los hermanos," Dolores repeated. "You don't know about them?"

Irritated, Stewart said that he bet they didn't know that his father kept rattlesnakes in his studio and let them bite him. He himself wasn't sure if the last part were true; he had hotly denied it when schoolmates had said they had heard this, but now it seemed appropriate to mention.

"He built his studio over their den on *purpose*," he told Enrique and Dolores. "He keeps some with him all the time."

"Now?" they exclaimed.

"No, not now. At home. In his studio. They can bite him and it feels like a mosquito to him. He could crawl into a den and come out unhurt."

"Brujo," Dolores muttered.

"No," Stewart said condescendingly. "He's not a witch. Anyone can get used to being bitten. You become immune to the venom."

"Why would anyone want to?" Enrique asked.

At dusk, Miguela called everyone in and they ate dinner: tortillas, beans, rice, and chile, and everyone ate quickly, saying little, although after dinner was over there was nothing to do but wait, which they did, sitting in the kitchen without turning the lights on. Enrique and Dolores whispered to each other in Spanish. Stewart was excited. He kept trying to see the expression on his father's face, but it was too dark. He could not remember when he'd last seen his father not wobbling around, dirty and unshaven, smelling of drink. And he must not have had a drink for a while, because usually when he didn't drink for a few days, he was sick and shaky and his face was the color of sand.

Now from somewhere in the distance, back towards the village, there came a faint broken whistling—bells and a reedy flute. Stewart heard his father catch his breath, and Enrique and Dolores jumped up and ran to the open doorway. Stewart followed and peered with them down the darkened village street. There were no streetlamps and no light fell from doorways and windows, but he could see the looming shadows of the houses. The music, which sounded to his child's ears like several giants whistling loudly off-key, grew louder very slowly. Then, down where the road stopped going uphill at the beginning of the village, a tiny dot of light appeared—like a single headlight approaching over a bumpy road without making any sound. But soon it was too high off the ground to be a headlight, and then it was followed by other dots, little wavering specks of light, gradually growing brighter and larger. Torches, Stewart finally realized. He had expected the procession to resemble a celebratory parade that stops at frequent intervals so that the band can play and the baton twirlers perform; this one came forward as steadily and as slowly as a line of funeral cars.

By this time he could also hear singing, a name to give only loosely to what he heard; the singers sounded very tired. Two singers began, then everyone else answered. It reminded Stewart of church, the responses one made to the priest. Stewart never answered and Rosario, if she caught him, exclaimed, "Who do you think you are? Did God make a special exception for you?" If he wanted to make her even angrier he would say, "I don't believe in God," but usually then Rosario would tell Ignacio to talk to him, and even when Stewart wanted to he could never resist Ignacio. In private rebellion he wouldn't think about God when he knelt in prayer; he would think about Ignacio.

The lights were only a few houses down now. By craning his neck Stewart could see over Enrique's head and what he thought he saw shocked him so greatly that he never afterward forgot it, even though his mistake was soon corrected. His vision seemed the explanation for his father's having brought him: behind the man carrying the first torch and the pipe players were children walking very slowly and stiffly, as if they had been walking for miles and miles, and behind them were grownups, who were hitting them over and over with whips.

"Why are they doing that?" he exclaimed, but even before his father hissed at him to be quiet he had realized that they weren't children, but men walking on their knees, as Enrique had been earlier.

Dolores and Enrique were whispering to each other. "Ése es Manuel Dominguez. No—es Alfredo Salazar."

Sidling behind Enrique, Stewart whispered, "Is your father in the procession?"

"I think so," Enrique said.

Dolores whispered, "¿Quién es el Señor?"

"El señor?" Stewart questioned.

"Only a very good man can be Jesus," Dolores said. Then she laughed and she and Enrique began to name all those they knew it could not be because of the bad things they had done.

The procession had reached the house now, and they stopped talking and went back to the doorway. Beneath the sound of the tinny flute, Stewart could hear very clearly the snapping of the lashes, and the shuffling forward of the men on their knees. Now that they were so close, he saw that the kneeling men, the penitents, wore hoods. Several men dragged crosses, which made a scraping sound along the dirt road. Except for the singing no one was saying anything and Stewart thought that maybe there was some trick way of hitting so that it didn't hurt.

"Ay, he is bloody, look!" Enrique whispered. "I bet there will be blood on the street."

"It isn't *real* blood," Stewart said.

He had spoken louder than he meant, and he felt his father's hand on his shoulder.

"You think it isn't real?" Jules asked softly.

In another little while the procession had passed the house and was almost out of sight where the road curved. Miguela turned on the light and offered to make them coffee before their trip back to town. When Jules said no, thank you, they would have to be going, she began to clear the dishes from the table. Stewart watched his father. His eyes were shiny and hard.

"It is a great privilege—muchas gracias a Ustedes," he said to Miguela. "You have been so kind. I know it is not often that outsiders are allowed to observe. We both—Stewart and I—we thank you humbly. I am sure it is an experience that Stewart will not forget. We also thank you for the lovely dinner. Make your goodbyes, Stewart, we have to be on our way."

Jules was talking in the falsely enthusiastic way he did when he visited the ranch house and had been drinking, but he was sober now, and instinctively Stewart looked nervously at Enrique.

"Can Stewart stay?" Enrique asked his mother. "We can take him to town tomorrow."

"Yes! Let him stay!" Dolores said.

But even before Miguela had begun to reply, Of course, he was welcome, Jules said, "Oh, no, he can't stay. It's Easter weekend. I want him at home with me."

Then they climbed into the truck and drove back through the village. Stewart sat in silence. Suddenly Jules swerved the truck so abruptly that Stewart was thrown against him.

"Sorry, Stew, didn't know it was coming up so soon."

"That what was?"

As far as Stewart could tell, they were heading directly into the trees.

"The road," Jules said. "Do you mean you can't see it?"

He laughed raucously and Stewart shrank back against the door—he was ashamed but he couldn't help it. Then Jules pulled the truck behind a clump of piñons, switched off the headlights, and shut off the engine. There was a moon—it was a clear night—and Stewart could see his father clearly.

"Whatever you see, whatever happens, you are not to make a sound, do you understand?" he said.

"Where are we going?"

"I said, do you understand?"

"How can I promise when I don't know what we're going to see?"

"If you knew, your promise wouldn't mean anything, would it? You must also promise never to tell a single soul what you see tonight. Do I have your promise?"

Stewart hunched against the door, and Jules said, "No one will lay a hand on you, if that's what you're worried about. Neither will I, unless you make noise. Now promise me."

"All right, I promise," Stewart mumbled. As he did so, he also swore to himself that this would be the last time he'd ever fear his father.

"Good," Jules said. "I admire you for it. You're only to talk if I ask you something. Understood?"

"Yes!"

"See that you keep your word. Now get out, and shut the door quietly."

As Stewart pushed the door closed, he saw his father lean over and take something out of the glove compartment and put it in his jacket pocket. Stewart couldn't see what shape it was—could it be a gun?

As they circled back past the village, snaking through the piñons on the slope above it, he looked down. Lights were on in many of the houses now, and he thought how no one in them knew that up above them an evil man and his son were creeping through the trees. He knew that they were going after the procession, and that they weren't supposed to see this part. Ignacio and Miguela had already done them a big favor in letting them watch as much as they had, Stewart knew. Ignacio must be in the procession.

They hadn't gone very much farther before they heard the flutes again. The procession seemed to be in front of them, as if, beyond the village, it had turned uphill; if they kept straight on they would run into it. The flutes made a sad sound—not like people playing instruments but like wounded birds trying to call. At first Stewart didn't think his father had heard it, because he kept on in the same direction, and Stewart was about to try to stop him when Jules took Stewart by the shoulder and turned him uphill.

He whispered, "Be as fast as you can, but stay quiet."

Jules now started into a lurching run straight up the slope—Stewart could scarcely keep up. He could have easily escaped at that point; Jules wasn't checking to see if he were following and he could have run right down into the road and gone straight to Miguela's house and told her that his father was after the procession and had a gun; Miguela would find someone to stop Jules—but Stewart wanted to see what his father was going to do. So he kept on, stumbling over rocks; once he stepped into a cactus and the spines pierced his tennis shoes, but he didn't feel it; that is, he felt it but it didn't hurt. Was that what his father felt when the rattle-snakes bit him? Was that why he did it—so that he could learn not to feel pain?

Thinking all these things, he bumped into his father, who had stopped and was crouched down, listening. Jules spun around, raising his arm, and Stewart cringed, but his father let his arm drop. They had reached the top of the hill; there was a small clear space in the middle, where a big hole had been dug. Some shovels protruded from the pile of the dirt that had been dislodged by the digging. Now that they had stopped moving, they could hear the flutes clearly again and, in a moment, the slap-slap of the whips. The procession was very close.

"We have to hurry," Jules whispered.

He ran, still crouching, approximately a quarter of the way around the hill, until they were opposite where the procession would appear. He crept close to the top, then lay flat under a piñon. He motioned to Stewart to do likewise. Stewart saw that, unless someone were to come right over to them, they would be hidden, yet by raising their heads they could see the bare top of the hill. A rock jutted into his stomach and another into his hip but he didn't dare move.

Later Stewart could not have said how long they waited. Because the men were walking on their knees it took a long time for them to ascend the hill. During that time Stewart felt lost in wonderment and a triumphant kind of joy to know that human beings really let other people do such things to them. He felt that he had been waiting his whole life to make certain of this. At last he could see the wavy lights of the first torches, then the men who were carrying them, and behind them the men dragging the crosses. When they reached the center of the clearing, one of the men gave his torch to another to hold and lifted the largest cross off of the shoulders of the man who had been dragging it. Relieved of the weight, this man tried to straighten up but couldn't and fell over. Someone else helped him to his feet and then he stood, wobbling. Like the other penitents, he wore a hood over his head.

Soon the rest of the procession had reached the top of the hill. The men who had "walked" kneeling continued to kneel, but the ones behind them weren't beating them anymore. Some of these now came forward and took the arms of the man who had dragged the cross. They led him, stumbling, towards the center of the clearing, where the hole was. The cross had been laid beside it. Even though he could hear movement, it seemed to Stewart that there was utter quiet. The man who had dragged the cross lay down upon it, his feet together, his arms spread out, like Jesus. Suddenly Stewart felt sick. Were they going to nail this pretend Christ to the cross? Was that what his father had brought him all this way to witness? He thought then that perhaps he was wrong, perhaps the men had not consented to be penitents at all, but were spellbound, or drugged by the ones with whips and torches.

He waited for these men to take out hammer and nails, afraid he wouldn't be able to stand it, even though more than anything he wanted to watch; even if he hid his eyes he would still hear the hammering and might scream or be sick to his stomach; he already felt sick, thinking about it. The men would discover him and his father and would nail them to crosses too, one on either side, like the thieves; he was sure now that this had been the trick of his father's question.

While Stewart was thinking this, other men came with ropes and instead of nailing the man to the cross tied him to it, around each wrist and his ankles. His arms were draped over the horizontal beam as if he had his arms around two friends' shoulders. He lay perfectly motionless as the men tied him. Then it was even quieter. More men came and helped to lift the cross and carry it like a stretcher up to the mound of dirt. They positioned it, then slid it into the hole. It sickened Stewart that they'd come up earlier to dig it, knowing what it was for. He wondered if they'd forced the same man they were now hanging from the cross to assist in the digging. Sometimes prisoners of war were forced to dig their own graves before being shot. Even if this man believed it the greatest honor in the world to be chosen as the Christ, Stewart thought, the rest of them must have believed him an idiot to think so. Several now braced the cross while the others shovelled the dirt back in. The man's feet were only a short distance from the ground, not high up, as in all the paintings Stewart had seen. As soon as the other men had finished stamping down the dirt around the cross, they backed off a little ways. A wind was blowing and the man's white pants, cut off above the knee, fluttered.

Before he thought, Stewart whispered, "Are they leaving him there to die?"

But Jules wasn't there—either to scold or to answer. When had he left and where had he gone? Stewart peered down the slope; a short ways below him he saw a dark pile and crept cautiously down to it: it turned out to be his father's clothes—his shirt, trousers, and jacket. Why had his father undressed? Stewart crawled back up the hill.

Around the cross, the men were still. Then one man, wearing the knee-length white trousers and a hood, threaded his way through the others. He was scanning the ground as he went. He picked something up—Stewart couldn't see what; what could he have lost or what could there be on the bare ground that he'd want?

He approached the cross and there seemed to be some whispering among others nearby but no one else moved. Then everything happened very quickly. The man reached up to the dangling feet and pounded at them, twice. There were two loud, horrible thuds. Simultaneously the man on the cross screamed, and then the first man was sprinting across the clearing towards Stewart, flinging something away—a rock—as he ran, and Stewart now screamed.

"Get up! Run!" Jules shouted harshly. He had torn off the hood and was fumbling among his discarded clothes. Men from the procession were pursuing him, shouting.

"Down the hill, Stewart! Now!"

Stewart ran blindly, sobbing, wanting to stop to be sick but not daring to. Behind him he heard a shot fired, and his father shouting, "Stay back!" Then his father running, catching up with him, dragging him back down and around the hill. But Stewart could also still hear the man on the cross screaming and he fought free from his father and shouted, "Ignacio! That's Ignacio!"

"Shut up!" his father hissed, dragging him faster until Stewart fell, tearing holes in the elbows of his shirt and the knees of his pants. He was choking on his sobs now. In between breaths he cried out, "Ignacio! Ignacio!" However, his father didn't attempt to silence him again until they reached the truck. Then he took him by the shoulders and said, "Stop, Stewart. Stop it, now." He was not speaking unkindly. "Get into the truck."

Jules backed down into the road without turning on the engine and coasted with the lights off until they were out of the village. Then he gave a strange laugh.

"Don't cry, Stewart. Don't you know that Ignacio was experiencing as close as any human can to what Christ felt on the cross? It's the supreme honor of the Brotherhood. You aren't looking at the thing in the right light. I was helping. The Brothers aren't allowed to use nails, but I know how much Ignacio wanted the chance to feel what his Savior felt. You've misunderstood. They say they want to know Christ's Passion themselves but how can you live something like that unless you do it all? The part can't stand for the whole—even a child must realize that."

Stewart didn't understand what his father was talking about; in any case he was incapable of answering; he felt as if, were he ever to open his mouth to speak to Jules again, he would choke to death. The wrong he would have to accuse him of was so large, and yet to Jules's mind seemingly so justifiable, that Stewart felt that no human voice could ever be loud enough to speak Jules's crime. It could only be reenacted: over and over and over and over, until one day its truth would simply be known.

Fortunately Jules didn't say another word the rest of the way back to town. He let Stewart out at the end of the road to the ranch, and Stewart tiptoed into the house and hid his torn and dirty clothes under his bed.

Rosario woke him, as she often did, with a cup of hot chocolate. She seemed distracted, but said only that Ignacio had gone to visit his brother. He wasn't around that evening, or the next day, Easter. Stewart didn't dare ask when Ignacio was coming back, although he was so ill at ease he had to force himself to eat. He was afraid that Rosario would suspect something if he didn't.

Then, on Monday morning, Ignacio was sitting in the kitchen when Stewart got up. One of his feet was heavily bandaged and a crutch rested against his chair. All of the color seemed to be sucked out of the room when Stewart saw him, and he stood in the doorway, unable to move.

"Hello, Stewart," Ignacio said.

Somehow Stewart walked over to him. When Ignacio reached out and took hold of his hands, Stewart began to sob.

"Stewart, what is it? Stewart, look at me."

"I thought you were dead!" Stewart sobbed.

"Dead!" Ignacio exclaimed. "Rosario, what have you been telling our poor boy?"

There was a heartiness in Ignacio's voice that Stewart knew was false only because he knew it had to be.

"I was working late in the shop on Friday and I climbed on the workbench to put a new bulb in the ceiling light. I was very stupid. I jumped off the bench without looking and I came down right on top of an upturned nail. I forgot I had left some old boards there that I meant to use over. The nail went all the way through my foot. It was very stupid of me. That's all, Stewart, my good friend. There's no reason to be so upset now, is there?"

"No," Stewart said, recognizing even then the irony of its being Ignacio's gentle wish to spare him that had saved him from the pity that had been about to engulf him, to obscure his purpose, and to merge his lot with everyone else's.

XXXIII SPARTA (HARMONY)

After what they started calling "Escape from the Naval Academy," dating everything from it as if it were A.D., Zoë and Rob were friends again the rest of the school year. He hadn't talked anymore the way he had that night; at least, if he brought up the same ideas, he made them sound like philosophy and Zoë had a hard time knowing why it had given her the creeps before.

Fortunately this time they were smart enough to keep their friendship to themselves. Rob never telephoned her, and she called him only after the bakery was closed. She waited until dark to go over, making sure no one saw her turning into Ivy Street. It was easy in winter; when daylight lasted longer, either they'd wait until very late or else she'd ride the bus to some place on the outskirts of Sparta and Rob would "borrow" his parents' car and pick her up. It was great, riding along in the spring air with the windows rolled down, out along the bay road, or west, towards the mountains. Sometimes they'd drive around all night—he'd drop her at the corner of Chesterfield and Metcalf just before dawn, then go back over to his parents' and park the car. He'd found the serial number and ordered an extra key from the dealer. His parents still didn't know he could drive it.

Zoë particularly didn't tell Bridget what was going on, even though Bridget seemed to have lost all curiosity where she was concerned. Her latest "heartthrob" was a sophomore at the college named Bruce and she was auditing a seminar so that she could "share his experiences." She seemed to think life was just one experience after another. At recess Zoë went with her out to the bamboo thicket behind the cupola so that Bridget could smoke—and, it seemed, confide her latest "exploits."

"I don't get it," she told Rob. "It doesn't even seem like she enjoys my company so why does she want to tell me all this stuff?"

"Maybe she wants you to envy her."

"She could care less what I think."

"Maybe she envies you," Rob suggested.

"Me! Why?"

"I can think of a lot of reasons. You're more attractive than she is, to begin with, and . . ."

"Are you crazy? Bridget's gorgeous!"

"I suppose. In a certain pre-Raphaelite way. But appearance isn't everything, you know. You have this aura about you, like you're connected to some other world."

"I do?"

"Take it from me. I know all about other worlds."

"Oh, I forgot."

It did seem as if Bridget had some ulterior motive in confiding her secrets; even when she was describing the most nauseatingly intimate details of her sex life with Bruce (Bruce the Goose, Rob called him), she seemed preoccupied, not exactly the way people did when they were lying, but similarly, flat in the way she talked. Bridget's stories didn't make Zoë wish she were having Bridget's experiences anymore, even though she would have liked to know what Bridget meant when she said that Bruce was the first man she'd "really made love with." When she asked her, Bridget said, "Oh, all the stars and fireworks and everything you always hear about." Great. Big help. Bridget listed a million details but the main thing, the actual substance of what she was saying, was always left out. Sometimes Zoë wondered if Bridget were depressed—but what would she be depressed about? She was madly in love with Bruce; she had already received an early acceptance to acting school; now that she'd let her hair grow out she really did look amazingly beautiful, whatever Rob might say; her parents let her do basically whatever she wanted—what could she be depressed about?

Maybe taking her cue from the Wycliffes, Monica had had a house key made for Zoë. She said, "After discussing it, your father and I have agreed that you're old enough to set your own limits. Ergo, no curfew, no restrictions, no nothing. It's up to you."

Monica could hardly look at her as she said this. Obviously they thought that she was sleeping with someone and that they were being all emancipated and liberal not to nose into her business. Little did they know. It would have been one thing if it were true, but all these months Rob had never so much as kissed her good night. Mostly she didn't think about it anymore; it was just that sometimes, seeing a couple at school kissing goodbye quickly before they went to class after lunch, or sitting close together in the front seat of their car, she would feel an ache, and would wonder if maybe one reason she and Rob didn't let anyone know they were seeing each other was because, if they had, they would have had to notice how bizarre it was, all the time they spent alone, driving around in the dark, sometimes stopping on a beach or in the woods, and just sitting there, sitting there and not talking. "Well, time to get back, I guess," Rob would say eventually. "I guess," she'd say. Then as soon as they were on the road they'd start talking again. *You mean you see him all the time and he's told you he loves you and you've never even kissed?*

It wasn't really true that she didn't think about it. All Rob had to do was look at her a way he had and she did, though later she wondered if she had secretly signalled him not to do more than look at her—but that was after she'd learned to analyze the life out of everything. That was what you did when there was nothing left.

Among everything else she and Rob talked about was Charlotte. Zoë was amazed how much sympathy Rob felt for her. They do *what*? They *drug* her? Since *when*? She told him she thought it was since Charlotte's four miscarriages, and he said, Can you imagine? Thinking four times that you were going to be a mother and each time having your hopes dashed? He actually said "hopes dashed," the kind of expression he never used unless he was too worked up to pay attention.

"Are you sure you've told me everything?" he kept asking, and she said, "Yes, why?" "Something's fishy," he said. "Something's fishy in Denmark. When you're up there this summer you really ought to find out what's what. Get to the bottom of things, Watson. Find the skeletons in the closet, Edgar. Are there closets in your grandmother's house? Find the fox in the attic. Any other animals while you're at it. There has to be some *reason* your mother has kept your grandmother drugged all this time—some nefarious thing she doesn't want her to remember. Don't you think?"

"Nefarious?"

"Evil. Dangerous."

"Where did you hear that word?"

"I don't recall the exact time and place where I first encountered it. It's been around for a while."

She'd asked Rob if he wanted to visit her in Harmony—Nick had a summer research job doing biochemistry and wasn't going to come—but Rob said he couldn't leave the bakery. It was frustrating; he complained all the time about how bored he was, but when she suggested he sell the business and do something else he said, "No, I couldn't do that," as if the reasons were obvious. She was sick of arguing with him about it.

June came, school ended, and Monica said she was free to do as she wished, but she did have to make up her mind. Vera Magoon wanted to visit her sister in North Carolina and if Zoë were in Harmony she could handle the cooking and oversee Charlotte's medication while Mrs. Magoon was gone; otherwise they'd have to hire a replacement. Zoë wanted to stay in Sparta to be near Rob, but she never saw him in the daytime—what would she do with herself? She looked halfheartedly for a job but didn't find one. And then, Bruce would be in Sparta for the summer, working as a bartender at the yacht club, no doubt so that he could spend his every free moment getting it on with Bridget. At least, if she went to Harmony, she wouldn't have to hear all the gory details of Bridget's sex life—what she and Bruce did in bed, how often, how long, how exciting he was because he would do everything, he wasn't a boy, he was a man, unlike certain French egotistical maniacs she wouldn't do the honor of mentioning. Bruce wasn't afraid of a woman desiring him; he understood how sex was about power—not in a bad way—it was like a conversation you had about power with your bodies; if it was real, if sex was real, then you could find out the most incredible things; it was as if the whole world were actually inside you and you could experience everything in history just through making love . . .

As usual Zoë wanted to ask Bridget what she meant, but she was afraid Bridget would answer with even more details, like the time she'd remarked that the things in *Lady Chatterley's Lover* didn't happen only in books, and then had to explain what actually happened in the book. Zoë got the feeling sometimes that Bridget wanted her to respond in some way she wasn't responding—but how? Did Bridget feel guilty? Was it like what had happened with the Pipe School—she had to turn herself in? But what did she expect Zoë to do?

On the way to Harmony, though, Zoë forgot about everything in Sparta and thought about Buell; she could never love him the way she loved Rob, but at least he wasn't afraid to show he liked her. She hadn't written to him as she'd promised, but she was sure he'd forgive her; maybe this summer they would make love—she could tell him she didn't have any expectations, in case that was what he were worried about.

The way her life was going, she should have known better than to count on anything. It didn't take more than a few seconds to figure out that the girl with Buell on the train platform was his girlfriend. Shelley. "Shelley what?" Zoë asked, feeling like a jerk. A couple of days later when Buell came over to mow the lawn when his grandfather wasn't feeling well, he told her that he and Shelley were *engaged*. She was going to nursing school and they'd get married when she was finished. How could this have happened since last summer, when absolutely nothing had happened with Rob?

Zoë hadn't plotted to take Charlotte off her medication. The very first morning Mrs. Magoon was away, Zoë put out the pill for Charlotte with her orange juice, although she didn't say anything about it, didn't stand there and say, "Now, Mrs. Robie, time for your medicine." She refused to talk to Charlotte like that. That first morning maybe Charlotte simply forgot. The second morning, Zoë set the pill on a saucer and the saucer on top of Charlotte's plate. She used the fancy dark blue Wedgwood so that the white pill would stand out. She was whipping eggs over the sink and could see Charlotte in the window. She saw Charlotte look at her, pick the pill up, and put it in the pocket of her housedress. Then she folded her hands in her lap and sat there.

Zoë stared at her grandmother's reflection, feeling as if she'd had an electric shock. Her heart was beating so fast that she could hardly breathe. She kept stirring the eggs until she had calmed down enough to turn around.

The same thing happened the next day, and the next. She put the pill on the saucer, but now she'd make sure she gave Charlotte a chance to hide it. Each time she turned around and the pill was gone her throat tightened up and she felt all hot. This went on for a week. During that time, Charlotte didn't act any differently, although she might have already had more energy.

Then, by accident, Zoë caught her. She had thought Charlotte had already hidden the pill, but she came back into the kitchen from the pantry just as Charlotte was dropping it into her pocket. Charlotte was sitting facing the pantry doorway and although Zoë immediately turned towards the sink there was no way that she could pretend not to have seen. Charlotte burst into tears.

"I'll do it," she said, wiping her eyes and retrieving the pill from her pocket and placing it on her tongue. "I couldn't help myself when you didn't watch me. Until now someone has always watched me."

"Grandmother, no, please . . ."

She couldn't stand it, Charlotte crying—and because she, her granddaughter, might scold her for misbehaving. She set down the cereal boxes and crouched beside Charlotte's chair.

"Don't cry, Grandmother. It's all right. I could care less if you take your medication or not. I knew you weren't taking it."

"You did?"

Charlotte's eyes were so clear, even through her tears. If Zoë hadn't been sure before that she was doing the right thing, she was positive now. It was like seeing someone who'd almost drowned making it back to the surface. To force Charlotte to take the pills again would be like pushing her back underwater and holding her there, just when she'd thought, I'm alive! I'm going to live!

"I won't tell anyone. I promise."

"But why would you keep such a secret for me?" Charlotte wondered.

This showed a change, too. Zoë couldn't remember Charlotte's ever questioning anything anyone said or did. When anything perplexed her, she thought of a quote from the Bible that covered the situation.

"Because I think it's wrong to make you take them. Maybe there was a reason once, but I can't see what it could be anymore. All they're doing is keeping you from being who you really are."

"Who I am?"

It was amazing, this whole new person beginning to appear. Charlotte had used to sound so resigned. After breakfast she stood up, reached for her apron, and said, "There's work to be done."

"Work?"

"Thaddeus will be coming home today. We must air out his room. And I expect that Henry and Samuel will not be long in arriving, once they know that their brother is home. If only Llewellyn. . . He went west, you know. I told him the Gold Rush was over, but he wouldn't listen. Always the dreamer. Of all the boys he was always the dreamiest. You were quite young when he left."

"I was?"

"Four or five—do you remember him at all?"

Zoë realized that Charlotte thought she was Monica, as if Charlotte had been transported back to before she started taking the drugs. She had changed so fast, though, it was incredible. It was as if hearing that Zoë wasn't going to turn her in had set her free all at once.

When Mrs. Magoon returned from North Carolina, Zoë convinced her that she didn't need to come back. She told her she enjoyed cooking; since she'd been careful after she "caught" Charlotte to flush one pill down the toilet every day, she would know when the prescription needed refilling. Furthermore, as time went on Charlotte became increasingly clear-headed, and she seemed to sense when it was unsafe to talk about her "boys."

One day, in passing, Charlotte mentioned the "family curse." She'd never wanted to marry, she said; she had hoped that the curse would stop with her.

"What curse?" Zoë exclaimed.

"Why, seeing," Charlotte replied. "Surely I've warned you about it, Harmony. You and . . ." She looked momentarily confused. "You and your daughter."

"You never told me about a curse."

"Should you happen to have a daughter. It strikes every other generation—my mother told me. You will be spared, but your daughter would not be."

"But what will happen to me—I mean, to her?"

"What I've been speaking of—the second sight. In my case it showed the future, but it can turn in the other direction. I don't know which is worse."

> She foresaw her own mother's death! [Zoë wrote to Rob]. She's never forgiven herself for not preventing it. That's the Howe family curse—seeing what you can't change; then you blame yourself forever.
>
> My grandmother has been telling me a lot about the past. She first met my grandfather when they were both six years old. Her mother did sewing for his mother. One day Adam (my grandfather) accused her of being a witch (because of her ancestor—I've told you that story) and made her go up with him to the widow's walk with a broom and try to fly. It's great up there, by the way. I wish you could see it. Considering that I've inherited the H. F. C. and might be a witch, I'm thinking of taking a broom up to the widow's walk some night to check it out.

"Get flight insurance," Rob wrote back. Zoë didn't tell him what Charlotte and Adam had seen through the telescope; he might interpret it as a hint.

> This is just the beginning, though. Right before my great-grandmother Louisa killed herself (she hung herself out in the barn, in case you forgot), she told my grandmother that my grandfather Adam's real father wasn't Henry Robie but some lawyer in town named Timothy Lowndes. (He's dead and doesn't have any descendants or I'd have new relatives—wouldn't it be great just to march up to someone's door and tell them you were their cousin?) My grandmother never told my grandfather, though; he was so proud of being Henry Robie's son that she was afraid he'd be mortified if he found out that he wasn't. Great-grandmother Louisa also told my grandmother Charlotte that she aborted two children after Adam was born—I mean, did it herself. Once she injected something and another time she threw herself down the stairs. She also told my grandmother that her mother (Ida, Charlotte's mother—I hope you can keep all these people straight) had nursed my grandfather when he was a baby—i.e., Ida nursed Charlotte *and* Adam and then twenty years later they got married, isn't that weird?
>
> It's so bizarre thinking about these things that happened before I

was born and how maybe they all led somehow to my grandmother's illness, which led to my mother being obsessed with her past and marrying my father who was obsessed with his past, which led to Nick and me growing up in a lunatic asylum, et cetera, et cetera, et cetera.

A week later, this news seemed minor. One afternoon, family archaeologist Zoë found the letters that Monica had stored in the attic: her and Seth's college correspondence, and Adam's letter telling Monica that he and Charlotte were brother and sister.

You're never going to believe what I've found out now, Rob. You were right about skeletons in the closet, all right. Get this. My grandfather Adam spent his whole life thinking that he was married to his own sister, but he never told her! If he'd told her, she could have told him it wasn't true, but he never said a word! He guessed from reading his father's will that Henry Robie was *Charlotte's* father, but he never knew that Henry wasn't also *his* father. It is *so* strange. I can't believe he thought this his whole life and never told a soul! For a long time he thought Charlotte knew and that that was why she'd had so many miscarriages (feeling it was a sin) but then he decided she didn't know and after that he had to live all alone with his guilt. I can't really even *think* about this, if you know what I mean.

As usual I'm sure my mother expected me and/or Nick to find this letter—why else would she leave it in the attic in a trunk? But what does she expect me to do about it? For one thing, I'm not sure she knows that Timothy Lowndes was Adam's father; my grandmother only remembered this since she's been off the drug. This means that my *mother* has spent twenty years believing that her parents *committed incest.* Can you imagine how warped that would make you? I don't know if she ever even told my father. It seems to me that it would have shown up in their letters if she had. I'm sure she wanted me and Nick to find out and feel like *we* were born with the stain on us.

If my mother doesn't know about Timothy Lowndes, it would probably be a great relief to her to hear about him, but then she'd want to know how I know and then she'd find out about Charlotte being off drugs. The main thing I can't decide, though, is whether I should say anything to my grandmother. Sometimes I feel as if I know so many secrets that my head is going to explode.

Wear a helmet [Rob wrote back]. Just kidding—I know what you mean. I know *exactly* what you mean. My advice: it goes against all my principles, but I don't think you should tell your grandmother what your grandfather thought. You feel bad because you can't change the past but I don't think you should. It's your life the news will change,

> not your grandmother's. It's as if you'd time-travelled back there and adjusted something, do you know what I mean? It's like you sneaked out from under the things people told you. That's what you have to do about all of history, I'm beginning to think. You have to experience it all *personally* before you can actually go on and have your own life. Do you know what I mean?

This summer Zoë was using the room Adam had used, and before him Henry Robie. She'd always slept in one of the smaller, flowery bedrooms in the back wing, but they made her too homesick for Rob's house now. Adam's room was painted a pale apricot and the furniture was dark and plain. It was in the back northeast corner of the main house so there was a cross-breeze, and on almost any night the white fluffy curtains blew into the room. During storms they snapped like untied sails, or were suddenly, ferociously sucked back against the screen, as if the storm were trying to pull the room out into it.

It was on a night like this that Samuel came back—Samuel Robie, Zoë's dead great-great uncle. Zoë knew the story everyone did—that he'd drowned when he was fifteen by floating over Harmony Falls, shouting back to his brother that he was fine. She'd always felt sad when she read the dates on his tombstone—she'd already lived longer than he had; it seemed so unfair.

That night thunder woke her; in the next lightning flash she saw a boy shutting the back window.

"Oh, don't!" she exclaimed, sitting up in bed. "I love storms!"

At the sound of her voice, he jumped and spun around.

"Who are you?" he demanded. "Where's Henry?"

"Where's who?"

Later it seemed to her that one of the strangest parts of the whole thing was the fact that she'd never once been scared. Maybe because of the thunderstorm—it was as if danger were finally, soothingly visible and so you could stop being afraid. And this was a storm to end all storms: lightning bolts cracked the sky in such rapid succession that the thunder was one continuous roar and water thudded into the room through every window, the curtains too soaked even to flap. She would have thought that waking to find a stranger in her room would have made her at least *nervous*, but some fear-erasing substance had filled her so that all she could feel was amazement.

"Henry who?" she repeated. "Who are you?"

She could see him only when the lightning flashed—her eyes didn't have a chance to adjust to the dark between flashes. She could tell that he was young—her age, more or less, tall and slender and dark-haired, and her first thought had been that it was Rob. But his voice was different and he had some kind of accent, though she couldn't really place it.

"I'm Samuel Robie," he said. "I must say, it is a quaint experience to introduce myself in my own house. Would you be so good as to inform me of my brother's whereabouts?"

"Your brother?"

"My brother Henry! You're sleeping in his bed! Surely this ruse has been played long enough. Have you a candle?"

"A candle?" she asked. If she'd been fully awake she might have figured it out sooner; instead she thought that he was Charlotte's *son* Samuel.

"Are you looking for Charlotte? Your mother?"

"My mother is not named Charlotte—who *are* you?"

But now she had realized who he was.

"I'm sorry, I don't have a candle," she said, sitting up straighter in bed. She didn't think it would be very smart to turn the electric light on. Electricity might not have been in people's houses yet when he was alive.

"What is your name and for what purpose are you here? Where is my brother sleeping?"

"My name is Zoë Carver. I'm Charlotte Robie's granddaughter."

"Who is this Charlotte you keep mentioning?"

"She married Henry's son, Adam. Well, maybe not exactly Henry's, but . . ."

"Henry's . . . You're daft," he said. "Why has Henry allowed a madwoman to take his place in his own bed?"

"I'm not a madwoman!" she exclaimed, laughing.

She was laughing because he sounded so much the way Rob sounded when he talked like a priggish aristocrat to be sarcastic.

"Henry's dead," she said. He had to know sometime. "He died in . . . well, I don't know the exact year. Long before I was born. I think he got syphilis. He was a sailor—you probably don't know. I hate to say it, but you're dead too. You drowned. You drowned in the Connecticut when you were fifteen."

"Oh, I'm sure," he said. "I don't mind if I tell you, miss, that the joke is in very poor taste. Where my brother found you. . . I'd know if you were from town. But you talk queer. Where are you from?"

He spoke less stuffily now that he was getting angry.

"*You* talk queer," she said. "I talk the way I do because I'm living in the last half of the twentieth century."

"It's 1875 and you know it."

"No, I don't know it," she said, "and, anyway, why should I believe you're really Sam? Someone could have put you up to this—someone who knew about you and Henry. I can't remember if I told Rob or not. Buell probably knows the story, but I can't imagine that he . . ."

"Would you kindly desist from chattering?"

He came to stand by the bed, and in the next lightning flash she saw that he was soaking wet. He was also incredibly handsome.

"You must be freezing!" she exclaimed.

"So would you be if you'd been washed downriver half a mile and had to . . . I can't fathom how it took me so very long to get home."

He sounded confused, and he sat down on the edge of the bed. He *felt* solid enough.

"And it was a bright sunny day. What time did the rain begin?"

Now he sounded troubled—she wished she hadn't told him he was dead.

"Maybe you got knocked on the head by something," she suggested. "That could mix up your sense of time."

"I can't understand why no one undertook to search for me," he went on. "Weren't they distressed? Didn't they wonder where I was? I cannot comprehend it."

"Henry thought you were playing a trick on him," she said, in a flash of inspiration. "That's why he didn't look for you. He was angry."

"Angry? But . . ."

"He thought you went over the falls on purpose. He said you waved and smiled at him."

"Over the falls? Why would I do that? Everyone knows it would be certain death. I remember being out in the boat with Henry and the sun was out . . . And then I don't remember anything else until I woke up on the bank downstream an hour or so ago. Come to think of it, how did I get past the falls? It seems to me Henry's been telling many stories."

Had he? Zoë wondered. Could Henry have murdered his brother and then made up the story he had told? Had he murdered Samuel but suppressed his memory of it? But how could she possibly learn the truth now? Even if she did, would it make any difference? She already knew too many things about the past that she couldn't change.

She thought she ought to talk some way that wouldn't sound too modern, but the only conversation she could think of from the right era was from *Huckleberry Finn*, and nothing in it seemed exactly appropriate. Samuel hadn't moved, so she threw the blankets back and got out of bed. The long white nightgown she was wearing—Charlotte had an endless supply of them—would seem right out of his century.

"Why don't you put on some dry clothes?" she asked, before she realized that she didn't have anything to give him. "Aren't you cold? You could get under the covers—there's plenty of room. You need to get out of your wet things, though—you'll catch your death of cold."

When she heard the Dracula-like thing she'd said she started to laugh, feeling very weird and flimsy.

"Sam," she said, "don't you realize that Henry's giving you a present? He's not playing a prank. Don't you see why he's not here?"

"I beg your pardon?"

"Aren't you cold?" she said again. She took him by the hand and led him towards the bed. He looked puzzled—when the lightning flashed so that she could see his expression—but he didn't resist. Rob had his chance, she thought. It was just too bad for him.

"Here, I'll do this," she said, and began unbuttoning his shirt. It was plain-looking and dark.

"Whatcha doin'?" he asked, sounding more like someone from present-day Harmony. He still didn't put up any resistance, though.

"What do you think I'm doing?"

"Seems to be you're divesting me of my clothes."

"Divesting . . ." she repeated.

She pushed the shirt back over his shoulders; he shrugged out of the sleeves. He sat on the bed and she knelt to untie his shoes. He had only one on. The wet knot was difficult to loosen. When she'd finished and began with the sock on the other foot, he said, "Careful, it's sore. Couldn't find the shoe anywhere."

All of a sudden the rain died down and she felt shy; before she'd figured out whether or not she actually had the nerve to start undoing his pants the moon was back, clouds scudding over it at breakneck speed, so that the room was lit intermittently with a rich, strange light. When she stood up, Sam was looking at her with a sort of smile. Did it mean, I bet you're not forward enough to take off the rest of my clothes? Did it mean, Are you crazy? I might as well see how crazy this girl is. Or could he not believe his good luck—something he'd always dreamed of—a girl inviting him into her bed?

She touched the waist of his pants (he probably called them trousers), but then took her hand away.

"You do this part," she whispered.

He did nothing, though. Stood still, instead, watching her. Maybe trying to see how big a fool she'd make of herself. She nearly said, "Okay, let me see what I can find for you that's dry"; she could pretend that all she'd ever meant was to give him dry clothes, but as she began to turn away, she felt so angry with herself—if she couldn't even be unselfconscious in front of a ghost . . . !

"Okay," she said quietly. Had people used that word back when Sam was alive?

Crossing her arms, she took hold of her nightgown on either side at the waist and pulled it up over her head. She freed her hands from the inside-out sleeves and dropped the nightgown to the floor. While she couldn't see, she'd wondered if Sam might have vanished when she got it off, but he was still there, staring at her. At first she thought he was in shock at her forwardness, but then she realized he was just too amazed to hide his curiosity. He wouldn't exactly have had *Playboy* to look at in those days. She was surprised how unembarrassed she felt—maybe because he was looking at her so admiringly.

"You say Henry asked you to come here?" he said finally, his voice bumpy.

She nodded, moving a little closer.

"What else?"

"What else?"

"What did he ask you to do?"

"Whatever you want."

"But I . . . if Henry sent you . . ."

Did he mean that he expected her to take the lead? How was she going to find a way out of that?

"All right," she said. "So I made that part up. Henry didn't send me. I asked him if I could come. When you didn't show up at dinner, he called me . . . I mean he sent me a message that tonight would be the perfect time."

"But who *are* you?" Samuel insisted. "I've never seen you before. Why would you want to . . ."

All this time he was studying her, memorizing the way she looked, as if he wanted to be sure he'd know exactly what to do when he finally touched her. No one had ever looked at her like that before. . . But what was she saying? No one besides Bridget and doctors had ever seen her with all her clothes off before. "Never mind who I am. It isn't important, is it? All you need to know is how long I've wanted . . . to do this. Never mind how I know you or how I came to be here. We're here, the two of us, and no one will disturb us. Isn't that all that counts?"

"You're not from these parts," Sam stated.

"So what?"

" 'So what?' " he repeated.

"Yes, so what? Does everyone have to be?" She stepped right up to him and lifted her arms and laid them around his neck. Whether from politeness, curiosity, or desire, or all of them, Samuel put his arms around her waist and pulled her towards him. His skin was cooler than hers, and his pants were cold and clammy. She shivered.

"I'll . . . I'll take them off," he stammered. "Don't you want to stay in the bed?"

She climbed back under the covers and pretended not to look while he finished undressing. He didn't turn his back to her, and she liked him more than ever that although he was shy it didn't make him embarrassed and secretive. When he got into the bed she held her arms out to him and he kissed her at once—it was obvious to her now that something in Rob had always been hesitating. He wouldn't risk *anything*—it was as if he were always waiting for the perfect time, but when would that be? It wasn't as if Samuel were in a hurry to get things over with; he was just *sure*. He did what he wanted to do. That was a simple thing to say—do what you want—but she could tell even though she'd never felt it from anyone before that it wasn't very common; to be brave enough to do what you wanted, to stop thinking all the time of what things *meant*. Samuel didn't hold anything back. It seemed so strange that the first person with whom she'd felt there were no boundaries at all wasn't even alive, although right now that seemed like any other quality a person might possess—just an adjective—like having brown hair or being tall. Although they hadn't said anything important to each other—if someone had been listening to them they'd think it was the most boring small talk, but it had felt as if every word had been a signpost leading them into each other's minds.

She sort of moaned when he first tried to push inside her—it didn't really hurt, even though he had to try several times before it worked—but because she was so surprised—one more thing nobody ever told you about. It didn't last very long the first time; Samuel groaned and shuddered and she heard herself suddenly cry out that she loved him; she hadn't even known she was going to say it. He said against her neck, "You do?"

"Would I have said it if I didn't?" She didn't know the answer.

He propped himself up to look down at her.

"Maybe I love you too," he said.

"This is one of those two kinds of reasoning," she said. "Maybe you've heard of them. One is where you reach a general conclusion from collecting evidence and one is where you know what will happen in any particular instance because you know the basic premise. Which do you think this is?"

"I've never been too swift at logic," Samuel said. "Henry knows that sort of thing. I never have the patience for it."

"What did you—I mean, do you—have the patience for?"

"Don't know," he said, moving off her and turning on his back. She turned on her side and nestled against him. He started stroking her hair. "Daydreaming—I'm a real hand at daydreaming. Teacher throws her eraser at me and it still don't wake me up."

"What do you daydream about?"

"For everything to be some other way. Everyone to act different. Myself to be someone else. Sometimes somewhere else."

"Where?"

"I don't know. Different, that's all. I think of things I want to tell people but when I do it's not what I meant."

"Do you feel that with me?"

"No, I don't. It's peculiar. A girl I never laid eyes on before . . . I know what you mean when you talk too."

"Kiss me again," she whispered. "Kiss me as if you'll never see me again."

"Never see you again? Why wouldn't I?"

"I don't know. Just in case."

"What kind of reasoning do you call that?" he asked, but he held her tightly and kissed her, and then they both got excited again and everything started all over. It was as if there were almost too much to feel—their lips and mouths trying to explain something to each other and his hands all over her, looking for something. Then when she started touching him she forgot he was touching her until she remembered with a shock and, remembering, forgot to move her hands. Except that the more she forgot, the more she remembered. Talk about no logic.

It was longer this time, and she could tell that something almost happened, but either he stopped too soon or she got nervous—but then the next time she got back to the beginning of that feeling right away and suddenly the wind blew the curtains into the room and while she was noticing that it just started to happen. "Sam!" she exclaimed. He stopped moving. "What? What's wrong?" "Nothing! Don't stop!" "Oh," he said, in a sigh, "Oh, I see . . ." and he moved again until he came too. "I love you," he whispered. "You won't ever forget me, will you?" she asked him. "Forget you? Don't be daft. I'll be right here when you wake up. Hush, now, go to sleep." He asked her what she'd said her name was as they drifted off.

A couple of hours later—it must have been almost dawn—she woke to hear him sobbing in a nightmare; she shook him awake and told him he'd been dreaming, but he kept insisting that it hadn't been a dream; he'd done something thinking he wouldn't die but it wasn't true, he was dead, but he wasn't allowed to admit it. He clung to her, shuddering; why had she told him he was dead when he first came in? "A bad joke—no reason. Something Henry and I dreamed up to scare you," she said. He was so cold, suddenly; and she pressed against him as tightly as she could until he warmed up, saying over and over, "It's all right, Sam, I'm here. Don't worry, it's all right."

In the morning he was gone. She didn't remember at first what had happened; she knew when she woke up only that she was happier than she remembered ever being; it was as if her mind were supported as softly and comfortably by some invisible certainty as her body was by the big four-poster bed. Something else felt different—then she realized that she wasn't wearing her nightgown. She sat up and saw it lying in a crumpled pile on the floor. At the sight, everything came back. Samuel had been there, or—she felt sick at the thought and immediately curled back up under the covers—she'd dreamed he had. It had seemed so real, though, how could it have been a dream? But it must have been. She felt like crying, except that she felt too hollow to cry. Everything she'd felt on waking up had not been true. Samuel had been a dream, and she pulled the covers over her head so that for as long as possible she could remember him in bed with her, the way he'd touched her, the things he'd said to her . . . She sat up in a sudden fury—how could all that have been only a *dream*?

She had never been so angry in her entire life. She didn't know what to do with herself. She threw back the covers and got out of bed—and then felt what she hadn't, lying down: an ache between her legs, a kind of soreness inside that she'd never felt before. Pulling the covers all the way back to the foot of the bed, she inspected the sheets and found several small stains. Nothing like the torrents of blood there were supposed to be the first time you slept with someone, but some discolored spots, like when she started getting her period. Could she have her period? But she'd just had it—it had been over for eight or nine days. Maybe something was wrong with her. She touched the stains, which were dry, but the sheet was stiff. She leaned across the bed and smelled the spots. They didn't smell like much—sweat, maybe. She felt between her legs to see if she was still bleeding, but she wasn't. She smelled her fingers—was it disgusting to do that? They smelled like the bed had, only much stronger. Naked still, shivering—the rain had cooled the air—she walked gingerly over to the window. There, on the bare floor where the rug stopped, was the muddy trace of a shoeprint. Just one.

"It happened!" she exclaimed aloud. "It happened! I can't believe it! It really happened!

She flung on her nightgown, ran to the door, and looked down the hallway. More footprints—one clear shoeprint and one smudged mark, coming from the stairs. She ran to the top of the stairway—the prints came up the stairs too.

"It happened!" she shouted, racing down.

"What did?" Charlotte asked, appearing from the kitchen.

"I'll tell you in a minute—I just have to see . . ."

The footprints came in the front door. There were no prints going out. That didn't mean anything, though. Samuel could have carried the shoe when he left. She turned back to look at Charlotte, then for the first time wondered what she must look like. She reached up to feel her hair. It was pretty tangled.

"The strangest thing happened last night," she said. "Samuel . . . not your son, but Great-grandfather Henry's brother Samuel Robie came to my room in the middle of the night."

She couldn't tell Charlotte everything; she didn't really mind if she guessed, but she couldn't just come out and tell her grandmother she'd made love for the first time in her life with her own dead great-great-uncle. Charlotte didn't know he was her great-great-uncle, but that was hardly the point.

"He didn't know he was dead," Zoë said. "He's still living in the nineteenth century. He didn't believe me when I told him he'd drowned."

"I don't suppose I'd believe you either," Charlotte replied, as if Zoë had done something improper.

"You mean I shouldn't have said anything? But, Grandmother, he woke up by the *river*, and . . ."

"How do you know he was dead? He was there in the room with you, wasn't he? You conversed."

"Yes, I know, but . . ."

"Do you know I'm alive? Do you know that you are?"

"I guess I can't prove it, in any kind of philosophical way, but . . ."

"I'm no philosopher," Charlotte retorted.

Zoë looked at her grandmother, the most certain person on the face of the earth at that moment.

"But how can he be dead and also alive? It makes no sense."

"Why should it? But it happened, didn't it? I told you you might go backwards. Now it's happened."

"Yes, but who will ever believe me?"

"Why, no one." Charlotte seemed amused. "If they haven't had the same experience . . ."

"But don't you . . . I mean, didn't you ever feel lonely, knowing you were the only one who knew something? Didn't it ever make you wonder if you'd made it up?"

"What a strange idea."

"It is? I think most people would wonder that."

"Would they?"

"I don't know," Zoë said sadly. "I'm just so afraid that he'll never come back—if he's dead."

Charlotte laughed. "I shouldn't fret about that if I were you. If you told him he was dead and he thinks he isn't, he'll be back. You wait and see. Nothing draws a man like the suspicion that you know something he doesn't. He won't rest content until you tell him everything you know, and *then* he won't rest content until he thinks he's convinced you that you never knew any such thing. Come along. Come into the kitchen, dear. Since it was so brisk this morning, I've laid a fire. As soon as the oven warms up, I'll put in the popovers. The batter's setting."

"I'll be there in a minute. I want to get dressed first."

Back upstairs, Zoë sat on the edge of the bed, then—just for a minute—got back under the covers. With her eyes closed, she could bring back the feeling of lying next to Sam, of having had company while sleeping, something she'd never thought about before. She had imagined only up to sex, not what would come after, what it was like falling asleep with another person. She had been lying on her back and Sam on his side with his arm across her. It had started raining again, but quietly, falling as if the universe were expressing its relief, and she had fallen asleep thinking that.

When she was making the bed, she found Sam's shoe. It had been knocked underneath and was still damp, smudged with mud. She sat down and held it for a while. It certainly didn't look like a modern shoe. She took it downstairs and showed it triumphantly to Charlotte, but all Charlotte said was, "Boys are always tracking mud in." After breakfast, Zoë thought to ask Charlotte if there were a picture of Samuel anywhere.

"Don't you remember, dear? All of the family portraits are in the front parlor. There's one of Henry and Samuel taken just before Samuel drowned. I believe it's over the piano."

Although she'd seen Samuel's face clearly only in the moments when the lightning flashed, Zoë recognized him instantly in the daguerreotype—he looked exactly like it. Was it possible that she'd seen the portrait before and simply hallucinated him? But how could she have hallucinated the physical things? She still felt sore. And the shoe—how could you hallucinate a wet, old-fashioned shoe that would stay behind when the rest of your hallucination vanished? It was as if Samuel had left it on purpose to give her the courage to believe in what she knew.

Once it was August, Zoë began to worry about Charlotte—how could she keep not taking the pills once Mrs. Magoon was back? She couldn't hold them in her mouth and not swallow them all through breakfast, and it would be risky either hiding them in her pocket or getting up to dispose of them. Finally she had what seemed like a brilliant and foolproof idea.

She took one of the pills with her the next time she went to Hanover and looked for a nonprescription drug that matched, which Charlotte could take every day. It was even easier than she'd expected. A new kind of aspirin capsule looked almost exactly the same—unless you studied them closely, you couldn't tell the pills apart. There was no writing on either one. And it couldn't hurt Charlotte to take one aspirin every day, at least not as much as taking the other stuff had. Since the prescription would have to be refilled a couple of times before next summer, Zoë went to several different drugstores in different towns and bought a year's supply. She explained to Charlotte what she had to do, and they hid the aspirins in a trunk in the attic. Mrs. Magoon had never thought to lock up the medicine—and by now Charlotte was adept at impersonating the docile, out-to-lunch old lady she'd been before she stopped taking the drugs. She'd protested at first when Sunday came around and Zoë insisted they go to church; she couldn't believe it when Zoë told her that she hadn't missed a Sunday for years. But then she thought it was funny—everyone impressed by how devout she was. She said it made her wonder what drug the rest of them were taking.

XXXIV CASCABEL FLATS

Nick was not in the snakehouse—he couldn't have padlocked himself in—but Zoë was so surprised not to find him there that she pounded on the door anyway, a shout of "Nick! Nick!" swelling in her throat until she coughed. She must have caught some of Monica's panic; maybe Nick wasn't putting on an act after all. She imagined the snakes inside, curled up like a row of Slinkies, their tongues licking vibrations from the air. But then she saw the tracks that curved around the building and headed towards the gully and knew that Nick had gone to Stewart's to get hold of Rob's letter. Well, she could keep pace with him in disentangling things, if that was what he wanted.

By the time she stepped back through the kitchen door, she knew exactly what she was going to do. There were the preliminaries: telling Monica Nick had gone for a walk; Monica's replying, "At least that's healthier." She had to hurry—Ellie and Pryce might be back at any time.

There's something I've always been meaning to tell you . . . she began. SOMETHING ALWAYS I WANT TELL YOU.

She shaped the signs slowly and distinctly.

"I don't know," Monica said, smiling. "Do I really want to hear this?"

NOT WORRY. NOT BAD.

"I shudder to think . . ."

YOUR MOTHER AND FATHER NOT REALLY . . .

"Zoë, can't this wait? I don't know that now is the time . . ."

NOT BROTHER AND SISTER.

When she drew her cupped hand down her cheek, signifying sister, Monica began to shake her head. At first once, but when Zoë redid the shapes, Monica twirled her head over and over, as if the movement were her natural condition and she'd been restraining it for years. She stopped when she thought of something. "You read my father's letter! I *knew* I should have destroyed it."

But, Mother, if I hadn't . . . IF NOT . . . *Your father's father was*

Timothy Lowndes, not Henry Robie, she signed, spelling out the names.

"Timothy Lowndes? The lawyer? Zoë, what story is this you're concocting?"

Her mother's hands were knotting and unknotting in her lap.

It's the truth. Zoë kept repeating it. *Louisa told Charlotte the night before she hanged herself.*

Zoë was standing by the glass doors again; the blue mountains were capped with snow. Monica, who had been sitting on the couch, jumped up now and began to pace around the room. She circled the couch, then the dining room table, tracing a figure-eight, then recommenced. Every few turns she'd stop and stare at Zoë, and Zoë would tell her something else. That it was Charlotte who'd told her these things that last summer before she died. "Oh, well, then . . ." Monica shrugged, resuming her pacing. Zoë reminded her that Charlotte's mind had been clear at that point. "That may be, but I never knew her that way," Monica replied. Zoë explained Charlotte's reason for never having told Adam—being a Robie meant so much to him; Monica retorted, "That's all very well, but one doesn't preserve one's husband's pride at the expense of his feeling depraved all his life."

It wasn't her fault! He never told her he thought she was Henry's daughter—he thought she already knew.

"How could she not know?"

She believed what her mother told her, that she didn't have a father.

"Well, that was a mistake."

I guess so.

Zoë could have reminded her mother that *she* had never bothered to ask Charlotte about it, never given her mother the chance to contradict Adam's story, but then she had kept to herself this fact that might have liberated Monica. She felt very patient with her mother now. When you'd spent thirty years thinking one thing and then someone came along and told you it wasn't true . . . It was how she'd feel if someone told her she wasn't responsible for Rob's being imprisoned in a mental hospital. What were you supposed to do? Turn around and say, "Oh, I'm not? Oh, well, so much for the last ten years then."

Monica might refuse to believe it now, but after a while it would seep into all her memories, altering them, and she'd see how many decisions she'd based on thinking something that wasn't true. Like marrying Seth—as if she'd had to perpetuate the hidden error handed down until she'd understood it. Now that she was free, would Monica pick up her pre-Seth self like a dropped stitch? So strange again to think that she and Nick wouldn't exist if it hadn't been for their mother's having acted on false information; after learning how unhappy her father had been when it was too late to help him, the only thing Monica could think of to do had been to be miserable herself. An amazing fallacy—but what was there to replace it?

Yet things were changing now, the error was coming undone, and still Zoë and Nick would be there, having sneaked into life. Didn't that give them a certain leeway?

Then Monica, trailing her hand the length of the dining room table like a child along a fence, softly said an amazing thing.

"I always wondered why Timothy Lowndes made me his heir."

WHAT? Zoë began to walk around too. She took the same route as Monica but in the opposite direction. They gave each other a peculiar look—the same peculiar look—each time they passed.

"I never mentioned it to anyone. I gave the money to a charity in his name. That poor man. I can see now that he tried to tell me. Poor old soul. I never gave him a chance."

WHEN?

They kept each other in sight as they circled the room. Monica's ability to understand sign language was improving by the minute.

"After my father died he came to see me. He had to bring me the letter. The poor soul must have known what it contained—he must have longed to tell me the truth."

So why didn't he?

"Poor thing," Monica said again. "Afraid, no doubt. As we're all afraid." She smiled fleetingly at Zoë. "We're all just so afraid—isn't it extraordinary? Why is it that we're created unable to face what we need to face?"

They had almost run into each other in the middle of the rug, and suddenly they both glimpsed what they looked like: as if they were playing a demented kind of musical chairs, with no music and too many seats even to pretend there was a shortage. They stood there on the rug, staring at each other, and then began to laugh. It was an incredible experience, to be laughing like that with her mother; whenever one of them stopped laughing, the other said something that set them off again. Zoë couldn't even remember her mother the way she'd been before.

"It's completely useless information you've provided me with, dear, I hope you appreciate that. What do you expect me to do? Dig up the Harmony graveyard and put everyone in their proper places?"

You could change your name to Monica Lowndes.

"Thank you, Zoë, that's very helpful."

Exhausted, they flung themselves on the couch and sat in a lovely, peaceful silence, looking out at the magical mountains, which gazed back calmly, surprised by nothing.

Around three, Pryce and Ellie bustled in, victorious with packages—the crowds were unbelievable; it was as if people were preparing for a siege instead of a holiday. Neither he nor Ellie had any idea that while they'd been gone Monica and Seth had been divorced and married other people; she and Nick had acquired a whole brigade of siblings . . . Monica was still tipsy from Zoë's news, and fell right in with Pryce and Ellie's hyped-up mood. In the kitchen Ellie unwrapped the roast to show Monica as if she were displaying a newborn baby—it was a real rib roast, not rump, which she'd thought she'd have to settle for, and Monica exclaimed, "It's simply the most beautiful roast I've ever seen! Don't you agree, Zoë?"

Beyond a shadow of a doubt.

"Where's Nick?" Ellie asked, looking back and forth between the two of them.

"He went for a walk."

He went to Stewart's.

"Aren't you both dying to hear about the chest?" Pryce interrupted.

"What chest?"

What chest?

"What chest! The one Ellie ordered from this ersatz cabinetmaker who's been the chief topic of our conversation for days!"

"Ignacio Ortega . . ."

He has been?

"Do you want to tell them or shall I?" Pryce asked.

"He's gone out of business!" Ellie shouted. "There was a sign on the door. "Shop Closed for Good.' That's what it said, word for word. 'For Good!' " She looked at Pryce, who held up his right hand.

"As God is my witness."

"Isn't that the most outrageous thing you've ever heard? Nothing else—not where to contact him, or anything about anyone taking over his business, or how we can get our deposits back . . ."

Suddenly Monica caught Zoë's eye and before they knew it they'd burst into uncontrollable laughter. What *had* happened to him? Zoë wondered. Had he ever even existed? He hadn't been at Stewart's party last night, either.

"Are you two drunk?" demanded Ellie.

"I admit I've been wondering the same thing," Pryce said.

"Not on any known inebriating substance," Monica said, smiling at Zoë.

"I'm beginning to feel as if we've stumbled into the Twilight Zone, aren't you, Pryce? Why did Nick go to Stewart's?"

I left something there, Zoë said.

"Last night?" Ellie asked, then looked uncomfortable.

Yesterday afternoon.

Everyone took the cue not to pursue the question. Ellie put away the groceries; then they all retreated to the living room and began "planning operations" for that evening. They'd just reached an unbreachable impasse in scheduling when Nancy Chamberlain rang up to let them know that they were welcome to camp out at her father's house if they had time to kill before church and didn't want to drive all the way back home. "What serendipity!" Ellie exclaimed. "The name of the day," Monica said. So that was settled.

Since there was really nothing to do for a couple of hours—the broth for the oyster stew took five minutes, and it was a little early to put the lamb in yet—Ellie proposed a game of Scrabble, which Pryce pronounced a "capital" idea. They were all talking like that, as if they were guests at an English manor house, making an occasion out of every occasion. Zoë wouldn't have been surprised if one of them had come out with "jolly good" or "bloody marvellous." Pryce "brewed up" some hot buttered rum and Ellie "brought forth" cheese and crackers and some slices of fruitcake. Zoë had plenty of time to think while she waited for the others to take their turns; it was clear now that it was Seth who had given Rob Nick's address. Rob had already written the letter when he went to visit Seth. Rob's visit had provoked Seth into asking Monica for a divorce and proposing to Lucy Chang Smith.

I want to know where Zoë is, Rob told Seth. Or maybe, since Seth might consider this pushy, Could you please tell me where Zoë is, Mr. Carver? Or, May I have your daughter's address, please? I assure you I wish her no harm. I can sympathize with your reluctance given the circumstances under which you last knew of me . . . Yes, certainly, if you prefer, I can leave you my telephone number and address, and she can contact me at her leisure . . . I beg your pardon, do I know Morse Code? She what? Zoë *what*?

Seth repeated it.

No, I'm afraid I didn't know.

Rob's voice trembled but he kept on bravely.

No. No one told me. No one told me *anything* in the hospital. They tried to get me to tell *them* things. Excuse me, I didn't intend to ramble on. I expect your information has come as somewhat of a shock . . . Would I care to what? Well, yes, that would be convenient. Excuse me, I meant I would appreciate the opportunity. I'm afraid I am somewhat out of the habit of engaging in conversation with intelligent human beings.

I'm familiar with the condition, Seth said. May I offer you a drink, Robert?

Yes, thank you, Mr. Carver. That would be very ingenious—I mean generous. You will have to excuse me. Since the shock treatments I appear to have a certain amount of difficulty with my adjectives.

Zoë had to keep herself from laughing aloud at this.

Seth had laughed too. Let me pour you a stiff Scotch—that will sort out the modifiers.

Rob looked pretty much the same. Maybe a little more solid, and he had a new nervous habit, tapped the fingers of both hands soundlessly on his knees even though he was aware of doing it and tried to stop himself.

Seth said, Unless I'm mistaken, you and I have never actually met.

Not officially, though I believe you saw me making a fool of myself in a school play called *The End of Slavery.* That was how I first came to know your daughter.

Actually he barely remembered this girl, Zoë Carver, though he knew everything went back to her somehow. Now her father told him that at the time he'd been sent to the hospital she had been stricken dumb. He tried to recall clearly the last occasion on which he had seen her, but couldn't. Had it been at the bakery?

Does she ever talk about me? he asked her father.

He thought that her father had a kind face; he looked sad, though. Rob couldn't remember anything specific that Zoë had said about him, though he did remember that she had always been trying to figure out why her parents were unhappy. He had spent a lot of time with her. He did have memories, but they were like single frames in a film with the sound turned off. That was interesting, he thought; she couldn't speak and in his memory the sound had been turned off.

Do you have any pictures of her? he asked.

Seth nodded and brought his photograph albums from the bedroom. Monica had made copies for him of every family picture they had ever taken—which was all, besides the contents of his study, that he'd removed from the Metcalf Street house. He opened the album to pictures of Zoë with Charlotte that Buell Magoon had taken that last summer Charlotte was alive. She and Charlotte were sitting together on the porch swing; she was wearing cut-offs and a T-shirt and Charlotte was wearing a blue-and-white-striped shirtwaist dress with little, darker blue flowers between the stripes. As usual Charlotte looked dainty and beautiful and she looked like a slob.

Rob felt a shock as he looked at her face. He recognized her, yet he still could not remember any experience of her. It seemed especially strange because she had a face you would never forget once you'd seen it—it took him a minute to describe it to himself, but then he had it—it looked as if other people had used it before her. It wasn't that she looked old; she looked as if she'd been other people before she'd become who she was now. Then he remembered having said that to her, one fall evening when they'd gone for a walk—she had been away somewhere for the summer, maybe visiting the pretty old lady in the photographs who Mr. Carver said was her grandmother. Rob felt that he had once known something about a grandmother of Zoë's, but he didn't recall any details.

In the photographs she was smiling mischievously—in some looking at her grandmother, in others at whoever had been taking the pictures. She looked very happy—not the way she'd looked in the other photographs, but it was better not to think about them, not until he had his chance to ask her what had really gone on between her and the photographer, and why she had shown him the pictures. Though not *shown* him—left on the coffee table (as if they weren't important) so that she wasn't even there when he noticed them. If only she'd stayed, if only he'd waited to ask if his assumption were correct (though what else could he assume?); if only . . . it was the longest *if* he allowed himself anymore, because it was the only *if* whose corollary he thought there was any hope of altering, but now he put it out of his mind; he studied the pictures of Zoë smiling, smiling and happy, though she also seemed to be listening, as if she were expecting someone to call her from inside the house.

He remembered her voice then. It had been kind of quavery—lively yet struggling not to be overwhelmed, like someone out in the surf having to leap up not to be swallowed by the next wave. You could maybe want to float, to drift off on her voice—if only she hadn't been on her guard, always anticipating the possibility of being drowned.

The pictures had been taken not long after Samuel came back, and Zoë remembered imagining, as she smiled at Buell, that when the photographs were developed Samuel would be in them; she had still felt his presence so clearly.

Trying to recall whether or not he'd found her attractive (he must have—why else would he have been such a wreck when he saw the photographs she'd posed for?), Rob retrieved an image he could tell by its solidity had been missing for years: he, maybe eleven, dressed in a suit, and two girls in spring dresses, standing around a table. He on one side, one girl across from him, the other at the head. Scissors, he said. *Scissors*?

one of the girls exclaimed, laughing. You're going to amputate someone's leg with *scissors*?

He had no idea what they'd been doing, but he knew who had said that. There was no mistaking that tone of completely delighted disbelief. You could live in absolute and total safety with someone who talked to you like that. It wasn't impossible that Zoë had been his girlfriend, though somehow he didn't think so. There had been some reason they hadn't acted on their attraction, though what it had been he could not imagine. He felt uncomfortable asking Zoë's father if he knew how his daughter had felt about him. So he said, I don't want to bother her if she's forgotten all about me.

Bother her, Seth said, in the imperative.

He had told the judge that he'd "done it" for her sake; he didn't remember saying that but he had many times heard his nauseating tape-recorded voice stating it. He had also said other things: he had been put on earth to "avenge the death of Christ," to "get even with all fathers on behalf of all sons . . ." He wondered if Zoë knew that part of it. Would he have talked to her about it? He wondered if he had made up that whole story so that he wouldn't have to talk about the photographs. In what order had things occurred? Was there a story that all religion was made up to obscure? Much as it sickened him to think of the photographs, they were the one thing he had told neither the lawyer, the judge, nor the hordes of doctors about, and, as a result, they remained his one lucid memory. Even though he'd looked at them only briefly before he'd burned them—set fire to them in the woods off Stark Road near where the bus let him off, before he went to his fateful meeting with his father—he could still see them as clearly as if he'd studied each one for years on end, though he didn't remember them as of *Zoë*; that was partly what had been so horrible: this person he knew and loved (he must have loved her) had been capable of *looking* like that. The face in those photographs bore no resemblance to the impishly smiling girl in the snapshots. There must be some kinds of emotional states, he thought, in which one recorded far more than one was conscious of experiencing at the time, because he could recall every detail of every photograph at will: the ecstasy on her face as she leaned back against the chair with her eyes closed, her hand, fallen languidly over the arm, holding an apple out of which a noticeable bite had been taken; some twisted, thoughtless symbolism to the picture; the others intended perhaps to derive from it—the ones in which she looked up beseechingly, begging, he could tell, not for mercy. It was better not to think about it.

In the hospital, after several years of tremendous frustration on both sides—he wouldn't recant and they couldn't seem to find a diagnosis of his "illness" that satisfied them, which, of course he told them, was because he wasn't ill—after a couple of years he'd come up with the brilliant idea of staging more outbreaks which they would be able to construe as similar to the "outbreak" during which he'd killed his father. First he'd attacked a nurse, careful to do it when there were orderlies around, since she wasn't very strong and he could have done her some real damage; it was a lucky coincidence that her name happened to be Mary—he told them she deserved to die for not having fought back on behalf of her son, and they got all kinds of mileage out of that. This was their cue to begin trying a whole pharmacy of drugs on him, which was the worst part of the whole thing; he couldn't think, and he was afraid he might tell them something he didn't want to; that was when his memory started to go bad. Yet he had always managed to keep the memory of the photographs separate; he took pride in having been able to do that, under the circumstances. What the photographs had to do with was between him and Zoë, if he ever saw her again, or between him and whomever had taken them. He had never been able even to guess at who it could have been—which had made it a hundred times more strange. They had been so close; how could she have been living an entire life he knew nothing about?

Fortunately he'd had just enough presence of mind, except when given the heaviest doses, to act after a while in ways that convinced the doctors that the drugs were having no effect. (So he'd imagined; he realized now that in fact they hadn't had much of one.) He stalked around the patients' common room whispering to the other zombies whatever he could remember from *The Antichrist* or *Thus Spake Zarathustra*—he was sure it would get back. He knew no one had read the books there and would think he was making up the lines. Every now and then he'd have to attack someone—he tried to stick with men he knew were fathers and saintly-looking women—that was how he'd become involved with Margaret. He had tried to strangle her during Crafts—he remembered very clearly that she had been making a potholder—one of those clumsy-looking ones you made with rings of material on a frame, the kind every kid had to make in kindergarten and every parent had to keep forever because they never fell apart. He hadn't attacked anyone for almost a year, he knew that, although he couldn't remember his reasoning for starting again—had he still been trying to convince them he was mentally ill? His plan: if they could pin a diagnosis on him and then think they'd medicated him out of it they'd let him out—though he hardly knew anymore why he wanted to get out. He was so used to thinking he wanted to that the thinking it had become sufficient in itself.

They let him read—not philosophy or religion now, but everything else. He took some correspondence courses in biology and physics—as much as was possible without a lab. If he ever got out of the hospital he might go to medical school. Specialize in amputations. No, not really, he told Margaret, who was always asking him, Are you serious? Do you mean it, Rob? Tell me the truth. And, if he already hadn't wanted to leave, meeting Margaret made him want to even less. Although it wasn't as simple as that.

He had waited, as usual, until there were orderlies nearby, and when they pulled him off her he'd made sure to stay violent enough so that they'd have to put him in solitary. Predictable as weather, they changed his medication. Margaret had been a new patient, brought in after a suicide attempt, and he hadn't been sure that she'd be there when he came back, but she was. Through ward gossip he learned that she'd tried to kill herself twice more since being admitted. Now the attendants watched her excruciatingly closely. Though they went on high alert when he first approached her, they didn't hear her say in a low voice, "I need to talk to you alone." It took almost a month before they were able to manage it. During that time, to throw off suspicion, they sat together at the group table, placidly making potholders, enough to hold on to every hot handle they might encounter for the rest of time, exclaiming over each other's choice of color. This was how they communicated—Do you have any more of that blue? I just love that yellow next to that red. But finally the day came when they sat in lounge chairs in a secluded part of the common room and no one bothered them. No doubt the prevailing medical opinion had been that their becoming friendly was a "healing experience" for both of them. Well, it was, though not in the way the doctors meant.

The first time they could really talk, Margaret said, I know you were faking that day you tried to strangle me. Why did you? Don't try to deny it.

All right, I won't.

What did you do it for? Don't you want to get out of here?

The only way I'll ever get out of here is if I convince them I'm really crazy so that they can then be convinced I'm cured.

I know you're in here for saying you killed your father—why did you lie?

He didn't ask her how she knew his background. There were plenty of awake-enough people who could have told her. It was a private mental hospital, so they tended to get your better quality of mental patient—

people not with boring, repetitive illnesses like banging their heads against the wall, but people with spasmodic, unclear maladies that kept the doctors intrigued. His father must have had a whopping insurance policy for his mother to have been able to maintain him there.

How can I be lying? He's dead.

You know there's no logic in that statement.

He had to laugh—it was the first time he remembered really laughing in the more than six years he'd been in there. Margaret reminded him of Zoë, the way Zoë's gleeful skepticism about everything had felt like a breakwater.

I just wish you'd succeeded, Margaret said, so I wouldn't have to do it myself. You've given me an idea, though. If I can stop making suicide attempts long enough to get out of here, I'll put myself in situations where I'll be likely to be murdered. It makes more sense that way, anyway.

Why?

That way I'd be being punished.

Why do you need to be punished?

Because I'm no good. I never have been. I just didn't think there was anything I could do about it until recently.

She spoke flatly, sounding almost bored.

What did you do?

Every time I read something about torture, I know I could have done that.

But, Margaret, being able to imagine something isn't the same as doing it.

Look who's talking, she said.

He was twenty-three or -four by then. She was a couple of years younger, very smart. Possibly brilliant, though who could tell in that environment. She was fluent in several languages. Her father had worked for some multinational corporation and she'd lived all over the place. She had always planned to train as an interpreter, until she'd realized she didn't have long to live. She didn't want to waste her parents' money.

Margaret was the first person he ever went to bed with. He didn't think he was her first, but it was none of his business if she didn't want to tell him. It hadn't been easy, finding a place, but it hadn't been impossible; he'd later decided that the attendants must have known and, directed by the doctors, looked the other way. For one thing, Margaret took birth control pills, and when she'd been in for a few months and had to renew the prescription no one made a fuss about it. Probably watched us on closed-circuit television, Rob thought.

Whether or not he was the first person Margaret had slept with, he was the only person she'd ever loved—she told him so and he believed her. She asked him if he loved her too, and he told her yes, he did, and it was true, but later he felt so sad that she'd always had to ask him. He didn't know why it had never occurred to him to tell her; it just hadn't. She asked him if he'd ever been in love with anyone else—he could tell it was important to her to think they were both doing something for the first time, and he said, "I don't think so," which was true, but which he would always regret having said.

Margaret spent about two and a half of the three years they were involved in the hospital. During the months when she was briefly out, she lived with her mother (her parents had been divorced not long after her first suicide attempt) but visited Rob every week—her home was sixty miles away. He had hated these visits, because she spent every single minute of them trying to persuade him to agree that he'd leave; he could convince the doctors that he was in good enough shape to leave any time he wanted.

Why are you doing this? she asked him, over and over.

Doing what? he replied.

Pretending like this!

Then one day a doctor sent for Rob and told him that Margaret had made an attempt on her life that had succeeded. That was exactly how they'd put it—it had taken Rob a moment to convert the statement's affirmative phrasing into its brutal sense. He looked at the doctor and then turned away, refusing to ask how she'd done it. Eventually he heard it on the grapevine: she'd hitchhiked until someone finally obliged by raping and then strangling her. Rob had made himself listen to the sickening details; it was the only punishment available at the moment, and he knew how arrogant and presumptuous it had been for him to consider anything he'd gone through before that to be punishment. He had *flattered* himself into thinking that he deserved to be punished, whereas Margaret had really *believed* it; she hadn't made a big song-and-dance about it; she'd tried and tried until finally she'd succeeded. He saw that if he were not to insult Margaret's memory he would have to leave the hospital.

Ironically the horrible depression that descended on him after Margaret's death helped to convince the doctors that he was "getting better." "Do you feel you could have prevented it?" they asked him. "Yes," he said. They thought that a paramount sign of health. He didn't add what he was thinking—"by admitting to her that I was sane." For the first time since he'd been in the hospital he felt how he was wasting his life. During his last two years, he finished up as much of a pre-medical degree as he could with limited lab experience. A dean from the college that administered the program came to see him and asked him so intelligently why he was in the hospital that he shrugged and said, "Habit." The dean offered him a job teaching introductory science courses when he got out. Meanwhile he had affairs with a couple of ward nurses. He felt nothing like what he'd felt for Margaret—how could he?—or for Zoë, although she was more of an icon to him by now than a real person, but he liked them and they helped him to recover from Margaret's death. One of them got fired because of it, but wrote him letters until he got out; after he'd taken care of the things he had to in Sparta, he thought he might go see her. Maybe. He wanted to see Zoë before he did anything else.

Rob looked at the album all the way back to when she had been in kindergarten. Seth came to sit on the couch to look at it with him. He identified everyone for Rob.

That's Zoë and Bridget on their donkeys in Mexico. Seth laughed. Don't they look invincible?

Then he closed his eyes and shook his head, trying to banish a different memory. He opened his eyes and looked at Rob. How could it have happened to her? I thought I'd warned her about life—what did I forget to tell her?

You didn't spend ten years in a mental hospital to get embarrassed when someone you hardly knew cried in your presence.

Don't blame yourself, Rob said. Parents always hide something—it's an instinct. All kids have to go looking for evil on their own.

Seth went into the bathroom. When he came out he said, Do you remember anything about that time, Robert? If you don't mind my asking.

Very little. I'm not even sure that what I do remember I actually remember or only think I do because I've been told so many times that it happened.

I think Zoë remembered everything for you, Seth said.

Rob nodded. That's why she can't talk, isn't it? At least partly. She got stuck with my feelings.

Take them back, Seth said, and he gave Rob Nick's address and phone number. Call—or write and then call. She'll be out there for ten days starting the twenty-second.

XXXV (CASCABEL FLATS) CASCABEL FLATS

Even if she'd *died*, Stewart thought later, scornfully, she'd have doubted he killed her. Did he intend what happened? Did he pretend to destroy her to shock her into speech or did he want to end her life? But why would he want to do that? Because she recognized him for what he was? Yet she wouldn't believe what she knew; she goaded and goaded him until he'd wanted to prove it to her. Yet the truth was he'd simply obliged her—he was an agreeable fellow. That his actions might be judged otherwise interested him only in that he knew people would always find other explanations for what he did than the true ones. They were too weak to believe in him. Everyone looked for him, trying to surprise him into revealing himself, yet when he complied they refused to believe that he existed: a willing force, incarnate, incontrovertible. It amused Stewart to see how people clung to the hope of redemption and yet rejected the logical conclusion: if redemption failed, someone had to be written into the program to carry out the necessary destruction.

When you loved a person, you would not abandon that person to die alone, would you? You'd do whatever you could to make the death as easy as possible. To think of a stranger holding that person's hand as he gasped for the last air he would ever breathe—you would never forgive yourself. Stewart would not have allowed a wounded animal to suffer; equally how could he stand by while others destroyed the place he had been born to, whose guardian he was, and without which he was nothing? If it had to die, he would hasten its death throes. Maybe someday, before the world died, people would recognize their conceit in thinking they did not domesticate rattlesnakes at their peril. How amusing that people assessed his motive as greed, as anger, as revenge—*motive* was such a modern invention, wasn't it? People inventing motives the way they reinvented the land, believing it cared for them when they did not care for it. For so long he had watched, waited and watched as *strangers* claimed title to the land, *his* land, prettied the wildness in it, bought and sold it, never seeing the fallacy. Wildness tamed would turn against them. But when he used their methods, played their game, they complained that the game was unfair.

The explanations people devised for his refusal to hand over his father's paintings testified to their capacity for invention: he wished to deny his father the renown that should rightly be his; he feared that the paintings' poor quality would relegate his father once and for all to the ranks of the amateurs; he entertained himself by defacing them, one at a time. Irene's claim that Jules had been embarked upon "great work" had convinced those who wished to believe, even though by her own admission she had never seen the paintings. People subscribed to the notion of Jules's mysterious inspiration, a subsidiary annunciation, a dilettante chosen as the instrument of glory. The idea that a unique talent had been harbored among them, disguised as a bibulous eccentric, pleased them, yet if they had known what his father's paintings revealed, would they have been so eager to look upon them? The truth the paintings bore witness to was not a truth people wanted to know: that any creator could endure loneliness only so long before he began to resent those he had fathered when they did not, as he had expected they would, relieve him of his loneliness.

Yet people said it was *Stewart* who sought revenge for his father's abandonment of him after his mother's death; this explanation annoyed Stewart the most. He felt no *personal* animosity towards his father—why could people not understand that? His purpose on earth was not individual, it was representative; as such he was not free to consider his own emotions—was that so difficult to comprehend?

Stewart concealed his father's paintings for one reason only: he was afraid that if what they recorded were to become public knowledge, people might reexamine the circumstances of his father's death. Someone would recognize Ignacio and ponder the fact that Jules had used him for a model; then someone would observe the nail through Ignacio's one foot and speculate upon Jules's lapse from tradition . . . Stewart did not fear human "justice," simply an untimely investigation into his father's death; it would interfere with the completion of his task. "You'll be repaid," he'd said to her, the sister of the credulous "rattlesnake farmer" to whom he had sold his father's studio; "I'll give you something," though when he had promised this he hadn't known what it would require of him—what she would require of him; how violent would have to be his insistence that he existed before she believed it—if she believed it even then.

After all these years, Stewart remained puzzled upon one point only: why Ignacio had never identified his torturer. That Ignacio knew who had pounded the nail through his foot Stewart had no doubt, yet Ignacio had never accused Jules, at least not publicly. He could have brought charges against him and yet he'd done nothing; why? Had he not wished it to be discovered that he'd invited an outsider to observe the procession? Had he *asked* Jules to help him move beyond simulation to identification, knowing that he could not ask that of his "brothers"? Had he decided Jules's treachery to be an appropriate punishment for the presumption of impersonating his Lord? Or had Ignacio spared Jules in order to spare Stewart the discomfort of seeing his father officially accused? Stewart also had never doubted that Ignacio knew that Jules had taken his son to watch the crucifixion of the one person he respected and loved. This certainty eventually led Stewart to wonder if Ignacio had done nothing because he had known that one day Stewart would avenge his wrong for him.

The coroner's verdict had been accurate as far as it went: accidental death by rattlesnake bite, possible suicide. Immediate cause of death: suffocation. But the whole story was to be found in the paintings (Stewart had not shown them all to Nick Carver's sister): the boy struggling to escape his father's grip; another in which the boy stretched his arms beseechingly towards the cross while his father attempted to drag him away—all excellent likenesses of Stewart at age eleven; he had been surprised to discover that his father was such an accomplished portraitist. His father's paintings, exhibited, would not only have endowed Stewart with a motive for revenge in people's minds, they might have untied the knot that bound everyone to their native hope that everything would be better, by and by, and this would not do, not just yet; his disguise depended upon the persistence of this hope.

Stewart remembered well his father's remark: "Don't cry, Stewart . . . It's the supreme honor of the brotherhood. You aren't looking at the thing in the right light. I was helping out . . ." He'd meant, So Ignacio wants the honor of feeling what Christ felt? Then let him feel it—everything: the horror, the protest, the writhing certainty of betrayal; all you've lived for washed from your mind like a dream you can never remember; the recognition, too late, that sacrifice never propitiates gods but merely whets their appetite. Maybe Jules had envied Ignacio his faith: his capacity to tolerate suffering as a part of the natural order of things. Neither the father nor the son possessed this capacity. Or Jules's motivation could have been as utilitarian as this: he needed to do something so violent in order to be able to paint again. And this was where his son would have come in: nothing of what he did would have been so horrible had it not been witnessed through a child's eyes, had the image to which people were hardened by familiarity not been brought to life again by a child's looking at it. If it was true that he had died also when he lost the child's mother—how could he feel again unless the child felt? Unless the child suffered?

Stewart remembered the drive back that night as an experience of absolute certainty: someday he would balance out what had been done to Ignacio. That was exactly how he thought of it—it was a question of equilibrium, not revenge. Only thus could he cure himself of the pity he felt for Ignacio—a pity that threatened to expand and engulf him, extending itself to everyone, to people he had never seen or dreamed of. Stewart knew what happened to people who let themselves feel pity like that. Yet he said to himself that it was not because he could not bear to feel the pity that he avoided it; it was because it would have interfered with what he had to do.

Though Stewart waited several years before he acted, it was not because he deliberated but because he could not conceive of a practical way to carry out his plan without casting suspicion upon himself. The fall after his trip into the mountains with Jules he had been sent away to boarding school; he was in the seventh grade. It wasn't until two years later, the summer before he began high school, that he finally came up with a workable idea.

His father, after Ignacio left the ranch, had hired a new foreman named Chandler; he was perhaps twenty-five at the most, and Stewart became friends with him. Chandler hunted rattlesnakes—he liked to see how many he could find and catch in a day, but he rarely killed them. When he did it was to use the skin for a hat band or the rattles for a necklace or a charm, not out of the lustful cruelty that led "hunters" to slaughter somnolent dens-full for sport. Chandler was fascinated by Jules's stories about his rattlesnakes—how he'd catch a few each year when they exited the den under his studio, bring them inside and let them go, making a game out of knowing where they were hidden, never disturbing them there. It would be a saner world, Jules liked to proclaim, if everyone kept a rattlesnake or two in their houses and learned to respect them. He fed his and claimed that it never took more than a couple of months before they trusted him enough to let him pick them up. This last Stewart was not sure he believed, but he did know that his father always kept at least three or four big diamondbacks, and once Chandler had taught Stewart to spot and catch rattlers, it didn't take him long to devise a plan that would turn Jules's vain boastfulness against him.

Every afternoon around three, Jules drove into town; he circulated among his favorite bars until they closed. Though he locked his studio, he kept a key at the ranch house, so it was easy enough for Stewart to ride over there one day, tether his horse in the arroyo, and go in. That first day he meant only to verify the number and size of snakes Jules kept, but in the process of searching the premises Stewart discovered a trunk beneath the bed. He slid it out—it wasn't heavy, but was locked; whatever the trunk contained had to be important if his father kept it locked in his own house, and Stewart considered forcing the lock but then decided he'd take the trunk with him next time. Whatever it held, he didn't want to leave for other people to find afterwards.

During his search he counted two large diamondbacks and four or five smaller ones. He wasn't concerned about replacing the exact number, but if his father had had no large snakes, for instance, drunk though he would be upon arriving home, he might have been alerted.

Stewart had timed everything more perfectly than he knew; the fateful cooperation of events affirmed his belief that he was merely acting according to plan. On Tuesday Chandler announced that the rest of the week he and the other hands would be riding fence. That gave Stewart three days of privacy in which to find the snakes he needed. Chandler had shown him the best places to hunt, and early Tuesday morning Stewart set out, before the day heated up and drove the rattlesnakes into hiding; he counted twenty-five before he rode home. Wednesday he retraced his steps and counted as many. To be safe, he caught them on Thursday, depositing them in the duffel bag he took his clothes to school in, in which he had cut a number of tiny airholes. He stored the bag of snakes overnight in one of the hacienda's unused rooms. At three-thirty the next afternoon, he saddled his own horse and another, which happened to have been left in the barn only because he'd been too lame to ride fence (though Stewart knew this was not happenstance). Besides the snakes, Stewart carried with him a long coil of rope, with which he intended somehow to fasten the trunk to the second horse's saddle. Again he tethered the horses in the arroyo; after making sure that his father's truck was gone, he entered the studio.

Whether or not it were true that his father had tamed them, Jules's snakes were easy to catch. Stewart used a pillowcase to carry them outside. When he let them go they seemed disoriented, but with persuasion and their eagerness to escape the midafternoon heat they soon disappeared. Next Stewart went to fetch the trunk. As he lifted it by its handle to carry it outside, the top fell open and tightly rolled canvases tumbled out; this startled Stewart so much that he cried out—he was certain that his father must be somewhere in the studio, observing his every move, having anticipated his deadly plan. Yet Stewart investigated both rooms thoroughly, concocting an explanation for his presence as he did so, and found no one. Returning to the trunk, he unrolled only three or four of the canvases before recognizing what his father had recorded on them. If his resolve had required strengthening, seeing the paintings would have strengthened it.

Instead, now, of attempting to transport the trunk, he emptied it and carried the canvases outside, replacing the trunk beneath the bed. He would be able to fit most of them into the duffel bag by rolling them around each other. He would have preferred to confine the wild snakes to the bedroom, where he could be sure that his father would encounter them, but there were no doors between the rooms, so he simply released the snakes and left the studio. Then he rode home. Abetting his purpose, the sky was clouding up, preparing for a summer thundershower; the water would obliterate the hoofprints and remove the last opportunity for anyone to suspect foul play. Jules's death could seem only the result of his own drunken stupidity, inevitable sooner or later. Not long after Stewart had arrived home, squared the horses away, and hidden the canvases in the back of a closet, the rain broke. He sat in the kitchen, admiring the wrathful hailstones pelting the courtyard; never had he felt so serene.

Chandler came home around six, eager to head into town to see a movie; Stewart enjoyed the film; he did not think about his father, did not worry about what would happen if his plan didn't work—if it didn't he would simply think of something else. He watched James Bond conquering evil, and afterwards accompanied Chandler to his favorite pool hall and shot a dozen games of eight-ball. They were both in bed by midnight; Stewart fell asleep at once.

It was Irene who discovered his father's body. Jules lay sprawled across the seat of his truck—on his way to seek help, it was surmised. He had received a large bite on the neck, and the swelling had constricted his windpipe and suffocated him.

A will was found, duly executed, and was filed at the courthouse. Everything was left to Stewart, with the exception of Jules's paintings, which, should he "not have destroyed them," were bequeathed to the local museum. Except for Irene's insistence to the contrary, everyone would have assumed that he had.

Stewart did not return to boarding school; in fact, he had never left home since. At his request Ignacio and Rosario moved back to the ranch and stayed until his marriage; Stewart would not have said that he was happy, but he wasn't unhappy either. He learned to assume his various roles as husband, entrepreneur, and member of the "old guard"; he watched his legend grow. This new companion entertained him—this millionaire descended from a sinning priest, married to his "childhood sweetheart"; if Stewart repudiated this rival, his denial merely contributed a new quality to the imposter's gallery of characteristics: he was "eccentric," "a recluse," "up to something." It was during this interval that he remodelled the kitchen and found the first Jules Beauregard's letter, and understood that the part he played was only the latest in a continuing pageant of revenge—sons against fathers, fathers against sons; he waited for the next act to be announced.

When Stewart met Nick Carver on the anniversary of Jules's death, though he knew at once that this newcomer would be cast in a supporting role in the next episode, he didn't immediately know what this was. One day Nick recounted his fruitless hunt for an affordable house, and that was when Stewart spied what came next: he'd sell the Carvers the studio; he knew there'd been a reason he'd refused to sell it before. Already he saw them living there; Nick's wife found it incredible that he should have forgotten that the studio had been built over a rattlesnake den; but why should he have remembered? He needed to remember only one thing: he existed because he existed; he could not be explained by reference to any other person or any event.

He had enjoyed Nick's companionship for a while, until Nick's innocence began to annoy him—did Nick really think it was possible to farm rattlesnakes and not expect to be bitten?—but his annoyance was nothing to the scorn he felt for Nick's wife, because she had the sense to suspect him yet prided herself on being able to parry whatever treacheries he might direct her way. He despised her, but not knowing what came next, he endured the identity she assigned him: the bored husband, the husband for whom, though he loved his wife, something was missing . . . It was ludicrous how far she was from understanding him. Nevertheless he let her think he sympathized with her, that he shared her wish to have a child, when in fact he and Judith had settled long ago that they would not reproduce; though this decision contradicted his wife's deepest instinct, she so believed in him that she agreed that this was no world into which to bring a child.

Stewart bore it as long as he could, and then after recoiling from Nick's wife's touch so instinctively he worried that his revulsion had superseded every other instinct. Perhaps he should have forced himself to follow where she wanted to go; he still could form no clear picture of what was to happen next. In fact, this was the only truly anxious period of Stewart's life—the interval between walking out on Nick's wife and in to encounter his sister; it was the only time he had fallen into the common lot of worrying that he might have misread the signals, that he might not have been following a destiny laid out for him but instead have succumbed to the illusion that he was. He subjected the impulse that directed him to innumerable painful questions; he searched everywhere for the direction to take, relentlessly climbing trail after trail, knowing at the beginning that they would not take him to the pass he sought but having to scale every crag just in case; that moment in which he finally spied the opening through which he would embark upon the next stage of his crusade was one he wouldn't forget: that instant of double recognition. (It could not have been other than double, however much she might wish to deny it.) So many strange emotions accompanied it—strange to him. He admired her—her knowing what he was and not shrinking from it—though not like her sister-in-law, not out of a foolish pride that she could outwit him. Though she would recoil and advance on the tide of her contradictory impulses, ultimately, he believed, she would have the courage to acknowledge him. He suddenly found himself so humanly weary of not being known; of residing always in his smug recognition of everyone's want of courage; what would it be like, for once, to be able to speak to someone who understood him? He found himself wanting things he had never before wanted with anyone—a life of his own here on earth, a child; a life not weighed down by the need to revenge himself on his father; a life, he imagined, like everyone else's. He wanted all life to go on, and for the world he had known and loved, however imperfect, to prevail.

But that was before he felt the pity again, its strangling coil tightening around his throat; it was unendurable. How did anyone endure it? The question of courage didn't enter in: if you could not breathe, you could not live—it was very simple. If for him this had to be the price of love, he could not pay it. He didn't believe that anyone could.

He hadn't been told that she couldn't speak and didn't realize that she hadn't until he noticed her family staring at him because he'd answered something she'd said with her hands.

XXXVI SPARTA

One Saturday afternoon in early March of her senior year in high school, Zoë was walking down Pearl Street towards Bridget's house. Bridget had called and asked if she felt like coming over and getting smashed. Her parents had gone to New York for the weekend and she felt lonely. She had dropped out of acting school after her first semester (too many stuck-up assholes who thought they were God's gift to the theater world) and was moping around home, still seeing Bruce the Goose and talking about "getting back to the land." She wanted to have a baby out in the woods without painkillers and grow all her own food. Her parents were out of their minds with anxiety, ranting and raving about her "need to reinvent the wheel."

Zoë and Rob had stopped being secretive about their friendship after last summer—the Summer Samuel Came Back, Zoë had dubbed it, though she'd never mentioned him to a living soul. She had, however, told Rob about Charlotte's not taking drugs anymore; and Charlotte wrote her in care of the bakery—great letters about her "boys" and what they were up to. This next summer Rob planned to take some time off and they'd go to Harmony together and come up with a plan for Charlotte to be off drugs officially.

At the moment she wasn't thinking about any of this, however. For one thing, it was a gorgeous day. The weather had warmed up and felt like spring, except with a slight, exciting edge still in the air, and she had taken off her sweater and tied it around her waist. Nothing was bothering her—not the prospect of hearing whatever Bridget was in a tizzy about now; not her daily anxiety that Charlotte (and her part in abetting her) would be discovered; not her constant irritation with Rob, though she was now rarely conscious of it. It was an awkward mental, physical sensation that was always there, like a sore you grew accustomed to and compensated for.

She didn't feel startled or surprised when a strange voice said, "Hello there, Zoë."

She stopped. A man dressed in a short-sleeved checked shirt and blue jeans was sitting in his open doorway, as if he'd been waiting for her. Although ten years had gone by since she'd seen him, she recognized him even before she realized which house it was.

It was Anders Ogilvy, poor Myra Ogilvy's father, or Myra Ogilvy's poor father, depending on how you looked at it. After the year they had all been in Mexico, Myra wasn't in school—she had gone to live with her mother in California; that was all anyone knew. There were rumors, but nothing specific. No one had been close friends with her.

"Hello," Zoë said. "You're Mr. Ogilvy, aren't you? Myra's father?"

"I have a daughter named Myra, yes," he said.

After that he didn't say anything; he seemed to be waiting for her to explain what she wanted, as if she were the one who'd begun the conversation. In the weird, detached mood she was in, however, it almost seemed to her as if she had, as if ever since she'd made herself go into his office at the Naval Academy (she thought of the library's upstairs room as his office) she'd been waiting to run into him.

He was looking at her in a sort of measuring way, as if trying to guess what size clothes she wore.

"Five dollars to take your picture," he said.

"What?" she exclaimed. She noticed for the first time that he had a camera on the step beside him.

"I said, 'Five dollars to take your picture,' " he repeated.

"You're a *photographer* now?"

"Now?"

"I just mean . . . I didn't know you were."

"Why should you have? What's your answer?"

She couldn't believe he was so rude—yet he was so unaware of it that it was as if he wasn't.

"I guess so. I don't care."

"Stand as you were before," he said, all businesslike. "Looking down at the sidewalk. Yes, that's right, but facing down the street." He snapped three or four shots. "Terrific."

He came down the steps and knelt at her feet, aiming the camera up at her face.

"Great light," he said.

He stood, backed down the sidewalk, and snapped three more of her head-on.

"That'll do it," he said.

"Am I allowed to look up now?" she asked sarcastically, but he didn't even hear her tone.

"I just told you I was finished."

She felt like hitting him, but she felt hypnotized at the same time—how could he really talk this way?

"Are you a professional photographer?"

"I don't depend upon it for my living, if that's what you imply."

"Do you have your own darkroom?"

"Naturally I have my own darkroom."

"Where? In the *basement*?"

"Yes." He was feeling in his back pocket. "Please wait a moment. My wallet's inside."

"You don't have to pay me." It made her feel as if she'd done something dirty.

"Don't be absurd. I couldn't have asked you otherwise." He went indoors.

While he was gone Zoë fought her impulse to leave—to run as fast as she could down to Bridget's and pound on the door . . . Quick, let me in! What's the matter? Bridget would exclaim. I'll tell you in a minute—just hurry! Then, when they were safe in the house, she'd say, The weirdest thing just happened, Bridget—Myra Ogilvy's father asked if he could take my picture—he's so creepy! Here I am, walking along Pearl Street, minding my own business, when this guy sitting on his steps says hello and then asks if he can take my picture, and it's him! Myra Ogilvy's father!

But she stood there until he came back with a five-dollar bill.

"I can't take that," she said.

For the first time he seemed disturbed.

"Then I can't use your photograph. I'll have to discard the film."

He picked the camera up and started opening the back.

"What are you doing? You'd ruin a whole roll of film just because I won't take your money? Forget it, I'll take it, since it means so much to you."

He snapped the camera shut.

"There's another possibility," he said.

"Another possibility of what?"

"You pose for me again. Consider the five a down payment."

"Again when? Right now?"

"Unless you'd prefer to wait. But in the house, for an hour or two. A real session."

"Are you serious? I don't have any experience."

"I prefer that," he said.

"Why? What would I have to do?"

"Whatever I tell you."

Most people would have laughed, saying such a thing, but he sounded put out that he'd been forced to explain something so obvious.

"I'm not very photogenic. I get pretty self-conscious in front of the camera."

"You weren't just now."

"You took it before I had a chance to be."

"That's what a good photographer does. He snaps the shutter at those moments when the subject loses self-consciousness. Some photographers rely on the odds—take enough shots, a few will be effective. In my book that's cheating. The real art lies in deploying the delicate relationship that exists between model and photographer." He stopped and added, like snapping a picture, "Interested?"

"Well, I can't right now," she said.

"Then whenever your schedule permits."

"Don't you have a schedule?"

"My time is my own."

"You don't work at the Naval Academy anymore?"

"How did you know I worked there?" he asked suspiciously.

"I knew Myra!" she exclaimed. "Don't you remember?"

"You knew Myra?"

"I used to play in the backyard—on her trampoline."

"My daughter never had a trampoline," Mr. Ogilvy said.

"But I jumped on it!"

"You must be mistaking someone else for Myra. I would never have allowed her to have a trampoline. They're quite dangerous."

"But . . ." Zoë began again, then stopped.

Had she mixed up someone else with Myra? But she could remember very clearly exactly where in the backyard it had been. Had Mr. Ogilvy had an accident and suffered brain damage?

"Where does Myra live, anyway?"

"Myra lives with her mother in California, last I heard."

"Last you heard!"

Mr. Ogilvy ignored this totally. He said, "How soon can you start?"

"Start? You mean, start posing? Well, it would have to be either weekends or Wednesday afternoons. Supposedly I'm doing an independent study—you're supposed to do something extracurricular, but so far I haven't come up with anything. I used to be in the drama workshop but I'm not anymore." She was just rattling on. She was sure that at any moment he'd tell her he'd been kidding. "Maybe posing for you would qualify."

"Wednesday afternoon would suit me. Three o'clock?"

"That would be fine."

"Excellent," he said.

"Okay, see you then."

He went inside and shut the door; he didn't say goodbye or wait for her to walk away. Was this really happening? What *had* just happened? Spooky Mr. Ogilvy had turned into a photographer and asked her to pose for him? She wouldn't show up—it would serve him right. Or if she wanted to be more polite (not that he deserved it) she could write him a note. She liked imagining him being angry or disappointed. Yet she couldn't understand how she could be feeling so resentful of someone she didn't even know. Was she angry at him after all these years just because he'd once locked her in his basement? That seemed ridiculous.

Bridget answered the doorbell wearing her bikini and holding a Bloody Mary. She had her hair up in a barrette so her curls fell all over her head. She looked like a pin-up.

"What took you so long? I thought you were coming right over."

"Sorry. I had to do something at home."

Zoë was shocked that she had lied as soon as she'd spoken, especially after what she'd rehearsed saying to Bridget, but now that she had she didn't take it back. She wished that Bridget had told her she was wearing her bathing suit.

Bridget was leading the way through the house to the backyard. A pitcher of Bloody Marys stood on the white ironwork table. There was some delicatessen rye bread, salami, and Swiss cheese.

"I haven't had lunch. Are you hungry? I presume you'd like a drink."

"Absolutely."

Bridget had poured her a glass and then they both made sandwiches.

"So, how are things with you lately?" she asked. "Anything exciting happening with good old Robert Went?"

"He bought a new dough mixer. It's speeded up his production enormously."

"How fascinating. I take it you don't want to talk about him."

"What's to talk about? Everything's the same."

Suddenly Bridget exclaimed, "I don't know why you waste your time on him! It doesn't seem to make you happy. It seems like you want more out of the relationship than he wants—wouldn't it be better just not to see him?"

"What do you mean, not see him? We're friends."

"You mean you're not interested in him romantically?"

"Oh, God, I don't even know anymore, it's been like this so long."

"Well, whatever makes you happy," Bridget said. "Probably I'm just thinking about my own situation."

"What situation? You mean with Bruce?"

There was a trial-and-error sound in Bridget's voice—usually she launched right into whatever was on her mind.

"Did you break up?"

"No, I'm still seeing him. I just . . . Oh, Zoë, I don't know if I should tell you."

Suddenly Bridget started to cry. Zoë was amazed—she couldn't remember the last time she'd seen Bridget cry. Was she drunk? But Zoë had seen her drunk before and she'd never cried.

"Tell me what? What is it?"

"Oh, God," Bridget said, wiping her eyes. "I can't believe I'm crying about this. *Again.* This is getting ridiculous!"

"*What* is?"

"It's just . . . oh, God. I'm in love." Bridget shook her head. "I'm not talking about Bruce. It's someone else at the college."

"But I thought you were still seeing Bruce."

"I am."

"But you're seeing this other guy too? Does Bruce know?"

"No! I'm not seeing him—he doesn't even know I'm alive. Furthermore, he's married."

"He's married?" Zoë stared at her. "Are you sure? I mean, who is it?"

"I'm too embarrassed to tell you," Bridget said. "Maybe when I've had another twenty drinks. I'd rather talk about it in the abstract for now, if you don't mind."

Bridget had never wanted to talk about anything "in the abstract" before in her life.

"I'm terrified my father's going to find out."

"Your father? Why would he find out?"

"The person *teaches* at the college, Zoë. He's not a student."

"Are you kidding?" Zoë tried to think of all the faculty members; there were some younger ones she hadn't met. "How did you get to know him?"

"Oh, I've known him for a long time. I even know his kids."

"His kids!" Who had kids? It must be someone Bridget babysat for. "Is it Mr. Warner?"

"No, it's not Mr. Warner," Bridget said, making a face. "What do you take me for?"

"I don't think he's that bad."

"I think he's a cold fish. However, that's beside the point. Don't try to guess, Zoë, please—I really want to tell you the general circumstances without you thinking of a particular person."

"Fine."

"Look, I know you already think of me as some kind of sleazeball . . ."

"I do not," Zoë said automatically.

"Okay, loose. Whatever. Don't deny it—I'm not pissed off—maybe you're even right. It's just that if I told you who it was I don't think you could understand how I could fall in love with him, and you wouldn't be able to think clearly about the situation."

"Okay. Just tell me one thing, though. Is it Mr. Steinkoenig?"

Bridget burst out laughing. "Come on. This person is older, but he's not a fossil. Besides, Mr. Steinkoenig doesn't have children."

"Is this guy unhappily married?"

"Yes, but he refuses to talk about it."

"I thought you said he doesn't know you exist."

"Figuratively speaking. He has no more feeling for me than a glow-worm."

Zoë laughed. Bridget laughed too.

"Well, it's true. He won't even let me talk about my feelings for him. He says I'm concocting a whole scenario in my head, quote unquote. My problem is, I can't decide if I think he's right or not. Sometimes I think he is, but other times I think he's just denying his feelings for me—if he admits he has them he might have to divorce his wife and I think he wants to wait until his kids have grown up and left home."

"How many kids does he have?"

Bridget sighed.

"I'm not even allowed to ask that?"

"Everything will be another clue you'll start thinking about. Let's just say he has more than one."

"Okay, let's just say that."

"Zoë, *please* don't be mad at me—I really need to talk to you about this. Part of why I think I'm attracted to him is because he has kids. You know how much I want to have them myself. Maybe it's because I never had any brothers or sisters, I don't know. Right now it just feels like the only thing worth doing. I've talked to Bruce about it, but he gets hysterical at the idea of being a father. He basically said he wouldn't see me anymore if I got pregnant.

"The thing is, though, since he said that, I have this kind of contempt for him. I don't even really feel like sleeping with him. I don't want to use birth control anymore—it doesn't seem right. Even though Bruce isn't revolted by women getting passionate over him like Bernard, I feel like not wanting me to have his kid is really the same thing."

"But he's only in college!"

"You sound like him," Bridget said, taking a gulp of her Bloody Mary. "Anyway, I told this other guy that he was just afraid to act on his feelings and do you know what he said? He smiled this self-satisfied professorial smile and said, 'Well, Bridget, I've been a coward all my life.' It makes me so goddamn sick. They all think it's fine to be anything as long as they admit it. My father's the same way. Hey, don't mind me, I'm an ax-murderer. Yes, that's right, I enjoy hacking people into tiny pieces." Bridget puffed on an imaginary pipe and smiled smugly.

Zoë laughed. "He sounds like a jerk."

"He *is* a jerk," Bridget exclaimed. "Of *course* he's a jerk. They *all* are. All they do their entire lives is sit on their duffs thinking they're the last bastion of the Western tradition, whatever the hell they think that is, and criticize. Have you ever noticed how they know what's wrong with absolutely everything in the entire universe? They act like they created the world and now they don't have any more responsibility for it. They want everyone else to do the dirty work."

"I guess that's true. That's why Rob said his father stopped teaching there."

"Well, I'm *positive* it's true," Bridget said. "With our background, how can we deal with the real world? We've been brought up in an ivory tower. We might as well be Rapunzel. We're totally unprepared to sully our precious selves by *doing* anything. We're stupid little intellectual snobs—we don't even realize it. Unless someone can quote Shakespeare to us we think they're idiots."

"We do?"

"*I* do. I know I do. I know I think everyone else is lower class—the clerks in the drugstores, gas station attendants, everyone in business or politics—anyone who soils his hands, so-called, by not contemplating his navel. I think that if you think about it you'll realize you have the same attitude. It's so ingrained in us we don't even question it. We'd probably have withdrawal symptoms if we went very long without seeing brick with ivy growing on it. It's pitiful."

Zoë laughed. "I know a baker," she said.

"Yeah, and look where he came from. It's probably why he opened the bakery—to try to get away from all the great *thinkers*. Even so, he can't just open a bakery, plain and simple. He has to have all these *reasons*, all the crap he said in the paper about existentialism and all that bullshit."

"He said that stuff because the interviewer was so stupid. He doesn't really think those things."

"Well, that proves my point. It's the same kind of snobbery, *exactly* the same, don't try to tell me it isn't."

Zoë shrugged. She didn't think it was as simple as Bridget said, but Bridget was in one of her moods when any disagreement would make her even more adamant. She was pouring them both more Bloody Marys, sloshing some out onto the table.

"Sorry there are no more goddamn celery stalks," she said.

She ripped a chunk of rye bread off the big round loaf. Where she'd torn it, it looked as if a giant mouse had been nibbling it. A giant mouse? A giant mouse was a rat. Zoë thought about mentioning this but didn't. She must be getting drunk herself. Bridget was well on the way to sloshdom. Zoë felt a sudden urge to tell Bridget about Mr. Ogilvy, but the secret was like an island in her melting mind, something more her own than she'd ever had before, and she didn't want to give that up.

She said to Bridget, "I don't understand why you're interested in him, if you think he's such a jerk."

"That, my dear, is what I wish I knew." Bridget stood up and lurched towards the house. "Be right back."

When she returned she hopped down the steps, hanging on to the railing singing, "I'm drunk. I'm drunk as a glorious skunk," to the tune of a song from *Mary Poppins*. She said, "I believe that when I so abruptly departed this scene you had just asked me precisely why I was interested in . . . this individual, when I believe him to be such a . . . jerk, was I believe the term you used. Well, in a way I don't know, but also in a way I do. I feel that if I can get him to turn his back on all his precious philosophy and supposed moral principles it will be a great victory. A victory for all mankind!" She laughed drunkenly. She seemed to have forgotten that she'd started out asking for advice. "I know it's wrong to try to get him to be unfaithful to his wife, to . . . for me to . . . Well, I can't explain it but somehow that's just the point. To knock him off his pedestal."

Bridget tripped into her seat. "Oh, Zoë," she said suddenly, all teary-eyed. "I don't know what I'd do without you. You're my best friend in the whole world! I would never want to do anything to hurt you. I know I haven't always been the best friend to you—I know sometimes I can be really self-centered . . . Oh God, I can't stand myself sometimes!"

Zoë stared at her. Bridget had started crying again.

"I hope we'll always be friends. I hope that nothing will ever change that."

"Why should it?"

"I don't know. I don't *know*. I just have this feeling that something's going to happen to pull us apart. I keep thinking of all the things we did as kids, trying to get lost on our bicycles, playing *nuns* in Mexico, do you *remember* that? And all the plans we had—how we were going to have all these houses and all these careers and travel all over the world, having different lovers in every location—do you remember?"

Zoë nodded.

"I guess we never knew how much real men could screw things up, did we?"

"What do you mean?"

"I mean, how they would get to be the main thing. At least, I didn't know that. Maybe you did. It's pretty sad. Even this insane passion that I feel right now—I'm sure that someday it will fade away, hard as I find that to believe. You go through all this turmoil when someday you won't even be able to remember feeling this way—it makes me feel I'm doing it for someone's amusement." Bridget shook her fist at the sky. "I mean, Zoë, I *like* men, but I swear to God something's wrong with them! What are they all so goddamn afraid of? Someday, somehow, if there's any justice at *all* in this universe then this man is going to feel the same way about me that I do about him!"

It was almost dark when Zoë left. They had gone inside about four when it started to get cold and eventually Bridget had fallen asleep curled up on the couch. Zoë read a magazine for a while, but when Bridget didn't wake up she covered her up with an afghan, wrote her a note, and left. That was Saturday. She didn't hear from Bridget once before the following Wednesday when, at three o'clock, she knocked on the door of Mr. Ogilvy's house. All Sunday, Monday, and Tuesday Zoë had been unable to think of anything else but her secret meeting. She kept telling herself that she had to write him a note and not go; what was she doing going over alone to his house considering the creepy things he'd done with her and Myra years ago, locking them in the basement and so on? Something had to be wrong with him for Myra never to write him; and then there was the business about the trampoline, not to mention the fact that he didn't work anymore and hadn't said why. People could retire fairly young from the navy and maybe that was all it was, but it seemed as if he'd made a point of not explaining anything. Maybe he'd been having a nervous breakdown when she knew him before and that was why he'd forgotten everything (and why he acted so strangely), but now he was fine. She thought that at least she ought to tell Bridget where she was going, in case she didn't show up for dinner, but she couldn't bear to.

Being asked to model by Mr. Ogilvy was the only grown-up thing that had ever happened to her, and she couldn't believe he would really hurt her. Finally she wrote a note saying where she'd gone and when and stuck it in her top desk drawer in an envelope marked, "To be opened in the event of my disappearance." She'd be home before Seth and Monica unless something did happen.

"I appreciate promptness," Mr. Ogilvy said when he opened the door. "Please come into the living room first. We didn't discuss your fee. I'd like to square that away before we start shooting."

His house was set up like hers inside, like Bridget's, like the Steinkoenigs', like most of the narrow old houses in Sparta. Stairs going up the wall as you came in, doors opening off the hallway on the opposite wall: living room, dining room, kitchen at the back. She remembered the marble-topped chest of drawers on the left.

"Take a look at this," Mr. Ogilvy said.

He handed her an eight-by-ten black and white photograph, a girl walking along a street, head bent, lost in thought.

"That's me? God, that's amazing! It hardly even looks like me."

"The profile's classic. You're a find," he said. "It's going to be very fruitful for me to work with you."

"I *hate* most pictures of myself. This is really . . . I'm amazed."

"I'll pay you twenty-five. Will that do?"

"Twenty-five dollars an *hour*?"

"Thirty, then."

"No, I didn't mean . . ."

"I won't go higher than that, not at first."

"No, of course not. That wasn't . . ."

"I tell you what. I'll pay you thirty the first five hours, thirty-five the next ten. If I use you more than that, we'll renegotiate."

Zoë multiplied quickly. It would be enough to buy a used car! She could drive up to see Charlotte. She could go anywhere—she'd never had that much money in her life. She felt like laughing hysterically.

"That sounds fine," she said.

"Good. Now that that's settled, you can change. Use the bedroom at the head of the stairs. There's a robe you can put on."

"A robe?" she repeated. She suddenly felt sick. It didn't sound as if he intended to photograph her in it. What should she do? You misunderstood, I'm not that kind . . . Of what? Meanwhile Mr. Ogilvy had turned away and was busy attaching an old-fashioned-looking camera to a tripod. Trying to think what to do, Zoë left and climbed the stairs. She had thought there was a possibility that he might want her to pose in the nude, but she hadn't dreamed that it would be right away. First she'd get to know him, and then one day, when they were already falling in love, he'd come over to her and slowly unbutton her blouse—she'd had the whole scene in her head. But it would be worse now if she told him she'd never posed in the nude before. He'd really think she was a prude. But how could he not know she hadn't? He knew she'd never posed at all. Maybe it embarrassed him too, and that was why he acted so cool about it. That was probably all it was.

In the bedroom she shut the door, and so she wouldn't have a chance to think undressed quickly, not looking at herself. Was she supposed to take *everything* off? It wasn't like the doctor's, when the nurse said, Take everything off but your socks, or Everything from the waist up. All he had said was "change." Maybe he really did mean just change. He *could* be going to photograph her in the robe. It was a beige silk kimono covered with purple irises. Where had he gotten it? Maybe it had belonged to Myra's mother. Or some former model, whose body was buried in the cellar. Had Myra really moved to California?

Zoë put on the robe, tied it tightly, and then sat on the bed stalling, like Bluebeard's wife, but she was afraid to wait too long. She went back into the living room—he wasn't there.

"In here," he called from the dining room.

He was arranging a dish of fruit on the table. At one end—it was a long dark shiny table like Charlotte's—he had set a place with an apple on a plate, a paring knife beside the apple.

"Sit here, please," he said. "Just drape the robe over the back of the chair and sit down as you would if you were sitting down to dinner."

Her heart was beating so fast she thought she might have a heart attack. He was so incredibly casual about it! Did he have girls model for him all the time? Or was he just trying to be matter-of-fact so that she wouldn't be embarrassed? Her hands were trembling so much she could hardly untie the belt. She didn't dare look at him to see if he were watching. When she'd finally undone the knot, she took the kimono off as fast as she possibly could so she wouldn't be able to think about it, then sat down. She looked at the edge of the table. She nearly died when she realized he would be able to see that her heart was pounding.

"Just gaze at the plate for now. Look at it as if you've been served the same thing to eat for months now, by servants you despise, and can't bear to begin eating again."

"What?" she asked, glancing at him. He wasn't even looking at her. He was fiddling with the camera. "Is this some symbolic thing about Eve?"

"Don't talk to me, please. Just do as I tell you. You said you've acted. Think about how bored you are."

"Fine," she said.

She hoped he heard her sarcasm—she hated him. How could he be so indifferent? She was sitting in front of him with all her clothes off, and he could give a shit. She despised him—he was destroying her innocence and he didn't even realize what he was doing. It was like murder, and she was just sitting there, being murdered. She despised him. She DESPISED him. She glanced up again—he was bent behind the camera.

"Head down," he said.

She did what he said but suddenly she felt so furious that she wasn't embarrassed anymore—she felt disoriented, though. For the last three days she had thought of people saying about her: she poses in the nude. She's having an affair with a married man. She didn't think he would make love to her for a while—he'd try to restrain his passion because of her youth but at last would confess that he was dying of love for her, he knew it was wrong, what he'd done, pretending he wanted to photograph her when all he really wanted was to make love to her, but she'd say reassuringly, "It's not wrong, Anders. It's what I want too." He'd look at her in joyous disbelief, then murmur, "Oh, my darling . . ." and lead her to the bed. She'd tell Bridget only after they'd already been lovers for several months. She hoped he would have some birth control.

"You look preoccupied, not bored," he said impatiently. "Please make an effort to look bored."

She'd like to tell him what to do with his stupid cameras. He had taken only one shot with the big camera; now he was snapping with a thirty-five millimeter from different angles. But if she showed him she was angry then he might guess what she'd been hoping for, and she'd rather die than have him guess that now. So she thought of hot summer afternoons when she and Bridget had walked all over town at a snail's pace and nothing in the world had seemed worth doing.

"Good," he said.

He took seven or eight more shots.

"Now, stretch. Raise your arms and close your eyes. Lean your head back against the chair."

She did exactly as he said. The more she did what he wanted, the more she hated him. It almost made her like doing what he ordered; soon he'd realize that she was doing it only because she despised him. She felt like she was insulting him by being naked in front of him and not giving a shit.

"Good. Excellent."

If she obeyed his every command, he wouldn't be able to resist ordering her to do everything.

"Hold that pose—I'm changing the lens."

She felt him hovering around her. She could actually feel the heat of his body, but she didn't budge. She didn't open her eyes.

He snapped several more shots, then said, "You can relax for a second. I need to change the film. Okay. Now. Pick the apple up and look out the window. Think of something pleasant."

Since the window looked onto the brick wall of the house next door it wasn't too easy. Then she realized she was thinking of the fantasies she'd had about him earlier. Well, so what? He couldn't *see* them, could he? But that made her think about Samuel. She switched those thoughts off. She couldn't think about Samuel; it would make her crazy, especially here. It would make her totally unable to accept the fact that she'd only been with him *once*.

"Now take a bite out of the apple and then drop the hand holding the apple to your side—yes, precisely like that."

Was the apple poisoned? Would he rape her when she passed out?

"Lean your head back against the chair again. Good. Don't slump, though. Straighten your back, arch your breasts—lovely."

She was made so ill by this remark that she closed her eyes tightly.

"Eyes open. Look at me."

"How do you want me to look?" She was trying to sound indifferent but it came out shaky.

"Look as if I've just caught you doing something you shouldn't, but you resent me for it."

"I don't know if . . ."

"Think of a time when you were scolded as a child. Unfairly. Everyone in the world has had that experience."

She tried to think of something, and at first nothing came to mind but then she remembered Seth accusing her of warping Robert—how hard she'd tried not to cry until he left the room. It was exactly how she felt towards Mr. Ogilvy right now.

"Perfect!" he exclaimed. "Absolutely perfect!"

Snap snap snap.

"You're a gem, Zoë. An absolute natural. We'll stop now—we've done enough for the first day. Don't want to wear you out."

"I'm not tired at all," she said.

"Well, I am." He laughed. He sounded almost like a normal person. "It's been quite a while since I've worked this hard. You're quite a challenge."

"I am?"

"Your expressions are so fleeting. Very volatile. Whole weathers of emotion cross your face every instant."

"They do?"

"I assure you."

He was rewinding the film. He took the cylinder out and put it in his pocket. Then he glanced at her, looking amused.

"You may dress now."

"Oh!"

She'd just been sitting there, naked. How could she have? She grabbed the robe and put it on and stood up, then hurried upstairs. He controlled everything! She couldn't control him. But she had to. He had to *want* to control her. When she came back down, he was sitting at a desk in the living room, writing out a check.

"Do you want me to come again?"

"Naturally. This was merely a warm-up."

"Am I allowed to ask you questions now?"

"What do you wish to know?"

"*Are* you doing some kind of series about Eve? I mean, with the apple and everything, it's sort of obvious."

"If it's obvious you don't require my commentary, then, do you?"

"No, but I just . . ."

"I'm interested in forcing people into a state of pure perception," he said impatiently. "You would think that by using ordinary objects—if I'd made you eat a banana instead of an apple, for instance—I would most effectively achieve that goal, but I've learned from experience that people immediately try to interpret visual images. However, if you take something they can immediately label, and then hit them with the image repeatedly there's a chance that eventually they'll see beyond it to something else."

"Like what?"

"That's the question, isn't it?"

She couldn't believe that was really what he was doing—it was like Rob feeding that reporter a line. What did he mean, This was merely a warm-up? She asked suddenly, "Did you used to take pictures of children?"

"What makes you ask that?"

"I just wondered. Maybe since the last time I was here I was a child."

"The last time . . . ? When were you here before?" He sounded as if she'd broken in.

"With Myra! We just talked about it the other day!"

"I'm afraid you must be mistaking the house. I'm sure you played with Myra somewhere else. I didn't allow her to have friends over."

"But . . ."

"I expect that my memory is more reliable than yours on the subject."

"But I've been in this house before!"

"If you have, it could only have been when I wasn't home, in express violation of my orders. I never allowed Myra to have friends over," he said again.

"Why not?"

"That's of no concern to you."

"Fine. But if I was here when you weren't here, how did you know my name?"

"When?"

"Saturday, when I walked by."

"You introduced yourself."

"I what? I did not! You said, 'Hello, Zoë,' otherwise I would never have seen you."

"Don't play games with me," he said. "I don't like that."

"I'm not! I swear, you knew my name."

He looked at her a minute. "You're having a reaction, aren't you?"

"What do you mean?"

"To posing. It's relatively common. The first time or two. You feel violated, I expect. It's understandable." He tapped the camera. "The prying eye."

She was too amazed that he could talk so coolly about it to feel amazed.

"It's addictive, though."

"What is?"

"If that prospect alarms you, I'd advise your not coming back."

"Don't *you* get addicted?" She couldn't believe it, but already the idea of not coming back was upsetting.

"I? Never. That will aggravate you—I know that from experience too. I expect you don't believe me, but think back on what I'm saying now, later on."

"Fine. I will. Do you want me to come at the same time next week?"

She thought he smiled to himself.

"That would be fine. Plan to stay a little longer if you can. I'd like to shoot a longer session. Sometimes something happens in a long session that can't in a short."

"What?"

"It's not easily explained. You'll know if it does."

What could he mean? Was he trying to tell her after all that he wanted her? Maybe he was extremely shy and this was the only way he knew to make friends with women. But by the time she'd walked home this seemed absurd. She had trouble remembering the way he'd actually spoken to her. Even more than with Rob, the person Mr. Ogilvy was when she thought about him and the person he seemed to be when she was with him didn't match. She needed more evidence; she had to understand whether he was really cold or just pretending to be. As the week went on she was so impatient that she could hardly stand it; she saw Rob that weekend as usual, but even that didn't distract her. She felt scornful of him, thinking of Anders Ogilvy, how masterful he was, the way he told her to do this and do that. It was impossible that he was as indifferent to her as he'd seemed—he'd just been hurt by his wife's leaving him; he needed someone who was as vulnerable as he was before he could trust a woman again.

The next weeks coasted by. Every Wednesday she showed up at his house at three and stayed for two or three hours. He said hello and she said hello, and then she went upstairs and undressed. She wanted to undress now. He had been right that she'd become addicted, but the fact that he'd known that gave her hope. If he knew how she'd feel then he must care about her. When she came downstairs she wore the robe loosely tied, impatient for him to say "All right," when he was ready to start shooting. From Wednesday to Wednesday, she felt as if she were in suspended animation; she could scarcely sleep and lay in bed running her hands up and down her body, whispering, "Anders, Anders." "My sweet love," he called her. He'd thought he was done with love, but knowing her had made him feel whole again.

For the first time in her life she fell behind in her school work. She got a D on a history test and thought, So this is what it feels like to be someone who gets Ds on tests. It amused her when Mr. Montgomery accosted her in the hallway and told her he'd been hearing worrisome rumors about her. Did her recent "poor performance" have anything to do with Mr. Went?

"With Rob? Of course not." She laughed. If he only knew. She refused to say anything else. Mr. Montgomery was dying of curiosity, but too bad. She was far beyond the reach of his theories. Whatever questions he was asking would have to be answered by someone else.

Six weeks went by before what Anders had said could happen in a long session happened. He must have photographed her in every room in the house, from every angle, in every possible position, always naked, but with a variety of props—no more Eve and the apple. He seemed to have given up on his quest to turn symbols back into real things—if that was what he'd meant—or maybe he felt he'd already succeeded. Once he actually tied her hands and feet to the bedposts with neckties and she thought that certainly this was it now; when he told her to close her eyes she was so convinced that finally he was going to touch her that when he began clicking the shutter and ordering her to do this or that in his usual voice tears came to her eyes. She prayed that he wouldn't see them—her hands weren't free to wipe her eyes. She was terrified that he would figure out what she was feeling, but he didn't seem to notice, or if he did he probably thought she was so moved by the experience of posing for him that she'd begun to weep. He wouldn't show her any of the photographs—he said that seeing them would "influence her adversely." She would try to look the way she thought she looked instead of doing what he said.

Then, that particular afternoon, as she was following his instructions, she did something he hadn't asked her to do. She wasn't aware at first that she had—that he had not spoken. She had felt such a strong urge to move in a certain way that she couldn't resist it, as if she had a cramp and had to release it. She thought he paused a moment, but then he kept snapping.

"Good," he said softly.

Before she thought about it, she knew where to move next.

"Lovely," he breathed. "Good girl."

It kept happening. She'd stand, sit, lie down, and he'd move around her, crouching, kneeling, towering above her, murmuring to her, now that he no longer had to tell her what to do—how could it have taken her so long to understand him? "Lovely, Zoë. Lovely. Ah. Exquisite. You're perfect. Beautiful." He caressed her with his praises, and she saw now why he'd had to treat her so coldly at first; it was how he'd pushed her into perfect harmony with his desires. All she wanted now was to do whatever he wanted and she knew that whatever she did would be what he wished. At one point she even left the room to pose on the stairs. He followed, eagerly clicking the shutter. He was entirely in her power. She was entirely in his. It went on for almost an hour, then suddenly she collapsed. She had never felt so exhausted in her life. She hadn't even known she was tired until she fell into an armchair, unable to move, her eyes closed. She was only gradually aware of his presence. Ordinarily, when they'd finished shooting, he was busy right away, labelling the rolls of film. He didn't want to talk to her—he was anxious for her to dress and leave. But now he was right next to her—she flicked her eyes open briefly. He was kneeling beside the chair.

"Didn't I tell you?"

"Yes."

"Lovely," he said, for the thousandth time, then leaned over and touched her cheek. Like a spider his fingers fluttered down her neck, across her breasts, and down the length of one leg. She closed her eyes and sighed. He ran his fingers back up the other leg. "Lovely," he whispered. He took his hand away and stood up. When she looked at him, he was standing in front of her, gazing at her, and she said, "Anders . . ." the way she'd imagined so many times. But the instant she said it the frame froze; she knew she'd made a mistake. She'd broken the spell by saying his name and he turned away as if she'd insulted him; she could tell that he hadn't been looking at her, he'd been looking at his *photographs*, his photographs come to life, as if he had invented her, as if she'd been a negative waiting to be developed. But where, then, was *she*?

Feeling—she didn't know how she felt—weak, frightened at how far from everything she'd ever known she was, she jumped up and ran upstairs. What should she do? What had she done? She didn't exist anymore—she felt alive now only when he was snapping pictures, and she knew it wouldn't be long until he became bored, now that she'd succumbed to his will. She had to escape before that happened. If she didn't . . . She didn't dare finish the thought. She couldn't come back. She would say, I'm never coming back, Anders. I never want to see you again. She had to leave while she still had the strength.

But when she went downstairs, he was sitting at his desk, writing out the check as usual, and it all seemed crazy—she didn't know what anything meant—could he really not give a damn about her as a person? No one could be that cold. If he hadn't taken her in his arms and told her he loved her it was only because she hadn't done or said the right thing yet—what was it? Did he want her to be more direct? To say, Anders, I love you—I want to be your mistress? But he'd reacted so harshly when all she'd said was his name—was it because she hadn't been straightforward enough? Did he want her to do his will even more completely? But how? Did he want to hurt her? Did he want her to want him to? Did he want her to plead with him to? But he didn't like it when she talked. Did he want her to hurt herself silently somehow while he watched?

She thanked him for the check—it was all she could think of to say. She had never cashed any of them. She kept them hidden in a shoebox in the back of her closet and took them out only to study his signature. By now he had paid her almost four hundred dollars. She didn't have a checking account; that was the reason she hadn't cashed them at first, but then she'd decided that she didn't want him to pay her. When he told her that none of his checks had come back, she'd say, I don't do this for money, Anders. However, he must never balance his checkbook or he'd have asked her about them by now.

The next week when she went upstairs to undress, she brought down the neckties from his bedroom; he understood, and this time tied her to the chair at the dining room table where she'd sat the first day. He began clicking close-ups (he never used the box camera anymore), concentrating first on her bound wrists, elbows, knees, and ankles, saying softly, "Tell me what you want me to do. Tell me what you want me to do to you."

"Everything," she whispered.

"Be specific."

He made her say all the words. If she hesitated he murmured, "Say it. Say it."

Finally she whispered, "I don't think I should be able to talk."

Again he understood, and he took a necktie and pulled it against her mouth from behind the chair until her mouth opened and the tie gagged her; then he knotted the necktie behind her head.

"Now tell me," he said, shooting close-ups of her face.

She moaned.

"Tell me with your eyes," he said. "You can't talk—tell me with your eyes."

She was feeling spasms in her abdomen and calves and a pressure behind her eyes so intense she thought she would black out as she looked at him, knowing nothing anymore except pure, absolute wanting—to go some place from which she could never come back. But the sessions always ended without her having reached this place.

She now scarcely slept at all, and when she did she had nightmares. She cut school as much as she dared, but she was afraid someone would write a note to Seth and Monica, so she made a Herculean effort and brought her grades back up. Bridget kept calling and leaving messages but Zoë hadn't returned them. Last week Bridget had written her a note asking her what she was pissed off about, but she hadn't answered it either. It was just like Bridget to assume that everything in the world had to do with her. Several times in the past weeks Zoë had canceled dates with Rob; he also wanted to know if he'd offended her in some way—it was incredible! Was the only person they ever thought about themselves?

After that last time gagged and bound in Eve's chair, as she thought of it, Zoë posed stiffly, and Anders was becoming impatient.

"What's happened to you? Everything was going so well. Maybe we need to take a break from each other."

"No, please. I'll be better next week. I'm just—I don't know—going through something."

"Well, don't go through it on my time, please."

However, the more she tried to do what she thought he wanted now, the less satisfied he became. "You're distracted," he snapped. "Go upstairs and dress. Let's try it with the robe on for a while—maybe that will correct the imbalance."

She didn't know what he meant. All she knew was that he *blamed* her; he acted as if posing for him, taking off her clothes, all the sick, submissive positions had been *her* idea—it was as if he'd poisoned her. There was something in him he could get rid of only by giving it to her—and willingly she'd taken anything he gave her since she wanted him to give her everything—but he would take nothing back and now how was she supposed to get rid of the poison?

It was now about a month before the end of school, another Saturday. As usual she could not sit still. She had to study for a trigonometry test but she absolutely could *not* stay in the house. What was she going to *do*? Go to Washington again? This time go directly to the Capitol and tell them it was all their fault? If they hadn't run the navy the way they had then Anders Ogilvy would be in love with her . . . Quick trip to the loony bin. No rescue by Rob this time.

No one was home—Monica was grocery shopping and Seth was in his office. Zoë left the house and walked down Main Street, but Harbor Place was crowded so she went up Academy Street and then across to the campus. She zigzagged back and forth along the diagonal brick paths, up the slope towards the administration building. The grass was deep spring green. The place was deserted. Probably a softball game going on on the back campus.

She walked around to the other side of the administration building towards Worthing Hall, where Seth's office was. Maybe she'd visit him—he could buy her a Coke at the coffee shop like the old days; she could pretend to be the person she'd been before she became depraved.

She climbed up to the third floor. There was no air conditioning—it grew hotter with every step. From the top of the stairs she could look down the hall three doors and see Seth's—it was shut. The top half was that ripply glass they had on bathroom windows; his name was stencilled on it like a doctor's, just "S. Carver." The professors here didn't believe it was necessary to advertise their rank and power. Quote unquote. Seth must not be there after all—he never kept the door shut when he was in. But as Zoë was about to turn, as in a bad dream, a grade-B bad dream, like the witch cackling at the exit to the maze, two shadows appeared behind the glass. One taller—Seth. Seth was with someone. The taller shadow reached for the shorter—abundant hair. She clutched at him, but he pushed her away.

The door began to open, and Zoë sprang away and raced down the stairs, not worrying about being quiet, wanting only to get away before she was caught. Outside, she bolted to the nearest large tree and hid behind it. Peering around, she could see the door. Would they both come out or only one of them? Then the door opened and Bridget came out. She was wearing a yellow seersucker sundress. She looked completely miserable. As she turned down the walk towards the administration building, she took a brush out of her purse and began to brush her hair. Zoë stepped out from behind the tree. She waited until Bridget saw her.

"Zoë!" she exclaimed.

Zoë didn't say anything. She could see that Bridget was trying to figure out if she knew. She wasn't going to say *anything.*

"I . . . Are you . . . Is everything all right?"

She just stood there. Bridget had come over to her and was standing there, holding her hairbrush down at her side.

Before Bridget had a chance to react, Zoë walked up to her and slapped her across the face. Once, twice, and then Bridget began to cry. She dropped her brush and put her hands up to protect herself, but she didn't fight back. Zoë kicked her and Bridget stumbled.

"Zoë, please listen."

"Shut up! Just shut up!"

"I tried to tell you. I wanted to tell you. I . . ."

"Shut up or I'll kill you!" Zoë screamed at the top of her lungs.

"Hey!" someone called out from the air somewhere.

She kept hitting Bridget everywhere—on the head, on her arms, in the stomach.

"Stop it, Zoë, stop it," Bridget sobbed. "I never wanted to hurt you. I never . . . I couldn't . . . I don't know what I've been thinking. Please . . . It's not the way you think. Nothing ever happened. He wouldn't."

"That's a lie! That's the biggest lie of all the lies you've ever told."

"It's *not.* Zoë, please . . . He wouldn't even . . ."

"Shut up!" she screamed.

Bridget turned and tried to run, dropping her purse, but Zoë grabbed her by the arm and kept swinging at her with the other arm. Seth had come out of the building now and was sprinting towards them.

"Zoë!" he shouted. "For God's sake, Zoë!"

She took one look at him, let go of Bridget, and ran as fast as she could down the walk. He came after her, but she'd reached the street before he did and from the sidewalk she turned and shouted, "Stay where you are! If you try to come any closer I'll throw myself in front of the next car. Believe me, I will."

He stopped but called, "Zoë, for God's sake, let me *talk* to you!"

"*Asshole!*" she shouted. "I'll never speak to you again!"

Then she darted across the street. She almost did get hit—a car had to slam on its brakes. The driver screamed at her out the window. "What are you trying to do, get yourself killed?" "What business is it of yours?" she shouted back. "Asshole!"

She ran down Green Street to Fairfax, then up to St. Stephen's Circle and down Chesterfield to Pearl. By the time she was pounding on Mr. Ogilvy's door, she could hardly breathe. Finally he opened it.

"I'm sorry, I don't recall . . ."

"Give me the pictures! All of them, and the negatives!"

"I beg your pardon?"

"I said, Give them to me!" she shouted.

"Why should I?" he asked. "Why are you here?"

"You pervert! You slimy sick pervert! God knows what happened to your daughter. I was insane ever to agree . . ."

"Come into the house," he said.

"Why? Are you afraid the neighbors will hear? Are you afraid they'll find out what a *pervert* you are?"

Now he was going to tie her up and hurt her, now he would have to. Take her down in the basement like before, but stab her. Not quickly, but cruelly, so she'd know. Her body would be found. Seth would commit suicide. Bridget wouldn't, not her, but she'd never be able to be really happy, she would never be able to forget.

"I never even cashed any of your checks!" she shouted as he pulled her into the hall and shut the door. She hoped he slapped her across the face the way she'd slapped Bridget. "Did you think I wanted your filthy money? Your filthy, sick money? Well, did you? Answer me!"

"What are you trying to express, Zoë?"

"If you try to blackmail me, I'll deny that I ever laid eyes on you."

"Blackmail you? What are you talking about? Why didn't you cash the checks?"

"You didn't even *notice*?"

"I pay my accountant to balance my checkbook every three months. I don't like to be bothered with it. You're speaking very strangely. You seem angry. Are you?"

"Oh, your perceptiveness amazes me. What a brilliant man. Get me the photographs. And the negatives. All of them. Right now. Otherwise I'm calling the police."

"The police? On what grounds?"

"I'll say you raped me. When they see some of the photographs, they'll believe it. Where are they?" When he didn't answer, she said, "The darkroom's in the basement." She headed down the hallway to the door. He took hold of her arm, but when she struggled, he let go. What an unbelievable coward he was. When she opened the door, he followed her downstairs, switching on the light. On the bottom step she stopped, too amazed to speak.

"Yes, it's my gallery," he said behind her. "They're all of you."

Every inch of wall space was taken up by photographs of her, from full-length shots to close-up sections of her body. But she couldn't take her eyes off the ones that showed her face. She looked so willing, so completely at his mercy—pleading with him to hurt her. She saw now that he had known—he'd known all along what she'd wanted.

"What do you do down here?" she said coldly—it was the only method she hadn't tried. But she knew it wouldn't do any good.

He shrugged. "Look at them. That's all. Look at them."

"You never meant to have a show, did you? You're not a real photographer. You never have had a show, have you?"

"No," he said quietly. "That is correct. I'm not a real photographer. I've never had a show. I'm lucky if every three years I can get someone to pose for me. Usually I have to pay them a lot more than I paid you." He shrugged and smiled. "They're generally a lot quicker to catch on."

"To what?"

"Need everything be spelled out?"

"Didn't you ever want me? Not even that time . . . that time you . . ."

"No, I never did. I never have. That's what Myra's mother always asked me—didn't I want her? She modelled for me too. There haven't been that many, six or seven in twenty years. I'm sure you'll agree that I never misled you."

"Oh, of course, I agree," she said.

Watching him, daring him to stop her, she began to tear down the photographs, carefully, taking her time, giving him time to pull her away from the wall and do what he had humiliated her into begging for, his complete and total indifference making her so frantic that she was ready to sacrifice everything, her *life*, to provoke a reaction from him.

"Why don't you get your camera? Wouldn't it be the perfect last shot for your series?"

"What are you going to do with them?"

"What!" she shouted. "You don't even have the courage to try to stop me?"

"Why should I try to stop you?" he asked.

"If I had a gun," she said, "I would shoot you. If I could kill you and not go to jail I would take pleasure in it. I really would. How do you feel about that?"

He shrugged. "You wouldn't do it."

"Oh, yes, I would. If I ever figure out a way to kill you without being caught, believe me, I'll do it."

"I'm sure you wish to believe that."

When she had cleared one entire wall, she gathered an armful of the photographs and went past him and back upstairs. In the living room, she stacked the photos on the couch. But in the climb up the stairs her anger had fallen away.

"How could you *do* that?" she said, crying now. "I just don't understand."

"Do you have to understand? Can't you simply accept what I say?"

"No!" she shouted at him. "No!"

Then she asked, "*Would* you sell some of them, if I asked you? To magazines?"

"Exhibit them?"

"Would you do it? *Please*?"

"I don't know. I can't promise."

"Any of them—you can use any of them. Please, Anders?"

"No."

"Then give me all the negatives."

"You know you can't check up on that."

"Stop it! Oh, just stop it! Stop it!" She collapsed onto the couch. "I just found out that my best friend is having an affair with my father. I saw them through the door to his office."

Anders Ogilvy didn't say anything.

"Did you even hear what I said?"

"Yes, I did. I'm sorry, I don't have anything to say."

"You don't have anything to say? You don't have anything to say! Oh, God, how can this be happening?"

Her mind was in flames; everything she looked at was sickeningly altered, distorted—the furniture, the tree outside the window . . . Mr. Ogilvy had infected everything and she would never again be able to look at anything without seeing its true, deep depravity.

She stood to confront him, whatever that would mean—she would force him to react, anything was better than this malicious paralyzed way he was, but she couldn't say anything; he had made her in his image, and it took every ounce of strength she had left just to turn away and sort through the photographs, choose eight or ten of the most suggestive poses, the ones most recognizably her, including a couple from the first day, with the apple. He said not a single word as she rummaged in his desk drawers for a manila envelope and slid the photographs into it and left.

The bakery was busy, a late Saturday afternoon rush. People stocking up on coffee cakes and sweet rolls for Sunday breakfast. Sundays the bakery was closed—Ha Ha: Rob quoting God's laughter—no end to which human beings would not go to force "Him" to reveal "Himself." Every table was occupied by customers drinking coffee and tea. Marcy Abbot, the seventh-grader working behind the counter, said distractedly to Zoë that Rob was out back. She protested when Zoë pushed past her and Todd Prendergast, the seventh-grader waiting tables, but Zoë ignored her. Rob was frantically frosting cinnamon rolls, wearing shorts and a navy blue T-shirt.

"Zoë!" he exclaimed. "Welcome to the madhouse! Want to ice the cupcakes?" Then he saw the way she looked. "What's *wrong*? What's *happened*?"

"I . . ."

But she couldn't talk here. The seventh-graders in the kitchen were watching them—she didn't even know their names. Rob had set down his decorating cone.

"Come upstairs. Come on. Jason, carry on. I'm going AWOL for a minute." Rob took her hand and led the way upstairs and down the hall into the living room. He sat down beside her on the flowered couch.

"I don't know how well I'm going to be able to talk," she said. Her voice was trembling and she was shaking so much that her teeth were starting to chatter. Rob put a hand on her knee. She looked at it, then laid her hand on his. He turned his so that their palms faced. They both held tightly.

"*Tell* me—*whatever* it is."

"Rob, I don't know—I don't know how. These things—all these things have been going on and I don't know how—I wanted—oh, Rob, this afternoon—Bridget—I found out—I think she and my father are having an affair. I went over to the campus and I caught them."

"Oh, Zoë—oh, no . . ."

Rob dropped her hand and jumped up as if Seth and Bridget were about to come in the room.

"Bridget and your *father*? Are you sure?"

He looked so shocked it made Zoë want to laugh.

"I haven't even told you the main thing. There's—oh, God—I don't know how to tell you. I've been . . . well, there's this man—I don't know why I even did this—but I've been—well, here . . ." She laid the envelope on the table.

"What's in there?"

"Photographs."

"Of Bridget and your father?" Rob half laughed. "Did you hire surveillance?"

"They're of me."

"Of you?"

He picked up the envelope.

"No, wait." She stood up. "I'll leave them, but don't look at them until after I'm gone. I needed to tell someone—I didn't have anyone to tell besides you. You're my best friend. You're my only friend, really." She laughed sharply, like an insane person. "I don't want you to despise me. Please, please say you won't despise me."

"Why would I despise you? Come on, Zoë, don't talk crazy. How could I despise you?"

"I don't know! I don't know! Just please don't—oh, please—oh, Rob, I have to go. I . . . Rob, please believe me. I love you. I'm in love with you. I always have been."

He was staring at her.

"Zoë!" he shouted, as she turned and ran down the hall, down the stairs, and out through the bakery while the seventh-graders stared after her like avenging angels. To this day she could feel them staring at her.

XXXVII CASCABEL FLATS

Zoë rehearsed the scenario thus: in the letter Rob would request a meeting; he had only now heard what had happened to her and he hoped that she could forgive him for whatever part he had played in her long silence. Although he had never tried to communicate with her, in part because he had been so incapacitated by drugs, he had to admit that he hadn't been sure she'd want to hear from him; now he saw that he should have realized she'd been waiting for nothing else . . . Could she forgive him?

They would meet, pick some neutral town out in the bland middle of the country where neither of them had ever been—I'll meet you in Middle America in front of the post office at noon (high noon as opposed to low noon) on January 6 . . . That's appropriate, isn't it? There would be some awkwardness at first, of course, but in the atmosphere of the local diner they would soon be chatting away about old times . . . You thought what? But how could you think that! I never once . . . Of course it was an accident! I just felt so *guilty* after seeing those photographs of you . . . If I had been able to *act* on my feelings . . . Yes, it was plain old fear, fear of transubstantiating my desires; everyone has to do that for themselves . . . Face it, Zoë, if I hadn't been such a coward, you would never have been driven to the lengths you were.

No—don't be silly—your father and Bridget had nothing to do with it. Yes, all right, so you lied about them, but you were *upset*, Zoë . . .

Nick came back from Stewart's shortly after dark; Stewart had given him a lift to the end of the driveway.

"He said he'd see the rest of you later," Nick said.

"Later where?" Ellie asked.

"At the service."

"The service!"

Nick's mood had changed completely—he was as giddy as Monica and Zoë now. Zoë heard him say to Monica, "I apologize, Mother—the divorce was such a shock after all this time. I felt as if my entire history were being revised before my eyes. It took a little getting used to. But I hope that whichever of your many admirers you decide to accept, if any, you'll be very happy."

Zoë managed to sign, *Did you get the letter?* but Nick said only, "Later."

Dinner was convivial despite an undertone of anxious expectation. Oyster stew, lamb with mint sauce, Monica's homemade clover leaf rolls, fruitcake for dessert. About eight-thirty they drove into town, where the snow-draped houses did look as if they were made of gingerbread, as Ellie had asserted—it was even less possible than before to make out their boundaries. Nick parked at Michael Chamberlain's house, down at the end of a dead end, and then they all headed on foot back towards the decorated part of town. Michael and company, Ellie had declared after knocking, must have already started.

After three or four blocks (although Zoë was guessing—there was no such thing as a block *out here*), the adornment began: at first an occasional house, but soon nearly every one, was outlined by the softly glowing lights, spaced at two or three feet intervals along the flat roof edges, atop walls, and on both sides of walkways as they had been at Stewart's the night before—showing Mary and Joseph the way to Bethlehem, wasn't that what Ellie had said? Evidently people *out here* weren't sure they'd made it yet. Some houses were as many-tiered as wedding cakes, their levels like battlements with crenellations afire, or maybe the campfires of a waiting army, staked out on a hill. There was that intent stillness to the night.

At intervals along the street people clustered around bonfires, their hands supplicating the flames, their voices trying out Christmas carols. A group began, "What child is thi-is who, laid to re-est, on Mary's la-ap is sle-ee-ping . . . ," the longing, wondering question shortly answered by the triumphant "This, *thi-is* is Christ the Ki-ing . . ." Doubt confronted by certainty, doubt by certainty, for two *thousand* years. A vibrant baritone underscored the other voices and suddenly Ellie exclaimed, "Good heavens, that's Michael Chamberlain! I had no idea he could sing like that. And there's Nancy!" as if it were somehow marvellous that someone they all knew should be part of the chorus.

When the song subsided they greeted the Chamberlains and walked along with the carollers, who paused next in front of a house so lavishly sprinkled with lights that it looked like a paint-by-number picture—take one lightning bolt, connect the dots: in a flash the whole would blaze into light.

"Hark, the herald angels sing," the group began, laying siege to the house, and Zoë pictured sharpshooters leveling on the carollers from darkened windows. "Enough!" their bullets would crack out, "Enough!" and the insurrection would begin at last. Nick had fallen behind the crowd with Zoë and now jostled her shoulder.

"Feel like adding your voice to the throng?" he asked. Then he looked at her, horrified. "My God, I'm sorry, Zoë! I must have thought . . . I don't know what I thought!"

Don't worry about it.

"Jesus, I must be more disoriented than I realized. In fact, how have you managed to take it so calmly? After all this time they're getting a divorce? Heaven and earth have split asunder, and you don't even seem fazed."

She shrugged. *It is going to be strange if they both marry again.*

"You're telling me. We may soon be the products of a *broken home.* We could have a *stepmother.*"

Or father.

"I know. I'm very worried."

Don't worry—I'll protect you.

"I'll protect you too. Shh!" he warned, as they began to laugh. "You don't want Mother to think we're actually *happy* about this, do you?"

The carollers, still unscathed, had advanced farther and were now singing, "Bring a torch, Jeannette, Isabella."

"Madame Alignac, fifth grade!" Nick exclaimed. "Un flambeau, Jeannette, Isabelle . . ." He put his arm through his sister's. "Often you—one—needs just to do *something.* Weighing a decision too closely—it doesn't pay." He smiled at her. "Do *you* know what I'm talking about?"

You read Rob's letter, didn't you? READ, R-O-B LETTER?

"Well, yes, I have to confess that I did." Nick extracted it, folded in half, from his back pocket. "I was going to give it to you."

WHAT SAY? She had moved her hands lethargically.

"You want me to tell you?"

Is it so bad?

"I really think you should read it yourself."

But you've already read it. Why won't you . . .

"All right, if you insist, but I hope you're ready for this," Nick said. "Robert wants to marry you."

She turned.

"That's right."

ALL HE SAY?

"Zoë, read the goddamn letter, will you? I've taken the sting out of it—have a little courage."

He led her to the nearest bonfire, unfolded the page, and handed it to her. She took it and held it up to the light. It was a sheet of notebook paper. Rob's "letter" took up three lines near the top.

"Dear Zoë," it said, "I think it's time we got married, don't you? Give me a call. Love, Rob."

He gave a phone number with an area code Zoë didn't recognize. No address. She stared at the familiar, though somewhat more elongated, handwriting. Surely he had to know by *now* that she couldn't talk. She pointed at the area code.

"I don't know where that is," Nick said. "I meant to check the phone book but I forgot."

How am I supposed to respond?

"It is rather terse."

Terse! She felt tears come to her eyes. Rob explained *nothing*. Nothing! She had been so sure that when she read his letter she would finally know what his motives had been, one way or the other, even though both alternatives had been unbearable . . .

"You're not obligated to answer it, you know."

Answer it! How?

Still Nick misunderstood. "I mean, no one would blame you for not taking a note like that seriously. The guy hasn't seen you for ten years—who does he think he is? Doesn't he know what happened to you? If I were you, I think I'd either ignore the letter or tell him what he can do with his proposal."

But he didn't—I don't . . . Nick, if I say no . . . Don't you understand?

"If you refuse him, what? He'll never give you another chance? Is that what you're saying? But, Zoë, this is nuts! You haven't heard from Robert in a decade—a decade in which he's been in a mental institution—and out of the blue he asks you to marry him and you're *considering* it? He acts as if he thinks you've been communicating the entire time!"

Maybe we have.

"What? Don't get mystical on me. You're starting to sound as crazy as he does. You're strung out because you've thought about him one way for so long, and now . . . It's how I felt hearing about Mom and Dad."

She shook her head.

"I'm not saying he's still crazy—I'm sure they wouldn't have let him out without good reason. But remember that Robert hasn't had to function in the real world since he was an adolescent. He's got to be frantic for some stability—where does he have to go in the world? If you want to see him, then just write him a neutral, friendly letter telling him that—he'll get the point."

Where would I send it?

"Oh, I see what you mean. Well, I could call for you and get his address."

I can't do it that way.

"What do you mean?"

I have to say yes or no.

"What! No, you don't!"

Yes, I do. You don't understand, Nick. All this time I've been waiting to find out what really happened, whether he meant to kill his father or not, but now I see that that would be cheating—that's why Rob's not telling me until I answer him.

"What?"

He's asking for a leap of faith. She had to spell out "faith."

"But, Zoë . . ."

Nick, stop arguing with me! It's hard enough as it is!

The others had finished singing "Good King Wenceslas" and, stalemated—the resisters skulking in their houses, too browbeaten after two thousand years to confront even this tawdry company—were now all strolling, strolling even though the cold was more penetrating by the minute—back in the direction of Michael Chamberlain's house. Nick walked beside Zoë in silence until they turned down the dead-end street.

"Zoë, let me say one other thing. I told Stewart Beauregard about Robert."

What? Why? Had he read the letter?

"I didn't mean to, actually. I was trying to warn him off somehow. The things he said . . ."

What things?

Nick grimaced. "He told me how well you expressed yourself."

Zoë smiled—Nick took it all so seriously.

"I told him to leave you alone."

And?

"He wanted to know if you'd asked me to say that. When I said no he said you were old enough to make up your own mind. So I told him about Robert."

Thinking, Nick meant, that if Stewart knew her history and what a shaky state she was in he would be moved to compassion. But that was just what she could count on Stewart not to be.

Had he read the letter? she asked again.

"The envelope was still sealed," Nick said.

That didn't matter, though; Stewart knew about Rob, which was what counted. It made it clearer than ever that he would have to tell her what Rob had refused to.

Inside, Nancy's husband took their coats and told them the pumpkin soup was on the verge of boiling. Pumpkin soup? It turned out to be sweet, topped with whipped cream, like liquid pumpkin pie. Michael, who had fallen behind to talk with a friend, puffed in now and rubbed his hands energetically in front of the spitting fire.

"What a lovely voice," he said to Monica, who had sung with the carollers. "Old-fashioned somehow, like the old music hall stars'."

"Probably because she hasn't used it for thirty years," Nick said.

"You might be right," Monica said. "I did sing in a choir in college."

"You never told us that!"

"No, I suppose I didn't."

"What else are we going to find out that you used to do? Rob banks? Compete in the Indianapolis 500?"

Monica smiled at Michael. "Such inquisitioners children are, don't you find?"

"Merciless."

He refused the soup, not "caring to dilute the excellent Kentucky bourbon" with which he'd been "bolstering his spirits" throughout the evening.

"Oh, for heaven's sake, Dad," Nancy said.

"My daughter maintains a personal interest in my liver," Michael remarked to Monica.

Monica winked at Nick and Zoë.

If she'd winked once in the last thirty years, they hadn't seen it.

Zoë felt heavy and sleepy—the too-warm room after the sharp cold; the lassitude induced by having her expectations aroused over and over again; the battle pitched but never joined; armies dissolving interminably into people simply going about their business. She sat down on the couch beside Pryce and laid her head on his shoulder, floated off on the murmur of talk: Michael Chamberlain's rambling on about the town, how he regretted the old order's passing, the advent of this new breed that imagined it could purchase the spirit of the place; there could be no *new* Eden, when would people learn to accept that? At least in the old days people had understood that you didn't get something for nothing . . . Nancy kept interrupting him, reminding him that their guests didn't know the individuals he spoke about, couldn't therefore be interested in the subject, why didn't he tell them instead the plot of his new mystery, crucifixion avenged up in the hills . . .

Why did she have to go back out in the cold again? Zoë wondered sleepily. Her thoughts grew slippery and she drowsed off; she dreamed she was back in the Naval Academy library, in Anders Ogilvy's office, except that when she opened the door to leave, the balcony was gone. Rob was down below, urging her to jump. She tried to tell him that something was missing—she was supposed to jump from the wall surrounding the whole *place*, not jump down in the middle of it—but he kept saying, "It will only hurt for a minute. A stab of pain, and then you'll be able to talk." "What do you mean?" she said. "I can already talk." "That's what you think," he said. Even in her dream she laughed, he sounded so much like Rob, and her laugh woke her up. Pryce was staring at her; Nick was staring at her—he had come to sit on the other end of the couch. On the other side of the room everyone else was still talking, conversationally clustered around the fire.

What? she signed.

"You talked in your sleep," Pryce said in an awestruck whisper.

Cut it out.

Nick looked almost sick with shock.

"You said, 'That's what you think,' " Pryce said.

The dream came back then.

I didn't say that. She meant that Rob had.

"Ask your brother. Didn't she say those exact words?"

Nick nodded. "Has she ever done that before?" he asked Pryce. He couldn't meet her eyes.

"Not to my knowledge. Zoë, maybe we . . ."

What?

"Let's go outside. Is it possible to walk to the church from here?"

Nick and Pryce were both speaking softly.

"I'll get our coats," Nick said.

"What plot are you three hatching over there?" Ellie interrupted. Zoë had seen it coming.

"We thought we'd walk up to the church," Nick said, in the forced casual way of someone trying to cross a border with false identification.

"It's only a quarter past eleven!"

"It won't hurt to be a little early."

"But it's ten minutes from here at the most!"

"Won't they be serving refreshments?"

"After, not before. Nick, I don't understand. What's the . . ."

"Do you two want to go?" Nick asked Zoë and Pryce. "Or maybe you'd prefer not to go at all. You can take the car—then you could come back for us . . ."

You think I'm going to talk if you leave me alone with Pryce? Zoë asked Nick, facing him so that Pryce couldn't see.

Ellie had stood and crossed the room. "Nick, what is the problem?"

Everyone else had now stopped talking.

"There is no problem."

"Did you change your mind about going?" Ellie asked Zoë.

No.

"Then what . . ."

"It's *nothing*, Ellie. Forget it."

Ellie stared at Nick and then her eyes filled with tears and she went into the bedroom where they'd all laid their coats. "Christ, I can't seem not to put my foot in it," Nick said under his breath.

Zoë glanced at Pryce—he was trying to catch Nick's eye from behind her back.

"Here's yours, and here's yours, and here's yours," Ellie said, dumping their coats in their laps.

"Ellie, I . . ." Nick began. Then he stood up and put his arm around her and kissed her. Ellie looked at him suspiciously, but something reassured her, and immediately her mood changed. It was amazing. She must really be in love with Nick, Zoë thought; how extraordinary. It was clear Nick loved Ellie too. Why had this always seemed so sinister?

They waited another twenty minutes. By a quarter to twelve they had pulled into the parking lot outside Nick and Ellie's church, which looked like a flying saucer with a central spire for antenna. Narrow panels of stained glass—abstract, not Biblical scenes—banded the center seam, as if the architects had decided that everyone knew the stories so well by now that they could be suggested merely by using the same materials in which they had formerly been represented. There was a coatroom off the entryway where everyone hung their coats—you couldn't call it a vestibule. Vestry, sacristy, nave, chapel—those provocative words could not be applied. Whatever meaning these entities had once possessed they'd now lost.

Rotating in place, people recited hello and Merry Christmas. Nick and Ellie led the way into the . . . not atrium, not tabernacle. Of course there were no pews. Metal folding chairs, most of them already taken, had been set up in a semicircle facing a wooden platform, which nothing identified as an altar, not even a plain, unoccupied cross. A wooden orange crate surrounded by hay stood in the center of the platform.

They found seats four rows back. Ellie slid in first, then Pryce, Monica, Nick, and Zoë. Zoë had the last seat in the row. Ellie was speaking to the woman beside her; leaning forward, Zoë saw Judith Beauregard.

She must have saved the seats. Stewart was sitting on the aisle, gazing forward. When Zoë sat back thinking, they put all those people between us but it won't do any good, Nick looked sharply at her, but she ignored him, instead watching the man who had come to stand on the platform and was gesturing for quiet; he was wearing a red flannel shirt, green tie, and herringbone tweed pants held up by suspenders; his whitening gray hair was drawn back into a ponytail. He announced that the Christmas committee, in keeping with Unitarian tastes—at which everyone laughed as at an in-joke—had planned a simple tableau and a reading from the nativity scene in John. "*Luke*, Zack!" someone called from the back. "Luke, sorry." He descended from the platform, gesturing towards the back of the room as he did, and amid laughter and murmuring a crowd of children appeared—a Mary and Joseph, Mary cradling a doll, the three Wise Men, and at least ten shepherds, each carrying, leading, or dragging a recalcitrant pet: dogs, cats, birds, hamsters, and, bringing up the rear, a boy in a shepherd's robe with a beautiful python draped around his arms and shoulders. Requisite gasps. The python seemed to be the only animal that wasn't terrified.

"That's a little much," Zoë heard behind her.

"What happened to the oxen and the sheep?"

"How are they going to keep it from eating the rabbits?"

Nick gave Zoë a disgusted look.

When the children had arranged themselves around the stage to a soundtrack of giggles, barks, and miaows, two more children, a boy and a girl, dressed as shepherds but not carrying animals, ascended the dais with Bibles. They opened them to marked places, then looked at each other indecisively. Misunderstanding cues, they both began to read, stopped, blushing as people laughed; they consulted in whispers; finally the girl began again.

"And in the sixth month the angel Gabriel was sent from God unto a city of Galilee, named Nazareth . . ."

"To a virgin," the girl added, as if she'd just thought of it, "espoused to a man whose name was Joseph, of the house of David; and the virgin's name was Mary."

They continued, alternating verses, taking up their lines with such adamancy that they seemed to be correcting each other's accounts.

"And Joseph also went up from Galilee," the boy repeated, "out of the city of Nazareth, into Judaea, unto the city of David, which is called Bethlehem . . ."

"To be taxed with Mary his espoused wife," the girl asserted, "being great with child."

"And so it was, that, while they were there, the days were accomplished that she should be delivered."

"And she brought forth her firstborn son, and wrapped him in swaddling clothes, and laid him in a manger; because there was no room for them at the inn."

This line delivered, they turned and looked conspicuously at the girl playing Mary, who kissed the doll she'd been rocking and laid it in the orange-crate manger. To the audience, the baby was now invisible in its wooden box, and they laughed. Zoë felt offended; couldn't they hear, even in this fake church, how the phrases resounded? Plaintive and yet somehow more ominous than she'd ever heard them, since even all the nondenominating and secularizing they had been able to administer had been without effect; the promise could not be eradicated: *Believe*, and you shall be saved; *believe*, and you will not walk alone in the valley of the shadow of death; *believe* that suffering signifies; *believe* that the Son's sacrifice can ease the Father's pain; *believe* that one evening long ago *one* child was born who will keep all the children who come after him from being sacrificed . . . It was an insidious contract, and the most inviting one ever offered; Stewart heard it, at the opposite end of the row, and Zoë knew that he, if no one else, understood what was at stake here tonight. How, knowing that, could she not follow wherever he led? If she didn't steal the child back from him, the contract would never be broken.

The reading had come to an end and as the audience, directed by Zack, began to sing "The First Noël," the children proceeded down from the dais, clutching squirming animals; suddenly there was a shriek.

"The snake!" someone screamed.

Multiple shrieks now, cries of "Is it poisonous?," "Stand on the chairs!," "Keep calm!" Zoë glanced at Nick, who shook his head again in absolute, hopeless disgust. Before pandemonium had a chance to take hold, however, the hapless snake was retrieved by its owner, who looked both mortified and furious.

At the refreshment table, Michael cornered Pryce again and Zoë took a Styrofoam cup of hot cider and went to examine the pictures hanging on the walls, children's drawings of nativity scenes. Clever church, to lay the whole burden of Christmas on the children. She paused before a picture of the Christ Child in the manger with his arms and legs sticking straight up in the air, Mary and Joseph on either side stiff as sentries.

"I didn't know you were a believer," Stewart said. He pressed against her back.

And you?

"You ask embarrassing questions." He lowered his voice. "You'll come tonight? When everyone's asleep, down the arroyo? You can find your way?"

Yes.

"Come to the barn behind the house—do you know where I mean?"

Zoë nodded again, glancing over Stewart's shoulder—Nick was coming. Stewart looked behind him, waved a welcoming hand, and continued rapidly, "I'll leave a light on in the house so you'll know where to climb out of the arroyo . . . Hello, Nick."

Nick nodded. He looked at Zoë.

"Quite a change from the midnight mass I grew up with," Stewart said. "How about you?"

Nick just stood there, and Stewart turned to Zoë.

"I *like* your brother, you know," he said. "Liked him from the first moment I saw him. Hard not to like someone so . . . friendly, don't you find? So eager to *be* liked."

"Zoë, please," Nick said.

"Please?" Stewart was amused. "You don't want your sister to talk to me?"

Nick had taken her arm but now dropped it. "I'll be over there," he said. "I'm obviously not wanted here."

"Forgive me, Father," Stewart murmured when Nick was out of hearing. "Forgive me, for I know not what I do." He bent close to her. "But that's no excuse, is it? You either do something or you don't—that's all we know. Except you don't really believe that, do you? You won't believe it until it's too late."

XXXVIII SPARTA

When she arrived home from the bakery, Zoë found an envelope from Seth on her desk. She wrote on it, "I'm not interested in anything you have to say," and slipped it through the banister on a step halfway up the third-floor stairs. She hadn't heard him but he might be lurking up in his study. Monica still wasn't home. The phone rang, but she was afraid it might be Rob and didn't answer it. At least now, though, she knew that Seth wasn't around. He would have picked it up. This was about four-thirty. She lay on the couch and fell asleep, to be woken about six by an ambulance siren, screaming down Chesterfield on its way to St. Luke's. She got up and went into the kitchen to see what was in the refrigerator and ate a slice of liverwurst and some leftover chocolate pudding.

At seven the phone rang again. This time she picked it up; she was going to have to talk to Rob—or Seth—eventually, but it was Monica calling from New York, where she was "between planes." That was what she said: "Zoë, dear, I'm between planes in New York." "You're what?" "Sweetheart, your grandmother died this morning." "She what?" "They think it was a heart attack—that's all I know right now. I'm sorry to have to tell you like this, especially since I have so little time to talk at the moment. My flight's just been announced. Could you please call Nick? And tell your father? I'll call later tonight, when I know better what's going on." "What do you mean, what's going on?" "Zoë, I don't . . ." "How do they know it was a heart attack?" "I don't know, sweetheart. I'll call you later, I promise. They're announcing my flight again—everyone's supposed to be on board. I'm sorry, dear. When I call back we can discuss arrangements." "Arrangements?" "For you to come up." "Come up there?" But Monica had said goodbye.

Zoë stood in the hallway with the receiver in her hand, listening again to her mother's words, but their meaning was a long way off, like a pinpoint appearing that you knew was the train you'd been waiting for even though you couldn't see it yet. It seemed as if there were something she had to do before what had happened would become visible.

Call Nick. She was supposed to call Nick. She dialed but there was no answer at the dorm. Of course not—it was Saturday night; everyone was out on a date. Who was Nick out with? Bridget, probably—since she couldn't get Seth she'd fall back on Nick. Why had Bridget been trying to steal her brother and her father?

Her grandmother was dead: Charlotte was dead. While Zoë had been thinking about something else, the news had crept closer and before she'd had a chance to move back from the edge it was on top of her, black and grinning with steel. She could hardly stand up; she was still in the hallway, holding the phone. She hung it up and sidled into the living room and fell into a chair. But then she was sick and had to jump back up and lurch down the hall to the bathroom. She barely made it. She'd realized that, while she'd been on campus, at Anders Ogilvy's and then at the bakery, driven by revenge, Charlotte had already been dead. If she hadn't done these things, Charlotte would still be alive.

As she rinsed out her mouth she remembered back to when she and Nick had found the letter from Monica announcing her and Seth's separation and how Nick had threatened to leave home but when she got sick he'd stayed. She started to cry. At least Nick loved her—or he had. How could even he love her anymore after what she'd done? If she told Rob that Charlotte was dead and that that was why she'd been so upset she'd lied about Seth and Bridget would he forgive her?

She dialed the bakery; no answer. Then she realized that if she hadn't lied, Rob would have been there. She'd call back and tell him the truth—not say, as she'd planned, that she'd given him the photographs because her grandmother had died but that her grandmother had died because she'd given him the photographs. She had been afraid that, by themselves, the photographs wouldn't justify her state of mind, so she'd thrown in Seth and Bridget. Now she saw that she'd wanted to punish Rob because he was the person she could hurt the most, and now she was being punished. "My grandmother's dead," she said aloud, "and it's my fault." This wasn't all, though; it wasn't over yet. Lightning flashed but thunder didn't break until you had forgotten you were waiting for it. Then it cracked open the sky right over your head.

She didn't know what she did for the next few hours. She tried the dorm several more times, she tried the bakery. She wanted to go over there—Rob might be there and refusing to answer the phone—but she was afraid that he might call while she was gone.

She called the Wycliffes', but Mr. Wycliffe answered and she hung up.

She remembered Seth's letter, lying unopened on the stairs, and she climbed the flight and a half and read it. Did she really think that he'd seduce her best friend—or, more to the point, allow himself to be seduced? He felt about Bridget as he did about her—protective and concerned, that was *all.* Why was she so eager to cast him in the role of villain? Bridget was acting out some sort of guilt complex—he didn't pretend to understand its aetiology—though in recollecting that childhood episode of their letters to teachers he realized that it must have been going on for some time. Probably all of everyone's lives. It had also become clear to him that Bridget compared herself unfavorably to Zoë and that Zoë's good opinion mattered more to Bridget than anyone else's. He could only think that, in attempting to seduce her (Zoë's) father, Bridget had been trying to "please" Zoë in some contorted manner by becoming the deceitful immoral person she believed Zoë thought she was. "You yourself know best whether or not this applies."

So he was saying that she was responsible for what Bridget had done too. It was the same thing he'd said years ago when he found out about the letters—"to involve a mentally unstable boy . . ." Why did everyone think she started everything and, furthermore, why was everyone always, forever, convinced that *she* was just fine?

Then a new anxiety hit her—where was *Seth*? Why would he have left the note and gone away again? Fighting some kind of undertow, she forced herself to climb the rest of the way up the stairs to the third floor. The study door was closed, but it always was. She knocked; when there was no answer she flung the door open—if he were lying there dead she'd rather know about it at once. But the room was empty—she could tell even before she switched on the light. Evidently she was going to have to suffer in silence a lot longer before knowing the full weight of everything she'd done.

She stood for a moment in the middle of the rug, looking at Seth's pipe rack, all the pipes arranged in a circle, their stems inserted into the metal ring, their polished wood bowls shining. She took one made of cherry from the rack and felt its silky surface. She or Nick had given it to him—they were always giving him pipes for his birthday. He probably couldn't believe it when once again he'd had another pipe-sized box to open, but he'd never once shown his disappointment. There they all were in a circle, their gifts to him.

Zoë turned off the light and sat in the windowseat. She looked down Metcalf at the cars driving by along Chesterfield. She thought about Samuel. He had been dead, and she had seen him—made love with him—yet she couldn't pretend that that meant Charlotte would come back.

No general conclusions could be drawn from any single inexplicable reappearance.

Monica called again at eleven. She was at the house in Harmony. She said she would have called earlier except that there had been things to see to.

"Are you all right?" Zoë asked.

"Oh, I'm as all right as I've ever been, which may not be saying much, now that I think about it."

Her mother sounded like a little girl trying to sound older.

"Is anyone with you? Mrs. Magoon or anyone?"

"Eldridge—Dr. Jewell—gave me a sleeping pill to take. I'll do that as soon as I hang up, though I can't imagine that it will have any effect. I can't imagine ever being able to sleep again, not after learning the manner of her death."

"The manner of her death?" Zoë repeated. "I thought you said she had a heart attack."

She had been standing again by the phone in the downstairs hallway. Now she carried it to the stairs and sat on the bottom step. She pressed one hand against her stomach.

"I didn't hear the whole story until I got here. All Vera knew when she called was heart attack."

"It wasn't a heart attack?"

"She did have one, yes, but it turns out that she hasn't been taking her medication. Dr. Mervyn and Dr. Jewell both think that the shock to her system may have provoked the heart attack."

Zoë squeezed her eyes shut and opened them again. "How do they know she wasn't taking her medication?"

"Verne found her in the attic—it's a miracle he even thought to look up there, but he was determined to ask her where she wanted him to transplant the day lilies. Mother was slumped over a trunk—Verne thought she might have been trying to move it. She'd been hiding her medication there. Vera can't understand how she concealed it, since she swears she watched her put it in her mouth and swallow it every morning. And no one can understand why she kept the pills instead of disposing of them. She must have been so confused, poor soul."

"But it was moving the trunk that triggered her heart attack?"

"That's a possibility, though both doctors think that coming off the medication so suddenly laid the groundwork. They want to do an autopsy to be sure."

"What?"

"I gave Dr. Mervyn my permission."

"How could you do that?"

"It may help other people, Zoë."

"Yes, but . . ." If possible, this was worse than hearing that Charlotte was dead—to think of strangers handling her body, what they would do to her.

"It can make no difference to her now."

If they did an autopsy, wouldn't they analyze the contents of her stomach and discover the aspirin and begin to put two and two together? How was it possible that they hadn't suspected already?

Suddenly Monica was crying.

"I've been stunned," she said. "I never realized . . . She made a *decision*. She took her life into her own hands—I can't tell you how that makes me feel. I'm so proud of her, Zoë. I never felt that about her before. I'm sorry. I don't mean to go on like this. I know how much you loved her, sweetheart. Are you all right? Were you able to get hold of Nick? Did you tell your father?"

"He hasn't come home. No one's answering at the dorm."

"Oh, Zoë, you're all *alone*?"

"You're all alone," she said.

"Yes, but . . ."

"It's your mother who died."

"I don't like the way you sound, Zoë. Where can your father possibly be at this hour? Would you at least call Bridget and ask her to come over and stay with you?"

"I don't need a babysitter."

"Zoë, please, don't fight me about this. I can't bear to think of you in the house alone. Please promise me you'll call someone."

"Okay, I'll call someone."

"You need to consider whether or not you want to come up for the funeral. It will be on Tuesday—they'll do the autopsy Monday. There's more than enough money in the joint account to cover your and Nick's tickets. Will you call me first thing in the morning? Or have your father call me, if you're already en route?"

"But I . . ."

"Zoë, *please*," she said.

What did her mother mean?

"Where is she?" she asked.

"Where's your grandmother?"

Zoë nodded, then realized she hadn't spoken and said, "Yes."

"At the hospital in Hanover."

At that moment Seth walked in.

"What is it? What's happened?" he asked when he saw her face.

Zoë put her hand over the receiver and said, "Grandma Charlotte died."

He flinched. "Is that your mother?"

Zoë nodded and he took the phone from her. She could tell by his responses that Monica was repeating the same information she'd given her.

"I was supposed to call Nick," Zoë said when Seth hung up, furious at feeling her throat tightening and her eyes watering, "but of course he's out. It's Saturday night. God knows when he'll be in. The funeral's on Tuesday. I think Mother wants us to come up tomorrow, though."

"Well, you don't have to decide tonight. Here, I'll try the dorm again and then I'll fix you a hot drink."

"Dad, it's hot already!"

He put the phone back on its table and put his arms around her. When he wouldn't let her go, she knew she wouldn't be able to resist. Through sobs she shouted at him, "It's my fault! That's what you don't understand—it's my fault!"

He stepped back so that he could see her. "What is, Zoë?"

"That Grandmother died! Didn't Mother tell you? She stopped taking her pills. They think that going off them caused her heart attack. But I'm the one who got her off her medication! Last summer, when Mrs. Magoon was in North Carolina."

Seth looked bewildered.

"Don't you understand? I killed her!"

"Zoë, come into the living room and sit down. Now say this again. You weaned your grandmother from her medication when you were in Harmony last summer? Is that what you're telling me?"

"Yes!"

"And, according to your mother, doctors speculate that being taken off the medication may have affected her heart?"

"Yes! That's what . . ."

"Did you force her to stop taking it?"

"Of course not! She stopped on her own but I caught her and didn't make her take it."

"Well, then . . ."

"But she couldn't have gone on not taking it without me. I helped her fool Mrs. Magoon. I bought an aspirin compound that looked like the drug and switched them. Mother thinks she was hiding the medication in the trunk but that was the last aspirin container. This summer I was going to figure out some way to convince Mom to let her stay off permanently."

Seth thought about this. Then he said, "May I ask you another question? Did anything happen to your grandmother, that you noticed, once she'd stopped taking the medication?"

"Yes! She was completely different. She was so lively—I wish Mother could have seen her. She told me on the phone that she's *proud* of Grandmother for having taken her life into her own hands."

"Then, Zoë, that's the more reason for saying nothing to your mother. It may be a moot issue if they're doing an autopsy, but if they discover nothing then let your mother think what she thinks. You didn't *kill* Charlotte—that's absurd. For one thing, she's been off the pills almost a year. All you did was to allow her her freedom. No one had ever done that for her in her life. Don't you think it's better that she ended her life alive instead of already half dead?"

"It's still my fault."

"In this case, thinking that may be a luxury you can't allow yourself. If being forgiven depends on making someone else feel responsible . . ."

"Who else would feel responsible?"

"Your mother, who else? If you were to tell her what a positive change was effected in your grandmother . . . Your mother's already had to live all these years with the knowledge that she might have made the wrong decision where your grandmother's treatment was concerned. If you tell her what you did, she may blame herself for the rest of her life."

"Are you serious?"

Seth actually laughed. "Zoë, sometimes I wonder . . . What sort of cold-blooded monsters do you take us for?"

"I don't know," she muttered.

He was shaking his head, looking at her incredulously, though kindly.

"I better call Nick," she said, embarrassed.

On the second ring a slurred voice answered.

" 's Jessica?" Zoë heard, when she asked for Nick.

"It's his sister."

" 'sn't here."

"Do you know where he is? It's an emergency."

"Not brother's keeper. Million apologies."

"Could you please leave a message for him to come home right away?"

"Home?"

"Home! Could you *please* just write that?"

"Take it easy, whosis?"

At this point Seth, who'd followed her into the hall and had been hovering impatiently, grabbed the phone.

"Who the *hell* am I speaking with? This is Seth Carver. What does it take to get you to give my son a message?

"It doesn't pay to be polite to idiots like that," he said, hanging up.

"He was drunk," she said.

"I believe I sobered him up some."

She let him make her hot chocolate. They'd been sitting in the kitchen for about twenty minutes when Nick came in. He was wearing a jacket and tie and looked very cheerful.

"I arrived just as Wilson was hanging up. It's a good thing—otherwise I never would have heard a word. Now, what's this about an emergency? Everybody miss my company so much?"

"Nick, it's not good news," Seth said.

Nick looked around the room. "Where's Mom?"

"Your grandmother just died. Your mother has already gone to Harmony."

"Shit," Nick said. He sat down at the table and looked at his hands. Zoë could tell he was stewed. Seth either didn't notice or pretended not to.

"Want some coffee?" she asked Nick softly.

He nodded, his lips pursed now, his chin quivering.

"There are arrangements to be discussed," Seth said. "Depending on whether or not you want to go to the funeral, which I understand is Tuesday."

"Can I get out of these clothes first? I think I still have some things upstairs."

Zoë knew he didn't want them to see him crying. After a couple of minutes, they heard the shower running in the upstairs bathroom. In ten minutes he reappeared in a T-shirt and jeans, his eyes red and his hair wet. He gulped the coffee.

"I remembered that I have my final lab test Monday morning. Since it's the end of the year it's almost impossible to reschedule. Do you think we could leave Monday afternoon?"

"We could take the flight Mom took. She got in about nine."

Nick slept in his old room and Sunday morning they made their reservations and phoned Monica. When Nick went back to campus, Zoë changed into a sundress—it was almost ninety already—then walked down to Mulberry Street.

Rob wasn't home—either that or not opening the door. She called him from the phone booth in front of Woolworth's, but if he was in he wasn't answering. If he *wasn't* home, where could he be? She tried his parents' house, but there was no answer there either. Maybe they'd all gone on a picnic, highly unlikely though that seemed.

She had a pen in her purse and walked down to the Harbor House and asked for a napkin. While she wrote the note she scanned the tables to make sure that Rob wasn't having brunch with Pete, the former baker.

> Rob,
>
> Do you want to go out to lunch somewhere? I'm sorry about yesterday—everything kind of ganged up on me at once. I'll try back around one.
>
> Zoë

She knew it was too casual, but she didn't like to say more when someone might come along and read it. It was a quarter to twelve—what was she going to do for an hour and fifteen minutes?

She walked over to the Naval Academy—they were having some kind of drill: forward and halt; turn, march; present arms; about face. She wished she were marching too; she envied the midshipmen having their every movement directed by someone else.

At one Rob still wasn't home, and the napkin was still in the door. Zoë was beginning to feel uneasy, not only because she wanted to see him so badly. Where could he be? He was *always* there, except when he went somewhere with her. He didn't even like to go down to the harbor by himself. It seemed incredible to her now that she could have known that about him and done what she had yesterday. She was the only person he talked to—the only person he *loved*, he'd told her so—and she'd tried to hurt him like that? What had she been hoping he would do, commit suicide? She had already started back down Mulberry Street towards the harbor when what she had been thinking registered—and then the imaginary calm she'd been in broke completely open and she was terrified, so full of a sick fear that she could hardly stand. She reached out and caught herself against the side of a house; the rough brick scraped her palm and the sensation brought to her such an unbearably clear picture of Rob that she turned against the wall and murmured, Oh, Rob, where *are* you? Please don't be dead, please—I can stand anything, but not that. Please, Rob, please, please . . . But already she was walking back towards the campus, pursuing some unclear idea of finding Nick and asking to borrow his car so that she could look for Rob. Seth would let her use the car but she didn't want to have to explain what she wanted it for. But Nick wasn't in his room; he wasn't in the lab; he wasn't in the library. No doubt with Jessica, whoever she was. But Zoë was too distraught to care.

All day followed this pattern—marching over and over the triangle between Metcalf Street (to try Rob on the phone), Mulberry Street, and the campus; Seth had told her to call him at his office when she felt hungry for dinner and he'd rustle something up or they'd go to the Chinaman. All day she tried to keep her sick terror from overwhelming her but it kept ricocheting back so suddenly and fiercely that she'd have to stop walking and lean against something. Should she go to the police? But what would she say to them? A person had to be gone longer than Rob had been to be officially considered missing.

At five she took the napkin out of the door and wrote on the other side:

> 5 p.m. Where are you? I tried your parents. My grandmother died—I need to see you. Could you please call me as soon as you get this?

After that she stayed home. She made grilled tuna fish and cheese sandwiches for herself and Seth and they ate them on the back porch. When Seth went up to his study, after asking her if she were all right—he was being very sweet and now she felt guilty about him and Bridget too—she mixed herself a gin and tonic and went back outside.

After a long time it got dark. The phone never rang. About ten Seth came downstairs and was startled to find her still sitting there.

"Do you think you could try to get some sleep?"

She went upstairs. At eleven-thirty she tiptoed downstairs and called the bakery. She came down to call every hour until daylight. In between she lay staring at the dark.

At seven she walked down to Mulberry Street—the note was still in the door, and she took it out. Maybe the police could do something after eight if he hadn't opened the bakery. Yet she felt so uncomfortable calling the police. It was hard to believe that she wasn't being melodramatic.

She went home and made coffee and at five past eight came back—nothing had changed. She had decided to go to school for the morning; if she came by at noon and the bakery was still closed there'd be time to go to the police before she and Nick had to leave for the airport. She'd left Seth a note telling him she'd gone to school and would be back by one.

She couldn't face riding to school with Archie Tannenbaum so she took the bus out to Hollister Point. It ran only three times a day: morning, noon, and rush hour. Hollister Day students hardly ever took it.

Through American history, she sat staring out the window at the cupola where she'd always imagined the consumptive Hollister daughter spending her last days—as if somehow the beauty of the setting would make dying not so bad. That now seemed like a stupid, romantic idea. Mr. Stead must have realized that she was more than usually out of it, because he left her alone, probably not wanting the hassle of trying to get her to respond to a question.

Just before the nine-twenty bell, Mr. Meyer, the assistant headmaster, opened the door to announce that there would be a special assembly at nine-thirty for the upper school.

"Oh, God, what now?" everyone groaned.

"Probably World War Three."

"At least we'll get to go home early."

People were joking all the way over from the classroom building to the converted barn where they had assemblies, staged plays, held dances, and organized anti-Vietnam rallies. Archie came up to her and told her he was sorry about her grandmother.

"You read my note?" She was wondering why he'd gone by the bakery yesterday afternoon.

"What note? When you didn't show I called your house to see if you were sick or just late. Woke up your old man, who told me what was going on. How did you get here?"

"On the bus."

Archie nodded knowingly.

"Your dad said you're flying up to New Hampshire this afternoon. You want me to drive you home after lunch?"

"Yeah, maybe. Thanks."

Inside the barn, it was obvious at once that the assembly had been called for something more serious than a reiteration of the no-smoking rules. The teachers were very subdued. Zoë caught Mr. Montgomery looking at her, although he looked away quickly, and for one insane moment she thought that the assembly was being held to announce that Charlotte had died. But people's grandparents died all the time without its being publicly announced. When everyone had crammed into the room, Mr. Curley, the headmaster, climbed onto the podium and raised his hands.

"Benediction!" someone shouted from the back. Everyone laughed and turned around, but the teachers hissed, "Shh!" The school had been called into special assembly a couple of times before for tragedies: an auto accident in which a seventh-grader had been killed; another time when one of the teachers lost her baby—a caesarean had been performed at the last minute but it had been too late. Mr. Curley had said he wanted them all to hear the actual details from "someone in authority" rather than have students gossiping and wondering. But special assemblies were also called when good things happened—when the Tannenbaums won the Bermuda Cup Race, or when some astronaut did something.

"Folks," Mr. Curley said now, "I don't have good news, I'm sorry."

Zoë thought how odd it was that he used almost the same words that Seth had used the night before to Nick.

"This is going to be difficult for some of you, I'm afraid."

"Get to the point," someone behind Zoë grumbled, though not so that Mr. Curley could hear.

"There's been an accident. A student who used to go here, Robert Went . . ."

Mr. Curley probably hadn't paused for more than a second, but it seemed to Zoë that in that interval she'd stopped breathing, her mind flashing forward to the knowledge that Rob was dead—so that she didn't hear the end of Mr. Curley's sentence. But the words were still hanging in her mind and she played them back.

"His father was killed Saturday evening."

Her shock at Rob's death had no time to change to pity and sadness for him and his father before Mr. Curley added, "Robert may have been involved."

Again he paused, and she wanted to shout at him, What *is* it? What happened? Is Rob a vegetable? Is he crippled for life? But he was already crippled for life.

"We have very few details as of yet, but apparently Robert was walking along Stark Road, which his father takes home from work every day—Mr. Went was working this Saturday—and Robert stepped out to wave at a place where . . . I'm sorry."

Mr. Curley's voice cracked. Zoë couldn't understand what was happening. Why was Mr. Curley so upset? Had he known Rob's father?

"In order to avoid hitting his son, Robert's father had no choice but to swerve. He lost control of the car and it rolled over a steep embankment. He died on the way to the hospital."

Still no one had reacted. Zoë could feel the paralysis in the room. "He died on the way to the hospital . . ." You read those words in the paper all the time, but she'd never heard anyone say them aloud.

Mr. Curley breathed out. "I'm afraid that isn't all," he said. "Apparently Robert . . . It seems he may have . . . What they're now trying to determine is whether or not . . ." He took another deep breath, trying to keep his voice from shaking. "It will be all over the papers tonight. I wanted those of you who knew him to hear it from me. Robert's in custody, and it looks as though he may be charged with manslaughter. At the minimum."

There was now absolute, total silence. But then someone said, "What!" and suddenly everyone was talking at once. One of the seventh-graders who worked for Rob started to cry. Then another. Mr. Curley called, "Please, silence. Please. I know you need to talk, but give me one minute. Remember that nothing—*nothing*—has been determined. Even if Robert should be charged, a charge is *not* a verdict and there is every reason to believe that another explanation will be forthcoming. Right now all they want to do is to keep Robert under observation. My point is that we must all make the utmost effort not to jump to any conclusions."

"Christ," Zoë heard Archie Tannenbaum swear.

"We all of us know Robert, and I am sure I can safely say that there's not a person among us who believes him capable of intentionally causing someone's death, least of all his own father's. As I said, I wanted you to hear the facts from me, since they are sure to be splashed over the evening papers as sensationalistically as possible. For now, all any of us can assume is that it was an accident."

"Then why don't the police assume that?" Archie called.

"I was coming to that," Mr. Curley said, and Archie said, "Sorry," then muttered, "I thought he was done."

"As I understand it, the main reason the D.A. is considering charging Robert is because of his own testimony."

Mr. Curley's voice sounded very tired now, as if he'd had to explain the same thing over a hundred times.

"He claims he did it on purpose. I need not tell you that there is every reason to mistrust his testimony, which is why Robert is being kept under guard in the psychiatric wing of St. Luke's instead of in jail. There's speculation that Rob's action was a suicide attempt that backfired. This is a lot to take in all at once, I know. I will be glad to answer questions in a moment. As you probably can imagine, the press will have a field day with all of this. Though I can keep reporters off the school grounds, I can't protect you from them elsewhere, and I'd like you to feel you have every right not to talk to them. I'd be very surprised if they don't try to ferret out information from among you, especially those of you who may have worked for him. So keep away from his bakery. Any of you who did work for him or are friends with him I would like to meet with separately after the general assembly has been dismissed. I promise to let all of you know the moment I know anything else. Later on, the other teachers and I will be discussing what the best means would be of offering our sympathy to Robert and his mother, and we'll let you know when the funeral will take place, since some of you may wish to go. Now, does anyone have questions? Or, if you prefer, speak to me afterwards. I'm sure you're all as upset and shocked as I am and I want you to try to trust that everything will soon be explained. I'm sorry to have to be the bearer of this news, but, as I said, I'd rather you'd hear it here, all together, than later, by yourselves. All right, please return to your classes now and do the best you can to continue with the work of the day."

Everyone was shuffling to their feet when Archie yelled out, "Did they read him his Miranda rights? They can't use his confession against him if they didn't. And why would they read rights at the scene of an accident?"

"Archie, I don't know," Mr. Curley said, raising his voice over the hubbub of people walking out. "I don't know the answer to these and other reasonable questions. I wish I did."

"A little knowledge is a dangerous thing," Archie muttered to himself. People were leaving, anxious to get outside. Teachers were zeroing in on Marcy Abbot and the other seventh-graders.

"Aren't you coming, Zo?" Archie asked.

She opened her mouth to answer him, but got something stuck in her throat and coughed. She shook her head.

"Oh, right, you'd be staying for the next meeting. Maybe I'll stay too."

She hadn't stopped shaking her head.

"Zoë?" a voice said.

She looked up: Mr. Montgomery. What had happened? The assembly hall was empty except for the seventh-graders up front around the podium with Mr. Curley and some other teachers. She blinked and stood up. Archie was looking at her strangely. She walked towards him, meaning to follow him.

"Hold on a minute," Mr. Montgomery said. "I'd prefer you didn't go back to class just yet."

She shrugged, trying not to look at him as he took her arm and helped her up the aisle as if she couldn't walk, then put his arm around her shoulders and said, "Let's walk a little. I don't have a class until next period."

She looked over her shoulder at Archie.

"Do you want to stay?" he asked. "I'll stay with you."

She shook her head. He thought she was reacting to one piece of bad news too many.

"I'd like to talk to Zoë alone, if she has no objection," Mr. Montgomery said.

"Do you?" Archie asked.

She shook her head again. Mr. Montgomery steered her outside, across the playing field, and down the reedy path to the river. She had no idea what he was saying—he might as well have been speaking Swahili—but the sound of his voice was comforting, the way the sentences billowed up and down. He talked all the way down to the river. When they had sat down on a half-rotted log by the bank, Mr. Montgomery said, "I don't know why it is that the worst things always seem to happen on the most beautiful days."

Was that true?

"Regardless of whether or no you and Rob have maintained your friendship—or what its nature is—I know that you must be experiencing many conflicting emotions right now. There was always something about the two of you that struck me as highly combustible—no," he said, raising a hand, "I'm not asking you for details. I'm sure you're not ready to go into it all yet."

Did he really imagine that someday she'd be discussing Rob with him, making up theories to explain why Rob had said he'd done something everyone was so sure he couldn't possibly have? Because with every step she'd taken since she'd heard, every breath she'd breathed in, she knew it was true, that it was this news she'd been waiting for all along: Rob killed his father. Rob killed his father. Rob killed his father to get even with her.

"Of course, should they pursue the idiocy of bringing the charge, which I don't believe for a minute—and, by the way, I think it outrageously irresponsible of Doug Curley even to suggest such a thing, whatever the paper may choose to print—but, as I was saying, *should* there be a charge, there will be the defense of temporary insanity. You should perhaps be prepared to be called as a witness."

Mr. Montgomery glanced at her. She could tell that he could hardly stand not to ask her questions.

"His apparent confession will probably be used in the end only as evidence that he was out of his mind. I'm not sure what I think about that, though." He stopped talking now. "Zoë, I'm quite sincere, you needn't answer, but . . . How long *is* it since you've seen Rob?"

She just shook her head. There was no longer any neutral response.

"I'm so disturbed to be reminded of what we talked about a year and a half ago—do you remember? Right after he opened the bakery. I believe I said to you then that Rob has been daring people all his life. That supposed accident when he was a child, then the bakery. Now this . . ."

She felt sorry for Mr. Montgomery for being so blind. He knew nothing about Charlotte, or Bridget and her designs, or Anders Ogilvy, or Rob's premonitions—how pitiful Mr. Montgomery was, thinking he knew so much. Why had she gone on a walk with him? Betraying Rob like this—Mr. Montgomery had tricked her.

My grandmother's being buried tomorrow, she opened her mouth to say. I am responsible for her death.

She wanted to shock Mr. Montgomery, say something that would make him just shut UP for once, but when she opened her mouth to speak the words she'd had in her mind, something got stuck in her throat and again she began to cough. This time she had to gasp for breath, as if someone were pressing hard on her windpipe to strangle her. She stared at Mr. Montgomery, trying to scream, I can't breathe! I can't breathe! but all that came out was a horrible croaking noise, no air in it, as if she were dying. I don't want to die! she tried to shout. I don't want to die!

"Zoë, good God, what is the matter?" Mr. Montgomery began hitting her between the shoulder blades. "Is something stuck in your throat?"

She shook her head wildly, twisting away from him. Then suddenly her throat opened and she gulped for air. The hand around her throat was gone.

"Are you all right?" he exclaimed.

I don't know, she started to say, I was just trying to . . . But instantly the words choked her; only when she took them back, pulled them out of her throat, or her lungs, back into her mind, promising that she wouldn't say them, was she allowed to breathe again. Yet she couldn't believe it—she couldn't *talk*?—and once again tried to say, Something's wrong with my throat; every time I try to say something . . . And once again the words piled up in her windpipe and choked her. She stared at Mr. Montgomery, as if he were doing this to her.

"Zoë, what *is* it?"

She pointed at her throat and shook her head.

"You can't talk?"

She shook her head again.

He looked at her, disturbed.

"Let's go back," he said.

Something was different in his voice now. He took her arm again and she felt like saying, I don't have a problem *walking*; it's just that I can't speak. But now even to imagine saying the words made her throat begin to clench up. Was she not even supposed to think of things she *might* say?

She avoided looking at Mr. Montgomery on the ten-minute walk back to school; fortunately the path through the reeds was narrow and they had to walk single file. He made her go first. When they reached the lawn below the cupola, he caught up with her.

"I think you shouldn't go back to class, Zoë. I don't want to alarm you further, but I'm afraid that you're going into some kind of shock."

Forgetting, she started to protest, I'm not in shock, I just can't talk! but her throat seized up so quickly that she staggered back as if someone had hit her. She had to swallow the words before she could breathe. But now she was infuriated. How could she not be able to talk? She would force herself. It was stupid. She would just *say* something. Anything.

I'm not going into shock. I'm fine. I just . . .

The words rose, stopped, blocked her throat. Drowning, she kept on, forcing more words up behind them.

I have to explain! I kept all these secrets and now everyone is dead! I lied to Rob! I told him my father was having an affair with Bridget! I left obscene photographs of myself for him to look at when I knew how he'd feel when he saw them! Now he's killed his father and it's my fault! He's gone insane and it's my fault! My grandmother's dead and it's my fault!

She had no memory of blacking out. All she remembered was waking up and seeing Mr. Montgomery bending over her, looking completely terrified. It reminded her right away of the time she'd fainted and woken up and thought she was in the play and called Rob "Louis." She laughed. Now Mr. Montgomery looked even more frightened. He thought she was going crazy; he loved talking about madness in books, but the minute he thought he'd encountered it in real life, forget it. Wait until she told Rob. Where was Rob? Oh, now she remembered, he was in the psychiatric ward at St. Luke's, accused of murdering his father. She laughed again.

Wait until you hear the nightmare I just had, she started to say to Mr. Montgomery, but at this the vise was clamped back on her throat and she sat up and retched. There wasn't much to vomit up—she'd hadn't eaten anything since six o'clock the night before.

Mr. Montgomery was looking around frantically. She could tell that he wanted to get help but was afraid to leave her alone. She wished she could have told him she was fine now—he didn't need to worry about her. It was just that when she'd first heard the news—Rob had killed his father—the impossible facts of loving someone and then of that person turning out to be a murderer had collided in her mind, two things that couldn't possibly be true simultaneously, but *were*. They'd moved closer and closer until they were squeezing together around her throat like white-knuckled hands. But she could see now that as long as she didn't talk it would be all right. She loved Rob and Rob had killed his father;

he'd said someone had to get revenge. If she never tried again to say it aloud, to say what she knew, and how she'd caused it, it would be all right. She hadn't said things when she should have said them—she'd wanted to know other people's *intentions* first, she'd wanted to know the ultimate intentions of the *universe* before she'd risk saying what *she* thought—so it made perfect sense that now her punishment would be silence. Even though she was perfectly comfortable where she was, so that Mr. Montgomery could relax she stood up.

"Can you walk?" he asked, then added quickly, "Don't try to talk."

They went into Mr. Curley's office. Mrs. Chernik, his ever-smiling secretary, asked what she could do for them.

"We need to make a private call. I'd like to use Doug's office—he's in class now, I think."

"Go right ahead," Mrs. Chernik said.

Inside, Mr. Montgomery shut the door. He gave Zoë a yellow legal pad and a pen.

"Please write down your phone number for me."

She wrote, "No one's home."

It was the first thing she'd ever said that way.

Mr. Montgomery looked at the pad.

"At work?"

"My mother is in New Hampshire. My grandmother just died. My father's probably at the college."

Mr. Montgomery looked at what she'd written, stared at her, and then, watching her the whole time as if she might try to run out of the room, opened Mr. Curley's desk drawers, looking for a phone book; when he couldn't find one he picked up the phone and dialed the operator. He got the number of the college, called the switchboard, and asked for Professor Carver's office.

"Dr. Carver," he said. "Jack Montgomery at Hollister Day. Your daughter is not well and I think it would be best if you could pick her up. If that's a problem, I . . .

"No, she's right here. No, I'm afraid she can't speak with you. That's part of the problem. Please, I can't explain more now. She's had a shock—there's been some bad news at the school. Now she tells me she's also just lost a grandmother. Please come as soon as you can. We'll be in the headmaster's office."

That was the first time Zoë realized that people treated you differently when you couldn't talk. The next few days were full of people either announcing or withholding information, but it was not often clear which they were doing. Monica (who'd flown back right after the funeral on

Tuesday afternoon) would be talking on the phone to someone and say, "Zoë doesn't know this, but . . ." All the while she'd be in her room at the top of the stairs, her door open. People were trying to let her know things without saying them to her, as if they thought it was unfair that they should be able to speak when she couldn't answer. In this way she learned that just before he'd died of massive internal bleeding in the ambulance, Rob's father had looked at Rob and said, "Why?" An attendant had witnessed this. When Mrs. Went had arrived at the hospital, Robert had turned to the police and *demanded* that they read him his rights so that whatever he said could be used against him. He'd had to argue with the policeman, who'd finally given in to his wishes in the hope of calming him down. Then, in front of his mother, the police, the doctor who'd pronounced his father dead, and a nurse, Rob said, "I did it on purpose. I am not crazy. I am not hysterical. I knew what I was doing. Unless you're completely irresponsible, you'll arrest me."

Instead they called the hospital psychiatrist and convinced Mrs. Went to sign a paper committing Rob for "observation" to the psychiatric ward. After they drove off with him, she went home and took an overdose of sleeping pills. Neighbors had found her—by a lucky fluke she'd invited friends in to dinner that night. "Of course one can't not wonder if she had that fact in the back of her mind when she took the pills," Zoë heard Monica say over the phone to someone. It was impossible to know whom she was speaking to. It couldn't have been Lydia Wycliffe—by that time Lydia had already called and made an enemy of Monica for life by telling her that her "adolescent of a husband" had tried to seduce her "innocent child"; Zoë had heard Monica relating the conversation later to Seth who told Monica the same story he'd told Zoë. Two days after this Lydia called again, hysterical, to ask if they'd heard from Bridget, who had disappeared, leaving behind only the vaguest of notes.

By the end of the week, Zoë had heard from Archie Tannenbaum (who came over bringing flowers, a box of chocolates, and a note that said, "In case I'm too much of a clod to say this aloud, I just really want you to know that I care about you a lot and am really sorry about all this stuff that's happened. You can count me your friend twenty-four hours a day—I mean it") that Bridget had called her parents from Utah to announce that she'd been married to a guitarist named Rolf whom she'd met on a cross-country bus. Her parents were out of their minds, but there was nothing they could do about it.

About a week after the accident, Zoë, listening from the top of the stairs, heard Monica say calmly to Seth that she hoped he didn't think she held him in any way responsible for Bridget's flight or for anything else, but she felt that she was now ready to ask him to move out of the house; they would see what they wanted to do, if anything, after that.

By figuring out the times, Zoë realized that the ambulance siren she'd heard when she was sitting up in Seth's study that past Saturday evening must have been the ambulance carrying Mr. Went's body to the hospital.

XXXIX CASCABEL FLATS

Another half hour of eating untransubstantiated cookies and drinking cider and they drove home. Nick had stalked up to Zoë as soon as Stewart disappeared and demanded to know what he'd been saying. *Nothing much*, she said. She'd been polite about it, though—hadn't wanted him to worry: he'd been her brother for a long time, after all, even if their family were now dissolved.

Home, she sank into a chair without taking off her coat, though she supposed she'd have to go through the ruse of going to bed. Ellie was aggressively solicitous; could she get anyone anything? A nightcap? Some hot chocolate? How about some eggnog? As if she were trying to compensate for the church refreshments not having performed their eucharistic service. Monica emerged from the curtained bathroom and bid everyone good night.

"And Merry Christmas," Pryce said.

"Yes, of course, Merry Christmas."

Ellie forced Zoë to come in the kitchen with her and whispered that Judith had told her after the service that she believed she'd had a miscarriage that morning. Judith had also apologized for what she'd said about Nick; having gathered from Ellie's reaction that she was hearing the information for the first time, Judith had checked with Stewart and realized that she hadn't gotten the story straight. "It's all fairly incredible," Ellie said, "but I prefer to believe her than to believe the alternative."

Then Nick and Ellie went to bed. Zoë was surprised, but nevertheless grateful when Pryce said simply, "Goodnight, Zoë," in a gentle, relinquishing voice, kissed her on the cheek, and turned out the light. While he'd been in the bathroom, she'd taken heavy socks out of her suitcase and left them with her snow boots and her pullover on the chair nearest the kitchen. When he'd been asleep for a while, she slid out of bed and shrugged the sweater on over her nightgown. In the kitchen she pulled on her socks and boots, then lifted Nick's big sheepskin jacket off its hook behind the kitchen door—it would be easier to walk in than her long coat. Outside there was no moon, but light reflected off the snow. However, before she headed down to the streambed she circled the house and looked in the glove compartment of the car—Nick had always kept a flashlight there; good that some things never changed. Then she found her way into the gully.

It went as smoothly as if she'd practiced it. She didn't need to use the flashlight because the tracks Nick had made that afternoon had left dark indentations in the snow. The misshapen pines leaned over the sides of the gulch like figures craning over an edge to see where something had fallen. It was incredibly quiet—except for her shuffling through the snow there was no sound at all; when she stopped and looked up at the sky the stars seemed to blink audibly. Right when she was beginning to wonder if she'd walked too far, Nick's tracks led up the embankment. Then, as Stewart had promised, she saw the light he'd left on in the house; it shimmered through the darkness, promising.

Halfway to the barn, Zoë saw that, hidden by a mound of snow so it couldn't be seen from the house, Stewart had also set out a candle in a paper bag like the ones in town: how ironic—a beacon signalling the way to the stable. The barn's sliding door had been left open a foot and she slipped through sideways, then stood, smelling the horses down at the other end. She could hear them breathing thickly. It wasn't warm in the barn, but wasn't as cold as outside. Then she heard Stewart's voice in the darkness. "Zoë, over here." She moved towards the sound. "I'm right here." Before she saw him he had taken her arm and begun to kiss her; she pulled away to catch her breath. Why was he in such a hurry? Did he think Judith suspected something?

"No time," he murmured. "Time's running out." He took her hand. "Up the ladder into the loft." It was warmer up there; Zoë smiled in recognition of the hay's sweet smell. She took the flashlight out of her coat pocket and handed it to Stewart.

"You want to *see*?" he asked, but switched it on and swept an arc around the room. "We can leave it on if you like—there are no windows up here." He set it upside down on a crossbeam halfway up the wall; the circle of light broke against the sloped wood ceiling. The sharp ends of nails aimed down at them from the rough surface.

"Tell me, why did you come?" Stewart asked. "Do you think I love you?"

Yes, she said.

"Well, you're right," he went on. "What is it people say? 'I loved you from the first moment I saw you'? You love me too, I know. I'm who you've always looked for, even though you gave up hope that you'd find me. But I'm here now—you didn't imagine me after all."

Stewart had helped her off with her coat and now spread it on the hay. He pulled off his boots, ceremonially, as if they shouldn't be involved. "Lie down," he said. When she didn't comply at once, he said, "What? You're not afraid, are you? You don't think I could hurt you, do you?"

No, but . . . It was happening so fast. She hadn't imagined it happening like this. She reached up to put her arms around his neck, but he leaned forward so that she stumbled and slid backwards into the hay. His hand was cold and his palm felt calloused against her breast, conscious with a hidden intent, and already she couldn't keep up; when he let his weight rest against her, she heard herself cry out, as if in eagerness, but it wasn't what she meant.

"You know how much I love you," he whispered. "I know you know." She tried to respond with her eyes, but she didn't know if he could see her. He kept talking more and more wildly, staring down at her, his eyes gleaming in the refracted light, but she couldn't make out his expression. "I'll never leave you," he muttered. "You believe me, don't you? Tell me you believe me."

Something about the way he said it disturbed her; she tried to believe the words but she felt frightened—yet she had no time to think about this because now he reached down to direct himself into her. She moaned a little, ambiguously, and he exclaimed, "No!" No, what? she tried to ask him, but his eyes were tightly closed; he was grimacing. She had thought that when finally they made love there would be no more descriptions of what she was feeling to choose among, and she felt despair to discover that even now she could not be sure what anything meant. He had not given her any time. Though temporarily she found and clung to the thought that Stewart was feeling too much to think about what she felt, no sooner did she satisfactorily describe what was happening and begin to respond in accordance than he would do something to make what she'd just decided seem irrelevant, even farcical—every time he began to lose himself he'd stop moving, eyes open now, and wait for her, saying angrily, "Stay with me! Stay with me!" I'm trying! she cried silently. I'm trying but I don't know where you are—where are you going? She had to prove that she trusted him, but how? "Don't leave me!" he cried out. "Look at me! Look at me!" She opened her eyes, which she had closed in order to be able to think more clearly. But I'm not! she shouted silently. I'll stay here always, I promise—I know I was afraid the last time but this time I'll stay no matter what I *will* accept you for who you are—and it was at this moment that she felt his hands circling her neck, a sweet gesture, a tender mastery, and she looked up at him submissively, trying to tell him that she'd waited her entire life to lose herself so completely, didn't he know that? But then his fingers pressed down and she widened her eyes, startled—a joke? A mistake? Smiling slightly, he lowered his face and pressed his lips against hers, then was kissing her deeply, and when she tried to move her head aside he pushed his tongue even farther into her mouth and shoved his thumbs against her windpipe. She could feel him pulsating now inside her. Frantically she tried to turn her head—didn't he realize she couldn't breathe? What was he thinking? How could he not realize what he was doing? She tried to see his expression, but his eyes were closed again, squeezed shut, as if helping his hands to squeeze out her breath. She felt pressure behind her eyes, in her ears, in her throat, choking her, and still he pushed his thumbs deeper. She was gagging and now Stewart lifted his face and looked down at her, his expression seeming purely interested.

In a childlike, sing-song voice, he said, "Don't resist. If you struggle it will only be worse. It will be over in a minute. I killed my father, you know. I've never told anyone, but I can tell you. Look at me—don't fight it. Things could have been different—you're the one who wants them this way."

But Zoë no longer heard the words. She knew only the threat in them, whatever they meant; there was no time to wonder anymore why he was shoving her life back down her throat; he *was,* that was all, and every cell in her body screamed at her to breathe—*breathe.* Nothing else matters—BREATHE. Because he had been in such a hurry, and because it was cold in the stable (although not now) Stewart had taken off only what clothing was necessary. He had removed his boots, but his jeans were around his knees and he had left her boots on and lifted her nightgown; his torso kept her pinned but his legs lay loosely between hers and, by twisting her hips she was able to get a purchase with her feet. She knew she would not have more than one chance—she was blacking out.

Slipping her left leg out from under him, she brought it close to her right and, bending her knees simultaneously, shoved them as hard as she could up between his. She was losing consciousness. But in the midst of her helpless horror at recognizing this she felt amazement when he loosened his grip and rolled on his back, doubled up in pain, clutching himself, groaning. It seemed laughable, his behaving in such a predictable way, the way she'd seen men double over during games, and as she scrambled away and crawled fast and awkwardly towards the ladder, gasping for air, she was amazed that her mind could spend even an instant on such a thought—simply because she could breathe now it was playing again; that was all it ever did. It entertained itself. As if reprimanded, it now presented her with a course of action; she grabbed Stewart's boots and flung them over the edge of the loft. She stepped onto the first rung of the ladder, began to climb down, and then paused while she could still see into the loft. Stewart was looking at her, lying on his side.

"I thought you were braver than this," he groaned. "You've disappointed me, Zoë."

She knew she ought to hurry; in a moment he would be up again and if he caught her he would never give her a second chance to escape, but she couldn't look away. She felt paralyzed by the ordinariness of the situation. He was talking to her; he wasn't trying to kill her; how could he have tried to kill her? It was absurd. Still on his side, Stewart had carefully begun to slide towards the ladder.

STOP.

He understood the gesture.

"Why? You're so seductive—you with all you know but your fear of saying it. It's too tantalizing. You ask too much."

He inched forward again but still she couldn't move.

"You can't believe I really meant to hurt you, can you?" he asked, his eyes glinting in the uneven light. "Don't you realize what I was doing? I was trying to shock you into speech. That's why I did what I did. You can't believe I meant to harm you."

She couldn't tell now whether or not he were moving. He seemed to be closer, but she couldn't remember when he had moved—the movement was so continuous. She lifted one foot to step down a rung, but couldn't make up her mind to leave. It was a fact that he had almost strangled her—she had been on the edge of blacking out—but did that mean he had really intended to *kill* her? He might be telling the truth. He could have been planning to release the pressure the instant she lost consciousness. If she'd done what he'd asked, not fought it, when she'd opened her eyes she might have said aloud, "What did you do that for?" but now she'd missed her chance, her one chance—what could she *do* now? She had waited, she had waited so long. How could he have meant to harm her? He was her child's father.

All this time Stewart's eyes held hers and she felt as if she were drifting, drifting downstream, at first slowly and majestically, then pulled forcefully as if within the stately current an unpredictable, rash tide began to exert its power; she understood that she was in danger yet the sensation of being moved with no effort on her part mesmerized her; suddenly she recognized it as exactly what she had always wanted to feel, what she had looked for all her life—nothing to think about anymore, life taking her where it wanted; the wildness had her now—the lost wildness that banished will and error.

Two things happened at once—or one immediately preceded the other; she would never be able to decide which. Stewart lunged for her, and Samuel's voice cried, "Look out!" Or else she heard the voice and then saw Stewart lunge.

She leapt back, caught a lower rung of the ladder as she slipped, which broke her fall; splinters of wood sliced her hands. Stewart had already swung around to vault down after her. She grabbed his boots and plunged out the door, hauled it closed, and heaved the boots as far away as she could into the darkness. He wouldn't be able to pursue her long through the snow in his socks. As she ran she heard the door slide open behind her.

"Don't turn around," Samuel said, she couldn't tell from where, except that he was close by. "Run."

She stopped only when she reached the top of the embankment. Then she turned briefly—Stewart wasn't in pursuit, at least not yet. But he must have made it back to the house—the light was off. Either that or Judith had woken and turned it off. She hoped so. She hoped she asked him what the hell he had been doing out in the snow at three a.m. Christmas morning.

"Hurry," Samuel urged her. "It's not safe."

She could feel his hand on her arm, helping her down the bank, and she swam back along the track—the snow seemed much deeper now. The air was harsh in her lungs. Her hands throbbed where she'd driven the splinters into them.

Samuel didn't say anything else until they came to where the tracks led back up out of the gully, but she felt him breathing with her. When she began stumbling up the slope, he reached down and helped her up. At the top she stood, panting—she had run, falling continually, most of the way—and looked at the house. It was dark and quiet.

"I can't go in there," he said softly.

She nodded, looking around for the sound. Did he know that she couldn't talk? Why couldn't she see him?

"Goodbye, Zoë," he said.

She reached towards the sound and it seemed to her that she felt warmth on her cheek, and then the night air was silent. Sam, she said in her mind. Just, "Sam." Then she walked slowly the rest of the way to the house, circled around back, and gently opened the kitchen door. Immediately it seemed too quiet, as if everyone were holding their breath. She had taken off her gloves to grip the knob and now stood on tiptoe, the fingers of her right hand folding around the key. She grimaced as the movement forced blood against the splinter, but she didn't have time to attend to it. All she could hear was her own breathing, nothing else. At least she hadn't been missed.

As she stepped back outside and carefully shut the door, Zoë realized for the first time how cold she was. It hadn't even seemed warm in the house. Her legs, above her boots and up to her thighs, were completely numb. She suppressed the impulse to begin chafing them; though she doubted anyone would hear her, she wanted to make as little noise as possible until she was inside the snakehouse; and even then she'd have to be quiet, since she was sure that Nick, asleep or awake, was always alert to any sound from that direction. Two windows of his and Ellie's bedroom faced the rattlesnake coop.

She hung the padlock on the latch and went in. She closed the door before she turned on the overhead light. As it shut, she patted the wall until she felt the light switch and flicked it up—nothing happened. She tried again—still nothing. Maybe the bulb was burnt out. She fingered her way along the wall towards the counter, where there was a high-intensity gooseneck lamp. But halfway there she stopped, realizing that the lights above the cages, which Nick left on all the time, were out too. The power had gone out. That was why it had seemed cold in the house and why it had been even quieter than usual. No refrigerator or furnace humming. It was cold here too. That explained why the light had been off in Stewart's house.

However, the generator was supposed to go on. The snakes had to be kept between seventy and eighty degrees; much below that they'd lose heat quickly. Even with her coat on Zoë could tell that it wasn't anywhere near the temperature they needed.

She reached into Nick's coat pocket, then remembered she'd left the flashlight behind. Could there be matches somewhere in the snakehouse? She kept forgetting to be careful of her hands; they ached and stung. Would the splinters leave scars? But what would that prove? Nothing against Stewart. If only she could see, she could try to pull them out. The generator was in the far corner under the counter—there would be no way she could see the controls without more light. A little came through the small windows above the counter, enough so that she could make out the bank of cages and the dim forms of the mute snakes, but not enough so that she could tell which was which. She thought she remembered where the big diamondback was, but if she made a mistake and was bitten first by a different snake, she might be too incapacitated to try again. Nick was so sure that it had to be a diamondback and that it would have to be a large one. It should strike somewhere where it could pierce a vein, like the wrist or the inside of the elbow; otherwise enough of the venom might not get into the blood. He had been adamant about its having to travel through the blood. She considered going back to the house for matches or another flashlight—there might be one somewhere in the kitchen—but she was worried now that the snake might already be too sluggish to bite, and any more delay would increase the likelihood of this. Besides, she'd wake someone up. She had to do it now, before she started being afraid.

Nothing like almost being strangled to get up your courage, she signed into the dark. But snakes had no sense of humor. It would be strange not to sign anymore, she was so used to it. Speech would always possess less integrity in comparison, but her hands might be out of commission for a while so it would be good timing. And now that she knew what could never be said, she could not betray herself.

Stepping back to the door, she pushed it open as wide as she could, but it wouldn't stay. She brought out the trash can, but it was empty and too light to resist the weight of the door.

Damn it, she said silently.

Then she thought of wedging one of her boots beneath the door; that seemed to work. With the additional light reflected off the snow, she could now make out the individual cages. The large Atrox was located in the middle of the top row. Yes, good, there it was, curled up tightly around itself in the corner. It must be very cold.

Undoing the latch, she slid the glass door down as far as it would go. No movement at all from the snake. She made as close to a hissing sound as she could. No response.

She blew on it. Nothing.

But what was she doing? It had to bite her in the right place or it would be worse than nothing. If it spun around and struck her in the face it wouldn't help in the least. The problem was, she couldn't really make out where its head was. And without seeing its head, she couldn't very well offer it her wrist. She was going to have to take it out of the cage.

Zoë felt along the wall above the counter for Nick's giant tongs, carefully closed them around the snake and lifted it out. She was astonished by its weight. She had been prepared for it to twist, struggling to free itself, as they all did when Nick lifted them, but it hung unprotesting, a long, limp upside-down U. She stretched it out on the counter.

Now she could locate the head, but she could also see that the snake was not moving. Was it dead? Could it have frozen so quickly? Were they all dead?

She lifted the Atrox behind its jaws, and with her other hand held its body. It didn't move, but she didn't know how to tell if it were dead or not.

Then she remembered how Nick preferred to kill them, by putting them in the freezer—and his story of once taking one out and, thinking it dead, leaving it in the sink for Ellie to deal with; he'd come back an hour later to find it coiled on top of the gas stove over the pilot light, rattling away at him as alive as you please. He hadn't had the heart to put it back in the freezer.

Maybe the Atrox would come back to life if she could warm it up. She picked it up again, involuntarily shuddering, a reflex of fear, even though she still didn't feel afraid, and looped it a couple of times around her arm. She wanted to close the door, and it would be easier to carry the snake with her than to try to find it again in the dark.

She worked her foot into her boot and when she stepped back the door fell shut. She waited until her eyes readjusted to the dimness, then sat down cross-legged on the floor, her back supported by the plywood platform the cages rested on. She arranged the snake in a coil in her lap, its head resting neatly on top; her nightgown sagged to the floor beneath its weight. She closed Nick's big sheepskin jacket around her and leaned back to wait. As she grew warmer, she felt very drowsy. She thought of how, soon, she would have to answer Rob. What would she say? The person she'd loved was gone—she knew that now—so that even if she could know, once and for all, what he'd done and why, it would make no difference; she couldn't know what the new Rob might do or what his reasons would be for what he did. So whom would she be marrying if she said yes to his proposal? Yet she had to think of the child—it needed a father—a father who would love it as his own, who would fight its ghostly father, if necessary, to keep that right. Rob had always said he'd rather adopt than have a child himself. The craziness wouldn't take hold that way.

She fell asleep and was woken by a flashlight in her face and Nick's voice exclaiming, "Jesus Christ, Zoë! Why the hell did you turn the generator off?"

She blinked, trying to see him. Then she felt the snake move. It raised its head and parted the lower edges of the coat where she hadn't been able to button it over her knees.

"Dear God!" Nick breathed.

Zoë looked down at the top of the snake's spade-shaped head—from above, the two knobs of its eyes made it look as if it were frowning.

"Zoë, sit absolutely and completely still, do you understand? I . . ."

Instead of obeying Nick, she began to undo the upper buttons of the coat. Nick, who'd been sidling along the counter, moaned, "Zoë! No!" at the same time that the snake curled into a defensive coil and began to rattle. But it was threatening Nick, not her. She couldn't believe it! She held her wrist right in front of its mouth but it ignored her completely and only lifted its head higher as if her arm were a branch or some other inanimate object that obstructed its view.

She couldn't see Nick—he still had the flashlight aimed at the two of them—but she pulled her hand back and signaled to him to leave.

"Zoë, are you out of your mind? I can't . . ."

She could tell that he didn't comprehend what he was seeing. Every time he spoke the snake tightened its coil and rattled more meaningfully. She began to sign *Go away*, but stopped herself. If Nick left, then the snake would probably settle right back down in her lap; it seemed perfectly content to stay there all night.

Instead she fingerspelled, T-O-N-G-S. She now had a plan. When Nick moved to capture the rattlesnake, it would strike at him, and she would somehow manage to get in the way. While Nick moved carefully along the counter, she shrugged free of the coat; the snake lowered itself back into her lap, though she could tell it was still watching Nick. Sure enough, as soon as he'd picked up the tongs and turned towards them, it began to rattle. Zoë felt the tail vibrating against her knee. The rattlesnake's Y-shaped tongue flicked in and out, sizing Nick up.

"Zoë, I'm not sure this will work. I don't understand why, but he doesn't seem to be aware of you—I think the best thing would be for you to knock him away from you; then I can use the L-stick to pin him down. I think there's the least risk that way."

No.

"No?"

She kept shaking her head.

"Zoë, do you comprehend the danger you're in? If he injected all his venom a bite from him on the face or chest could kill you. You might not even make it to the hospital. Please. Do you understand what I'm saying?"

Yes, of course.

"For God's sake, do as I say! Knock him away from you! Try to stand up at the same time."

No.

Nick said incredulously, "You *want* him to bite you?"

Yes, that's right.

"Oh, Zoë, my God . . ."

Why not? You were going to.

"Oh, who knows what I was going to do!"

She laid her left hand on top of the coiled snake; it was warm now, alive with her warmth. She moved her hand up until she cupped it behind its head—it didn't stir.

"That's it!" Nick whispered. "That's *it*! Tighten your hand right where you have it and he won't be able to turn."

She opened her fist and stroked the snake's brown and gray scales. "Zoë, for the love of God!"

At the sound of his voice, the snake reared into striking position. Nick shouted, "Enough!"

He took a step and she lifted her arm. Perfect timing. Just as Nick extended the tongs to grab the snake, it lunged at him and she thrust her arm full length between it and Nick. Only after it had already happened did Zoë realize that the rattlesnake had sunk its fangs full-length into her arm. By this time Nick had grabbed it and heaved it into its cage and pushed up the door. Zoë was surprised that he didn't say, Now you stay in your room until I tell you to come out! She was sorry for having tricked the snake, but was distracted from this regret by the fact that her right arm felt as if someone were holding a thousand lighted matches to the skin. Nick had ripped off the cord of his bathrobe and was tying it around her upper arm. He was too furious to say a word. At that moment Ellie called down from the kitchen door,

"What's taking so long, Nick? Isn't the generator on?"

"Call the hospital!" he shouted back. "Tell them to expect a rattlesnake bite!"

"Jesus! Oh, Nick, where are you bitten? I can't . . ."

"I'm not! Zoë is! Ellie, do it!"

"Zoë?" they heard, but then the kitchen door slammed—Pryce and Monica wouldn't be asleep much longer, if in fact they still were.

Nick had taken a box from the shelf under the counter.

"Zoë, I'm going to cut into your arm with a razor blade. Can you hold the flashlight with your other hand?"

She nodded. She was beginning to feel sick to her stomach. When Nick came back with the razor, he handed her the flashlight. She directed the light upon her arm. It looked a little swollen, and she could see two blood-specked punctures where the fangs had entered.

"The tourniquet is probably irrelevant," Nick said, "as this may also be. I think he did hit a vein. Don't worry, Zoë, you're going to be all right." Clenching his lips between his teeth to control his own nausea, he sliced lengthwise along the inside of her arm.

"Nick, Stewart Beauregard tried to strangle me," she said.

It was even more unbelievable, said aloud. Her voice didn't sound at all the way she'd remembered it—the words didn't even sound like words. But Nick seemed to understand well enough.

"This is hardly a time for jokes," he said. "I don't know what the hell you think . . ."

Then his face snapped up from her arm, frozen, gaping.

"I'm not joking," she said, although it was strange; now that she'd spoken she felt indifferent as to whether or not Nick believed her. "He killed his father—he told me." Though not like Rob—whatever Rob had done. She smiled weakly at Nick. "I'm also pregnant."

How quickly did the hormones begin their new production schedule? At the very instant of conception? Was that why the venom had worked? If that was the case, then no matter how many birth control pills Nick had taken the bite wouldn't have done *him* any good. Right about the time Stewart had closed his fingers around her throat, her chemistry had already started to change.

"Zoë . . ." Nick choked out. He was trying to squeeze the blood out of the cuts.

Ellie appeared at the door. "I've called them," she said, her voice shaking. "Where is she bitten? How did it happen?"

Glancing up at Ellie, Zoë saw that the sky had begun to lighten.

"Just on the arm," she said.

"What?" Ellie said. "Who . . . ?" Then she started to scream.

This woke Nick from his trance. "Take it easy!" he shouted.

"But she talked!" Ellie shrieked. "Zoë talked! What . . . ?"

"She's in no state to be asked questions, for God's sake, Ellie! Run back up and start the car. I'll help her around to the driveway."

Ellie, protesting inarticulately, stumbled up the bank. Nick lifted Zoë to her feet—she felt very faint and sick now. Pryce appeared at the kitchen door and they heard him choke out to Ellie, "Is she alive?"

"She can talk!" Ellie shouted at him. "We have to take her to the hospital!"

"But what . . ."

Zoë began to laugh. She could talk and so they had to rush her to the hospital. They were arguing with each other like the three crones after Perseus stole their one eye.

"Ellie and Pryce can take me, Nick," she said. Her voice sounded so loud. "You have to get the generator running. You can still revive the other snakes."

They were near the top of the slope now, but when she spoke Nick stopped and turned away.

"What? What's the matter? Can't you understand me?"

Then she thought that maybe she'd hurt his feelings by suggesting that he might have forgotten about the snakes. She remembered what he'd said when he'd first come into the snakehouse.

"Nick, I didn't turn the generator off, honest. It was off when I went in. I wouldn't do that."

He turned and stared at her. "Are you crazy? How can you think I was thinking about that? It's not . . . Zoë, it's not . . ." He couldn't finish.

"Don't cry, Nick," she said, wondering at the strange shape the sound of his name made in the winter air. "There's nothing to cry about."

"Oh, Zoë . . ."

He grabbed her and clung to her, sobbing against her hair. She patted him on the back with her left arm. Suddenly he pulled away and looked at her, and if she hadn't been feeling so dizzy she would have laughed at the mixture of expressions on his face: pain and love and bewilderment and joy and—what most amazed her—an incredible relief at having heard her say his name. Was that really all that people wanted?

"It's as if you've come back from the dead," he murmured, putting his arms back around her. "Promise me you'll never leave like that again."

She crossed her fingers behind his back and said, "I promise."

A NOTE ON THE TYPE

The text of this book was set in Sabon, a typeface designed by Jan Tschichold (1902–1974), the well-known German typographer. Because it was designed in Frankfurt, Sabon was named for the famous Frankfurt typefounder Jacques Sabon, who died in 1580 while manager of the Egenolff foundry. Based loosely on the original designs of Claude Garamond (c. 1480–1561), Sabon is unique in that it was explicitly designed for hot-metal composition on both the Monotype and Linotype machines as well as for film composition.

Composed by American–Stratford Graphic Services, Inc.,
Brattleboro, Vermont

Printed and bound by The Haddon Craftsmen, Inc.,
Scranton, Pennsylvania

Typography and binding design
by Dorothy S. Baker